COLLECTED
STORIES

SAUL BELLOW

COLLECTED STORIES

Preface by
JANIS BELLOW

Introduction by
JAMES WOOD

VIKING

To Beena Kamlani, whose kindly function is to face me in the right direction.
Her respectful and grateful author. —S. B.

VIKING
Published by the Penguin Group
Penguin Putnam Inc., 375 Hudson Street, New York, New York 10014, U.S.A.
Penguin Books Ltd, 80 Strand, London WC2R ORL, England
Penguin Books Australia Ltd, Ringwood, Victoria, Australia
Penguin Books Canada Ltd, 10 Alcorn Avenue, Toronto, Ontario, Canada M4V 3B2
Penguin Books, (N.Z.) Ltd, 182–190 Wairau Road, Auckland 10, New Zealand

Penguin Books Ltd, Registered Offices: Harmondsworth, Middlesex, England

First published in 2001 by Viking Penguin, a member of Penguin Putnam Inc.

10   9   8   7   6   5   4   3   2   1

PREFACE

Yesterday my husband and I took our year-old daughter, Naomi Rose, for a stroll in the neighborhood. The weather was ferociously cold—what the forecasters in these parts unaccountably describe as "blustery." To escape the icy wind we headed for the Brookline Booksmith. Now when Saul ducks into a bookstore, chances are he's going to be there for some time. I pulled Rosie out of her snowsuit and attempted to distract her with the dust jacket of *Ravelstein*. "Who's this, Naomi Rose? Who's the man in the picture?" And turning to point at Saul, she answered in that bell-like infant voice of hers that could be heard all through the store, "Dad, dad, dad." Now Dad was muffled in turtle fleece to the eyebrows, but his face emerged to give her a most delicious smile.

This morning, as I begin to write, I imagine Rosie the reader, a couple of decades deeper into the century. When Rosie is ready for Saul's books, what memories will there be of Dad at his desk? And does memory need an assist? Will someone produce an accurate portrait of her father at work? Why not begin, I ask myself, with this little preface? To say for Rosie's sake, and for scores of others who will never see the man sitting down to write—this is how it was done.

Proximity has been my privilege. I was there, for instance, when "The Bellarosa Connection" was born.

It began innocently enough. In the first week of May 1988 en route from Chicago to Vermont we stopped in Philadelphia, where Saul gave a lecture, "A Jewish Writer in America," for the Jewish Publication Society. In the weeks before he delivered this talk, and for the remainder of that month—during the drive from Philadelphia to Vermont; while exploring Dartmouth, where he was a visiting lecturer; and later in Vermont; where we were doing battle with the blackflies to lay in a garden—our conversation was about nothing but the fate of the Jews in the twentieth century. Just then Saul was facing the final revisions on "A Theft," and he was wrestling with *A Case of Love*—a novel he would never finish. Meanwhile, he was waiting to hear whether "A Theft" had been accepted by *The New Yorker*. Both *Esquire* and the *Atlantic Monthly* had already decided the story was too long. It wasn't in Saul to mope alone by the telephone. Every morning over breakfast he diverted me with puns or entertained me with possible subjects for stories, and often he came downstairs to say that he had dreamed up a new way to jump-start *A Case of Love*. Why not introduce an eccentric Parisian pianist of the old school who would teach his heroine about love? We were reading and rereading the proofs of "A Theft." Saul habitually revises well beyond the last moment. The ending wasn't right—too many ideas, not enough movement. He would rework it by day and each night I would type and retype the latest pages. In the middle of May we got word that *The New Yorker* had also turned down his story, but Saul was too busy to be checked by bad news. He was reflecting deeply on what should come next, and the weather wasn't being cooperative. Now I ought to explain that Saul is extremely weather-sensitive. High-pressure azure skies—those of late May and early June—have always turned him on. But in that spring of '88 the gloomy rain fell day after day. Saul would light a fire in the kitchen, drink his coffee, and then slosh out to the studio through the blackfly-infested soppy grass. He wasn't writing, he told me; he was going there "to brood." And he added, "That's how I've always done things—you separate yourself from editors, lawyers, publishers. You set down your burdens and you brood."

Our Vermont friends and neighbors Herb and Libby Hillman, looking to lift our sagging spirits, invited us to dinner. Over Libby's homemade bread and roast chicken, the conversation turned once again to the Jewish question, and Saul introduced an idea we had been debating since his Philadelphia lecture. Should the Jews feel shame over the Holocaust? Is there a particular disgrace in being victimized? I was ferociously opposed to this suggestion. As we awaited dessert we let go of the argument. The smell of chocolate announced that the drowsy end of the evening was upon us. Serious subjects gave way to gags, jokes, old chestnuts. But as we were getting ready to leave, our host, a retired chemist specializing in house paints, began to tell the story of one of his colleagues. This man, now dying of lung cancer after a lifetime of exposure to toxins, had been a European refugee in the early forties. I have to admit: while I was scraping the last of the chocolate from my plate, my mind was already on the rain and the slippery ride home. I was not attending as closely as I might have been.

May 24: The first fine day of the season. When Saul came back from the studio for lunch he had that shining-eyed look that made me anticipate his announcement: "I'm on to something new. I don't want to talk about it just yet." Next day as we were driving into Brattleboro for our weekly supplies, he elaborated: "I haven't found a shape for the new story yet, but it's based on what Herb told us over dinner." Did I remember the details? No. But fortunately, Saul did: A refugee is imprisoned by the Italian Fascists, but prior to his imprisonment, having become aware that his arrest is imminent, he has written overseas to the Broadway impresario Billy Rose on the advice of a friend. (In the story as Saul eventually wrote it, the hero makes no such appeal to Billy Rose and in fact has never even heard of him.) A mysterious plan is concocted while he waits in his prison cell. He learns that his door will be left open at a certain hour on a certain night. Someone will meet him in the street behind the prison and indicate that he has been sent by Billy Rose. There will be money and instructions about which city to go to until the next contact appears. All happens as planned, and with the aid of these emissaries he escapes to the States. There, he is denied entry because of the quotas, but makes it to Cuba. Years later when he is back in the United States he tries to contact Billy Rose and to thank him in person. But it seems Rose, who has helped a lot of people, will have nothing to do with the refugees he has saved, perhaps fearing that they will lean on him or mooch from him indefinitely. The rescued man is quite shaken by the cold shoulder he gets from Broadway Billy.

Such were the bare bones of the story, as sketched by Saul that day on the way to town, a story no longer about Herb's friend, but already about a character—Harry Fonstein—"Surviving Harry," as Saul would later call him, borrowing from John Berryman's "Dreamsong" (dedicated to Saul) about "Surviving Henry." Saul, it turned out, knew quite a lot about Billy Rose. For in his Greenwich Village days he had known Bernie Wolfe, who was Rose's ghostwriter. A Wolfe-like character might become the intermediary between Rose and the protagonist. Wolfe had been a very bright, very savvy and strange man who took an unusual interest in New York people and their obscure motivations. Such a man would be sympathetic to the Fonstein character. Saul then told me a story about going to Wolfe's place in the Village and noticing an old, worn woman dusting and scrubbing the apartment. On Saul's way out Wolfe turned to him and said, "That lady is my mother." He hadn't introduced her or paid her any heed. Why make the confession then? Oh, people had ideas about being open in those Village days, Saul added. They prized their singularity. At that time they worried a great deal about their mental health. What a contrast such low-level American antics would provide to the somber seriousness of the European story.

Saul had also seen Billy Rose in Jerusalem. What did he look like? I asked. "Well, he was small, Jewish; he might have been handsome but for the tense lines in his face. He looked strained, greedy, dissatisfied with himself."

When we got to town Saul borrowed a book on Billy Rose from the library. We couldn't turn up any information about Wolfe.

The next day the sun shone again, and when Saul returned from work he said only, "I've figured out a way to write this story."

On May 29 we dawdled to the studio together, and Saul read me the first few pages—handwritten on lined yellow legal-size paper. What struck me at first was how intently he had listened to Herb's tale. Saul had remembered that the protagonist was in Italy when he had been imprisoned. In Rome the man had managed to become a clerk at a hotel. Thanks to his gift for languages and his false papers, he had such freedom of movement that he'd even found himself at a gathering where Hitler had made an appearance. And so on. Now I've always prided myself on my attentiveness—to Saul I am a "genius noticer." This time it didn't matter that I'd been less than alert: Saul had been fully present. When he is on to a story, his capacity for hearing and absorbing details expands exponentially. I realized then that a writer does not need to be tuned in all the time. In fact—forgive me, Henry James—being "someone upon whom nothing is lost" is too distracting. A writer keeps to himself, broods, sits quietly. But from the moment when he attaches himself to a story, everything is re-arranged. Suddenly, as Saul puts it, the wakeful writer has "feelers all over the place."

From an after-dinner story came one luminous strand of silk, and over the next few days and then weeks I watched as Saul wove event, accident, memory, and thought—what he had read, what we had discussed, and the contents of his dreams—into that oriental carpet of a novella "The Bellarosa Connection." This mingling of elements, however, has very little to do with facts, with autobiography. It is so rare and complex and strange a use of human material that even if I were to unravel every thread that found its way into the work, and to describe the process by which each was carded and dyed and woven and tied, I would still come no closer to the secret of its composition.

Saul had already decided that the story would have two central characters: not only this European Jew, Fonstein, who made his escape, but an American Jew as well. He wanted his reader to be able to feel the difference in tone between the two men's lives. He could mine his own experience and call upon his memories of Wolfe for the American, but who would be the model for his European character? On June 2, Saul told me a long story about his stepmother's nephew. Over the winter he had learned that this nephew was dead, and he had been oppressed by the fact that the death had occurred some time ago, and that he hadn't known that the man was gone. At one time he had been very fond of this chess-playing sober young refugee. They had sought each other out at his stepmother's boring Sunday gatherings. What does it mean to say that you are close to someone, Saul wondered, when you discover that you are relying only on scraps of memory about that person? From these musings came Saul's notion of the "warehouse of good intentions." Someone occupies a place in your life, takes on some special significance—what it is, you can't really say. But you have made a real connection—this person has come to stand for something in your life. Time goes by, you haven't seen the party, you don't know what has happened to him, he may even be dead for all you know, and yet you hang on to the idea of the unique importance of that individual. What a shock to discover that memories have become a stand-in for that warehoused person.

So much of our conversation about the Jewish question revolved around memory. Now it would be Saul's memories of this late immigrant arrival with his singsong Polish accent, his gift for languages, and his business smarts that would give flavor to his European character, Harry Fonstein. The American narrator in "The Bellarosa Connection" would find out about the death of Fonstein in much the same way that Saul learned of the death of his stepmother's nephew.

When pieces of life begin to find their way into the work, there is always something magical about the manner in which they are lifted from the recent—or distant—past or the here and now, and then kneaded and shaped and subtly transformed into narrative. Saul *did* have a nightmare like the one that wakes his narrator. He described what it felt like to be overcome by midnight dread, to be in that pit without the strength to climb out. And he *did* have a stepmother who parted her hair in the middle and baked delicious strudel. And while lecturing in Philadelphia we *had* visited a grand old mansion much like the home Saul's narrator would find himself uncomfortably, awkwardly inhabiting. And there are so many bits that never find their way into the narrative. Here's one I loved: The European, Harry Fonstein, tells the American about the way he grieved for his mother, whom he had buried in Ravenna, by speaking of his aversion to a particular shade of blue-gray. This was the color of the shroud in which he had buried his mother. In our hotel room in Philadelphia, Saul and I had been talking about the way certain colors impress you. He had told me then that his own mother had been buried in a blue-gray shroud.

To watch these details working their way into or out of the novella is nothing like the cutting and pasting of actual events. Biographers, beware: Saul wields a wand, not scissors. He is no fact-collector. Better to imagine Prospero at play. Or to picture Saul as he lights out for the studio: a small boy with his satchel and his piece of fruit.

Most mornings we linger. Work will wait. We tour the "giardino" and see which flowers have appeared. This June there is a white anemone of which Saul is enormously proud (there's never been another before or since—the moles seem to get at the bulbs). The giant red-orange poppies are budding, the peonies will flower this year in time for Saul's birthday, and there's one early bright purple cosmos blossom. We admire a fat sassy snake curling among the wild columbines. "The whole world is an ice cream cone to him," Saul laughs as he disappears into his studio.

Everything must be taken up nimbly, easily, or not at all. You can't read Saul without being aware of the laughter running beneath every word. He has always been playful. Now he is also firm and spare. There is also the matter of taste. Sometimes a detail is borrowed because the flavor is right (like Charlus and the telephone in the narrator's mansion—never mind the anachronism). Saul generally steers clear of puzzles and riddles. Lovers of word games must look to Joyce or Nabokov for the serious pleasures of the anagrammist. What we find instead is Stendhalian brio—laughter, whimsy, lightness of touch. Odd, perhaps, that I should speak of laughter in considering what is essentially Saul's darkest look at one of the century's most serious subjects. But "Bellarosa" wasn't born in anger. Everything that moved Saul deeply at that time found its way into the novella, and what moved him deeply, no matter how serious, was a source of energy and ultimately of pleasure. This was a time when we were often up toward dawn—discussing the story, his memories of New Jersey or of Greenwich Village, and most often the history of the Jews. But perhaps because we were young lovers then my memories of that spring are anything but dark. Saul was writing this powerful, even horrible book with intense heat and joy, dipping into his brightest colors.

That's not to say the writing always came easily or that the work went on un-interrupted. By early June Saul had begun turning the yellow pages into manu-script. I remember hearing the sound of the typewriter one morning, and feeling a thrill that his breakfast forecast—"I think I've got something here"—was being realized. He was working in the house, and when I took him his tea, I stood by and listened for another volley of staccato fire. Saul hunts down his words with the keys of his Remington. He revises as he types, and spots of si-lence are followed by these racy rattling rhythmical bursts. He looks forward to this cup of hot tea with one round slice of lemon floating on top. The proper drink for a European Jew on an overcast day, Saul first observed when he visited the empty Jewish quarters of Polish cities. The lemon stands for the sun; the sugar and caffeine give the jolt you need when the surge from your morning cof-fee subsides. How he was managing to write at all was fairly mysterious, since he would accept no protection from distractions. And there had been many: a visit from a neighbor; phone calls from an agent, a lawyer, a friend (I could always tell from the roars of laughter when it was Allan Bloom on the line). After each interruption the study door would close and the wonderful *ack-ack-ack* of the typewriter would begin again.

A week before his birthday on June 10, Saul read me the first dozen typed pages of the story. The account of Fonstein's escape from the Italian prison made me hold my breath then, and every time I've heard it since. The narrator would be an older man, recounting a story that had been told to him by Fonstein years earlier.

Though Saul was bushed, he was putting on speed so as to have as much done as possible before we took off for Paris and Rome in the middle of the month. What? Europe, now? Well, we would see Bloom in Paris, and in Italy the Scanno Prize was being offered to Saul. The details of the award—a bag of gold coins, a stay in a hunting lodge in the remote Abruzzi region—had too much of the flavor of adventure to resist. Saul never takes it easy when he is overworked and beginning to feel run down. He continued to ride his mountain bike, to chop up the fallen limbs of an apple tree, to remove boulder-sized rocks from the garden, to carry in logs for the morning fire. I was convinced he had a horseshoe over his head that spring. He tripped while cutting brush and scraped his face; he had a gashed shin to show for a tumble from his mountain bike; his eye was bloodshot; there was a bleeding nose. Of course he worked the morning of the nosebleed, lying down on the futon in the studio whenever the bleeding started, and then getting up to scrawl out a new paragraph. When he hadn't returned for lunch I carried a bite out to him and found him typing vigorously, his face and his T-shirt covered with blood. Composing for Saul is an aerobic activity. He sweats when he writes, and peels off layers of clothing. When he is concentrating particularly hard, he screws up his left eye and emits a sound that's a cross between the panting of a long-distance runner and a breathy whistle: "Windy suspirations of forced breath."

Saul's birthday—at least for the fourteen years I have celebrated it with him—is always a his-kind-of-working-weather day—blue skies, copper sun, the atmospheric high of high pressure. But there would be no writing today. I should add that time off is something unheard of for Saul. No holidays, no Sabbaths. A birthday is like any other day—a chance to type another couple of pages. He was, however, high as a kite. Family was on the way, and at his request I was baking a devil's food chocolate cake with chocolate icing and toasted coconut.

A brief break from words is never a sign that the mental wheels aren't racing round and round. Two days later Saul returned from his morning's work and announced: "I started my story again from scratch. There are times when it takes over, you know." At dinner I pressed him about the new beginning and he became very expansive: there were too many ideas piled on at the start—too much to expect the reader to digest all at once. All this stuff about the American versus the European Jew. This must unfold gradually. What the story is really about is memory and faith. There is no religion without remembering. As Jews we remember what was told to us at Sinai; at the Seder we remember the Exodus; Yiskor is about remembering a father, a mother. We are told not to forget the Patriarchs; we admonish ourselves, "If I forget thee, O Jerusalem . . ." And we are constantly reminding God not to forget his Covenant with us. This is what the "chosenness" of the Chosen People is all about. We are chosen to be God's privileged mind readers. All of it, what binds us together, is our history, and we are a people because we remember.

Saul then told me that his narrator was beginning to come to life. He had decided not to give him a name. This elderly man, narrator X, is starting to lose his memory. He is walking down the street one day, humming "Way down upon the . . ." and he can't remember the name of the river—it torments him, he's in agony over this loss of a word, he feels ready to stop a passerby, to do anything to recover the word (this actually did happen to Saul during the winter in Chicago, while strolling around downtown on his way back from the dentist, and until Suwannee came to him he was beside himself). The narrator can't afford such a lapse because, as Saul explained, his whole life has been built around memory. He will be the founder of this institute—the Mnemosyne Institute—that helps business people sharpen their memories. In order to put it all together and make a coherent picture, he is going to take it upon himself to remember what Fonstein's life had been, to write a memoir about this European refugee.

Over the next couple of days we pored over an essay about Nietzsche's idea of the will to power that Saul felt was central to his thoughts about the American half of the story. The "nihilism of stone" that Nietzsche talks about has degenerated, in Saul's formulation, into a "nihilism of sleaze." Now the will to power supposedly releases creative energy. Is the Hollywood of Billy Rose, the Las Vegas of Fonstein's cardplaying son, the chaos of American life the best we are able to come up with by way of new creation? Perhaps the narrator of "The Bellarosa Connection" means to oppose the idea that human life has become an utterly meaningless chaos with memory—which is another way of saying faith.

The spring that had begun with cold and rain was ending in a heat wave. It was pushing 90 degrees on June 13, and as I made for the pond at high noon I found Saul heading the same way, bending the long grasses and parting the wildflowers. When we met before the green water we had the following exchange: "Was it a good morning?" I asked.

"Yes. I started something new."

"What?!"

"I'm loosened up now, I'm just writing something I had it in mind to write."

Stripped of our clothes (yes, Rosie, your parents were young and wild once upon a time), we went for the first swim of the season, Saul leading the way into the deliciously cold water. Then, as we were drying ourselves on the rocks in the blazing sun, Saul asked: "You want to hear some of it?" I don't know what I was expecting. Probably a new beginning for "Bellarosa." But when he opened the composition book he had brought down to the pond, he began to read the first several thousand words of something *completely* new—what would eventually become *Marbles*, a novel he has written and rewritten for close to a decade now, and has never, to this day, completed.

When thinking of Saul at work, I have before my eyes the image of a juggler—luminous airborne balls, each one a different color, turning against an azure sky, kept aloft by the infinite skill of a magician, who is at once relaxed, wry, and concentrating intensely. Hand him a telephone, ask him a practical question about dinner, or invite him on a walk and he's still working those airborne balls. If you were aware of them, and walking behind him on that road, you would see them circling overhead.

—Janis Bellow

INTRODUCTION

1

Every writer is eventually called a "beautiful writer," just as all flowers are eventually called pretty. Any prose above the most ordinary is applauded; and "stylists" are crowned every day, of steadily littler kingdoms. Amidst this busy relativity, it is easy to take for granted the immense stylistic powers of Saul Bellow, who, with Faulkner, is the greatest modern American writer of prose.

But again, many writers are called "great"; the word is everywhere, industrially farmed. In Bellow's case it means greatly abundant, greatly precise, greatly various, rich, and strenuous. It means prose as a registration of the joy of life: the happy rolling freedom of his daring, uninsured sentences. These qualities are present in Bellow's stories as fully as in his novels. Any page from this selection yields a prose of august raciness, ripe with inheritance (the rhythms of Melville and Whitman, Lawrence and Joyce, and behind them, Shakespeare). This prose sometimes cascades in poured adjectives (a river, in "The Old System," seen as "crimped, green, blackish, glassy") and at other times darts with lancing metaphorical wit ("his baldness was total, like a purge"). Controlling these different modes of expression is a firm intelligence, always tending to peal into comic, metaphysical wryness—as in the description of Behrens, the florist, in "Something to Remember Me By": "Amid the flowers, he alone had no color—something like the price he paid for being human."

Bellow is a great portraitist of the human form, Dickens's equal at the swift creation of instant gargoyles; everyone remembers Valentine Gersbach in *Herzog*, with his wooden leg, "bending and straightening gracefully like a gondolier." In these stories, more eagerly chased by form than the novels, Bellow is even more swift and compactly appraising. In "What Kind of Day Did You Have?" we encounter Victor Wulpy, the great art critic and theorist, who is disheveled and "wore his pants negligently": "By the way his entire face expanded when he spoke emphatically you recognized that he was a kind of tyrant in thought"; in "Cousins," Cousin Riva: "I remembered Riva as a full-figured, dark-haired, plump, straight-legged woman. Now all the geometry of her figure had changed. She had come down in the knees like the jack of a car, to a diamond posture"; in "A Silver Dish," Pop, who fights with his son on the ground and then suddenly becomes still: "His eyes stuck out and his mouth was open, sullen. Like a stout fish"; in "Him with His Foot in His Mouth," Professor Kippenberg, a great scholar with bushy eyebrows "like caterpillars from the Tree of Knowledge"; in "Zetland," Max Zetland, with a "black cleft" in his chin, an "unshavable pucker"; and McKern, the drunk brought home by the young narrator of "Something to Remember Me By," and laid out naked on a sofa: "I looked in at McKern, who had thrown down the coat and taken off his drawers. The parboiled face, the short nose pointed sharply, the life signs in the throat, the broken look of his neck, the black hair of his belly, the short cylinder between his legs ending in a spiral of loose skin, the white shine of the shins, the tragic expression of his feet."

What function do these exuberant physical sketches have? First, there is joy, simple joy, to be had from reading the sentences. The description of Professor Kippenberg's bushy eyebrows as resembling caterpillars from the Tree of Knowledge is not just a fine joke; when we laugh, it is with appreciation for a species of wit that is properly called metaphysical. We delight in the curling process of invention whereby seemingly incompatible elements—eyebrows and caterpillars and Eden; or women's hips and car jacks—are combined. Thus, although we feel after reading Bellow that most novelists do not really bother to attend closely enough to people's shapes and dents, his portraiture does not exist merely as realism. We are encouraged not just to see the lifelikeness of Bellow's characters, but to partake in a creative joy, the creator's joy in *making* them look like this. This is not just how people look; they are also sculptures, pressed into by the artist's quizzical and ludic force. In "Mosby's Memoirs," for instance, a few lines describe a Czech pianist performing Schönberg. "This man, with muscular baldness, worked very hard upon the keys." Certainly, we quickly have a vision of this "muscular baldness"; we know what this looks like. But then Bellow adds: "the muscles of his forehead rising in protest against *tabula rasa*—the bare skull," and suddenly we have entered the surreal, the realm of play: how strange and comic, the idea that the muscles of the man's head are somehow rebelling against the bareness, the blankness, the *tabula rasa,* of his bald head!

But of course, Bellow does also make us see the human form, does open our senses and discipline our sensibilities, as Flaubert told Maupassant the writer should: "There is a part of everything which is unexplored," said Flaubert, "because we are accustomed to using our eyes only in association with the memory of what people before us have thought of the thing we are looking at. Even the smallest thing has something in it which is unknown." Bellow exposes this unknown quality, either by force of metaphorical wit (hips like a car jack) or by noticing, with unexpected tenderness of vision, what we have grown accustomed to overlooking: the "white shine" of poor McKern's shins as he lies on the bed, or Pop's bald head, as remembered by his son in "A Silver Dish": "the sweat was sprinkled over his scalp—more drops than hairs."

And seeing is important, lays an injunction on us, in these stories. Many of them are narrated by men who are remembering childhood experiences, or at least younger days, and are using powers of visual recall to conjure forth vivid characters and heroes. Physical detail, exactly rendered, is memory's quarry and makes its own moral case: it is how we bring the dead back to life, give them a second life in our minds. In fact, these memories become, through force of evocation, a first life again and begin to jostle us as the actually living do. In "Cousins," the narrator agrees to intervene in a relative's court case because his family memories exert a pressure over him: "I did it for Cousin Metzger's tic. For the three bands of Neapolitan ice cream. For the furious upright growth of Cousin Shana's ruddy hair, and the avid veins of her temples and in the middle of her forehead. For the strength with which her bare feet advanced as she mopped the floor and spread the pages of the *Tribune* over it."

Bellow's way of seeing his characters also tells us something about his metaphysics. In his fictional world, people do not stream with motives; as novelists go, he is no depth psychologist. Instead, his characters are embodied souls, stretched essences. Their bodies are their confessions, their moral camouflage faulty and peeling: they have the bodies they deserve. Victor Wulpy, a tyrant in thought, has a large, tyrannical head; Max Zetland, a reproving, witholding father, has an unshavable cleft or pucker in his chin, and when he smokes, "he held in the smoke of his cigarettes." It is perhaps for this reason that Bellow is rarely found describing young people; even his middle-aged characters seem old. For in a sense he turns all his characters into old people, since the old helplessly wear their essences on their bodies, they are seniors in moral struggle. Aunt Rose, in "The Old System," has a body almost literally eaten into by history: "She had a large bust, wide hips, and old-fashioned thighs of those corrupted shapes that belong to history."

Like Dickens, and to some extent like Tolstoy and Proust, Bellow sees humans as the embodiments of a single dominating essence or law of being, and makes repeated reference to his characters' essences, in a method of leitmotif. As, in *Anna Karenina*, Stiva Oblonsky always has a smile, and Anna a light step, and Levin a heavy tread, each attribute the accompaniment of a particular temperament, so Max Zetland has his reproving pucker, and Sorella, in "The

Bellarosa Connection," her forceful obesity, and so on. In *Seize the Day*, probably the finest of Bellow's shorter works, Tommy Wilhelm sees the great crowds walking in New York and seems to see "in every face the refinement of one particular motive or essence—*I labor, I spend, I strive, I design, I love, I cling, I uphold, I give way, I envy, I long, I scorn, I die, I hide, I want.*"

Bellow has written that when we read "the best nineteenth and twentieth-century novelists, we soon realize that they are trying in a variety of ways to establish a definition of human nature," and his own work, his own way of seeing essential human types, may be added to that grand project.

2

Bellow's stories seem to divide into two kinds: long, loose-edged stories, which read as if they began life as novels (such as "Cousins"), and short, almost classical tales, which often recount the events of a single day ("Something to Remember Me By," "A Silver Dish," "Looking for Mr. Green"). Yet in both types of story the same kind of narrative prose is at work, one that tends toward the recollection of distant events and tends also toward a version of stream of consciousness. Here, the unnamed narrator of "Zetland" recalls Max Zetland, his friend's father:

> Max Zetland was a muscular man who weighed two hundred pounds, but these were only scenes—not dangerous. As usual, the morning after, he stood at the bathroom mirror and shaved with his painstaking brass Gillette, made neat his reprehending face, flattened his hair like an American executive, with military brushes. Then, Russian style, he drank his tea through a sugar cube, glancing at the *Tribune*, and went off to his position in the Loop, more of less *in Ordnung*. A normal day. Descending the back stairs, a short cut to the El, he looked through the window of the first floor at his Orthodox parents in the kitchen. Grandfather sprayed his bearded mouth with an atomizer—he had asthma. Grandmother made orange-peel candy. Peels dried all winter on the steam radiators. The candy was kept in shoeboxes and served with tea.
>
> Sitting in the El, Max Zetland wet his finger on his tongue to turn the pages of the thick newspaper . . . Tin pagoda roofs covered the El platforms. Each riser of the long staircase advertised Lydia Pinkham's Vegetable Compound. Iron loss made young girls pale. Max Zetland himself had a white face, white-jowled, a sarcastic bear, but acceptably pleasant, entering the merchandising palace on Wabash Avenue . . .

The narrator, who is not related to Max Zetland, is writing about Max Zetland as if he himself had been there, as if he were recalling the daily scene, and he is using a style of writing that Joyce perfected in *Ulysses*—a jumble of different recollected details, a life-sown prose logging impressions with broken speed, in which the perspective keeps on expanding and contracting, as memory does: at one moment, we see Grandfather caught in a moment of dynamism, spraying his bearded mouth with an atomizer, and then in the next we hear that Grandmother made candy from orange peel and that this peel spent all winter drying on the radiators. At one moment we see the advertisements for Lydia Pinkham's Vegetable Compound, the next we see Max entering his workplace. The prose moves between different temporalities, between the immediate and the traditional, the shortlived and the longlived. The narrator of "Something to Remember Me By" writes that at home, inside the house, they lived by "an archaic rule; outside, the facts of life." Bellow's prose moves in similar ways, between the "archaic" or traditional, and the immediate, dynamic "facts of life."

Detail feels modern in Bellow because it is so often the remembered *impression* of a detail, filtered through a consciousness; and yet his details still have an unmodern solidity. At the risk of sounding apocalyptic, one might say that Bellow reprieved realism for a generation, the generation that came after the Second World War, that he held its neck back from the blade of the postmodern; and he did this by revivifying traditional realism with modernist techniques. His prose is densely "realistic," yet it is hard to find in it any of the usual conventions of realism or even of storytelling. His people do not walk out of the house and into other houses—they are, as it were, tipped from one recalled scene to another—and his characters do not have obviously "dramatic" conversations. It is almost impossible to find in these stories sentences along the lines of "He put down his drink and left the room." These are at once traditional and very untraditional stories, both "archaic" and radical.

Curiously enough, the stream of consciousness, for all its reputation as the great accelerator of description, actually slows down realism, asks it to dawdle over tiny remembrances, tiny details and lusters, to circle and return. The stream of consciousness is properly the ally of the short story, of the anecdote, the fragment—and it is no surprise that the short story and the stream of consciousness appear in strength in literature at about the same time, toward the end of the nineteenth century: in Hamsun and in Chekhov, and a little later in Bely and Babel.

3

"At home, inside the house, an archaic rule; outside, the facts of life." This is the axis on which many of these stories run, both at the level of the shifting prose and at the larger level of meaning. For most of the heroes and narrators of these stories, Chicago, where "the facts of life" reign, exists as both torment and spur. Chicago is American, modern; but life at home, as for Max Zetland, is traditional, "archaic," respectably Jewish, with memories and habits of Russian life. (Bellow was nearly born in Russia, of course; his father came from there to Lachine, Quebec, in 1913, and Bellow was born in June 1915.) In these tales, Bellow returns again and again to the city of his childhood, massive, industrial, peopled, where the El "ran like the bridge of the elect over the damnation of the slums," a city both brutal and poetic, "blue with winter, brown with evening, crystal with frost." Chicago, this agglomeration of human fantasies—the protagonist of "Looking for Mr. Green" realizes that the city represents a collective agreement of will—must be reckoned with and recorded as exactly and lyrically as the humans who throng these characters' memories. But Chicago is also a realm of confusion and vulgarity, a place inimical to the life of the mind and the proper expansion of the imagination. The narrator of "Zetland" remembers that he and young Zetland (Max's son) would read Keats to each other while rowing on the city lagoon: "Books in Chicago were obtainable. The public library in the twenties had many storefront branches along the car lines. Summers, under flipping gutta-percha fan blades, boys and girls read in the hard chairs. Crimson trolley cars swayed, cowbellied, on the rails. The country went broke in 1929. On the public lagoon, rowing, we read Keats to each other while the weeds bound the oars."

"While the reeds bound the oars"—Chicago always threatens to entangle the Bellovian character, as also does his family, to stifle him. In these stories, Bellow's characters are repeatedly tempted by visions of escape—sometimes mystical, sometimes religious, and often Platonic (Platonic in the sense that the real world, the Chicago world, is felt to be not the real world but only a place where the soul is in exile, a place of mere appearances). Woody, in "A Silver Dish" is suffused with the "secret certainty that the goal set for this earth was that it should be filled with good, saturated with it," and sits and listens religiously to all the Chicago bells ringing on Sunday. Yet the story he recalls is a tale of shameful theft and trickery, an utterly secular story. The narrator of "Him with His Foot in His Mouth," is attracted by the visions of Swedenborg, and to the idea that "the Divine Spirit" has "withdrawn in our time from the outer, visible world." Yet his tale is couched as a letter of apology and confession to a peaceful woman he once cruelly insulted. The narrator of "Cousins" admits that he has "never given up the habit of referring all truly important observations to that original self or soul" (referring here to the Platonic idea that man has an original soul from which he has been exiled, and back to which he must again find a path). But again, the spur of his revelations is completely secular—a shameful court case involving a crooked cousin.

Bellow's argument, if that word is not too bullying, would seem to be that a purely religious or intellectual vision—a theoretical intelligence—is weightless, even dangerous, without the human data provided both by a city like Chicago and by the ordinary strategies and culpabilities of families and friends. Zetland, who, we are told, has "no interest in surface phenomena," abandons the pure thought of analytic logic after moving to New York and reading Melville. Victor Wulpy may be a great art critic, but he cannot tell Katrina, his lover, that he loves her, even though it is what she most earnestly longs to hear. It falls to a charlatan and producer of science fiction films, Larry Wrangel, correctly to remark on the painful limits of Victor's all-knowing mind.

Bellow's characters all yearn to make something of their lives in the religious sense, and yet this yearning is not written up religiously or solemnly. It is written up comically: our metaphysical cloudiness, and our fierce, clumsy attempts to make these clouds yield rain, are full of hilarious pathos in his work. In this regard, Bellow is perhaps most tenderly suggestive in his lovely late story "Something to Remember Me By." The narrator, now old, recalls a single day from his adolescence, in Depression-dug Chicago. He was, he recalls, a kid dreamy with religious and mystical ideas of a distinctly Platonic nature: "Where, then, is the world from which the human form comes?" he asks rhetorically. On his job delivering flowers in the city, he always used to take one of his philosophical or mystical texts with him. On the day under remembrance, he becomes the victim of a cruel prank. A woman lures him into her bedroom, encourages him to remove his clothes, throws them out of the window, and then flees. The clothes disappear, and it is his task then to get home, an hour away across freezing Chicago, to the house where his mother is dying and his stern father waits for him, with "blind Old Testament rage"—"at home, inside the house, an archaic rule; outside, the facts of life."

The boy is clothed by the local barman and earns his fare home by agreeing to take one of the bar's regulars, a drunk called McKern, to McKern's apartment. Once there, the boy lays out the drunk and then cooks supper for McKern's two motherless young daughters—he cooks pork cutlets, the fat splattering his hands and filling the little apartment with pork smoke. "All that my upbringing held in horror geysered up, my throat filling with it, my guts griping," he tells us. But he does it. Eventually, the boy finds his own way home, where his father, as expected, beats him. Along with his clothes, he has lost his treasured book, which was also thrown out of the window. But, he reflects, he will buy the book again, with money stolen from his mother. "I knew where my mother secretly hid her savings. Because I looked into all books, I had found the money in her *mahzor,* the prayer book for the High Holidays, the days of awe."

There are coiled ironies here. Forced by the horridly secular confusions of his day ("the facts of life," indeed) to steal, the boy will take this money to buy more mystical and unsecular books, books that will no doubt religiously or philosophically instruct him that this life, the life he is leading, is not the real life! And why does the boy even know about his mother's hiding place? Because he looks "into all books." His bookishness, his unworldliness, are the reasons that he knows how to perform the worldly business of stealing! And where does he steal this money from? From a sacred text ("the archaic rule," indeed). So then, the reader thinks, who is to say that *this* life, the life our narrator has been so vividly telling us about, with all its embarrassments and Chicago vulgarities, is not real? Not only real, but also religious in its way—for the day he has just painfully lived has also been a kind of day of awe, in which he has learned much—a secular High Holiday, complete with the sacrificial burning of goyish pork.

It might be said that all of these beautiful stories throw out at us, in burning centrifuge, the secular-religious questions: What are our days of awe? And how shall we know them?

—James Wood

CONTENTS

BY THE ST. LAWRENCE

NOT *THE* ROB REXLER?

Yes, Rexler, the man who wrote all those books on theater and cinema in Weimar Germany, the author of *Postwar Berlin* and of the controversial study of Bertolt Brecht. Quite an old man now and, it turns out, though you wouldn't have guessed it from his work, physically handicapped—not disabled, only slightly crippled in adolescence by infantile paralysis. You picture a tall man when you read him, and his actual short, stooped figure is something of a surprise. You don't expect the author of those swift sentences to have an abrupt neck, a long jaw, and a knot-back. But these are minor items, and in conversation with him you quickly forget his disabilities.

Because New York has been his base for half a century, it is assumed that he comes from the East Side or Brooklyn. In fact he is a Canadian, born in Lachine, Quebec, an unlikely birthplace for a historian who has written so much about cosmopolitan Berlin, about nihilism, decadence, Marxism, national socialism, and who described the trenches of World War I as "man sandwiches" served up by the leaders of the great powers.

Yes, he was born in Lachine to parents from Kiev. His childhood was divided between Lachine and Montreal. And just now, after a near-fatal illness, he had had a curious desire or need to see Lachine again. For this reason he accepted a lecture invitation from McGill University despite his waning interest in (and a growing dislike for) Bertolt Brecht. Tired of Brecht and his Marxism—his Stalinism—he stuck with him somehow. He might have canceled the trip. He was still convalescent and weak. He had written to his McGill contact, "I've been playing hopscotch at death's door, and since I travel alone I have to arrange for wheelchairs between the ticket counter and the gate. Can I count on being met at Dorval?"

He counted also on a driver to take him to Lachine. He asked him to park the Mercedes limo in front of his birthplace. The street was empty. The low brick house was the only one left standing. All the buildings for blocks around had been torn down. He told the driver, "I'm going to walk down to the river. Can you wait for about an hour?" He anticipated correctly that his legs would soon tire and that the empty streets would be cold, too. Late October was almost wintry in these parts. Rexler was wearing his dark-green cloaklike Salzburg loden coat.

There was nothing familiar to see at first, you met no people here. You were surprised by the bigness and speed of the St. Lawrence. As a kid you were hemmed in by the dinky streets. The river now had opened up, and the sky also, with long static autumn clouds. The rapids were white, the water reeling over the rocks. The old Hudson's Bay Trading Post was now a community center. Opposite, in gloomy frames of moss and grime, there stood a narrow provincial stone church. And hadn't there been a convent nearby? He did not look for it. Downriver he made out Caughnawaga, the Indian reservation, on the far shore. According to Parkman, a large party of Caughnawaga Mohawks, crossing hundreds of miles on snowshoes, had surprised and massacred the settlers of Deerfield, Massachusetts, during the French-Indian wars. Weren't those Indians Mohawks? He couldn't remember. He believed that they were one of the Iroquois nations. For that matter he couldn't say whether his birthplace was on Seventh Avenue or on Eighth. So many landmarks were gone. The tiny synagogue had become a furniture warehouse. There were neither women nor children in the streets. Immigrant laborers from the Dominion Bridge Company once had lived in the cramped houses. From the narrow front yard (land must have been dear), where Rexler's mother more than seventy years ago had set him cross-strapped in his shawl to dig snow with the black stove shovel, you could see the wide river surface—it had been there all the while, beyond the bakeries and sausage shops, kitchens and bedrooms.

Beside the Lachine Canal, where the "kept" water of the locks was still and green, various reasons for Rexler's return began to take shape. When asked how he was doing—and it was only two months ago that the doctors had written him off; the specialist had told him, "Your lungs were whited out. I wouldn't have given two cents for your life"—Rexler answered, "I have no stamina. I put out some energy and then I can't bend down to tie my shoelaces."

Why then did he take this trying trip? Was it sentimentality, was it nostalgia? Did he want to recall how his mother, mute with love, had bundled him in woolens and set him down in the snow with a small shovel? No, Rexler wasn't at all like that. He was a tough-minded man. It was toughness that had drawn him decades ago to Bert Brecht. Nostalgia, subjectivism, inwardness—all that was in the self-indulgence doghouse now. But he was making no progress toward an answer. At his age the reprieve from death could be nothing but short. It was noteworthy that the brick and stucco that had walled in the Ukrainian-, Sicilian-, and French-Canadian Dominion Bridge Company laborers also cut them off from the St. Lawrence in its platinum rush toward the North Atlantic. To have looked at their bungalows again wouldn't have been worth the fatiguing trip, the wear and tear of airports, the minor calvary of visiting-lecturer chitchat.

Anyway, he saw death as a magnetic field that every living thing must enter. He was ready for it. He had even thought that since he had been unconscious under the respirator for an entire month, he might just as well have died in the hospital and avoided further trouble. Yet here he was in his *birthplace.* Intensive-care nurses had told him that the electronic screens monitoring his heart had run out of graphs, squiggles, and symbols at last and, foundering, flashed out nothing but question marks. That would have been the way to go, with all the machines confounded, from unconsciousness to nonconsciousness. But it wasn't over yet, and now this valetudinarian native son stood in Monkey Park beside the locks shadowed with the autumn green of the banked earth and asked himself whether all this was a justified expense of his limited energy.

> *The cook, she's nam' was Rosie*
> *She cam' from Mo'real*
> *And was chambermaid on a lumber barge*
> *In the Grand Lachine Canal.*

Rexler had more than once thought of opening an office to help baffled people who could remember only one stanza of a ballad or song. For a twenty-five-dollar fee you would provide the full text.

He remembered that when a barge was in the locks, the Lachinois, loafing unemployed or killing time, would chat or joke with the crew. He had been there himself, waving and grinning at the wisecracks. His boy's body was clean then. As such things are reckoned he had still been normal during his final childhood holiday in Lachine. Toward the end of that summer he came down with polio and his frame was contorted into a monkey puzzle. Next, adolescence turned him into a cripple gymnast whose skeleton was the apparatus he worked out on like an acrobat in training. This was how reality punished you for your innocence. It turned you into a crustacean. But in his early years, until the end of the twenties, his body was still well formed and smooth. Then his head grew heavy, his jawline lengthened, his sideburns were thick pillars. But he had taken pains to train himself away from abnormality, from the outlook and the habits of a cripple. His long eyes were mild. He walked with a virile descending limp, his weight coming down on the advancing left foot. "Not personally responsible for the way life operates" was what he tacitly declared.

This, more or less, was Rexler, the last of the tribe that had buzzed across the Atlantic early in the century and found limited space in streets that shut out the river. They lived among the French, the Indians, the Sicilians, and the Ukrainians.

His aunt Rozzy, who was fond of him, often rescued him in July from the St. Dominick Street slum in Montreal. His older cousins in Lachine, already adults, all with witty strong faces, seemed to like his company. "Take the boy with you," Aunt Rozzy would say when she dispatched them on errands.

He tooted all over Lachine with them in their cars and trucks.

These were solid detailed recollections, nothing dreamlike about them. Rexler knew therefore that he must have come back to them repeatedly over many years. Again and again the cousins, fully mature at twenty, or even at sixteen. The eldest, Cousin Ezra, was an insurance adjuster. Next in age was Albert, a McGill law student. And then Matty, less tough than his big brothers. The youngest was Reba. She had the odor stout girls often have, Rexler used to think—a distinctive sexy scent. They were all, for that matter, sexy people. Except, of course, the parents. But Ezra and Albert, even Matty, varied their business calls with visits to girls. They joked with them in doorways. Sometimes with a Vadja, sometimes a Nadine. Ezra, who was so stern about business, buying and trading building lots—the insurance was a sideline—would laugh after he had cranked his Ford and say as he jumped into the seat, "How did you like that one, Robbie?" And, playful, he surprised Rexler by gripping his thigh. Ezra had a leathery pleasant face. His complexion, like his father's, was dark and he had vertical furrows under each ear; an old country doctor had cured him surgically of swellings caused by milk from a tubercular cow. But even the scars were pleasant to see. Ezra had an abrupt way of clearing his nose by snorting. He trod the pedals of the Ford. His breath was virile—a little salty or perhaps sour. Over Rexler he had great seniority—more an uncle than a cousin. And when Ezra was silent, having business thoughts, all laughing was shut down. He brought his white teeth together and a sort of gravity came over him. No Yiddish jokes then, or Hebrew with double meanings. He was a determined man out to make good. At his death he left an estate in the millions.

Rexler had never visited his grave or the graves of the others. They all lay together somewhere on a mountainside—Westmount, would that be, or Outremont? Ezra and Albert quarreled when Reba died. Ezra had been away and Albert buried her in a remote cemetery. "I want my dead together." Ezra was angry at what he saw as disrespect to the parents. Rexler, recalling this, made a movement of his crippled back, shrugging off the piety. It was not his cup of tea. But then why did he recall it so particularly?

On a June day he had gone in the car with Albert across the Grand Trunk tracks where the parents owned rental property. They had been here no more than fifteen years and they didn't know twenty words of the language, yet they were buying property. Only the immediate family were in on this. They were secretive. At Rexler's age—seven or eight years old—he wouldn't have understood. But when he was present they were guarded nevertheless. As a result, he did come to understand. Such a challenge was sure to provoke him.

Cousin Albert put you off with his shrewd look of amusement. For women he had a lewd eye. And at McGill he had picked up a British manner. He said "By Jove." He also said "Topping." Joe Cohen, an MP in Ottawa, had chosen Albert to be a student clerk. Clerking for Joe Cohen, he was made. In time he would become a partner in Cohen's firm. He'll stop saying "By Jove," and say instead "What's the deal?" was Cousin Ezra's true prophecy. But Ezra had airs of his own. The look of the firstborn, for example. A few thousand years of archaic gravity would settle on him. The advantage of being in remote Lachine was that he could freely improvise from the Old Testament.

Anyway, Rexler was in the family's second Ford with Albert on the far side of the tracks, over toward Dorval, and Albert parked in front of a large bungalow. It had a spacious white porch, round pillars, and a swing hanging on chains.

"I have to go in," said Albert. "I'll be a while."

"Long?"

"As long as it takes."

"Can I go out and walk back and forth?"

"I'd like you to stay in the auto."

He went in, Rexler remembered, and the wait was interminable. The sun came through the June leaves. Dark periwinkle grew in all the shady places and young women came and went on the broad porch. They walked arm in arm or sat together on the swing or in white wooden Adirondack chairs. Rexler moved into the driver's seat and played with the wheel and the choke—or was it the spark lever? Crouching, he worked the pedals with his hands. A cloven hoof would be a good fit on the ovals of the clutch and brake.

Then it became tiresome to wait.

Then Rexler was fretful.

He might have been alone for as long as an hour.

Did he, Rexler now wondered, have any idea as to what was keeping Albert? He may have had. All those young women passing through the screen door, promenading, swinging between the creaking chains.

Without haste Albert stepped between the green plots to the Ford. Smiling, a pretense of regret in his look, he said, "There was more business to do than usual." He mentioned a lease. Baloney, of course. It wasn't what he said but how he spoke that mattered. He had a lippy sort of look and somehow, to Rexler, his mouth had become an index: lippy, but the eyes were at variance with the lower face. Those eyes reflected the will of an upper power center. This was Rexler's early manner of observation. His eagerness, his keenness for this had weakened with time and, in his seventies, he did not care about Albert's cunning, his brothels, his secret war against his brother Ezra.

At the first candy store Albert parked the Ford and gave Rexler a copper two-cent piece—a helmeted woman with a trident and shield. With this coin Rexler bought two porous squares of blond molasses candy. He understood that he was being bribed, though he couldn't have explained exactly why. He would not in any case have said a word to Aunt Rozzy about the house with all the girls. Such outside street things never were reported at home. He chewed the candy to a fine dust while Albert entered a cottage to make the rent collection for his mother. Not a thing a university man liked doing. Although where money came from didn't much matter.

Albert was in a better humor when he came out and gave little Rexler a joyride through the pastures and truck gardens, turning back just short of Dorval. Returning, they saw a small crowd at the level crossing of the Grand Trunk. There had been an accident. A man had been killed by a fast train. The tracks had not yet been cleared and for the moment a line of cars was held up and Rexler, standing on the running board of the Model T, was able to see—not the corpse, but his organs on the roadbed—first the man's liver, shining on the white, egg-shaped stones, and a little beyond it his lungs. More than anything, it was the lungs—Rexler couldn't get over the twin lungs crushed out of the man by the train when it tore his body open. Their color was pink and they looked inflated still. Strange that there should be no blood, as if the speed of the train had scattered it.

Albert didn't have the curiosity to find out who the dead man was. He must not have wanted to ask. The Ford had stopped running and he set the spark and jumped down to crank it again. When the engine caught, the fender shuddered and then the file of cars crept over the planks. The train was gone—nothing but an empty track to the west.

"So, where did you get lost such a long time?" said Aunt Rozzy.

Albert said, "A man was killed at the Grand Trunk crossing."

That was answer enough.

Rexler was sent down to the garden in the yard to pick tomatoes. Even more than the fruit itself, the vines and leaves carried the strong tomato odor. You could smell it on your fingers. Uncle Mikhel had staked the plants and bound them with strips of cloth torn from old petticoats and undershirts. Though his hands were palsied, Uncle Mikhel could weed and tie knots. His head, too, made involuntary movements but his eyes looked at you steadily, wide open. His face was tightly held by the close black beard. He said almost nothing. You heard the crisping of his beard against the collar oftener than his voice. He stared, you expected him to say something; instead he went on staring with an involuntary wag of the head. The children had a great respect for him. Rexler remembered him with affection. Each of his olive-brown eyes had a golden flake on it like the scale of a smoked fish. If his head went back and forth it was not because he was denying anything, he was warding off a tremor.

"Why doesn't the boy eat?" Aunt Rozzy said to Albert at dinner. "Did he let you stuff yourself with candy?"

"Why aren't you eating your soup, Robbie?" Albert asked. His smile was narrow. Albert was not at all afraid that he, Rexler, would mention the girls on the porch swing or his long wait in the car. And even if something were to slip out, it would be no more than his mother already suspected.

"I'm just not hungry."

Shrewd Albert smiled even more narrowly at the boy, bearing down on him. "I think it was the accident that took away his appetite. A man was killed on the tracks as we were coming home."

"God in heaven," said Aunt Rozzy.

"He burst open," said Albert. "We came to a stop and there were his insides—heart, liver. . . ."

His lungs! The lungs reminded Rexler of the water wings used by children learning to swim.

"Who was the man?"

"A drunkard," said Aunt Rozzy.

Uncle Mikhel interrupted. "He may have been a railway worker."

Out of respect for the old man no more was said, for Uncle Mikhel was once a CPR laborer. He had been a conscript on the eastern front during the Russian war with Japan. He deserted, reached western Canada somehow, and for years was employed by the railroad, laying tracks. He saved his *groschen,* as he liked to say, and sent for his family. And now, surrounded by grown sons, he was a patriarch at his own table in his own huge kitchen with large oil paintings out of the junk shop hanging on the walls. There were baskets of fruit, sheep in the fold, and Queen Victoria with her chin resting on her wrist.

Cousin Albert had turned things around with sparkling success and seemed to be saying to little Rexler, "See how it's done?"

But Rexler was transfixed by the chicken soup. As a treat, Aunt Rozzy had served him the gizzard. It had been opened by her knife so that it showed two dense wings ridged with lines of muscle, brown and gray at the bottom of the dish. He had often watched the hens upside down, hanging by trussed feet, first fluttering, then more gently quivering as they bled to death. The legs too went into the soup.

Aunt Rozzy, his father's sister, had the family face but her look was more sharp and severe by far. There was nothing so red as her nose in zero weather. She had cruelly thick legs and her hindquarters were wildly overdeveloped, so that walking must have been a torment. She certainly did not put herself out to be loved, for she was wicked to everyone. Except, perhaps, little Rexler.

"Did you see what happened? What did you see?"

"The man's heart."

"What else?"

"His liver, and the lungs."

Those spongy soft swelled ovals patched pink and red.

"And the body?" she said to Albert.

"Maybe dragged by the train," he said, unsmiling this time.

Aunt Rozzy lowered her voice and said something about the dead. She was fanatically Orthodox. Then she told Rexler that he didn't have to eat his dinner. She was not a lovable woman, but the boy loved her and she was aware of it. He loved them all. He even loved Albert. When he visited Lachine he shared Albert's bed, and in the morning he would sometimes stroke Albert's head, and not even when Albert fiercely threw off his hand did he stop loving him. The hair grew in close rows, row after row.

These observations, Rexler was to learn, were his whole life—his being—and love was what produced them. For each physical trait there was a corresponding feeling. Paired, pair by pair, they walked back and forth, in and out of his soul.

Aunt Rozzy had the face, the fiery face of a hanging judge, and she was determined to fix the blame for the accident on the victim. The dead man himself. And Rexler, walking in Monkey Park and beginning to feel the strain of his excursion, the weakness of his legs, sat down with the experienced delicacy of a cripple on the first bench he came to.

Cousin Reba, always ready to disagree with her mother, said, "We can't assume he was drunk. He may have been absentminded." But Aunt Rozzy with an even more flaming face seemed to believe that if he was innocent his death was all the more deserved. She sounded like Bertolt Brecht when he justified the murder of Bukharin. The one thing to be proud of, according to the playwright, the only true foundation of self-respect, was not to be taken in by illusions and sentiments. The only items in the book of rules were dead items. If you didn't close the book, if you still harked back to the rules, you deserved to die.

How deep can the life of a modern man be? Very deep, if he is hard enough to see innocence as a fault, if, as Brecht held, he wipes out the oughts which the gullible still buy and expels pity from politics.

The destruction of the dwarf brick houses opened the view of the river, as huge as a plain, but swift nevertheless, and this restoration of things as they had been when first seen by explorers opened Rexler himself to an unusual degree, so that he began to consider how desirable it could be to settle nearby so that he might see it every day—to buy or rent, to have a view of the rapids and the steely speed . . . why not? He was a native son, and he had no present attachments in New York. But he knew this was an impracticable fancy. He could not (for how long?) spend his final years with no more company than the river. Since giving up his Brecht studies, he had no occupation. Brecht was light on the subject of death. If he was to live with Stalinism this lightness was essential. Hence the joys of the knife, as in "Mackie Messer," so many years on the hit parade. All that pre-Hitler Weimar stuff. It was Stalin, whom Brecht had backed, who should have won in 1932. But Rexler did not intend to go public with such views. He was too ill, too old to make enemies. If he turned polemical the intelligentsia would be sure to say that he was a bitter aging hunchback. No, for him it was private life from now on.

He didn't want to think about the books and articles that had made his Lachine cousins so proud of him. "Just look how Robbie overcame the polio and made something of himself," Cousin Ezra would tell his growing children.

Nobody could say exactly how extensive Cousin Ezra's real-estate holdings were.

But toward the end, dying of leukemia, Ezra greeted Rexler by throwing his arms wide. He sat up in his hospital bed and exclaimed, "A *maloch* has walked into my room." His color was his father's exactly—very dark and with pleasant folds, and he had become the Old Testament patriarch through and through—an Abraham bargaining with the Lord God to spare Sodom and Gomorrah or buying the cave of Machpelah to bury his wife.

"Angel," Ezra said with delicacy because of the mound on Rexler's back: not exactly a pair of folded wings. The truth at that time was that Rexler looked like one of the cast of a Brecht–Kurt Weill production: hands sunk in his trousers' pockets and his skeptical head—it was too heavy, it listed—needing cleverly poised feet to support it. His hair was gray, something like the color of drying oregano. What did his dying cousin make of him, of his reputation as a scholar and a figure in New York theatrical circles? Rexler had gone against the mainstream in the arts, and his radical side was the side that had won.

All those years of error, as it now seemed to Rexler. Hands clasped behind his back he tramped, limped, along the Lachine Canal, thinking that his dying cousin Ezra gave him high marks for his struggle against paralysis.

Here in Lachine, Rexler had had a second family. After Uncle Mikhel and Aunt Rozzy died and Ezra had assumed the role of patriarch, Albert had refused to acknowledge him as such. "*I* recognized, *I* was willing." In this matter Rexler saw that he had relied on the mainstream. It was an inconsistency.

Strictly speaking, the child with normal spine and arms and legs was transformed into the deformed man in the loden coat, the theatrical hat pulled down over the thick sideburns.

It had been better on balance to be a revolutionary than a cripple.

"Have I ever told you, Robbie, that we are descended from the tribe of Naphtali?" said Ezra.

"How do we know that?"

"Oh, these things are known. It was passed on to me and I pass it on to you."

In a month's time Ezra was dead. Years ago he had exhumed Reba's body and she was buried beside her parents. They were all to be together. Twenty years later Matty joined them. Only Albert remained. At eighty he was still an *homme à femmes*. But they wouldn't stay put when they found out what was expected of them. Now he was no longer a seducer, he was a petitioner or suppliant. The meanness, however, hadn't gone out of him. Only he was weakened, he couldn't enforce anything, and he played humble. The last of his wives had left him within a year. Back to Baltimore.

Albert sent for Rexler. He was by now the last of the Rexlers. "Only the two of us left," said Albert. "I'm so glad you came. The family doted on you."

"When I got polio my childish charm was shot down."

"Of course it was very hard. But you fought back. You became a distinguished man. I used to give copies of your books to my literate clients."

Evidence of wasted years, Rexler thought, if anyone wished to make a case against him. However, you don't waste the time of a dying man with disclosures, confessions, repudiations. "One day I went with you in the Model T," said Rexler, "and you parked in front of a clapboard house across the tracks. Then you went in. Was that a whorehouse?"

"Why do you ask?"

"Because you were there for such a long time and I played with the pedals and the steering wheel."

Albert smiled forgivingly. It was himself that he forgave. "There were a couple of houses."

"On this one there was a veranda."

"I wouldn't have paid much attention. . . ."

"And on the way home there was an accident on the Grand Trunk tracks. A man was killed."

"Was he?"

Albert had no memory of it.

"Minutes before we crossed. His liver was in the roadbed."

"The things kids will remember."

Rexler was about to describe his surprise at seeing a man's organs on the ties and stones on the roadbed but he caught himself in time luckily. Albert's skin cancer had metastasized and he hadn't far to go. His still-shrewd eyes communicated this to Rexler, who backed off, thinking that for Albert that afternoon, when he and the girl had lain chest to chest, his heart and lungs pressing upon hers, had added up to a different sum. Rexler had come to say good-bye to his cousin, whom he wouldn't be seeing again. Albert was wasted; his legs forked under the covers like winter branches, and his courtroom voice was as dim as a child's toy xylophone. He sent for me, Rexler reminded himself, not to talk about my memories, and I think I look alien to him, that seeing me is a disappointment.

In the upside-down intravenous flask a pellucid drop was about to pass into his spoiled blood. If other things could be as clear as that fluid. Probably Albert had asked one of his daughters to telephone me because he remembered how things once were. The uncritical affectionate child. He hoped I might bring back something. But all he got from me was a cripple at his bedside. Yet Rexler had tried to offer him something. Let's see if we can ratchet up some of that old-time feeling. Perhaps Albert *had* got something out of it. But Albert had taken no conscious notice of the man hit by the train. There never was a conversation about that and now Albert too was buried with the rest of the family—"my dead," as Ezra spoke of them. Rexler, who didn't even know where the cemetery was and would never go to visit it, walked lopsided in the sunny grass of Monkey Park beside the canal locks. Deep-voiced, either humming or groaning, he turned his mind again to the lungs in the roadbed as pink as a rubber eraser and the other organs, the baldness of them, the foolish oddity of the shapes, almost clownish, almost a denial or a refutation of the high-ranking desires and subtleties. How finite they looked.

His deformity, the shelf of his back and the curved bracket of his left shoulder, gave added protection to his hoarded organs. A contorted coop or bony armor must have been formed by his will on the hint given that afternoon at the scene of the accident. Don't tell me, Rexler thought, that everything depends on these random-looking parts—and that to preserve them I was turned into some kind of human bivalve?

The Mercedes limo had come to the canal for him and he got in, turning his thoughts to the afternoon lecture he didn't particularly want to give.

A SILVER DISH

WHAT DO YOU DO about death—in this case, the death of an old father? If you're a modern person, sixty years of age, and a man who's been around, like Woody Selbst, what do you do? Take this matter of mourning, and take it against a contemporary background. How, against a contemporary background, do you mourn an octogenarian father, nearly blind, his heart enlarged, his lungs filling with fluid, who creeps, stumbles, gives off the odors, the moldiness or gassiness, of old men. I *mean!* As Woody put it, be realistic. Think what times these are. The papers daily give it to you—the Lufthansa pilot in Aden is described by the hostages as being on his knees, begging the Palestinian terrorists not to execute him, but they shoot him through the head. Later they themselves are killed. And still others shoot others, or shoot themselves. That's what you read in the press, see on the tube, mention at dinner. We know now what goes daily through the whole of the human community, like a global death-peristalsis.

Woody, a businessman in South Chicago, was not an ignorant person. He knew more such phrases than you would expect a tile contractor (offices, lobbies, lavatories) to know. The kind of knowledge he had was not the kind for which you get academic degrees. Although Woody had studied for two years in a seminary, preparing to be a minister. Two years of college during the Depression was more than most high school graduates could afford. After that, in his own vital, picturesque, original way (Morris, his old man, was also, in his days of nature, vital and picturesque), Woody had read up on many subjects, subscribed to *Science* and other magazines that gave real information, and had taken night courses at De Paul and Northwestern in ecology, criminology, existentialism. Also he had traveled extensively in Japan, Mexico, and Africa, and there was an African experience that was especially relevant to mourning. It was this: on a launch near the Murchison Falls in Uganda, he had seen a buffalo calf seized by a crocodile from the bank of the White Nile. There were giraffes along the tropical river, and hippopotamuses, and baboons, and flamingos and other brilliant birds crossing the bright air in the heat of the morning, when the calf, stepping into the river to drink, was grabbed by the hoof and dragged down. The parent buffaloes couldn't figure it out. Under the water the calf still thrashed, fought, churned the mud. Woody, the robust traveler, took this in as he sailed by, and to him it looked as if the parent cattle were asking each other dumbly what had happened. He chose to assume that there was pain in this, he read brute grief into it. On the White Nile, Woody had the impression that he had gone back to the pre-Adamite past, and he brought home to South Chicago his reflections. He brought also a bundle of hashish from Kampala. In this he took a chance with the customs inspectors, banking perhaps on his broad build, frank face, high color. He didn't look like a wrongdoer, a bad guy; he looked like a good guy. But he liked taking chances. Risk was a wonderful stimulus. He threw down his trench coat on the customs counter. If the inspectors searched the pockets, he was prepared to say that the coat wasn't his. But he got away with it, and the Thanksgiving turkey was stuffed with hashish. This was much enjoyed. That was practically the last feast at which Pop, who also relished risk or defiance, was present. The hashish Woody had tried to raise in his backyard from the African seeds didn't take. But behind his warehouse, where the Lincoln Continental was parked, he kept a patch of marijuana. There was no harm at all in Woody, but he didn't like being entirely within the law. It was simply a question of self-respect.

After that Thanksgiving, Pop gradually sank as if he had a slow leak. This went on for some years. In and out of the hospital, he dwindled, his mind wandered, he couldn't even concentrate enough to complain, except in exceptional moments on the Sundays Woody regularly devoted to him. Morris, an amateur who once was taken seriously by Willie Hoppe, the great pro himself, couldn't execute the simplest billiard shots anymore. He could only conceive shots; he began to theorize about impossible three-cushion combinations. Halina, the Polish woman with whom Morris had lived for over forty years, was too old herself now to run to the hospital. So Woody had to do it. There was Woody's mother, too—a Christian convert—needing care; she was over eighty and frequently hospitalized. Everybody had diabetes and pleurisy and arthritis and cataracts and cardiac pacemakers. And everybody had lived by the body, but the body was giving out.

There were Woody's two sisters as well, unmarried, in their fifties, very Christian, very straight, still living with Mama in an entirely Christian bungalow.

Woody, who took full responsibility for them all, occasionally had to put one of the girls (they had become sick girls) in a mental institution. Nothing severe. The sisters were wonderful women, both of them gorgeous once, but neither of the poor things was playing with a full deck. And all the factions had to be kept separate—Mama, the Christian convert; the fundamentalist sisters; Pop, who read the Yiddish paper as long as he could still see print; Halina, a good Catholic. Woody, the seminary forty years behind him, described himself as an agnostic. Pop had no more religion than you could find in the Yiddish paper, but he made Woody promise to bury him among Jews, and that was where he lay now, in the Hawaiian shirt Woody had bought for him at the tilers' convention in Honolulu. Woody would allow no undertaker's assistant to dress him, but came to the parlor and buttoned the stiff into the shirt himself, and the old man went down looking like Ben-Gurion in a simple wooden coffin, sure to rot fast. That was how Woody wanted it all. At the graveside, he had taken off and folded his jacket, rolled up his sleeves on thick freckled biceps, waved back the little tractor standing by, and shoveled the dirt himself. His big face, broad at the bottom, narrowed upward like a Dutch house. And, his small good lower teeth taking hold of the upper lip in his exertion, he performed the final duty of a son. He was very fit, so it must have been emotion, not the shoveling, that made him redden so. After the funeral, he went home with Halina and her son, a decent Pole like his mother, and talented, too—Mitosh played the organ at hockey and basketball games in the Stadium, which took a smart man because it was a rabble-rousing kind of occupation—and they had some drinks and comforted the old girl. Halina was true blue, always one hundred percent for Morris.

Then for the rest of the week Woody was busy, had jobs to run, office responsibilities, family responsibilities. He lived alone; as did his wife; as did his mistress: everybody in a separate establishment. Since his wife, after fifteen years of separation, had not learned to take care of herself, Woody did her shopping on Fridays, filled her freezer. He had to take her this week to buy shoes. Also, Friday night he always spent with Helen—Helen was his wife de facto. Saturday he did his big weekly shopping. Saturday night he devoted to Mom and his sisters. So he was too busy to attend to his own feelings except, intermittently, to note to himself, "First Thursday in the grave." "First Friday, and fine weather." "First Saturday; he's got to be getting used to it." Under his breath he occasionally said, "Oh, Pop."

But it was Sunday that hit him, when the bells rang all over South Chicago—the Ukrainian, Roman Catholic, Greek, Russian, African Methodist churches, sounding off one after another. Woody had his offices in his warehouse, and there had built an apartment for himself, very spacious and convenient, in the top story. Because he left every Sunday morning at seven to spend the day with

Pop, he had forgotten by how many churches Selbst Tile Company was surrounded. He was still in bed when he heard the bells, and all at once he knew how heartbroken he was. This sudden big heartache in a man of sixty, a practical, physical, healthy-minded, and experienced man, was deeply unpleasant. When he had an unpleasant condition, he believed in taking something for it. So he thought: What shall I take? There were plenty of remedies available. His cellar was stocked with cases of Scotch whisky, Polish vodka, Armagnac, Moselle, Burgundy. There were also freezers with steaks and with game and with Alaskan king crab. He bought with a broad hand—by the crate and by the dozen. But in the end, when he got out of bed, he took nothing but a cup of coffee. While the kettle was heating, he put on his Japanese judo-style suit and sat down to reflect.

Woody was moved when things were *honest.* Bearing beams were honest; undisguised concrete pillars inside high-rise apartments were honest. It was bad to cover up anything. He hated faking. Stone was honest. Metal was honest. These Sunday bells were very straight. They broke loose, they wagged and rocked, and the vibrations and the banging did something for him—cleansed his insides, purified his blood. A bell was a one-way throat, had only one thing to tell you and simply told it. He listened.

He had had some connections with bells and churches. He was, after all, something of a Christian. Born a Jew, he was a Jew facially, with a hint of Iroquois or Cherokee, but his mother had been converted more than fifty years ago by her brother-in-law, the Reverend Doctor Kovner. Kovner, a rabbinical student who had left the Hebrew Union College in Cincinnati to become a minister and establish a mission, had given Woody a partly Christian upbringing. Now, Pop was on the outs with these fundamentalists. He said that the Jews came to the mission to get coffee, bacon, canned pineapple, day-old bread, and dairy products. And if they had to listen to sermons, that was okay—this was the Depression and you couldn't be too particular—but he knew they sold the bacon.

The Gospels said it plainly: "Salvation is from the Jews."

Backing the Reverend Doctor were wealthy fundamentalists, mainly Swedes, eager to speed up the Second Coming by converting all Jews. The foremost of Kovner's backers was Mrs. Skoglund, who had inherited a large dairy business from her late husband. Woody was under her special protection.

Woody was fourteen years of age when Pop took off with Halina, who worked in his shop, leaving his difficult Christian wife and his converted son and his small daughters. He came to Woody in the backyard one spring day and said, "From now on you're the man of the house." Woody was practicing with a golf club, knocking off the heads of dandelions. Pop came into the yard in his good suit, which was too hot for the weather, and when he took off his fedora the skin of his head was marked with a deep ring and the sweat was sprinkled over his scalp—more drops than hairs. He said, "I'm going to move out." Pop was anxious, but he was set to go—determined. "It's no use. I can't live a life like this." Envisioning the life Pop simply *had* to live, his free life, Woody was able to picture him in the billiard parlor, under the El tracks in a crap game, or playing poker at Brown and Koppel's upstairs. "You're going to be the man of the house," said Pop. "It's okay. I put you all on welfare. I just got back from Wabansia Avenue, from the relief station." Hence the suit and the hat. "They're sending out a caseworker." Then he said, "You got to lend me money to buy gasoline—the caddie money you saved."

Understanding that Pop couldn't get away without his help, Woody turned over to him all he had earned at the Sunset Ridge Country Club in Winnetka. Pop felt that the valuable life lesson he was transmitting was worth far more than these dollars, and whenever he was conning his boy a sort of high-priest expression came down over his bent nose, his ruddy face. The children, who got their finest ideas at the movies, called him Richard Dix. Later, when the comic strip came out, they said he was Dick Tracy.

As Woody now saw it, under the tumbling bells, he had bankrolled his own desertion. Ha ha! He found this delightful; and especially Pop's attitude of "That'll teach you to trust your father." For this was a demonstration on behalf of real life and free instincts, against religion and hypocrisy. But mainly it was aimed against being a fool, the disgrace of foolishness. Pop had it in for the Reverend Doctor Kovner, not because he was an apostate (Pop couldn't have cared less), not because the mission was a racket (he admitted that the Reverend Doctor was personally honest), but because Doctor Kovner behaved foolishly, spoke like a fool, and acted like a fiddler. He tossed his hair like a Paganini (this was Woody's addition; Pop had never even heard of Paganini). Proof that he was not a spiritual leader was that he converted Jewish women by stealing their hearts. "He works up all those broads," said Pop. "He doesn't even know it himself, I swear he doesn't know how he gets them."

From the other side, Kovner often warned Woody, "Your father is a dangerous person. Of course, you love him; you should love him and forgive him, Voodrow, but you are old enough to understand he is leading a life of wice."

It was all petty stuff: Pop's sinning was on a boy level and therefore made a big impression on a boy. And on Mother. Are wives children, or what? Mother often said, "I hope you put that brute in your prayers. Look what he has done to us. But only pray for him, don't see him." But he saw him all the time. Woodrow was leading a double life, sacred and profane. He accepted Jesus Christ as his personal redeemer. Aunt Rebecca took advantage of this. She made him work. He had to work under Aunt Rebecca. He filled in for the janitor at the mission and settlement house. In winter, he had to feed the coal furnace, and on some nights he slept near the furnace room, on the pool table. He also picked the lock of the storeroom. He took canned pineapple and cut bacon from the flitch with his pocketknife. He crammed himself with uncooked bacon. He had a big frame to fill out.

Only now, sipping Melitta coffee, he asked himself: Had he been so hungry? No, he loved being reckless. He was fighting Aunt Rebecca Kovner when he took out his knife and got on a box to reach the bacon. She didn't know, she couldn't prove that Woody, such a frank, strong, positive boy, who looked you in the eye, so direct, was a thief also. But he was also a thief. Whenever she looked at him, he knew that she was seeing his father. In the curve of his nose, the movements of his eyes, the thickness of his body, in his healthy face, she saw that wicked savage Morris.

Morris, you see, had been a street boy in Liverpool—Woody's mother and her sister were British by birth. Morris's Polish family, on their way to America, abandoned him in Liverpool because he had an eye infection and they would all have been sent back from Ellis Island. They stopped awhile in England, but his eyes kept running and they ditched him. They slipped away, and he had to make out alone in Liverpool at the age of twelve. Mother came of better people. Pop, who slept in the cellar of her house, fell in love with her. At sixteen, scabbing during a seamen's strike, he shoveled his way across the Atlantic and jumped ship in Brooklyn. He became an American, and America never knew it. He voted without papers, he drove without a license, he paid no taxes, he cut every corner. Horses, cards, billiards, and women were his lifelong interests, in ascending order. Did he love anyone (he was so busy)? Yes, he loved Halina. He loved his son. To this day, Mother believed that he had loved her most and always wanted to come back. This gave her a chance to act the queen, with her plump wrists and faded Queen Victoria face. "The girls are instructed never to admit him," she said. The Empress of India speaking.

Bell-battered Woodrow's soul was whirling this Sunday morning, indoors and out, to the past, back to his upper corner of the warehouse, laid out with such originality—the bells coming and going, metal on naked metal, until the bell circle expanded over the whole of steel-making, oil-refining, power-producing midautumn South Chicago, and all its Croatians, Ukrainians, Greeks, Poles, and respectable blacks heading for their churches to hear Mass or to sing hymns.

Woody himself had been a good hymn singer. He still knew the hymns. He had testified, too. He was often sent by Aunt Rebecca to get up and tell a churchful of Scandihoovians that he, a Jewish lad, accepted Jesus Christ. For this she paid him fifty cents. She made the disbursement. She was the bookkeeper, fiscal chief, general manager of the mission. The Reverend Doctor didn't know a thing about the operation. What the Doctor supplied was the fervor. He was genuine, a wonderful preacher. And what about Woody himself? He also had fervor. He was drawn to the Reverend Doctor. The Reverend Doctor taught him to lift up his eyes, gave him his higher life. Apart from this higher life, the rest was Chicago—the ways of Chicago, which came so natural that nobody thought to question them. So, for instance, in 1933 (what ancient, ancient times!), at the Century of Progress World's Fair, when Woody was a coolie and pulled a rickshaw, wearing a peaked straw hat and trotting with powerful, thick legs, while the brawny red farmers—his boozing passengers—were laughing their heads off and pestering him for whores, he, although a freshman at the seminary, saw nothing wrong, when girls asked him to steer a little business their way, in making dates and accepting tips from both sides. He necked in Grant Park with a powerful girl who had to go home quickly to nurse her baby. Smelling of milk, she rode beside him on the streetcar to the West Side, squeezing his rickshaw puller's thigh and wetting her blouse. This was the Roosevelt Road car. Then, in the apartment where she lived with her mother, he couldn't remember that there were any husbands around. What he did remember was the strong milk odor. Without inconsistency, next morning he did New Testament Greek: The light shineth in darkness—*to fos en te skotia fainei*—and the darkness comprehended it not.

And all the while he trotted between the shafts on the fairgrounds he had one idea, nothing to do with these horny giants having a big time in the city: that the goal, the project, God's purpose was (and he couldn't explain why he thought so; all evidence was against it)—that this world should be a love world, that it should eventually recover and be entirely a world of love. He wouldn't have said this to a soul, for he could see himself how stupid it was—personal and stupid. Nevertheless, there it was at the center of his feelings. And at the same time, Aunt Rebecca was right when she said to him, strictly private, close to his ear even, "You're a little crook, like your father."

There was some evidence for this, or what stood for evidence to an impatient person like Rebecca. Woody matured quickly—he had to—but how could you expect a boy of seventeen, he wondered, to interpret the viewpoint, the feelings, of a middle-aged woman, and one whose breast had been removed? Morris told him that this happened only to neglected women, and was a sign. Morris said that if titties were not fondled and kissed, they got cancer in protest. It was a cry of the flesh. And this had seemed true to Woody. When his imagination tried the theory on the Reverend Doctor, it worked out—he couldn't see the Reverend Doctor behaving in that way to Aunt Rebecca's breasts! Morris's theory kept Woody looking from bosoms to husbands and from husbands to bosoms. He still did that. It's an exceptionally smart man who isn't marked forever by the sexual theories he hears from his father, and Woody wasn't all that smart. He knew this himself. Personally, he had gone far out of his way to do right by women in this regard. What nature demanded. He and Pop were common, thick men, but there's nobody too gross to have ideas of delicacy.

The Reverend Doctor preached, Rebecca preached, rich Mrs. Skoglund preached from Evanston, Mother preached. Pop also was on a soapbox. Everyone was doing it. Up and down Division Street, under every lamp, almost, speakers were giving out: anarchists, Socialists, Stalinists, single-taxers, Zionists, Tolstoyans, vegetarians, and fundamentalist Christian preachers—you name it. A beef, a hope, a way of life or salvation, a protest. How was it that the accumulated gripes of all the ages took off so when transplanted to America?

And that fine Swedish immigrant Aase (Osie, they pronounced it), who had been the Skoglunds' cook and married the eldest son, to become his rich, religious widow—she supported the Reverend Doctor. In her time she must have been built like a chorus girl. And women seem to have lost the secret of putting up their hair in the high basketry fence of braid she wore. Aase took Woody under her special protection and paid his tuition at the seminary. And Pop said . . . But on this Sunday, at peace as soon as the bells stopped banging, this velvet autumn day when the grass was finest and thickest, silky green: before the first frost, and the blood in your lungs is redder than summer air can make it and smarts with oxygen, as if the iron in your system was hungry for it, and the chill was sticking it to you in every breath . . . Pop, six feet under, would never feel this blissful sting again. The last of the bells still had the bright air streaming with vibrations.

On weekends, the institutional vacancy of decades came back to the warehouse and crept under the door of Woody's apartment. It felt as empty on Sundays as churches were during the week. Before each business day, before the trucks and the crews got started, Woody jogged five miles in his Adidas suit. Not on this day still reserved for Pop, however. Although it was tempting to go out and run off the grief. Being alone hit Woody hard this morning. He thought: Me and the world; the world and me. Meaning that there always was some activity to interpose, an errand or a visit, a picture to paint (he was a creative amateur), a massage, a meal—a shield between himself and that troublesome solitude which used the world as its reservoir. But Pop! Last Tuesday, Woody had gotten into the hospital bed with Pop because he kept pulling out the intravenous needles. Nurses stuck them back, and then Woody astonished them all by climbing into bed to hold the struggling old guy in his arms. "Easy, Morris, Morris, go easy." But Pop still groped feebly for the pipes.

When the tolling stopped, Woody didn't notice that a great lake of quiet had come over his kingdom, the Selbst Tile warehouse. What he heard and saw was an old red Chicago streetcar, one of those trams the color of a stockyard steer.

Cars of this type went out before Pearl Harbor—clumsy, big-bellied, with tough rattan seats and brass grips for the standing passengers. Those cars used to make four stops to the mile, and ran with a wallowing motion. They stank of carbolic or ozone and throbbed when the air compressors were being charged. The conductor had his knotted signal cord to pull, and the motorman beat the foot gong with his mad heel.

Woody recognized himself on the Western Avenue line and riding through a blizzard with his father, both in sheepskins and with hands and faces raw, the snow blowing in from the rear platform when the doors opened and getting into the longitudinal cleats of the floor. There wasn't warmth enough inside to melt it. And Western Avenue was the longest car line in the world, the boosters said, as if it was a thing to brag about. Twenty-three miles long, made by a draftsman with a T square, lined with factories, storage buildings, machine shops, used-car lots, trolley barns, gas stations, funeral parlors, six-flats, utility buildings, and junkyards, on and on from the prairies on the south to Evanston on the north. Woodrow and his father were going north to Evanston, to Howard Street, and then some, to see Mrs. Skoglund. At the end of the line they would still have about five blocks to hike. The purpose of the trip? To raise money for Pop. Pop had talked him into this. When they found out, Mother and Aunt Rebecca would be furious, and Woody was afraid, but he couldn't help it.

Morris had come and said, "Son, I'm in trouble. It's bad."

"What's bad, Pop?"

"Halina took money from her husband for me and has to put it back before old Bujak misses it. He could kill her."

"What did she do it for?"

"Son, you know how the bookies collect? They send a goon. They'll break my head open."

"Pop! You know I can't take you to Mrs. Skoglund."

"Why not? You're my kid, aren't you? The old broad wants to adopt you, doesn't she? Shouldn't I get something out of it for my trouble? What am I— outside? And what about Halina? She puts her life on the line, but my own kid says no."

"Oh, Bujak wouldn't hurt her."

"Woody, he'd beat her to death."

Bujak? Uniform in color with his dark-gray work clothes, short in the legs, his whole strength in his tool-and-die-maker's forearms and black fingers; and beat-looking—there was Bujak for you. But, according to Pop, there was big, big violence in Bujak, a regular boiling Bessemer inside his narrow chest. Woody could never see the violence in him. Bujak wanted no trouble. If anything, maybe he was afraid that Morris and Halina would gang up on him and kill him, screaming. But Pop was no desperado murderer. And Halina was a calm, serious woman. Bujak kept his savings in the cellar (banks were going out of business). The worst they did was to take some of his money, intending to put it back. As Woody saw him, Bujak was trying to be sensible. He accepted his sorrow. He set minimum requirements for Halina: cook the meals, clean the house, show respect. But at stealing Bujak might have drawn the line, for money was different, money was vital substance. If they stole his savings he might have had to take action, out of respect for the substance, for himself—self-respect. But you couldn't be sure that Pop hadn't invented the bookie, the goon, the theft—the whole thing. He was capable of it, and you'd be a fool not to suspect him. Morris knew that Mother and Aunt Rebecca had told Mrs. Skoglund how wicked he was. They had painted him for her in poster colors—purple for vice, black for his soul, red for hell flames: a gambler, smoker, drinker, deserter, screwer of women, and atheist. So Pop was determined to reach her. It was risky for everybody. The Reverend Doctor's operating costs were met by Skoglund Dairies. The widow paid Woody's seminary tuition; she bought dresses for the little sisters.

Woody, now sixty, fleshy and big, like a figure for the victory of American materialism, sunk in his lounge chair, the leather of its armrests softer to his fingertips than a woman's skin, was puzzled and, in his depths, disturbed by certain blots within him, blots of light in his brain, a blot combining pain and amusement in his breast (how did *that* get there?). Intense thought puckered the skin between his eyes with a strain bordering on headache. Why had he let Pop have his way? Why did he agree to meet him that day, in the dim rear of the poolroom?

"But what will you tell Mrs. Skoglund?"

"The old broad? Don't worry, there's plenty to tell her, and it's all true. Ain't I trying to save my little laundry-and-cleaning shop? Isn't the bailiff coming for the fixtures next week?" And Pop rehearsed his pitch on the Western Avenue car. He counted on Woody's health and his freshness. Such a straightforward-looking body was perfect for a con.

Did they still have such winter storms in Chicago as they used to have? Now they somehow seemed less fierce. Blizzards used to come straight down from Ontario, from the Arctic, and drop five feet of snow in an afternoon. Then the rusty green platform cars, with revolving brushes at both ends, came out of the barns to sweep the tracks. Ten or twelve streetcars followed in slow processions, or waited, block after block.

There was a long delay at the gates of Riverview Park, all the amusements covered for the winter, boarded up—the dragon's-back high-rides, the Bobs, the Chute, the Tilt-a-Whirl, all the fun machinery put together by mechanics and electricians, men like Bujak the tool-and-die maker, good with engines. The blizzard was having it all its own way behind the gates, and you couldn't see far

inside; only a few bulbs burned behind the palings. When Woody wiped the vapor from the glass, the wire mesh of the window guards was stuffed solid at eye
level with snow. Looking higher, you saw mostly the streaked wind horizontally
driving from the north. In the seat ahead, two black coal heavers, both in leather
Lindbergh flying helmets, sat with shovels between their legs, returning from a
job. They smelled of sweat, burlap sacking, and coal. Mostly dull with black
dust, they also sparkled here and there.

There weren't many riders. People weren't leaving the house. This was a day
to sit, legs stuck out beside the stove, mummified by both the outdoor and the
indoor forces. Only a fellow with an angle, like Pop, would go and buck such
weather. A storm like this was out of the compass, and you kept the human scale
by having a scheme to raise fifty bucks. Fifty soldiers! Real money in 1933.

"That woman is crazy for you," said Pop.

"She's just a good woman, sweet to all of us."

"Who knows what she's got in mind. You're a husky kid. Not such a kid,
either."

"She's a religious woman. She really has religion."

"Well, your mother isn't your only parent. She and Rebecca and Kovner
aren't going to fill you up with their ideas. I know your mother wants to wipe
me out of your life. Unless I take a hand, you won't even understand what life is.
Because they don't know—those silly Christers."

"Yes, Pop."

"The girls I can't help. They're too young. I'm sorry about them, but I can't
do anything. With you it's different."

He wanted me to be like himself—an American.

They were stalled in the storm, while the cattle-colored car waited to have the
trolley reset in the crazy wind, which boomed, tingled, blasted. At Howard
Street they would have to walk straight into it, due north.

"You'll do the talking at first," said Pop.

Woody had the makings of a salesman, a pitchman. He was aware of this
when he got to his feet in church to testify before fifty or sixty people. Even
though Aunt Rebecca made it worth his while, he moved his own heart when he
spoke up about his faith. But occasionally, without notice, his heart went away
as he spoke religion and he couldn't find it anywhere. In its absence, sincere behavior got him through. He had to rely for delivery on his face, his voice—on
behavior. Then his eyes came closer and closer together. And in this approach of
eye to eye he felt the strain of hypocrisy. The twisting of his face threatened to
betray him. It took everything he had to keep looking honest. So, since he
couldn't bear the cynicism of it, he fell back on mischievousness. Mischief was
where Pop came in. Pop passed straight through all those divided fields, gap after gap, and arrived at his side, bent-nosed and broad-faced. In regard to Pop,

you thought of neither sincerity nor insincerity. Pop was like the man in the song: he wanted what he wanted when he wanted it. Pop was physical; Pop was digestive, circulatory, sexual. If Pop got serious, he talked to you about washing under the arms or in the crotch or of drying between your toes or of cooking supper, of baked beans and fried onions, of draw poker or of a certain horse in the fifth race at Arlington. Pop was elemental. That was why he gave such relief from religion and paradoxes, and things like that. Now, Mother *thought* she was spiritual, but Woody knew that she was kidding herself. Oh, yes, in the British accent she never gave up she was always talking to God or about Him—please God, God willing, praise God. But she was a big substantial bread-and-butter down-to-earth woman, with down-to-earth duties like feeding the girls, protecting, refining, keeping them pure. And those two protected doves grew up so overweight, heavy in the hips and thighs, that their poor heads looked long and slim. And mad. Sweet but cuckoo—Paula cheerfully cuckoo, Joanna depressed and having episodes.

"I'll do my best by you, but you have to promise, Pop, not to get me in Dutch with Mrs. Skoglund."

"You worried because I speak bad English? Embarrassed? I have a mockie accent?"

"It's not that. Kovner has a heavy accent, and she doesn't mind."

"Who the hell are those freaks to look down on me? You're practically a man and your dad has a right to expect help from you. He's in a fix. And you bring him to her house because she's bighearted, and you haven't got anybody else to go to."

"I got you, Pop."

The two coal trimmers stood up at Devon Avenue. One of them wore a woman's coat. Men wore women's clothing in those years, and women men's, when there was no choice. The fur collar was spiky with the wet, and sprinkled with soot. Heavy, they dragged their shovels and got off at the front. The slow car ground on, very slow. It was after four when they reached the end of the line, and somewhere between gray and black, with snow spouting and whirling under the street lamps. On Howard Street, autos were stalled at all angles and abandoned. The sidewalks were blocked. Woody led the way into Evanston, and Pop followed him up the middle of the street in the furrows made earlier by trucks. For four blocks they bucked the wind and then Woody broke through the drifts to the snowbound mansion, where they both had to push the wrought-iron gate because of the drift behind it. Twenty rooms or more in this dignified house and nobody in them but Mrs. Skoglund and her servant Hjordis, also religious.

As Woody and Pop waited, brushing the slush from their sheepskin collars and Pop wiping his big eyebrows with the ends of his scarf, sweating and freezing, the chains began to rattle and Hjordis uncovered the air holes of the glass storm door by turning a wooden bar. Woody called her "monk-faced." You no longer see women like that, who put no female touch on the face. She came plain, as God made her. She said, "Who is it and what do you want?"

"It's Woodrow Selbst. Hjordis? It's Woody."

"You're not expected."

"No, but we're here."

"What do you want?"

"We came to see Mrs. Skoglund."

"What for do you want to see her?"

"Just tell her we're here."

"I have to tell her what you came for, without calling up first."

"Why don't you say it's Woody with his father, and we wouldn't come in a snowstorm like this if it wasn't important."

The understandable caution of women who live alone. Respectable old-time women, too. There was no such respectability now in those Evanston houses, with their big verandas and deep yards and with a servant like Hjordis, who carried at her belt keys to the pantry and to every closet and every dresser drawer and every padlocked bin in the cellar. And in High Episcopal Christian Science Women's Temperance Evanston, no tradespeople rang at the front door. Only invited guests. And here, after a ten-mile grind through the blizzard, came two tramps from the West Side. To this mansion where a Swedish immigrant lady, herself once a cook and now a philanthropic widow, dreamed, snowbound, while frozen lilac twigs clapped at her storm windows, of a new Jerusalem and a Second Coming and a Resurrection and a Last Judgment. To hasten the Second Coming, and all the rest, you had to reach the hearts of these scheming bums arriving in a snowstorm.

Sure, they let us in.

Then in the heat that swam suddenly up to their mufflered chins Pop and Woody felt the blizzard for what it was; their cheeks were frozen slabs. They stood beat, itching, trickling in the front hall that *was* a hall, with a carved-newel-post staircase and a big stained-glass window at the top. Picturing Jesus with the Samaritan woman. There was a kind of Gentile closeness to the air. Perhaps when he was with Pop, Woody made more Jewish observations than he would otherwise. Although Pop's most Jewish characteristic was that Yiddish was the only language he could read a paper in. Pop was with Polish Halina, and Mother was with Jesus Christ, and Woody ate uncooked bacon from the flitch. Still, now and then he had a Jewish impression.

Mrs. Skoglund was the cleanest of women—her fingernails, her white neck, her ears—and Pop's sexual hints to Woody all went wrong because she was so intensely clean, and made Woody think of a waterfall, large as she was, and grandly built. Her bust was big. Woody's imagination had investigated this. He thought she kept things tied down tight, very tight. But she lifted both arms once to raise a window and there it was, her bust, beside him, the whole un-bindable thing. Her hair was like the raffia you had to soak before you could weave with it in a basket class—pale, pale. Pop, as he took his sheepskin off, was in sweaters, no jacket. His darting looks made him seem crooked. Hardest of all for these Selbsts with their bent noses and big, apparently straightforward faces was to look honest. All the signs of dishonesty played over them. Woody had often puzzled about it. Did it go back to the muscles, was it fundamentally a jaw problem—the projecting angles of the jaws? Or was it the angling that went on in the heart? The girls called Pop Dick Tracy, but Dick Tracy was a good guy. Whom could Pop convince? Here Woody caught a possibility as it flitted by. Precisely because of the way Pop looked, a sensitive person might feel remorse for condemning unfairly or judging unkindly. Just because of a face? Some must have bent over backward. Then he had them. Not Hjordis. She would have put Pop into the street then and there, storm or no storm. Hjordis was religious, but she was wised-up, too. She hadn't come over in steerage and worked forty years in Chicago for nothing.

Mrs. Skoglund, Aase (Osie), led the visitors into the front room. This, the biggest room in the house, needed supplementary heating. Because of fifteen-foot ceilings and high windows, Hjordis had kept the parlor stove burning. It was one of those elegant parlor stoves that wore a nickel crown, or miter, and this miter, when you moved it aside, automatically raised the hinge of an iron stove lid. That stove lid underneath the crown was all soot and rust, the same as any other stove lid. Into this hole you tipped the scuttle and the anthracite chestnut rattled down. It made a cake or dome of fire visible through the small isinglass frames. It was a pretty room, three-quarters paneled in wood. The stove was plugged into the flue of the marble fireplace, and there were parquet floors and Axminster carpets and cranberry-colored tufted Victorian upholstery, and a kind of Chinese étagère, inside a cabinet, lined with mirrors and contain-ing silver pitchers, trophies won by Skoglund cows, fancy sugar tongs and cut-glass pitchers and goblets. There were Bibles and pictures of Jesus and the Holy Land and that faint Gentile odor, as if things had been rinsed in a weak vinegar solution.

"Mrs. Skoglund, I brought my dad to you. I don't think you ever met him," said Woody.

"Yes, Missus, that's me, Selbst."

Pop stood short but masterful in the sweaters, and his belly sticking out, not soft but hard. He was a man of the hard-bellied type. Nobody intimidated Pop. He never presented himself as a beggar. There wasn't a cringe in him anywhere. He let her see at once by the way he said "Missus" that he was independent and that he knew his way around. He communicated that he was able to handle himself with women. Handsome Mrs. Skoglund, carrying a basket woven out of her own hair, was in her fifties—eight, maybe ten years his senior.

"I asked my son to bring me because I know you do the kid a lot of good. It's natural you should know both of his parents."

"Mrs. Skoglund, my dad is in a tight corner and I don't know anybody else to ask for help."

This was all the preliminary Pop wanted. He took over and told the widow his story about the laundry-and-cleaning business and payments overdue, and explained about the fixtures and the attachment notice, and the bailiff's office and what they were going to do to him; and he said, "I'm a small man trying to make a living."

"You don't support your children," said Mrs. Skoglund.

"That's right," said Hjordis.

"I haven't got it. If I had it, wouldn't I give it? There's bread lines and soup lines all over town. Is it just me? What I have I divvy with. I give the kids. A bad father? You think my son would bring me if I was a bad father into your house? He loves his dad, he trusts his dad, he knows his dad is a good dad. Every time I start a little business going I get wiped out. This one is a good little business, if I could hold on to that little business. Three people work for me, I meet a payroll, and three people will be on the street, too, if I close down. Missus, I can sign a note and pay you in two months. I'm a common man, but I'm a hard worker and a fellow you can trust."

Woody was startled when Pop used the word "trust." It was as if from all four corners a Sousa band blew a blast to warn the entire world: "Crook! This is a crook!" But Mrs. Skoglund, on account of her religious preoccupations, was remote. She heard nothing. Although everybody in this part of the world, unless he was crazy, led a practical life, and you'd have nothing to say to anyone, your neighbors would have nothing to say to you, if communications were not of a practical sort, Mrs. Skoglund, with all her money, was unworldly—two-thirds out of this world.

"Give me a chance to show what's in me," said Pop, "and you'll see what I do for my kids."

So Mrs. Skoglund hesitated, and then she said she'd have to go upstairs, she'd have to go to her room and pray on it and ask for guidance—would they sit down and wait. There were two rocking chairs by the stove. Hjordis gave Pop a grim look (a dangerous person) and Woody a blaming one (he brought a dangerous stranger and disrupter to injure two kind Christian ladies). Then she went out with Mrs. Skoglund.

As soon as they left, Pop jumped up from the rocker and said in anger, "What's this with the praying? She has to ask God to lend me fifty bucks?"

Woody said, "It's not you, Pop, it's the way these religious people do."

"No," said Pop. "She'll come back and say that God wouldn't let her."

Woody didn't like that; he thought Pop was being gross and he said, "No, she's sincere. Pop, try to understand: she's emotional, nervous, and sincere, and tries to do right by everybody."

And Pop said, "That servant will talk her out of it. She's a toughie. It's all over her face that we're a couple of chiselers."

"What's the use of us arguing," said Woody. He drew the rocker closer to the stove. His shoes were wet through and would never dry. The blue flames fluttered like a school of fishes in the coal fire. But Pop went over to the Chinese-style cabinet or étagère and tried the handle, and then opened the blade of his penknife and in a second had forced the lock of the curved glass door. He took out a silver dish.

"Pop, what is this?" said Woody.

Pop, cool and level, knew exactly what this was. He relocked the étagère, crossed the carpet, listened. He stuffed the dish under his belt and pushed it down into his trousers. He put the side of his short thick finger to his mouth.

So Woody kept his voice down, but he was all shook up. He went to Pop and took him by the edge of his hand. As he looked into Pop's face, he felt his eyes growing smaller and smaller, as if something were contracting all the skin on his head. They call it hyperventilation when everything feels tight and light and close and dizzy. Hardly breathing, he said, "Put it back, Pop."

Pop said, "It's solid silver; it's worth dough."

"Pop, you said you wouldn't get me in Dutch."

"It's only insurance in case she comes back from praying and tells me no. If she says yes, I'll put it back."

"How?"

"It'll get back. If I don't put it back, you will."

"You picked the lock. I couldn't. I don't know how."

"There's nothing to it."

"We're going to put it back now. Give it here."

"Woody, it's under my fly, inside my underpants. Don't make such a noise about nothing."

"Pop, I can't believe this."

"For cry-ninety-nine, shut your mouth. If I didn't trust you I wouldn't have let you watch me do it. You don't understand a thing. What's with you?"

"Before they come down, Pop, will you dig that dish out of your long johns."

Pop turned stiff on him. He became absolutely military. He said, "Look, I order you!"

Before he knew it, Woody had jumped his father and begun to wrestle with him. It was outrageous to clutch your own father, to put a heel behind him, to force him to the wall. Pop was taken by surprise and said loudly, "You want Halina killed? Kill her! Go on, you be responsible." He began to resist, angry, and they turned about several times, when Woody, with a trick he had learned in a Western movie and used once on the playground, tripped him and they fell to the ground. Woody, who already outweighed the old man by twenty pounds, was on top. They landed on the floor beside the stove, which stood on a tray of decorated tin to protect the carpet. In this position, pressing Pop's hard belly, Woody recognized that to have wrestled him to the floor counted for nothing. It was impossible to thrust his hand under Pop's belt to recover the dish. And now Pop had turned furious, as a father has every right to be when his son is violent with him, and he freed his hand and hit Woody in the face. He hit him three or four times in midface. Then Woody dug his head into Pop's shoulder and held tight only to keep from being struck and began to say in his ear, "Jesus, Pop, for Christ's sake remember where you are. Those women will be back!" But Pop brought up his short knee and fought and butted him with his chin and rattled Woody's teeth. Woody thought the old man was about to bite him. And because he was a seminarian, he thought: Like an unclean spirit. And held tight. Gradually Pop stopped thrashing and struggling. His eyes stuck out and his mouth was open, sullen. Like a stout fish. Woody released him and gave him a hand up. He was then overcome with many many bad feelings of a sort he knew the old man never suffered. Never, never. Pop never had these groveling emotions. There was his whole superiority. Pop had no such feelings. He was like a horseman from Central Asia, a bandit from China. It was Mother, from Liverpool, who had the refinement, the English manners. It was the preaching Reverend Doctor in his black suit. You have refinements, and all they do is oppress you? The hell with that.

The long door opened and Mrs. Skoglund stepped in, saying, "Did I imagine, or did something shake the house?"

"I was lifting the scuttle to put coal on the fire and it fell out of my hand. I'm sorry I was so clumsy," said Woody.

Pop was too huffy to speak. With his eyes big and sore and the thin hair down over his forehead, you could see by the tightness of his belly how angrily he was fetching his breath, though his mouth was shut.

"I prayed," said Mrs. Skoglund.

"I hope it came out well," said Woody.

"Well, I don't do anything without guidance, but the answer was yes, and I feel right about it now. So if you'll wait, I'll go to my office and write a check. I asked Hjordis to bring you a cup of coffee. Coming in such a storm."

And Pop, consistently a terrible little man, as soon as she shut the door, said, "A check? Hell with a check. Get me the greenbacks."

"They don't keep money in the house. You can cash it in her bank tomorrow. But if they miss that dish, Pop, they'll stop the check, and then where are you?"

As Pop was reaching below the belt, Hjordis brought in the tray. She was very sharp with him. She said, "Is this a place to adjust clothing, Mister? A men's washroom?"

"Well, which way is the toilet, then?" said Pop.

She had served the coffee in the seamiest mugs in the pantry, and she bumped down the tray and led Pop along the corridor, standing guard at the bathroom door so that he shouldn't wander about the house.

Mrs. Skoglund called Woody to her office and after she had given him the folded check said that they should pray together for Morris. So once more he was on his knees, under rows and rows of musty marbled-cardboard files, by the glass lamp by the edge of the desk, the shade with flounced edges, like the candy dish. Mrs. Skoglund, in her Scandinavian accent—an emotional contralto—raising her voice to Jesus-uh Christ-uh, as the wind lashed the trees, kicked the side of the house, and drove the snow seething on the windowpanes, to send light-uh, give guidance-uh, put a new heart-uh in Pop's bosom. Woody asked God only to make Pop put the dish back. He kept Mrs. Skoglund on her knees as long as possible. Then he thanked her, shining with candor (as much as he knew how), for her Christian generosity and he said, "I know that Hjordis has a cousin who works at the Evanston YMCA. Could she please phone him and try to get us a room tonight so that we don't have to fight the blizzard all the way back? We're almost as close to the Y as to the car line. Maybe the cars have even stopped running."

Suspicious Hjordis, coming when Mrs. Skoglund called to her, was burning now. First they barged in, made themselves at home, asked for money, had to have coffee, probably left gonorrhea on the toilet seat. Hjordis, Woody remembered, was a woman who wiped the doorknobs with rubbing alcohol after guests had left. Nevertheless, she telephoned the Y and got them a room with two cots for six bits.

Pop had plenty of time, therefore, to reopen the étagère, lined with reflecting glass or German silver (something exquisitely delicate and tricky), and as soon as the two Selbsts had said thank you and good-bye and were in midstreet again up to the knees in snow, Woody said, "Well, I covered for you. Is that thing back?"

"Of course it is," said Pop.

They fought their way to the small Y building, shut up in wire grille and re-sembling a police station—about the same dimensions. It was locked, but they made a racket on the grille, and a small black man let them in and shuffled them upstairs to a cement corridor with low doors. It was like the small-mammal house in Lincoln Park. He said there was nothing to eat, so they took off their wet pants, wrapped themselves tightly in the khaki army blankets, and passed out on their cots.

First thing in the morning, they went to the Evanston National Bank and got the fifty dollars. Not without difficulties. The teller went to call Mrs. Skoglund and was absent a long time from the wicket. "Where the hell has he gone?" said Pop.

But when the fellow came back, he said, "How do you want it?"

Pop said, "Singles." He told Woody, "Bujak stashes it in one-dollar bills."

But by now Woody no longer believed Halina had stolen the old man's money.

Then they went into the street, where the snow-removal crews were at work. The sun shone broad, broad, out of the morning blue, and all Chicago would be releasing itself from the temporary beauty of those vast drifts.

"You shouldn't have jumped me last night, Sonny."

"I know, Pop, but you promised you wouldn't get me in Dutch."

"Well, it's okay. We can forget it, seeing you stood by me."

Only, Pop had taken the silver dish. Of course he had, and in a few days Mrs. Skoglund and Hjordis knew it, and later in the week they were all waiting for Woody in Kovner's office at the settlement house. The group included the Reverend Doctor Crabbie, head of the seminary, and Woody, who had been flying along, level and smooth, was shot down in flames. He told them he was innocent. Even as he was falling, he warned that they were wronging him. He denied that he or Pop had touched Mrs. Skoglund's property. The missing object—he didn't even know what it was—had probably been misplaced, and they would be very sorry on the day it turned up. After the others were done with him, Dr. Crabbie said that until he was able to tell the truth he would be suspended from the seminary, where his work had been unsatisfactory anyway. Aunt Rebecca took him aside and said to him, "You are a little crook, like your father. The door is closed to you here."

To this Pop's comment was "So what, kid?"

"Pop, you shouldn't have done it."

"No? Well, I don't give a care, if you want to know. You can have the dish if you want to go back and square yourself with all those hypocrites."

"I didn't like doing Mrs. Skoglund in the eye, she was so kind to us."

"Kind?"

"Kind."

"Kind has a price tag."

Well, there was no winning such arguments with Pop. But they debated it in various moods and from various elevations and perspectives for forty years and more, as their intimacy changed, developed, matured.

"Why did you do it, Pop? For the money? What did you do with the fifty bucks?" Woody, decades later, asked him that.

"I settled with the bookie, and the rest I put in the business."

"You tried a few more horses."

"I maybe did. But it was a double, Woody. I didn't hurt myself, and at the same time did you a favor."

"It was for me?"

"It was too strange of a life. That life wasn't *you,* Woody. All those women . . . Kovner was no man, he was an in-between. Suppose they made you a minister? Some Christian minister! First of all, you wouldn't have been able to stand it, and second, they would have thrown you out sooner or later."

"Maybe so."

"And you wouldn't have converted the Jews, which was the main thing they wanted."

"And what a time to bother the Jews," Woody said. "At least *I* didn't bug them."

Pop had carried him back to his side of the line, blood of his blood, the same thick body walls, the same coarse grain. Not cut out for a spiritual life. Simply not up to it.

Pop was no worse than Woody, and Woody was no better than Pop. Pop wanted no relation to theory, and yet he was always pointing Woody toward a position—a jolly, hearty, natural, likable, unprincipled position. If Woody had a weakness, it was to be unselfish. This worked to Pop's advantage, but he criticized Woody for it, nevertheless. "You take too much on yourself," Pop was always saying. And it's true that Woody gave Pop his heart because Pop was so selfish. It's usually the selfish people who are loved the most. They do what you deny yourself, and you love them for it. You give them your heart.

Remembering the pawn ticket for the silver dish, Woody startled himself with a laugh so sudden that it made him cough. Pop said to him after his expulsion from the seminary and banishment from the settlement house, "You want in again? Here's the ticket. I hocked that thing. It wasn't so valuable as I thought."

"What did they give?"

"Twelve-fifty was all I could get. But if you want it you'll have to raise the dough yourself, because I haven't got it anymore."

"You must have been sweating in the bank when the teller went to call Mrs. Skoglund about the check."

"I was a little nervous," said Pop. "But I didn't think they could miss the thing so soon."

That theft was part of Pop's war with Mother. With Mother, and Aunt Rebecca, and the Reverend Doctor. Pop took his stand on realism. Mother represented the forces of religion and hypochondria. In four decades, the fighting never stopped. In the course of time, Mother and the girls turned into welfare personalities and lost their individual outlines. Ah, the poor things, they became dependents and cranks. In the meantime, Woody, the sinful man, was their dutiful and loving son and brother. He maintained the bungalow—this took in roofing, pointing, wiring, insulation, air-conditioning—and he paid for heat and light and food, and dressed them all out of Sears, Roebuck and Wieboldt's, and bought them a TV, which they watched as devoutly as they prayed. Paula took courses to learn skills like macramé-making and needlepoint, and sometimes got a little job as recreational worker in a nursing home. But she wasn't steady enough to keep it. Wicked Pop spent most of his life removing stains from people's clothing. He and Halina in the last years ran a Cleanomat in West Rogers Park—a so-so business resembling a Laundromat—which gave him leisure for billiards, the horses, rummy and pinochle. Every morning he went behind the partition to check out the filters of the cleaning equipment. He found amusing things that had been thrown into the vats with the clothing—sometimes, when he got lucky, a locket chain or a brooch. And when he had fortified the cleaning fluid, pouring all that blue and pink stuff in from plastic jugs, he read the *Forward* over a second cup of coffee, and went out, leaving Halina in charge. When they needed help with the rent, Woody gave it.

After the new Disney World was opened in Florida, Woody treated all his dependents to a holiday. He sent them down in separate batches, of course. Halina enjoyed this more than anybody else. She couldn't stop talking about the address given by an Abraham Lincoln automaton. "Wonderful, how he stood up and moved his hands, and his mouth. So real! And how beautiful he talked." Of them all, Halina was the soundest, the most human, the most honest. Now that Pop was gone, Woody and Halina's son, Mitosh, the organist at the Stadium, took care of her needs over and above Social Security, splitting expenses. In Pop's opinion, insurance was a racket. He left Halina nothing but some out-of-date equipment.

Woody treated himself, too. Once a year, and sometimes oftener, he left his business to run itself, arranged with the trust department at the bank to take care of his gang, and went off. He did that in style, imaginatively, expensively. In Japan, he wasted little time on Tokyo. He spent three weeks in Kyoto and stayed at the Tawaraya Inn, dating from the seventeenth century or so. There he slept on the floor, the Japanese way, and bathed in scalding water. He saw the dirtiest strip show on earth, as well as the holy places and the temple gardens. He visited also Istanbul, Jerusalem, Delphi, and went to Burma and Uganda and Kenya on safari, on democratic terms with drivers, Bedouins, bazaar merchants. Open, lavish, familiar, fleshier and fleshier but still muscular (he jogged, he lifted weights)—in his naked person beginning to resemble a Renaissance courtier in full costume—becoming ruddier every year, an outdoor type with freckles on his back and spots across the flaming forehead and the honest nose. In Addis Ababa he took an Ethiopian beauty to his room from the street and washed her, getting into the shower with her to soap her with his broad, kindly hands. In Kenya he taught certain American obscenities to a black woman so that she could shout them out during the act. On the Nile, below Murchison Falls, those fever trees rose huge from the mud, and hippos on the sandbars belched at the passing launch, hostile. One of them danced on his spit of sand, springing from the ground and coming down heavy, on all fours. There, Woody saw the buffalo calf disappear, snatched by the crocodile.

Mother, soon to follow Pop, was being lightheaded these days. In company, she spoke of Woody as her boy—"What do you think of my Sonny?"—as though he was ten years old. She was silly with him, her behavior was frivolous, almost flirtatious. She just didn't seem to know the facts. And behind her all the others, like kids at the playground, were waiting their turn to go down the slide: one on each step, and moving toward the top.

Over Woody's residence and place of business there had gathered a pool of silence of the same perimeter as the church bells while they were ringing, and he mourned under it, this melancholy morning of sun and autumn. Doing a life survey, taking a deliberate look at the gross side of his case—of the other side as well, what there was of it. But if this heartache continued, he'd go out and run it off. A three-mile jog—five, if necessary. And you'd think that this jogging was an entirely physical activity, wouldn't you? But there was something else in it. Because, when he was a seminarian, between the shafts of his World's Fair rickshaw, he used to receive, pulling along (capable and stable), his religious experiences while he trotted. Maybe it was all a single experience repeated. He felt truth coming to him from the sun—a communication that was also light and warmth. It made him very remote from his horny Wisconsin passengers, those farmers whose whoops and whore cries he could hardly hear when he was in one of his states. And again out of the flaming of the sun would come to him a secret certainty that the goal set for this earth was that it should be filled with good, saturated with it. After everything preposterous, after dog had eaten dog, after the crocodile death had pulled everyone into his mud. It wouldn't conclude as Mrs. Skoglund, bribing him to round up the Jews and hasten the Second Coming, imagined it, but in another way. This was his clumsy intuition. It went no further. Subsequently, he proceeded through life as life seemed to want him to do it.

There remained one thing more this morning, which was explicitly physical, occurring first as a sensation in his arms and against his breast and, from the pressure, passing into him and going into his breast.

It was like this: When he came into the hospital room and saw Pop with the sides of his bed raised, like a crib, and Pop, so very feeble, and writhing, and toothless, like a baby, and the dirt already cast into his face, into the wrinkles— Pop wanted to pluck out the intravenous needles and he was piping his weak death noise. The gauze patches taped over the needles were soiled with dark blood. Then Woody took off his shoes, lowered the side of the bed, and climbed in and held him in his arms to soothe and still him. As if he were Pop's father, he said to him, "Now, Pop. Pop." Then it was like the wrestle in Mrs. Skoglund's parlor, when Pop turned angry like an unclean spirit and Woody tried to appease him, and warn him, saying, "Those women will be back!" Beside the coal stove, when Pop hit Woody in the teeth with his head and then became sullen, like a stout fish. But this struggle in the hospital was weak—so weak! In his great pity, Woody held Pop, who was fluttering and shivering. From those people, Pop had told him, you'll never find out what life is, because they don't know what it is. Yes, Pop—well, what is it, Pop? Hard to comprehend that Pop, who was dug in for eighty-three years and had done all he could to stay, should now want nothing but to free himself. How could Woody allow the old man to pull the intravenous needles out? Willful Pop, he wanted what he wanted when he wanted it. But what he wanted at the very last Woody failed to follow, it was such a switch.

After a time, Pop's resistance ended. He subsided and subsided. He rested against his son, his small body curled there. Nurses came and looked. They disapproved, but Woody, who couldn't spare a hand to wave them out, motioned with his head toward the door. Pop, whom Woody thought he had stilled, had only found a better way to get around him. Loss of heat was the way he did it. His heat was leaving him. As can happen with small animals while you hold them in your hand, Woody presently felt him cooling. Then, as Woody did his best to restrain him, and thought he was succeeding, Pop divided himself. And when he was separated from his warmth, he slipped into death. And there was his elderly, large, muscular son, still holding and pressing him when there was nothing anymore to press. You could never pin down that self-willed man. When he was ready to make his move, he made it—always on his own terms. And always, always, something up his sleeve. That was how he was.

THE BELLAROSA
CONNECTION

AS FOUNDER OF the Mnemosyne Institute in Philadelphia, forty years in the
trade, I trained many executives, politicians, and members of the defense establishment, and now that I am retired, with the Institute in the capable hands
of my son, I would like to *forget* about remembering. Which is an Alice-in-
Wonderland proposition. In your twilight years, having hung up your gloves (or
sheathed your knife), you don't want to keep doing what you did throughout
your life: a change, a change—your kingdom for a change! A lawyer will walk
away from his clients, a doctor from his patients, a general will paint china, a
diplomatist turn to fly-fishing. My case is different in that I owe my worldly
success to the innate gift of memory—a tricky word, "innate," referring to the
hidden sources of everything that really matters. As I used to say to clients,
"Memory is life." That was a neat way to impress a member of the National Security Council whom I was coaching, but it puts me now in an uncomfortable
position because if you have worked in memory, which is life itself, there is no
retirement except in death.

There are other discomforts to reckon with: This gift of mine became the
foundation of a commercial success—an income from X millions soundly invested and an antebellum house in Philadelphia furnished by my late wife, a
woman who knew everything there was to know about eighteenth-century furniture. Since I am not one of your stubborn defensive rationalizers who deny
that they misuse their talents and insist that they can face God with a clear conscience, I force myself to remember that I was not born in a Philadelphia house
with twenty-foot ceilings but began life as the child of Russian Jews from New
Jersey. A walking memory file like me can't trash his beginnings or distort his

early history. Sure, in the universal process of self-revision anybody can be carried away from the true facts. For instance, Europeanized Americans in Europe will assume a false English or French correctness and bring a disturbing edge of self-consciousness into their relations with their friends. I have observed this. It makes an unpleasant impression. So whenever I was tempted to fake it, I asked myself, "And how are things out in New Jersey?"

The matters that concern me now had their moving axis in New Jersey. These are not data from the memory bank of a computer. I am preoccupied with feelings and longings, and emotional memory is nothing like rocketry or gross national products. What we have before us are the late Harry Fonstein and his late wife, Sorella. My pictures of them are probably too clear and pleasing to be true. Therefore they have to be represented pictorially first and then *wiped out and reconstituted*. But these are technical considerations, having to do with the difference between literal and affective recollection.

If you were living in a house of such dimensions, among armoires, hangings, Persian rugs, sideboards, carved fireplaces, ornamented ceilings—with a closed garden and a bathtub on a marble dais fitted with a faucet that would not be out of place in the Trevi Fountain—you would better understand why the recollection of a refugee like Fonstein and his Newark wife might become significant.

No, he, Fonstein, wasn't a poor schlepp; he succeeded in business and made a fair amount of dough. Nothing like my Philadelphia millions, but not bad for a guy who arrived after the war via Cuba and got a late start in the heating business—and, moreover, a gimpy Galitzianer. Fonstein wore an orthopedic shoe, and there were other peculiarities: His hair looked thin, but it was not weak, it was a strong black growth, and although sparse it was vividly kinky. The head itself was heavy enough to topple a less determined man. His eyes were dark and they were warm, so perhaps it was their placement that made them look shrewd as well. Perhaps it was the expression of his mouth—not severe, not even unkind—which worked together with the dark eyes. You got a smart inspection from this immigrant.

We were not related by blood. Fonstein was the nephew of my stepmother, whom I called Aunt Mildred (a euphemistic courtesy—I was far too old for mothering when my widower father married her). Most of Fonstein's family were killed by the Germans. In Auschwitz he would have been gassed immediately, because of the orthopedic boot. Some Dr. Mengele would have pointed his swagger stick to the left, and Fonstein's boot might by now have been on view in the camp's exhibition hall—they have a hill of cripple boots there, and a hill of crutches and of back braces and one of human hair and one of eyeglasses. Objects that might have been useful in German hospitals or homes.

Harry Fonstein and his mother, Aunt Mildred's sister, had escaped from Poland. Somehow they had reached Italy. In Ravenna there were refugee relatives, who helped as well as they could. The heat was on Italian Jews too, since Mussolini had adopted the Nuremberg racial laws. Fonstein's mother, who was a diabetic, soon died, and Fonstein went on to Milan, traveling with phony papers while learning Italian as fast as he was able. My father, who had a passion for refugee stories, told me all this. He hoped it would straighten me out to hear what people had suffered in Europe, in the real world.

"I want you to see Mildred's nephew," my old man said to me in Lakewood, New Jersey, about forty years ago. "Just a young fellow, maybe younger than you. Got away from the Nazis, dragging one foot. He's just off the boat from Cuba. Not long married."

I was at the bar of paternal judgment again, charged with American puerility. When would I shape up, at last! At the age of thirty-two, I still behaved like a twelve-year-old, hanging out in Greenwich Village, immature, drifting, a layabout, shacking up with Bennington girls, a foolish intellectual gossip, nothing in his head but froth—the founder, said my father with comic bewilderment, of the Mnemosyne Institute, about as profitable as it was pronounceable.

As my Village pals liked to say, it cost no more than twelve hundred dollars a year to be poor—or to play at poverty, yet another American game.

Surviving-Fonstein, with all the furies of Europe at his back, made me look bad. But he wasn't to blame for that, and his presence actually made my visits easier. It was only on the odd Sunday that I paid my respects to the folks at home in green Lakewood, near Lakehurst, where in the thirties the Graf Hindenburg Zeppelin had gone up in flames as it approached its fatal mooring mast, and the screams of the dying could be heard on the ground.

Fonstein and I took turns at the chessboard with my father, who easily beat us both—listless competitors who had the architectural weight of Sunday on our caryatid heads. Sorella Fonstein sometimes sat on the sofa, which had a transparent zippered plastic cover. Sorella was a New Jersey girl—correction: lady. She was very heavy and she wore makeup. Her cheeks were downy. Her hair was done up in a beehive. A pince-nez, highly unusual, a deliberate disguise, gave her a theatrical air. She was still a novice then, trying on these props. Her aim was to achieve an authoritative, declarative manner. However, she was no fool.

Fonstein's place of origin was Lemberg, I think. I wish I had more patience with maps. I can visualize continents and the outlines of countries, but I'm antsy about exact locations. Lemberg is now Lvov, as Danzig is Gdansk. I never was strong in geography. My main investment was in memory. As an undergraduate showing off at parties, I would store up and reel off lists of words fired at me by a circle of twenty people. Hence I can tell you more than you will want to know about Fonstein. In 1938 his father, a jeweler, didn't survive the confiscation by the Germans of his investments (valuable property) in Vienna. When the war had broken out, with Nazi paratroopers dressed as nuns spilling from planes, Fonstein's sister and her husband hid in the countryside, and both were caught and ended in the camps. Fonstein and his mother escaped to Zagreb and eventually got to Ravenna. It was in the north of Italy that Mrs. Fonstein died, and she was buried in a Jewish cemetery, perhaps the Venetian one. Then and there Fonstein's adolescence came to an end. A refugee with an orthopedic boot, he had to consider his moves carefully. "He couldn't vault over walls like Douglas Fairbanks," said Sorella.

I could see why my father took to Fonstein. Fonstein had survived the greatest ordeal of Jewish history. He still looked as if the worst, even now, would not take him by surprise. The impression he gave was unusually firm. When he spoke to you he engaged your look and held it. This didn't encourage small talk. Still, there were hints of wit at the corners of his mouth and around the eyes. So you didn't want to play the fool with Fonstein. I sized him up as a Central European Jewish type. He saw me, probably, as an immature unstable Jewish American, humanly ignorant and loosely kind: in the history of civilization, something new in the way of human types, perhaps not so bad as it looked at first.

To survive in Milan he had to learn Italian pretty damn quick. So as not to waste time, he tried to arrange to speak it even in his dreams. Later, in Cuba, he acquired Spanish too. He was gifted that way. In New Jersey he soon was fluent in English, though to humor me he spoke Yiddish now and then; it was the right language for his European experiences. I had had a tame war myself— company clerk in the Aleutians. So I listened, stooped over him (like a bishop's crook; I had six or eight inches on him), for he was the one who had seen real action.

In Milan he did kitchen work, and in Turin he was a hall porter and shined shoes. By the time he got to Rome he was an assistant concierge. Before long he was working on the Via Veneto. The city was full of Germans, and as Fonstein's German was good, he was employed as an interpreter now and then. He was noticed by Count Ciano, Mussolini's son-in-law and foreign minister.

"So you knew him?"

"Yes, but he didn't know me, not by name. When he gave a party and needed extra translators, I was sent for. There was a reception for Hitler—"

"You mean you saw Hitler?"

"My little boy says it that way too: 'My daddy saw Adolf Hitler.' Hitler was at the far end of the *grande salle*."

"Did he give a speech?"

"Thank God I wasn't close by. Maybe he made a statement. He ate some pastry. He was in military uniform."

"Yes, I've seen pictures of him on company manners, acting sweet."

"One thing," said Fonstein. "There was no color in his face."

"He wasn't killing anybody that day."

"There was nobody he couldn't kill if he liked, but this was a reception. I was happy he didn't notice me."

"I think I would have been grateful too," I said. "You can even feel love for somebody who can kill you but doesn't. Horrible love, but it is a kind of love."

"He would have gotten around to me. My trouble began with this reception. A police check was run, my papers were fishy, and that's why I was arrested."

My father, absorbed in his knights and rooks, didn't look up, but Sorella Fonstein, sitting in state as obese ladies seem to do, took off her pince-nez (she had been copying a recipe) and said, probably because her husband needed help at this point in his story, "He was locked up."

"Yes, I see."

"You *can't* see," said my stepmother. "Nobody could guess who saved him."

Sorella, who had been a teacher in the Newark school system, made a teacherly gesture. She raised her arm as though to mark a check on the blackboard beside a student's sentence. "Here comes the strange element. This is where Billy Rose plays a part."

I said, "Billy Rose, in Rome? What would he be doing there? Are we talking about Broadway Billy Rose? You mean Damon Runyon's pal, the guy who married Fanny Brice?"

"He can't believe it," said my stepmother.

In Fascist Rome, the child of her sister, her own flesh and blood, had seen Hitler at a reception. He was put in prison. There was no hope for him. Roman Jews were then being trucked to caves outside the city and shot. But he was saved by a New York celebrity.

"You're telling me," I said, "that Billy was running an underground operation in Rome?"

"For a while, yes, he had an Italian organization," said Sorella. Just then I needed an American intermediary. The range of Aunt Mildred's English was limited. Besides, she was a dull lady, slow in all her ways, totally unlike my hasty, vivid father. Mildred had a powdered look, like her own strudel. Her strudel was the best. But when she talked to you she lowered her head. She too had a heavy head. You saw her parted hair oftener than her face.

"Billy Rose did good things too," she said, nursing her fingers in her lap. On Sundays she wore a green, beaded dark dress.

"*That* character! I can't feature it. The Aquacade man? He saved you from the Roman cops?"

"From the Nazis." My stepmother again lowered her head when she spoke. It was her dyed and parted hair that I had to interpret.

"How did you find this out?" I asked Fonstein.

"I was in a cell by myself. Those years, every jail in Europe was full, I guess. Then one day, a stranger showed up and talked to me through the grille. You know what? I thought maybe Ciano sent him. It came in my mind because this Ciano could have asked for me at the hotel. Sure, he dressed in fancy uniforms and walked around with his hand on a long knife he carried in his belt. He was a playactor, but I thought he was civilized. He was pleasant. So when the man stood by the grille and looked at me, I went over and said, 'Ciano?' He shook one finger back and forth and said, 'Billy Rose.' I had no idea what he meant. Was it one word or two? A man or a woman? The message from this Italianer was: 'Tomorrow night, same time, your door will be open. Go out in the corridor. Keep turning left. And nobody will stop you. A person will be waiting in a car, and he'll take you to the train for Genoa.' "

"Why, that little operator! Billy had an underground all to himself," I said. "He must've seen Leslie Howard in *The Scarlet Pimpernel*."

"Next night, the guard didn't lock my door after supper, and when the corridor was empty I came out. I felt as if I had whiskey in my legs, but I realized they were holding me for deportation, the SS was at work already, so I opened every door, walked upstairs, downstairs, and when I got to the street there was a car waiting and people leaning on it, speaking in normal voices. When I came up, the driver pushed me in the back and drove me to the Trastevere station. He gave me new identity papers. He said nobody would be looking for me, because my whole police file had been stolen. There was a hat and coat for me in the rear seat, and he gave me the name of a hotel in Genoa, by the waterfront. That's where I was contacted. I had passage on a Swedish ship to Lisbon."

Europe could go to hell without Fonstein.

My father looked at us sidelong with those keen eyes of his. He had heard the story many times.

I came to know it too. I got it in episodes, like a Hollywood serial—the Saturday thriller, featuring Harry Fonstein and Billy Rose, or Bellarosa. For Fonstein, in Genoa, while he was hiding in great fear in a waterfront hotel, had no other name for him. During the voyage, nobody on the refugee ship had ever heard of Bellarosa.

When the ladies were in the kitchen and my father was in the den, reading the Sunday paper, I would ask Fonstein for further details of his adventures (his torments). He couldn't have known what mental files they were going into or that they were being cross-referenced with Billy Rose—one of those insignificant-significant characters whose name will be recognized chiefly by show-biz historians. The late Billy, the business partner of Prohibition hoodlums, the sidekick of Arnold Rothstein; multimillionaire Billy, the protégé of Bernard Baruch, the young shorthand prodigy whom Woodrow Wilson, mad for shorthand, invited to the White House for a discussion of the rival systems of Pitman and Gregg; Billy the producer, the consort of Eleanor Holm, the mermaid queen of the New York World's Fair; Billy the collector of Matisse, Seurat, and so forth . . . nationally syndicated Billy, the gossip columnist. A Village pal of mine was a member of his ghostwriting team.

This was the Billy to whom Harry Fonstein owed his life.

I spoke of this ghostwriter—Wolfe was his name—and thereafter Fonstein may have considered me a possible channel to Billy himself. He never had met Billy, you see. Apparently Billy refused to be thanked by the Jews his Broadway underground had rescued.

The Italian agents who had moved Fonstein from place to place wouldn't talk. The Genoa man referred to Bellarosa but answered none of Fonstein's questions. I assume that Mafia people from Brooklyn had put together Billy's Italian operation. After the war, Sicilian gangsters were decorated by the British for their work in the Resistance. Fonstein said that with Italians, when they had secrets to keep, tiny muscles came out in the face that nobody otherwise saw. "The man lifted up his hands as if he was going to steal a shadow off the wall and stick it in his pocket." Yesterday a hit man, today working against the Nazis.

Fonstein's type was *edel*—well-bred—but he also was a tough Jew. Sometimes his look was that of a man holding the lead in the hundred-meter breast-stroke race. Unless you shot him, he was going to win. He had something in common with his Mafia saviors, whose secrets convulsed their faces.

During the crossing he thought a great deal about the person who had had him smuggled out of Italy, imagining various kinds of philanthropists and idealists ready to spend their last buck to rescue their people from Treblinka.

"How was I supposed to guess what kind of man—or maybe a committee, the Bellarosa Society—did it?"

No, it was Billy acting alone on a spurt of feeling for his fellow Jews and squaring himself to outwit Hitler and Himmler and cheat them of their victims. On another day he'd set his heart on a baked potato, a hot dog, a cruise around Manhattan on the Circle Line. There were, however, spots of deep feeling in flimsy Billy. The God of his fathers still mattered. Billy was as spattered as a Jackson Pollock painting, and among the main trickles was his Jewishness, with other streaks flowing toward secrecy—streaks of sexual weakness, sexual humiliation. At the same time, he had to have his name in the paper. As someone said, he had a buglike tropism for publicity. Yet his rescue operation in Europe remained secret.

Fonstein, one of the refugee crowd sailing to New York, wondered how many others among the passengers might have been saved by Billy. Nobody talked much. Experienced people begin at a certain point to keep their own counsel and refrain from telling their stories to one another. Fonstein was eaten alive by his fantasies of what he would do in New York. He said that at night when the

ship rolled he was like a weighted rope, twisting and untwisting. He expected
that Billy, if he had saved scads of people, would have laid plans for their future
too. Fonstein didn't foresee that they would gather together and cry like Joseph
and his brethren. Nothing like that. No, they would be put up in hotels or
maybe in an old sanitarium, or boarded with charitable families. Some would
want to go to Palestine; most would opt for the U.S.A. and study English, perhaps finding jobs in industry or going to technical schools.

But Fonstein was detained at Ellis Island. Refugees were not being admitted
then. "They fed us well," he told me. "I slept in a wire bin, on an upper bunk. I
could see Manhattan. They told me, though, that I'd have to go to Cuba. I still
didn't know who Billy was, but I waited for his help.

"And after a few weeks a woman was sent by Rose Productions to talk to me.
She dressed like a young girl—lipstick, high heels, earrings, a hat. She had legs
like posts and looked like an actress from the Yiddish theater, about ready to begin to play older roles, disappointed and sad. She called herself a *dramatisten*
and was in her fifties if not more. She said my case was being turned over to the
Hebrew Immigrant Aid Society. They would take care of me. No more Billy
Rose."

"You must have been shook up."

"Of course. But I was even more curious than dashed. I asked her about the
man who rescued me. I said I would like to give Billy my thanks personally.
She brushed this aside. Irrelevant. She said, 'After Cuba, maybe.' I saw that she
doubted it would happen. I asked, did he help lots of people. She said, 'Sure he
helps, but himself he helps first, and you should hear him scream over a dime.'
He was very famous, he was rich, he owned the Ziegfeld Building and was continually in the papers. What was he like? Tiny, greedy, smart. He underpaid the
employees, and they were afraid of the boss. He dressed very well, and he was a
Broadway character and sat all night in cafés. 'He can call up Governor Dewey
and talk to him whenever he likes.'

"That was what she said. She said also, 'He pays me twenty-two bucks, and if
I even hint a raise I'll be fired. So what then? Second Avenue is dead. For Yiddish radio there's a talent oversupply. If not for the boss, I'd fade away in the
Bronx. Like this, at least I work on Broadway. But you're a greener, and to you
it's all a blank.'

" 'If he hadn't saved me from deportation, I'd have ended like others in my
family. I owe him my life.'

" 'Probably so,' she agreed.

" 'Wouldn't it be normal to be interested in a man you did that for? Or at
least have a look, shake a hand, speak a word?'

" 'It would have *been* normal,' she said. 'Once.'

"I began to realize," said Fonstein, "that she was a sick person. I believe she had TB. It wasn't the face powder that made her so white. White was to her what yellow color is to a lemon. What I saw was not makeup—it was the Angel of Death. Tubercular people often are quick and nervous. Her name was Missus Hamet—*khomet* being the Yiddish word for a horse collar. She was from Galicia, like me. We had the same accent."

A Chinese singsong. Aunt Mildred had it too—comical to other Jews, uproarious in a Yiddish music hall.

" 'HIAS will get work for you in Cuba. They take terrific care of you fellas. Billy thinks the war is in a new stage. Roosevelt is for King Saud, and those Arabians hate Jews and keep the door to Palestine shut. That's why Rose changed his operations. He and his friends are now chartering ships for refugees. The Romanian government will sell them to the Jews at fifty bucks a head, and there are seventy thousand of them. That's a lot of moola. Better hurry before the Nazis take over Romania.' "

Fonstein said very reasonably, "I told her how useful I might be. I spoke four languages. But she was hardened to people pleading, ingratiating themselves with their lousy gratitude. Hey, it's an ancient routine," said Fonstein, standing on the four-inch sole of his laced boot. His hands were in his pockets and took no part in the eloquence of his shrug. His face was, briefly, like a notable face in a museum case, in a dark room, its pallor spotlighted so that the skin was stippled, a curious effect, like stony gooseflesh. Except that he was not on show for the brilliant deeds he had done. As men go, he was as plain as seltzer.

Billy didn't want his gratitude. First your suppliant takes you by the knees. Then he asks for a small loan. He wants a handout, a pair of pants, a pad to sleep in, a meal ticket, a bit of capital to go into business. One man's gratitude is poison to his benefactor. Besides, Billy was fastidious about persons. In principle they were welcome to his goodwill, but they drove him to hysteria when they put their moves on him.

"Never having set foot in Manhattan, I had no clue," said Fonstein. "Instead there were bizarre fantasies, but what good were those? New York is a collective fantasy of millions. There's just so much a single mind can do with it."

Mrs. Horsecollar (her people had had to be low-caste teamsters in the Old Country) warned Fonstein, "Billy doesn't want you to mention his name to HIAS."

"So how did I get to Ellis Island?"

"Make up what you like. Say that a married Italian woman loved you and stole money from her husband to buy papers for you. But no leaks on Billy."

Here my father told Fonstein, "I can mate you in five moves." My old man would have made a mathematician if he had been more withdrawn from human affairs. Only, his motive for concentrated thought was winning. My father wouldn't apply himself where there was no opponent to beat.

I have my own fashion of testing my powers. Memory is my field. But also my faculties are not what they once were. I haven't got Alzheimer's, *absit omen* or *nicht da gedacht*—no sticky matter on my recollection cells. But I am growing slower. Now who was the man that Fonstein had worked for in Havana? Once I had instant retrieval for such names. No electronic system was in it with me. Today I darken and grope occasionally. But thank God I get a reprieve—Fonstein's Cuban employer was Salkind, and Fonstein was his legman. All over South America there were Yiddish newspapers. In the Western Hemisphere, Jews were searching for surviving relatives and studying the published lists of names. Many DPs were dumped in the Caribbean and in Mexico. Fonstein quickly added Spanish and English to his Polish, German, Italian, and Yiddish. He took engineering courses in a night school instead of hanging out in bars or refugee cafés. To tourists, Havana was a holiday town for gambling, drinking, and whoring—an abortion center as well. Unhappy single girls came down from the States to end their love pregnancies. Others, more farsighted, flew in to look among the refugees for husbands and wives. Find a spouse of a stable European background, a person schooled in suffering and endurance. Somebody who had escaped death. Women who found no takers in Baltimore, Kansas City, or Minneapolis, worthy girls to whom men never proposed, found husbands in Mexico, Honduras, and Cuba.

After five years, Fonstein's employer was prepared to vouch for him, and sent for Sorella, his niece. To imagine what Fonstein and Sorella saw in each other when they were introduced was in the early years beyond me. Whenever we met in Lakewood, Sorella was dressed in a suit. When she crossed her legs and he noted the volume of her underthighs, an American observer like me could, and would, picture the entire woman unclothed, and depending on his experience of life and his acquaintance with art, he might attribute her type to an appropriate painter. In my mental picture of Sorella I chose Rembrandt's Saskia over the nudes of Rubens. But then Fonstein, when he took off his surgical boot, was . . . well, he had imperfections too. So man and wife could forgive each other. I think my tastes would have been more like those of Billy Rose—water nymphs, Loreleis, or chorus girls. Eastern European men had more sober standards. In my father's place, I would have had to make the sign of the cross over Aunt Mildred's face while getting into bed with her—something exorcistic (far-fetched) to take the curse off. But you see, I was not my father, I was his spoiled American son. Your stoical forebears took their lumps in bed. As for Billy, with his trousers and shorts at his ankles, chasing girls who had come to be auditioned, he would have done better with Mrs. Horsecollar. If he'd forgive her bagpipe udders and estuary leg veins, she'd forgive his unheroic privates, and they could pool their wretched mortalities and stand by each other for better or worse.

Sorella's obesity, her beehive coif, the preposterous pince-nez—a "lady" put-on—made me wonder: What *is* it with such people? Are they female impersonators, drag queens?

This was a false conclusion reached by a middle-class boy who considered himself an enlightened bohemian. I was steeped in the exciting sophistication of the Village.

I was altogether wrong, dead wrong about Sorella, but at the time my perverse theory found some support in Fonstein's story of his adventures. He told me how he had sailed from New York and gone to work for Salkind in Havana while learning Spanish together with English and studying refrigeration and heating in a night school. "Till I met an American girl, down there on a visit."

"You met Sorella. And you fell in love with her?"

He gave me a hard-edged Jewish look when I spoke of love. How do you distinguish among love, need, and prudence?

Deeply experienced people—this continually impresses me—will keep things to themselves. Which is all right for those who don't intend to go beyond experience. But Fonstein belonged to an even more advanced category, those who don't put such restraints on themselves and feel able to enter the next zone; in that next zone, their aim is to convert weaknesses and secrets into burnable energy. A first-class man subsists on the matter he destroys, just as the stars do. But I am going beyond Fonstein, needlessly digressing. Sorella wanted a husband, while Fonstein needed U.S. naturalization papers. *Mariage de convenance* was how I saw it.

It's always the falsest formulation that you're proudest of.

Fonstein took a job in a New Jersey shop that subcontracted the manufacture of parts in the heating-equipment line. He did well there, a beaver for work, and made rapid progress in his sixth language. Before long he was driving a new Pontiac. Aunt Mildred said it was a wedding present from Sorella's family. "They are *so* relieved," Mildred told me. "A few years more, and Sorella would be too old for a baby." One child was what the Fonsteins had, a son, Gilbert. He was said to be a prodigy in mathematics and physics. Some years down the line, Fonstein consulted me about the boy's education. By then he had the money to send him to the best schools. Fonstein had improved and patented a thermostat, and with Sorella's indispensable help he became a rich man. She was a tiger wife. Without her, he was to tell me, there would have been no patent. "My company would have stolen me blind. I wouldn't be the man you're looking at today."

I then examined the Fonstein who stood before me. He was wearing an Italian shirt, a French necktie, and his orthopedic boot was British-made—bespoke on Jermyn Street. With that heel he might have danced the flamenco. How different from the crude Polish article, boorishly ill-made, in which he had hobbled across Europe and escaped from prison in Rome. *That* boot, as he dodged the Nazis, he had dreaded to take off, nights, for if it had been stolen he would have been caught and killed in his short-legged nakedness. The SS would not have bothered to drive him into a cattle car.

How pleased his rescuer, Billy Rose, should have been to see the Fonstein of today: the pink, white-collared Italian shirt, the rue de Rivoli tie, knotted under Sorella's instruction, the easy hang of the imported suit, the good color of his face, which, no longer stone white, had the full planes and the color of a ripe pomegranate.

But Fonstein and Billy never actually met. Fonstein had made it his business to see Billy, but Billy was never to see Fonstein. Letters were returned. Sometimes there were accompanying messages, never once in Billy's own hand. Mr. Rose wished Harry Fonstein well but at the moment couldn't give him an appointment. When Fonstein sent Billy a check accompanied by a note of thanks and the request that the money be used for charitable purposes, it was returned without acknowledgment. Fonstein came to his office and was turned away. When he tried one day to approach Billy at Sardi's he was intercepted by one of the restaurant's personnel. You weren't allowed to molest celebrities here.

Finding his way blocked, Fonstein said to Billy in his Galician-Chinese singsong, "I came to tell you I'm one of the people you rescued in Italy." Billy turned toward the wall of his booth, and Fonstein was escorted to the street.

In the course of years, long letters were sent. "I want nothing from you, not even to shake hands, but to speak man to man for a minute."

It was Sorella, back in Lakewood, who told me this, while Fonstein and my father were sunk in a trance over the chessboard. "Rose, that special party, won't see Harry," said Sorella.

My comment was "I break my head trying to understand why it's so important for Fonstein. He's been turned down? So he's been turned down."

"To express gratitude," said Sorella. "All he wants to say is 'Thanks.' "

"And this wild pygmy absolutely refuses."

"Behaves as if Harry Fonstein never existed."

"Why, do you suppose? Afraid of the emotions? Too Jewish a moment for him? Drags him down from his standing as a full-fledged American? What's your husband's opinion?"

"Harry thinks it's some kind of change in the descendants of immigrants in this country," said Sorella.

And I remember today what a pause this answer gave me. I myself had often wondered uncomfortably about the Americanization of the Jews. One could begin with physical differences. My father's height was five feet six inches, mine was six feet two inches. To my father, this seemed foolishly wasteful somehow. Perhaps the reason was biblical, for King Saul, who stood head and shoulders above the others, was *verrucht*—demented and doomed. The prophet Samuel had warned Israel not to take a king, and Saul did not find favor in God's eyes.

Therefore a Jew should not be unnecessarily large but rather finely made, strong but compact. The main thing was to be deft and quick-witted. That was how my father was and how he would have preferred me to be. My length was superfluous, I had too much chest and shoulders, big hands, a wide mouth, a band of black mustache, too much voice, excessive hair; the shirts that covered my trunk had too many red and gray stripes, idiotically flashy. Fools ought to come in smaller sizes. A big son was a threat, a parricide. Now Fonstein, despite his short leg, was a proper man, well arranged, trim, sensible, and clever. His development was hastened by Hitlerism. Losing your father at the age of fourteen brings your childhood to an end. Burying your mother in a foreign cemetery, no time to mourn, caught with false documents, doing time in the slammer ("sitting" is the Jewish term for it: *"Er hat gesessen"*). A man acquainted with grief. No time for froth or moronic laughter, for vanities and games, for climbing the walls, for effeminacies or infantile plaintiveness.

I didn't agree, of course, with my father. We were bigger in my generation because we had better nutrition. We were, moreover, less restricted, we had wider liberties. We grew up under a larger range of influences and thoughts—we were the children of a great democracy, bred to equality, living it up with no pales to confine us. Why, until the end of the last century, the Jews of Rome were still locked in for the night; the Pope ceremonially entered the ghetto once a year and spat ritually on the garments of the chief rabbi. Were we giddy here? No doubt about it. But there were no cattle cars waiting to take us to camps and gas chambers.

One can think of such things—and think and *think*—but nothing is resolved by these historical meditations. To *think* doesn't settle anything. No idea is more than an imaginary potency, a Los Alamos mushroom cloud (destroying nothing, making nothing) rising from blinding consciousness.

And Billy Rose wasn't big; he was about the size of Peter Lorre. But oh! he was American. There was a penny-arcade jingle about Billy, the popping of shooting galleries, the rattling of pinballs, the weak human cry of the Times Square geckos, the lizard gaze of sideshow freaks. To see him as he was, you have to place him against the whitewash glare of Broadway in the wee hours. But even such places have their grandees—people whose defects can be converted to seed money for enterprises. There's nothing in this country that you can't sell, nothing too weird to bring to market and found a fortune on. And once you got as much major real estate as Billy had, then it didn't matter that you were one of the human deer that came uptown from the Lower East Side to graze on greasy sandwich papers. Billy? Well, Billy had bluffed out mad giants like Robert Moses. He bought the Ziegfeld Building for peanuts. He installed Eleanor Holm in a mansion and hung the walls with masterpieces. And he went on from there. They'd say in feudal Ireland that a proud man is a lovely man (Yeats's Parnell), but in glamorous New York he could be lovely because the columnists said he was—George Sokolsky, Walter Winchell, Leonard Lyons, the "Midnight Earl"—and also Hollywood pals and leaders of nightclub society. Billy was all over the place. Why, he was even a newspaper columnist, and syndicated. True, he had ghostwriters, but he was the mastermind who made all the basic decisions and vetted every word they printed.

Fonstein was soon familiar with Billy's doings, more familiar than I ever was or cared to be. But then Billy had saved the man: took him out of prison, paid his way to Genoa, installed him in a hotel, got him passage on a neutral ship. None of this could Fonstein have done for himself, and you'd never in the world hear him deny it.

"Of course," said Sorella, with gestures that only a two-hundred-pound woman can produce, because her delicacy rests on the mad overflow of her behind, "though my husband has given up on making contact, he hasn't stopped, and he can't stop being grateful. He's a dignified individual himself, but he's also a very smart man and has got to be conscious of the kind of person that saved him."

"Does it upset him? It could make him unhappy to be snatched from death by a kibitzer."

"It gets to him sometimes, yes."

She proved quite a talker, this Sorella. I began to look forward to our conversations as much for what came out of her as for the intrinsic interest of the subject. Also I had mentioned that I was a friend of Wolfe, one of Billy's ghosts, and maybe she was priming me. Wolfe might even take the matter up with Billy. I informed Sorella up front that Wolfe would never do it. "This Wolfe," I told her, "is a funny type, a little guy who seduces big girls. Very clever. He hangs out at Birdland and dotes on Broadway freaks. In addition, he's a Yale-trained intellectual heavy, or so he likes to picture himself; he treasures his kinks and loves being deep. For instance, his mother also is his cleaning lady. He told me recently as I watched a woman on her knees scrubbing out his pad, 'The old girl you're looking at is my mother.' "

"Her own dear boy?" said Sorella.

"An only child," I said.

"She must love him like anything."

"I don't doubt it for a minute. To him, that's what's deep. Although Wolfe is decent, under it all. He has to support her anyway. What harm is there in saving ten bucks a week on the cleaning? Besides which he builds up his reputation as a weirdo nihilist. He wants to become the Thomas Mann of science fiction. That's his real aim, he says, and he only dabbles in Broadway. It amuses him to write Billy's columns and break through in print with expressions like: 'I'm going to hit him on his pointy head. I'll give him such a *hit!* '"

Sorella listened and smiled, though she didn't wish to appear familiar with these underground characters and their language or habits, with Village sex or Broadway sleaze. She brought the conversation back to Fonstein's rescue and the history of the Jews.

She and I found each other congenial, and before long I was speaking as openly to her as I would in a Village conversation, let's say with Paul Goodman at the Casbah, not as though she were merely a square fat lady from the dark night of petty-bourgeois New Jersey—no more than a carrier or genetic relay to produce a science savant of the next generation. She had made a respectable ("contemptible") marriage. However, she was also a tiger wife, a tiger mother. It was no negligible person who had patented Fonstein's thermostat and rounded up the money for his little factory (it *was* little at first), meanwhile raising a boy who was a mathematical genius. She was a spirited woman, at home with ideas. This heavy tailored lady was extremely well informed. I wasn't inclined to discuss Jewish history with her—it put my teeth on edge at first—but she overcame my resistance. She was well up on the subject, and besides, damn it, you couldn't say no to Jewish history after what had happened in Nazi Germany. You had to listen. It turned out that as the wife of a refugee she had set herself to master the subject, and I heard a great deal from her about the technics of annihilation, the large-scale-industry aspect of it. What she occasionally talked about while Fonstein and my father stared at the chessboard, sealed in their trance, was the black humor, the slapstick side of certain camp operations. Being a French teacher, she was familiar with Jarry and *Ubu Roi,* Pataphysics, Absurdism, Dada, Surrealism. Some camps were run in a burlesque style that forced you to make these connections. Prisoners were sent naked into a swamp and had to croak and hop like frogs. Children were hanged while starved, freezing slave laborers lined up on parade in front of the gallows and a prison band played Viennese light opera waltzes.

I didn't want to hear this, and I said impatiently, "All right, Billy Rose wasn't the only one in show biz. So the Germans did it too, and what they staged in Nuremberg was bigger than Billy's rally in Madison Square Garden—the 'We Will Never Die' pageant."

I understood Sorella: the object of her researches was to assist her husband. He was alive today because a little Jewish promoter took it into his queer head to organize a Hollywood-style rescue. I was invited to meditate on themes like: Can Death Be Funny? or Who Gets the Last Laugh? I wouldn't do it, though. First those people murdered you, then they forced you to brood on their crimes. It suffocated me to do this. Hunting for causes was a horrible imposition added to the original "selection," gassing, cremation. I didn't want to think of the history and psychology of these abominations, death chambers and furnaces. Stars are nuclear furnaces too. Such things are utterly beyond me, a pointless exercise.

Also my advice to Fonstein—given mentally—was: Forget it. Go American.

Work at your business. Market your thermostats. Leave the theory side of it to your wife. She has a taste for it, and she's a clever woman. If she enjoys collecting a Holocaust library and wants to ponder the subject, why not? Maybe she'll write a book herself, about the Nazis and the entertainment industry. Death and mass fantasy.

My own suspicion was that there was a degree of fantasy embodied in Sorella's obesity. She was biologically dramatized in waves and scrolls of tissue. Still, she was, at bottom, a serious woman fully devoted to her husband and child. Fonstein had his talents; Sorella, however, had the business brain. And Fonstein didn't have to be told to go American. Together this couple soon passed from decent prosperity to real money. They bought property east of Princeton, off toward the ocean, they educated the boy, and when they had sent him away to camp in the summer, they traveled. Sorella, the onetime French teacher, had a taste for Europe. She had had, moreover, the good luck to find a European husband.

Toward the close of the fifties they went to Israel, and as it happened, business had brought me to Jerusalem too. The Israelis, who culturally had one of everything in the world, had invited me to open a memory institute.

So, in the lobby of the King David, I met the Fonsteins. "Haven't seen you in years!" said Fonstein.

True, I had moved to Philadelphia and married a Main Line lady. We lived in a brownstone mansion, which had a closed garden and an 1817 staircase photographed by *American Heritage* magazine. My father had died; his widow had gone to live with a niece. I seldom saw the old lady and had to ask the Fonsteins how she was. Over the last decade I had had only one contact with the Fonsteins, a telephone conversation about their gifted boy.

This year, they had sent him to a summer camp for little science prodigies.

Sorella was particularly happy to see me. She was sitting—at her weight I suppose one generally is more comfortable seated—and she was unaffectedly pleased to find me in Jerusalem. My thought about the two of them was that it was good for a DP to have ample ballast in his missus. Besides, I believe that he loved her. My own wife was something of a Twiggy. One never does strike it absolutely right. Sorella, calling me "Cousin," said in French that she was still a *femme bien en chair*. I wondered how a man found his way among so many creases. But that was none of my business. They looked happy enough.

The Fonsteins had rented a car. Harry had relations in Haifa, and they were going to tour the north of the country. Wasn't it an extraordinary place! said Sorella, dropping her voice to a theatrical whisper. (What was there to keep secret?) Jews who were electricians and bricklayers, Jewish policemen, engineers, and sea captains. Fonstein was a good walker. In Europe he had walked a thousand miles in his Polish boot. Sorella, however, was not built for sight-seeing.

"I should be carried in a litter," she said. "But that's not a trade for Israelis, is it?" She invited me to have tea with her while Fonstein looked up hometown people—neighbors from Lemberg.

Before our tea, I went up to my room to read the *Herald Tribune*—one of the distinct pleasures of being abroad—but I settled down with the paper in order to think about the Fonsteins (my two-in-one habit—like using music as a background for reflection). The Fonsteins were not your predictable, disposable distant family relations who labeled themselves by their clothes, their conversation, the cars they drove, their temple memberships, their party politics. Fonstein for all his Jermyn Street boots and Italianate suits was still the man who had buried his mother in Venice and waited in his cell for Ciano to rescue him. Though his face was silent and his manner "socially advanced"—this was the only term I could apply: far from the Jewish style acquired in New Jersey communities—I believe that he was thinking intensely about his European origin and his American transformation: Part I and Part II. Signs of a tenacious memory in others seldom escape me. I always ask, however, what people are doing with their recollections. Rote, mechanical storage, an unusual capacity for retaining facts, has a limited interest for me. Idiots can have that gift. Nor do I care much for nostalgia and its associated sentiments. In most cases, I dislike it. Fonstein was *doing* something with his past. This was the lively, the active element of his still look. But you no more discussed this with a man than you asked how he felt about his smooth boot with the four-inch sole.

Then there was Sorella. No ordinary woman, she broke with every sign of ordinariness. Her obesity, assuming she had some psychic choice in the matter, was a sign of this. She might have willed herself to be thinner, for she had the strength of character to do it. Instead she accepted the challenge of size as a Houdini might have asked for tighter knots, more locks on the trunk, deeper rivers to escape from. She was, as people nowadays say, "off the continuum"— her graph went beyond the chart and filled up the whole wall. In my King David reverie, I put it that she had had to wait for an uncle in Havana to find a husband for her—she had been a matrimonial defective, a reject. To come out of it gave her a revolutionary impulse. There was going to be no sign of her early humiliation, not in *any* form, no bitter residue. What you didn't want you would shut out decisively. You had been unhealthy, lumpish. Your fat had made you pale and clumsy. Nobody, not even a lout, had come to court you. What do you do now with this painful record of disgrace? You don't bury it, nor do you transform it; you *annihilate* it and then use the space to draw a more powerful design. You draw it in freedom because you can afford to, not because there's anything to hide. The new design, as I saw it, was not an invention. The Sorella I saw was not constructed but revealed.

I put aside the *Herald Tribune* and went down in the elevator. Sorella had settled herself on the terrace of the King David. She wore a dress of whitish beige. The bodice was ornamented with a large square of scalloped material. There was something military and also mystical about this. It made me think of the Knights of Malta—a curious thing to be associated with a Jewish lady from New Jersey. But then the medieval wall of the Old City was just across the valley. In 1959 the Israelis were still shut out of it; it was Indian country then. At the moment, I wasn't thinking of Jews and Jordanians, however. I was having a civilized tea with a huge lady who was also distinctly, authoritatively dainty. The beehive was gone. Her fair hair was cropped, she wore Turkish slippers on her small feet, which were innocently crossed under the beaten brass of the tray table. The Vale of Hinnom, once the Ottoman reservoir, was green and blossoming. What I have to say here is that I was aware of—I directly experienced—the beating of Sorella's heart as it faced the challenge of supply in so extensive an organism. This to me was a bold operation, bigger than the Turkish waterworks. I felt my own heart signifying admiration for hers—the extent of the project it had to face.

Sorella put me in a tranquil state.

"Far from Lakewood."

"That's the way travel is now," I said. "We've done something to distance. Some transformation, some bewilderment."

"And you've come here to set up a branch of your institute—do these people need one?"

"They think they do," I said. "They have a modified Noah's ark idea. They don't want to miss out on anything from the advanced countries. They have to keep up with the world and be a complete microcosm."

"Do you mind if I give you a short, friendly test?"

"Go right ahead."

"Can you remember what I was wearing when we first met in your father's house?"

"You had on a gray tailored suit, not too dark, with a light stripe, and jet earrings."

"Can you tell me who built the Graf Zeppelin?"

"I can—Dr. Hugo Eckener."

"The name of your second-grade teacher, fifty years ago?"

"Miss Emma Cox."

Sorella sighed, less in admiration than in sorrow, in sympathy with the burden of so much useless information.

"That's pretty remarkable," she said. "At least your success with the Mnemosyne Institute has a legitimate basis—I wonder, do you recall the name of the woman Billy Rose sent to Ellis Island to talk to Harry?"

"That was Mrs. Hamet. Harry thought she was suffering from TB."

"Yes, that's correct."

"Why do you ask?"

"Over the years I had some contact with her. First she looked us up. Then I looked her up. I cultivated her. I liked the old lady, and she found me also sympathetic. We saw a lot of each other."

"You put it all in the past tense."

"That's where it belongs. A while back, she passed away in a sanitarium near White Plains. I used to visit her. You might say a bond formed between us. She had no family to speak of. . . ."

"A Yiddish actress, wasn't she?"

"True, and she was personally theatrical, but not only from nostalgia for a vanished art—the Vilna Troupe, or Second Avenue. It was also because she had a combative personality. There was lots of sophistication in that character, lots of purpose. Plenty of patience. Plus a hell of a lot of stealth."

"What did she need the stealth for?"

"For many years she kept an eye on Billy's doings. She put everything in a journal. As well as she could, she maintained a documented file—notes on comings and goings, dated records of telephone conversations, carbon copies of letters."

"Personal or business?"

"You couldn't draw a clear line."

"What's the good of all this material?"

"I can't say exactly."

"Did she hate the man? Was she trying to get him?"

"Actually, I don't believe she was. She was very tolerant—as much as she could be, leading a nickel-and-dime life and feeling mistreated. But I don't think she wanted to nail him by his iniquities. He was a celeb, to her—that was what she called him. She ate at the Automat; he was a celeb, so he took his meals at Sardi's, Dempsey's, or in Sherman Billingsley's joint. No hard feelings over it. The Automat gave good value for your nickels, and she used to say she had a healthier diet."

"I seem to recall she was badly treated."

"So was everybody else, and they all said they detested him. What did your friend Wolfe tell you?"

"He said that Billy had a short fuse. That he was a kind of botch. Still, it made Wolfe ecstatic to have a Broadway connection. There was glamour in the Village if you were one of Billy's ghosts. It gave Wolfe an edge with smart girls who came downtown from Vassar or Smith. He didn't have first-class intellectual credentials in the Village, he wasn't a big-time wit, but he was eager to go forward, meaning that he was prepared to take abuse—and they had plenty of it to give—from the top wise-guy theoreticians, the heavyweight pundits, in order to get an education in modern life—which meant you could combine Kierkegaard and Birdland in the same breath. He was a big chaser. But he didn't abuse or sponge on girls. When he was seducing, he started the young lady off on a box of candy. The next stage, always the same, was a cashmere sweater—both candy and cashmere from a guy who dealt in stolen goods. When the affair was over, the chicks were passed on to somebody more crude and lower on the totem pole. . . ."

Here I made a citizen's arrest, mentally—I checked myself. It was the totem pole that did it. A Jew in Jerusalem, and one who was able to explain where we were at—how Moses had handed on the law to Joshua, and Joshua to the Judges, the Judges to the Prophets, the Prophets to the Rabbis, so that at the end of the line, a Jew from secular America (a diaspora within a diaspora) could jive glibly about the swinging Village scene of the fifties and about totem poles, about Broadway lowlife and squalor. Especially if you bear in mind that this particular Jew couldn't say what place he held in this great historical procession. I had concluded long ago that the Chosen were chosen to read God's mind. Over the millennia, this turned out to be a zero-sum game.

I wasn't about to get into that.

"So old Mrs. Hamet died," I said, in a sad tone. I recalled her face as Fonstein had described it, whiter than confectioners' sugar. It was almost as though I had known her.

"She wasn't exactly a poor old thing," said Sorella. "Nobody asked her to participate, but she was a player nevertheless."

"She kept this record—why?"

"Billy obsessed her to a bizarre degree. She believed that they belonged together because they were similar—defective people. The unfit, the rejects, coming together to share each other's burden."

"Did she want to be Mrs. Rose?"

"No, no—that was out of the question. He only married celebs. She had no PR value—she was old, no figure, no complexion, no money, no status. Too late even for penicillin to save her. But she did make it her business to know everything about him. When she let herself go, she was extremely obscene. Obscenity was linked to everything. She certainly knew all the words. She could sound like a man."

"And she thought she should tell you? Share her research?"

"Me, yes. She approached us through Harry, but the friendship was with me. Those two seldom met, almost never."

"And she left you her files?"

"A journal plus supporting evidence."

"Ugh!" I said. The tea had steeped too long and was dark. Lemon lightened the color, and sugar was just what I needed late in the afternoon to pick me up.

I said to Sorella, "Is this journal any good to you? You don't need any help from Billy."

"Certainly not. America, as they say, has been good to us. However, it's quite a document she left. I think you'd find it so."

"If I cared to read it."

"If you started, you'd go on, all right."

She was offering it. She had brought it with her to Jerusalem! And why had she done that? Not to show to me, certainly. She couldn't have known that she was going to meet me here. We had been out of touch for years. I was not on good terms with the family, you see. I had married a Wasp lady, and my father and I had quarreled. I was a Philadelphian now, without contacts in New Jersey. New Jersey to me was only a delay en route to New York or Boston. A psychic darkness. Whenever possible I omitted New Jersey. Anyway, I chose not to read the journal.

Sorella said, "You may be wondering what use I might make of it."

Well, I wondered, of course, why she hadn't left Mrs. Hamet's journal at home. Frankly, I didn't care to speculate on her motives. What I understood clearly was that she was oddly keen to have me read it. Maybe she wanted my advice. "Has your husband gone through it?" I said.

"He wouldn't understand the language."

"And it would embarrass you to translate it."

"That's more or less it," said Sorella.

"So it's pretty hairy in places? You said she knew the words. Clinical stuff didn't scare Mrs. Hamet, did it."

"In these days of scientific sex studies, there's not much that's new and shocking," said Sorella.

"The shock comes from the source. When it's someone in the public eye."

"Yes, I figured that."

Sorella was a proper person. She was not suggesting that I share any lewdnesses with her. Nothing was further from her than evil communications. She had never in her life seduced anyone—I'd bet a year's income on that. She was as stable in character as she was immense in her person. The square on the bosom of her dress, with its scalloped design, was like a repudiation of all trivial mischief. The scallops themselves seemed to me to be a kind of message in cursive characters, warning against kinky interpretations, perverse attributions.

She was silent. She seemed to say: Do you doubt me?

Well, this was Jerusalem, and I am unusually susceptible to places. In a moment I had touched base with the Crusaders, with Caesar and Christ, the kings of Israel. There was also the heart beating in her (in me too) with the persistence of fidelity, a faith in the necessary continuation of a radical mystery—don't ask me to spell it out.

I wouldn't have felt this way in blue-collar Trenton.

Sorella was too big a person to play any kind of troublemaking games or to create minor mischief. Her eyes were like vents of atmospheric blue, and their backing (the camera obscura) referred you to the black of universal space, where there is no object to reflect the flow of invisible light.

Clarification came in a day or two, from an item in that rag the *Post*. Expected soon in Jerusalem were Billy Rose and the designer, artistic planner, and architectural sculptor Isamu Noguchi. Magnificent Rose, always a friend of Israel, was donating a sculpture garden here, filling it with his collection of masterpieces. He had persuaded Noguchi to lay it out for him—or, if that wasn't nifty enough, to preside over its creation, for Billy, as the reporter said, had the philanthropic impulses but was hopeless with the aesthetic requirements. Knew what he wanted; even more, he knew what he *didn't* want.

Any day now they would arrive. They would meet with Jerusalem planning officials, and the prime minister would invite them to dinner.

I couldn't talk to Sorella about this. The Fonsteins had gone to Haifa. Their driver would take them to Nazareth and the Galil, up to the Syrian border. Gennesaret, Capernaum, the Mount of the Beatitudes were on the itinerary. There was no need for questions; I now understood what Sorella was up to. From the poor old Hamet lady, possibly (that sapper, that mole, that dedicated researcher), she had had advance notice, and it wouldn't have been hard to learn the date of Billy's arrival with the eminent Noguchi. Sorella, if she liked, could read Billy the riot act, using Mrs. Hamet's journal as her promptbook. I wondered just how this would happen. The general intention was all I could make out. If Billy was ingenious in getting maximum attention (half magnificence, half baloney and smelling like it), if Noguchi was ingenious in the department of beautiful settings, it remained to be seen what Sorella could come up with in the way of ingenuity.

Technically, she was a housewife. On any questionnaire or application she would have put a check in the housewife box. None of what goes with that—home decoration, the choice of place mats, flatware, wallpapers, cooking utensils, the control of salt, cholesterol, carcinogens, preoccupation with hairdressers and nail care, cosmetics, shoes, dress lengths, the time devoted to shopping malls, department stores, health clubs, luncheons, cocktails—none of these things, or forces, or powers (for I see them also as powers, or even spirits), could keep a woman like Sorella in subjection. She was no more a housewife than Mrs. Hamet had been a secretary. Mrs. Hamet was a dramatic artist out of work, a tubercular, moribund, and finally demonic old woman. In leaving her dynamite journal to Sorella, she made a calculated choice, dazzlingly appropriate.

Since Billy and Noguchi arrived at the King David while Sorella and Fonstein were taking time off on the shore of Galilee, and although I was busy with

Mnemosyne business, I nevertheless kept an eye on the newcomers as if I had been assigned by Sorella to watch and report. Predictably, Billy made a stir among the King David guests—mainly Jews from the United States. To some, it was a privilege to see a legendary personality in the lobby and the dining room, or on the terrace. For his part, he didn't encourage contacts, didn't particularly want to know anybody. He had the high color of people who are observed—the cynosure flush.

Immediately he made a scene in the pillared, carpeted lobby. El Al had lost his luggage. A messenger from the prime minister's office came to tell him that it was being traced. It might have gone on to Jakarta. Billy said, "You better fuckin' find it fast. I *order* you! All I got is this suit I traveled in, and how'm I supposed to shave, brush my teeth, change socks, underpants, and sleep without pajamas?" The government would take care of this, but the messenger was forced to hear that the shirts were made at Sulka's and the suits by the Fifth Avenue tailor who served Winchell, or Jack Dempsey, or top executives at RCA. The designer must have chosen a model from the bird family. The cut of Billy's jacket suggested the elegance of thrushes or robins, dazzling fast walkers, fat in the breast and folded wings upcurved. There the analogy stopped. The rest was complex vanity, peevish haughtiness, cold outrage—a proud-peewee performance, of which the premises were that he was a considerable figure, a Broadway personage requiring special consideration, and that he himself owed it to his high show-biz standing to stamp and scream and demand and threaten. Yet all the while, if you looked close at the pink, histrionic, Oriental little face, you saw a small but distinct private sector. It contained quite different data. Billy looked as if he, the *personal* Billy, had other concerns, arising from secret inner reckonings. He had come up from the gutter. That was okay, though, in America the land of opportunity. If he had some gutter in him still, he didn't have to hide it much. In the U.S.A. you could come from nowhere and still stand tall, especially if you had the cash. If you pushed Billy he'd retaliate, and if you can retaliate you've got your self-respect. He could even be a cheapie, it wasn't worth the trouble of covering up. He didn't give a shit who thought what. On the other hand, if he wanted a memorial in Jerusalem, a cultural beauty spot, *that* noble gift was a Billy Rose concept, and don't you forget it. Such components made Billy worth looking at. He combed his hair back like George Raft, or that earlier dude sweetheart Rudolph Valentino. (In the Valentino days, Billy had been a tunesmith in Tin Pan Alley—had composed a little, stolen a little, promoted a whole lot; he still held valuable copyrights.) His look was simultaneously weak and strong. He could claim nothing classic that a well-bred Wasp might claim—a man, say, whose grandfather had gone to Groton, whose remoter ancestors had had the right to wear a breastplate and carry a sword. Weapons were a no-no for Jews in those remoter times, as were blooded horses.

Or the big wars. But the best you could do in the present age if you were of privileged descent was to dress in drab expensive good taste and bear yourself with what was left of the Brahmin or Knickerbocker style. By now that, too, was tired and hokey. For Billy, however, the tailored wardrobe was indispensable— like having an executive lavatory of your own. He couldn't present himself without his suits, and this was what fed his anger with El Al and also his despair. This, as he threw his weight around, was how I read him. Noguchi, in what I fancied to be a state of Zen calm, also watched silently as Billy went through his nerve-storm display.

In quieter moments, when he was in the lounge drinking fruit juice and reading messages from New York, Billy looked as if he couldn't stop lamenting the long sufferings of the Jews and, in addition, his own defeats at the hands of fellow Jews. My guess was that his defeats by lady Jews were the most deeply wounding of all. He could win against men. Women, if I was correctly informed, were too much for him.

If he had been an old-time Eastern European Jew, he would have despised such sex defeats. His main connection being with his God, he would have granted no such power to a woman. The sexual misery you read in Billy's looks was an American torment—straight American. Broadway Billy was, moreover, in the pleasure business. Everything, on his New York premises, was resolved in play, in jokes, games, laughs, put-ons, cock teases. And his business efforts were crowned with money. Uneasy lies the head that has no money crown to wear. Billy didn't have to worry about *that*.

Combine these themes, and you can understand Billy's residual wistfulness, his resignation to forces he couldn't control. What he could control he controlled with great effectiveness. But there was so much that counted—how it counted! And how well he knew that he could do nothing about it.

The Fonsteins returned from Galilee sooner than expected. "Gorgeous, but more for the Christians," Sorella said to me. "For instance, the Mount of Beatitudes." She also said, "There wasn't a rowboat big enough for me to sit in. As for swimming, Harry went in, but I didn't bring a bathing suit."

Her comment on Billy's lost luggage was "It must have embarrassed the hell out of the government. He came to build them a major tourist attraction. If he had kept on hollering, I could see Ben-Gurion himself sitting down at the sewing machine to make him a suit."

The missing bags by then had been recovered—fine-looking articles, like slim leather trunks, brass-bound, and monogrammed. Not from Tiffany, but from the Italian manufacturer who would have supplied Tiffany if Tiffany had sold luggage (obtained through contacts, like the candy and cashmeres of Wolfe the ghostwriter: why should you pay full retail price just because you're a multimillionaire?). Billy gave a press interview and complimented Israel on being part of the modern world. The peevish shadow left his face, and he and Noguchi went out every day to confer on the site of the sculpture garden. The atmosphere at the King David became friendlier. Billy stopped hassling the desk clerks, and the clerks for their part stopped lousing him up. Billy on arrival had made the mistake of asking one of them how much to tip the porter who carried his briefcase to his suite. He said he was not yet at home with the Israeli currency. The clerk had flared up. It made him indignant that a man of such wealth should be miserly with nickels and dimes, and he let him have it. Billy saw to it that the clerk was disciplined by the management. When he heard of this, Fonstein said that in Rome a receptionist in a class hotel would never in the world have made a scene with one of the guests.

"Jewish assumptions," he said. "Not clerks and guests, but one Jew letting another Jew have it—plain talk."

I had expected Harry Fonstein to react strongly to Billy's presence—a guest in the same hotel at prices only the affluent could afford. Fonstein, whom Billy had saved from death, was no more than an undistinguished Jewish American, two tables away in the restaurant. And Fonstein was strong-willed. Under no circumstances would he have approached Billy to introduce himself or to confront him: "I am the man your organization smuggled out of Rome. You brought me to Ellis Island and washed your hands of me, never gave a damn about the future of this refugee. Cut me at Sardi's." No, no, not Harry Fonstein. He understood that there is such a thing as making too much of the destiny of an individual. Besides, it's not really in us nowadays to extend ourselves, to become involved in the fortunes of anyone who happens to approach us.

"Mr. Rose, I am the person you wouldn't see—couldn't fit into your schedule." A look of scalding irony on Fonstein's retributive face. "Now the two of us, in God's eye of terrible judgment, are standing here in this holy city . . ."

Impossible words, an impossible scenario. Nobody says such things, nor would anyone seriously listen if they were said.

No, Fonstein contented himself with observation. You saw a curious light in his eyes when Billy passed, talking to Noguchi. I can't recall a moment when Noguchi replied. Not once did Fonstein discuss with me Billy's presence in the hotel. Again I was impressed with the importance of keeping your mouth shut, the kind of fertility it can induce, the hidden advantages of a buttoned lip.

I did ask Sorella how Fonstein felt at finding Billy here after their trip north.

"A complete surprise."

"Not to you, it wasn't."

"You figured that out, did you?"

"Well, it took no special shrewdness," I said. "I now feel what Dr. Watson must have felt when Sherlock Holmes complimented him on a deduction Holmes had made as soon as the case was outlined to him. Does your husband know about Mrs. Hamet's file?"

"I told him, but I haven't mentioned that I brought the notebook to

Jerusalem. Harry is a sound sleeper, whereas I am an insomniac, so I've been up half the night reading the old woman's record, which damns the guy in the suite upstairs. If I didn't have insomnia, this would keep me awake."

"All about his deals, his vices? Damaging stuff?"

Sorella first shrugged and then nodded. I believe that she herself was perplexed, couldn't quite make up her mind about it.

"If he were thinking of running for president, he wouldn't like this information made public."

"Sure. But he isn't running. He's not a candidate. He's Broadway Billy, not the principal of a girls' school or pastor of the Riverside Church."

"That's the truth. Still, he is a public person."

I didn't pursue the subject. Certainly Billy was an oddity. On the physical side (and in her character too), Sorella also was genuinely odd. She was so much bigger than the bride I had first met in Lakewood that I couldn't keep from speculating on her expansion. She made you look twice at a doorway. When she came to it, she filled the space like a freighter in a canal lock. In its own right, consciousness—and here I refer to my own conscious mind—was yet another oddity. But the strangeness of souls is certainly no news in this day and age.

Fonstein loved her, that was a clear fact. He respected his wife, and I did too. I wasn't poking fun at either of them when I wondered at her size. I never lost sight of Fonstein's history, or of what it meant to be the survivor of such a destruction. Maybe Sorella was trying to incorporate in fatty tissue some portion of what he had lost—members of his family. There's no telling what she might have been up to. All I can say is that it (whatever it was at bottom) was accomplished with some class or style. Exquisite singers can make you forget what hillocks of suet their backsides are. Besides, Sorella did dead sober what delirious sopranos put over on us in a state of false Wagnerian intoxication.

Her approach to Billy, however, was anything but sober, and I doubt that any sober move would have had an effect on Billy. What she did was to send him several pages, three or four items copied from the journal of that poor consumptive the late Mrs. Hamet. Sorella made sure that the clerk put it in Billy's box, for the material was explosive, and in the wrong hands it might have been deadly.

When this was a fait accompli, she told me about it. Too late now to advise her not to do it. "I invited him to have a drink," she said to me.

"Not the three of you . . . ?"

"No. Harry hasn't forgotten the bouncer scene at Sardi's—you may remember—when Billy turned his face to the back of the booth. He'd never again force himself on Billy or any celebrity."

"Billy might still ignore you."

"Well, it's in the nature of an experiment, let's say."

I put aside for once the look of social acceptance so many of us have mastered perfectly and let her see what I thought of her "experiment." She might talk "Science" to her adolescent son, the future physicist. I was not a child you could easily fake out with a prestigious buzzword. Experiment? She was an ingenious and powerful woman who devised intricate, glittering, bristling, needling schemes. What she had in mind was confrontation, a hand-to-hand struggle. The laboratory word was a put-on. "Boldness," "Statecraft," "Passion," "Justice" were the real terms. Still, she may not herself have been clearly aware of this. And then, I later thought, the antagonist *was* Broadway Billy Rose. And she didn't expect him to meet her on the ground she had chosen, did she? What did he care for her big abstractions? He was completely free to say, "I don't know what the fuck you're talking about, and I couldn't care less, lady."

Most interesting—at least to an American mind.

I went about my Mnemosyne business in Jerusalem at a seminar table, unfolding my methods to the Israelis. In the end, Mnemosyne didn't take root in Tel Aviv. (It did thrive in Taiwan and Tokyo.)

On the terrace next day, Sorella, looking pleased and pleasant over her tea, said, "We're going to meet. But he wants me to come to his suite at five o'clock."

"Doesn't want to be seen in public, discussing this . . . ?"

"Exactly."

So she did have real clout, after all. I was sorry now that I hadn't taken the opportunity to read Mrs. Hamet's record. (So much zeal, malice, fury, and tenderness I missed out on.) And I didn't even feel free to ask why Sorella thought Billy had agreed to talk to her. I was sure he wouldn't want to discuss moral theory upstairs. There weren't going to be any revelations, confessions, speculations. People like Billy didn't worry about their deeds, weren't in the habit of accounting to themselves. Very few of us, for that matter, bother about accountability or keep spreadsheets of conscience.

What follows is based on Sorella's report and supplemented by my observations. I don't have to say, "If memory serves." In my case it serves, all right. Besides, I made tiny notes, while she was speaking, on the back pages of my appointment book (the yearly gift to depositors in my Philadelphia bank).

Billy's behavior throughout was austere-to-hostile. Mainly he was displeased. His conversation from the first was negative. The King David suite wasn't up to his standards. You had to rough it here in Jerusalem, he said. But the state was young. They'd catch up by and by. These comments were made when he opened the door. He didn't invite Sorella to sit, but at her weight, on her small feet, she wasn't going to be kept standing, and she settled her body in a striped chair, justifying herself by the human sound she made when she seated herself—exhaling as the cushions exhaled.

This was her first opportunity to look Billy over, and she had a few unforeseeable impressions: so this was Billy from the world of the stars. He was very well dressed, in the clothes he had made such a fuss about. At moments you had the feeling that his sleeves were stuffed with the paper tissue used by high-grade cleaners. I had mentioned that there was something birdlike about the cut of his coat, and she agreed with me, but where I saw a robin or a thrush, plump under the shirt, she said (through having installed a bird feeder in New Jersey) that he was more like a grosbeak; he even had some of the color. One eye was set a little closer to the nose than the other, giving a touch of Jewish pathos to his look. Actually, she said, he was a little like Mrs. Hamet, with the one sad eye in her consumptive, theatrical death-white face. And though his hair was groomed, it wasn't absolutely in place. There was a grosbeak disorder about it.

"At first he thought I was here to put the arm on him," she said.

"Money?"

"Sure—probably money."

I kept her going, with nods and half words, as she described this meeting. Of course: blackmail. A man as deep as Billy could call on years of savvy; he had endless experience in handling the people who came to get something out of him—anglers, con artists, crazies.

Billy said, "I glanced over the pages. How much of it is there, and how upset am I supposed to be about it?"

"Deborah Hamet gave me a stack of material before she died."

"Dead, is she?"

"You know she is."

"I don't know anything," said Billy, meaning that this was information from a sector he cared nothing about.

"Yes, but you do," Sorella insisted. "That woman was mad for you."

"That didn't have to be my business, her emotional makeup. She was part of my office force and got her pay. Flowers were sent to White Plains when she got sick. If I had an idea how she was spying, I wouldn't have been so considerate— the dirt that wild old bag was piling up against me."

Sorella told me, and I entirely believed her, that she had come not to threaten but to discuss, to explore, to sound out. She refused to be drawn into a dispute. She could rely on her bulk to give an impression of the fullest calm. Billy had a quantitative cast of mind—businessmen do—and there was lots of woman here. He couldn't deal even with the slenderest of girls. The least of them had the power to put the sexual whammy (Indian sign) on him. Sorella herself saw this. "If he could change my gender, then he could fight me." This was a hint at the masculinity possibly implicit in her huge size. But she had tidy wrists, small feet, a feminine, lyrical voice. She was wearing perfume. She set her lady self before him, massively. . . . What a formidable, clever wife Fonstein had. The protection he lacked when he was in flight from Hitler he had found on our side of the Atlantic.

"Mr. Rose, you haven't called me by name," she said to him. "You read my letter, didn't you? I'm Mrs. Fonstein. Does that ring a bell?"

"And why should it . . . ?" he said, refusing recognition.

"I married Fonstein."

"And my neck size is fourteen. So what?"

"The man you saved in Rome—one of them. He wrote so many letters. I can't believe you don't remember."

"Remember, forget—what's the difference to me?"

"You sent Deborah Hamet to Ellis Island to talk to him."

"Lady, this is one of a trillion incidents in a life like mine. Why should I recollect it?"

Why, yes, I see his point. These details were like the scales of innumerable shoals of fish—the mackerel-crowded seas: like the particles of those light-annihilating masses, the dense matter of black holes.

"I sent Deborah to Ellis Island—so, okay. . . ."

"With instructions for my husband never to approach you."

"It's a blank to me. But so what?"

"No personal concern for a man you rescued?"

"I did all I could," said Billy. "And for that point of time, that's more than most can say. Go holler at Stephen Wise. Raise hell with Sam Rosenman. Guys were sitting on their hands. They would call on Roosevelt and Cordell Hull, who didn't care a damn for Jews, and they were so proud and happy to be close enough to the White House, even getting the runaround was such a delicious privilege. FDR snowed those famous rabbis when they visited him. He blinded them with his footwork, that genius cripple. Churchill also was in on this with him. The goddamn white paper. So? There were refugees by the hundred thousands to ship to Palestine. Or there wouldn't have been a state here today. That's why I gave up the single-party rescue operation and started to raise money to get through the British blockade in those rusty Greek tramp ships. . . . Now what do you want from me—that I didn't receive your husband! What's the matter? I see you did all right. Now you have to have special recognition?"

The level, as Sorella was to say to me, being dragged down, down, downward, the greatness of the events being beyond anybody's personal scope. . . . At times she would make such remarks.

"Now," Billy asked her, "what do you want with this lousy scandal stuff collected by that cracked old bitch? To embarrass me in Jerusalem, when I came to start this major project?"

Sorella said that she raised both her hands to slow him down. She told him she had come to have a sensible discussion. Nothing threatening had been hinted. . . .

"No! Except that Hamet woman was collecting poison in bottles, and you have the whole collection. Try and place this material in the papers—you'd have to be crazy in the head. If you did try, the stuff would come flying back on you faster than shit through a tin whistle. Look at these charges—that I bribed Robert Moses's people to put across my patriotic Aquacade at the Fair. Or I hired an arsonist to torch a storefront for revenge. Or I sabotaged Baby Snooks because I was jealous of Fanny's big success, and I even tried to poison her. Listen, we still have libel laws. That Hamet was one sick lady. And you— you should stop and think. If not for me, where would you be, a woman like you . . . ?" The meaning was, a woman deformed by obesity.

"Did he say *that?*" I interrupted. But what excited me was not what *he* said. Sorella stopped me in my tracks. I never knew a woman to be so candid about herself. What a demonstration this was of pure objectivity and self-realism. What it signified was that in a time when disguise and deception are practiced so extensively as to numb the powers of awareness, only a major force of personality could produce such admissions. "I *am* built like a Mack truck. My flesh *is* boundless. An Everest of lipoids," she told me. Together with this came, unspoken, an auxiliary admission: she confessed that she was guilty of self-indulgence. This deformity, my outrageous size, an imposition on Fonstein, the brave man who loves me. Who else would want me? All this was fully implicit in the plain, unforced style of her comment. Greatness is the word for such candor, for such an admission, made so naturally. In this world of liars and cowards, there *are* people like Sorella. One waits for them in the blind faith that they *do* exist.

"He was reminding me that he had saved Harry. For me."

Translation: The SS would have liquidated him pretty quick. So except for the magic intervention of this little Lower East Side rat, the starved child who had survived on pastrami trimmings and pushcart apples . . .

Sorella went on. "I explained to Billy: it took Deborah's journal to put me through to him. He had turned his back on us. His answer was, 'I don't need entanglements—what I did, I did. I have to keep down the number of relationships and contacts. What I did for you, take it and welcome, but spare me the relationship and all the rest of it.' "

"I can understand that," I said.

I can't tell you how much I relished Sorella's account of this meeting with Billy. These extraordinary revelations, and also the comments on them that were made. In what he said there was an echo of George Washington's Farewell Address. Avoid entanglements. Billy had to reserve himself for his deals, devote himself body and soul to his superpublicized bad marriages; together with the squalid, rich residences he furnished; plus his gossip columns, his chorus lines, and the awful pursuit of provocative, teasing chicks whom he couldn't do a thing with when they stopped and stripped and waited for him. He had to be free to work his curse out fully. And now he had arrived in Jerusalem to put a top dressing of Jewish grandeur on his chicken-scratch career, on this poor punished N.Y. soil of his. (I am thinking of the tiny prison enclosures—a few black palings—narrow slices of ground preserved at the heart of Manhattan for leaves and grass.) Here Noguchi would create for him a Rose Garden of Sculpture, an art corner within a few kilometers of the stunned desert sloping toward the Dead Sea.

"Tell me, Sorella, what were you after? The objective."

"Billy to meet with Fonstein."

"But Fonstein gave up on him long ago. They must pass each other at the King David every other day. What would be simpler than to stop and say, 'You're Rose? I'm Harry Fonstein. You led me out of Egypt *b'yad hazzakah*."

"What is that?"

"With a mighty hand. So the Lord God described the rescue of Israel—part of my boyhood basic training. But Fonstein has backed away from this. While you . . ."

"I made up my mind that Billy was going to do right by him."

Yes, sure, of course; roger; I read you. Something is due from every man to every man. But Billy hadn't heard and didn't want to hear about these generalities.

"If you lived with Fonstein's feelings as I have lived with them," said Sorella, "you'd agree he should get a chance to complete them. To finish out."

In a spirit of high-level discussion, I said to her, "Well, it's a nice idea, only nobody expects to complete their feelings anymore. They have to give up on closure. It's just not available."

"For some it is."

So I was obliged to think again. Sure—what about the history of Sorella's own feelings? She had been an unwanted Newark French teacher until her Havana uncle had a lucky hunch about Fonstein. They were married, and thanks to him, she obtained her closure, she became the tiger wife, the tiger mother, grew into a biological monument and a victorious personality . . . a figure!

But Billy's reply was: "So what's it got to do with me?"

"Spend fifteen minutes alone with my husband," she said to him.

Billy refused her. "It's not the kind of thing I do."

"A handshake, and he'll say thanks."

"First of all, I warned you already about libel, and as for the rest, what do you think you're holding over me anyway? I wouldn't do this. You haven't convinced me that I must. I don't like things from the past being laid on me. This happened one time, years ago. What's it got to do with now—1959? If your husband has a nice story, that's his good luck. Let him tell it to people who go for stories. I don't care for them. I don't care for my own story. If I had to listen to it, I'd break out in a cold sweat. And I wouldn't go around and shake everybody's hand unless I was running for mayor. That's why I never would run. I shake when I close a deal. Otherwise, my hands stay in my pockets."

Sorella said, "Since Deborah Hamet had given me the goods on him and the worst could be assumed, he stood up to me on the worst basis, with all the bruises on his reputation, under every curse—grungy, weak, cheap, perverted. He made me take him for what he was—a kinky little kike finagler whose life history was one disgrace after another. Take this man: He never flew a single mission, never hunted big game, never played football or went down in the Pacific. Never even tried suicide. And this reject was a celeb! . . . You know, Deborah had a hundred ways to say celeb. Mostly she cut him down, but a celeb is still a celeb—you can't take that away. When American Jews decided to make a statement about the War Against the Jews, they had to fill Madison Square Garden with big-name celebs singing Hebrew and 'America the Beautiful.' Hollywood stars blowing the shofar. The man to produce this spectacular and arrange the press coverage was Billy. They turned to him, and he took total charge. . . . How many people does the Garden hold? Well, it was full, and everybody was in mourning. I suppose the whole place was in tears. The *Times* covered it, which is the paper of record, so the record shows that the American Jewish way was to assemble twenty-five thousand people, Hollywood style, and weep publicly for what had happened."

Continuing her report on her interview with Billy, Sorella said that he adopted what negotiators call a bargaining posture. He behaved as though he had reason to be proud of his record, of the deals he had made, and I suppose that he was standing his ground behind this front of pride. Sorella hadn't yet formulated her threat. Beside her on a chair that decorators would have called a love seat there lay (and he saw) a large manila envelope. It contained Deborah's papers—what else would she have brought to his suite? To make a grab for this envelope was out of the question. "I outreached him and outweighed him," said Sorella. "I could scratch him as well, and also shriek. And the very thought of a scene, a scandal, would have made him sick. Actually, the man was looking sick. His calculation in Jerusalem was to make a major gesture, to enter Jewish history, attaining a level far beyond show biz. He had seen only a sample of the Hamet/Horsecollar file. But imagine what the newspapers, the world tabloid press, could do with this material.

"So he was waiting to hear my proposition," said Sorella.

I said, "I'm trying to figure out just what you had in mind."

"Concluding a chapter in Harry's life. It should be concluded," said Sorella. "It was a part of the destruction of the Jews. On our side of the Atlantic, where we weren't threatened, we have a special duty to come to terms with it. . . ."

"Come to terms? Who, Billy Rose?"

"Well, he involved himself in it actively."

I recall that I shook my head and said, "You were asking too much. You couldn't have gotten very far with him."

"Well, he did say that Fonstein suffered much less than others. He wasn't in Auschwitz. He got a major break. He wasn't tattooed with a number. They didn't put him to work cremating the people that were gassed. I said to Billy that the Italian police must have been under orders to hand Jews over to the SS and that so many were shot in Rome, in the Ardeatine Caves."

"What did he say to this?"

"He said, 'Look, lady, why do *I* have to think about all of that? I'm not the kind of guy who's expected to. This is too much for me.' I said, 'I'm not asking you to make an enormous mental effort, only to sit down with my husband for fifteen minutes.' 'Suppose I do,' he said. 'What's your offer?' 'I'll hand over Deborah's whole file. I've got it right here.' 'And if I don't play ball?' 'Then I'll turn it over to some other party, or parties.' Then he burst out, 'You think you've got me by the knackers, don't you? You're taking an unfair terrible advantage of me. I don't want to talk dirty to a respectable person, but I call this kicking the shit out of a man. Right now I'm in an extrasensitive position, considering what's my purpose in Jerusalem. I want to contribute a memorial. Maybe it would be better not to leave any reminder of my life and I should be forgotten altogether. So at this moment you come along to take revenge from the grave for a jealous woman. I can imagine the record this crazy put together, about deals I made—I know she got the business part all wrong, and the bribery and arson would never stick. So that leaves things like the private clinical junk collected from show girls who bad-mouthed me. But let me say one thing, Missus: Even a geek has his human rights. Last of all, I haven't got all that many secrets left. It's all been told.' 'Almost all,' I said."

I observed, "You sure did bear down hard on him."

"Yes, I did," she admitted. "But he fought back. The libel suits he threatened were only bluff, and I told him so. I pointed out how little I was asking. Not even a note to Harry, just a telephone message would be enough, and then fifteen minutes of conversation. Mulling it over, with his eyes cast down and his little hands passive on the back of a sofa—he was on his feet, he wouldn't sit down, that would seem like a concession—he refused me again. Once and for all he said he wouldn't meet with Harry. 'I already did for him all I'm able to do.' 'Then you leave me no alternative,' I said."

On the striped chair in Billy's suite, Sorella opened her purse to look for a handkerchief. She touched herself on the temples and on the folds of her arms, at the elbow joint. The white handkerchief looked no bigger than a cabbage moth. She dried herself under the chin.

"He must have shouted at you," I said.

"He began to yell at me. It was what I anticipated, a screaming fit. He said no matter what you did, there was always somebody waiting with a switchblade to cut you, or acid to throw in your face, or claws to rip the clothes off you and leave you naked. That fucking old Hamet broad, whom he kept out of charity—as if her eyes weren't kooky enough, she put on those giant crooked round goggles. She hunted up those girls who swore he had the sexual development of a ten-year-old boy. It didn't matter for shit, because he was humiliated all his life long and you couldn't do more than was done already. There was relief in having no more to cover up. He didn't care what Hamet had written down, that bitch-eye mummy, spitting blood and saving the last glob for the man she hated most. As for me, I was a heap of fat filth!"

"You don't have to repeat it all, Sorella."

"Then I won't. But I did lose my temper. My dignity fell apart."

"Do you mean that you wanted to hit him?"

"I threw the document at him. I said, 'I don't *want* my husband to talk to the likes of you. You're not fit . . .' I aimed Deborah's packet at him. But I'm not much good at throwing, and it went through the open window."

"What a moment! What did Billy do then?"

"All the rage was wiped out instantly. He picked up the phone and got the desk. He said, 'A very important document was dropped from my window. I want it brought up right now. You understand? Immediately. This minute.' I went to the door. I don't suppose I wanted to make a gesture, but I am a Newark girl at bottom. I said, 'You're the filth. I want no part of you.' And I made the Italian gesture people used to make in a street fight, the edge of the palm on the middle of my arm."

Inconspicuously, and laughing as she did it, she made a small fist and drew the edge of her other hand across her biceps.

"A very American conclusion."

"Oh," she said, "from start to finish it was a one hundred percent American event, of our own generation. It'll be different for our children. A kid like our Gilbert, at his mathematics summer camp? Let him for the rest of his life do nothing but mathematics. Nothing could be more different from either East Side tenements or the backstreets of Newark."

All this had happened toward the end of the Fonsteins' visit, and I'm sorry now that I didn't cancel a few Jerusalem appointments for their sake—take them to dinner at Dagim Benny, a good fish restaurant. It would have been easy enough for me to clear the decks. What, to spend more time in Jerusalem with a couple from New Jersey named Fonstein? Yes is the answer. Today it's a matter of regret. The more I think of Sorella, the more charm she has for me.

I remember saying to her, "I'm sorry you didn't hit Billy with that packet."

My thought, then and later, was that she was too much hampered by fat under the arms to make an accurate throw.

She said, "As soon as the envelope left my hands I realized that I longed to get rid of it, and of everything connected with it. Poor Deborah—Mrs. Horsecollar, as you like to call her. I see that I was wrong to identify myself with her cause, her tragic life. It makes you think about the high and the low in people. Love is supposed to be high, but imagine falling for a creature like Billy. I didn't want a single thing that man could give Harry and me. Deborah recruited me, so I would continue her campaign against him, keep the heat on from the grave. He was right about that."

This was our very last conversation. Beside the King David driveway, she and I were waiting for Fonstein to come down. The luggage had been stowed in the Mercedes—at that time, every other cab in Jerusalem was a Mercedes-Benz. Sorella said to me, "How do you see the whole Billy business?"

In those days I still had the Villager's weakness for theorizing—the profundity game so popular with middle-class boys and girls in their bohemian salad days. Ring anybody's bell, and he'd open the window and empty a basin full of thoughts on your head.

"Billy views everything as show biz," I said. "Nothing is real that isn't a show. And he wouldn't perform in your show because he's a producer, and producers don't perform."

To Sorella, this was not a significant statement, so I tried harder. "Maybe the most interesting thing about Billy is that he wouldn't meet with Harry," I said. "He wasn't able to be the counterexample in a case like Harry's. Couldn't begin to measure up."

Sorella said, "That may be a little more like it. But if you want my basic view, here it is: The Jews could survive everything that Europe threw at them. I mean the lucky remnant. But now comes the next test—America. Can they hold their ground, or will the U.S.A. be too much for them?"

This was our final meeting. I never saw Harry and Sorella again. In the sixties, Harry telephoned once to discuss Cal Tech with me. Sorella didn't want Gilbert to study so far from home. An only child, and all of that. Harry was full of the boy's perfect test scores. My heart doesn't warm to the parents of prodigies. I react badly. They're riding for a fall. I don't like parental boasting. So I was unable to be cordial toward Fonstein. My time just then was unusually valuable. Horribly valuable, as I now judge it. Not one of the attractive periods in the development (gestation) of a success.

I can't say that communication with the Fonsteins ceased. Except in Jerusalem, we hadn't had any. I *expected*, for thirty years, to see them again. They were excellent people. I admired Harry. A solid man, Harry, and very brave. As for Sorella, she was a woman with great powers of intelligence, and in these democratic times, whether you are conscious of it or not, you are continually in quest of higher types. I don't have to draw you maps and pictures. Everybody knows what standard products and interchangeable parts signify, understands the operation of the glaciers on the social landscape, planing off the hills, scrubbing away the irregularities. I'm not going to be tedious about this. Sorella was outstanding (or as one of my grandchildren says, "standing out"). So of course I meant to see more of her. But I saw nothing. She was in the warehouse of intentions. I was going to get around to the Fonsteins—write, telephone, have them for Thanksgiving, for Christmas. Perhaps for Passover. But that's what the Passover phenomenon is now—it never comes to pass.

Maybe the power of memory was to blame. Remembering them so well, did I need actually to *see* them? To keep them in a mental suspension was enough. They were a part of the permanent cast of characters, in absentia permanently. There wasn't a thing for them to do.

The next in this series of events occurred last March, when winter, with a grunt, gave up its grip on Philadelphia and began to go out in trickles of grimy slush. Then it was the turn of spring to thrive on the dirt of the city. The season at least produced crocuses, snowdrops, and new buds in my millionaire's private back garden. I pushed around my library ladder and brought down the poems of George Herbert, looking for the one that runs ". . . how clean, how pure are Thy returns," or words to that effect; and on my desk, fit for a Wasp of great wealth, the phone started to ring as I was climbing down. The following Jewish conversation began:

"This is Rabbi X [or Y]. My ministry"—what a Protestant term: he must be Reform, or Conservative at best; no Orthodox rabbi would say "ministry"—"is in Jerusalem. I have been approached by a party whose name is Fonstein. . . ."

"Not Harry," I said.

"No. I was calling to ask *you* about locating Harry. The Jerusalem Fonstein says that he is Harry's uncle. This man is Polish by birth, and he is in a mental institution. He is a very difficult eccentric and lives in a world of fantasy. Much of the time he hallucinates. His habits are dirty—filthy, even. He's totally without resources and well known as a beggar and local character who makes prophetic speeches on the sidewalk."

"I get the picture. Like one of our own homeless," I said.

"Precisely," said Rabbi X or Y, in that humane tone of voice one has to put up with.

"Can we come to the point?" I asked.

"Our Jerusalem Fonstein swears he is related to Harry, who is very rich. . . ."

"I've never seen Harry's financial statement."

"But in a position to help."

I went on, "That's just an opinion. At a hazard . . ." One does get pompous. A solitary, occupying a mansion, living up to his surroundings. I changed my tune; I dropped the "hazard" and said, "It's been years since Harry and I were in touch. You can't locate him?"

"I've tried. I'm on a two-week visit. Right now I'm in New York. But L.A. is my destination. Addressing . . ." (He gave an unfamiliar acronym.) Then he went on to say that the Jerusalem Fonstein needed help. Poor man, absolutely bananas, but under all the tatters, physical and mental (I paraphrase), humanly so worthy. Abused out of his head by persecution, loss, death, and brutal history; beside himself, crying out for aid—human and supernatural, no matter in what mixture. There may have been something phony about the rabbi, but the case, the man he was describing, was a familiar type, was real enough.

"And you, too, are a relative?" he said.

"Indirectly. My father's second wife was Harry's aunt."

I never loved Aunt Mildred, nor even esteemed her. But, you understand, she had a place in my memory, and there must have been a good reason for that.

"May I ask you to find him for me and give him my number in L.A.? I'm carrying a list of family names and Harry Fonstein will recognize, will identify him. Or will not, if the man is *not* his uncle. It would be a mitzvah."

Christ, spare me these mitzvahs.

I said, "Okay, Rabbi, I'll trace Harry, for the sake of this pitiable lunatic."

The Jerusalem Fonstein gave me a pretext for getting in touch with the Fonsteins. (Or at least an incentive.) I entered the rabbi's number in my book, under the last address I had for Fonstein. At the moment, there were other needs and duties requiring my attention; besides, I wasn't yet ready to speak to Sorella and Harry. There were preparations to make. This, as it appears under my ballpoint, reminds me of the title of Stanislavski's famous book, *An Actor Prepares*—again, a datum relating to my memory, a resource, a vocation, to which a lifetime of cultivation has been devoted, and which in old age also oppresses me.

For just then (meaning now: "Now, now, very now") I was, I am, having difficulties with it. I had had a failure of memory the other morning, and it had driven me almost mad (not to hold back on an occurrence of such importance). I had had a dental appointment downtown. I drove, because I was already late and couldn't rely on the radio cab to come on time. I parked in a lot blocks away, the best I could do on a busy morning, when closer lots were full. Then, walking back from the dentist's office, I found (under the influence of my walking rhythm, I presume) that I had a tune in my head. The words came to me:

Way down upon the . . .
Way down upon the . . .
. . . upon the ———— River . . .

But what was the river called! A song I'd sung from childhood, upwards of seventy years, part of the foundation of one's mind. A classic song, known to all Americans. Of my generation anyway.

I stopped at the window of a sports shop, specializing, as it happened, in horsemen's boots, shining boots, both men's and women's, plaid saddle blankets, crimson coats, fox-hunting stuff—even brass horns. All objects on display were ultrasignificantly distinct. The colors of the plaid were especially bright and orderly—enviably orderly to a man whose mind was at that instant shattered.

What was that river's name!

I could easily recall the rest of the words:

There's where my heart is yearning ever,
That's where the old folks stay.
All the world is [am?] sad and dreary
Everywhere I roam.
O darkies, how my heart grows weary . . .

And the rest.

All the world *was* dark and dreary. Fucking-A right! A chip, a plug, had gone dead in the mental apparatus. A forerunning omen? Beginning of the end? There are psychic causes of forgetfulness, of course. I've lectured on those myself. Not everyone, needless to say, would take such a lapsus so to heart. A bridge was broken: I could not cross the ———— River. I had an impulse to hammer the window of the riding shop with the handle of my umbrella, and when people ran out, to cry to them, "Oh, God! You must tell me the words. I can't get past 'Way down upon the . . . upon the!' " They would—I saw it—throw that red saddle cloth, a brilliant red, threads of fire, over my shoulders and take me into the shop to wait for the ambulance.

At the parking lot, I wanted to ask the cashier—out of desperation. When she said, "Seven dollars," I would begin singing the tune through the round hole in the glass. But as the woman was black, she might be offended by "O darkies." And could I assume that she, like me, had been brought up on Stephen Foster? There were no grounds for this. For the same reason, I couldn't ask the car jockey either.

But at the wheel of the car, the faulty connection corrected itself, and I began to shout, "Swanee—Swanee—Swanee," punching the steering wheel. Behind the windows of your car, what you do doesn't matter. One of the privileges of liberty car ownership affords.

Of course! The Swanee. Or Suwannee (spelling preferred in the South). But this was a crisis in my mental life. I had had a double purpose in looking up George Herbert—not only the appropriateness of the season but as a test of my memory. So, too, my recollection of *Fonstein* v. *Rose* is in part a test of memory, and also a more general investigation of the same, for if you go back to the assertion that memory is life and forgetting death ("mercifully forgetting," the commonest adverb linked by writers with the participle, reflecting the preponderance of the opinion that so much of life *is* despair), I have established at the very least that I am still able to keep up my struggle for existence.

Hoping for victory? Well, what would a victory be?

I took Rabbi X/Y's word for it that the Fonsteins had moved away and were unlocatable. Probably they had, like me, retired. But whereas I am in Philadelphia, hanging in there, as the idiom puts it, they had very likely abandoned that ground of struggle the sullen North and gone to Sarasota or to Palm Springs. They had the money for it. America was good to Harry Fonstein, after all, and delivered on its splendid promises. He had been spared the worst we have here—routine industrial or clerical jobs and bureaucratic employment. As I wished the Fonsteins well, I was pleased for them. My much-appreciated-in-absentia friends, so handsomely installed in my consciousness.

Not having heard from me, I assumed, they had given up on me, after three decades. Freud has laid down the principle that the *un*conscious does not recognize death. But as you see, consciousness is freaky too.

So I went to work digging up forgotten names of relatives from my potato-patch mind—Rosenberg, Rosenthal, Sorkin, Swerdlow, Bleistiff, Fradkin. Jewish surnames are another curious subject, so many of them imposed by German, Polish, or Russian officialdom (expecting bribes from applicants), others the invention of Jewish fantasy. How often the name of the rose was invoked, as in the case of Billy himself. There were few other words for flowers in the pale. *Margaritka,* for one. The daisy. Not a suitable family name for anybody.

Aunt Mildred, my stepmother, had been cared for during her last years by relatives in Elizabeth, the Rosensafts, and my investigations began with them. They weren't cordial or friendly on the phone, because I had seldom visited Mildred toward the last. I think she began to claim that she had brought me up and even put me through college. (The funds came from a Prudential policy paid for by my own mother.) This was a venial offense, which gave me the reasons for being standoffish that I was looking for. I wasn't fond of the Rosensafts either. They had taken my father's watch and chain after he died. But then one can live without these objects of sentimental value. Old Mrs. Rosensaft said she had lost track of the Fonsteins. She thought the Swerdlows in Morristown might know where Harry and Sorella had gone.

Information gave me Swerdlow's number. Dialing, I reached an answering machine. The voice of Mrs. Swerdlow, affecting an accent more suitable to upper-class Morristown than to her native Newark, asked me to leave my name, number, and the date of the call. I hate answering machines, so I hung up. Besides, I avoid giving my unlisted number.

As I went up to my second-floor office that night holding the classic Philadelphia banister, reflecting that I was pretty sick of the unshared grandeur of this mansion, I once more considered Sarasota or the sociable Florida Keys. Elephants and acrobats, circuses in winter quarters, would be more amusing. Moving to Palm Springs was out of the question. And while the Keys had a large homosexual population, I was more at home with gay people, thanks to my years in the Village, than with businessmen in California. In any case, I couldn't bear much more of these thirty-foot ceilings and all the mahogany solitude. This mansion demanded too much from me, and I was definitely conscious of a strain. My point had long ago been made—I could achieve such a dwelling place, possess it in style. Now take it away, I thought, in a paraphrase of the old tune "I'm so tired of roses, take them all away." I decided to discuss the subject again with my son, Henry. His wife didn't like the mansion; her tastes were modern, and she was satirical, too, about the transatlantic rivalry of parvenu American wealth with the titled wealth of Victorian London. She had turned me down dead flat when I tried to give the place to them.

What I was thinking was that if I could find Harry and Sorella, I'd join them in retirement, if they'd accept my company (forgiving the insult of neglect). For me it was natural to wonder whether I had not exaggerated (urged on by a desire for a woman of a deeper nature) Sorella's qualities in my reminiscences, and I gave further thought to this curious personality. I never had forgotten what she had said about the testing of Jewry by the American experience. Her interview with Billy Rose had itself been such an American thing. Again Billy: Weak? Weak! Vain? Oh, very! And trivial for sure. Creepy Billy. Still, in a childish way, big-minded—spacious; and spacious wasn't just a boast adjective from "America the Beautiful" (the spacious skies) but the dropping of fifteen to twenty actual millions on a rest-and-culture garden in Jerusalem, the core of Jewish history, the navel of the earth. This gesture of oddball magnificence was American. American and Oriental.

And even if I didn't in the end settle near the Fonsteins, I could pay them a visit. I couldn't help asking why I had turned away from such a terrific pair— Sorella, so mysteriously obese; Fonstein with his reddish skin (once stone white), his pomegranate face. I may as well include myself, as a third—a tall old man with a structural curl at the top like a fiddlehead fern or a bishop's crook.

Therefore I started looking for Harry and Sorella not merely because I had promised Rabbi X/Y, nor for the sake of the crazy old man in Jerusalem who was destitute. If it was only money that he needed, I could easily write a check or ask my banker to send him one. The bank charges eight bucks for this convenience, and a phone call would take care of it. But I preferred to attend to things in my own way, from my mansion office, dialing the numbers myself, bypassing the Mnemosyne Institute and its secretaries.

Using old address books, I called all over the place. (If only cemeteries had switchboards. "Hello, Operator, I'm calling area code 000.") I didn't want to involve the girls at the Institute in any of this, least of all in my investigations. When I reached a number, the conversation was bound to be odd, and a strain on the memory of the Founder. "Why, how are you?" somebody would ask whom I hadn't seen in three decades. "Do you remember my husband, Max? My daughter, Zoe?" Would I know what to say?

Yes, I would. But then again, why should I? How nice oblivion would be in such cases, and I could say, "Max? Zoe? No, I can't say that I do." On the fringes of the family, or in remote, time-dulled social circles, random memories can be an affliction. What you see first, retrospectively, are the psychopaths, the uglies, the cheapies, the stingies, the hypochondriacs, the family bores, humanoids, and tyrants. These have dramatic staying power. Harder to recover are the kind eyes, gentle faces, of the comedians who wanted to entertain you, gratis, divert you from troubles. An important part of my method is that memory chains are constructed thematically. Where themes are lacking there can be little or no recall. So, for instance, Billy, our friend Bellarosa, could not easily place Fonstein because of an unfortunate thinness of purely human themes—as contrasted with business, publicity, or sexual themes. To give a strongly negative example, there are murderers who can't recall their crimes because they have no interest in the existence or nonexistence of their victims. So, students, only pertinent themes assure full recollection.

Some of the old people I reached put me down spiritedly: "If you remember so much about me, how come I haven't seen you since the Korean War! . . ." "No, I can't tell you anything about Salkind's niece Sorella. Salkind came home to New Jersey after Castro took over. He died in an old people's nursing racket setup back in the late sixties."

One man commented, "The pages of calendars crumble away. They're like the dandruff of time. What d'you want from me?"

Calling from a Philadelphia mansion, I was at a disadvantage. A person in my position will discover, in contact with people from Passaic, Elizabeth, or Paterson, how many defenses he has organized against vulgarity or the lower grades of thought. I didn't want to talk about Medicare or Social Security checks or hearing aids or pacemakers or bypass surgery.

From a few sources I heard criticisms of Sorella. "Salkind was a bachelor, had no children, and that woman should have done something for the old fella."

"He never married?"

"Never," said the bitter lady I had on the line. "But he married *her* off, for his own brother's sake. Anyway, they've all checked out, so what's the diff."

"And you can't tell me where I might find Sorella?"

"I could care less."

"No," I said. "You couldn't care less."

So the matchmaker himself had been a lifelong bachelor. He had disinterestedly found a husband for his brother's daughter, bringing together two disadvantaged people.

Another lady said about Sorella, "She was remote. She looked down on my type of conversation. I think she was a snob. I tried to sign her up once for a group tour in Europe. My temple sisterhood put together a real good charter-flight package. Then Sorella told me that French was her second language, and she didn't need anybody to interpret for her in Paris. I should have told her, 'I knew you when no man would give you a second look and would even take back the first look if he could.' So that's how it was. Sorella was too good for everybody. . . ."

I saw what these ladies meant (this was a trend among my informants). They accused Mrs. Fonstein of being uppish, too grand. Almost all were offended. She preferred the company of Mrs. Hamet, the old actress with the paraffin-white tubercular face. Sorella was too grand for Billy too; hurling Mrs. Hamet's deadly dossier at him was the gesture of a superior person, a person of intelligence and taste. Queenly, imperial, and inevitably isolated. This was the consensus of all the gossips, the elderly people I telephoned from the triple isolation of my Philadelphia residence.

The Fonsteins and I were meant to be company for one another. They weren't going to force themselves on me, however. They assumed that I was above them socially, in upper-class Philadelphia, and that I didn't want their friendship. I don't suppose that my late wife, Deirdre, would have cared for Sorella, with her pince-nez and high manner, the working of her intellect and the problems of her cumulous body—trying to fit itself into a Hepplewhite chair in our dining room. Fonstein would have been comparatively easy for Deirdre to be with. Still, if I was not an assimilationist, I was at least an avoider of uncomfortable mixtures, and in the end I am stuck with these twenty empty rooms.

I can remember driving with my late father through western Pennsylvania. He was struck by the amount of land without a human figure in it. So much space! After long silence, in a traveler's trance resembling the chessboard trance, he said, "Ah, how many Jews might have been settled here! Room enough for everybody."

At times I feel like a socket that remembers its tooth.

As I made call after call, I was picturing my reunion with the Fonsteins. I had them placed mentally in Sarasota, Florida, and imagined the sunny strolls we might take in the winter quarters of Ringling or Hagenbeck, chatting about events long past at the King David Hotel—Billy Rose's lost suitcases, Noguchi's

Oriental reserve. In old manila envelopes I found color snapshots from Jerusalem, among them a photograph of Fonstein and Sorella against the background of the Judean desert, the burning stones of Ezekiel, not yet (even today) entirely cooled, those stones of fire among which the cherubim had walked. In that fierce place, two modern persons, the man in a business suit, the woman in floating white, a married couple holding hands—her fat palm in his inventor's fingers. I couldn't help thinking that Sorella didn't have a real biography until Harry entered her life. And he, Harry, whom Hitler had intended to kill, had a biography insofar as Hitler had marked him for murder, insofar as he had fled, was saved by Billy, reached America, invented a better thermostat. And here they were in color, the Judean desert behind them, as husband and wife in a once-upon-a-time Coney Island might have posed against a painted backdrop or sitting on a slice of moon. As tourists in the Holy Land where were they, I wondered, biographically speaking? How memorable had this trip been for them? The question sent me back to myself and, Jewish style, answered itself with yet another question: What was there worth remembering?

When I got to the top of the stairs—this was the night before last—I couldn't bring myself to go to bed just yet. One does grow weary of taking care of this man-sized doll, the elderly retiree, giving him his pills, pulling on his socks, spooning up his cornflakes, shaving his face, seeing to it that he gets his sleep. Instead of opening the bedroom door, I went to my second-floor sitting room.

To save myself from distraction by concentrating every kind of business in a single office, I do bills, bank statements, legal correspondence on the ground floor, and my higher activities I carry upstairs. Deirdre had approved of this. It challenged her to furnish each setting appropriately. One of my diversions is to make the rounds of antiques shops and look at comparable pieces, examining and pricing them, noting what a shrewd buyer Deirdre had been. In doing this, I build a case against remaining in Philadelphia, a town in which a man finds little else to do with himself on a dull afternoon.

Even the telephone in my second-story room is a French instrument with a porcelain mouthpiece—blue-and-white Quimper. Deirdre had bought it on the boulevard Haussmann, and Baron Charlus might have romanced his boyfriends with it, speaking low and scheming intricately into this very phone. It would have amused him, if he haunted objects of common use, to watch me dialing the Swerdlows' number again, pursuing my Fonstein inquiries.

On this art nouveau article—for those who escape from scientific ignorance (how *do* telephones operate?) with the aid of high-culture toys—I tried Morristown again, and this time Hyman Swerdlow himself answered. As soon as I heard his voice, he appeared before me, and presently his wife also was reborn in my memory and stood beside him. Swerdlow, who was directly related to Fonstein, had been an investment counselor. Trained on Wall Street, he settled in stylish New Jersey. He was a respectable, smooth person, very quiet in manner, "understated," to borrow a term from the interior decorators. His look was both saturnine and guilt-free. He probably didn't like what he had made of his life, but there was no way to revise that now. He settled for good manners—he was very polite, he wore Brooks Brothers grays and tans. His tone was casual. One could assimilate now *without* converting. You didn't have to choose between Jehovah and Jesus. I had known old Swerdlow. His son had inherited an ancient Jewish face from him, dark and craggy. Hyman had discovered a way to drain the Jewish charge from it. What replaced it was a look of perfect dependability. He was well spoken. He could be trusted with your pension funds. He wouldn't dream of making a chancy investment. His children were a biochemist and a molecular biologist, respectively. His wife could now devote herself to her watercolor box.

I believe the Swerdlows were very intelligent. They may even have been deeply intelligent. What had happened to them couldn't have been helped.

"I can't tell you anything about Fonstein," Swerdlow said. "I've somehow lost track. . . ."

I realized that, like the Fonsteins, Swerdlow and his wife had isolated themselves. No deliberate choice was made. You went your own way, and you found yourself in Greater New York but beyond the bedroom communities, decently situated. Your history, too, became one of your options. Whether or not having a history was a "consideration" was entirely up to you.

Cool Swerdlow, who of course remembered me (I was rich, I might have become an important client; there was, however, no reproach detectable in his tone), now was asking what I wanted with Harry Fonstein. I said that a mad old man in Jerusalem needed Fonstein's help. Swerdlow dropped his inquiry then and there. "We never did develop a relationship," he said. "Harry was very decent. His wife, however, was somewhat overpowering."

Decoded, this meant that Edna Swerdlow had not taken to Sorella. One learns soon enough to fill in the simple statements to which men like Swerdlow limit themselves. They avoid putting themselves out and they shun (perhaps even hate) psychological elaboration.

"When did you last see the Fonsteins?"

"During the Lakewood period," said tactful Swerdlow—he avoided touching upon my father's death, possibly a painful subject. "I think it was when Sorella talked so much about Billy Rose."

"They were involved with him. *He* refused to be drawn in. . . . So you heard them talking about it?"

"Even sensible people lose their heads over celebrities. What claim did Harry have on Billy Rose, and why *should* Billy have done more than he did? A man like Rose has to ration the number of people he can take on."

"Like a sign in an elevator—'Maximum load twenty-eight hundred pounds'?"

"If you like."

"When I think of the Fonstein-Billy thing," I said, "I'm liable to see European Jewry also. What was all *that* about? To me, the operational term is Justice. Once and for all it was seen that this expectation, or reliance, had no foundation. You had to forget about Justice . . . whether, taken seriously for so long, it could be taken seriously still."

Swerdlow could not allow me to go on. This was not his kind of conversation. "Put it any way you like—how does it apply to Billy? What was *he* supposed to do about it?"

Well, I didn't expect Billy to take this, or anything else, upon himself. From Hyman Swerdlow I felt that speaking of Justice was not only out of place but off the wall. And if the Baron Charlus had been listening, haunting his telephone with the Quimper mouthpiece, he would have turned from this conversation with contempt. I didn't greatly blame myself, and I certainly did not feel like a fool. At worst it had been inappropriate to call Swerdlow for information and then, without preparation, swerve wildly into such a subject, trying to carry him with me. These were matters I thought about privately, the subjective preoccupations of a person who lived alone in a great Philadelphia house in which he felt out of place, and who had lost sight of the difference between brooding and permissible conversation. I had no business out of the blue to talk to Swerdlow about Justice or Honor or the Platonic Ideas or the expectations of the Jews. Anyway, his tone now made it clear that he wanted to get rid of me, so I said, "This Rabbi X/Y from Jerusalem, who speaks better than fair English, got me to promise that I would locate Fonstein. He said he hadn't been able to find him."

"Are you sure that Fonstein isn't listed in the directory?"

No, I wasn't sure, was I? I hadn't looked. That was just like me, wasn't it? "I assumed the rabbi *had* looked," I said. "I feel chastened. I shouldn't have taken the man's word for it. *He* should have looked. I took it for granted. You're probably right."

"If I can be of further use . . . ?"

By pointing out how he would have gone about finding Fonstein, Swerdlow showed me how lopsided I was. Sure it was stupid of me not to look in the phone directory. Smart, smart, but a dope, as the old people used to say. For the Fonsteins *were* listed. Information gave me their number. There they were, as accessible as millions of others, in small print, row on row on row, the endless listings.

I dialed the Fonsteins, braced for a conversation—my opening words prepared, my excuses for neglecting them made with warmth, just such warmth as I actually felt. Should they be inclined to blame me—well, I was to blame.

But they were out, or had unplugged their line. Elderly people, they probably turned in early. After a dozen rings, I gave up and went to bed myself. And when I got into bed—without too much fear of being alone in this huge place, not that there aren't plenty of murdering housebreakers in the city—I picked up a book, preparing to settle in for a long read.

Deirdre's bedside books had now become mine. I was curious to know how she had read herself to sleep. What had been on her mind became important to me. In her last years she had turned to such books as *Koré Kosmu*, the *Hermetica* published by Oxford, and also selections from the Zohar. Like the heroine of Poe's story "Morella." Odd that Deirdre had said so little about it. She was not a secretive lady, but like many others she kept her own counsel in matters of thought and religion. I loved to see her absorbed in a book, mummied up on her side of the antique bed, perfectly still under the covers. A pair of lamps on each side were like bronze thornbushes. I was always after Deirdre to get sensible reading lights. Nothing could persuade her—she was obstinate when her taste was challenged—and three years after she passed away I was still shopping: Those sculpture brambles never will be replaced.

Some men fall asleep on the sofa after dinner. This often results in insomnia, and as I hate to be up in the night, my routine is to read in bed until midnight, concentrating on passages marked by Deirdre and on her notes at the back of the book. It has become one of my sentimental rituals.

But on this night I passed out after a few sentences, and presently I began to dream.

There is great variety in my dreams. My nights are often busy. I have anxious dreams, amusing dreams, desire dreams, symbolic dreams. There are, however, dreams that are all business and go straight to the point. I suppose we have the dreams we deserve, and they may even be prepared in secret.

Without preliminaries, I found myself in a hole. Night, a dark plain, a pit, and from the start I was already trying to climb out. In fact, I had been working at it for some time. This was a dug hole, not a grave but a trap prepared for me by somebody who knew me well enough to anticipate that I would fall in. I could see over the edge, but I couldn't crawl out because my legs were tangled and caught in ropes or roots. I was clawing at the dirt for something I could grip. I had to rely on my arms. If I could hoist myself onto the edge, I might free the lower body. Only, I was already exhausted, winded, and if I did manage to pull myself out, I'd be too beat to fight. My struggles were watched by the person who had planned this for me. I could see his boots. Down the way, in a similar ditch, another man was also wearing himself out. He wasn't going to make it either. Despair was not principally what I felt, nor fear of death. What made the dream terrible was my complete conviction of error, my miscalculation of strength, and the recognition that my forces were drained to the bottom. The whole structure was knocked flat. There wasn't a muscle in me that I hadn't called on, and for the first time I was aware of them all, down to the tiniest, and the best they could do was not enough. I couldn't call on myself, couldn't meet the demand, couldn't put out. There's no reason why I should ask you to feel this with me, and I won't blame you for avoiding it; I've done that myself. I always avoid extremes, even during sleep. Besides, we all recognize the burden of my dream: Life so diverse, the Grand Masquerade of Mortality shriveling to a hole in the ground. Still, that did not exhaust the sense of the dream, and the remainder is essential to the interpretation of what I've set down about Fonstein, Sorella, or Billy even. I couldn't otherwise have described it. It isn't so much a dream as a communication. I was being shown—and I was aware of this in sleep—that I had made a mistake, a lifelong mistake: something wrong, false, now fully manifest.

Revelations in old age can shatter everything you've put in place from the beginning—all the wiliness of a lifetime of expertise and labor, interpreting and reinterpreting in patching your fortified delusions, the work of the swarm of your defensive shock troops, which will go on throwing up more perverse (or insane) barriers. All this is bypassed in a dream like this one. When you have one of these, all you can do is bow to the inevitable conclusions.

Your imagination of strength is connected to your apprehensions of brutality, where that brutality is fully manifested or absolute. Mine is a New World version of reality—granting me the presumption that there is anything real about it. In the New World, your strength *doesn't* give out. That was the reason why your European parents, your old people, fed you so well in this land of youth. They were trained in submission, but you were free and bred in liberty. You were equal, you were strong, and here you could not be put to death, as Jews *there* had been.

But your soul brought the truth to you so forcibly that you woke up in your fifty-fifty bed—half Jewish, half Wasp—since, thanks to the powers of memory, you were the owner of a Philadelphia mansion (too disproportionate a reward), and there the dream had just come to a stop. An old man resuming ordinary consciousness opened his still-frightened eyes and saw the bronze brier-bush lamp with bulbs glowing in it. His neck on two pillows, stacked for reading, was curved like a shepherd's crook.

It wasn't the dream alone that was so frightful, though that was bad enough; it was the accompanying revelation that was so hard to take. It wasn't death that had scared me, it was disclosure: I wasn't what I thought I was. I really didn't understand merciless brutality. And whom should I take this up with now? Deirdre was gone; I can't discuss things like this with my son—he's all administrator and executive. That left Fonstein and Sorella. Perhaps.

Sorella had said, I recall, that Fonstein, in his orthopedic boot, couldn't vault over walls and escape like Douglas Fairbanks. In the movies, Douglas Fairbanks was always too much for his enemies. They couldn't hold him. In *The Black Pirate* he disabled a sailing vessel all by himself. Holding a knife, he slid down the mainsail, slicing it in half. You couldn't have locked a man like that in a cattle car; he would have broken out. Sorella wasn't speaking of Douglas Fairbanks, nor did she refer to Fonstein only. Her remark was ultimately meant for me. Yes, she was talking of me and also of Billy Rose. For Fonstein was Fonstein—he was Mitteleuropa. I, on the other hand, was from the Eastern Seaboard—born in New Jersey, educated at Washington Square College, a big mnemonic success in Philadelphia. I was a Jew of an entirely different breed. And therefore (yes, go on, you can't avoid it now) closer to Billy Rose and his rescue operation, the personal underground inspired by *The Scarlet Pimpernel*—the Hollywood of Leslie Howard, who acted the Pimpernel, substituted for the Hollywood of Douglas Fairbanks. There was no way, therefore, in which I could grasp the real facts in the case of Fonstein. I hadn't understood *Fonstein* v. *Rose,* and I badly wanted to say this to Harry and Sorella. You pay a price for being a child of the New World.

I decided to switch off the lamp, which, fleetingly, was associated with the thicket in which Abraham-*avinu* had found a ram caught by the horns—as you see, I was bombarded from too many sides. Now illuminated particles of Jewish history were coming at me.

An old man has had a lifetime to learn to control his jitters in the night. Whatever I was (and that, at this late stage, still remained to be seen), I would need strength in the morning to continue my investigation. So I had to take measures to avoid a fretful night. Great souls may welcome insomnia and are happy to think of God or Science in the dead of night, but I was too disturbed to think straight. An important teaching of the Mnemosyne System, however, is to learn to make your mind a blank. You will yourself to think nothing. You expel all the distractions. Tonight's distractions happened to be very serious. I had discovered for how long I had shielded myself from unbearable imaginations— no, not imaginations, but recognitions—of murder, of relish in torture, of the ground bass of brutality, without which no human music ever is performed.

So I applied my famous method. I willed myself to think nothing. I shut out all thoughts. When you think nothing, consciousness is driven out. Consciousness being gone, you are asleep.

I conked out. It was a mercy.

In the morning, I found myself being supernormal. At the bathroom sink I rinsed my mouth, for it was parched (the elderly often suffer from such dryness). Shaved and brushed, I exercised on my ski machine (mustn't let the muscles go slack) and then I dressed and, when dressed, stuck my shoes under the revolving brush. Once more in rightful possession of a fine house, where Francis X. Biddle was once a neighbor and Emily Dickinson a guest at tea (there were other personages to list), I went down to breakfast. My housekeeper came from the kitchen with granola, strawberries, and black coffee. First the coffee, more than the usual morning fix.

"How did you sleep?" said Sarah, my old-fashioned caretaker. So much discretion, discernment, wisdom of life rolled up in this portly black lady. We didn't communicate in words, but we tacitly exchanged information at a fairly advanced level. From the amount of coffee I swallowed she could tell that I was shamming supernormalcy. From my side, I was aware that possibly I was crediting Sarah with very wide powers because I missed my wife, missed contact with womanly intelligence. I recognized also that I had begun to place my hopes and needs on Sorella Fonstein, whom I now was longing to see. My mind persisted in placing the Fonsteins in Sarasota, in winter quarters with the descendants of Hannibal's elephants, amid palm trees and hibiscus. An idealized Sarasota, where my heart apparently was yearning ever.

Sarah put more coffee before me in my study. Probably new lines had appeared in my face overnight—signs indicating the demolition of a long-standing structure. (How *could* I have been such a creep!)

At last my Fonstein call was answered—I was phoning on the half hour.

A young man spoke. "Hello, who is this?"

How clever of Swerdlow to suggest trying the old listed number.

"Is this the Fonstein residence?"

"That's what it is."

"Would you be Gilbert Fonstein, the son?"

"I would not," the young person said, breezy but amiable. He was, as they say, laid back. No suggestion that I was deranging him (Sorella entered into this—she liked to make bilingual puns). "I'm a friend of Gilbert's, house-sitting here. Walk the dog, water the plants, set the timed lights. And who are you?"

"An old relative—friend of the family. I see that I'll have to leave a message. Tell them that it has to do with another Fonstein who lives in Jerusalem and claims to be an uncle or cousin to Harry. I had a call from a rabbi—X/Y—who feels that something should be done, since the old guy is off the wall."

"In what way?"

"He's eccentric, deteriorated, prophetic, psychopathic. A decaying old man, but he's still ebullient and full of protest. . . ."

I paused briefly. You never can tell whom you're talking to, seen or unseen. What's more, I am one of those suggestible types, apt to take my cue from the other fellow and fall into his style of speech. I detected a certain freewheeling charm in the boy at the other end, and there was an exchange of charm for charm. Evidently I wanted to engage this young fellow's interest. In short, to imitate, to hit it off and get facts from him.

"This old Jerusalem character says he's a Fonstein and wants money?" he said. "You sound as if you yourself were in a position to help, so why not wire money."

"True. However, Harry could identify him, check his credentials, and naturally would want to hear that he's turned up alive. He may have been on the dead list. Are you only a house-sitter? You sound like a friend of the family."

"I see we're going to have a talk. Hold a minute while I find my bandanna. It's starting to be allergy time, and my whole head is raw. . . . Which relative are you?"

"I run an institute in Philadelphia."

"Oh, the memory man. I've heard of you. You go back to the time of Billy Rose—*that* flake. Harry disliked talking about it, but Sorella and Gilbert often did. . . . Can you hold on till I locate the handkerchief? Wiping my beard with Kleenex leaves crumbs of paper."

When he laid down the phone, I used the pause to place him plausibly. I formed an image of a heavy young man—a thick head of hair, a beer paunch, a T-shirt with a logo or slogan. *Act Up* was now a popular one. I pictured a representative member of the youth population seen on every street in every section of the country and even in the smallest of towns. Rough boots, stone-washed jeans, bristly cheeks—something like Leadville or Silverado miners of the last century, except that these young people were not laboring, never would labor with picks. It must have diverted him to chat me up. An old gent in Philadelphia, moderately famous and worth lots of money. He couldn't have imagined the mansion, the splendid room where I sat holding the French phone, expensively rewired, an instrument once the property of a descendant of the Merovingian nobility. (I wouldn't give up on the Baron Charlus.)

The young man was not a hang-loose, hippie handyman untroubled by intelligence, whatever else. I was certain of that. He had much to tell me. Whether he was malicious I had no way of saying. He was manipulative, however, and he had already succeeded in setting the tone of our exchange. Finally, he had information about the Fonsteins, and it was information I wanted.

"I do go back a long way," I said. "I've been out of touch with the Fonsteins for too many years. How have they arranged their retirement? Do they divide their year between New Jersey and a warm climate? Somehow I fancy them in Sarasota."

"You need a new astrologer."

He wasn't being satirical—protective rather. He now treated me like a senior citizen. He gentled me.

"I was surprised lately when I reckoned up the dates and realized the Fonsteins and I last met about thirty years ago, in Jerusalem. But emotionally I was in contact—that does happen." I tried to persuade him, and I felt in reality that it was true.

Curiously, he agreed. "It would make a dissertation subject," he said. "Out of sight isn't necessarily out of mind. People withdraw into themselves, and then they work up imaginary affections. It's a common American condition."

"Because of the continental U.S.A.—the terrific distances?"

"Pennsylvania and New Jersey are neighboring states."

"I do seem to have closed out New Jersey mentally," I admitted. "You sound as though you have studied . . . ?"

"Gilbert and I were at school together."

"Didn't he do physics at Cal Tech?"

"He switched to mathematics—probability theory."

"There I'm totally ignorant."

"That makes two of us," he said, adding, "I find you kind of interesting to talk to."

"One is always looking for someone to have a real exchange with."

He seemed to agree. He said, "I'm inclined to make the time for it, whenever possible."

He had described himself as a house-sitter, without mentioning another occupation. In a sense I was a house-sitter myself, notwithstanding that I owned the property. My son and his wife may also have seen me in such a light. A nice corollary was that my soul played the role of sitter in my body.

It did in fact cross my mind that the young man wasn't altogether disinterested. That I was undergoing an examination or evaluation. So far, he had told me nothing about the Fonsteins except that they didn't winter in Sarasota and that Gilbert had studied mathematics. He didn't say that he himself had attended Cal Tech. And when he said that out of sight wasn't invariably out of mind, I thought his dissertation, if he had written one, might have been in the field of psychology or sociology.

I recognized that I was half afraid of asking direct questions about the Fonsteins. By neglecting them, I had compromised my right to ask freely. There were things I did and did not want to hear. The house-sitter sensed this, it amused him, and he led me on. He was light and made sporty talk, but I began to feel there was a grim side to him.

I decided that it was time to speak up, and I said, "Where can I reach Harry and Sorella, or is there a reason you can't give out their number?"

"I haven't got one."

"Please don't talk riddles."

"They can't be reached."

"What are you telling me! Did I put it off too long?"

"I'm afraid so."

"They're dead, then."

I was shocked. Something essential in me caved in, broke down. At my age, a man is well prepared to hear news of death. What I felt most sharply and immediately was that I had abandoned two extraordinary people whom I had always said I valued and held dear. I found myself making a list of names: Billy is dead; Mrs. Hamet, dead; Sorella, dead; Harry, dead. All the principals, dead.

"Were they sick? Did Sorella have cancer?"

"They died about six months ago, on the Jersey Turnpike. The way it's told, a truck and trailer went out of control. But I wish I didn't have to tell you this, sir. As a relative, you'll take it hard. They were killed instantly. And thank God, because their car folded on them and it took welders to cut the bodies free— This must be hard for somebody who knew them well."

He was, incidentally, giving me the business. To some extent, I had it coming. But at any moment during these thirty years, any of us might have died in an instant. I too might have. And he was wrong to assume that I was a Jew of the old type, bound to react sentimentally to such news as this.

"You *are* a senior citizen, you said. You'd have to be, given the numbers."

My voice was low. I said I was one. "Where were the Fonsteins going?"

"They were driving from New York, bound for Atlantic City."

I saw the bloodstained bodies delivered from the car and stretched out on the grass slope—the police flares, the crush of diverted traffic and the wavering of the dark, gassed atmosphere, the sucking shrieks of the ambulance, the paramedics and their body bags. Last summer's heat was tormenting. You might say the dead sweated blood.

If you're deciding which is the gloomiest expressway in the country, the Jersey Pike is certainly a front-runner. This was no place for Sorella, who loved Europe, to be killed. Harry's forty American years of compensation for the destruction of his family in Poland suddenly were up.

"Why were they going to Atlantic City?"

"Their son was there, having trouble."

"Was he gambling?"

"It was pretty widely known, so I'm able to say. After all, he wrote a mathematical study on winning at blackjack. Math mavens say it's quite a piece of work. On the real-life side, he's gotten into trouble over this."

They were rushing to the aid of their American son when they were killed.

"It must be very dreary to hear this," the young man said.

"I looked forward to seeing them again. I'd been promising myself to resume contact."

"I don't suppose death is the worst . . . ," he said.

I wasn't about to go into eschatology with this kid on the telephone and start delineating the various grades of evil. Although, God knows, the phone may encourage many forms of disclosure, and you may hear as much if not more from the soul by long distance as face to face.

"Which one was driving?"

"Mrs. Fonstein was, and maybe being reckless."

"I see—an emergency, and a mother in a terrible hurry. Was she still huge?"

"The same for years, and right up against the wheel. But there weren't many people like Sorella Fonstein. You don't want to criticize."

"I'm not criticizing," I said. "I would have gone to the funeral to pay my respects."

"Too bad you didn't come and speak. It wasn't much of a memorial service."

"I might have told the Billy Rose story to a gathering of friends in the chapel."

"There was no gathering," the young man said. "And did you know that when Billy died, they say that he couldn't be buried for a long time. He had to wait until the court decided what to do about the million-dollar tomb provision in his will. There was a legal battle over it."

"I never heard."

"Because you don't read the *News*, or *Newsday*. Not even the *Post*."

"Was *that* what happened!"

"He was kept on ice. This used to be discussed by the Fonsteins. They wondered about the Jewish burial rules."

"Does Gilbert take any interest in his Jewish background—for instance, in his father's history?"

Gilbert's friend hesitated ever so slightly—just enough to make me think that he was Jewish himself. I don't say that he disowned being a Jew. Evidently he didn't want to reckon with it. The only life he cared to lead was that of an American. So hugely absorbing, that. So absorbing that one existence was too little for it. It could drink up a hundred existences, if you had them to offer, and reach out for more.

"What you just asked is—I translate—whether Gilbert is one of those science freaks with minimal human motivation," he said. "You have to remember what a big thing gambling is to him. It never could be *my* thing. You couldn't pay me to go to Atlantic City, especially since the double-deck disaster. They put a double-deck bus on the road, filled with passengers bound for the casino. It was too high to clear one of the viaducts, and the top was torn away."

"Did many die? Were heads sheared off?"

"You'd have to check the *Times* to find out."

"I wouldn't care to. But where is Gilbert now? He inherited, I suppose."

"Well, sure he did, and right now he's in Las Vegas. He took a young lady with him. She's trained in his method, which involves memorizing the deck in every deal. You keep mental lists of cards that have been played, and you apply various probability factors. They tell me that the math of it is just genius."

"The system depends on memorizing?"

"Yes. That's up your alley. Is Gilbert the girl's lover? is the next consideration. Well, this wouldn't work without sex interest. The gambling alone wouldn't hold a young woman for long. Does she enjoy Las Vegas? How could she not? It's the biggest showplace in the world—the heart of the American entertainment industry. Which city today is closest to a holy city—like Lhasa or Calcutta or Chartres or Jerusalem? Here it could be New York for money, Washington for power, or Las Vegas attracting people by the millions. Nothing to compare with it in the history of the whole world."

"Ah," I said. "It's more in the Billy Rose vein than in the Harry Fonstein vein. But how is Gilbert making out?"

"I haven't finished talking about the sex yet," said the bitter-witty young man. "Is the gambling a turn-on for sex, or does sex fuel the gambling? Figuring it as a sublimation. Let's assume that for Gilbert, abstraction is dominant. But past a certain abstraction point, people are said to be definitely mad."

"Poor Sorella—poor Harry! Maybe it was their death that threw him."

"I can't make myself responsible for a diagnosis. My own narcissistic problem is plenty severe. I confess I expected a token legacy, because I was damn near a family member and looked after Gilbert."

"I see."

"You don't see. This brings my faith in feelings face to face with the real conditions of existence."

"Your feelings for Fonstein and Sorella?"

"The feelings Sorella led me to believe she had for me."

"Counting on you to take care of Gilbert."

"Well . . . this has been a neat conversation. Good to talk to a person from the past who was so fond of the Fonsteins. We'll all miss them. Harry had the dignity, but Sorella had the dynamism. I can see why you'd be upset—your timing was off. But don't pine too much."

On this commiseration, I cradled the phone, and there it was, on its high mount, a conversation piece from another epoch sitting before a man with an acute need for conversation. Stung by the words of the house-sitter. I also considered that owing to Gilbert, the Fonsteins from their side had avoided me—he was so promising, the prodigy they had had the marvelous luck to produce and who for mysterious reasons (Fonstein would have felt them to be mysterious American reasons) had gone awry. They wouldn't have wanted me to know about this.

As for pining—well, that young man had been putting me on. He was one of those lesser devils that come out of every pore of society. All you have to do is press the social soil. He was taunting me—for my Jewish sentiments. Dear, dear! Two more old friends gone, just when I was ready after thirty years of silence to open my arms to them: Let's sit down together and recall the past and speak again of Billy Rose—"sad stories of the death of kings." And the "sitter" had been putting it to me, existentialist style. Like: Whose disappearance will fill you with despair, sir? Whom can you not live without? Whom do you painfully long for? Which of your dead hangs over you daily? Show me where and how death has mutilated you. Where are your wounds? Whom would you pursue beyond the gates of death?

What a young moron! Doesn't he think I know all that?

I had a good mind to phone the boy back and call him on his low-grade cheap-shot nihilism. But it would be an absurd thing to do if improvement of the understanding (*his* understanding) was my aim. You can never dismantle all these modern mental structures. There are so many of them that they face you like an interminable vast city.

Suppose I were to talk to him about the roots of memory in feeling—about the themes that collect and hold the memory; if I were to tell him what retention of the past really means. Things like: "If sleep is forgetting, forgetting is also sleep, and sleep is to consciousness what death is to life. So that the Jews ask even God to remember, *'Yiskor Elohim.'*"

God doesn't forget, but your prayer requests him particularly to remember your dead. But how was I to make an impression on a kid like that? I chose instead to record everything I could remember of the Bellarosa Connection, and set it all down with a Mnemosyne flourish.

THE OLD SYSTEM

IT WAS a thoughtful day for Dr. Braun. Winter. Saturday. The short end of December. He was alone in his apartment and woke late, lying in bed until noon, in the room kept very dark, working with a thought—a feeling: Now you see it, now you don't. Now a content, now a vacancy. Now an important individual, a force, a necessary existence; suddenly nothing. A frame without a picture, a mirror with missing glass. The feeling of necessary existence might be the aggressive, instinctive vitality we share with a dog or an ape. The difference being in the power of the mind or spirit to declare *I am*. Plus the inevitable inference *I am not*. Dr. Braun was no more pleased with being than with its opposite. For him an age of equilibrium seemed to be coming in. How nice! Anyway, he had no project for putting the world in rational order, and for no special reason he got up. Washed his wrinkled but not elderly face with freezing tap water, which changed the nighttime white to a more agreeable color. He brushed his teeth. Standing upright, scrubbing the teeth as if he were looking after an idol. He then ran the big old-fashioned tub to sponge himself, backing into the thick stream of the Roman faucet, soaping beneath with the same cake of soap he would apply later to his beard. Under the swell of his belly, the tip of his parts, somewhere between his heels. His heels needed scrubbing. He dried himself with yesterday's shirt, an economy. It was going to the laundry anyway. Yes, with the self-respecting expression human beings inherit from ancestors for whom bathing was a solemnity. A sadness.

But every civilized man today cultivated an unhealthy self-detachment. Had learned from art the art of amusing self-observation and objectivity. Which, since there had to be something amusing to watch, required art in one's conduct. Existence for the sake of such practices did not seem worthwhile. Mankind was in a confusing, uncomfortable, disagreeable stage in the evolution of its consciousness. Dr. Braun (Samuel) did not like it. It made him sad to feel that the thought, art, belief of great traditions should be so misemployed. Elevation? Beauty? Torn into shreds, into ribbons for girls' costumes, or trailed like the tail of a kite at Happenings. Plato and the Buddha raided by looters. The tombs of Pharaohs broken into by desert rabble. And so on, thought Dr. Braun as he passed into his neat kitchen. He was well pleased by the blue-and-white Dutch dishes, cups hanging, saucers standing in slots.

He opened a fresh can of coffee, much enjoyed the fragrance from the punctured can. Only an instant, but not to be missed. Next he sliced bread for the toaster, got out the butter, chewed an orange; and he was admiring long icicles on the huge red, circular roof tank of the laundry across the alley, the clear sky, when he discovered that a sentiment was approaching. It was said of him, occasionally, that he did not love anyone. This was not true. He did not love anyone steadily. But unsteadily he loved, he guessed, at an average rate.

The sentiment, as he drank his coffee, was for two cousins in upstate New York, the Mohawk Valley. They were dead. Isaac Braun and his sister Tina. Tina was first to go. Two years later, Isaac died. Braun now discovered that he and Cousin Isaac had loved each other. For whatever use or meaning this fact might have within the peculiar system of light, movement, contact, and perishing in which he tried to find stability. Toward Tina, Dr. Braun's feelings were less clear. More passionate once, but at present more detached.

Isaac's wife, after he died, had told Braun, "He was proud of you. He said, 'Sammy has been written up in *Time,* in all the papers, for his research. But he never says a word about his scientific reputation!' "

"I see. Well, computers do the work, actually."

"But you have to know what to put into these computers."

This was more or less the case. But Braun had not continued the conversation. He did not care much for being *first* in his field. People were boastful in America. Matthew Arnold, a not entirely appetizing figure himself, had correctly observed this in the U.S. Dr. Braun thought this native American boastfulness had aggravated a certain weakness in Jewish immigrants. But a proportionate reaction of self-effacement was not praiseworthy. Dr. Braun did not want to be interested in this question at all. However, his cousin Isaac's opinions had some value for him.

In Schenectady there were two more Brauns of the same family, living. Did Dr. Braun, drinking his coffee this afternoon, love them too? They did not elicit such feelings. Then did he love Isaac more because Isaac was dead? There one might have something.

But in childhood, Isaac had shown him great kindness. The others, not very much.

Now Braun remembered certain things. A sycamore tree beside the Mohawk

River. Then the river couldn't have been so foul. Its color, anyhow, was green, and it was powerful and dark, an easy, level force—crimped, green, blackish, glassy. A huge tree like a complicated event, with much splitting and thick chalky extensions. It must have dominated an acre, brown and white. And well away from the leaves, on a dead branch, sat a gray-and-blue fish hawk. Isaac and his little cousin Braun passed in the wagon—the old coarse-tailed horse walking, the steady head in blinders, working onward. Braun, seven years old, wore a gray shirt with large bone buttons and had a short summer haircut. Isaac was dressed in work clothes, for in those days the Brauns were in the secondhand business—furniture, carpets, stoves, beds. His senior by fifteen years, Isaac had a mature business face. Born to be a man, in the direct Old Testament sense, as that bird on the sycamore was born to fish in water. Isaac, when he had come to America, was still a child. Nevertheless his old-country Jewish dignity was very firm and strong. He had the outlook of ancient generations on the New World. Tents and kine and wives and maidservants and manservants. Isaac was handsome, Braun thought—dark face, black eyes, vigorous hair, and a long scar on the cheek. Because, he told his scientific cousin, his mother had given him milk from a tubercular cow in the old country. While his father was serving in the Russo-Japanese War. Far away. In the Yiddish metaphor, on the lid of hell. As though hell were a cauldron, a covered pot. How those old-time Jews despised the goy wars, their vainglory and obstinate *Dummheit*. Conscription, mustering, marching, shooting, leaving the corpses everywhere. Buried, unburied. Army against army. Gog and Magog. The czar, that weak, whiskered arbitrary and woman-ridden man, decreed that Uncle Braun would be swept away to Sakhalin. So by irrational decree, as in *The Arabian Nights,* Uncle Braun, with his greatcoat and short humiliated legs, little beard, and great eyes, left wife and child to eat maggoty pork. And when the war was lost, Uncle Braun escaped through Manchuria. Came to Vancouver on a Swedish ship. Labored on the railroad. He did not look so strong, as Braun remembered him in Schenectady. His chest was deep and his arms long, but the legs like felt, too yielding, as if the escape from Sakhalin and trudging in Manchuria had been too much. However, in the Mohawk Valley, monarch of used stoves and fumigated mattresses—dear Uncle Braun! He had a small, pointed beard, like George V, like Nick of Russia. Like Lenin, for that matter. But large, patient eyes in his wizened face, filling all of the space reserved for eyes.

A vision of mankind Braun was having as he sat over his coffee Saturday afternoon. Beginning with those Jews of 1920.

Braun as a young child was protected by the special affection of his cousin Isaac, who stroked his head and took him on the wagon, later the truck, into the countryside. When Braun's mother had gone into labor with him, it was Isaac whom Aunt Rose sent running for the doctor. He found the doctor in the saloon. Faltering, drunken Jones, who practiced among Jewish immigrants before those immigrants had educated their own doctors. He had Isaac crank the Model T. And they drove. Arriving, Jones tied Mother Braun's hands to the bedposts, a custom of the times.

Having worked as a science student in laboratories and kennels, Dr. Braun had himself delivered cats and dogs. Man, he knew, entered life like these other creatures, in a transparent bag or caul. Lying in a bag filled with transparent fluid, a purplish water. A color to mystify the most rational philosopher. What is this creature that struggles for birth in its membrane and clear fluid? Any puppy in its sac, in the blind terror of its emergence, any mouse breaking into the external world from this shining, innocent-seeming blue-tinged transparency!

Dr. Braun was born in a small wooden house. They washed him and covered him with mosquito netting. He lay at the foot of his mother's bed. Tough Cousin Isaac dearly loved Braun's mother. He had great pity for her. In intervals of his dealing, of being a Jewish businessman, there fell these moving reflections of those who were dear to him.

Aunt Rose was Dr. Braun's godmother, held him at his circumcision. Bearded, nearsighted old Krieger, fingers stained with chicken slaughter, cut away the foreskin.

Aunt Rose, Braun felt, was the original dura mater—the primal hard mother. She was not a big woman. She had a large bust, wide hips, and old-fashioned thighs of those corrupted shapes that now belong to history. Which hampered her walk. Together with poor feet, broken by the excessive female weight she carried. Her face was red, her black hair powerful. She had a straight sharp nose. To cut through mercy like a cotton thread. In the light of her eyes Braun recognized the joy she took in her hardness—hardness of reckoning, hardness of tactics, hardness of dealing and of speech. She was building a kingdom with the labor of Uncle Braun and the strength of her obedient sons. The Brauns had their shop, they had real estate. They had a hideous synagogue of such red brick as seemed to grow in upstate New York by the will of the demon spirit charged with maintaining the ugliness of America in that epoch—which saw to it that a particular comic ugliness should influence the soul of man. In Schenectady, in Troy, in Gloversville, Mechanicville, as far west as Buffalo. There was a sour-paper mustiness in this synagogue. Uncle Braun not only had money, he also had some learning and he was respected. But it was a quarrelsome congregation. Every question was disputed. There were rivalries and rages; slaps were given, families stopped speaking. Pariahs, thought Braun, with the dignity of princes among themselves.

Silent, with silent eyes crossing and recrossing the red water tank bound by twisted cables, from which ragged icicles hung down and white vapor rose, Dr. Braun extracted a moment four decades gone in which Cousin Isaac had said, with one of those archaic looks he had, that the Brauns were descended from the tribe of Naphtali.

"How do we know?"

"People—families—*know.*"

Dr. Braun was reluctant, even at the age of ten, to believe such things. But Isaac, who was almost old enough to be Braun's uncle, said: "You'd better not forget it."

As a rule, Isaac was gay with young Braun. Laughing against the tension of the scar that forced his mouth to one side. His eyes, black, soft, but also skeptical. His breath had a bitter fragrance that translated itself to Braun as masculine earnestness and gloom. All the sons in the family had the same sort of laugh. They sat on the open porch, Sundays, laughing, while Uncle Braun read aloud the Yiddish matrimonial advertisements. "Attractive widow, thirty-five, with dark charms, owning her own dry-goods business in Hudson, excellent cook, Orthodox, well-bred, refined. Plays the piano. Two intelligent, well-behaved children, eight and six."

All but Tina, the obese sister, took part in this satirical Sunday pleasure. Behind the screen door, she stood in the kitchen. Below was the yard, where crude flowers grew—zinnias, plantain lilies, trumpet vine on the chicken shed.

Now the country cottage appeared to Braun, in the Adirondacks. A stream. So beautiful! Trees, full of great strength. Wild strawberries, but you must be careful about the poison ivy. In the drainage ditches, polliwogs. Braun slept in the attic with Cousin Mutt. Mutt danced in his undershirt in the morning, naked beneath, and sang an obscene song:

> "*I stuck my nose up a nanny goat's ass*
> *And the smell was enough to blind me.*"

He was leaping on bare feet, and his thing bounded from thigh to thigh. Going into saloons to collect empty bottles, he had learned this. A ditty from the stokehold. Origin, Liverpool or Tyneside. Art of the laboring class in the machine age.

An old mill. A pasture with clover flowers. Braun, seven years old, tried to make a clover wreath, pinching out a hole in the stems for other stems to pass through. He meant the wreath for fat Tina. To put it on her thick savory head, her smoky black harsh hair. Then in the pasture, little Braun overturned a rotten stump with his foot. Hornets pursued and stung him. He screamed. He had painful crimson lumps all over his body. Aunt Rose put him to bed and Tina came huge into the attic to console him. An angry fat face, black eyes, and the dilated nose breathing at him. Little Braun, stung and burning. She lifted her dress and petticoat to cool him with her body. The belly and thighs swelled before him. Braun felt too small and frail for this ecstasy. By the bedside was a chair, and she sat. Under the dizzy heat of the shingled roof, she rested her legs upon him, spread them wider, wider. He saw the barbarous and coaly hair. He saw the red within. She parted the folds with her fingers. Parting, her dark nostrils opened, the eyes looked white in her head. She motioned that he should press his child's genital against her fat-flattened thighs. Which, with agonies of incapacity and pleasure, he did. All was silent. Summer silence. Her sexual odor. The flies and gnats stimulated by delicious heat or the fragrance. He heard a mass of flies tear themselves from the windowpane. A sound of detached adhesive. Tina did not kiss, did not embrace. Her face was menacing. She was defying. She was drawing him—taking him somewhere with her. But she promised nothing, told him nothing.

When he recovered from his stings, playing once more in the yard, Braun saw Isaac with his fiancée, Clara Sternberg, walking among the trees, embracing very sweetly. Braun tried to go with them, but Cousin Isaac sent him away. When he still followed, Cousin Isaac turned him roughly toward the cottage. Little Braun then tried to kill his cousin. He wanted with all his heart to club Isaac with a piece of wood. He was still struck by the incomparable happiness, the luxury of that pure murderousness. Rushing toward Isaac, who took him by the back of the neck, twisted his head, held him under the pump. He then decreed that little Sam Braun must go home, to Albany. He was far too wild. Must be taught a lesson. Cousin Tina said in private, "Good for *you*, Sam. I hate him, too." She took Braun with her dimpled, inept hand and walked down the road with him in the Adirondack dust. Her gingham-fitted bulk. Her shoulders curved, banked, like the earth of the hill-cut road. Together, they hampered her walk. The excessive weight of her body was too much for her feet.

Later she dieted. Became for a while thinner, more civilized. Everyone was more civilized. Little Braun became a docile, bookish child. Did very well at school.

All clear? Quite clear to the adult Braun, considering his fate no more than the fate of others. Before his tranquil look, the facts arranged themselves—rose, took a new arrangement. Remained awhile in the settled state and then changed again. We were getting somewhere.

Uncle Braun died angry with Aunt Rose. He turned his face to the wall with his last breath to rebuke her hardness. All the men, his sons, burst out weeping. The tears of the women were different. Later, too, their passion took other forms. They bargained for more property. And Aunt Rose defied Uncle Braun's will. She collected rents in the slums of Albany and Schenectady from properties he had left to his sons. She dressed herself in the old fashion, calling on black tenants or the Jewish rabble of tailors and cobblers. To her, the old Jewish words for these trades—*Schneider, Schuster*—were terms of contempt. Rents belonging mainly to Isaac she banked in her own name. Riding ancient streetcars in the factory slums, she did not need to buy widow's clothes. She had always worn suits, and they had always been black. Her hat was three-cornered, like the town crier's. She let the black braid hang behind, as though she were in her own kitchen. She had trouble with bladder and arteries, but ailments did not keep her at home and she had no use for doctoring and drugs. She blamed Uncle Braun's death on Bromo-Seltzer, which, she said, had enlarged his heart.

Isaac did not marry Clara Sternberg. Though he was a manufacturer, her father turned out on inquiry to have started as a cutter and her mother had been a housemaid. Aunt Rose would not tolerate such a connection. She took long trips to make genealogical inquiries. And she vetoed all the young women, her judgments severe without limit. "A false dog." "Candied poison." "An open ditch. A sewer. A born whore!"

The woman Isaac eventually married was pleasant, mild, round, respectable, the daughter of a Jewish farmer.

Aunt Rose said, "Ignorant. A common man."

"He's honest, a hard worker on the land," said Isaac. "He recites the Psalms even when he's driving. He keeps them under his wagon seat."

"I don't believe it. A son of Ham like that. A cattle dealer. He stinks of manure." And she said to the bride in Yiddish, "Be so good as to wash thy father before bringing him to the synagogue. Get a bucket of scalding water, and 20 Mule Team Borax and ammonia, and a horse brush. The filth is ingrained. Be sure to scrub his hands."

The rigid madness of the Orthodox. Their haughty, spinning, crazy spirit.

Tina did not bring her young man from New York to be examined by Aunt Rose. Anyway, he was neither young, nor handsome, nor rich. Aunt Rose said he was a minor hoodlum, a slugger. She had gone to Coney Island to inspect *his* family—a father who sold pretzels and chestnuts from a cart, a mother who cooked for banquets. And the groom himself—so thick, so bald, so grim, she said, his hands so common and his back and chest like fur, a fell. He was a beast, she told young Sammy Braun. Braun was a student then at Rensselaer Polytechnic and came to see his aunt in her old kitchen—the great black-and-nickel stove that stood there, the round table on its oak pedestal, the dark-blue-and-white check of the oilcloth, a still life of peaches and cherries salvaged from the secondhand shop. And Aunt Rose, more feminine with her corset off and a gaudy wrapper over her thick Victorian undervests, camisoles, bloomers. Her stockings were gartered below the knee and the wide upper portions, fashioned for thighs, drooped down, flimsy, nearly to her slippers.

Tina was then handsome, if not pretty. In high school she took off eighty pounds. Then she went to New York City without getting her diploma. What did *she* care for such things! said Rose. And how did she get to Coney Island by herself? Because she was perverse. Her instinct was for freaks. And there she met this beast. This hired killer, this second Lepke of Murder, Inc. Upstate, the old woman read the melodramas of the Yiddish press, which she embroidered with her own ideas of wickedness.

But when Tina brought her husband to Schenectady, installing him in her father's secondhand shop, he turned out to be a big innocent man. If he had ever had guile, he lost it with his hair. His baldness was total, like a purge. He had a sentimental, dependent look. Tina protected him. Here Dr. Braun had sexual thoughts, about himself as a child and about her childish bridegroom. And scowling, smoldering Tina, her angry tenderness in the Adirondacks, and how she was beneath, how hard she breathed in the attic, and the violent strength and obstinacy of her crinkled, sooty hair.

Nobody could sway Tina. That, thought Braun, was probably the secret of it. She had consulted her own will, kept her own counsel for so long, that she could accept no other guidance. Anyone who listened to others seemed to her weak.

When Aunt Rose lay dead, Tina took from her hand the ring Isaac had given her many years ago. Braun did not remember the entire history of that ring, only that Isaac had loaned money to an immigrant who disappeared, leaving this jewel, which was assumed to be worthless but turned out to be valuable. Braun could not recall whether it was ruby or emerald; nor the setting. But it was the one feminine adornment Aunt Rose wore. And it was supposed to go to Isaac's wife, Sylvia, who wanted it badly. Tina took it from the corpse and put it on her own finger.

"Tina, give that ring to me. Give it here," said Isaac.

"No. It was hers. Now it's mine."

"It was not Mama's. You know that. Give it back."

She outfaced him over the body of Aunt Rose. She knew he would not quarrel at the deathbed. Sylvia was enraged. She did what she could. That is, she whispered, "*Make* her!" But it was no use. He knew he could not recover it. Besides, there were too many other property disputes. His rents were deposited in Aunt Rose's savings account.

But only Isaac became a millionaire. The others simply hoarded, old-immigrant style. He never sat waiting for his legacy. By the time Aunt Rose died, Isaac was already worth a great deal of money. He had put up an ugly apartment building in Albany. To him, an achievement. He was out with his men at dawn. Having prayed aloud while his wife, in curlers, pretty but puffy with sleepiness, sleepy but obedient, was in the kitchen fixing breakfast. Isaac's Orthodoxy only increased with his wealth. He soon became an old-fashioned Jewish paterfamilias. With his family he spoke a Yiddish unusually thick in old Slavic and Hebrew expressions. Instead of "important people, leading citizens," he said *"Anshe ha-ir,"* Men of the City. He, too, kept the Psalms near. As active, worldly Jews for centuries had done. One copy lay in the glove compartment of his Cadillac. To which his great gloomy sister referred with a twist of the face—she had become obese again, wider and taller, since those Adirondack days. She said, "He reads the Tehillim aloud in his air-conditioned Caddy when there's a long freight train at the crossing. That crook! He'd pick God's pocket!"

One could not help thinking what fertility of metaphor there was in all of these Brauns. Dr. Braun himself was no exception. And what the explanation might be, despite twenty-five years of specialization in the chemistry of heredity, he couldn't say. How a protein molecule originating in an invisible ferment might carry such propensities of ingenuity, and creative malice and negative power, be capable of printing a talent or a vice upon a billion hearts. No wonder Isaac Braun cried out to his God when he sat sealed in his great black car and the freights rumbled in the polluted shimmering of this once-beautiful valley

Answer me when I call, O God of my
righteousness.

"But what do you think?" said Tina. "Does he remember his brothers when there is a deal going? Does he give his only sister a chance to come in?"

Not that there was any great need. Cousin Mutt, after he was wounded at Iwo Jima, returned to the appliance business. Cousin Aaron was a CPA. Tina's husband, bald Fenster, branched into housewares in his secondhand shop. Tina was back of that, of course. No one was poor. What irritated Tina was that Isaac would not carry the family into real-estate deals, where the tax advantages were greatest. The big depreciation allowances, which she understood as legally sanctioned graft. She had her money in savings accounts at a disgraceful two and a half percent, taxed at the full rate. She did not trust the stock market.

Isaac had tried, in fact, to include the Brauns when he built the shopping center at Robbstown. At a risky moment, they abandoned him. A desperate moment, when the law had to be broken. At a family meeting, each of the Brauns had agreed to put up twenty-five thousand dollars, the entire amount to be given under the table to Ilkington. Old Ilkington headed the board of directors of the Robbstown Country Club. Surrounded by factories, the club was moving farther into the country. Isaac had learned this from the old caddie master when he gave him a lift, one morning of fog. Mutt Braun had caddied at Robbstown in the early twenties, had carried Ilkington's clubs. Isaac knew Ilkington, too, and had a private talk with him. The old goy, now seventy, retiring to the British West Indies, had said to Isaac, "Off the record. One hundred thousand. And I don't want to bother about Internal Revenue." He was a long, austere man with a marbled face. Cornell 1910 or so. Cold but plain. And, in Isaac's opinion, fair.

Developed as a shopping center, properly planned, the Robbstown golf course was worth half a million apiece to the Brauns. The city in the postwar boom was spreading fast. Isaac had a friend on the zoning board who would clear everything for five grand. As for the contracting, he offered to do it all on his own. Tina insisted that a separate corporation be formed by the Brauns to make sure the building profits were shared equally. To this Isaac agreed. As head of the family, he took the burden upon himself. He would have to organize it all. Only Aaron the CPA could help him, setting up the books. The meeting, in Aaron's office, lasted from noon to three P.M. All the difficult problems were examined. Four players, specialists in the harsh music of money, studying a score. In the end, they agreed to perform.

But when the time came, ten A.M. on a Friday, Aaron balked. He would not do it. And Tina and Mutt also reneged. Isaac told Dr. Braun the story. As arranged, he came to Aaron's office carrying the twenty-five thousand dollars for Ilkington in an old briefcase. Aaron, now forty, smooth, shrewd, and dark, had the habit of writing tiny neat numbers on his memo pad as he spoke to you. Dark fingers quickly consulting the latest tax publications. He dropped his voice very low to the secretary on the intercom. He wore white-on-white shirts and silk-brocade ties, signed "Countess Mara." Of them all, he looked most like Uncle Braun. But without the beard, without the kingly pariah derby, without the gold thread in his brown eye. In many externals, thought scientific Braun, Aaron and Uncle Braun were drawn from the same genetic pool. Chemically, he was the younger brother of his father. The differences within were due possibly to heredity. Or perhaps to the influence of business America.

"Well?" said Isaac, standing in the carpeted office. The grandiose desk was superbly clean.

"How do you know Ilkington can be trusted?"

"I think he can."

"*You* think. He could take the money and say he never heard of you in all his life."

"Yes, he might. But we talked that over. We have to gamble."

Probably on his instructions, Aaron's secretary buzzed him. He bent over the instrument and out of the corner of his mouth he spoke to her very deliberately and low.

"Well, Aaron," said Isaac. "You want me to guarantee your investment? Well? Speak up."

Aaron had long ago subdued his thin tones and spoke in the gruff style of a man always sure of himself. But the sharp breaks, mastered twenty-five years ago, were still there. He stood up with both fists on the glass of his desk, trying to control his voice.

He said through clenched teeth, "I haven't slept!"

"Where is the money?"

"I don't have that kind of cash."

"No?"

"You know damn well. I'm licensed. I'm a certified accountant. I'm in no position . . ."

"And what about Tina—Mutt?"

"I don't know anything about them."

"Talked them out of it, didn't you? I have to meet Ilkington at noon. Sharp. Why didn't you tell me sooner?"

Aaron said nothing.

Isaac dialed Tina's number and let the phone ring. Certain that she was there, gigantically listening to the steely, beady drilling of the telephone. He let it ring, he said, about five minutes. He made no effort to call Mutt. Mutt would do as Tina did.

"I have an hour to raise this dough."

"In my bracket," Aaron said, "the twenty-five would cost me more than fifty."

"You could have told me this yesterday. Knowing what it means to me."

"You'll turn over a hundred thousand to a man you don't know? Without a receipt? Blind? Don't do it."

But Isaac had decided. In our generation, Dr. Braun thought, a sort of playboy capitalist has emerged. He gaily takes a flier in rebuilt office machinery for Brazil, motels in East Africa, high-fidelity components in Thailand. A hundred thousand means little. He jets down with a chick to see the scene. The governor of a province is waiting in his Thunderbird to take the guests on jungle expressways built by graft and peons to a surf-and-champagne weekend where the executive, youthful at fifty, closes the deal. But Cousin Isaac had put his stake together penny by penny, old style, starting with rags and bottles as a boy; then fire-salvaged goods; then used cars; then learning the building trades. Earth moving, foundations, concrete, sewage, wiring, roofing, heating systems. He got his money the hard way. And now he went to the bank and borrowed seventy-five thousand dollars, at full interest. Without security, he gave it to Ilkington in Ilkington's parlor. Furnished in old goy taste and disseminating an old goy odor of tiresome, silly, respectable things. Of which Ilkington was clearly so proud. The applewood, the cherry, the wing tables and cabinets, the upholstery with a flavor of dry paste, the pork-pale colors of gentility. Ilkington did not touch Isaac's briefcase. He did not intend, evidently, to count the bills, or even to look. He offered Isaac a martini. Isaac, not a drinker, drank the clear gin. At noon. Like something distilled in outer space. Having no color. He sat there sturdily but felt lost—lost to his people, his family, lost to God, lost in the void of America. Ilkington drank a shaker of cocktails, gentlemanly, stony, like a high slab of something generically human, but with few human traits familiar to Isaac. At the door he did not say he would keep his word. He simply shook hands with Isaac, saw him to the car. Isaac drove home and sat in the den of his bungalow. Two whole days. Then on Monday, Ilkington phoned to say that the Robbstown directors had decided to accept his offer for the property. A pause. Then Ilkington added that no written instrument could replace trust and decency between gentlemen.

Isaac took possession of the country club and filled it with a shopping center. All such places are ugly. Dr. Braun could not say why this one struck him as especially brutal in its ugliness. Perhaps because he remembered the Robbstown Club. Restricted, of course. But Jews could look at it from the road. And the elms had been lovely—a century or older. The light, delicate. And the Coolidge-era sedans turning in, with small curtains at the rear window, and holders for artificial flowers. Hudsons, Auburns, Bearcats. Only machinery. Nothing to feel nostalgic about.

Still, Braun was startled to see what Isaac had done. Perhaps in an unconscious assertion of triumph—in the vividness of victory. The green acres reserved, it was true, for mild idleness, for hitting a little ball with a stick, were now paralyzed by parking for five hundred cars. Supermarket, pizza joint, chop suey, Laundromat, Robert Hall clothes, a dime store.

And this was only the beginning. Isaac became a millionaire. He filled the Mohawk Valley with housing developments. And he began to speak of "my people," meaning those who lived in the buildings he had raised. He was stingy with land, he built too densely, it was true, but he built with benevolence. At six in the morning, he was out with his crews. He lived very simply. Walked humbly with his God, as the rabbi said. A Madison Avenue rabbi, by this time. The little synagogue was wiped out. It was as dead as the Dutch painters who would have appreciated its dimness and its shaggy old peddlers. Now there was a *temple* like a World's Fair pavilion. Isaac was president, having beaten out the father of a famous hoodlum, once executioner for the Mob in the Northeast. The worldly rabbi with his trained voice and tailored suits, like a Christian minister except for the play of Jewish cleverness in his face, hinted to the old-fashioned part of the congregation that he had to pour it on for the sake of the young people. America. Extraordinary times. If you wanted the young women to bless Sabbath candles, you had to start their rabbi at twenty thousand dollars, and add a house and a Jaguar.

Cousin Isaac, meantime, grew more old-fashioned. His car was ten years old. But he was a strong sort of man. Self-assured, a dark head scarcely thinning at the top. Upstate women said he gave out the positive male energy they were beginning to miss in men. He had it. It was in the manner with which he picked up a fork at the table, the way he poured from a bottle. Of course, the world had done for him exactly what he had demanded. That meant he had made the right demand and in the right place. It meant his reading of life was metaphysically true. Or that the Old Testament, the Talmud, and Polish Ashkenazi Orthodoxy were irresistible.

But that wouldn't altogether do, thought Dr. Braun. There was more there than piety. He recalled his cousin's white teeth and scar-twisted smile when he was joking. "I fought on many fronts," Cousin Isaac said, meaning women's bellies. He often had a sound American way of putting things. Had known the back stairs in Schenectady that led to the sheets, the gripping arms and spreading thighs of workingwomen. The Model T was parked below. Earlier, the horse waited in harness. He got great pleasure from masculine reminiscences. Recalling Dvorah the greenhorn on her knees, hiding her head in pillows while her buttocks soared, a burst of kinky hair from the walls of whiteness, and her feeble voice crying, *"Nein."* But she did not mean it.

Cousin Mutt had no such anecdotes. Shot in the head at Iwo Jima, he came back from a year in the hospital to sell Zenith, Motorola, and Westinghouse appliances. He married a respectable girl and went on quietly amid a bewildering expansion and transformation of his birthplace. A computer center taking over the bush-league park where a scout had him spotted before the war as material for the majors. On most important matters, Mutt went to Tina. She told him what to do. And Isaac looked out for him, whenever possible buying appliances through Mutt for his housing developments. But Mutt took his problems to Tina. For instance, his wife and her sister played the horses. Every chance they got, they drove to Saratoga, to the trotting races. Probably no great harm in this. The two sisters with gay lipstick and charming dresses. And laughing continually with their pretty jutting teeth. And putting down the top of the convertible.

Tina took a mild view of this. Why shouldn't they go to the track? Her fierceness was concentrated, all of it, on Braun the millionaire.

"That whoremaster!" she said.

"Oh, no. Not in years and years," said Mutt.

"Come, Mutt. I know whom he's been balling. I keep an eye on the Orthodox. Believe me, I do. And now the governor has put him on a commission. Which is it?"

"Pollution."

"Water pollution, that's right. Rockefeller's buddy."

"Well, you shouldn't, Tina. He's our brother."

"He feels for *you.*"

"Yes, he does."

"A multimillionaire—lets you go on drudging in a little business? He's heartless. A heartless man."

"It's not true."

"What? He never had a tear in his eye unless the wind was blowing," said Tina.

Hyperbole was Tina's greatest weakness. They were all like that. The mother had bred it in them.

Otherwise, she was simply a gloomy, obese woman, sternly combed, the hair tugged back from her forehead, tight, so that the hairline was a fighting barrier. She had a totalitarian air—and not only toward others. Toward herself, also. Absorbed in the dictatorship of her huge person. In a white dress, and with the ring on her finger she had seized from her dead mother. By a putsch in the bedroom.

In her generation—Dr. Braun had given up his afternoon to the hopeless pleasure of thinking affectionately about his dead—in her generation, Tina was also old-fashioned for all her modern slang. People of her sort, and not only the women, cultivated charm. But Tina consistently willed for nothing, to have no appeal, no charm. Absolutely none. She never tried to please. Her aim must have been majesty. Based on what? She had no great thoughts. She built on her own nature. On a primordial idea, hugely blown up. Somewhat as her flesh in its dress of white silk, as last seen by Cousin Braun some years ago, was blown up. Some sub-suboffice of the personality, behind a little door of the brain where the restless spirit never left its work, had ordered this tremendous female form, all of it, to become manifest. With dark hair on the forearms, conspicuous nostrils in the white face, and black eyes staring. Her eyes had an affronted expression; sometimes a look of sulphur; a clever look, also a malicious look—they had all the looks, even the look of kindness that came from Uncle Braun. The old man's sweetness. Those who try to interpret humankind through its eyes are in for much strangeness—perplexity.

The quarrel between Tina and Isaac lasted for years. She accused him of shaking off the family when the main chance came. He had refused to cut them in. He said that they had all deserted him at the zero hour. Eventually, the brothers made it up. Not Tina. She wanted nothing to do with Isaac. In the first phase of enmity she saw to it that he should know exactly what she thought of him. Brothers, aunts, and old friends told him what she was saying about him: He was a crook, Mama had lent him money; he would not repay; that was why she had collected those house rents. Also, Isaac had been a silent partner of Zaikas, the Greek, the racketeer from Troy. She said that Zaikas had covered for Isaac, who was implicated in the state-hospital scandal. Zaikas took the fall, but Isaac had to put fifty thousand dollars in Zaikas's box at the bank. The Stuyvesant Bank, that was. Tina said she even knew the box number. Isaac said little to these slanders, and after a time they stopped.

And it was when they stopped that Isaac actually began to feel the anger of his sister. He felt it as head of the family, the oldest living Braun. After he had not seen his sister for two or three years, he began to remind himself of Uncle

Braun's affection for Tina. The only daughter. The youngest. Our baby sister. Thoughts of the old days touched his heart. Having gotten what he wanted, Tina said to Mutt, he could redo the past in sentimental colors. Isaac would remember that in 1920 Aunt Rose wanted fresh milk, and the Brauns kept a cow in the pasture by the river. What a beautiful place. And how delicious it was to crank the Model T and drive at dusk to milk the cow beside the green water. Driving, they sang songs. Tina, then ten years old, must have weighed two hundred pounds, but the shape of her mouth was very sweet, womanly—perhaps the pressure of the fat, hastening her maturity. Somehow she was more feminine in childhood than later. It was true that at nine or ten she sat on a kitten in the rocker, unaware, and smothered it. Aunt Rose found it dead when her daughter stood up. "You huge thing," she said to her daughter, "you animal." But even this Isaac recollected with amused sadness. And since he belonged to no societies, never played cards, never spent an evening drinking, never went to Florida, never went to Europe, never went to see the State of Israel, Isaac had plenty of time for reminiscences. Respectable elms about his house sighed with him for the past. The squirrels were Orthodox. They dug and saved. Mrs. Isaac Braun wore no cosmetics. Except a touch of lipstick when going out in public. No mink coats. A comfortable Hudson seal, yes. With a large fur button on the belly. To keep her, as he liked her, warm. Fair, pale, round, with a steady innocent look, and hair worn short and symmetrical. Light brown, with kinks of gold. One gray eye, perhaps, expressed or came near expressing slyness. It must have been purely involuntary. At least there was not the slightest sign of conscious criticism or opposition. Isaac was master. Cooking, baking, laundry, all housekeeping, had to meet his standard. If he didn't like the smell of the cleaning woman, she was sent away. It was an ample old-fashioned respectable domestic life on an Eastern European model completely destroyed in 1939 by Hitler and Stalin. Those two saw to the eradication of the old conditions, made sure that certain modern race notions became social realities. Maybe the slightest troubling ambiguity in one of Cousin Sylvia's eyes was the effect of a suppressed historical comment. As a woman, Dr. Braun considered, she had more than a glimmering of this modern transformation. Her husband was a multimillionaire. Where was the life this might have bought? The houses, servants, clothes, and cars? On the farm she had operated machines. As his wife, she was obliged to forget how to drive. She was a docile, darling woman, and she was in the kitchen baking sponge cake and chopping liver, as Isaac's mother had done. Or should have done. Without the mother's flaming face, the stern meeting brows, the rigorous nose, and the club of powerful braid lying on her spine. Without Aunt Rose's curses.

In America, the abuses of the Old World were righted. It was appointed to be the land of historical redress. However, Dr. Braun reflected, new uproars filled the soul. Material details were of the greatest importance. But still the largest strokes were made by the spirit. Had to be! People who said this were right.

Cousin Isaac's thoughts: a web of computations, of frontages, elevations, drainage, mortgages, turn-around money. And since, in addition, he had been a strong, raunchy young man, and this had never entirely left him (it remained only as witty comment), his piety really did appear to be put on. Superadded. The Psalm-saying at building sites. *When I consider the heavens, the work of Thy fingers . . . what is Man that Thou art mindful of him?* But he evidently meant it all. He took off whole afternoons before high holidays. While his fair-faced wife, flushed with baking, noted with the slightly biblical air he expected of her that he was bathing, changing upstairs. He had visited the graves of his parents and announced on his return, "I've been to the cemetery."

"Oh," she said with sympathy, the one beautiful eye full of candor. The other fluttering with a minute quantity of slyness.

The parents, stifled in the clay. Two crates, side by side. Grass of burning green sweeping over them, and Isaac repeating a prayer to the God of Mercy. And in Hebrew with a Baltic accent, at which modern Israelis scoffed. September trees, yellow after an icy night or two, now that the sky was blue and warm, gave light instead of shadow. Isaac was concerned about his parents. Down there, how were they? The wet, the cold, above all the worms worried him. In frost, his heart shrank for Aunt Rose and Uncle Braun, though as a builder he knew they were beneath the frost line. But a human power, his love, affected his practical judgment. It flew off. Perhaps as a builder and housing expert (on two of the governor's commissions, not one) he especially felt his dead to be unsheltered. But Tina—they were her dead, too—felt he was still exploiting Papa and Mama and that he would have exploited her, too, if she had let him.

For several years, at the same season, there was a scene between them. The pious thing before the Day of Atonement was to visit the dead and to forgive the living—forgive and ask forgiveness. Accordingly, Isaac went annually to the old home. Parked his Cadillac. Rang the bell, his heart beating hard. He waited at the foot of the long, enclosed staircase. The small brick building, already old in 1915 when Uncle Braun had bought it, passed to Tina, who tried to make it modern. Her ideas came out of *House Beautiful*. The paper with which she covered the slanted walls of the staircase was unsuitable. It did not matter. Tina, above, opened the door, saw the masculine figure and scarred face of her brother and said, "What do you want?"

"Tina! For God's sake, I've come to make peace."

"What peace! You swindled us out of a fortune."

"The others don't agree. Now, Tina, we are brother and sister. Remember Father and Mother. Remember . . ."

She cried down at him, "You son of a bitch, I *do* remember! Now get the hell out of here."

Banging the door, she dialed her brother Aaron, lighting one of her long cigarettes. "He's been here again," she said. "What shit! He's not going to practice his goddamn religion on me."

She said she hated his Orthodox cringe. She could take him straight. In a deal. Or a swindle. But she couldn't bear his sentiment.

As for herself, she might smell like a woman, but she acted like a man. And in her dress, while swooning music came from the radio, she smoked her cigarette after he was gone, thundering inside with great flashes of feeling. For which, otherwise, there was no occasion. She might curse him, thought Dr. Braun, but she owed him much. Aunt Rose, who had been such a harsh poet of money, had left her daughter needs—such needs! Quiet middle-age domestic decency (husband, daughter, furnishings) did nothing for needs like hers.

So when Isaac Braun told his wife that he had visited the family graves, she knew that he had gone again to see Tina. The thing had been repeated. Isaac, with a voice and gesture that belonged to history and had no place or parallel in upstate industrial New York, appealed to his sister in the eyes of God, and in the name of souls departed, to end her anger. But she cried from the top of the stairs, "Never! You son of a bitch, never!" and he went away.

He went home for consolation, and walked to the synagogue later with an injured heart. A leader of the congregation, weighted with grief. Striking breast with fist in old-fashioned penitence. The new way was the way of understatement. Anglo-Saxon restraint. The rabbi, with his Madison Avenue public-relations airs, did not go for these European Judaic, operatic fist-clenchings. Tears. He made the cantor tone it down. But Isaac Braun, covered by his father's prayer shawl with its black stripes and shedding fringes, ground his teeth and wept near the ark.

These annual visits to Tina continued until she became sick. When she went into the hospital, Isaac phoned Dr. Braun and asked him to find out how things really stood.

"But I'm not a medical doctor."

"You're a scientist. You'll understand it better."

Anyone might have understood. She was dying of cancer of the liver. Cobalt radiation was tried. Chemotherapy. Both made her very sick. Dr. Braun told Isaac, "There is no hope."

"I know."

"Have you seen her?"

"No. I hear from Mutt."

Isaac sent word through Mutt that he wanted to come to her bedside.

Tina refused to see him.

And Mutt, with his dark sloping face, unhandsome but gentle, dog-eyed, softly urged her, "You should, Tina."

But Tina said, "No. Why should I? A Jewish deathbed scene, that's what he wants. No."

"Come, Tina."

"No," she said, even firmer. Then she added, "I hate him." As though explaining that Mutt should not expect her to give up the support of this feeling. And a little later she added, in a lower voice, as though speaking generally, "I can't help him."

But Isaac phoned Mutt daily, saying, "I have to see my sister."

"I can't get her to do it."

"You've got to explain it to her. She doesn't know what's right."

Isaac even telephoned Fenster, though, as everyone was aware, he had a low opinion of Fenster's intelligence. And Fenster answered, "She says you did us all dirt."

"I? She got scared and backed out. I had to go it alone."

"You shook us off."

Quite simplemindedly, with the directness of the biblical fool (this was how Isaac saw him, and Fenster knew it), he said, "You wanted it all for yourself, Isaac."

That they should let him, ungrudgingly, enjoy his great wealth, Isaac told Dr. Braun, was too much to expect. And he admitted that he was very rich. He did not say how much money he had. This was a mystery to the family. The old people said, "He himself don't know."

Isaac confessed to his cousin Dr. Braun, "I never understood her." He was much moved, even then, a year later.

Cousin Tina had discovered that one need not be bound by the old rules. That, Isaac's painful longing to see his sister's face being denied, everything was put into a different sphere of advanced understanding, painful but truer than the old. From her bed she appeared to be directing this research.

"You ought to let him come," said Mutt.

"Because I'm dying?"

Mutt, plain and dark, stared at her, his black eyes momentarily vacant as he chose an answer. "People recover," he said.

But she said, with peculiar indifference to the fact, "Not this time." She had already become gaunt in the face and high in the belly. Her ankles were swelling. She had seen this in others and understood the signs.

"He calls every day," said Mutt.

She had had her nails done. A dark-red, almost maroon color. One of those odd twists of need or desire. The ring she had taken from her mother was now loose on the finger. And, reclining on the raised bed, as if she had found a moment of ease, she folded her arms and said, pressing the lace of the bed jacket with her fingertips, "Then give Isaac my message, Mutt. I'll see him, yes, but it'll cost him money."

"Money?"

"If he pays me twenty thousand dollars."

"Tina, that's not right."

"Why not! For my daughter. She'll need it."

"No, she doesn't need that kind of dough." He knew what Aunt Rose had left. "There's plenty and you know it."

"If he's got to come, that's the price of admission," she said. "Only a fraction of what he did us out of."

Mutt said simply, "He never did me out of anything." Curiously, the shrewdness of the Brauns was in his face, but he never practiced it. This was not because he had been wounded in the Pacific. He had always been like that. He sent Tina's message to Isaac on a piece of business stationery, BRAUN APPLIANCES, 42 CLINTON. Like a contract bid. No word of comment, not even a signature.

For 20 grand cash Tina says yes otherwise no.

In Dr. Braun's opinion, his cousin Tina had seized upon the force of death to create a situation of opera, which at the same time was a situation of parody. As he stated it to himself, there was a feedback of mockery. Death the horrid bridegroom, waiting with a consummation life had never offered. Life, accordingly, she devalued, filling up the clear light remaining (which should be reserved for beauty, miracle, nobility) with obese monstrosity, rancor, failure, self-torture.

Isaac, on the day he received Tina's terms, was scheduled to go out on the river with the governor's commission on pollution. A boat was sent by the Fish and Game Department to take the five members out on the Hudson. They would go south as far as Germantown, where the river, with mountains on the west, seems a mile wide. And back again to Albany. Isaac would have canceled this inspection, he had so much thinking to do, was so full of things. "Overthronged" was the odd term Braun chose for it, which seemed to render Isaac's state best. But Isaac could not get out of this official excursion. His wife made him take his Panama hat and wear a light suit. He bent over the side of the boat, hands clasped tight on the dark-red, brass-jointed rail. He breathed through his teeth. At the back of his legs, in his neck, his pulses beating; and in the head an arterial swell through which he was aware, one-sidedly, of the air streaming, and gorgeous water. Two young professors from Rensselaer lectured on the geology and wildlife of the upper Hudson and on the industrial and community problems of the region. The towns were dumping raw sewage into the Mohawk and the Hudson. You could watch the flow from giant pipes. Cloacae, said the professor with his red beard and ruined teeth. Much dark metal in his mouth, pewter ridges instead of bone. And a pipe with which he pointed to the turds yellowing the river. The cities, spilling their filth. How dispose of it? Methods were discussed—treatment plants. Atomic power. And finally he presented an ingenious engineering project for sending all waste into the interior of the earth, far under the crust, thousands of feet into deeper strata. But even if pollution were stopped today, it would take fifty years to restore the river. The fish had persisted but at last abandoned their old spawning grounds. Only a savage scavenger eel dominated the water. The river great and blue in spite of the dung pools and the twisting of the eels.

One member of the governor's commission had a face remotely familiar, long and high, the mouth like a latch, cheeks hollow, the bone warped in the nose, and hair fading. Gentle. A thin person. His thoughts on Tina, Isaac had missed his name. But looking at the printed pages prepared by the staff, he saw that it was Ilkington Junior. This quiet, likable man examining him with such meaning from the white bulkhead, long trousers curling in the breeze as he held the metal rail behind him.

Evidently he knew about the hundred thousand dollars.

"I think I was acquainted with your father," Isaac said, his voice very low.

"You were, indeed," said Ilkington. He was frail for his height; his skin was pulled tight, glistening on the temples, and a reddish blood lichen spread on his cheekbones. Capillaries. "The old man is well."

"Well. I'm glad."

"Yes. He's well. Very feeble. He had a bad time, you know."

"I never heard."

"Oh, yes, he invested in hotel construction in Nassau and lost his money."

"All of it?" said Isaac.

"All his legitimate money."

"I'm very sorry."

"Lucky he had a little something to fall back on."

"He did?"

"He certainly did."

"Yes, I see. That *was* lucky."

"It'll last him."

Isaac was glad to know and appreciated the kindness of Ilkington's son in telling him. Also the man knew what the Robbstown Country Club had been worth to him, but did not grudge him, behaved with courtesy. For which Isaac, filled with thankfulness, would have liked to show gratitude. But what you showed, among these people, you showed with silence. Of which, it seemed to Isaac, he was now beginning to appreciate the wisdom. The native, different wisdom of Gentiles, who had much to say but refrained. What was this Ilkington Junior? He looked into the pages again and found a paragraph of biography. Insurance executive. Various government commissions. Probably Isaac could have discussed Tina with such a man. Yes, in heaven. On earth they would never discuss a thing. Silent impressions would have to do. Incommunicable diversities, kindly but silent contact. The more they had in their heads, the less people seemed to know how to tell it.

"When you write to your father, remember me to him."

Communities along the river, said the professor, would not pay for any sort of sewage-treatment plants. The federal government would have to arrange it. Only fair, Isaac considered, since Internal Revenue took away to Washington billions in taxes and left small change for the locals. So they pumped the excrements into the waterways. Isaac, building along the Mohawk, had always taken this for granted. Building squalid settlements of which he was so proud. . . . Had been proud.

He stepped onto the dock when the boat tied up. The state game commissioner had taken an eel from the water to show the inspection party. It was writhing toward the river in swift, powerful loops, tearing its skin on the planks, its crest of fin standing. *Treph!* And slimy black, the perishing mouth open.

The breeze had dropped and the wide water stank. Isaac drove home, turning on the air conditioner of his Cadillac. His wife said, "What was it like?"

He had no answer to give.

"What are you doing about Tina?"

Again, he said nothing.

But knowing Isaac, seeing how agitated he was, she predicted that he would go down to New York City for advice. She told this later to Dr. Braun, and he saw no reason to doubt it. Clever wives can foretell. A fortunate husband will be forgiven his predictability.

Isaac had a rabbi in Williamsburg. He was Orthodox enough for that. And he did not fly. He took a compartment on the *Twentieth Century* when it left Albany just before daybreak. With just enough light through the dripping gray to see the river. But not the west shore. A tanker covered by smoke and cloud divided the bituminous water. Presently the mountains emerged.

They wanted to take the old crack train out of service. The carpets were filthy, the toilets stank. Slovenly waiters in the dining car. Isaac took toast and coffee, rejecting the odors of ham and bacon by expelling breath. Eating with his hat on. Racially distinct, as Dr. Braun well knew. A blood group characteristically eastern Mediterranean. The very fingerprints belonging to a distinctive family of patterns. The nose, the eyes long and full, the skin dark, slashed near the mouth by a Russian doctor in the old days. And looking out as they rushed past Rhinecliff, Isaac saw, with the familiarity of hundreds of journeys, the grand water, the thick trees—illuminated space. In the compartment, in captive leisure, shut up with the foul upholstery, the rattling door. The old arsenal, Bannerman's Island, the playful castle, yellow-green willows around it, and the water sparkling, as green as he remembered it in 1910—one of the forty million foreigners coming to America. The steel rails, as they were then, the twisting currents and the mountain round at the top, the wall of rock curving steeply into the expanding river.

From Grand Central, carrying a briefcase with all he needed in it, Isaac took the subway to his appointment. He waited in the anteroom, where the rabbi's bearded followers went in and out in long coats. Dressed in business clothes, Isaac, however, seemed no less archaic than the rest. A bare floor. Wooden seats, white stippled walls. But the windows were smeared, as though the outside did not matter. Of these people, many were survivors of the German Holocaust. The rabbi himself had been through it as a boy. After the war, he had lived in Holland and Belgium and studied sciences in France. At Montpellier. Biochemistry. But he had been called—summoned—to these spiritual duties in New York; Isaac was not certain how this had happened. And now he wore the full beard. In his office, sitting at a little table with a green blotting pad, and a pen and note paper. The conversation was in the *jargón*—in Yiddish.

"Rabbi, my name is Isaac Braun."

"From Albany. Yes, I remember."

"I am the eldest of four—my sister, the youngest, the *muzínka,* is dying."

"Are you sure of this?"

"Of cancer of the liver, and with a lot of pain."

"Then she is. Yes, she is dying." From the very white, full face, the rabbi's beard grew straight and thick in rich bristles. He was a strong, youthful man, his stout body buttoned tightly, straining in the shiny black cloth.

"A certain thing happened soon after the war. An opportunity to buy a valuable piece of land for building. I invited my brothers and my sister to invest with me, Rabbi. But on the day . . ."

The rabbi listened, his white face lifted toward a corner of the ceiling, but fully attentive, his hands pressed to the ribs, above the waist.

"I understand. You tried to reach them that day. And you felt abandoned."

"They deserted me, Rabbi, yes."

"But that was also your good luck. They turned their faces from you, and this made you rich. You didn't have to share."

Isaac admitted this but added, "If it hadn't been one deal, it would have been another."

"You were destined to be rich?"

"I was sure to be. And there were so many opportunities."

"Your sister, poor thing, is very harsh. She is wrong. She has no ground for complaint against you."

"I am glad to hear that," said Isaac. "Glad," however, was only a word, for he was suffering.

"She is not a poor woman, your sister?"

"No, she inherited property. And her husband does pretty well. Though I suppose the long sickness costs."

"Yes, a wasting disease. But the living can only will to live. I am speaking of Jews. They wanted to annihilate us. To give our consent would have been to turn from God. But about your problem: Have you thought of your brother Aaron? He advised the others not to take the risk."

"I know."

"It was to his interest that she should be angry with you, and not with him."

"I realize that."

"He is guilty. He is sinning against you. Your other brother is a good man."

"Mutt? Yes, I know. He is decent. He barely survived the war. He was shot in the head."

"But is he still himself?"

"Yes, I believe so."

"Sometimes it takes something like that. A bullet through the head." The rabbi paused and turned his round face, the black quill beard bent on the folds of shiny cloth. And then, as Isaac told him how he went to Tina before the High Holidays, he looked impatient, moving his head forward, but his eyes turning sideward. "Yes. Yes." He was certain that Isaac had done the right things. "Yes. You have the money. She grudged you. Unreasonable. But that's how it seems to her. You are a man. She is only a woman. You are a rich man."

"But, Rabbi," said Isaac, "now she is on her deathbed, and I have asked to see her."

"Yes? Well?"

"She wants money for it."

"Ah? Does she? Money?"

"Twenty thousand dollars. So that I can be let into the room."

The burly rabbi was motionless, white fingers on the armrests of the wooden chair. "She knows she is dying, I suppose?" he said.

"Yes."

"Yes. Our Jews love deathbed jokes. I know many. Well. America has not changed everything, has it? People assume that God has a sense of humor. Such jokes made by the dying in anguish show a strong and brave soul, but skeptical. What sort of woman is your sister?"

"Stout. Large."

"I see. A fat woman. A chunk of flesh with two eyes, as they used to say. Staring at the lucky ones. Like an animal in a cage, perhaps. Separated. By sensual greed and despair. A fat child like that—people sometimes behave as though they were alone when such a child is present. So those little monster souls have a strange fate. They see people as people are when no one is looking. A gloomy vision of mankind."

Isaac respected the rabbi. Revered him, thought Dr. Braun. But perhaps he was not old-fashioned enough for him, notwithstanding the hat and beard and gabardine. He had the old tones, the manner, the burly poise, the universal calm judgment of the Jewish moral genius. Enough to satisfy anyone. But there was also something foreign about him. That is, contemporary. Now and then there was a sign of the science student, the biochemist from the south of France, from Montpellier. He would probably have spoken English with a French accent, whereas Cousin Isaac spoke like anyone else from upstate. In Yiddish they had the same dialect—White Russian. The Minsk region. The Pripet Marshes, thought Dr. Braun. And then returned to the fish hawk on the brown and chalky sycamore beside the Mohawk. Yes. Perhaps. Among these recent birds, finches, thrushes, there was Cousin Isaac with more scale than feather in his wings. A more antique type. The ruddy brown eye, the tough muscles of the jaw working under the skin. Even the scar was precious to Dr. Braun. He knew the man. Or rather, he had the longing of having known. For these people were dead. A useless love.

"You can afford the money?" the rabbi asked. And when Isaac hesitated, he said, "I don't ask you for the figure of your fortune. It is not my concern. But could you give her the twenty thousand?"

And Isaac, looking greatly tried, said, "If I had to."

"It wouldn't make a great difference in your fortune?"

"No."

"In that case, why shouldn't you pay?"

"You think I should?"

"It's not for me to tell you to give away so much money. But you gave—you gambled—you trusted the man, the goy."

"Ilkington? That was a business risk. But Tina? So you believe I should pay?"

"Give in. I would say, judging the sister by the brother, there is no other way."

Then Isaac thanked him for his time and his opinion. He went out into the broad daylight of the street, which smelled of muck. The tedious mortar of tenements, settled out of line, the buildings swaybacked, with grime on grime, as if built of cast-off shoes, not brick. The contractor observing. The ferment of sugar and roasting coffee was strong, but the summer air moved quickly in the damp under the huge machine-trampled bridge. Looking about for the subway entrance, Isaac saw instead a yellow cab with a yellow light on the crest. He first told the driver, "Grand Central," but changed his mind at the first corner and said, "Take me to the West Side Air Terminal." There was no fast train to Albany before late afternoon. He could not wait on Forty-second Street. Not today. He must have known all along that he would have to pay the money. He had come to get strength by consulting the rabbi. Old laws and wisdom on his side. But Tina from the deathbed had made too strong a move. If he refused to come across, no one could blame him. But he would feel greatly damaged. How would he live with himself? Because he made these sums easily now. Buying and selling a few city lots. Had the price been fifty thousand dollars, Tina would have been saying that he would never see her again. But twenty thousand—the figure was a shrewd choice. And Orthodoxy had no remedy. It was entirely up to him.

Having decided to capitulate, he felt a kind of deadly recklessness. He had never been in the air before. But perhaps it was high time to fly. Everyone had lived enough. And anyway, as the cab crept through the summer lunchtime crowds on Twenty-third Street, there seemed plenty of humankind already.

On the airport bus, he opened his father's copy of the Psalms. The black Hebrew letters only gaped at him like open mouths with tongues hanging down, pointing upward, flaming but dumb. He tried—forcing. It did no good. The tunnel, the swamps, the auto skeletons, machine entrails, dumps, gulls, sketchy Newark trembling in fiery summer, held his attention minutely. As though he were not Isaac Braun but a man who took pictures. Then in the plane running with concentrated fury to take off—the power to pull away from the magnetic earth, and more: When he saw the ground tilt backward, the machine rising from the runway, he said to himself in clear internal words, *"Shema Yisroel,"* Hear, O Israel, God alone is God! On the right, New York leaned gigantically seaward, and the plane with a jolt of retracted wheels turned toward the river. The Hudson green within green, and rough with tide and wind. Isaac released the breath he had been holding, but sat belted tight. Above the marvelous bridges, over clouds, sailing in atmosphere, you know better than ever that you are no angel.

The flight was short. From Albany airport, Isaac phoned his bank. He told Spinwall, with whom he did business there, that he needed twenty thousand dollars in cash. "No problem," said Spinwall. "We have it."

Isaac explained to Dr. Braun, "I have passbooks for my savings accounts in my safe-deposit box."

Probably in individual accounts of ten thousand dollars, protected by federal deposit insurance. He must have had bundles of these.

He went through the round entrance of the vault, the mammoth delicate door, circular, like the approaching moon seen by space navigators. A taxi waited as he drew the money and took him, the dollars in his briefcase, to the hospital. Then at the hospital, the hopeless flesh and melancholy festering and drug odors, the splashy flowers and wrinkled garments. In the large cage elevator that could take in whole beds, pulmotors, and laboratory machines, his eyes were fixed on the silent, beautiful Negro woman dreaming at the control as they moved slowly from lobby to mezzanine, from mezzanine to first. The two were alone, and since there was no going faster, he found himself observing her strong, handsome legs, her bust, the gold wire and glitter of her glasses, and the sensual bulge in her throat, just under the chin. In spite of himself, struck by these as he slowly rose to his sister's deathbed.

At the elevator, as the gate opened, was his brother Mutt.

"Isaac!"

"How is she?"

"Very bad."

"Well, I'm here. With the money."

Confused, Mutt did not know how to face him. He seemed frightened. Tina's power over Mutt had always been great. Though he was three or four years her senior. Isaac somewhat understood what moved him and said, "That's all right, Mutt, if I have to pay. I'm ready. On her terms."

"She may not even know."

"Take it. Say I'm here. I want to see my sister, Mutt."

Unable to look at Isaac, Mutt received the briefcase and went in to Tina. Isaac moved away from her door without glancing through the slot. Because he could not stand still, he moved down the corridor, hands clasped behind his back. Past the rank of empty wheelchairs. Repelled by these things which were made for weakness. He hated such objects, hated the stink of hospitals. He was sixty years old. He knew the route he, too, must go, and soon. But only knew, did not yet feel it. Death still was at a distance. As for handing over the money, about which Mutt was ashamed, taking part unwillingly in something un-just, grotesque—yes, it was far-fetched, like things women imagined they wanted in pregnancy, hungry for peaches, or beer, or eating plaster from the walls. But as for himself, as soon as he handed over the money, he felt no more concern for it. It was nothing. He was glad to be rid of it. He could hardly understand this about himself. Once the money was given, the torment stopped. Nothing at all. The thing was done to punish, to characterize him, to convict him of something, to put him in a category. But the effect was just the opposite. What category? Where was it? If she thought it made him suffer, it did not. If she thought she understood his soul better than anyone—his poor dying sister; no, she did not.

And Dr. Braun, feeling with them this work of wit and despair, this last attempt to exchange significance, rose, stood, looking at the shafts of ice, the tatters of vapor in winter blue.

Then Tina's private nurse opened the door and beckoned to Isaac. He hur-ried in and stopped with a suffocated look. Her upper body was wasted and yel-low. Her belly was huge with the growth, and her legs, her ankles were swollen. Her distorted feet had freed themselves from the cover. The soles like clay. The skin was tight on her skull. The hair was white. An intravenous tube was taped to her arm, and other tubes from her body into excretory jars beneath the bed. Mutt had laid the briefcase before her. It had not been unstrapped. Fleshless, hair coarse, and the meaning of her black eyes impossible to understand, she was looking at Isaac.

"Tina!"

"I wondered," she said.

"It's all there."

But she swept the briefcase from her and in a choked voice said, "No. Take it." He went to kiss her. Her free arm was lifted and tried to embrace him. She was too feeble, too drugged. He felt the bones of his obese sister. Death. The end. The grave. They were weeping. And Mutt, turning away at the foot of the bed, his mouth twisted open and the tears running from his eyes. Tina's tears were much thicker and slower.

The ring she had taken from Aunt Rose was tied to Tina's wasted finger with dental floss. She held out her hand to the nurse. It was all prearranged. The nurse cut the thread. Tina said to Isaac, "Not the money. I don't want it. You take Mama's ring."

And Dr. Braun, bitterly moved, tried to grasp what emotions were. What good were they! What were they for! And no one wanted them now. Perhaps the cold eye was better. On life, on death. But, again, the cold of the eye would be proportional to the degree of heat within. But once humankind had grasped its own idea, that it was human and human through such passions, it began to exploit, to play, to disturb for the sake of exciting disturbance, to make an uproar, a crude circus of feelings. So the Brauns wept for Tina's death. Isaac held his mother's ring in his hand. Dr. Braun, too, had tears in his eyes. Oh, these Jews—these Jews! Their feelings, their hearts! Dr. Braun often wanted nothing more than to stop all this. For what came of it? One after another you gave over your dying. One by one they went. You went. Childhood, family, friendship, love were stifled in the grave. And these tears! When you wept them from the heart, you felt you justified something, understood something. But what did you understand? Again, *nothing!* It was only an intimation of understanding. A promise that mankind might—*might,* mind you—eventually, through its gift which might—*might* again!—be a divine gift, comprehend why it lived. Why life, why death.

And again, why these particular forms—these Isaacs and these Tinas? When Dr. Braun closed his eyes, he saw, red on black, something like molecular processes—the only true heraldry of being. As later, in the close black darkness when the short day ended, he went to the dark kitchen window to have a look at stars. These things cast outward by a great begetting spasm billions of years ago.

A THEFT

CLARA VELDE, to begin with what was conspicuous about her, had short blond hair, fashionably cut, growing upon a head unusually big. In a person of an inert character a head of such size might have seemed a deformity; in Clara, because she had so much personal force, it came across as ruggedly handsome. She needed that head; a mind like hers demanded space. She was big-boned; her shoulders were not broad but high. Her blue eyes, exceptionally large, grew prominent when she brooded. The nose was small—ancestrally a North Sea nose. The mouth was very good but stretched extremely wide when she grinned, when she wept. Her forehead was powerful. When she came to the threshold of middle age, the lines of her naïve charm deepened; they would be permanent now. Really, everything about her was conspicuous, not only the size and shape of her head. She must have decided long ago that for the likes of her there could be no cover-up; she couldn't divert energy into disguises. So there she was, a rawboned American woman. She had very good legs—who knows what you would have seen if pioneer women had worn shorter skirts. She bought her clothes in the best shops and was knowledgeable about cosmetics. Nevertheless the backcountry look never left her. She came from the sticks; there could be no mistake about that. Her people? Indiana and Illinois farmers and small-town businessmen who were very religious. Clara was brought up on the Bible: prayers at breakfast, grace at every meal, psalms learned by heart, the Gospels, chapter and verse—old-time religion. Her father owned small department stores in southern Indiana. The children were sent to good schools. Clara had studied Greek at Bloomington and Elizabethan-Jacobean literature at Wellesley. A disappointing love affair in Cambridge led to a suicide attempt. The family decided not to bring her back to Indiana. When she threatened to swallow more sleeping pills they allowed her to attend Columbia University, and she lived in New York under close supervision—the regimen organized by her parents. She, however, found ways to do exactly as she pleased. She feared hellfire but she did it just the same.

After a year at Columbia she went to work at Reuters, then she taught in a private school and later wrote American feature articles for British and Australian papers. By the age of forty she had formed a company of her own—a journalistic agency specializing in high fashion for women—and eventually she sold this company to an international publishing group and became one of its executives. In the boardroom she was referred to by some as "a good corporate person," by others as "the czarina of fashion writing." By now she was also the attentive mother of three small girls. The first of these was conceived with some difficulty (the professional assistance of gynecologists made it possible). The father of these children was Clara's fourth husband.

Three of the four had been no more than that—men who fell into the husband class. Only one, the third, had been something like the real thing. That was Spontini the oil tycoon, a close friend of the billionaire leftist and terrorist Giangiacomo F., who blew himself up in the seventies. (Some Italians said, predictably, that the government had set him up to explode.) Mike Spontini was not political, but then he wasn't born rich, like Giangiacomo, whose role model had been Fidel Castro. Spontini made his own fortune. His looks, his town houses and châteaus and yachts, would have qualified him for a role in *La Dolce Vita*. Scores of women were in pursuit. Clara had won the fight to marry him but lost the fight to keep him. Recognizing at last that he was getting rid of her, she didn't oppose this difficult, arbitrary man and surrendered all property rights in the settlement—a nonsettlement really. He took away the terrific gifts he had made her, down to the last bracelet. No sooner had the divorce come through than Mike was bombed out by two strokes. He was half paralyzed now and couldn't form his words. An Italian Sairey Gamp type took care of him in Venice, where Clara occasionally went to see him. Her ex-husband would give her an animal growl, one glare of rage, and then resume his look of imbecility. He would rather be an imbecile on the Grand Canal than a husband on Fifth Avenue.

The other husbands—one married in a full-dress church wedding, the others routine City Hall jobs—were . . . well, to be plain about it, gesture-husbands. Velde was big and handsome, indolent, defiantly incompetent. He worked on the average no longer than six months at any job. By then everybody in the organization wanted to kill him.

His excuse for being in and out of work was that his true talent was for campaign strategies. Elections brought out the best in him: getting media attention for his candidate, who never, ever, won in the primaries. But then, he disliked being away from home, and an election is a traveling show. "Very sweet" went one of Clara's summaries to Laura Wong, the Chinese American dress designer who was her confidante. "An affectionate father as long as the kids don't bother him, what Wilder mostly does is sit reading paperbacks—thrillers, science fiction, and pop biographies. I think he feels that all will be well as long as he keeps sitting there on his cushions. To him inertia is the same as stability. Meantime I run the house single-handed: mortgage, maintenance, housemaids, au pair girls from France or Scandinavia—Austrian the latest. I dream up projects for the children, I do the school bit, do the dentist and the pediatrician, plus playmates, outings, psychological tests, doll dressing, cutting and pasting valentines. What else . . . ? Work with their secret worries, sort out their quarrels, encourage their minds, wipe tears. Love them. Wilder just goes on reading P. D. James, or whoever, till I'm ready to snatch the book and throw it in the street."

One Sunday afternoon she did exactly that—opened the window first and skimmed his paperback into Park Avenue.

"Was he astonished?" asked Ms. Wong.

"Not absolutely. He sees how provoking he is. What he doesn't allow is that I have reason to be provoked. He's *there,* isn't he? What else do I want? In all the turbulence, he's the point of calm. And for all the wild times and miseries I had in the love game—about which he has full information—he's the answer. A sexy woman who couldn't find the place to put her emotionality, and appealing to brilliant men who couldn't do what she really wanted done."

"And he *does* do?"

"He's the overweening overlord, and for no other reason than sexual performance. It's stud power that makes him so confident. He's not the type to think it out. *I* have to do that. A sexy woman may delude herself about the gratification of a mental life. But what really settles everything, according to him, is masculine bulk. As close as he comes to spelling it out, his view is that I wasted time on Jaguar nonstarters. Lucky for me I came across a genuine Rolls-Royce. But he's got the wrong car," she said, crossing the kitchen with efficient haste to take the kettle off the boil. Her stride was powerful, her awkward, shapely legs going too quickly for the heels to keep pace. "Maybe a Lincoln Continental would be more like it. Anyway, no woman wants her bedroom to be a garage, and least of all for a boring car."

What was a civilized lady like Laura Wong making of such confidences? The raised Chinese cheek with the Chinese eye let into it, the tiny degree of heaviness of the epicanthic fold all the whiter over the black of the eye, and the light of that eye, so foreign to see and at the same time superfamiliar in its sense . . . What could be more human than the recognition of this familiar sense? And yet Laura Wong was very much a New York lady in her general understanding of things. She did not confide in Clara as fully as Clara confided in her. But then who did, who *could* make a clean breast so totally? What Ms. Wong's rich eyes suggested, Clara in her awkwardness tried in fact to say. To do.

"Yes, the books," said Laura. "You can't miss that." She had also seen Wilder Velde pedaling his Exercycle while the TV ran at full volume.

"He can't understand what's wrong, since what I make looks like enough for us. But I don't earn *all* that much, with three kids in private schools. So family money has to be spent. That involves my old parents—sweet old Bible Hoosiers. I can't make him see that I can't afford an unemployed husband, and there isn't a headhunter in New York who'll talk to Wilder after one look at his curriculum vitae and his job record. Three months here, five months there. Because it's upsetting me, and for *my* sake, my bosses are trying to place him somewhere. I'm important enough to the corporation for that. If he loves elections so much, maybe he should run for office. He *looks* congressional, and what do I care if he screws up in the House of Representatives. I've been with congressmen, I even married one, and he's no dumber than they are. But he won't admit that anything is wrong; he's got that kind of confidence in himself—so much that he can even take a friendly interest in the men I've been involved with. They're like failed competitors to the guy who won the silver trophy. He's proud to claim a connection with the famous ones, and when I went to visit poor Mike in Venice, he flew with me."

"So he isn't jealous," said Laura Wong.

"The opposite. The people I've been intimate with, to him are like the folks in a history book. And suppose Richard III or Metternich had gotten into *your* wife's pants when she was a girl? Wilder is a name-dropper, and the names he most enjoys dropping are the ones he came into by becoming my husband. Especially the headliners . . ."

Laura Wong was of course aware that it was not for her to mention the most significant name of all, the name that haunted all of Clara's confidences. That was for Clara herself to bring up. Whether it was appropriate, whether she could summon the strength to deal with the most persistent of her preoccupations, whether she would call on Laura to bear with her one more time . . . these were choices you had to trust her to make tactfully.

". . . whom he sometimes tapes when they're being interviewed on CBS or the MacNeil/Lehrer programs. Teddy Regler always the foremost."

Yes, there was the name. Mike Spontini mattered greatly, but you had to see him still in the husband category. Ithiel Regler stood much higher with Clara than any of the husbands. "On a scale of ten," she liked to say to Laura, "he *was* ten."

"Is ten?" Laura had suggested.

"I'd not only be irrational but psycho to keep Teddy in the active present tense," Clara had said. This was a clouded denial. Wilder Velde continued to be judged by a standard from which Ithiel Regler could never be removed. It did not make, it never could make, good sense to speak of irrationality and reckless-ness. Clara never would be safe or prudent, and she wouldn't have dreamed of expelling Ithiel's influence—not even if God's angel had offered her the option. She might have answered: You might as well try to replace my own sense of touch with somebody else's. And the matter would have had to stop there.

So Velde, by taping Ithiel's programs for her, proved how unassailable he was in his position as the final husband, the one who couldn't in the scheme of things be bettered. "And I'm glad the man thinks that," said Clara. "It's best for all of us. He wouldn't believe that I might be unfaithful. You've got to admire *that*. So here's a double-mystery couple. Which is the more mysterious one? Wilder actually enjoys watching Ithiel being so expert and smart from Washing-ton. And meantime, Laura, I have no sinful ideas of being unfaithful. I don't even think about such things, they don't figure in my conscious mind. Wilder and I have a sex life no marriage counselor in the world could fault. We have three children, and I'm a loving mother, I bring them up conscientiously. But when Ithiel comes to town and I see him at lunch, I start to flow for him. He used to make me come by stroking my cheek. It can happen when he talks to me. Or even when I see him on TV or just hear his voice. *He* doesn't know it—I think not—and anyway Ithiel wouldn't want to do harm, interfere, dominate or exploit—that's not the way he is. We have this total, delicious connection, which is also a disaster. But even to a woman raised on the Bible, which in the city of New York in this day and age is a pretty remote influence, you couldn't call my attachment an evil that rates punishment after death. It's not the sex of-fenses that will trip you up, because by now nobody can draw the line between natural and unnatural in sex. Anyway, it couldn't be a woman's hysteria that would send her to hell. It would be something else. . . ."

"What else?" Laura asked. But Clara was silent, and Laura wondered whether it wasn't Teddy Regler who should be asked what Clara considered a mortal sin. He had known Clara so well, over so many years, that perhaps he could explain what she meant.

This Austrian au pair girl, Miss Wegman—Clara gave herself the pleasure of siz-ing her up. She checked off the points: dressed appropriately for an interview, hair freshly washed, no long nails, no conspicuous polish. Clara herself was got-ten up as a tailored matron, in a tortoiseshell-motif suit and a white blouse with a ruff under the chin. From her teaching days she commanded a taskmistress's way of putting questions ("Now, Willie, pick up the *Catiline* and give me the tense of *abutere* in Cicero's opening sentence"): it was the disciplinarian's armor worn by a softy. This Austrian chick made a pleasing impression. The father was a Viennese bank official and the kid was correct, civil and sweet. You had to put it out of your head that Vienna was a hatchery of psychopaths and Hitlerites. Think instead of that dear beauty in the double suicide with the crown prince. This child, who had an Italian mother, was called Gina. She spoke English fluently and probably wasn't faking when she said she could assume responsibility for three little girls. Not laying secret plans to con everybody, not actually full of dislike for defiant, obstinate, mutely resistant kids like Clara's eldest, Lucy, a stout little girl needing help. A secretly vicious young woman could do terrible damage to a kid like Lucy, give her wounds that would never heal. The two little skinny girls laughed at their sister. They scooped up their snickers in their hands while Lucy held herself like a Roman soldier. Her face was heated with boredom and grievances.

The foreign young lady made all the right moves, came up with the correct answers—why not? since the questions made them obvious. Clara realized how remote from present-day "facts of life" and current history her "responsible" assumptions were—those were based on her small-town Republican churchgoing upbringing, the nickel-and-dime discipline of her mother, who clicked out your allowance from the bus conductor's changemaker hanging from her neck. Life in that Indiana town was already as out of date as ancient Egypt. The "decent people" there were the natives from whom television evangelists raised big money to pay for their stretch limos and Miami-style vices. Those were Clara's preposterous dear folks, by whom she had felt stifled in childhood and for whom she now felt a boundless love. In Lucy she saw her own people, rawboned, stubborn, silent—she saw herself. Much could be made of such beginnings. But how did you coach a kid like this, what could you do for her in New York City?

"Now—is it all right to call you Gina?—what was your purpose, Gina, in coming to New York?"

"To perfect my English. I'm registered in a music course at Columbia. And to learn about the U.S.A."

A well-brought-up and vulnerable European girl would have done better to go to Bemidji, Minnesota. Any idea of the explosive dangers girls faced here? They could be blown up from within. When she was young (and not only then), Clara had made reckless experiments—all those chancy relationships; anything might have happened; much did; and all for the honor of running risks. This led her to resurvey Miss Wegman, to estimate what might be done to a face like hers, its hair, her figure, the bust—to the Arabian Nights treasure that nubile girls (innocent up to a point) were sitting on. So many dangerous attractions—and such ignorance! Naturally Clara felt that she herself would do everything (up to a point) to protect a young woman in her household, and everything possible meant using all the resources of an experienced person. At the same time it was a fixed belief with Clara that no *in*experienced woman of mature years could be taken seriously. So could it be a serious Mrs. Wegman back in Vienna, the mother, who had given this Gina permission to spend a year in Gogmagogsville? In the alternative, a rebellious Gina was chancing it on her own. Again, for the honor of running risks.

Clara, playing matron, lady of the house, nodded to agree with her own thoughts, and this nod may have been interpreted by the girl to mean that it was okay, she was as good as hired. She'd have her own decent room in this vast Park Avenue co-op apartment, a fair wage, house privileges, two free evenings, two afternoons for the music-history classes, parts of the morning while the children were at school. Austrian acquaintances, eligible young people, were encouraged to visit, and American friends vetted by Clara. By special arrangement, Gina could even give a small party. You can be democratic and still have discipline.

The first months, Clara watched her new au pair girl closely, and then she was able to tell friends at lunch, people in the office, and even her psychiatrist, Dr. Gladstone, how lucky she had been to find this Viennese Miss Wegman with darling manners. What a desirable role model she was, and also such a calming influence on the hyperexcitable tots. "As you have said, Doctor, they set off hysterical tendencies in one another."

You didn't expect replies from these doctors. You paid them to lend you their ears. Clara said as much to Ithiel Regler, with whom she remained very much in touch—frequent phone calls, occasional letters, and when Ithiel came up from Washington they had drinks, even dinner from time to time.

"If you think this Gladstone is really helping . . . I suppose some of those guys *can* be okay," said Ithiel, neutral in tone. With him there was no trivial meddling. He never tried to tell you what to do, never advised on family matters.

"It's mostly to relieve my heart," said Clara. "If you and I had become husband and wife that wouldn't have been necessary. I might not be so overcharged. But even so, we have open lines of communication to this day. In fact, you went through a shrink period yourself."

"I sure did. But my doctor had even more frailties than me."

"Does that matter?"

"I guess not. But it occurred to me one day that he couldn't tell me how to be Teddy Regler. And nothing would go well unless I *was* Teddy Regler. Not that I make cosmic claims for precious Teddy, but there never was anybody else for me to be."

Because he thought things out he spoke confidently, and because of his confidence he sounded full of himself. But there was less conceit about Ithiel than people imputed to him. In company, Clara, speaking as one who knew, really *knew* him—and she made no secret of that—would say, when his name was mentioned, when he was put down by some restless spirit or other, that Ithiel Regler was more plainspoken about his own faults than anybody who felt it necessary to show him up.

At this turn in their psychiatry conversation, Clara made a move utterly familiar to Ithiel. Seated, she inclined her upper body toward him. "*Tell* me!" she said. When she did that, he once more saw the country girl in all the dryness of her ignorance, appealing for instruction. Her mouth would be slightly open as he made his answer. She would watch and listen with critical concentration. "Tell!" was one of her code words.

Ithiel said, "The other night I watched a child-abuse program on TV, and after a while I began to think how much they were putting under that heading short of sexual molestation or *deadly* abuse—mutilation and murder. Most of what they showed was normal punishment in my time. So today I could be a child-abuse case and my father might have been arrested as a child-beater. When he was in a rage he was transformed—he was like moonshine from the hills compared to store-bought booze. The kids, all of us, were slammed two-handed, from both sides simultaneously, and without mercy. So? Forty years later I have to watch a TV show to see that I, too, was abused. Only, I loved my late father. Beating was only an incident, a single item between us. I still love him. Now, to tell you what this signifies: I can't apply the going terms to my case without damage to reality. My father beat me passionately. When he did it, I hated him like poison and murder. I also loved him with a passion, and I'll *never* think myself an abused child. I suspect that your psychiatrist would egg me on to hate, not turn hate into passivity. So he'd be telling me from the height of his theoretical assumptions how Teddy Regler should be Teddy Regler. The real Teddy, however, rejects this grudge against a dead man, whom he more than half expects to see in the land of the dead. If that were to happen, it would be because we loved each other and wished for it. Besides, after the age of forty a moratorium has to be declared—earlier, if possible. You can't afford to be a damaged child forever. That's my argument with psychiatry: it encourages you to build on abuses and keeps you infantile. Now the heart of this whole country aches for itself. There may be occult political causes for this as well. Foreshadowings of the fate of this huge superpower . . ."

Clara said, "*Tell!*" and then she listened like a country girl. That side of her would never go away, thank God, Ithiel thought; while Clara's secret observation was, How well we've come to understand each other. If only we'd been like this twenty years back.

It wasn't as if she hadn't been able to follow him in the early years. She always had understood what Ithiel was saying. If she hadn't, he wouldn't have taken the trouble to speak—why waste words? But she also recognized the comic appeal of being the openmouthed rube. Gee! Yeah! Of course! And I could kick myself in the head for not having thought of this myself! But all the while the big-city Clara had been in the making, stockpiling ideas for survival in Gogmagogsville.

"But let me tell you," she said, "what I was too astonished to mention when we were first acquainted . . . when we lay in bed naked in Chelsea, and you sent thoughts going around the world, but then they always came back to *us,* in bed. In *bed,* which in my mind was for rest, or sex, or reading a novel. And back to *me,* whom you never overlooked, wherever your ideas may have gone."

This Ithiel, completely black-haired then, and now grizzled, had put some weight on. His face had filled, rounded out at the bottom. It had more of an urn shape. Otherwise his looks were remarkably unchanged. He said, "I really didn't have such a lot of good news about the world. I think you were hunting among the obscure things I talked about for openings to lead back to your one and only subject: love and happiness. I often feel as much curiosity about love and happiness now as you did then listening to my brainstorms."

Between jobs, Ithiel had been able to find time to spend long months with Clara—in Washington, his main base, in New York, on Nantucket, and in Montauk. After three years together, she had actually pressured him into buying an engagement ring. She was at that time, as she herself would tell you, terribly driven and demanding (as if she wasn't now). "I needed a symbolic declaration at least," she would say, "and I put such heat on him, saying that he had dragged me around so long as his girl, his lay, that at last I got this capitulation from him." He took Clara to Madison Hamilton's shop in the diamond district and bought her an emerald ring—the real thing, conspicuously clear, color perfect, top of its class, as appraisers later told Clara. Twelve hundred dollars he paid for it, a big price in the sixties, when he was especially strapped. He was like that, though: hard to convince, but once decided, he dismissed the cheaper items. "Take away all this other shit," he muttered. Proper Mr. Hamilton probably had heard this. Madison Hamilton was a gentleman, and reputable and dignified in a decade when some of those qualities were still around: "Before our fellow Americans had lied themselves into a state of hallucination—bullshitted themselves into inanity," said Ithiel. He said also, still speaking of Hamilton, who sold antique jewelry, "I think the weird moniker my parents gave me predisposed me favorably toward vanishing types like Hamilton—Wasps with good manners. . . . For all I know, he might have been an Armenian, passing."

Clara held out her engagement finger, and Ithiel put on the ring. When the check was written and Mr. Hamilton asked for identification, Ithiel was able to show not only a driver's license but a Pentagon pass. It made a great impression. At that time Ithiel was flying high as a wunderkind in nuclear strategy, and he might have gone all the way to the top, to the negotiating table in Geneva, facing the Russians, if he had been less quirky. People of great power set a high value on his smarts. Well, you only had to look at the size and the evenness of his dark eyes—"The eyes of Hera in my Homeric grammar," said Clara. "Except that he was anything but effeminate. No way!" All she meant was that he had a classic level look.

"At Hamilton's that afternoon, I wore a miniskirt suit that showed my knees touching. I haven't got knock-knees, just this minor peculiarity about the inside of my legs. . . . If this is a deformity, it did me good. Ithiel was crazy about it."

At a later time, she mentioned this as "the unforeseen usefulness of anomalies." She wrote that on a piece of paper and let it drift about the house with other pieces of paper, so that if asked what it meant, she could say she had forgotten.

Although Ithiel now and again might mention "game theory" or "MAD," he wouldn't give out information that might be classified, and she didn't even try to understand what he did in Washington. Now and then his name turned up in the *Times* as a consultant on international security, and for a couple of years he was an adviser to the chairman of a Senate committee. She let politics alone, asking no questions. The more hidden his activities, the better she felt about him. Power, danger, secrecy made him even sexier. No loose talk. A woman could feel safe with a man like Ithiel.

It was marvelous luck that the little apartment in Chelsea should be so near Penn Station. When he blew into town he telephoned, and in fifteen minutes he was there, holding his briefcase. It was his habit when he arrived to remove his necktie and stuff it in among his documents. It was her habit when she hung up the phone to take the ring from its locked drawer, admire it on her finger, and kiss it when the doorbell rang.

No, Ithiel didn't make a big public career, he wasn't a team player, he had no talent for administration; he was too special in his thinking, and there was no chance that he would reach cabinet level. Anyway, it was too easy for him to do well as a free agent; he wouldn't latch on to politicians with presidential ambitions: the smart ones never would make it. "And besides," he said, "I like to stay mobile." A change of continent when he wanted fresh air. He took on such assignments as pleased the operator in him, the behind-the-scenes Teddy Regler: in the Persian Gulf, with a Japanese whiskey firm looking for a South American market, with the Italian police tracking terrorists. None of these activities compromised his Washington reputation for dependability. He testified before congressional investigative committees as an expert witness.

In their days of intimacy, Clara more than once helped him to make a deadline. Then they were Teddy and Clara, a superteam working around the clock. He knew how dependable she was, a dervish for work, how quickly she grasped unfamiliar ideas, how tactful she could be. From her side, she was aware how analytically deep he could go, what a range of information he had, how good his reports were. He outclassed everybody, it seemed to her. Once, at the Hotel

Cristallo in Cortina d'Ampezzo, they did a document together, to the puncturing rhythm of the tennis court below. He had to read the pages she was typing for him over the transatlantic telephone. While he spoke, he let her run ahead on the machine. He could trust her to organize his notes and write them up in a style resembling his own (not that style mattered in Washington). All but the restricted material. She'd do any amount of labor—long dizzy days at the tinny lightweight Olivetti—to link herself with him.

As she told Ms. Wong, she had seen a book many years ago in the stacks of the Columbia library. A single title had detached itself from the rest, from thousands: *The Human Pair*. Well, the big-boned blond student doing *research* and feeling (unaware) so volcanic that one of her controls was to hold her breath—at the sight of those gilded words on the spine of a book was able to breathe again. She breathed. She didn't take the book down; she didn't want to read it. "I wanted *not* to read it."

She described this to Laura Wong, who was too polite to limit her, too discreet to direct her confidences into suitable channels. You had to listen to everything that came out of Clara's wild head when she was turned on. Ms. Wong applied these personal revelations to her own experience of life, as anybody else would have done. She had been married too. Five years an American wife. Maybe she had even been in love. She never said. You'd never know.

"The full title was *The Human Pair in the Novels of Thomas Hardy*. At school I loved Hardy, but now all I wanted of that book was the title. It came back to me at Cortina. Ithiel and I were the Human Pair. We took a picnic lunch up to the forest behind the Cristallo—cheese, bread, cold cuts, pickles, and wine. I rolled on top of Ithiel and fed him. Later I found out when I tried it myself how hard it is to swallow in that position.

"I now feel, looking back, that I was carrying too much of an electrical charge. It's conceivable that the world-spirit gets into mere girls and makes them its demon interpreters. I mentioned this to Ithiel a while back—he and I are old enough now to discuss such subjects—and he said that one of his Russian dissident pals had been talking to him about something called 'superliterature'— literature being the tragedy or comedy of private lives, while superliterature was about the possible end of the world. Beyond personal history. In Cortina I thought I was acting from personal emotions, but those emotions were so devouring, fervid, that they may have been suprapersonal—a wholesome young woman in love expressing the tragedy or comedy of the world concluding. A fever using love as its carrier.

"After the holiday we drove down to Milan. Actually, that's where I met Spontini. We were at a fancy after-dinner party, and he said, 'Let me give you a ride back to your hotel.' So Ithiel and I got into his Jaguar with him, and we were escorted by carloads of cops, fore and aft. He was proud of his security; this was when the Red Brigades were kidnapping the rich. It wasn't so *easy* to be rich—rich enough for ransom. Mike said, 'For all I know, my own friend Giangiacomo may have a plan to abduct me. Not Giangiacomo personally but the outfit he belongs to.'

"On that same trip Ithiel and I also spent some time with Giangiacomo the billionaire revolutionist himself. He was a kind, pleasant man, good-looking except for his preposterous Fidel Castro getup, like a little kid from Queens in a cowboy suit. He wore a forage cap, and in a corner of his fancy office there was a machine gun on the floor. He invited Ithiel and me to his château, about eighty kilometers away, eighteenth-century rococo: it might have been a set for *The Marriage of Figaro,* except for the swimming pool with algae in it and a sauna alongside, in the dank part of the garden far down the hill. At lunch, the butler was leaning over with truffles from Giangiacomo's own estate to grate over the *crème veloutée,* and he couldn't because Giangiacomo was waving his arms, going on about revolutionary insurgency, the subject of the book he was writing. Then, when Ithiel told him that there were no views like his in Karl Marx, Giangiacomo said, 'I never read Marx, and it's too late now to do it; it's urgent to act.' He drove us back to Milan in the afternoon at about five hundred miles an hour. Lots of action, let me tell you. I covered my emerald and gripped it with my right hand, to protect it, maybe, in a crash.

"Next day, when we flew out, Giangiacomo was at the airport in battle dress with a group of boutique girls, all in minis. A year or two later he blew himself up while trying to dynamite power lines. I was sad about it."

When they returned to New York in stuffy August, back to the apartment in Chelsea, Clara cooked Ithiel a fine Italian dinner of veal with lemon and capers, as good as, or better than, the Milan restaurants served, or Giangiacomo's chef at the lovely toy château. At work in the narrow New York galley-style kitchen, Clara was naked and wore clogs. To make it tender, she banged the meat with a red cast-iron skillet. In those days she wore her hair long. Whether she was dressed or nude, her movements always were energetic; she didn't know the meaning of slow-time.

Stretched on the bed, Ithiel studied his dangerous documents (all those forbidden facts) while she cooked and the music played; the shades were down, the lights were on, and they enjoyed a wonderful privacy. "When I was a kid and we went on holidays to the Jersey coast during the war," Clara recalled, "we had black window blinds because of the German submarines hiding out there under the Atlantic, but we could play our radios as loud as we wanted." She liked to fancy that she was concealing Ithiel and his secret documents—not that the deadly information affected Ithiel enough to change the expression of his straight profile: "concentrating like Jascha Heifetz." Could anybody have been tailing him? Guys with zoom lenses or telescopic sights on the Chelsea rooftops?

Ithiel smiled, and pooh-poohed this. He wasn't that important. "I'm not rich like Spontini." They might rather be trained on Clara, zeroing in on a Daughter of Albion without a stitch on, he said.

In those days he came frequently from Washington to visit his young son, who lived with his mother on East Tenth Street. Ithiel's ex-wife, who now used her maiden name, Etta Wolfenstein, went out of her way to be friendly to Clara, chatted her up on the telephone. Etta had informants in Washington, who kept an eye on Ithiel. Ithiel was indifferent to gossip. "I'm not the president," he would say to Clara, "that bulletins should go out about my moods and movements."

"I shouldn't have blamed Ithiel for taking a woman out to dinner now and then in Washington. He needed plain, ordinary quiet times. I turned on so much power in those days. Especially after midnight, my favorite time to examine my psyche—what love was; and death; and hell and eternal punishment; and what Ithiel was going to cost me in the judgment of God when I closed my eyes on this world forever. All my revivalist emotions came out after one A.M., whole nights of tears, anguish and hysteria. I drove him out of his head. To put a stop to this, he'd have to marry me. Then he'd never again have to worry. All my demon power would be at his service. But meanwhile if he got an hour's sleep toward morning and time enough to shave before his first appointment, he'd swallow his coffee, saying that he looked like Lazarus in his shroud. He was vain of his good looks too," said Clara to Ms. Wong. "Maybe that's why I chose that kind of punishment, to put rings under his eyes. Once he said that he had to outline a piece of legislation for the Fiat people—they were trying to get a bill passed in Congress—and they'd think he'd spent the night at an orgy and now couldn't get his act together."

Clara wasn't about to tell Teddy that in Milan when Mike Spontini had invited her to sit in front with him, she had found the palm of his hand waiting for her on the seat, and she had lifted herself up immediately and given him her evening bag to hold. In the dark his fingers soon closed on her thigh. Then she pushed in the cigarette lighter and he guessed what she would do with it when the coil was hot, so he stopped, he let her be. You didn't mention such incidents to the man you were with. It was anyway commonplace stuff to a man who thought world politics continually.

In the accounts heard by Ms. Wong (who had so much American sensitivity, despite her air of Oriental distance and the Chinese cut of her clothes), Clara's frankness may have made *her* seem foreign. Clara went beyond the conventions of American openness. The emerald ring appeased her for a time, but Ithiel was not inclined to move forward, and Clara became more difficult. She told him she had decided that they would be buried in the same grave. She said, "I'd rather go into the ground with the man I loved than share a bed with somebody indifferent. Yes, I think we should be in the same coffin. Or two coffins, but the one who dies last will be on the top. Side by side is also possible. Holding hands, if that could be arranged." Another frequent topic was the sex and the name of their first child. An Old Testament name was what she preferred—Zebulon or Gad or Asher or Naftali. For a girl, Michal, perhaps, or Naomi. He vetoed Michal because she had mocked David for his naked victory dance, and then he refused to take part in such talk at all. He didn't want to make any happy plans. He was glum with her when she said that there was a lovely country cemetery back in Indiana with big horse chestnuts all around.

When he went off to South America on business, she learned from Etta Wolfenstein that he had taken a Washington secretary with him for assistance and (knowing Teddy) everything else. To show him what was what, Clara had an affair with a young Jean-Claude just over from Paris, and within a week he was sharing her apartment. He was very good-looking, but he seldom washed. His dirt was so ingrained that she couldn't get him clean in the shower stall. She had to take a room at the Plaza to force him into the tub. Then for a while she could bear the smell of him. He appealed to her to help get a work permit, and she took him to Steinsalz, Ithiel's lawyer. Later Jean-Claude refused to return her house key, and she had to go to Steinsalz again. "Have your lock changed, dear girl," said Steinsalz, and he asked whether she wanted Ithiel billed for these consultations. He was a friend and admired Ithiel.

"But Ithiel told me you never charged him for your services."

Clara had discovered how amused New Yorkers were by her ignorance.

"Since you took up with this Frenchie, have you missed anything around the house?"

She seemed slow to understand, but that was simply a put-on. She had locked the emerald ring in her deposit box (this, too, an act suggestive of burial).

She said firmly, "Jean-Claude is no bum."

Steinsalz liked Clara too, for her passionate character. Somehow he knew, also, that her family had money—a real-estate fortune, and this gained her a certain consideration with him. Jean-Claude was not the Steinsalz type. He advised Clara to patch up her differences with Ithiel. "Not to use sex for spite," he said. Clara could not help but look at the lawyer's lap, where because he was obese his sex organ was outlined by the pressure of his fat. It made her think of one of those objects that appeared when art lovers on their knees made rubbings on a church floor. The figure of a knight dead for centuries.

"Then why can't Ithiel stay faithful?"

Steinsalz's first name was Bobby. He was a great economist. He ran a million-dollar practice, and it cost him not a cent. He sublet a corner office space from a flashy accountant and paid him in legal advice.

Steinsalz said, "Teddy is a genius. If he didn't prefer to hang loose, he could name his position in Washington. He values his freedom, so that when he wanted to visit Mr. Leakey in the Olduvai Gorge, he just picked up and went. He thinks no more about going to Iran than I do about Coney Island. The shah likes to talk to him. He sent for him once just to be briefed on Kissinger. I tell you this, Clara, so that you won't hold Ithiel on too short a leash. He truly appreciates you, but he irks easy. A little consideration of his needs would fill him with gratitude. A good idea is not to get too clamorous around him. Let me tell you, there are curators in the zoo who give more thought to the needs of a fruit bat than any of us give our fellowman."

Clara answered him, "There are animals who come in pairs. So suppose the female pines?"

That was a good talk, and Clara remembered Steinsalz gratefully.

"Everybody knows how to advise lovers," said Steinsalz. "But only the lovers can say what's what."

A bookish bachelor, he lived with his eighty-year-old mother, who had to be taken to the toilet in her wheelchair. He liked to list the famous men he had gone to high school with—Holz the philosopher, Buchman the Nobel physicist, Lashover the crystallographer. "And yours truly, whose appellate briefs have made legal history."

Clara said, "I sort of loved old Steinsalz too. He was like a Santa Claus with an empty sack who comes down your chimney to steal everything in the house—that's one of Ithiel's wisecracks, about Steinsalz and property. In his own off-the-wall way, Steinsalz was generous."

Clara took advice from the lawyer and made peace with Ithiel on his return. Then the same mistakes overtook them. "I was a damn recidivist. When Jean-Claude left I was glad of it. Getting into the tub with him at the Plaza was a kind of frolic—a private camp event. They say the Sun King stank. If so, Jean-Claude could have gone straight to the top of Versailles. But my family are cleanliness freaks. Before she would sit in your car, my granny would force you to whisk-broom the seat, under the floor mat too, to make sure her serge wouldn't pick up any dust." By the way, Clara locked up the ring not for fear that Jean-Claude would steal it but to protect it from contamination by her wrongful behavior in bed.

But when Ithiel came back, his relations with Clara were not what they had been. Two outside parties had come between them, even though Ithiel seemed indifferent to Jean-Claude. Jealous and hurt, Clara could not forgive the little twit from Washington, of whom Etta Wolfenstein had given her a full picture. That girl was stupid but had very big boobs. When Ithiel talked about his mission to Betancourt in Venezuela, Clara was unimpressed. An American woman in love was far more important than any South American hotshot. "And did you take your little helper along to the president's palace to show off her chest development?"

Ithiel sensibly said, "Let's not beat on each other too much," and Clara repented and agreed. But soon she set up another obstacle course of tests and rules, and asserted herself unreasonably. When Ithiel had his hair cut, Clara said, "That's not the way I like it, but then I'm not the one you're pleasing." She'd say, "You're grooming yourself more than you used to. I'm sure Jascha Heifetz doesn't take such care of his hands." She made mistakes. You didn't send a man with eyes from Greek mythology to the bathroom to cut his fingernails, even if you did have a horror of clippings on the carpet—she'd forget that she and Ithiel were the Human Pair.

But at the time she couldn't be sure that Ithiel was thinking as she did about "Human." To sound him out, she assumed a greater interest in politics and got him to talk about Africa, China, and Russia. What emerged was the insignificance of the personal factor. Clara repeated and tried out words like Kremlin or Lubyanka in her mind (they sounded like the living end) while she heard Ithiel tell of people who couldn't explain why they were in prison, never rid of lice and bedbugs, never free from dysentery and TB, and finally hallucinating. They make an example of them, she thought, to show that nobody is anybody, everybody is expendable. And even here, when Ithiel was pushed to say it, he admitted that here in the U.S., the status of the individual was weakening and probably in irreversible decline. Felons getting special consideration was a sign of it. He could be remote about such judgments, as if his soul were one of a dozen similar souls in a jury box, hearing evidence: to find us innocent would be nice, but guilty couldn't shock him much. She concluded that he was in a dangerous moral state and that it was up to her to rescue him from it. The Human Pair was also a rescue operation.

"A terrible crisis threatened to pinch us both to death."

At the time, she was not advanced enough to think this to a conclusion. Later she would have known how to put it: You couldn't separate love from being. You could Be, even though you were alone. But in that case, you loved only yourself. If so, everybody else was a phantom, and then world politics was a shadow play. Therefore she, Clara, was the only key to politics that Ithiel was likely to find. Otherwise he might as well stop bothering his head about his grotesque game theories, ideology, treaties, and the rest of it. Why bother to line up so many phantoms?

But this was not a time for things to go well. He missed the point, although it was as big as a boulder to her. They had bad arguments—"It was a mistake not to let him sleep"—and after a few oppressive months, he made plans to leave the country with yet another of his outlandish lady friends.

Clara heard, again from Etta Wolfenstein, that Ithiel was staying in a fleabag hotel in the Forties west of Broadway, where he'd be hard to find. " 'Safety in sleaze,' Etta said—*She* was a piece of work." He was to meet the new girlfriend at Kennedy next afternoon.

At once Clara went uptown in a cab and walked into the cramped lobby, dirty tile like a public lavatory. She pressed with both hands on the desk and lied that she was Ithiel's wife, saying that he had sent her to check him out and take his luggage. "They believed me. You're never so cool as when you're burned up completely. They didn't even ask for identification, since I paid cash and tipped everybody five bucks apiece. When I went upstairs I was astonished that he could bring himself to sit down on such a bed, much less sleep in those grungy sheets. The morgue would have been nicer."

Then she returned to her apartment with his suitcase—the one they took to Cortina, where she had been so happy. She waited until after dark, and he turned up at about seven o'clock. Cool with her, which meant that he was boiling.

"Where do you get off, pulling this on me?"

"You didn't say you were coming to New York. You were sneaking out of the country."

"Since when do I have to punch the clock in and out like an employee!"

She stood up to him without fear. In fact she was desperate. She shouted at him the Old Testament names of their unborn children. "You're betraying Michal and Naomi."

As a rule, Ithiel was self-possessed to an unusual degree, "unless we were making love. It was cold anger at first," as Clara was to tell it. "He spoke like a man in a three-piece suit. I reminded him that the destiny of both our races depended on those children. I said they were supposed to be a merger of two high types. I'm not against other types, but they'd be there anyway, and more numerous— I'm no racist."

"I can't have you check me out of my hotel and take my suitcase. Nobody is going to supervise me. And I suppose you went through my things."

"I wouldn't do that. I was protecting you. You're making the mistake of your life."

At that moment Clara's look was hollow. You saw the bones of her face, especially the orbital ones. The inflammation of her eyes would have shocked Ithiel if he hadn't been bent on teaching her a lesson. Time to draw the line, was what he was saying to himself.

"You're not going back to that horrible hotel!" she said when he picked up his bag.

"I have a reservation in another place."

"Teddy, take off your coat. Don't go now, I'm in a bad way. I love you with my soul." She said it again, when the door swung shut after him.

He told himself it would set a bad precedent to let her control him with her fits.

The luxury of the Park Avenue room didn't sit well with him—the gilded wall fixtures, the striped upholstery, the horror of the fresco painting, the bed turned back like the color photograph in the brochure, with two tablets of chocolate mint on the night table. The bathroom was walled with mirrors, the brightwork shone, and he felt the life going out of him. He went to the bed and sat on the edge but did not lie down. It was not in the cards for him to sleep that night. The phone rang—it was a mean sound, a thin rattle—and Etta said, "Clara has swallowed a bottle of sleeping pills. She called me and I sent the ambulance. You'd better go to Bellevue; you may be needed. Are you alone there?"

He went immediately to the hospital, hurrying through gray corridors, stopping to ask directions until he found himself in the waiting space for relatives and friends, by a narrow horizontal window. He saw bodies on stretchers, no one resembling Clara. A young man in a dog collar presently joined him. He said he was Clara's minister.

"I didn't realize that she had one."

"She often comes to talk to me. Yes, she's in my parish."

"Has her stomach been pumped?"

"That—oh, yes. But she took a big dose, and they're not certain yet. You're Ithiel Regler, I suppose?"

"I am."

The young minister asked no other questions. No discussions occurred. You couldn't help but be thankful for his tact. Also for the information he brought from the nurses. Word came in the morning that she would live. They were moving her upstairs to a women's ward.

When she was able, she sent word through her clergyman friend that she didn't want to see Ithiel, had no wish to hear from him, ever. After a day of self-torment in the luxury of the hotel on Park Avenue, he canceled his trip to Europe. He fended off the sympathy of Etta Wolfenstein, avid to hear about his torments, and went back to Washington. The clergyman made a point of seeing him off at Penn Station. There he was, extra tall, in his dickey and clerical collar. Baldness had just come over him, he had decided not to wear a hat, and he kept reaching for vanished or vanishing tufts of hair. Ithiel was made uncomfortable by his sympathy. Because the young man had nothing at all to tell him except that he shouldn't blame himself. He may have been saying: "You with your sins, your not very good heart. I with my hair loss." This took no verbal form. Only a mute urgency in his decent face. He said, "She's ambulatory already. She goes around the ward and tapes back their IV needles when they work loose. She's a help to old derelicts."

You can always get a remedy, you can tap into solace when you need it, you can locate a mental fix. America is generous in this regard. The air is full of helpful hints. Ithiel was too proud to accept any handy fix. Like: "Suicide is a power move." "Suicide is punitive." "The poor kids never mean it." "It's all the drama of rescue." You could tell yourself such things; they didn't mean a damn. In all the world, now, there wasn't a civilized place left where a woman would say, "I love you with my soul." Only this backcountry girl was that way still. If no more mystical sacredness remained in the world, she hadn't been informed yet. Straight-nosed Ithiel, heading for Washington and the Capitol dome, symbolic of a nation swollen with world significance, set a greater value on Clara than on anything in *this* place, or any place. He thought, This is what I opted for, and this is what I deserve. Walking into that room at the Regency, I got what I had coming.

It was after this that Clara's marriages began—first the church wedding in her granny's gown, the arrangements elaborate, Tiffany engravings, Limoges china, Lalique glassware. Mom and Dad figured that after two suicide attempts, the fullest effort must be made to provide a stable life for their Clara. They were dear about it. There were no economies. Husband One was an educational psychologist who tested schoolchildren. His name was a good one—Monserrat. On the stationery she had printed, Clara was Mme de Monserrat. But as she was to say to Ithiel: "This marriage was like a Thanksgiving turkey. After a month the bird is drying out and you're still eating breast of turkey. It needs more and more Russian dressing, and pretty soon the sharpest knife in the city won't slice it." If there was anything she could do to perfection, it was to invent such descriptions. "Pretty soon you're trying to eat threads of bird meat," she said.

Her second husband was a southern boy who went to Congress and even ran in a few presidential primaries. They lived out in Virginia for about a year, and she saw something of Ithiel in Washington. She was not very kind to him then. "Frankly," she told him at lunch one day, "I can't imagine why I ever wanted to embrace you. I look at you, and I say, Yuch!"

"There probably is a *yuch* aspect to me," said Ithiel, perfectly level. "It does no harm to learn about your repulsive side."

She couldn't flap him. In the glance she then gave him, there was a glimmer of respect.

"I was a little crazy," she would say later.

At that time she and her southern husband were trying to have a child. She telephoned Ithiel and described the difficulties they were having. "I thought maybe you would oblige me," she said.

"Out of the question. It would be grotesque."

"A child with classic Greek eyes. Listen, Teddy, as I sit here, what do you think I'm doing to myself? Where do you suppose my hand is, and what am I touching?"

"I've already done my bit for the species," he said. "Why breed more sinners?"

"What do you suggest?"

"These utility husbands are not the answer."

"But for you and me, it wasn't in the cards, Ithiel. Why did you have so many women?"

"For you there were quite a few men—maybe it has something to do with democracy. There are so many eligibles, such handsome choices. Mix with your equals. And why limit yourself?"

"Okay, but it comes out so unhappy. . . . And why shouldn't I be pregnant by you? Alistair and I aren't compatible that way. Haven't you forgiven me for what I said that day about your being *yuch?* I was just being perverse. Ithiel, if you were here now . . ."

"But I'm not going to be."

"Just for procreation. There are even surrogate mothers these days."

"I can see a black dude motorcycle messenger in boots, belt, and helmet, waiting with a warm box for the condom full of sperm. 'Here you are, Billy. Rush this to the lady.' "

"You shouldn't make fun. You should think of the old Stoic who told his buddies when they caught him in the act, 'Mock not, I plant a Man.' Oh, I talk this way to make an impression on you. It's not real. I ask you—and now I'm serious—what should I do?"

"It should be Alistair's child."

But she divorced Alistair and married Mike Spontini, whom she had threatened in Milan to burn with the dashboard lighter coil. For Spontini she had real feeling, she said. "Even though I caught him humping another woman just before we were married."

"He wasn't meant to be a husband."

"I thought once he got to know my quality I'd mean more to him. He'd finally *see* it. I don't say that I'm better than other women. I'm not superior. I'm nutty, also. But I am in touch with the *me* in myself. There's so much I could do for a man that I loved. How *could* Mike, in my bed, with the door unlocked and me in the house, ball such an awful tramp as that? *Tell* me."

"Well, people have to be done with disorder, finally, and by the time they're done they're also finished. When they back off to take a new leap, they realize they've torn too many ligaments. It's all over."

Mike Spontini intended to do right by Clara. He bought a handsome place in Connecticut with a view of the sea. He never invested badly, never lost a penny. He doubled his money in Connecticut. The Fifth Avenue apartment was a good deal too. In the country, Clara became a gardener. She must have hoped that there was sympathetic magic in flowers and vegetables, or that the odor of soil would calm Mike's jetting soul, bring down his fever. The marriage lasted three years. He paid the wretchedness fee, he did bad time, as convicts say, then he filed for divorce and liquidated the real estate. It took a stroke to stop Mad Mike. The left side of his face was disfigured in such a manner (this was Clara speaking) that it became a fixed commentary on the life strategy he had followed: "his failed concept." But Clara was strong on loyalty, and she was loyal even to a stricken ex-husband. You don't cut all bonds after years of intimacy. After his stroke, she arranged a birthday party for him at the hospital; she sent a cake to the room. However, the doctor asked her not to come.

When you were down, busted, blasted, burnt out, dying, you saw the best of Clara.

So it was odd that she should also have become an executive, highly paid and influential. She could make fashionable talk, she dressed with originality, she knew a lot and at first hand about decadence, but at any moment she could set aside the "czarina" and become the hayseed, the dupe of traveling salesmen or grifters who wanted to lure her up to the hayloft. In her you might see suddenly a girl from a remote town, from the vestigial America of one-room schoolhouses, constables, covered-dish suppers, one of those communities bypassed by technology and urban development. Her father, remember, was still a vestryman, and her mother sent checks to TV fundamentalists. In a sophisticated boardroom Clara could be as plain as cornmeal mush, and in such a mood, when she opened her mouth, you couldn't guess whether she would speak or blow bubble gum. Yet anybody who had it in mind to get around her was letting himself in for lots of bad news.

She was prepared always to acknowledge total ignorance, saying, as she had so often said to Ithiel Regler, "*Tell* me!" The girl from the backwoods was also sentimental; she kept souvenirs, family photographs, lace valentines, and she cherished the ring Ithiel had bought her. She held on to it through four marriages. When she had it appraised for insurance, she found that it had become very valuable. It was covered for fifteen thousand dollars. Ithiel had never been smart about money. He was a bad investor—unlucky, careless. On Forty-seventh Street twenty years ago, Madison Hamilton had goofed, uncharacteristically, in pricing his emerald. But Clara was careless as well, for the ring disappeared while she was carrying Patsy. Forgotten on a washstand, maybe, or stolen from a bench at the tennis club. The loss depressed her; her depression deepened as she searched for it in handbags, drawers, upholstery crevices, shag rugs, pill bottles.

Laura Wong remembered how upset Clara had been. "*That* put you back on the couch," she said, with Oriental gentleness.

Clara had been hoping to free herself from Dr. Gladstone. She had said as much. "Now that I'm expecting for the third time I should be able to go it alone at last. A drink with Ithiel when I'm low does more for me. I've already got more doctors than any woman should need. Gladstone will ask me why this Ithiel symbol should still be so powerful. And what will there be to say? When the bag of your Hoover fills with dust, you replace it with another. Why not get rid of feeling-dust too. Yet . . . even a technician like Gladstone knows better. What he wants is to desensitize me. I was ready to die for love. Okay, I'm still living, have a husband, expect another baby. I'm as those theology people say, all those divinity fudges: *situated.* If, finally, you get situated, why go into mourning over a ring?"

In the end Clara did telephone Ithiel to tell him about the emerald. "Such a link between us," she said. "And it makes me guilty to bother you with it now, when things aren't going well for you with Francine."

"Never so bad that I can't spare some words of support," said Ithiel, so dependable. He disliked grieving over his own troubles. And he was so highly organized—as if living up to the classic balance of his face; such a pair of eyes seemed to call for a particular, maybe even an administered, sort of restraint. Ithiel could be hard on himself. He blamed himself about Clara and for his failed marriages, including the present one. And yet the choices he made showed him to be reckless too. He was committed to high civility, structure, order; nevertheless he took chances with women, he was a gambler, something of an anarchist. There was anarchy on both sides. Nevertheless, his attachment, his feeling for her was—to his own surprise—permanent. His continually increasing respect for her came over the horizon like a moon taking decades to rise.

"Seven marriages between us, and we still love each other," she said. Ten years before, it would have been a risky thing to say, it would have stirred a gust of fear in him. Now she was sure that he would agree, as indeed he did.

"That is true."

"How do you interpret the ring, then?"

"I don't," said Ithiel. "It's a pretty bad idea to wring what happens to get every drop of meaning out of it. The way people twist their emotional laundry is not to be believed. *I* don't feel that you wronged me by losing that ring. You say it was insured?"

"Damn right."

"Then file a claim. The companies charge enough. Your premiums must be out of sight."

"I'm really torn up about it," said Clara.

"That's your tenth-century soul. Much your doctor can do about that!"

"He helps, in some respects."

"Those guys!" said Ithiel. "If a millipede came into the office, he'd leave with an infinitesimal crutch for each leg."

Reporting this conversation to Ms. Wong, Clara said, "That did it. That's the anarchist in Ithiel busting out. It gives me such a boost to chat with him even for five minutes."

The insurance company paid her fifteen thousand dollars, and then, a year later, the missing ring turned up.

In one of her fanatical fits of spring cleaning, she found it beneath the bed, above the caster, held in the frame to which the small braking lever was attached. It was on her side of the bed. She must have been groping for a paper tissue and knocked it off the bedside table. For what purpose she had been groping, now that it was discovered, she didn't care to guess. She held the ring to her face, felt actually as if she were inhaling the green essence of this ice—no, ice was diamond; still, this emerald also was an ice. In it Ithiel's pledge was frozen. Or else it represented the permanent form of the passion she had had for this man. The hot form would have been red, like a node inside the body, in the sexual parts. That you'd see as a ruby. The cool form was this concentrate of clear green. This was not one of her fancies; it was as real as the green of the ocean, as the mountains in whose innards such gems are mined. She thought these locations (the Atlantic, the Andes) as she thought the inside of her own body. In her summary fashion, she said, "Maybe what it comes to is that I am an infant mine." She had three small girls to prove it.

The insurance company was not notified. Clara was not prepared to return the money. By now it simply wasn't there. It had been spent on a piano, a carpet, yet another set of Limoges china—God knows what else. So the ring couldn't be reinsured, but that didn't matter much. Exultingly glad, she told Ithiel on the telephone, "*In*credible, where that ring fell! Right under me, as I lay there suffering over it. I could have touched it by dropping my arm. I could have poked it with my finger."

"How many of us can say anything like that?" said Ithiel. "That you can lie in bed and have the cure for what ails you within reach."

"Only you don't know it . . ." said Clara. "I thought you'd be pleased."

"Oh, I am. I think it's great. It's like adding ten years to your life to have it back."

"I'll have to take double good care of it. It's not insurable. . . . I'm never sure how important an item like this ring can be to a man who has to think about the Atlantic Alliance and all that other stuff. Deterrence, nuclear theater forces . . . completely incomprehensible to me."

"If only the answers were under my bed," said Ithiel. "But you shouldn't think I can't take a ring seriously, or that I'm so snooty about world significance or Lenin's 'decisive correlation of forces'—that you're just a kid and I indulge you like a big daddy. I like you better than I do the president, or the national security adviser."

"Yes, I can see that, and why, humanly, you'd rather have me to deal with."

"Just think, if you didn't do your own spring cleaning, your help might have found the ring."

"My help wouldn't dream of going under the bed at any season of the year; that's why I took time off from the office. I had to work around Wilder, who's been reading John le Carré. Sitting in the middle of his female household like a Sioux Indian in his wickiup. Like Sitting Bull. All the same, he's often very sweet. Even when he acts like the reigning male. And he'd be totally at sea if I weren't . . . oops!"

"If you weren't manning the ship," said Ithiel.

Well, it was a feminine household, and for that reason perhaps Gina felt less foreign in New York. She said that she loved the city, it had so many accommodations for women specifically. Everybody who arrived, moreover, already knew the place because of movies and magazines, and when John Kennedy said he was a Berliner, all of Berlin could have answered, "So? We are New Yorkers." There was no such thing as being strange here, in Gina's opinion.

"That's what *you* think, baby" was Clara's response, although it was not made to Gina Wegman, it was made to Ms. Wong. "And let's hope she never finds out what this town can do to a young person. But when you think about such a pretty child and the Italian charm of her looks, so innocent—although innocence is a tricky thing to prove. You can't expect her to forget about being a girl just because the surroundings are so dangerous."

"Do you let her ride the subway?"

"*Let* her!" said Clara. "When the young things go into the street, where's your control over them? All I can do is pray she'll be safe. I told her if she was going to wear a short skirt she should also put on a coat. But what good is advice without a slum background? What a woman needs today is some slum experience. However, it's up to me to keep an eye on the child, and I must assume she's innocent and doesn't *want* to be rubbed up against in the rush hours by dirty-sex delinquents."

"It's hard to be in the responsible-adult position," said Laura.

"It's the old-time religion in me. Stewardship." Clara said this partly in fun. Yet when she invoked her background, her formative years, she became for a moment the girl with the wide forehead, the large eyes, the smallish nose, who had been forced by her parents to memorize long passages from Galatians and Corinthians.

"She suits the children," said Ms. Wong.

"They're very comfortable with her, and there's no strain with Lucy." For Clara, Lucy was the main thing. At this stage she was so sullen—overweight, shy of making friends, jealous, resistant, troubled. Hard to move. Clara had often suggested that Lucy's hair be cut, the heavy curls that bounded her face. "The child has hair like Jupiter," said Clara in one of her sessions with Laura. "Sometimes I think she must be as strong—potentially—as a hod carrier."

"Wouldn't she like it short and trim, like yours?"

"I don't want a storm over it," said Clara.

The child was clumsy certainly (although her legs were going to be good—you could already see that). But there was a lot of power under this clumsiness. Lucy complained that her little sisters united against her. It looked that way, Clara agreed. Patsy and Selma were graceful children, and they made Lucy seem burly, awkward before the awkward age. She would be awkward after it too, just as her mother had been, and eruptive, defiant and prickly. When Clara got through to her (the superlarge eyes of her slender face had to bear down on the kid till she opened up—"You can always talk to Mother about what goes on, what's cooking inside"), then Lucy sobbed that all the girls in her class snubbed and made fun of her.

"Little bitches," said Clara to Ms. Wong. "Amazing how early it all starts. Even Selma and Patsy, affectionate kids, are developing at Lucy's expense. Her 'grossness'—you know what a word 'gross' is with children—makes ladies of them. And the little sisters are far from dumb, but I believe Lucy is the one with the brains. There's something *major* in Lucy. Gina Wegman agrees with me. Lucy acts like a small she-brute. It's not just that Roman hairdo. She's greedy and bears grudges. God, she does! That's where Gina comes in, because Gina has so much class, and Gina *likes* her. As much as I can, with executive responsibilities and bearing the brunt of the household, I mother those girls. Also, I have sessions with the school psychologists—I was once married to one of those characters—and discussions with other mothers. Maybe putting them in the 'best' schools is a big mistake. The influence of the top stockbrokers and lawyers in town has to be overcome there. I'm saying it as I see it. . . ."

What Clara couldn't say, because Laura Wong's upbringing was so different from her own (and it was her own that seemed the more alien), had to do with Matthew 16:18: "the gates of hell shall not prevail against it"—*it* being love, against which no door can be closed. This was more of the primitive stuff that Clara had brought from the backcountry and was part of her confused inner life. Explaining it to her confidante would be more trouble than it was worth, if you considered that in the end Ms. Wong would still be in the dark—the second dark being darker than the first. Here Clara couldn't say it as she saw it.

"There's a lot of woman in that child. A handsome, powerful woman. Gina Wegman intuits the same about her," said Clara.

She was much drawn to Gina, only it wouldn't be wise to make a younger friend of her; that would lie too close to adoption and perhaps cause rivalry with the children. You had to keep your distance—avoid intimacies, avoid confidences especially. Yet there was nothing wrong with an occasional treat, as long as the treat was educational. For instance, you asked the au pair girl to bring some papers to your office, and then you could show her around the suite, give her a nice tea. She let Gina attend a trade briefing on shoulder pads and hear arguments for this or that type of padding, the degree of the lift, the desirability of a straighter line in the hang of one's clothes; the new trends in size in the designs of Armani, Christian Lacroix, Sonia Rykiel. She took the girl to a show of the latest spring fashions from Italy, where she heard lots of discussion about the desirability of over-the-knee boots, and of the layering of the skirts of Gianni Versace over puffy knickers. Agitprop spokesmen putting across short garments of puckered silk, or jackets of cunningly imitated ocelot, or simulated beaver capes—all this the ingenious work of millionaire artisans, billionaire designer commissars. Gina came suitably dressed, a pretty girl, very young. Clara couldn't say how this fashion display impressed her. It was best, Clara thought, to underplay the whole show: the luxurious setting, the star cast of Italians, and the pomp of the experts—somewhat subdued by the presence of the impassive czarina.

"Well, what should I say about these things?" said Clara, again confiding to Laura Wong. "This glitter is our living, and nice women grow old and glum, cynical too, in all this glitz of fur, silk, leather, cosmetics, et cetera, of the glamour trades. Meanwhile my family responsibilities are what count. How to protect my children."

"And you wanted to give your Gina a treat," said Ms. Wong.

"And I'm glad about the playfulness," said Clara. "We have to have that. But the sums it costs! And who gets what! Besides, Laura, if it has to be slathered onto women . . . If a woman is beautiful and you add beautiful dress, that's one thing: you're adding beauty to beauty. But if the operation comes from the outside only, it has curious effects. And that's the way it generally happens. Of course there will be barefaced schemers or people in despair looking glorious. But in most cases of decoration, the effect is hell. It's a variation on that Auden line I love so much about 'the will of the insane to suffer.' " When she had said this she looked blankly violent. She had gone further than she had intended, further than Ms. Wong was prepared to follow. Here Clara might well have added the words from Matthew 16.

Her Chinese American confidante was used to such sudden zooming. Clara was not being stagy when she expressed such ideas about clothing; she was brooding audibly, and very often she had Ithiel Regler in mind, the women he had gone off with, the women he had married. Among them were several "fancy women"—she meant that they were overdressed sexpots, gaudy and dizzy, "ground-dragging titzers," on whom a man like Ithiel should never have squandered his substance. And he had been married three times and had two children. What a waste! Why should there have been seven marriages, five children! Even Mike Spontini, for all his powers and attractions, had been a waste—a Mediterranean, an Italian husband who came back to his wife when he saw fit, that is, when he was tired of business and of playing around. *All* the others had been

dummy husbands, humanly unserious—you could get no real masculine resonance out of any of them.

What a pity! thought Laura Wong. Teddy Regler should have married Clara.
Apply any measure—need, sympathy, feeling, you name it—and the two pro-
files (that was Laura's way of putting it) were just about identical. And Ithiel was
doing very badly now. Just after Gina became her au pair girl, Clara learned
from the Wolfenstein woman, Teddy's first wife, who had her scouts in Washington, that the third Mrs. Regler had hired a moving van and emptied the
house one morning as soon as Teddy left for the office. Coming home in the
evening, he found nothing but the bed they had shared the night before
(stripped of bedding) and a few insignificant kitchen items. Francine, the third
wife, had had no child to take care of. She had spent her days wandering around
department stores. That much was true. He didn't let her feel that she was sharing his life. Yet the man was stunned, wiped out—depressed, then ill. He had
been mourning his mother. Francine had made her move a week after his
mother's funeral. One week to the day.

Clara and Laura together had decided that Francine couldn't bear his grieving. She had no such emotions herself, and she disliked them. "Some people just
can't grasp grief," was what Clara said. Possibly, too, there was another man in
the picture, and it would have been awkward, after an afternoon with this man,
to come home to a husband absorbed in dark thoughts or needing consolation.
"I can easily picture this from the wife's side," said Laura. Her own divorce had
been a disagreeable one. Her husband, a man named Odo Fenger, a dermatolo-
gist, had been one of those ruddy, blond, fleshy baby-men who have to engross
you in their emotions (eyes changing from baby blue to whiskey blue) and so
centuple the agonies of breaking away. So why *not* send a van to the house and
move straight into the future—future being interpreted as never (never in this
life) meeting the other party again. "That Francine didn't have it in her to see
him through, after the feeling had been killed out of *her*. Each age has its
own way of dealing with these things. As you said before, in the Renaissance you
used poison. When the feeling is killed, the other party becomes physically
unbearable."

Clara didn't entirely attend to what Laura was saying. Her only comment
was, "I suppose there *has* been progress. Better moving than murdering. At least
both parties go on living."

By now Ms. Wong wanted no husbands, no children. She had withdrawn
from all that. But she respected Clara Velde. Perhaps her curiosity was even
deeper than her respect, and she was most curious about Clara and Ithiel Regler.
She collected newspaper clippings about Regler and like Wilder Velde didn't
miss his TV interviews, if she could help it.

When Clara heard about Francine and her moving van, she flew down to

Washington as soon as she could get to the shuttle. Gina was there to take charge of the children. Clara never felt so secure as when dependable Gina was looking after them. As a backup Clara had Mrs. Peralta, the cleaning woman, who had also become a family friend.

Clara found Ithiel in a state of sick dignity. He was affectionate with her but reserved about his troubles, thanked her somewhat formally for her visit, and told her that he would rather not go into the history of his relations with Francine.

"Just as you like," said Clara. "But you haven't got anybody here; there's just me in New York. I'll look after you if you should need it."

"I'm glad you've come. I've been despondent. What I've learned, though, is that when people get to talking about their private troubles, they go into a winding spiral about relationships, and they absolutely stupefy everybody with boredom. I'm sure that I can turn myself around."

"Of course. You're resilient," said Clara, proud of him. "So we won't say too much about it. Only, that woman didn't have to wait until your mother was dead. She might have done it earlier. You don't wait until a man is down, then dump on him."

"Shall we have a good dinner? Middle Eastern, Chinese, Italian, or French? I see you're wearing the emerald."

"I hoped you'd notice. Now tell me, Ithiel, are you giving up your place? Did she leave it very bare?"

"I can camp there until some money comes in and then refit the living room."

"There ought to be somebody taking care of you."

"If there's one thing I can do without, it's this picture of poor me, deep in the dumps, and some faithful female who makes my heart swell with gratitude." Being rigorous with his heart gave him satisfaction.

"He likes to look at the human family as it is," Clara was to explain.

"You wouldn't marry a woman who did value you," said Clara at dinner. "Like Groucho Marx saying he wouldn't join a club that accepted him for membership."

"Let me tell you," said Ithiel, and she understood that he had drawn back to the periphery in order to return to the center from one of his strange angles. "When the president has to go to Walter Reed Hospital for surgery and the papers are full of sketches of his bladder and his prostate—I can remember the horrible drawings of Eisenhower's ileitis—then I'm glad there are no diagrams of my vitals in the press and the great public isn't staring at my anus. For the same reason, I've always discouraged small talk about my psyche. It's only fair that Francine shouldn't have valued me. I would have lived out the rest of my life with her. I was patient. . . ."

"You mean you gave up, you resigned yourself."

"I was affectionate," Ithiel insisted.

"You had to fake it. You saw your mistake and were ready to pay for it. She didn't give a squat for your affection."

"I was faithful."

"No, you were licked," said Clara. "You went to your office hideaway and did your thing about Russia or Iran. Those crazy characters from Libya or Lebanon are *some* fun to follow. What did she do for fun?"

"I suppose that every morning she had to decide where to go with her credit cards. She liked auctions and furniture shows. She bought an ostrich-skin outfit, complete with boots and purse."

"What else did she do for fun?"

Ithiel was silent and reserved, moving crumbs back and forth with the blade of his knife. Clara thought, She cheated on him. Precious Francine had no idea what a husband she had. And what did it matter what a woman like that did with her gross organs. Clara didn't get a rise out of Ithiel with her suggestive question. She might just as well have been talking to one of those Minoans dug up by Evans or Schliemann or whoever, characters like those in the silent films, painted with eye-lengthening makeup. If Clara was from the Middle Ages, Ithiel was from antiquity. Imagine a low-down woman who felt that *he* didn't appreciate *her!* Why, Ithiel could be the Gibbon or the Tacitus of the American Empire. *He* wouldn't have thought it, but she remembered to this day how he would speak about Keynes's sketches of Clemenceau, Lloyd George, and Woodrow Wilson. If he wanted, he could do with Nixon, Johnson, Kennedy, or Kissinger, with the shah or de Gaulle, what Keynes had done with the Allies at Versailles. World figures had found Ithiel worth their while. Sometimes he let slip a comment or a judgment: "Neither the Russians nor the Americans can manage the world. Not capable of organizing the future." When she came into her own, Clara thought, she'd set up a fund for him so he could write his views.

She said, "If you'd like me to stay over, Wilder has gone to Minnesota to see some peewee politician who needs a set of speeches. Gina is entertaining a few friends at the house."

"Do I look as if I needed friendly first aid?"

"You are *down*. What's the disgrace in that?"

Ithiel drove her to the airport. For the moment the parkways were empty. Ahead were airport lights, and in the slanting planes seated travelers by the thousands came in, went up.

Clara asked what job he was doing. "Not who you're doing it for, but the subject."

He said he was making a survey of the opinions of émigrés on the new Soviet regime—he seemed glad to change the subject, although he had always been a bit reluctant to talk politics to her. Politics were not her thing, he didn't like to waste words on uncomprehending idle questioners, but he seemed to have his emotional reasons tonight for saying just what it was that he was up to. "Some of the smartest émigrés are saying that the Russians didn't announce liberalization until they had crushed the dissidents. Then they co-opted the dissidents' ideas. After you've gotten rid of your enemies, you're ready to abolish capital punishment—that's how Alexander Zinoviev puts it. And it wasn't only the KGB that destroyed the dissident movement but the whole party organization, and the party was supported by the Soviet people. They strangled the opposition, and now they're pretending to be *it*. You have the Soviet leaders themselves criticizing Soviet society. When it has to be done, they take over. And the West is thrilled by all the reforms."

"So we're going to be bamboozled again," said Clara.

But there were other matters, more pressing, to discuss on the way to the airport. Plenty of time. Ithiel drove very slowly. The next shuttle flight wouldn't be taking off until nine o'clock. Clara was glad they didn't have to rush.

"You don't mind my wearing this ring tonight?" said Clara.

"Because this is a bad time to remind me of the way it might have gone with us? No. You came down to see how I was and what you could do for me."

"Next time, Ithiel, if there is a next time, you'll let me check the woman out. You may be big in political analysis . . . No need to finish *that* sentence. Besides, my own judgment hasn't been one hundred percent."

"If anybody were to ask me, Clara, I'd say that you were a strange case—a woman who hasn't been corrupted, who has developed a moral logic of her own, worked it out independently by her own solar power and from her own feminine premises. You hear I've had a calamity and you come down on the next shuttle. And how few people take this Washington flight for a human purpose. Most everybody comes on business. Some to see the sights, a few because of the pictures at the National Gallery, a good percentage to get laid. How many come because they're deep?"

He parked his car so that he could walk with her to the gate.

"You're a dear man," she said. "We have to look out for each other."

On the plane, she pulled her seat belt tight in order to control her feelings, and she opened a copy of *Vogue,* but only to keep her face in it. No magazine now had anything to tell her.

When she got back to Park Avenue, the superintendent's wife, a Latino lady, was waiting. Mrs. Peralta was there too. Clara had asked the cleaning lady to help Gina entertain (to keep an eye on) her friends. The elevator operator–doorman was with the ladies, a small group under the marquee. The sidewalks of Park Avenue are twice as broad as any others, and the median strip was nicely planted with flowers of the season. When the doorman helped Clara from the yellow cab, the women immediately began to tell her about the huge bash Gina had given. "A real mix of people," said Mrs. Peralta.

"And the girls?"

"Oh, we were careful with them, kept them away from those East Harlem types. We're here because Mr. Regler called to say what flight you'd be on."

"I asked him to do that," said Clara.

"I don't think Gina thought so many were coming. Friends, and friends of friends, of her boyfriend, I guess."

"Boyfriend? Now, who would he be? This is news to me."

"I asked Marta Elvia to come and see for herself," said Antonia Peralta. Marta Elvia, the super's wife, was related somehow to Antonia.

They were taken up in the elevator. Marta Elvia, eight months pregnant and filling up much of the space, was saying what a grungy mob had turned up. It was an open house.

"But tell me, quickly, who is the boyfriend?" said Clara.

The man was described as coming from the West Indies; he was French-speaking, dark-skinned, very good-looking, "arrogant-like," said Mrs. Peralta.

"And how long has he been coming to the house?"

"Couple of weeks, just."

When she entered the living room, Clara's first impression was: So this is what can be done here. It doesn't have to be the use I put it to. She had limited the drawing room to polite behavior.

The party was mostly over; there were only four or five couples left. As Clara described it, the young women looked gaudy. "The room was more like a car of the West Side subway. Lots of muscle on the boys, as if they did aerobics. And I used to be able to identify the smell of pot, but I'm in the dark, totally, on the new drugs. Crack is completely beyond me; I can't even say what it is, much less describe how it works and does it have a smell. The whole scene was like a mirage to me, how they were haberdashed. Gina's special friend, Frederic, was a good-looking boy, black, and he did have an attractive French accent. Gina tried to behave as if nothing at all was wrong, and she couldn't quite swing that. I wasn't going to fuss at her, though. At the back of the apartment, I had three children sleeping. At a time like this your history books come back to you—how a pioneer woman dealt with an Indian war party when her husband was away. So I put myself out to make time pass pleasantly, toned down the music, ventilated the smoke, and soon the party petered out."

While Mrs. Peralta was cleaning up, Clara had a talk with Gina Wegman. She said she had imagined a smaller gathering—a few acquaintances, not a random sample of the street population.

"Frederic asked if he could bring some friends."

Well, Clara was willing to believe that this was simply a European misconception of partying in New York—carefree musical young people, racially mixed, dancing to reggae music. In Vienna, as elsewhere, such pictures of American life were on TV—America as the place where you let yourself go.

"Anyway, I must tell you, Gina, that I can't allow this kind of thing—like scenes from some lewd dance movie."

"I'm sorry, Mrs. Velde."

"Where did you meet Frederic?"

"Through friends from Austria. They work at the UN."

"Is that where he works too?"

"I never asked."

"And do you see a lot of him? You don't have to answer—I can tell you're taken with him. You never asked what he does? He's not a student?"

"It never came up."

Clara thought, judging by Gina's looks, that what came up was Gina's skirt. Clara herself knew all too well how that was. We've been through it. What can be more natural in a foreign place than to accept exotic experiences? Otherwise why leave home at all?

Clifford, a convict in Attica, still sent Clara a Christmas card without fail. She hadn't seen him in twenty-five years. They had no other connection. Frederic, to go by appearances, wouldn't even have sent a card. Generational differences. Clifford had been a country boy.

We must see to it that it doesn't end badly, was what Clara told herself.

But then we must learn what sort of person Gina is, really, she thought. What makes her tick, and if this is the whole sum of what she wants. I didn't take her for a little hot-pants type.

"I suppose things are done differently in Vienna," Clara said. "As to bringing strangers into the house . . ."

"No. But then you're personally friendly with the colored lady who works here."

"Mrs. Peralta is no stranger."

"She brings her children here at Thanksgiving, and they eat with the girls at the same table."

"And why not? But yes," said Clara, "I can see that this is a mixture that might puzzle somebody just over from Europe for the first time. My husband and I are not rashists. . . ." (This was a pronunciation Clara could not alter.) "However, Mrs. Peralta is a trusted member of this household."

"But Frederic's friends might steal . . . ?"

"I haven't accused anyone. You couldn't vouch for anybody, though. You've just met these guests yourself. And haven't you noticed the security arrangements—the doors, the buzzer system, everybody inspected?"

Gina said, speaking quietly and low, "I noticed. I didn't apply it to myself."

Not *herself*. Gina hadn't considered Frederic in this light. And she couldn't allow him to be viewed with suspicion. Clara gave her a good mark for loyalty. Ten on a scale of ten, she thought, and warmed toward Gina. "It's not a color question. The corporation I'm in has even divested itself in South Africa." This was not a strong statement. To Clara, South Africa was about as close as Xanadu. But she said to herself that they were being diverted into absurdities, and what she and Gina were telling each other was only so much fluff. The girl had come to New York to learn about such guys as Frederic, and there wasn't all that much to learn. This was simply an incident, and not even a good incident. Just a lot of exciting trouble. Then she made a mental note to take all this up with Ithiel and also get his opinion on divestiture.

"Well," she said, "I'm afraid I'm going to set a limit on the size of the group you can entertain."

The girl nodded. That made sense. She couldn't deny it.

No more scolding. And a blend of firmness and concern for the girl. If she were to send her away, the kids would cry. And I'd miss her myself, Clara admitted. So she stood up (mistress terminating a painful interview was how Clara perceived it; she saw that she really had come to depend on certain lady-of-the-house postures). When Gina had gone to her room, Clara ran a check: the Jensen ashtray, the silver letter opener, mantelpiece knickknacks; and for the *n*th time she wished that there were someone to share her burdens. Wilder was no good to her that way. If he got fifty speech commissions he couldn't make up the money he had sunk in mining stocks—Homestake and Sunshine. Supposedly, precious metals were a hedge, but there was less and less principal for the shrinking hedge to hedge.

The inspection over, Clara talked to Antonia Peralta before Antonia turned on the noisy vacuum cleaner. How often had Gina's young man been in the apartment? Antonia jabbed at her cheek with a rigid finger, meaning that a sharp lookout was necessary. Her message was: "Count on me, Mrs. Velde." Well, she was part of a pretty smart subculture. Between them, she and Marta Elvia would police the joint. On Gina Wegman herself Antonia Peralta did not comment. But then she wasn't always around, she had her days off. And remember, Antonia hadn't cleaned under the bed. And if she *had* been thorough she would have found the missing ring. In that case, would she have handed it over? She was an honest lady, according to her lights, but there probably were certain corners into which those lights never were turned. The insurance company had paid up, and Clara would have been none the wiser if Antonia had silently pocketed a lost object. No, the Spanish ladies were honest enough. Marta Elvia was bonded, triple certified, and Antonia Peralta had never taken so much as a handkerchief.

"In my own house," Clara was to explain later, "I object to locking up valuables. A house where there is no basic trust is not what I call a house. I just can't live with a bunch of keys, like a French or Italian person. Women have told me that they couldn't sleep nights if their jewelry weren't locked up. *I* couldn't sleep if it were."

She said to Gina, "I'm taking your word for it that nothing bad will happen." She was bound to make this clear, while recognizing that there was no way to avoid giving offense.

Gina had no high looks, no sharp manner. She simply said, "Are you telling me not to have Frederic here?"

Clara's reaction was, Better here than *there*. She tried to imagine what Frederic's pad must be like. That was not too difficult. She had, after all, herself been a young woman in New York. Gina was giving her a foretaste of what she would have to face when her own girls grew up. Unless heaven itself were to decree that Gogmagogsville had gone far enough, and checked the decline—time to lower the boom, send in the Atlantic to wash it away. Not a possibility you could count on.

"By no means," said Clara. "I will ask you, though, to take full charge when Antonia is off."

"You don't want Frederic here when the children are with me?"

"Right."

"He wouldn't harm them."

Clara did not see fit to say more.

She spoke to Ms. Wong about it, stopping at her place after work for a brief drink, a breather on the way home. Ms. Wong had an unsuitably furnished Madison Avenue apartment, Scandinavian design, not an Oriental touch about it except some Chinese prints framed in blond wood. Holding her iced Scotch in a dampening paper napkin, Clara said, "I hate to be the one enforcing the rules on that girl. I feel for her a lot more than I care to."

"You identify all that much with her?"

"She's got to learn, of course," said Clara. "Just as I did. And I don't think much of mature women who have evaded it. But sometimes the schooling we have to undergo is too rough."

"Seems to you *now* . . ."

"No, it takes far too much out of a young girl."

"You're thinking of three daughters," said Ms. Wong, accurate enough.

"I'm thinking how it is that you have to go on for twenty years before you understand—maybe understand—what there was to preserve."

Somewhat dissatisfied with her visit to Laura (it was so *New York!*), she walked home, there to be told by Mrs. Peralta that she had found Gina and Frederic stretched out on the living room sofa. Doing what? Oh, only petting, but the young man with the silk pillows under his combat boots. Clara could see why Antonia should be offended. The young man was putting down the Veldes and their fine upholstery, spreading himself about and being arrogant.

And perhaps it wasn't even that. He may not have reached *that* level of intentional offensiveness.

"You talk to the girl?"

"I don't believe I will. No," said Clara, and risked being a contemptible American in Mrs. Peralta's eyes, one of those people who let themselves be run over in their own homes. Largely to herself, Clara explained, "I'd rather put up with him here than have the girl do it in his pad." No sooner had she said this than she was dead certain that there was nothing to keep Gina from doing whatever they did in both places. She would have said to Gina, "Making the most of New York—this not-for-Vienna behavior. No boys lying on top of you in your mother's drawing room." "Land of opportunity," she might have said, but she said this only to herself after thinking matters through, considering deeply in a trancelike private stillness and moistening the center of her upper lip with the tip of her tongue. Why did it go so dry right at the center? Imagining sexual things sometimes did that to her. She didn't envy Gina; the woman who had made such personal sexual disclosures to Ms. Wong didn't have to envy anyone. No, she was curious about this pretty, plump girl. She sensed that she was a deep one. *How* deep was what Clara was trying to guess when she went so still.

And so she closed her eyes briefly, nodding, when Marta Elvia, who sometimes waited for her in the lobby, pressed close with her pregnant belly to say that Frederic had come in at one o'clock and left just before Mrs. Velde was expected.

(There were anomalies in Clara's face when you saw it frontally. Viewing it in profile, you would find yourself trying to decide which of the Flemish masters would have painted her best.)

"Thanks, Marta Elvia," she said. "I've got the situation under control."

She shouldn't have been so sure about it, for that very evening when she was dressing for dinner—a formal corporate once-a-year affair—she was standing before the long mirror in her room, when suddenly she knew that her ring had been stolen. She kept it in the top drawer of her dresser—unlocked, of course. Its place was a dish Jean-Claude had given her years ago. The young Frenchman, Ithiel's temporary replacement recklessly chosen in anger, had called this gift a *vide-poches*. At bedtime you emptied your pockets into it. It was meant for men; women didn't use that kind of object; but it was one of those mementos Clara couldn't part with—she kept schoolday valentines in a box, too. She looked, of course, into the dish. The ring wasn't there. She hadn't expected it to be. She expected nothing. She said that the sudden knowledge that it was gone came over her like death and she felt as if the life had been vacuumed out of her.

Wilder, already in evening clothes, was reading one of his thrillers in a corner where the back end of the grand piano hid him. With her rapid, dry decision-maker's look, Clara went to the kitchen, where the kids were at dinner. Under

Gina's influence they behaved so well at table. "May I see you for a moment?" said Clara, and Gina immediately got up and followed her to the master bedroom. There Clara shut both doors, and lowering her head so that she seemed to be examining Gina's eyes, "Well, Gina, something has happened," she said. "My ring is gone."

"You mean the emerald that was lost and found again? Oh, Mrs. Velde, I am sorry. Is it gone? I'm sure you have looked. Did Mr. Velde help you?"

"I haven't told him yet."

"Then let's look together."

"Yes, let's. But it's always in the same place, in this room. In that top drawer under my stockings. Since I found it again, I've been extra careful. And of course I want to examine the shag rug. I want to crawl and hunt for it. But I'd have to take off this tight dress to get on my knees. And my hair is fixed for going out."

Gina, stooping, combed through the carpet near the dresser. Clara, silent, let her look, staring down, her eyes superdilated, her mouth stern. She said, at last, "It's no use." She had let Gina go through the motions.

"Should you call the police to report it?"

"I'm not going to do that," said Clara. She was not so foolish as to tell the young woman about the insurance. "Perhaps that makes you feel better, not having the police."

"I think, Mrs. Velde, you should have locked up your valuable objects."

"In my own home, I shouldn't have to."

"Yes, but there are other people also to consider."

"I consider, Gina, that a woman has a right in her own bedroom . . . it's for a woman *herself* to decide who comes in. I made it explicit what the household rules were. I would have vouched for you, and you must vouch for your friend."

Gina was shaken. Both women trembled. After all, thought Clara, a human being can be sketched in three or four lines, but then when the sockets are empty, no amount of ingenuity can refill them. Not her brown, not my blue.

"I understand you," said Gina with an air of being humiliated by a woman whose kindness she counted on. "Are you sure the ring isn't misplaced again?"

"Are *you* sure . . . ?" Clara answered. "And try to think of my side of it. That was an engagement ring from a man who loved me. It's not just an object worth *x* dollars. It's also a life support, my dear." She was about to say that it was involved with her very grip on existence, but she didn't want any kind of cry to come out or to betray a fear of total slippage. She said instead, "The ring was here yesterday. And a person I don't know wandering around the house and—why not?—coming into my room . . ."

"Why don't you say it?" said Gina.

"I'd have to be a fool not to. To be too nice for such things, I'd have to be a moron. Frederic was here all afternoon. Has he got a job somewhere?"

The girl had no answer to this.

"You can't say. But you don't believe he's a thief. You don't think he'd put you in this position. And don't try to tell me he's being accused because of his color."

"I didn't try. People *are* nasty about the Haitians."

"You'd better go and talk to him. If he's got the ring, tell him he has to return it. I want you to produce it tomorrow. Marta Elvia can sit with the girls if you have to go out tonight. Where does he live?"

"One hundred twenty-eighth Street."

"And a telephone? You can't go up there alone after dark. Not even by day. Not alone. And where does he hang out? I can ask Antonia's husband to take you by cab. . . . Now Wilder's coming down the corridor, and I've got to go."

"I'll wait here for the concierge."

"For Marta Elvia. I'll talk to her on the way out. *You* wouldn't steal, Gina. And Mrs. Peralta has been here eight years without a coffee spoon missing."

Later Clara took it out on herself: What did I do to that girl, like ordering her to go to Harlem, where she could be raped or killed, because of my goddamn ring, the rottenest part of town in the rotten middle of the night, frantic mad and (what it comes down to) over Ithiel, who balked at marrying me twenty years ago! A real person understands how to cut losses, not let her whole life be wound around to the end by a single desire, because under it all is the uglitude of this one hang-up. Four husbands and three kids haven't cured me of Ithiel. And finally this love-toy emerald, personal sentimentality, makes me turn like a maniac on this Austrian kid. She may think I grudge her the excitement of her romance with that disgusting girl-fucker who used her as his cover to get into the house and now sticks her with this theft.

Nevertheless Clara had fixed convictions about domestic and maternal responsibilities. She had already gone too far in letting Gina bring Frederic into the apartment and infect the whole place, spraying it with sexual excitement. And, as it now turned out, even become involved in crime. A fling in the U.S.A. was all very well for a young lady from bourgeois Vienna—like the poor Russian hippie, that diplomat's son who fell in love with Mick Jagger. "Tell Mick Jagger good-bye," he said, boarding the plane. This city had become the center, the symbol of worldwide adolescent revolt.

In the middle of the corporate evening Clara was attacked by one of her fierce migraines, and a head as conspicuous as hers, dominating a dinner table, affected everybody when it began to ache, so that the whole party stood up when she rose and hurried out. The Veldes went straight home. Swallowing a handful of white pills from the medicine chest, Clara went immediately to Gina's room. To her relief, the girl was there, in bed. The reading lamp was on, but she wasn't reading, only sitting up, her hands thoughtfully folded.

"I'm glad you didn't go to Harlem!"

"I reached Frederic on the phone. He was with some of our UN friends."

"And you'll see him tomorrow . . . ?"

"I didn't mention the ring. But I am prepared to move out. You told me I had to bring it back or leave."

"Going where . . . !" Clara was taken by surprise. Next she was aware of the girl's brown gaze, the exceptional fixity of it. Unshed tears were killing her. "But if Frederic gives back the ring, you'll stay." While she was speaking, Clara with some shame recognized how dumb she sounded. It was the hereditary peasant in her saying this. The guy would deny the theft, and if eventually he admitted it, he still would not return the ring. This very moment he might be taking a thousand bucks for it. These people came up from the tropical slums to outsmart New York, and with all the rules crumbling here as elsewhere, so that nobody could any longer be clear in his mind about anything, they could do it.

Left standing were only property rights. With murder in second place. A stolen ring. A corpse to account for. Such were the only universals recognized, and very few others could be acknowledged. So where did love fit in? Love was down in the catacombs, those catacombs being the personal neuroses of women like herself.

She said to Gina, as one crypto lover to another, "What will you do?"

Gina said, but without resentment, not a hint of accusation in her voice, "That I can't say. I've only had a couple of hours to think. There are places."

She'd move in with her Haitian, Clara guessed, plausibly enough. But this was not sayable. Clara was learning to refrain. You didn't *say* everything. "Discover silence," she instructed herself.

Next day she rushed home from work in a cab and found Marta Elvia babysitting. Clara had already been in touch with an agency, and there was a new girl coming tomorrow. Best she could do on short notice. Lucy was upset, predictably, and Clara had to take her aside for special explanations. She said, "Gina suddenly had to go. It was an emergency. She didn't *want* to. When she can, she'll come back. It's not *your* fault." There was no guessing just how rattled Lucy was. She was silent, stoical.

Clara had rehearsed this on the telephone with the psychiatrist, Dr. Gladstone.

"With working parents," she said to Lucy, "such problems do come up."

"But Daddy isn't working now."

You're telling *me!* thought Clara. He was doping out the upcoming primaries in New Hampshire.

As soon as possible, she went to see Dr. Gladstone. He was about to take one of his holidays and would be away three weeks. They had discussed this absence in the last session. In the waiting room, she studied the notes she had prepared: Where is Gina? How can I find out, keep track? Protect?

She acknowledged to Dr. Gladstone that she was in a near-hysterical state over the second disappearance, the theft. She was discovering that she had come to base her stability entirely on the ring. Such dependency was fearful. He asked how she saw this, and how Ithiel figured in it. She said, "The men I meet don't seem to be real persons. Nobody really is anybody. There may be more somebodies than I've been able to see. I don't want to write off about one half of our species. And concentrated desire for so many years may have affected my judgment. Anyway, for me, what a man is seems to be defined by Ithiel. Also, I am *his* truest friend, and he understands that and responds emotionally."

Involuntarily Clara fell into Dr. Gladstone's way of talking. To herself, she would never say "responds emotionally." As the sessions were short, she adopted his lingo to save time, notwithstanding the danger of false statements. Hope brought her here, every effort must be made, but when she looked, looked with all her might at Dr. Gladstone, she could not justify the trust she was asked to place in that samurai beard, the bared teeth it framed, the big fashionable specs, his often baseless confidence in his science. However, it would take the better part of a year to acquaint a new doctor with the fundamentals of her case. She was stuck with this one.

"And I'm very worried about Gina. How do I find out what's happening to her? Should I hire a private investigator? A girl like that survive in Spanish Harlem? No way."

"An expensive proposition," said Dr. Gladstone. "Any alternatives in mind?"

"Wilder does nothing. *He* could get on the case. Like shadow her, make practical use of the thrillers he's read. But he's negotiating with some hopeless wimp who wants to go for the White House."

"Let's get back to the theft, if it *is* a theft."

"It *has* to be. I didn't misplace it again."

"However, it gave you daily anxiety. Why did it occupy so big a place in you?"

"What did I come up with last time we discussed it? I cheated the insurance company and had the ring *and* the money. You could call that white-collar crime. It all added to the importance of my emerald, but I would never have guessed that it would be so shattering to lose it."

"I can suggest a coincidence," said the doctor. "At this bad moment for you I am going on a holiday. My support is removed. And my name is Glad*stone*. Is that why you take the loss so hard?"

Astonished, she gave him a real stare, not a fitting or becoming one. She said, "You may be a stone, but you're not a gem."

When she returned to her office she telephoned Ithiel, her only dependable adviser, to discuss matters.

"I wish you were coming up to New York," she said. "I used to call on Steinsalz when things were urgent."

"He was a great loss to me too."

"He took such interest in people. Short of lending them money. He'd treat you to dinner but never lend a cent. He did listen, though."

"It so happens," said Ithiel (when he was being methodical, a sort of broken flatness entered his voice), "that I have a lunch date next Tuesday with a man in New York."

"Let's say half past three, then?"

Their customary meeting place was St. Patrick's cathedral, near Clara's office, a central location and a shelter in bad weather. "Like a drop for secret agents," Ithiel said. They left the cathedral and went directly to the Helmsley Palace. A quiet corner of the bar was still available at that early hour. "This is on my Gold Card," said Clara. "Now let's see how you look—somewhere between a Spanish grandee and a Mennonite."

Then with executive rapidity she set forth the main facts.

"What's your opinion of Frederic—an occasional stealer or a pro?"

"I think he improvises," said Clara. "Dope? Probably."

"You could find out about his police record, if any. Then ask the Austrian consulate about her. Not telephone her folks in Vienna."

"I knew it would be a relief to talk to you. Now tell me . . . about the ring."

"A loss, I'd guess. Write it off."

"I suppose I'll have to. I indulged myself about it, and look at the trouble it made. There's nothing appropriate. For instance, this luxury bar that fits neither you nor me. In my true feelings you and I are as naked as Adam and Eve. I'm not being suggestive, either. It's not an erotic suggestion, just a simile."

Talk like this, the hint of wildness in it, had the effect of forcing him into earnestness. She could see him applying his good mind to her difficulties, like a person outside pressing his forehead on the windowpane to see what's going on.

As she figured it, he counted on the executive Clara to gain on the subjective Clara. She *did* have the ability to put her house in order. Yet his sympathy for the subjective, personal Clara was very strong. Considering the greater tumult in her, she had done better than he. Even now her life was more coherent than his.

"For a few hundred bucks, I think you can find out where the girl is. Investigators are easy to hire."

"Tell me! I can see why General Haig and such people call on you to analyze the Iranians or the Russians. By the way, Wilder thought you were great on TV with Dobrynin, week before last."

When Ithiel smiled, his teeth were so good you suspected Hollywood dentistry, but they were all his own.

"Dobrynin has some genius, of a low kind. He convinces Americans that Russians are exactly like them. Sometimes he behaves as if he were the senior senator from a fifty-first, all-Russian state. Just a slight accent, but the guys from the Deep South have one also. He sold Gorbachev on this completely, and Gorbachev is selling the whole U.S.A. Which craves to be sold. Deceived, if you prefer."

"Like me, in a way, about the Human Pair."

"You're close to that girl, I see."

"Very close. It would be easy for you to put her down as a well-brought-up kid with a taste for low sex. Resembling me. You'd be wrong. Too bad you can't see her yourself. Your opinion would interest me."

"So she isn't like you?"

"I sure hope not." Clara made a gesture, as if saying, Wipe out these Helmsley Palace surroundings and listen to me. "Don't forget my two suicide attempts. I have a spoonful of something wild in my mixture, my whole sense of . . ."

"Of life . . ."

"Listen to me. You have no idea really how wild and how mixed, or how much territory it takes in. The territory stretches over into death. When I'm drunk with agitation—and it is like being drunk—there's one pulse in me that's a death-beat pulse, and it tempts me to make out with death. It says, Why wait! When I get as intense as that, existence won't hold me. That's the internal horror side of the thing. I'm open to seduction by death. Now you're going to remind me that I'm the mother of three kids."

"Exactly what I was about to do."

"There's no one in the world but you that I'd say this to. You're the one human being I fully confide in. Neither do you have secrets from me. Whatever you didn't admit I saw for myself."

"You certainly did, Clara."

"But we'll never be man and wife. Oh, you don't have to say anything. You love me, but the rest is counterindicated. It's one of those damn paradoxes that have to be waited out. There may even be a parallel to it in your field, in politics. We have the power to destroy ourselves, and maybe the desire, and we keep ourselves in permanent suspense—waiting. Isn't that wild, too? You could tell *me*. You're the expert. You're going to write the book of books about it."

"Now you're making fun of me."

"Not really, Ithiel. If it is the book of books on the subject, it should be written. You may be the man to write it, and I'm not making fun. For *me* it would be funny. Think of a great odalisque, nude and beautiful. And now think of her in eyeglasses and writing books on a lap board."

Over the table they smiled briefly at each other.

"But I want to get back to Gina," said Clara. "You're going to find me a dependable investigator to check out Frederic, and the rest of it. I doubt that she is like me, except in taking chances. But when I told her that the ring was given by a man who loved me, the fact registered completely. What I didn't add was that I bullied you into giving it to me. Don't deny it. I twisted your arm. Then I sentimentalized it. Then I figured out that you continued to love me *because* we didn't marry. And now the ring . . . The girl understands about the ring. The love part of it."

Teddy was stirred, and looked aside. He wasn't ready, and perhaps never would be ready, to go further. No, they never would be man and wife. When they stood up to go, they kissed like friends.

"You'll get me an investigator with a little class . . . the minimum sleaze?"

"I'll tell the man to go to your office, so you can look him over."

"A few things have to be done for you too," said Clara. "That Francine left you in bad shape. You have that somber look that you get when you're up against it."

"Is that what you mean by the Mennonite?"

"There were plenty of Mennonites in Indiana—I can tell that you didn't have any business in New York today except me."

Within ten days she had Gina's address—a fourth-floor walk-up on East 128th Street, care of F. Vigneron. She had a phone number as well. Call? No, she wouldn't speak to her yet. She brought her executive judgment to bear on this, and the advice from this source was to send a note. In her note, she wrote that the children asked for Gina often. Lucy missed her. Even so, she had done Lucy good. You could see the improvements. There was a lot of woman in that small girl, already visible. Then, speaking for herself, she said that she was sorry to have come down so hard on a matter that needn't be spelled out now. She had left Gina few options. She had had no choice but to go. The mystery was why she had gone "uptown" when other choices were possible. However, Gina owed her no explanations. And Clara hoped that she would not feel that she had to turn away from her forever or decide that she, Clara, was an enemy. Anything but a hostile judge, Clara respected her sense of honor.

Asked for a reference on her unlisted mental line, Clara, when reached, would have said about Gina: soft face, soft bust, brown bourgeois-maiden gaze, but firm at decision time. Absolutely ten on a scale of ten.

But in the note she sent to Gina she went on, ladylike, matronly and fair-minded, to wish her well, and concluded, "You should have had some notice, and I believe it only fair that the month should have been rounded out, so since I am not absolutely certain of the correct address, I will leave an envelope with Marta Elvia. Two hundred dollars in cash."

Frederic Vigneron would send her for the money, if he got wind of it.

Gottschalk, the private eye, did his job responsibly; that was about the best that could be said of him. Perhaps half an eye. And not much more ear. Still, he did obtain the facts she asked for. He said of the building in East Harlem, "Of course the city can't run around and condemn every joint it should, or there'd be lots more street people sleeping in the West Side Terminal. But I wouldn't want any nieces of mine living there."

Having done what you could, you went ahead with your life: showered and powdered with talcum in the morning, put on underthings and stockings, chose a skirt and blouse for the day, made up your face for the office, took in the paper, and, if Wilder was sleeping in (he did often), ground your coffee and as the water dripped turned the pages of the *Times* professionally. For a group of magazines owned by a publishing corporation, she was the lady overseeing women's matters. Almost too influential to have a personal life, as she sometimes observed to Ms. Wong. High enough in the power structure, you can be excused from having one, "an option lots of people are glad to exercise."

Nobody called for the money envelope. Marta Elvia's instructions were to give it to Gina only. After a period of keen interest, Clara stopped asking about it. Gottschalk, doing little, sent an occasional memo: "Status quo unchanged." To go with his Latin, Clara figured that Gina had found a modus vivendi with her young Haitian. The weeks, week after week, subdued Clara. You can say that you're waiting only if there is something definite to wait for. During this time it often seemed there wasn't anything. And, "I never feel so bad as when the life I lead stops being characteristic—when it could be anybody else's life," she told Laura Wong.

But coming home one afternoon after a session with Dr. Gladstone (things were so bad that she was seeing him regularly again), she entered her bedroom for an hour's rest before the kids returned from ballet class. She had dropped her shoes and was crawling toward the pillows, her mouth open in the blindness of fatigue, surrendering to the worst of feelings, when she saw that her ring had been placed on the night table. It had been set on a handkerchief, a new object from a good shop. She slipped on her ring and lunged for the phone across the bed, rapidly punching out Marta Elvia's number.

"Marta Elvia," she said, "has anybody been here today? Did anybody come to leave an article for me?" Fifteen years in the U.S. and the woman still spoke incomplete English. "Listen," said Clara. "Did Gina come here today? Did you or anybody let Gina into the apartment? . . . No? Somebody did come in, and Gina gave up her house keys when she left. . . . Sure she could have made a duplicate—she or her boyfriend. . . . Of course I should have changed the lock. . . . No, nothing was taken. On the contrary, the person gave back something. I'm glad I didn't change the lock."

Now Marta Elvia was upset that an outside somebody had got in. Security in this building was one hundred percent. She was sending her husband up to make sure the door hadn't been jimmied open.

"No, no!" said Clara. "There hasn't been illegal entry. What a wild idea!"

Her own ideas at this moment were not less wild. She rang Gina's number in East Harlem. What she got was an answering machine, from which came Frederic's voice, whose Frenchy slickness was offensive. (Clara disliked those telephone devices anyway, and her prejudice extended to the sound of the signal—in this instance a pig squeal.) "This is Mrs. Wilder Velde calling Miss Wegman." Inasmuch as Gina might have prevailed by reasonable means over him, Clara was ready to revise her opinion of Frederic too. (On her scale of ten, she could upgrade him from less than zero to one.)

Next Clara phoned Gottschalk and entered on his tape her request that he call back. She then tried Laura Wong, and finally Wilder in New Hampshire. It was primary time up there; his candidate lagged far behind the field, and you couldn't expect Wilder to be in his hotel room. Ithiel was in Central America. There was no one to share the recovery of the ring with. The strongest lights in the house were in the bathroom, and she turned them on, pressing against the sink to examine the stone and the setting, making sure that the small diamonds were all there. Since Mrs. Peralta had been in that day, she tried her number— she had a crying need to talk with somebody—and this time actually succeeded. "Did anybody come into the house today?"

"Only deliveries, by the service elevator."

During this unsatisfactory conversation Clara had a view of herself in the hall mirror—a bony woman, not young, blond but not fair, gaunt, a long face, a hollow cheek, not rejoicing, and pressing the ringed hand under the arm that held the phone. The big eyes ached, and looked it. Feeling so high, why did she appear so low? But did she think that recovering the ring would make her young?

What she believed—and it was more than a belief; there was triumph in it—was that Gina Wegman had come into the bedroom and placed the ring on the nightstand.

And how had Gina obtained the ring, what had she had to promise, or sacrifice, or pay? Maybe her parents had wired money from Vienna. Suppose that her only purpose during four months had been nothing but restitution, and that the girl had done her time in East Harlem for no other reason? It struck Clara that if Gina had stolen the emerald back from Frederic and run away, then leaving a message on his machine had been a bad mistake. He might put it all together and come after Gina with a gun. There was even a private eye in this quickly fermenting plot. Except that Gottschalk was no Philip Marlowe in a Raymond Chandler story. Nevertheless he was a detective of some kind. He must be licensed to carry a gun. And everybody's mind ran in these psychopathic-melodrama channels streaming with blood, or children's finger-paints, or blood that naïve people took for fingerpaint. The fancy (or hope) that Gottschalk would kill Frederic in a shoot-out was so preposterous that it helped Clara to calm herself.

When she received Gottschalk in her office next day, she was wearing the ring and showed it to him. He said, "That's a high-value object. I hope you don't take public transportation to work." She looked disdainful. There was a livery service. He didn't seem to realize how high her executive bracket was. But he said, "There are people in top positions who insist on using the subway. I could name you a Wall Street woman who goes to work disguised as a bag lady so it isn't worthwhile to hassle her."

"I believe Gina Wegman entered my apartment yesterday and left the emerald by my bed."

"Must've been her."

Gottschalk's personal observation was that Mrs. Velde hadn't slept last night.

"It couldn't have been the *man,*" she said. "What's your professional conclusion about him?"

"Casual criminal. Not enough muscle for street crime."

"She didn't marry him, did she?"

"I could run a check on that. My guess is no."

"What you can find out for me is whether she's still on One hundred twenty-eighth Street. If she grabbed the ring and brought it back, he may do her some harm."

"Well, ma'am, he's been in the slammer a few times for petty stuff. He wouldn't do anything major." Frederic had been one of those boat people lucky enough to reach Florida a few years back. So much Clara knew.

"After stealing your ring, he didn't even know how to fence it."

Clara said, "I have to find out where she's living. I have to see the girl. Get hold of her. I'll pay a bonus—within reason."

"Send her to your house?"

"That might embarrass her—the girls, Mrs. Peralta, my husband. Say I want to have lunch with her. Ask her whether she received my note."

"Let me look into it."

"Quickly. I don't want this dragging on."

"Top priority," said Gottschalk.

She counted on the suite of offices to impress him, and she was glad now that she had paid his bills promptly. Keeping on his good side, taking care from every standpoint to be a desirable client. As for Gottschalk, he was exactly what she had ordered from Ithiel—minimum sleaze. Not much more.

"I'd like a progress report by Friday," she said.

That afternoon she met with Ms. Wong. Moved to talk. And with the gesture of a woman newly engaged, she held out her hand, saying, "Here's the ring. I thought it had gone into the muck for good. It's getting to be a fairy-tale object. With me it's had the funny effect of those trick films they used to show kids—first a building demolished by dynamite. They show it coming down. Then they reverse it in slow motion, and it's put together again."

"Done by means of a magic ring?" said Ms. Wong.

It occurred to Clara that Laura was a mysterious lady too. She was exotic in externals, but in what she said she was perfectly conventional. While your heart was moved, she would still murmur along. If you came and told her you were going to kill yourself, what would she do? Probably nothing. Yet one must talk.

"I can't say what state I'm in," said Clara, "whether I'm pre-dynamite or post-dynamite. I don't suppose I look demolished. . . ."

"Certainly not."

"Yet I feel as if something had come down. There are changes. Gina, for instance, was a girl I took into the house to help with the kids. Little was ever said. I didn't think well of her Caribbean romance, or sex experiment. Just another case of being at sea among collapsing cultures—I sound like Ithiel now, and I don't actually take much stock in the collapsing-culture bit: I'm beginning to see it instead as the conduct of life without input from your soul. Essential parts of people getting mislaid or crowded out—don't ask me for specifics; I can't give them. They're always flitting by me. But what I started to say was how I've come to love that girl. Just as she immediately understood Lucy, how needy Lucy was, in one minute she also got the whole meaning of this ring. And on the decision to get it back for me she left the house. Moving to East Harlem, yet."

"If her Vienna family had a notion . . ."

"I intend to do something for her. That's a special young woman. I certainly will do something. I have to think what it should be. Now, I don't expect her to describe what she went through, and I don't intend to ask her. There are things I wouldn't want anybody to ask me," said Clara. Clifford from Attica was on her mind. On the whole, she kept this deliberately remote, yet if pressed she could recover quite a lot from her memory.

"Have you any idea . . . ?" said Laura Wong.

"About her, not yet, not until I've spoken to her. About myself, however, I do have different views as a result of this. Twice losing and recovering this ring is a sign, a message. It forces me to interpret. For instance, when Francine came in a van and emptied Ithiel's house—that woman is about as human as a toilet plunger!—Ithiel didn't turn to me. He didn't come and say, 'You're unhappy with Wilder. And between us we've had seven marriages. Now, shouldn't you and I . . . ?' "

"Clara, you wouldn't have done that?" said Laura. For once her voice was more real. Clara was struck by the difference.

"I *might* have done it. So far it's been change and change and change. There's pleasure change, and acquisitive change, and there's the dynamic of . . . oh, I don't know. Perhaps of power. Is there no point of rest? Won't the dynamic ever let you go? I felt that Ithiel might be a point of rest. Or I for him. But that was simply goofy. I have an anti-rest character. I think there's too much basic discord in me."

"So the ring stood for hope of Teddy Regler," said Laura Wong.

"The one exception. Teddy. A repeatedly proven exception. There must be others, but I never came across them."

"And do you think . . . ?"

"He'll ever accomplish his aim? I can't say. He can't, either. What he says is that no trained historian will ever do it, only a singular person with a singular eye. Looking at the century with his singular inborn eye, with a genius for observing politics: That's about the way he says it, and perhaps he'll take hold one day and do a wrap-up of the century, the wrap-up of wrap-ups. As for me," said Clara, "I have the kids, with perhaps Wilder thrown in as a fourth child. The last has been unacceptable. What I'd most like now is a quiet life."

"The point of rest?"

"No, I don't expect that. A quiet life in lieu of the point of rest. The point of rest might have been with Ithiel. I have to settle for what I can get—peaceful evenings. Let there be a convent atmosphere, when the kids have gone to bed and I can disconnect the phones and concentrate on Yeats or somebody like that. Not to be too ambitious; it would be enough to get rid of your demons— they're like patients who drift in and out of the mental hospital. In short, come to terms with my anti-rest character."

"So all these years you've never given up hope that Teddy Regler and you . . ."

"Might make a life together, in the end . . . ?" said Clara. Something caused her to hesitate. As they had always done in problematic situations, her eyes turned sideways, looking for an exit, and her country-girl mouth was open but silent.

On Madison Avenue, walking uptown, Clara was thinking, saying to herself in her contralto grumble, This is *totally* off the wall. There's no limit, is there? She wanted me to say that Ithiel and I were finished, so that she could put her own moves on him. Everybody feels free to picture what they like, and I talked Ithiel up until he became too desirable for her to resist, and how long has the little bitch been dreaming of having him for herself! No way! Clara was angry, but she was also laughing about this. So I choose friends, so I choose lovers, so I choose husbands and bankers and accountants and psychiatrists and ministers, all the way down the line. And just now lost my principal confidante. But I have to spin her off very slowly, for if I cut the relationship, she's in a position to hurt me with Wilder. There's also the insurance company, remember, the real owner of this ring. Also, she's so gifted professionally. We still need her layouts.

Meanwhile she had in mind an exceptional, a generous action.

From her office next day, on her private line, she had a preliminary talk about it with Ithiel, just back from Central America. Naturally she couldn't tell him what her goal was. She began by describing the return of her ring, all the strange circumstances. "This very minute, I'm looking at it. Wearing it, I don't feel especially girlish. I'm more like contemplating it."

She could see Ithiel trying on this new development, matching the contemplative Clara against the Clara who had once sunk her long nails into his forearm and left scars that he might have shown General Haig or Henry Kissinger if he had wanted to emphasize a point about violence. He had quite a sense of humor, Ithiel did. He enjoyed telling how, in a men's room at the White House, Mr. Armand Hammer was at the next urinal, and about the discussion on Soviet intentions they had had between the opening and the closing zips.

Or thinking back to the passionate Clara, or to the Clara who had wanted them buried side by side or even in the same grave. This had lately begun to amuse him.

From her New York office, she had continued to talk. So far he had had little to say other than to congratulate her on the recovery of this major symbol, Madison Hamilton's emerald. "This Gina is a special young woman, Ithiel," she told him. "You would have expected such behavior from a Sicilian or a Spanish woman, and not a contemporary, either, but a romantic Stendhal character—a Happy Few type, or a young woman of the Italian Renaissance in one of those Venetian chronicles the Elizabethans took from."

"Not what you would expect from the Vienna of Kurt Waldheim," he said.

"You've got it. And a young person of that quality shouldn't go on tending kids in New York—Gogmagogsville. Now, what I want to suggest is that she go to Washington."

"And you'd like me to find her a job?"

"That wouldn't be easy. She has a student visa, not a green card. I need to get her away from here."

"Save her from the Haitian. I see. However, she may not want to be saved."

"I'll have to find out how she sees it. My hunch is that the Haitian episode is over and she's ready for some higher education. . . ."

"And that's where I come in, isn't it?"

"Don't be light with me about this. I'm asking you to take me seriously. Remember what you said to me not long ago about my moral logic, worked out on my own feminine premises under my own power. . . . Now, I've never known you to talk through your hat on any real subject."

She had been centered, unified, concentrated, heartened, oriented by his description of her, and she couldn't let him withdraw any part of it.

"What I saw was what I said. Years of observation to back it. Does she want to come to Washington?"

"Well, Ithiel, I haven't had an opportunity to ask her. But . . . so that you'll understand me, I've come to love that girl. I've examined minutely every aspect of what probably happened, and I believe that the man stole the ring because their relationship was coming to an end. Their affair was about over. So he made her an accessory to the theft and she went with him only to get my emerald back."

Ithiel said, "And why do you believe this . . . this scenario of yours—that she was through with him, and he was so cunning, and she had such a great sense of honor, or responsibility? All of it sounds more like *you* than like any sample of the general population."

"But what I'm telling you," she said with special emphasis, "is that Gina isn't a sample from the population, and that I love her."

"And you want us to meet. And she'll come under my influence. She'll fall in love with me. So you and I will increase our number. She'll enlist with us. And she and I will cherish each other, and you will have the comfort of seeing me in safe hands, and this will be your blessing poured over the two of us."

"Teddy, you're making fun of me," she said, but she knew perfectly well that he wasn't making fun, that wasn't where the accent fell, and his interpretation was more or less correct, as far as it went.

"We'll never get each other out of trouble," said Ithiel. "Not the amount of trouble we're in. And even that is not so exceptional. And we all know what to expect. Only a few mavericks fight on. That's you I'm speaking of. I like to think that I'm at home with what is real. Your idea of the real is different. Maybe it's deeper than mine. Now, if your young lady has her own reasons for moving down here to Washington, I'll be happy to meet her for your sake and talk to her. But the sort of arrangements that are ideal for your little children—play school, parties, and concerned teachers—can't be extended to the rest of us."

"Oh, Teddy, I'm not such a fool as you take me for," Clara said.

After this conversation, she drew up a memo pad to try to summarize Ithiel's underlying view: The assumptions we make as to one another's motives are so circumscribed, our understanding of the universe and its forces is so false, that the more we analyze, the more injury we do. She knew perfectly well that this memo, like all the others, would disappear. She'd ask herself, "What was I thinking after my talk with Teddy?" and she'd never see this paper anymore.

Now she had to arrange a meeting with Gina Wegman, and that turned out to be a difficult thing to do. She would never have anticipated that it would be so hard. She repeatedly called Gottschalk, who said he was in touch with Gina. He hadn't actually seen her yet. He now had a midtown number for her and occasionally was able to reach her. "Have you said that I'd like a meeting?" said Clara. She thought, It's shame. The poor kid is ashamed.

"She said she was extremely busy, and I believe there's a plan for her to go home."

"To Austria?"

"She speaks English okay, only I'm not getting a clear signal."

Unkindly, Clara muttered that if he'd keep his glasses clean he'd see more. Also, to increase his importance and his fees, he was keeping information from her—or pretending that he had more information than he actually did have. "If you'd give me the number, I could try a direct call," she said. "Now, is the young man with her, there in midtown?"

"That wouldn't be my guess. I think she's with friends, relatives, and I think she's going back to Vienna real soon. I'll give you her number, but before you call her, let me have a few hours more to get supplementary information for you."

"Fine," said Clara, and as soon as Gottschalk was off the line she dialed Gina. She reached her at once. As simple as that.

"Oh, Mrs. Velde. I meant to call you," said Gina. "I was a little put off by that Mr. Gottschalk. He's a detective, and I worried about your attitude, that you thought it was a police matter."

"He's not police at all, he's strictly private. I needed to find out. I would never have threatened. I wanted to know where you were. The man's a moron. Never mind about him. Is it true, Gina, that you're going to Vienna?"

The young woman said, "Tonight, Lufthansa. Via Munich."

"Without seeing me? Why, that's not possible. I must have made you angry. But it's not anger that I feel toward you; just the opposite. And we have to meet before you leave. You must be rushed with last-minute things." Horrified to be losing her, and dilated with heat and breath, her heart swelling suddenly, she was hardly able to speak because of the emotional stoppage of her throat. "Won't you make some time for me, Gina? There's so much to work out, so much between us. Why the rush home?"

"And I would very much like to see you, Mrs. Velde. The hurry is my engagement and marriage."

Clara wildly guessed, She's pregnant. "Are you marrying Frederic?" she said. It was a charged question, nearly a prayer: Don't let her be as crazy as that. Gina was not prepared to answer. She seemed to be considering. But presently she said, "I wouldn't have to go to Vienna, in that case. My fiancé is a man from my father's bank."

Whether or not to explain herself must have been the issue. Explanations, in

Clara's opinion, should be made. Gina had been wavering, but now she agreed, she decided to see Clara after all. Yes, she was going to do it. "Some friends are giving me a cocktail send-off. That's on Madison in the low Seventies. Maybe half an hour beforehand? . . . In your way, you *were* very kind," Clara heard the girl saying.

"Let's make it at the Westbury, then. When? At four o'clock."

Kind, in my way . . . Signifying what? She feels I was crude. But these side issues could be dealt with later. Right now Clara's appointment with Dr. Gladstone must be canceled. Since the fee would have to be paid notwithstanding, he'd have an hour to think deep analytic thoughts, ponder identity problems, Clara told herself with more than a drop of hatred. Was there anybody who was somebody? How was a man like Gladstone to know! Plumbers was what Ithiel called these Gladstone types. He was fond of reminding her that he had quit analysis because nobody was able to tell him what it took to be Ithiel Regler. This sounded haughty, but actually it was the only reasonable thing. It was no more than true. It applied to her as well.

That she should be so firm and assertive was strange, seeing that she was in a fever, trying to regulate an outflow of mingled soiled emotions. In the cab—one of ten thousand cars creeping uptown—she leaned her long neck backward to relieve it of the weight of her head and to control the wildness of her mind, threatened with panic. These gridlocks on Madison Avenue, these absolutely unnecessary mobs, the vehicles that didn't have to be here, carrying idle shoppers or old people with no urgent purpose except to break out of confinement or go and scold someone. Clara was suffocated by this stalling and delay. She exploded engines in her mind, got out at corners and pulled down stoplights with terrible strength. Five of the thirty minutes Gina could give her were already down the drain. Two blocks from the Westbury, she could no longer bear the traffic, and she got out and trotted the rest of the way, the insides of her knees rubbing together as they always did when she was in a rush.

She passed through the four-quartered door into the lobby and there was Gina Wegman just getting up from the tall chair, and how beautiful the girl looked in her round black glossy straw hat with a half veil dropped onto the bridge of her nose. She certainly wasn't gotten up to look contrite, in a dress that showed off her bust and the full lines of her bottom. On the other hand, she wasn't defiant, either. Lively, yes, and brilliant too. She approached Clara with an affectionate gesture so that when they kissed on the cheek Clara captured part of what a passionate man might feel toward a girl like this.

Clara, as she blamed her lateness on the rush hour, was at the same instant dissatisfied with the dress she had put on that day—those big flowers were a mistake, a bad call, and belonged in her poor-judgment closet.

They sat down in the cocktail lounge. At once one of those smothering New York waiters was upon them. Clara wasted no time on him. She ordered a Campari, and as he wrote down the drinks, she said, "Bring them and then don't bother us; we have to cover lots of ground." Then she leaned toward Gina—two heads of fine hair, each with its distinct design. The girl put up her veil. "Now, Gina . . . *tell* me," said Clara.

"The ring looks wonderful on your hand. I'm glad to see it there."

No longer the au pair girl waiting to be spoken to, she held herself like a different person—equal-equal, and more. It was a great thing she had done in America.

"How did you get it into the house?"

"Where did you find it?" asked Gina.

"What does *that* mean?" Clara wanted to know. In her surprise, she fell back on the country girl's simpleminded flat tone of challenge and suspicion. "It was on my night table."

"Yes. Okay then," said Gina.

"One thing I feel terrible about is the hard assignment I gave you. Just about impossible," said Clara. "The alternative was to turn the case over to the police. I suppose you know by now that Frederic has a criminal record—no serious crimes, but they had him on Rikers Island and in the Bronx jail. That would have made trouble, an investigation would have been hard on you, and I wouldn't do that." She lowered her hand to her legs and felt the startling prominence of the muscles at the knee.

Gina did not look embarrassed by this mention of Rikers Island. She must have taken a decision not to be.

Clara never would find out what the affair with Frederic was about. Gina went no further than to acknowledge that her boyfriend had taken the ring. "He said he was walking around the apartment . . ." Imagine, a man like that, lewd and klepto, at large in her home! "He saw the ring, so he put it in his pocket, not even thinking. I said it was given to you by someone you loved, who loved you"—so she definitely *did* understand about the love!—"and I felt responsible because it was me that brought Frederic into the house."

"That made him look blank, I suppose."

"He said that people on Park Avenue didn't understand anything. They didn't like trouble and relied on security to protect them. Once you got past the security arrangements in the lobby, why, they were just as helpless as chickens. Lucky if they weren't killed. No idea of defense."

Clara's gaze was clear and sober. Her upturned nose added dryness to her look. She said, "I have to agree. In my own place I didn't feel that I should lock away the valuables. But he may be right about Park Avenue. This is a class of people that won't think and can't admit. So it is lucky that somebody more vicious than Frederic didn't get in. Maybe Haitians are more lighthearted than some others in Harlem or the Bronx."

"Your class of Park Avenue people?"

"Yes," said Clara. She looked great-eyed again, grimly thinking, My God, what will my kids be up against! "I should thank the man for only stealing, I suppose."

"We have no time to talk about this side of it," said Gina.

These minutes in the bar seemed to be going according to Gina's deliberate plan. Frederic was not to be discussed. Suddenly Clara's impulse was to come down hard on Gina. Why, she was like the carnal woman in the Book of Proverbs who eats and drinks and wipes away all signs of lust with her napkin. But she couldn't sustain this critical impulse. Who could say how the girl got sucked in and how she managed, or what she had to do to recover the ring from such a fellow. I *owe* her. Also, with the kids she was trustworthy. Now then, what are we looking at here? There is some pride in this Gina. She stood up to the New York scene, a young upper-class Vienna girl. There *is* a certain vain-glory playing through. It's false to do the carnal woman number on her. Let's not get so Old Testament. My regular Christmas card from Attica is still arriving. Before marrying this man from Daddy's bank the girl owed herself some excitement, and Gogmagogsville is the ideal place for it. Dr. Gladstone might have pointed out that Clara's thoughts were taking on a hostile color—envious of youth, perhaps. She didn't think so. Nobody, but nobody, can withstand modern temptations. (Try and print your personal currency, and see what you can get for it.) She still felt that her affection for the girl was not misplaced. "Are you sure you want to go flying back—would you think of staying?"

"What should I stay for?"

"I only wondered. If you wanted a different experience of America, you might find it in Washington, D.C."

"What would I be doing there?"

"Serious work. And don't be put off by 'serious'; it wouldn't be dull. I did some of it myself in Cortina d'Ampezzo years ago and had one of the greatest summers of my life. This friend of mine in Washington, the one I did it for, may possibly be a dark horse in the history of the American mind. I think perhaps he's the one with the gifts to put it all in perspective. Everything. If you met him, you'd agree that he was a fascinating man. . . ." Here Clara stopped herself. Without warning, she had sped into a complex intersection, a cloverleaf without a single sign. A pause was imposed on her, and she considered in a silence of many levels where her enthusiasm for this Austrian girl—a pretty girl and a sound one, basically (maybe)—was leading. Did she want to give Ithiel to her? She wanted to reward Gina. All right. And she wanted to find a suitable woman for Ithiel. It was a scandal, the wives he chose. (Or my husbands; not much better.) Again, all right. But what about Frederic? What had she done that she had to veto all discussion of the Haitian connection? And why was this conversation with Clara cramped into twenty minutes? Why was she not invited to the farewell cocktail party? Who would be there?

Now came any number of skeptical scenarios: Gina's parents had come to America to take her home. They had paid Frederic off, and an incidental part of the deal was that he should surrender the ring. Clara could readily imagine such a package. The girl had plenty of reasons to keep Clara away from her friends—possibly her parents. Brash Clara with her hick candor might have put the case point-blank to the rich parents with all their Mitteleuropa culture (bullshit culture, Ithiel might have said). Oh, let them have their party undisturbed. But she wasn't about to send Gina to Washington all done up in gift wrapping—only the present with ribbons would have been Ithiel, handed over to this young woman. No way! Clara decided. Let me be as crude as she accused me of being. I am sure not going to make a marriage to rankle me for life. She stopped the matchmaking pitch she had begun, in her softheaded goodness. Yes, Gina was an unusual girl—that conviction was unchanged—but if Teddy Regler was the man in prospect, no.

"I haven't met him, have I?" Gina said.

"No."

Nor will you ever.

"You'd like to do something for me, wouldn't you?" Gina spoke in earnest.

"Yes, if there were something feasible," said Clara.

"You're a generous woman—exceptionally so. I'm not in a position to go to Washington. Otherwise I might be glad to. And I have to leave you soon, I'm sorry to say. I really am sorry. There's no time to talk about it, but you have meant a lot to me."

That's one thing, Clara was thinking. The people you mean a lot to just haven't got the time to speak to you about it. "Let me tell you quickly," said Clara, "since it has to be quick, what I've been thinking of the stages a woman like me has gone through in her life. Stage one: Everybody is kindly, basically good; you treat 'em right, they'll treat you right—that's baby time. Stage two: Everybody is a brute, butcher, barbarian, rapist, crook, liar, killer, and monster. Stage three: Cynicism *also* is unacceptable, and you begin to put together an improved judgment based on minimal leads or certain selected instances. I don't know what, if anything, you can make of that. . . . Now, before you leave you're going to satisfy my curiosity at least on one point: how you got the ring back. If it cost you money, I want to pay every cent of it. I insist. Tell me how much, and to whom. And how did you get into the apartment? Nobody saw you. Not with a key?"

"Don't talk about costs; there's no money owing," said Gina. "The one thing

I have to tell you is how the ring got to your bedside. I went to Lucy's school and gave it to her."

"You gave an emerald to Lucy! To a young child?"

"I made sure to arrive before her new sitter came for her, and I explained to Lucy what had to be done: Here's your mother's ring, it has to be put on her night table, and here's a nice Madeira handkerchief to put it on."

"What else did you say?"

"There wasn't much else that needed saying. She knew the ring was lost. Well, it was found now. I folded the handkerchief around the ring and put it in her schoolbag."

"And she understood?"

"She's a lot like you."

"How's that? *Tell* me!"

"The same type as you. You mentioned that to me several times. Did I think so? And presently I did begin to think so."

"You could trust her to carry it out, and not to say, not to tell. Why, I was beside myself when the ring turned up on the handkerchief. Where did it drop from! Who could have done it! I even wondered if a burglar had been hired to come in and put it there. Not a word from the kid. She looked straight ahead like a Roman sentry. You asked her not to say?"

"Well, yes. It was better that way. It never occurred to you to ask her about it?"

"How would that ever come up?" said Clara. Not once. My own kid, capable of that.

"I told her to come down to the street again and report to me afterward," said Gina. "I walked behind them from school—Lucy and the new girl, who doesn't know me. And in about fifteen minutes Lucy came to me at the corner and said she had put it where I told her. . . . You're pleased, aren't you?"

"I'm mystified. I'm moved. Frankly, Gina, I don't believe you and I will ever meet again. . . ." The girl didn't disagree, and Clara said, "So I'm going to speak my mind. You weren't going to describe or discuss your experiences in New York—in Harlem: I suppose you were being firm according to your private lights. Your intimacies are your business, but the word I used to describe your attitude was 'vainglory'—the pride of a European girl in New York who gets into a mess and takes credit for getting herself out. But it's far beyond that." Tears fell from Clara's eyes as she took Gina's hand. "I see how you brought it all together through my own child. You gave her something significant to do, and she was equal to it. Most amazing to me is the fact that she didn't talk, she only watched. That level of observation and control in a girl of ten . . . how do you suppose it feels to discover that?"

Gina had been getting ready to stand up, but she briefly sat down again. She said, "I think you found the right word—right for both of us. When I came to be interviewed, the vainglory was all around—you were waving it over me. I wondered whether the lady of the house was like that in America. But you're not an American lady of the house. You have a manner, Mrs. Velde. As if you were directing traffic. 'Turn left, go right—do this, do that.' You have definite ideas."

"Pernickety, maybe?" said Clara. "Did I hurt your feelings?"

"If that means bossy, no. My feelings weren't hurt when I knew you better. You were firm, according to *your* lights. I decided that you were a complete person, and the orders you gave you gave for that reason."

"Oh, wait a minute, I don't see any complete persons. In luckier times I'm sure complete persons did exist. But now? Now that's just the problem. You look around for something to take hold of, and where is it?"

"I see it in you," said Gina. She stood up and took her purse. "You may be reluctant to believe it, because of the disappointment and confusion. Which people are the lost people? This is the hardest thing of all to decide, even about oneself. The day of the fashion show we had lunch, and you made a remark like 'Nobody is anybody.' You were just muttering, talking about your psychiatrist. But when you started to talk about the man in Washington just now, there was no nobody-anybody problem. And when the ring was stolen, it wasn't the lost property that upset you. Lost people lose 'valuables.' You only lost this particular ring." She set her finger on the stone.

How abnormal for two people, one of them young, to have such a mental conversation. Maybe life in New York had forced a girl like Gina to be mental. Clara wondered about that. "Good-bye, Gina."

"Good-bye, Mrs. Velde." Clara was rising, and Gina put her arm about her. They embraced. "With all the disorder, I can't see how you keep track. You do, though. I believe you pretty well know who you are." Gina quickly left the lounge.

Minutes ago (which might have been hours), Clara had entertained mean feelings toward the girl. She intended, even, to give her a hard time, to stroll back with her to her destination, fish for an invitation to the cocktail farewell, talk to her parents, embarrass her with her friends. That was before she understood what Gina had done, how the ring had been returned. But now, when Clara came out of the revolving door, and as soon as she had the pavement under her feet, she started to cry passionately. She hurried, crying, down Madison Avenue, not like a person who belonged there but like one of the homeless, doing grotesque things in public, one of those street people turned loose from an institution. The main source of tears came open. She found a handkerchief and held it to her face in her ringed hand, striding in an awkward hurry. She might have been treading water in New York harbor—it felt that way, more a sea than a pavement, and for all the effort and the motions that she made she wasn't getting anywhere, she was still in the same place. When he described me to myself in Washington, I should have taken Ithiel's word for it, she was thinking. He knows what the big picture is—the big, *big* picture; he doesn't flatter, he's realistic and he's truthful. I do seem to have an idea who it is that's at the middle of me. There may not be more than one in a zillion, more's the pity, that do have. And my own child possibly one of those.

LOOKING FOR
MR. GREEN

Whatsoever thy hand findeth to do,
do it with thy might. . . .

HARD WORK? No, it wasn't really so hard. He wasn't used to walking and stair-climbing, but the physical difficulty of his new job was not what George Grebe felt most. He was delivering relief checks in the Negro district, and although he was a native Chicagoan this was not a part of the city he knew much about—it needed a depression to introduce him to it. No, it wasn't literally hard work, not as reckoned in foot-pounds, but yet he was beginning to feel the strain of it, to grow aware of its peculiar difficulty. He could find the streets and numbers, but the clients were not where they were supposed to be, and he felt like a hunter inexperienced in the camouflage of his game. It was an unfavorable day, too—fall, and cold, dark weather, windy. But, anyway, instead of shells in his deep trench-coat pocket he had the cardboard of checks, punctured for the spindles of the file, the holes reminding him of the holes in player-piano paper. And he didn't look much like a hunter, either; his was a city figure entirely, belted up in this Irish conspirator's coat. He was slender without being tall, stiff in the back, his legs looking shabby in a pair of old tweed pants gone through and fringy at the cuffs. With this stiffness, he kept his head forward, so that his face was red from the sharpness of the weather; and it was an indoors sort of face with gray eyes that persisted in some kind of thought and yet seemed to avoid definiteness of conclusion. He wore sideburns that surprised you somewhat by the tough curl of the blond hair and the effect of assertion in their length. He was not so mild as he looked, nor so youthful; and nevertheless there was no effort on his part to seem what he was not. He was an educated man; he was a bachelor; he was in some ways simple; without lushing, he liked a drink; his luck had not been good. Nothing was deliberately hidden.

He felt that his luck was better than usual today. When he had reported for work that morning he had expected to be shut up in the relief office at a clerk's job, for he had been hired downtown as a clerk, and he was glad to have, instead, the freedom of the streets and welcomed, at least at first, the vigor of the cold and even the blowing of the hard wind. But on the other hand he was not getting on with the distribution of the checks. It was true that it was a city job; nobody expected you to push too hard at a city job. His supervisor, that young Mr. Raynor, had practically told him that. Still, he wanted to do well at it. For one thing, when he knew how quickly he could deliver a batch of checks, he would know also how much time he could expect to clip for himself. And then, too, the clients would be waiting for their money. That was not the most important consideration, though it certainly mattered to him. No, but he wanted to do well, simply for doing-well's sake, to acquit himself decently of a job because he so rarely had a job to do that required just this sort of energy. Of this peculiar energy he now had a superabundance; once it had started to flow, it flowed all too heavily. And, for the time being anyway, he was balked. He could not find Mr. Green.

So he stood in his big-skirted trench coat with a large envelope in his hand and papers showing from his pocket, wondering why people should be so hard to locate who were too feeble or sick to come to the station to collect their own checks. But Raynor had told him that tracking them down was not easy at first and had offered him some advice on how to proceed. "If you can see the postman, he's your first man to ask, and your best bet. If you can't connect with him, try the stores and tradespeople around. Then the janitor and the neighbors. But you'll find the closer you come to your man the less people will tell you. They don't want to tell you anything."

"Because I'm a stranger."

"Because you're white. We ought to have a Negro doing this, but we don't at the moment, and of course you've got to eat, too, and this is public employment. Jobs have to be made. Oh, that holds for me too. Mind you, I'm not letting myself out. I've got three years of seniority on you, that's all. And a law degree. Otherwise, you might be back of the desk and I might be going out into the field this cold day. The same dough pays us both and for the same, exact, identical reason. What's my law degree got to do with it? But you have to pass out these checks, Mr. Grebe, and it'll help if you're stubborn, so I hope you are."

"Yes, I'm fairly stubborn."

Raynor sketched hard with an eraser in the old dirt of his desk, left-handed, and said, "Sure, what else can you answer to such a question. Anyhow, the trouble you're going to have is that they don't like to give information about anybody. They think you're a plainclothes dick or an installment collector, or summons-server or something like that. Till you've been seen around the neighborhood for a few months and people know you're only from the relief."

It was dark, ground-freezing, pre-Thanksgiving weather; the wind played hob with the smoke, rushing it down, and Grebe missed his gloves, which he had left in Raynor's office. And no one would admit knowing Green. It was past three o'clock and the postman had made his last delivery. The nearest grocer, himself a Negro, had never heard the name Tulliver Green, or said he hadn't. Grebe was inclined to think that it was true, that he had in the end convinced the man that he wanted only to deliver a check. But he wasn't sure. He needed experience in interpreting looks and signs and, even more, the will not to be put off or denied and even the force to bully if need be. If the grocer did know, he had got rid of him easily. But since most of his trade was with reliefers, why should he prevent the delivery of a check? Maybe Green, or Mrs. Green, if there was a Mrs. Green, patronized another grocer. And was there a Mrs. Green? It was one of Grebe's great handicaps that he hadn't looked at any of the case records. Raynor should have let him read files for a few hours. But he apparently saw no need for that, probably considering the job unimportant. Why prepare systematically to deliver a few checks?

But now it was time to look for the janitor. Grebe took in the building in the wind and gloom of the late November day—trampled, frost-hardened lots on one side; on the other, an automobile junk yard and then the infinite work of Elevated frames, weak-looking, gaping with rubbish fires; two sets of leaning brick porches three stories high and a flight of cement stairs to the cellar. Descending, he entered the underground passage, where he tried the doors until one opened and he found himself in the furnace room. There someone rose toward him and approached, scraping on the coal grit and bending under the canvas-jacketed pipes.

"Are you the janitor?"

"What do you want?"

"I'm looking for a man who's supposed to be living here. Green."

"What Green?"

"Oh, you maybe have more than one Green?" said Grebe with new, pleasant hope. "This is Tulliver Green."

"I don't think I c'n help you, mister. I don't know any."

"A crippled man."

The janitor stood bent before him. Could it be that he was crippled? Oh, God! what if he was. Grebe's gray eyes sought with excited difficulty to see. But no, he was only very short and stooped. A head awakened from meditation, a strong-haired beard, low, wide shoulders. A staleness of sweat and coal rose from his black shirt and the burlap sack he wore as an apron.

"Crippled how?"

Grebe thought and then answered with the light voice of unmixed candor, "I don't know. I've never seen him." This was damaging, but his only other choice was to make a lying guess, and he was not up to it. "I'm delivering checks for the relief to shut-in cases. If he weren't crippled he'd come to collect himself. That's why I said crippled. Bedridden, chair-ridden—is there anybody like that?"

This sort of frankness was one of Grebe's oldest talents, going back to childhood. But it gained him nothing here.

"No suh. I've got four buildin's same as this that I take care of. I don' know all the tenants, leave alone the tenants' tenants. The rooms turn over so fast, people movin' in and out every day. I can't tell you."

The janitor opened his grimy lips, but Grebe did not hear him in the piping of the valves and the consuming pull of air to flame in the body of the furnace. He knew, however, what he had said.

"Well, all the same, thanks. Sorry I bothered you. I'll prowl around upstairs again and see if I can turn up someone who knows him."

Once more in the cold air and early darkness he made the short circle from the cellarway to the entrance crowded between the brickwork pillars and began to climb to the third floor. Pieces of plaster ground under his feet; strips of brass tape from which the carpeting had been torn away marked old boundaries at the sides. In the passage, the cold reached him worse than in the street; it touched him to the bone. The hall toilets ran like springs. He thought grimly as he heard the wind burning around the building with a sound like that of the furnace, that this was a great piece of constructed shelter. Then he struck a match in the gloom and searched for names and numbers among the writings and scribbles on the walls. He saw WHOODY-DOODY GO TO JESUS, and zigzags, caricatures, sexual scrawls, and curses. So the sealed rooms of pyramids were also decorated, and the caves of human dawn.

The information on his card was, TULLIVER GREEN—APT 3D. There were no names, however, and no numbers. His shoulders drawn up, tears of cold in his eyes, breathing vapor, he went the length of the corridor and told himself that if he had been lucky enough to have the temperament for it he would bang on one of the doors and bawl out "Tulliver Green!" until he got results. But it wasn't in him to make an uproar and he continued to burn matches, passing the light over the walls. At the rear, in a corner off the hall, he discovered a door he had not seen before and he thought it best to investigate. It sounded empty when he knocked, but a young Negress answered, hardly more than a girl. She opened only a bit, to guard the warmth of the room.

"Yes suh?"

"I'm from the district relief station on Prairie Avenue. I'm looking for a man named Tulliver Green to give him his check. Do you know him?"

No, she didn't; but he thought she had not understood anything of what he had said. She had a dream-bound, dream-blind face, very soft and black, shut off. She wore a man's jacket and pulled the ends together at her throat. Her hair was parted in three directions, at the sides and transversely, standing up at the front in a dull puff.

"Is there somebody around here who might know?"

"I jus' taken this room las' week."

He observed that she shivered, but even her shiver was somnambulistic and there was no sharp consciousness of cold in the big smooth eyes of her handsome face.

"All right, miss, thank you. Thanks," he said, and went to try another place.

Here he was admitted. He was grateful, for the room was warm. It was full of people, and they were silent as he entered—ten people, or a dozen, perhaps more, sitting on benches like a parliament. There was no light, properly speaking, but a tempered darkness that the window gave, and everyone seemed to him enormous, the men padded out in heavy work clothes and winter coats, and the women huge, too, in their sweaters, hats, and old furs. And, besides, bed and bedding, a black cooking range, a piano piled towering to the ceiling with papers, a dining-room table of the old style of prosperous Chicago. Among these people Grebe, with his cold-heightened fresh color and his smaller stature, entered like a schoolboy. Even though he was met with smiles and goodwill, he knew, before a single word was spoken, that all the currents ran against him and that he would make no headway. Nevertheless he began. "Does anybody here know how I can deliver a check to Mr. Tulliver Green?"

"Green?" It was the man that had let him in who answered. He was in short sleeves, in a checkered shirt, and had a queer, high head, profusely overgrown and long as a shako; the veins entered it strongly from his forehead. "I never heard mention of him. Is this where he live?"

"This is the address they gave me at the station. He's a sick man, and he'll need his check. Can't anybody tell me where to find him?"

He stood his ground and waited for a reply, his crimson wool scarf wound about his neck and drooping outside his trench coat, pockets weighted with the block of checks and official forms. They must have realized that he was not a college boy employed afternoons by a bill collector, trying foxily to pass for a relief clerk, recognized that he was an older man who knew himself what need was, who had had more than an average seasoning in hardship. It was evident enough if you looked at the marks under his eyes and at the sides of his mouth.

"Anybody know this sick man?"

"No suh." On all sides he saw heads shaken and smiles of denial. No one knew. And maybe it was true, he considered, standing silent in the earthen, musky human gloom of the place as the rumble continued. But he could never really be sure.

"What's the matter with this man?" said shako-head.

"I've never seen him. All I can tell you is that he can't come in person for his money. It's my first day in this district."

"Maybe they given you the wrong number?"

"I don't believe so. But where else can I ask about him?" He felt that this persistence amused them deeply, and in a way he shared their amusement that he should stand up so tenaciously to them. Though smaller, though slight, he was his own man, he retracted nothing about himself, and he looked back at them, gray-eyed, with amusement and also with a sort of courage. On the bench some man spoke in his throat, the words impossible to catch, and a woman answered with a wild, shrieking laugh, which was quickly cut off.

"Well, so nobody will tell me?"

"Ain't nobody who knows."

"At least, if he lives here, he pays rent to someone. Who manages the building?"

"Greatham Company. That's on Thirty-ninth Street."

Grebe wrote it in his pad. But, in the street again, a sheet of wind-driven paper clinging to his leg while he deliberated what direction to take next, it seemed a feeble lead to follow. Probably this Green didn't rent a flat, but a room. Sometimes there were as many as twenty people in an apartment; the real-estate agent would know only the lessee. And not even the agent could tell you who the renters were. In some places the beds were even used in shifts, watchmen or jitney drivers or short-order cooks in night joints turning out after a day's sleep and surrendering their beds to a sister, a nephew, or perhaps a stranger, just off the bus. There were large numbers of newcomers in this terrific, blight-bitten portion of the city between Cottage Grove and Ashland, wandering from house to house and room to room. When you saw them, how could you know them? They didn't carry bundles on their backs or look picturesque. You only saw a man, a Negro, walking in the street or riding in the car, like everyone else, with his thumb closed on a transfer. And therefore how were you supposed to tell? Grebe thought the Greatham agent would only laugh at his question.

But how much it would have simplified the job to be able to say that Green was old, or blind, or consumptive. An hour in the files, taking a few notes, and he needn't have been at such a disadvantage. When Raynor gave him the block of checks Grebe asked, "How much should I know about these people?" Then Raynor had looked as though Grebe were preparing to accuse him of trying to make the job more important than it was. Grebe smiled, because by then they were on fine terms, but nevertheless he had been getting ready to say something like that when the confusion began in the station over Staika and her children.

Grebe had waited a long time for this job. It came to him through the pull of an old schoolmate in the Corporation Counsel's office, never a close friend, but suddenly sympathetic and interested—pleased to show, moreover, how well he had done, how strongly he was coming on even in these miserable times. Well, he was coming through strongly, along with the Democratic administration itself. Grebe had gone to see him in City Hall, and they had had a counter lunch or beers at least once a month for a year, and finally it had been possible to swing the job. He didn't mind being assigned the lowest clerical grade, nor even being a messenger, though Raynor thought he did.

This Raynor was an original sort of guy and Grebe had taken to him immediately. As was proper on the first day, Grebe had come early, but he waited long, for Raynor was late. At last he darted into his cubicle of an office as though he had just jumped from one of those hurtling huge red Indian Avenue cars. His thin, rough face was wind-stung and he was grinning and saying something breathlessly to himself. In his hat, a small fedora, and his coat, the velvet collar a neat fit about his neck, and his silk muffler that set off the nervous twist of his chin, he swayed and turned himself in his swivel chair, feet leaving the ground, so that he pranced a little as he sat. Meanwhile he took Grebe's measure out of his eyes, eyes of an unusual vertical length and slightly sardonic. So the two men sat for a while, saying nothing, while the supervisor raised his hat from his miscombed hair and put it in his lap. His cold-darkened hands were not clean. A steel beam passed through the little makeshift room, from which machine belts once had hung. The building was an old factory.

"I'm younger than you; I hope you won't find it hard taking orders from me," said Raynor. "But I don't make them up, either. You're how old, about?"

"Thirty-five."

"And you thought you'd be inside doing paperwork. But it so happens I have to send you out."

"I don't mind."

"And it's mostly a Negro load we have in this district."

"So I thought it would be."

"Fine. You'll get along. *C'est un bon boulot.* Do you know French?"

"Some."

"I thought you'd be a university man."

"Have you been in France?" said Grebe.

"No, that's the French of the Berlitz School. I've been at it for more than a year, just as I'm sure people have been, all over the world, office boys in China and braves in Tanganyika. In fact, I damn well know it. Such is the attractive power of civilization. It's overrated, but what do you want? *Que voulez-vous?* I get *Le Rire* and all the spicy papers, just like in Tanganyika. It must be mystifying, out there. But my reason is that I'm aiming at the diplomatic service. I have a cousin who's a courier, and the way he describes it is awfully attractive. He rides in the *wagon-lits* and reads books. While we— What did you do before?"

"I sold."

"Where?"

"Canned meat at Stop and Shop. In the basement."

"And before that?"

"Window shades, at Goldblatt's."

"Steady work?"

"No, Thursdays and Saturdays. I also sold shoes."

"You've been a shoe-dog too. Well. And prior to that? Here it is in your folder." He opened the record. "Saint Olaf's College, instructor in classical languages. Fellow, University of Chicago, 1926–27. I've had Latin, too. Let's trade quotations—'Dum spiro spero.'"

" 'De dextram misero.' "

" 'Alea jacta est.' "

" 'Excelsior.' "

Raynor shouted with laughter, and other workers came to look at him over the partition. Grebe also laughed, feeling pleased and easy. The luxury of fun on a nervous morning.

When they were done and no one was watching or listening, Raynor said rather seriously, "What made you study Latin in the first place? Was it for the priesthood?"

"No."

"Just for the hell of it? For the culture? Oh, the things people think they can pull!" He made his cry hilarious and tragic. "I ran my pants off so I could study for the bar, and I've passed the bar, so I get twelve dollars a week more than you as a bonus for having seen life straight and whole. I'll tell you, as a man of culture, that even though nothing looks to be real, and everything stands for something else, and that thing for another thing, and that thing for a still further one—there ain't any comparison between twenty-five and thirty-seven dollars a week, regardless of the last reality. Don't you think that was clear to your Greeks? They were a thoughtful people, but they didn't part with their slaves."

This was a great deal more than Grebe had looked for in his first interview with his supervisor. He was too shy to show all the astonishment he felt. He laughed a little, aroused, and brushed at the sunbeam that covered his head with its dust. "Do you think my mistake was so terrible?"

"Damn right it was terrible, and you know it now that you've had the whip of hard times laid on your back. You should have been preparing yourself for trouble. Your people must have been well-off to send you to the university. Stop me, if I'm stepping on your toes. Did your mother pamper you? Did your father give in to you? Were you brought up tenderly, with permission to go and find out what were the last things that everything else stands for while everybody else labored in the fallen world of appearances?"

"Well, no, it wasn't exactly like that." Grebe smiled. *The fallen world of appearances!* no less. But now it was his turn to deliver a surprise. "We weren't rich. My father was the last genuine English butler in Chicago—"

"Are you kidding?"

"Why should I be?"

"In a livery?"

"In livery. Up on the Gold Coast."

"And he wanted you to be educated like a gentleman?"

"He did not. He sent me to the Armour Institute to study chemical engineering. But when he died I changed schools."

He stopped himself, and considered how quickly Raynor had reached him. In no time he had your valise on the table and all your stuff unpacked. And afterward, in the streets, he was still reviewing how far he might have gone, and how much he might have been led to tell if they had not been interrupted by Mrs. Staika's great noise.

But just then a young woman, one of Raynor's workers, ran into the cubicle exclaiming, "Haven't you heard all the fuss?"

"We haven't heard anything."

"It's Staika, giving out with all her might. The reporters are coming. She said she phoned the papers, and you know she did."

"But what is she up to?" said Raynor.

"She brought her wash and she's ironing it here, with our current, because the relief won't pay her electric bill. She has her ironing board set up by the admitting desk, and her kids are with her, all six. They never are in school more than once a week. She's always dragging them around with her because of her reputation."

"I don't want to miss any of this," said Raynor, jumping up. Grebe, as he followed with the secretary, said, "Who is this Staika?"

"They call her the 'Blood Mother of Federal Street.' She's a professional donor at the hospitals. I think they pay ten dollars a pint. Of course it's no joke, but she makes a very big thing out of it and she and the kids are in the papers all the time."

A small crowd, staff and clients divided by a plywood barrier, stood in the narrow space of the entrance, and Staika was shouting in a gruff, mannish voice, plunging the iron on the board and slamming it on the metal rest.

"My father and mother came in a steerage, and I was born in our house, Robey by Huron. I'm no dirty immigrant. I'm a U.S. citizen. My husband is a gassed veteran from France with lungs weaker'n paper, that hardly can he go to the toilet by himself. These six children of mine, I have to buy the shoes for their feet with my own blood. Even a lousy little white Communion necktie, that's a couple of drops of blood; a little piece of mosquito veil for my Vadja so she won't be ashamed in church for the other girls, they take my blood for it by Goldblatt. That's how I keep goin'. A fine thing if I had to depend on the relief. And there's plenty of people on the rolls—fakes! There's nothin' *they* can't get, that can go and wrap bacon at Swift and Armour anytime. They're lookin' for them by the Yards. They never have to be out of work. Only they rather lay in their lousy beds and eat the public's money." She was not afraid, in a predominantly Negro station, to shout this way about Negroes.

Grebe and Raynor worked themselves forward to get a closer view of the woman. She was flaming with anger and with pleasure at herself, broad and huge, a golden-headed woman who wore a cotton cap laced with pink ribbon. She was barelegged and had on black gym shoes, her Hoover apron was open and her great breasts, not much restrained by a man's undershirt, hampered her arms as she worked at the kid's dress on the ironing board. And the children, silent and white, with a kind of locked obstinacy, in sheepskins and lumberjackets, stood behind her. She had captured the station, and the pleasure this gave her was enormous. Yet her grievances were true grievances. She was telling the truth. But she behaved like a liar. The look of her small eyes was hidden, and while she raged she also seemed to be spinning and planning.

"They send me out college caseworkers in silk pants to talk me out of what I got comin'. Are they better'n me? Who told them? Fire them. Let 'em go and get married, and then you won't have to cut electric from people's budget."

The chief supervisor, Mr. Ewing, couldn't silence her and he stood with folded arms at the head of his staff, bald—bald-headed, saying to his subordinates like the ex–school principal he was, "Pretty soon she'll be tired and go."

"No she won't," said Raynor to Grebe. "She'll get what she wants. She knows more about the relief even than Ewing. She's been on the rolls for years, and she always gets what she wants because she puts on a noisy show. Ewing knows it. He'll give in soon. He's only saving face. If he gets bad publicity, the commissioner'll have him on the carpet, downtown. She's got him submerged; she'll submerge everybody in time, and that includes nations and governments."

Grebe replied with his characteristic smile, disagreeing completely. Who would take Staika's orders, and what changes could her yelling ever bring about?

No, what Grebe saw in her, the power that made people listen, was that her cry expressed the war of flesh and blood, perhaps turned a little crazy and certainly ugly, on this place and this condition. And at first, when he went out, the spirit of Staika somehow presided over the whole district for him, and it took color from her; he saw her color, in the spotty curb fires, and the fires under the El, the straight alley of flamey gloom. Later, too, when he went into a tavern for a shot of rye, the sweat of beer, association with West Side Polish streets, made him think of her again.

He wiped the corners of his mouth with his muffler, his handkerchief being inconvenient to reach for, and went out again to get on with the delivery of his checks. The air bit cold and hard and a few flakes of snow formed near him. A train struck by and left a quiver in the frames and a bristling icy hiss over the rails.

Crossing the street, he descended a flight of board steps into a basement grocery, setting off a little bell. It was a dark, long store and it caught you with its stinks of smoked meat, soap, dried peaches, and fish. There was a fire wrinkling and flapping in the little stove, and the proprietor was waiting, an Italian with a long, hollow face and stubborn bristles. He kept his hands warm under his apron.

No, he didn't know Green. You knew people but not names. The same man might not have the same name twice. The police didn't know, either, and mostly didn't care. When somebody was shot or knifed they took the body away and didn't look for the murderer. In the first place, nobody would tell them anything. So they made up a name for the coroner and called it quits. And in the second place, they didn't give a goddamn anyhow. But they couldn't get to the bottom of a thing even if they wanted to. Nobody would get to know even a tenth of what went on among these people. They stabbed and stole, they did every crime and abomination you ever heard of, men and men, women and women, parents and children, worse than the animals. They carried on their own way, and the horrors passed off like a smoke. There was never anything like it in the history of the whole world.

It was a long speech, deepening with every word in its fantasy and passion and becoming increasingly senseless and terrible: a swarm amassed by suggestion and invention, a huge, hugging, despairing knot, a human wheel of heads, legs, bellies, arms, rolling through his shop.

Grebe felt that he must interrupt him. He said sharply, "What are you talking about! All I asked was whether you knew this man."

"That isn't even the half of it. I been here six years. You probably don't want to believe this. But suppose it's true?"

"All the same," said Grebe, "there must be a way to find a person."

The Italian's close-spaced eyes had been queerly concentrated, as were his muscles, while he leaned across the counter trying to convince Grebe. Now he gave up the effort and sat down on his stool. "Oh—I suppose. Once in a while. But I been telling you, even the cops don't get anywhere."

"They're always after somebody. It's not the same thing."

"Well, keep trying if you want. I can't help you."

But he didn't keep trying. He had no more time to spend on Green. He slipped Green's check to the back of the block. The next name on the list was FIELD, WINSTON.

He found the backyard bungalow without the least trouble; it shared a lot with another house, a few feet of yard between. Grebe knew these two-shack arrangements. They had been built in vast numbers in the days before the swamps were filled and the streets raised, and they were all the same—a board-walk along the fence, well under street level, three or four ball-headed posts for clotheslines, greening wood, dead shingles, and a long, long flight of stairs to the rear door.

A twelve-year-old boy let him into the kitchen, and there the old man was, sitting by the table in a wheelchair.

"Oh, it's d' Government man," he said to the boy when Grebe drew out his checks. "Go bring me my box of papers." He cleared a space on the table.

"Oh, you don't have to go to all that trouble," said Grebe. But Field laid out his papers: Social Security card, relief certification, letters from the state hospital in Manteno, and a naval discharge dated San Diego, 1920.

"That's plenty," Grebe said. "Just sign."

"You got to know who I am," the old man said. "You're from the Govern-ment. It's not your check, it's a Government check and you got no business to hand it over till everything is proved."

He loved the ceremony of it, and Grebe made no more objections. Field emptied his box and finished out the circle of cards and letters.

"There's everything I done and been. Just the death certificate and they can close book on me." He said this with a certain happy pride and magnificence. Still he did not sign; he merely held the little pen upright on the golden-green corduroy of his thigh. Grebe did not hurry him. He felt the old man's hunger for conversation.

"I got to get better coal," he said. "I send my little gran'son to the yard with my order and they fill his wagon with screening. The stove ain't made for it. It fall through the grate. The order says Franklin County egg-size coal."

"I'll report it and see what can be done."

"Nothing can be done, I expect. You know and I know. There ain't no little ways to make things better, and the only big thing is money. That's the only sunbeams, money. Nothing is black where it shines, and the only place you see black is where it ain't shining. What we colored have to have is our own rich. There ain't no other way."

Grebe sat, his reddened forehead bridged levelly by his close-cut hair and his cheeks lowered in the wings of his collar—the caked fire shone hard within the isinglass-and-iron frames but the room was not comfortable—sat and listened while the old man unfolded his scheme. This was to create one Negro million-aire a month by subscription. One clever, good-hearted young fellow elected every month would sign a contract to use the money to start a business employ-ing Negroes. This would be advertised by chain letters and word of mouth, and every Negro wage earner would contribute a dollar a month. Within five years there would be sixty millionaires.

"That'll fetch respect," he said with a throat-stopped sound that came out like a foreign syllable. "You got to take and organize all the money that gets thrown away on the policy wheel and horse race. As long as they can take it away from you, they got no respect for you. Money, that's d' sun of human-kind!" Field was a Negro of mixed blood, perhaps Cherokee, or Natchez; his skin was reddish. And he sounded, speaking about a golden sun in this dark room, and looked—shaggy and slab-headed—with the mingled blood of his face and broad lips, and with the little pen still upright in his hand, like one of the underground kings of mythology, old judge Minos himself.

And now he accepted the check and signed. Not to soil the slip, he held it down with his knuckles. The table budged and creaked, the center of the gloomy, heathen midden of the kitchen covered with bread, meat, and cans, and the scramble of papers.

"Don't you think my scheme'd work?"

"It's worth thinking about. Something ought to be done, I agree."

"It'll work if people will do it. That's all. That's the only thing, anytime. When they understand it in the same way, all of them."

"That's true," said Grebe, rising. His glance met the old man's.

"I know you got to go," he said. "Well, God bless you, boy, you ain't been sly with me. I can tell it in a minute."

He went back through the buried yard. Someone nursed a candle in a shed, where a man unloaded kindling wood from a sprawl-wheeled baby buggy and two voices carried on a high conversation. As he came up the sheltered passage he heard the hard boost of the wind in the branches and against the house fronts, and then, reaching the sidewalk, he saw the needle-eye red of cable tow-ers in the open icy height hundreds of feet above the river and the factories—those keen points. From here, his view was obstructed all the way to the South Branch and its timber banks, and the cranes beside the water. Rebuilt after the Great Fire, this part of the city was, not fifty years later, in ruins again, factories boarded up, buildings deserted or fallen, gaps of prairie between. But it wasn't desolation that this made you feel, but rather a faltering of organization that set free a huge energy, an escaped, unattached, unregulated power from the giant raw place. Not only must people feel it but, it seemed to Grebe, they were com-pelled to match it. In their very bodies. He no less than others, he realized. Say that his parents had been servants in their time, whereas he was supposed not to be one. He thought that they had never done any service like this, which no one visible asked for, and probably flesh and blood could not even perform. Nor could anyone show why it should be performed; or see where the performance would lead. That did not mean that he wanted to be released from it, he realized with a grimly pensive face. On the contrary. He had something to do. To be compelled to feel this energy and yet have no task to do—that was horrible; that was suffering; he knew what that was. It was now quitting time. Six o'clock. He could go home if he liked, to his room, that is, to wash in hot water, to pour a drink, lie down on his quilt, read the paper, eat some liver paste on crackers before going out to dinner. But to think of this actually made him feel a little sick, as though he had swallowed hard air. He had six checks left, and he was determined to deliver at least one of these: Mr. Green's check.

So he started again. He had four or five dark blocks to go, past open lots, condemned houses, old foundations, closed schools, black churches, mounds, and he reflected that there must be many people alive who had once seen the neighborhood rebuilt and new. Now there was a second layer of ruins; centuries of history accomplished through human massing. Numbers had given the place forced growth; enormous numbers had also broken it down. Objects once so new, so concrete that it could never have occurred to anyone they stood for other things, had crumbled. Therefore, reflected Grebe, the secret of them was out. It was that they stood for themselves by agreement, and were natural and not unnatural by agreement, and when the things themselves collapsed the agreement became visible. What was it, otherwise, that kept cities from looking peculiar? Rome, that was almost permanent, did not give rise to thoughts like these. And was it abidingly real? But in Chicago, where the cycles were so fast and the familiar died out, and again rose changed, and died again in thirty years, you saw the common agreement or covenant, and you were forced to think about appearances and realities. (He remembered Raynor and he smiled. Raynor was a clever boy.) Once you had grasped this, a great many things became intelligible. For instance, why Mr. Field should conceive such a scheme. Of course, if people were to agree to create a millionaire, a real millionaire would come into existence. And if you wanted to know how Mr. Field was inspired to think of this, why, he had within sight of his kitchen window the chart, the very bones of a successful scheme—the El with its blue and green confetti of signals. People consented to pay dimes and ride the crash-box cars, and so it was a success. Yet how absurd it looked; how little reality there was to start with. And yet Yerkes, the great financier who built it, had known that he could get people to agree to do it. Viewed as itself, what a scheme of a scheme it seemed, how close to an appearance. Then why wonder at Mr. Field's idea? He had grasped a principle. And then Grebe remembered, too, that Mr. Yerkes had established the Yerkes Observatory and endowed it with millions. Now how did the notion come to him in his New York museum of a palace or his Aegean-bound yacht to give money to astronomers? Was he awed by the success of his bizarre enterprise and therefore ready to spend money to find out where in the universe being and seeming were identical? Yes, he wanted to know what abides; and whether flesh is Bible grass; and he offered money to be burned in the fire of suns. Okay, then, Grebe thought further, these things exist because people consent to exist with them—we have got so far—and also there is a reality which doesn't depend on consent but within which consent is a game. But what about need, the need that keeps so many vast thousands in position? You tell me that, you *private* little gentleman and *decent* soul—he used these words against himself scornfully. Why is the consent given to misery? And why so painfully ugly? Because there is *something* that is dismal and permanently ugly? Here he sighed and gave it up, and thought it was enough for the present moment that he had a real check in his pocket for a Mr. Green who must be real beyond question. If only his neighbors didn't think they had to conceal him.

This time he stopped at the second floor. He struck a match and found a door. Presently a man answered his knock and Grebe had the check ready and showed it even before he began. "Does Tulliver Green live here? I'm from the relief."

The man narrowed the opening and spoke to someone at his back.

"Does he live here?"

"Uh-uh. No."

"Or anywhere in this building? He's a sick man and he can't come for his dough." He exhibited the check in the light, which was smoky—the air smelled of charred lard—and the man held off the brim of his cap to study it.

"Uh-uh. Never seen the name."

"There's nobody around here that uses crutches?"

He seemed to think, but it was Grebe's impression that he was simply waiting for a decent interval to pass.

"No, suh. Nobody I ever see."

"I've been looking for this man all afternoon"—Grebe spoke out with sudden force—"and I'm going to have to carry this check back to the station. It seems strange not to be able to find a person to *give* him something when you're looking for him for a good reason. I suppose if I had bad news for him I'd find him quick enough."

There was a responsive motion in the other man's face. "That's right, I reckon."

"It almost doesn't do any good to have a name if you can't be found by it. It doesn't stand for anything. He might as well not have any," he went on, smiling. It was as much of a concession as he could make to his desire to laugh.

"Well, now, there's a little old knot-back man I see once in a while. He might be the one you lookin' for. Downstairs."

"Where? Right side or left? Which door?"

"I don't know which. Thin-face little knot-back with a stick."

But no one answered at any of the doors on the first floor. He went to the end of the corridor, searching by matchlight, and found only a stairless exit to the yard, a drop of about six feet. But there was a bungalow near the alley, an old house like Mr. Field's. To jump was unsafe. He ran from the front door, through the underground passage and into the yard. The place was occupied. There was a light through the curtains, upstairs. The name on the ticket under the broken, scoop-shaped mailbox was Green! He exultantly rang the bell and pressed against the locked door. Then the lock clicked faintly and a long staircase opened before him. Someone was slowly coming down—a woman. He had the impression in the weak light that she was shaping her hair as she came, making herself presentable, for he saw her arms raised. But it was for support that they were raised; she was feeling her way downward, down the wall, stumbling. Next he wondered about the pressure of her feet on the treads; she did not seem to be wearing shoes. And it was a freezing stairway. His ring had got her out of bed, perhaps, and she had forgotten to put them on. And then he saw that she was not only shoeless but naked; she was entirely naked, climbing down while she talked to herself, a heavy woman, naked and drunk. She blundered into him. The contact of her breasts, though they touched only his coat, made him go back against the door with a blind shock. See what he had tracked down, in his hunting game!

The woman was saying to herself, furious with insult, "So I cain't fuck, huh? I'll show that son of a bitch kin I, cain't I."

What should he do now? Grebe asked himself. Why, he should go. He should turn away and go. He couldn't talk to this woman. He couldn't keep her standing naked in the cold. But when he tried he found himself unable to turn away.

He said, "Is this where Mr. Green lives?"

But she was still talking to herself and did not hear him.

"Is this Mr. Green's house?"

At last she turned her furious drunken glance on him. "What do you want?"

Again her eyes wandered from him; there was a dot of blood in their enraged brilliance. He wondered why she didn't feel the cold.

"I'm from the relief."

"Awright, what?"

"I've got a check for Tulliver Green."

This time she heard him and put out her hand.

"No, no, for *Mr.* Green. He's got to sign," he said. How was he going to get Green's signature tonight!

"I'll take it. He cain't."

He desperately shook his head, thinking of Mr. Field's precautions about identification. "I can't let you have it. It's for him. Are you Mrs. Green?"

"Maybe I is, and maybe I ain't. Who want to know?"

"Is he upstairs?"

"Awright. Take it up yourself, you goddamn fool."

Sure, he was a goddamn fool. Of course he could not go up because Green would probably be drunk and naked, too. And perhaps he would appear on the landing soon. He looked eagerly upward. Under the light was a high narrow brown wall. Empty! It remained empty!

"Hell with you, then!" he heard her cry. To deliver a check for coal and clothes, he was keeping her in the cold. She did not feel it, but his face was burning with frost and self-ridicule. He backed away from her.

"I'll come tomorrow, tell him."

"Ah, hell with you. Don't never come. What you doin' here in the nighttime? Don' come back." She yelled so that he saw the breadth of her tongue. She stood astride in the long cold box of the hall and held on to the banister and the wall. The bungalow itself was shaped something like a box, a clumsy, high box pointing into the freezing air with its sharp, wintry lights.

"If you are Mrs. Green, I'll give you the check," he said, changing his mind.

"Give here, then." She took it, took the pen offered with it in her left hand, and tried to sign the receipt on the wall. He looked around, almost as though to see whether his madness was being observed, and came near to believing that someone was standing on a mountain of used tires in the auto-junking shop next door.

"But are you Mrs. Green?" he now thought to ask. But she was already climbing the stairs with the check, and it was too late, if he had made an error, if he was now in trouble, to undo the thing. But he wasn't going to worry about it. Though she might not be Mrs. Green, he was convinced that Mr. Green was upstairs. Whoever she was, the woman stood for Green, whom he was not to see this time. Well, you silly bastard, he said to himself, so you think you found him. So what? Maybe you really did find him—what of it? But it was important that there was a real Mr. Green whom they could not keep him from reaching because he seemed to come as an emissary from hostile appearances. And though the self-ridicule was slow to diminish, and his face still blazed with it, he had, nevertheless, a feeling of elation, too. "For after all," he said, "he *could* be found!"

COUSINS

JUST BEFORE THE SENTENCING of Tanky Metzger in a case memorable mainly to his immediate family, I wrote a letter—I was induced, pressured, my arm was twisted—to Judge Eiler of the Federal Court. Tanky and I are cousins, and Tanky's sister Eunice Karger kept after me to intercede, having heard that I knew Eiler well. He and I became acquainted years ago when he was a law student and I was presiding over a television program on Channel Seven which debated curious questions in law. Later I was toastmaster at a banquet of the Chicago Council on Foreign Relations, and a picture in the papers showed Eiler and me in dinner jackets shaking hands and beaming at each other.

So when Tanky's appeal was turned down, as it should have been, Eunice got me on the telephone. First she had a cry so passionate that it shook me up in spite of myself. When her control returned she said that I must use my influence. "Lots of people say that you're friends with the judge."

"Judges aren't that way. . . ." I corrected myself: "Some judges may be, but Eiler isn't."

Eunice only pressed harder. "Please, Ijah, don't brush me off. Tanky could get up to fifteen years. I'm not in a position to spell out the entire background. About his associates, I mean. . . ." I knew quite well what she meant; she was speaking of his Mob connections. Tanky had to keep his mouth shut if he didn't want the associates to order his execution.

I said, "I more or less get the point."

"Don't you feel for him?"

"How could I not."

"You've led a very different life from the rest, Ijah, but I've always said how fond you were of the Metzgers."

"It's true."

"And loved our father and our mother, in the old days."

"I'll never forget them."

She lost control again, and why she sobbed so hard, no expert, not even the most discerning, could exactly specify. She didn't do it from weakness. That I can say with certainty. Eunice is not one of your fragile vessels. She is forceful like her late mother, tenacious, determined. Her mother had been honorably direct, limited and primitive.

It was a mistake to say, "I'll never forget them," for Eunice sees herself as her mother's representative here among the living, and it was partly on Shana's account that she uttered such sobs. Sounds like this had never come over this quiet office telephone line of mine. What a disgrace to Shana that her son should be a convicted felon. How would the old woman have coped with such a wound! Still refusing to surrender her mother to death, Eunice (alone!) wept for what Shana would have suffered.

"Remember that my mother idolized you, Ijah. She said you were a genius."

"That she did. It was an intramural opinion. The world didn't agree."

Anyway, here was Eunice pleading for Raphael (Tanky's real name). For his part, Tanky didn't care a damn about his sister.

"Have you been in touch, you two?"

"He doesn't answer letters. He hasn't been returning calls. Ijah! I want him to know that I care!"

Here my feelings, brightened and glowing in the recollection of old times, grew dark and leaden on me. I wish Eunice wouldn't use such language. I find it hard to take. Nowadays WE CARE is stenciled on the walls of supermarkets and loan corporations. It may be because her mother knew no English and also because Eunice stammered when she was a kid that it gives her great satisfaction to be so fluent, to speak as the most advanced Americans now speak.

I couldn't say, "For Christ's sake don't talk balls to me." Instead I had to comfort her because she was heartsick—a layer cake of heartsickness. I said, "You may be sure he knows how you feel."

Gangster though he may be.

No, I can't swear that Cousin Raphael (Tanky) actually is a gangster. I mustn't let his sister's clichés drive me (madden me) into exaggeration. He associates with gangsters, but so do aldermen, city officials, journalists, big builders, fundraisers for charitable institutions—the Mob gives generously. And gangsters aren't the worst of the bad guys. I can name greater evildoers. If I had been a Dante, I'd have worked it all out in full detail.

I asked Eunice pro forma why she had approached me. (I didn't need to be a clairvoyant to see that Tanky had put her up to it.) She said, "Well, you are a public personality."

She referred to the fact that many years ago I invented the famous-trials TV program, and appeared also as moderator, or master of ceremonies. I was then in a much different phase of existence. Having graduated near the top of my law-school class, I had declined good positions offered by leading firms because I felt too active, or kinetic (hyperkinetic). I couldn't guarantee my good behavior in any of the prestigious partnerships downtown. So I dreamed up a show called *Court of Law,* in which significant, often notorious, cases from the legal annals were retried by brilliant students from Chicago, Northwestern, De Paul, or John Marshall. Cleverness, not institutional rank, was where we put the accent. Some of our most diabolical debaters were from the night schools. The opportunities for dialectical subtlety, imposture, effrontery, eccentric display, nasty narcissism, madness, and other qualifications for the practice of law were obvious. My function was to pick entertaining contestants (defense and prosecution), to introduce them, to keep up the pace—to set the tone. With the help of my wife (my then wife, who was a lawyer, too), I chose the cases. She was attracted by criminal trials with civil rights implications. My preference was for personal oddities, mysteries of character, ambiguities of interpretation—less likely to make a good show. But I proved to have a knack for staging these dramas. Before the program I always gave the contestants an early dinner at Fritzel's on Wabash Avenue. Always the same order for me—a strip steak, rare, over which I poured a small pitcher of Roquefort salad dressing. For dessert, a fudge sundae, with which I swallowed as much cigarette ash as chocolate. I wasn't putting on an act. This early exuberance and brashness I later chose to subdue; it presently died down. Otherwise I might have turned into "a laff riot," in the language of *Variety,* a zany. But I saw soon enough that the clever young people whom I would lead in debate (mainly hustlers about to take the bar exam, already on the lookout for clients and avid for publicity) were terribly pleased by my odd behavior. The Fritzel dinner loosened up the participants. During the program I would guide them, goad them, provoke, pit them against one another, override them. At the conclusion, my wife Sable (Isabel: I called her Sable because of her dark coloring) would read the verdict and the decision of the court. Many of our debaters have since become leaders of the bar, rich celebrities. After our divorce, Sable married first one and then another of them. Eventually she made it big in communications—on National Public Radio.

Judge Eiler, then a young lawyer, was more than once a guest on the program.

So to my cousins I remained thirty years later the host and star of *Court of Law,* a media personality. Something magical, attributes of immortality. Almost as though I had made a ton of money, like a Klutznik or a Pritzker. And now I learned that to Eunice I was not only a media figure, but a mystery man as well. "In the years when you were gone from Chicago, didn't you work for the CIA, Ijah?"

"I did not. For five years, out in California, I was in the Rand Corporation, a think tank for special studies. I did research and prepared reports and analyses. Much the kind of thing the private group I belong to here now does for banks. . . ."

I wanted to dispel the mystery—scatter the myth of Ijah Brodsky. But of course words like "research" and "analysis" only sounded to her like spying.

A few years ago, when Eunice came out of the hospital after major surgery, she told me she had no one in all the world to talk to. She said that her husband, Earl, was "not emotionally supportive" (she hinted that he was close-fisted). Her daughters had left home. One was in the Peace Corps and the other, about to graduate from medical school, was too busy to see her. I asked Eunice out to dinner—drinks first in my apartment on Lake Shore Drive. She said, "All these dark old rooms, dark old paintings, these Oriental rugs piled one on top of the other, and books in foreign languages—and living alone" (meaning that I didn't have horrible marital fights over an eight-dollar gas bill). "But you must have girls—lady friends?"

She was hinting at the "boy question." Did the somber luxury I lived in disguise the fact that I had turned queer?

Oh, no. Not that, either. Just singular (to Eunice). Not even a different drummer. I do no marching.

But, to return to our telephone conversation, I finally got it out of Eunice that she had called me at the suggestion of Tanky's lawyer. She said, "Tanky is flying in tonight from Atlantic City"—gambling—"and asked to meet you for dinner tomorrow."

"Okay, say that I'll meet him at the Italian Village on Monroe Street, upstairs in one of the little private rooms, at seven P.M. To ask the headwaiter for me."

I hadn't really talked with Tanky since his discharge from the army, in 1946, when conversation was still possible. Once, at O'Hare about ten years ago, we ran into each other when I was about to board a plane and he was on the incoming flight. He was then a power in his union. (Just what this signified I have lately learned from the papers.) Anyway, he spotted me in the crowd and introduced me to the man he was traveling with. "I want you to meet my famous cousin, Ijah Brodsky," he said. At which moment I was gifted with a peculiar vision: I saw how we might have appeared to a disembodied mind above us both. Tanky was built like a professional football player who had gotten lucky and in middle age owned a ball club of his own. His wide cheeks were like rosy Meissen. He sported a fair curly beard. His teeth were large and square. What are the right words for Tanky at this moment? Voluminous, copious, full of vitamins, potent, rich, insolent. By way of entertainment he was putting his cousin on display—bald Ijah with the eyes of an orangutan, his face flat and round, transmitting a naïveté more suited to a brute from the zoo—long arms, orange hair. I was someone who emitted none of the signals required for serious consideration, a man who was not concerned with the world's work in any category which made full sense. It passed through my thoughts that once, early in the century, when Picasso was asked what young men in France were doing, he answered, *"La jeunesse, c'est moi."* But I had never been in a position to illustrate or represent *anything*. Tanky, in fun, was offering me to his colleague as an intellectual, and while I don't mind being considered clever, I confess I do feel the disgrace of being identified as an intellectual.

By contrast, consider Tanky. He had done well out of his rackets. He was one of those burly people who need half an acre of cloth for a suit, who eat New York sirloin strip steaks at Eli's, put together million-dollar deals, fly to Palm Springs, Las Vegas, Bermuda. Tanky was saying, "In our family, Ijah was the genius. One of them, anyway; we had a couple or three."

I was no longer the law-school whiz kid for whom a brilliant future had been predicted—so much was true. The tone of derision was justified, insofar as I had enjoyed being the family's "rose of expectancy."

As for Tanky's dark associate, I have no idea who he may have been—maybe Tony Provenzano, or Sally (Bugs) Briguglio, or Dorfman of the Teamsters Union insurance group. It was not Jimmy Hoffa. Hoffa was then in jail. Besides, I, like millions of others, would have recognized him. We knew him personally, for after the war Tanky and I had both been employed by our cousin Miltie Rifkin, who at that time operated a hotel in which Hoffa was supposed to have an interest. Whenever Hoffa and his gang came to Chicago, they stayed there. I was then tutoring Miltie's son Hal, who was too fast and foxy to waste time on books. Longing to see action, Hal was only fourteen when Miltie put him in charge of the hotel bar. It amused his parents one summer to let him play manager, so that when liquor salesmen approached him, Miltie could say, "You'll have to see my son Hal; he does the buying. Ask for the young fellow who looks like Eddie Cantor." They would find a fourteen-year-old boy in the office. I was there to oversee Hal, while teaching him the rules governing the use of the ablative (he was a Latin School pupil). I kept an eye on him. A smart little kid of whom the parents were immensely proud.

Necessarily I spent much time in the bar, and so became acquainted with the Hoffa contingent. Goons, mostly, apart from Harold Gibbons, who was highly urbane and in conversation, at least with me, bookish in his interests. The others were very tough indeed, and Cousin Miltie made the mistake of trying to hold his own with them, man to man, a virile brute. He was not equal to this self-imposed challenge. He could be harsh, he accepted nihilism in principle, but the high-powered executive will simply was not there. Miltie couldn't say, as Caesar did to a sentry who had orders not to let him pass, "It's easier for me to kill you than to argue." Hoffas are like that.

Tanky, then just out of the service, was employed by Miltie to search out tax-delinquent property for him. It was one of Miltie's side rackets. Evictions were common. So it was through Miltie Rifkin that Cousin Tanky (Raphael) met Red Dorfman, the onetime boxer who acted as broker between Hoffa and organized crime in Chicago. Dorfman, then a gym teacher, inherited Tanky from his father, from Red, the old boxer. A full set of gang connections was part of the legacy.

These were some of the people who dominated the world in which it was my intention to conduct what are often called "higher activities." To "long for the best that ever was": this was not an abstract project. I did not learn it over a seminar table. It was a constitutional necessity, physiological, temperamental, based on sympathies which could not be acquired. Human absorption in faces, deeds, bodies, drew me toward metaphysics. I had these peculiar metaphysics as flying creatures have their radar. Maturing, I found the metaphysics in my head. And school, as I have just told you, had little to do with it. As a commuting university student sitting for hours on the elevated trains that racketed, bobbled, squealed, pelted at top speed over the South Side slums, I boned up on Plato, Aristotle, or St. Thomas for Professor Perry's class.

But never mind these preoccupations. Here in the Italian Village was Tanky, out on a $500,000 bond, waiting to be sentenced. He didn't look good. He didn't have fast colors after all. His big face was swelled out by years of brutal business. The amateur internist in me diagnosed hypertension—250 over 165 were the numbers I came up with. His inner man was toying with a stroke as the alternative to jail. Tanky kept the Edwardian beard trimmed, for his morale, and that very morning, as this was no time to show white hairs, the barber might have given it a gold rinse. The kink of high vigor had gone out of it, however. Tanky wouldn't have cared for my sympathy. He was well braced, a man ready to take his lumps. The slightest hint that I was sorry would have irritated him. Experienced sorry-feelers will understand me, though, when I say that there was a condensed mass of troubles on his side of the booth. This mass emitted signals for which I lacked the full code.

An old-time joint opposite the First National, where I have my office on the fifty-first floor (those upswept incurves rising, rising), the Italian Village is one of the few restaurants in the city with private recesses for seduction or skulduggery. It dates back to the twenties and is decorated like a saint's-day carnival in Little Italy, with strings of electric bulbs and wheels of lights. It also suggests a shooting gallery. Or an Expressionist stage set. Prohibition fading away, the old Loop was replaced by office buildings, and the Village became a respectable place, known to all the stars of the musical world. Here visiting divas and great baritones gorged on risotto after singing at the Lyric. Signed photos of artists hung on the walls. Still, the place retained its Al Capone atmosphere—sauce as red as blood, the foot smell of cheeses, the dishes of invertebrates raked up from sea mud.

Little was said of a personal nature. I worked across the street? Tanky said. Yes. Had he asked what my days were like, I would have begun by saying that I was up at six to play indoor tennis to start the blood circulating, and that when I got to the office I read the *New York Times,* the *Wall Street Journal, The Economist,* and *Barron's,* and scanned certain printouts and messages prepared by my secretary. Having noted the outstanding facts, I put them all behind me and devoted the rest of the morning to my private interests.

But Cousin Tanky did not ask how my days were spent. He mentioned our respective ages—I am ten years his senior—and said that my voice had deepened as I grew older. Yes. My basso profundo served no purpose except to add depth to small gallantries. When I offer a chair to a lady at a dinner party, she is enveloped in a deep syllable. Or when I comfort Eunice, and God knows she needs it, my incoherent rumble seems to give assurance of stability.

Tanky said, "For some reason you keep track of all the cousins, Ijah."

The deep sound I made in reply was neutral. I didn't think it would be right, even by so much as a hint, to refer to his career in the union or to his recent trial.

"Tell me what happened to Miltie Rifkin, Ijah. He gave me a break when I got out of the army."

"Miltie now lives in the Sunbelt. Married to the switchboard operator from the hotel."

Now, Tanky might have given *me* fascinating information about Miltie, for I know that Cousin Miltie had been dying to draw Hoffa deeper into the hotel operation. Hoffa had such reservoirs of money behind him, all those billions in the pension fund. Miltie was stout, near obese, with a handsome hawk face, profile-proud, his pampered body overdressed, bedizened, his glance defiant and contentious. A clever moneymaker, he was choleric by temperament and, in his fits, dangerously quick to throw punches. It was insane of him to fight so much. His former wife, Libby, weighing upward of 250 pounds, hurrying about the hotel on spike heels, was what we used to call a "suicide blond" (dyed by her own hand). Catering, booking, managing, menacing, bawling out the *garde-manger,* firing housekeepers, hiring bartenders, Libby was all made up like a Kabuki performer. In trying to restrain Miltie (they were less man and wife than business partners), she had her work cut out for her. Several times Miltie complained to Hoffa about one of his goons, whose personal checks were not clearing. The goon—his name escapes me, but for parking purposes he had a clergy sticker on the windshield of his Chrysler—knocked Miltie down in the lobby, then choked him nearly to death. This occurrence came to the attention of Robert F. Kennedy, who was then out to get Hoffa, and Kennedy issued a subpoena for Cousin Miltie to testify before the McClellan Committee. To give evidence against Hoffa's people would have been madness. Libby cried out when word came that a subpoena was on its way: "Now see what you've done. They'll chop you to bits!"

Miltie fled. He drove to New York, where he loaded his Cadillac on the *Queen Elizabeth*. He didn't flee alone. The switchboard operator kept him company. They were guests in Ireland of the American ambassador (linked through Senator Dirksen and the senator's special assistant, Julius Farkash). While staying at the U.S. embassy, Miltie bought land for what was to have become the new Dublin airport. He bought, however, in the wrong location. After which, he and his wife-to-be flew to the Continent in a transport plane carrying the Cadillac. They did crossword puzzles during the flight. Landing in Rome . . .

I spared Tanky these details, many of which he probably knew. Besides, the man had seen so much action that they wouldn't have been worth mentioning. It would have been an infraction of something to speak of Hoffa or to refer to the evasion of a subpoena. Tanky, of course, had been forced to say no to the usual federal immunity offer. It would have been fatal to accept it. One understands this better now that the FBI wiretaps and other pieces of evidence in the Williams-Dorfman trial have been made public. Messages like: "Tell Merkle that if he doesn't sell us the controlling interest in his firm on our terms, we'll waste him. Not only him. Say that we'll also hack up his wife and strangle his kids. And while you're at it, pass the word to his lawyer that we'll do the same to him and his wife, and his kids."

Tanky personally was no killer. He was Dorfman's man of business, one of his legal and financial team. He was, however, sent to intimidate people who were slow to cooperate or repay. He crushed his cigar on the fine finish of desks, and broke the framed photographs of wives and children (which I think in some cases a good idea). Millions of dollars had to be involved. He didn't get violent over trifles.

And naturally it would have been offensive to speak of Hoffa, for Tanky might be one of the few who knew how Hoffa had disappeared. I myself, reading widely (with the motives of a concerned cousin), was persuaded that Hoffa had entered a car on his way to a "reconciliation" meeting in Detroit. He was immediately knocked on the head and probably murdered in the backseat. His body was shredded in one machine, and incinerated in another.

Much knowledge of such happenings was in Tanky's looks, in the puffiness of his face—an edema of deadly secrets. This knowledge made him dangerous. Because of it he would go to prison. The organization, convinced that he was steadfast, would take care of him. What he needed from me was nothing but a private letter to the judge. "Your honor, I submit this statement to you on behalf of the defendant in *U.S.* v. *Raphael Metzger*. The family have asked me to intercede as a friend of the court, and I do so fully convinced that the jury has done its job well. I shall try to persuade you, however, to be lenient in sentencing.

Metzger's parents were decent, good people. . . ." Adding, perhaps, "I knew him in his infancy" or "I was present at his circumcision."

These are not matters to bring to the court's attention: that he was a whopping kid; that nothing so big was ever installed in a high chair; or that he still wears the expression he was born with, one of assurance, of cheerful insolence. His is a case of the Spanish proverb:

Genio y figura
Hasta la sepultura.

The divine or, as most would prefer to say, the genetic stamp visible even in corruption and ruin. And we belong to the same genetic pool, with a certain difference in scale. My frame is much narrower. Nevertheless, some of the same traits are there, creases in the cheeks, a turn at the end of the nose, and most of all, a tendency to fullness in the underlip—the way the mouth works toward the sense-world. You could identify these characteristics also in family pictures from the old country—the Orthodox, totally different human types. Yet the cheekbones of bearded men, a band of forehead under a large skullcap, the shock of a fixed stare from two esoteric eyes, are recognizable still in their descendants.

Cousins in an Italian restaurant, looking each other over. It was no secret that Tanky despised me. How could it be a secret? Cousin Ijah Brodsky, speaking strange words, never really making sense, acting from peculiar motives, obviously flaky. Studied the piano, was touted as some kind of prodigy, made a sensation in the Kimball Building (the Noah's ark of stranded European music masters), worked at Compton's Encyclopedia, edited a magazine, studied languages—Greek, Latin, Russian, Spanish—and also linguistics.

I had taken America up in the wrong way. There was only one language for a realist, and that was Hoffa language. Tanky belonged to the Hoffa school—in more than half its postulates, virtually identical with the Kennedy school. If you didn't speak real, you spoke phony. If you weren't hard, you were soft. And let's not forget that at one time, when his bosses were in prison, Tanky, their steward, managed an institution that owns more real estate than the Chase Manhattan Bank.

But to return to Cousin Ijah: music, no; linguistics, no; he next distinguished himself at the University of Chicago Law School, after he had been disappointed in the university's metaphysicians. He didn't practice law, either; that was just another phase. A star who never amounted to anything. He fell in love with a concert harpist who had only eight fingers. Unrequited, it didn't pan out; she was faithful to her husband. Ijah's wife, who organized the TV show, had been as shrewd as the devil. She couldn't make anything of him, either. Ambitious, she dismissed him when it became plain that Ijah was not cut out for a team player, lacked the instincts of a go-getter. She was like Cousin Miltie's wife, Libby, and thought of herself as one of an imperial pair, the dominant one.

What was Tanky to make of someone like Ijah? Ijah was *not* passive. Ijah *did* have a life plan. But this plan was incomprehensible to his contemporaries. In fact, he didn't appear to have any contemporaries. He had contacts with the living. Not quite the same thing.

The principal characteristic of our existence is *suspense.* Nobody—nobody at all—can say how it's going to turn out.

What was curious and comical to Tanky was that Ijah should be so highly respected and connected. This deep-toned Ijah, a member of so many upper-class clubs and associations, was a gentleman. Tanky's cousin a *gentleman!* Ijah's bald head with the reasonably composed face was in the papers. He obviously made pretty good money (peanuts to Tanky). Maybe he would be reluctant to disclose to a federal judge that he was closely related to a convicted felon. If that was what Tanky thought, he was mistaken.

Years ago, Ijah was a kind of wild-ass type. His TV show was like a Second City act, a Marx Brothers routine. It went on in a fever of absurdities.

Ijah's conduct is much different now. Today he's quiet, he's a gentleman. What does it take to be a gentleman? It used to require hereditary lands, breeding, conversation. Toward the end of the last century, Greek and Latin did it, and I have some of each. If it comes to that, I enjoy an additional advantage in that I don't have to be anti-Semitic or strengthen my credentials as a civilized person by putting down Jews. But never mind that.

"Your Honor, it may be instructive to hear the real facts in a case you have tried. On the bench, one seldom learns what the wider human circumstances are. As Metzger's cousin, I can be amicus curiae in a larger sense.

"I remember Tanky in his high chair. Tanky is what he was called on the Schurz High football squad. To his mother he was R'foel. She called him Folya, or Folka, for she was a village woman, born behind the pale. A tremendous infant, strapped in, struggling with his bonds. A powerful voice and a strong color. Like other infants he must have fed on Pablum or farina, but Cousin Shana also gave him more potent things to eat. She cooked primitive dishes like calf's-foot jelly in her kitchen, and I remember eating stewed lungs, which had a spongy texture, savory but chewy, much gristle. The family lived on Hoyne Street in a brick bungalow with striped awnings, alternating broad bands of white and cantaloupe. Cousin Shana was a person of great force, and she kept house as it had been kept for hundreds of years. She was a wide woman, a kind of human blast furnace. Her style of conversation was exclamatory. She began by saying, in Yiddish, 'Hear! Hear! Hear! Hear!' And then she told you her opinion. It may be that persons of her type have become extinct in America. She made an immense

impression on me. We were fond of each other, and I went to the Metzgers' because I was at home there, and also to see and hear primordial family life.

"Shana's aunt was my grandmother. My paternal grandfather was one of a
dozen men who had memorized the whole of the Babylonian Talmud (or was it
the Jerusalem one? here I am ignorant). All my life I have asked, 'Why do that?'
But it was done.

"Metzger's father sold haberdashery in the Boston Store down in the Loop. In
the Austro-Hungarian Empire he had been trained as a cutter and also as a designer of men's clothing. A man of many skills, he was always nicely dressed,
stocky, bald except for a lock at the front, combed to swerve to the right. Some
men are mutely bald; his baldness was expressive; stressful lumps would form in
his skin, which dissolved with the return of calm. He said little; he grinned and
beamed instead, and if there is a celestial meridian of good nature, it intersected
his face. He had guileless abbreviated teeth with considerable spaces between
them. What else? He was a stickler for respect. Nobody was to take his amia-
bility for granted. When his temper rose, failure to find words gave him a stifled
look, while large lumps came up under his scalp. One seldom saw this, however.
He suffered from a tic of the eyelids. Also, to show his fondness (to boys) he
used harmless Yiddish obscenities—a sign that he took you into his confidence.
You would be friends when you were old enough.

"Just one thing more, Your Honor, if you care about the defendant's personal
background. Cousin Metzger, his father, enjoyed stepping out in the evening,
and he often came to play cards with my father and my stepmother. In winter
they drank tea with raspberry preserves; in summer I was sent to the drugstore
to buy a quart brick of three-layered ice cream—vanilla, chocolate, and straw-
berry. You asked for 'Neapolitan.' It was a penny-ante poker game and often
went on past midnight."

"I understand you're a friend of Gerald Eiler," said Tanky.

"Acquaintance. . . ."

"Ever been to his house?"

"About twenty years ago. But the house is gone, and so is his wife. I also used
to meet him at parties, but the host who gave them passed away. About half of
that social circle is in the cemetery."

As usual, I gave more information than my questioner had any use for, using
every occasion to transmit my sense of life. My father before me also did this.
Such a habit can be irritating. Tanky didn't care who was in the cemetery.

"You knew Eiler before he was on the bench?"

"Oh, long before. . . ."

"Then you might be just the guy to write to him about me."

By sacrificing an hour at my desk I might spare Tanky a good many years of
prison. Why shouldn't I do it for old times' sake, for the sake of his parents,

whom I held in such affection. I *had* to do it if I wanted to continue these exercises of memory. My souvenirs would stink if I let Shana's son down. I had no space to work out whether this was a moral or a sentimental decision.

I might also write to Eiler to show off the influence I so queerly had. Tanky's interpretation of my motives would make a curious subject. Did I want to establish that, bubble brain though I seemed to him, there were sound reasons why a letter from me might carry weight with a veteran of the federal judiciary like Eiler? Or prove that *I* had lived right? He would never concede me that. Anyway, with a long sentence hanging over him, he was in no mood to study life's mysteries. He was sick, deadly depressed.

"It's pretty snazzy across the street over at First National."

Below, in the plaza, is the large Chagall mosaic, costing millions, the theme of which is the Soul of Man in America. I often doubt that old Chagall had the strength necessary to take such a reading. He is too levitational. Too many fancies.

I explained: "The group I'm with advises bankers on foreign loans. We specialize in international law—political economy and so forth."

Tanky said, "Eunice is very proud of you. She sends me clippings about how you're speaking to the Council on Foreign Relations. Or you're sitting in the same box with the governor at the opera. Or were the escort of Mrs. Anwar Sadat when she got an honorary degree. And you play tennis, indoors, with *politicians.*"

How was it that Cousin Ijah's esoteric interests gave him access to these prominent people—art patrons, politicians, society ladies, dictators' widows? Tanky came down heavy on the politicians. About politicians he knew more than I ever would, knew the *real* guys; he had done business with the machine people, he had cash-flow relations with them. He could tell *me* who took from whom, which group owned what, who supplied the schools, hospitals, the county jail and other institutions, who milked public housing, handed out the franchises, made the sweetheart deals. Unless you were a longtime insider, you couldn't find the dark crossings used by the mob and the machine. They were occasionally revealed. Very recently two hit men tried to kill a Japanese dope supplier in his car. Tokyo Joe Eto is his name. He was shot three times in the skull and ballistics experts are unable to explain why not a single bullet penetrated the brain. Having nothing more to lose, Tokyo Joe named the killers, one of whom proved to be a deputy on the county sheriff's payroll. Were other city or county payrollers moonlighting for the Mafia? Nobody proposed to investigate. Cousin Tanky knew the answers to many such questions. Hence the gibing look he gave me in the booth. But even that look was diluted, much below full strength. Facing the shades of the prison house, he was not well. We had our share of wrongdoers in the family, but few who made it to the penitentiary. He didn't mean to discuss this with me, however. All he wanted was that I should use such influence as I might have. It was worth a try. Another iron in the fire. As for my motive in agreeing to intercede, it was too obscure to be worth the labor of examination. Sentiment. Eccentric foolery. Vanity.

"Okay, Raphael. I'll try a letter to the judge."

I did it for Cousin Metzger's tic. For the three bands of Neapolitan ice cream. For the furious upright growth of Cousin Shana's ruddy hair, and the avid veins of her temples and in the middle of her forehead. For the strength with which her bare feet advanced as she mopped the floor and spread the pages of the *Tribune* over it. It was also for Cousin Eunice's stammer, and for the elocution lessons that cured it, for the James Whitcomb Riley recitations she gave to the captive family and the determination of the "a-a-a-a" with which she stood up to the challenge of "When the Frost Is on the Punkin." I did it because I had been present at Cousin Tanky's circumcision and heard his cry. And because his cumbersome body was now wrapped in defeat. The curl had gone out of his beard. He looked like Death's sparring partner and his cheeks were battered under the eyes. And if he thought that *I* was the sentimentalist and *he* the nihilist, he was mistaken. I myself have some experience of evil and of the dissolution of the old bonds of existence; of the sores that have broken out on the body of mankind, which I, however, have the impulse to touch with my own hands.

I wrote the letter because the cousins are the elect of my memory.

"Raphael Metzger's parents, Your Honor, were hardworking, law-abiding people, not so much as a traffic violation on their record. Over fifty years ago, when the Brodskys came to Chicago, the Metzgers sheltered them for weeks. We slept on the floor, as penniless immigrants did in those days. We children were clothed and bathed and fed by Mrs. Metzger. This was before the birth of the defendant. Admittedly, Raphael Metzger became a tough guy. Still, he has committed no violent crimes and it is possible, with such a family background, that he may yet become a useful citizen. In presentencing hearings, doctors have testified that he suffers from emphysema and also from high blood pressure. If he has to serve a sentence in one of the rougher prisons, his health may be irreparably damaged."

This last was pure malarkey. A good federal prison is like a sanatorium. I have been told by more than one ex-convict: "They made a new man out of me in jail. They fixed my hernia and operated my cataracts, they gave me false teeth and fitted me with a hearing aid. On my own, I could never afford it."

A veteran like Eiler has received plenty of clemency letters. Thousands of them are sent by civic leaders, by members of the Congress, and, sure as shooting, by other federal judges, all of them using the low language of high morals—payola letters putting in a good word for well-connected constituents or political buddies, or old friends in the rackets. You can leave it to Judge Eiler to read between the lines.

I may even have been effective. Tanky got a short sentence. Eiler certainly understood that Tanky was acting on instructions from the higher-ups. If there were kickbacks, he didn't keep much of the money. Presumably a few bucks did stick to his fingers, but he never would have owned four large homes, like some of his bosses. I take it, too, that the judge was aware of secret investigations then going on and of indictments being prepared by grand juries. The government was after bigger game. These are not matters which Eiler will ever discuss with me. When we meet, we talk music or tennis, sometimes foreign trade. We gossip about the university. But Eiler was aware that a stiff sentence might have endangered Tanky's life. He would have been suspected of giving information to get out sooner. It is generally agreed that Tanky's patron, Dorfman, was killed last year after his conviction in the Nevada bribery case because he would have been sent to prison for life and he might therefore well have chosen to make a deal with the authorities. Dorfman was shot in the head last winter by two men, executed with smooth skill in a parking lot. The TV cameras took many close-ups of the bloodstained slush. Nobody bothered to wash it away, and in my fantasy the rats came at night to lap it. Expecting to die, Dorfman made no arrangement to protect himself. He hired no bodyguards. A free-for-all shoot-out between bodyguards and hit men might have brought reprisals against his family. So he silently endured the emotions of a doomed man, as he waited for the inevitable hit.

A word about how people think of such things in Chicago, about this life to which all have consented. Buy cheap, sell dear is the very soul of business. The foundations of political stability, of democracy, according even to its eminent philosophers, are swindle and fraud. Now, smoothness in fraud arranges immunity for itself. The top executives, the lawyers at the nucleus of power, the spreaders of the most fatal nets—*they* are never shredded and incinerated, *they* never leave the blood of their brains in parking lots. Therefore Chicagoans accord a certain respect to those four-mansion crooks who risk their lives in crimes of high visibility. We are looking at the fear of death that defines your essential bourgeois. The Chicago public doesn't examine its attitudes as closely as this, but there you are: the Mob big shot has prepared his soul for execution. He *must.* For such elementary reminders that justice in some form still exists the plain man is grateful. (I am having a moment of impotent indignation; let's drop it.)

I have to relate that I was embarrassed by the delivery of a case of Lafite-Rothschild prior to the sentencing. I hadn't yet mailed my letter to the judge. As a member (inactive) of the bar, I record this impropriety with discomfort. Nobody need know. Zimmerman's liquor truck brought me a dozen delicious bottles too conscience-contaminated to be drunk. I gave them to hostesses, as dinner gifts. At least Tanky knew good wine.

At the Italian Village I had ordered Nozzole, a decent Chianti which Tanky barely tasted. Too bad he didn't allow himself to become tipsy. I might have made him an amusing cousinly confidence (off the record for us both). I, too, am involved in the lending of big sums. Tanky dealt in millions. As one who prepares briefing documents, I am involved with the lending of billions to Mexico, Brazil, Poland, and other hopeless countries. That very day, the representative of a West African state had been sent into my office to discuss aspects of his country's hard-currency problems; in particular, restrictions on the importing of European luxury products, especially German and Italian automobiles used by the executive class (in which they made Sunday excursions with their ladies and all the kids to watch the public executions—the big entertainment of the week: he told this to me in his charming Sorbonnish English).

But Tanky would never have responded with confidences about the outfit. So I never did get a chance to open this potentially intriguing exchange between two Jewish cousins who dealt in megabucks.

Where this private, confidential wit might have been, there occurred instead a deep silence. Gulfs of silence are what give a basso profundo like mine its oceanic resonance when talk resumes.

It should be said that it's not my office work that most absorbs me. I am consumed by different interests, passions. I am coming to that.

With time off for good behavior, Tanky would have only about eight full months to serve in a decent jail in the Sunbelt, where as a trained accountant he could reckon on being assigned light work, mostly fooling with computers. You would have thought that this would satisfy him. No, he was restless and pressing. He apparently thought that Eiler might have a soft spot for low-rumbling, off-the-wall Cousin Ijah. He may even have concluded that Ijah "had something" on the judge, if I know anything about the way minds work in Chicago.

In any case, Cousin Eunice telephoned again, to say, "I *must* see you." In her own behalf, she would have said, "I'd *like* to see you." So I knew it was Tanky. What now?

I recognized that I couldn't refuse. I was trapped. For when Coolidge was president the Brodskys had slept on Cousin Shana's floor. We were hungry and she fed us. The words of Jesus and the prophets can never be extracted from the blood of certain people.

Mind, I absolutely agree with Hegel (lectures at Jena, 1806) that the whole mass of ideas that have been current until now, "the very bonds of the world," are dissolving and collapsing like a vision in a dream. A new emergence of Spirit is—or had better be—at hand. Or as another thinker and visionary has put it, mankind was long supported by an unheard music which buoyed it, gave it flow, continuity, coherence. But this humanistic music has ceased, and now there is a different, barbarous music welling up, and a different elemental force has begun to manifest itself, without form as yet.

That, too, is a good way to put the matter: a cosmic orchestra sending out music has suddenly canceled its performance. And where, with regard to the cousins, does that leave us? I confine myself to cousins. I do have brothers, but one of them is a foreign service officer whom I never see, while the other operates a fleet of taxicabs in Tegucigalpa and has written off Chicago altogether. I am blockaded in a small historical port, as it were. I can't sail forth; I can't even extricate myself from the ties of Jewish cousinhood. It may be that the dissolution of the bonds of the world affects Jews in different ways. The whole mass of ideas that have been current until now, the very bonds of the world . . .

What has Tanky to do with bonds or ties? Years in the underworld. Despises his sister. Thinks his cousin Ijah a creep. Here before us is a life to which all have consented. But not Cousin Ijah. Why is he a holdout? What sphere does he think *he* is from? If he doesn't get into the action so gratifying for the most significant and potent people around, where does he satisfy his instincts?

Well, we met in the Italian Village to drink Nozzole. The Village has three stories and three dining rooms, which I call Inferno, Purgatorio, and Paradiso. We ate our veal limone in Paradiso. In his need, Tanky turned to Ijah. Jewish consanguinity—a special phenomenon, an archaism of which the Jews, until the present century stopped them, were in the course of divesting themselves. The world as it was dissolving apparently collapsed on top of them, and the divestiture could not continue.

Okay, now I take Eunice to lunch atop the First National skyscraper, one of the monuments of the most curious present (how weird can these presents get?). I show her the view, and far, far below us is the Italian Village, a thin slice of old-world architecture from Hansel-and-Gretel time. The Village is squeezed on one side by the green opulent swellings of the new Xerox headquarters and on the other by the Bell Savings Corporation.

I am painfully aware that Eunice has had cancer surgery. I know that there is a tormenting rose of scar tissue under her blouse, and she told me when we last met about the pains in her armpit and her terror of recurrence. Her command of medical terminology, by the way, is terrific. And you never get a chance to forget how much behavioral science she has studied. To counteract old affections and pity, I round up in self-defense any number of negative facts about the Metzger family. First, brutal Tanky. Then the fact that old Metzger used to frequent burlesque prick-tease shows when he could spare an hour from his duties at the Boston Store, and I would see him in those horny dark joints on South State Street when I was cutting school. But that was not so negative. It was more touching than sinful. It was his way of coming to life; it was artificial resuscitation. A man of any sexual delicacy may feel himself hit in the genitals by a two-by-four after doing his conjugal duty in the bungalow belt. Cousin Shana was a dear soul but there was nothing of the painted erotic woman about her. Anyway,

South State Street was nothing but meat-and-potatoes lewdness in meat-and-potatoes Chicago. In the refined Orient, even in holy cities, infinitely more corrupt exhibitions were offered to the public.

Then I tried to see what I might convict Cousin Shana of, and how I might disown even her. Toward the end of her life, owner of a large apartment building, she hitchhiked on Sheridan Road to save bus fare. So as to leave more money to Eunice she starved herself, some of the cousins said. They added that she, Eunice, would need every penny of it because her husband, Earl, a Park District employee, deposited his weekly check as soon as he was paid, locked it in his personal savings account. Rejected all financial responsibility. Eunice put the children through school entirely on her own. She was a psychologist with the Board of Education. Mental testing was her profession. (Her *racket*, Tanky might have called it.)

Eunice and I sit down at our reserved table atop the First National Bank and she transmits Tanky's new request. Eagerness to serve her brother consumes her. She is a mother like her own mother, all-sacrificing, and a sister to match. Tanky, who would get to see Eunice once in five years, is now in frequent communication with her. She brings his messages to me. I am like the great fish in the Grimm fairy tale. The fisherman freed him from his net and has been granted three wishes. We are now at wish number two. The fish is listening in the executive dining room. What does Tanky ask? Another letter to the judge, requesting more frequent medical examinations, a visit to a specialist, a special diet. "The stuff he has to eat makes him sick."

The great fish should now say, "Beware!"

Instead he says, "I can try."

He speaks in his deeper tones, a beautiful depth, three notes bowed out on the double bass, or the strange baryton—an ancient stringed instrument, part guitar, part bass viol; Haydn, who loved the baryton, wrote moving trios for it.

Eunice said, "My special assignment is to get him out of there alive."

To resume his existence deeper within the sphere of illicit money, operating out of hotels of the Las Vegas type, looking well (in sickness) amid glittering fixtures designed to make everybody the picture of perfect health.

Eunice was crowded with masses of feeling for which there was no language. She transferred her articulate powers to accessible themes. What made communication difficult was that she was very proud of the special vocabulary she had mastered. She was vain of her degree in educational psychology. "I am a professional person," she said. She got this in as often as possible. She was the fulfillment of her mother's obscure, powerful drive, her ambition for her child. Eunice was not pretty, but to Shana she was infinitely dear. She had been as daintily dressed as other small girls, in print party dresses with underpants (visible) of the same print material, in the fashion of the twenties. Among other kids her age she was, however, a giantess. Besides, the strain of stammering would congest her face. But then she learned to speak bold declarative sentences and these absorbed and contained the terrible energy of her stammer. With formidable discipline, she had harnessed the forces of her curse.

She said, "You've always been willing to advise me. I always felt I could turn to you. I'm grateful, Ijah, that you have so much compassion. It's no secret that my husband is not a supportive individual. He says no to everything I suggest. All money has to be totally separate. 'I keep mine, you hang on to yours,' he tells me. He wouldn't educate the girls beyond high school—as much education as he got. I had to sell Mother's building—I took the mortgage myself. It's a shame that the rates were so low then. They're sky high now. Financially, I took a bath on that deal."

"Didn't Raphael advise you?"

"He said I was crazy to spend my whole inheritance on the girls. What would I do in old age? Earl made the same argument. Nobody should be dependent. He says we must all stand on our own two feet."

"You're unusually devoted to your daughters. . . ."

I knew only the younger one—Carlotta—who had the dark bangs and the arctic figure of an Eskimo. With me this is not a pejorative. I am fascinated by polar regions and their peoples. Carlotta had long, sharp, painted nails, her look was febrile, her conversation passionate and inconsequent. At a family dinner I attended, she played the piano so crashingly that conversation was out of the question, and when Cousin Pearl asked her to play more softly she burst into tears and locked herself in the toilet. Eunice told me that Carlotta was going to resign from the Peace Corps and join an armed settlement on the West Bank.

Annalou, the older daughter, had steadier ambitions. Her grades hadn't been good enough for the better medical schools. Cousin Eunice now gave me an astonishing account of her professional education. "I had to pay extra," she said. "Yes, I had to commit myself to make a big donation to the school."

"Did you say the Talbot Medical School?"

"That's what I said. Even to get to talk to the director, a payoff was necessary. You need a clearance from a trustworthy person. I had to promise Scharfer—"

"Which Scharfer?"

"Our cousin Scharfer the fund-raiser. You have to have a go-between. Scharfer said he would arrange the interview if I would make a gift first to *his* organization."

"Under the table, at a medical school?" I said.

"Otherwise I couldn't get into the director's office. Well, I made a contribution to Scharfer of twelve-five. His price. And then I had to pledge myself to Talbot for fifty thousand dollars."

"Over and above tuition?"

"Over and above. You can guess what a medical degree is worth, the income it guarantees. A small school like Talbot, no endowment, has no funding. You can't hire decent faculty unless you're competitive in salaries, and you can't get accreditation without an adequate faculty."

"So you had to pay?"

"I made a down payment of half, with the balance promised before graduation. No degree until you deliver. It's one of those concealed interfaces the general public never gets to see."

"Were you able to manage all this?"

"Even though Annalou was president of her class, word came that they were expecting the final installment. It made me pretty desperate. Bear in mind that I held a five percent mortgage, and the rate is now about fourteen. Earl wouldn't even talk to me about it. I took the problem to my psychiatrist. His advice was to write to the school director. We formulated a statement—a promise to make good on the twenty-five. I said that I was a person of 'the highest integrity.' When I went to my lawyer to check out the language, he advised against 'highest.' Just 'integrity' was enough. So I wrote, 'On my word as a person of known integrity.' Then Annalou was allowed to graduate, on the strength of this."

"*And . . . ?*" I said.

My question puzzled her. "A twenty-cent stamp saved me a fortune."

"You're not going to pay?"

"I wrote the *letter . . .*" she said.

A difference of emphasis separated us. She sat straighter, rejecting the back of the chair, stiffening herself upward from the base of the spine. Little Eunice had become severely bony, just an old broad, except for the attraction of nobility, the high, prominent profile, the face charged with her mother's color, part blood, part irrationality. Put together, if you can, the contemporary "smarts" she took pride in with these glimpses of patrician antiquity.

But if one of us was an anachronism, it was myself. Again, Cousin Ijah, holding out. With what motive? For unspecified reasons, I didn't congratulate Eunice on her exploit. She longed for me to tell her what a clever thing she had done, how dandy it was, and I seemed determined to disappoint her. What could my puzzling balkiness mean?

"Those words, 'high integrity,' saved you twenty-five thou . . . ?"

"Just 'integrity.' I told you, Ijah, I cut out the 'high.' "

Well, why shouldn't Eunice, too, make advantageous use of a fine word? All the words were up for grabs. Her grasp of politics was better than mine. I didn't like to see the word "integrity" fucked up. I suppose the best reason I could advance was the defense of poetry. That was a stupid reason, given that she was defending her one-breasted body. A metastasis would bankrupt her.

The subject was changed. We talked a little about her husband. He had been busy in Grant Park, on the lakefront. Because of the alarming jump in the crime rate, the park board had decided to cut down concealing shrubbery and demolish the old-style comfort stations. Rapists used the bushes for cover, and women had been stabbed to death in the toilets, so now there were cans of the sentry-box type, admitting only one person at a time. Karger was administering the new installations. So Eunice said with pride, although the account she gave of her husband, when all references were assembled, did not make a favorable impression. Weirdly close-mouthed, he dismissed all attempts at conversation. Conversation not worthwhile. Maybe he was right, I saw his point. On the plus side, he didn't give a damn what people thought of him. He was a stand-up eccentric. His independence appealed to me. He had no act going, anyway.

"I have to pay half the rent," said Eunice. "And also the utilities."

I didn't buy her hard-luck story. "Why do you stay together?"

She explained, "I'm covered by his Blue Cross–Blue Shield. . . ." Most people would have been convinced by this explanation. My response was neutral; I was taking it all under consideration.

When lunch ended, she asked to see what my office was like. "My cousin the genius," she said, very pleased by the size of the room. I must be important to rate so much space on the fifty-first floor of a great building. "I won't ask what you do with all these gadgets, documents, and books. For instance, these huge green books. I'm sure it bores you to have to explain."

The huge faded green books, dating from the beginning of the century, had nothing at all to do with my salaried functions. When I read them I was playing hooky. They were two volumes in the series of reports of the Jesup Expedition, published by the American Museum of Natural History. Siberian ethnography. Fascinating. I was beguiled of my griefs (considerable griefs) by these monographs. Two tribes, the Koryak and the Chukchee, as described by Jochelson and Bogoras, absorbed me totally. Just as old Metzger had been drawn magnetically from the Boston Store (charmed from his clerk's duties) by bump-and-grinders, so I neglected office work for these books. Political radicals Waldemar Jochelson and Waldemar Bogoras (curious Christian names for a pair of Russian Jews) were exiled to Siberia in the 1890s and, in the region where the Soviets later established the worst of their labor camps, Magadan and Kolyma, the two Waldemars devoted years to the study of the native tribes.

About this arctic desert, purified by frosts as severe as fire, I read for my relief as if I were reading the Bible. In winter darkness, even within a Siberian settlement you might be lost if the wind blew you down, for the speed of the snow was such as to bury you before you could recover your feet. If you tied up your dogs you would find them sometimes smothered when you dug them out in the morning. In this dark land you entered the house by a ladder inside the chimney. As the snows rose, the dogs climbed up to smell what was cooking. They fought for places at the chimney tops and sometimes fell into the cauldron. There were photographs of dogs crucified, a common form of sacrifice. The powers of darkness surrounded you. A Chukchee informant told Bogoras that there were invisible enemies who beset human beings from all sides, demanding spirits whose mouths were always gaping. The people cringed and gave ransom, buying protection from these raving ghosts.

The geography of mental travel can't be the same from century to century; the realms of gold move away. They float into the past. Anyway, a wonderful silence formed around me in my office as I read about these tribes and their spirits and shamans—it doubled, quadrupled. It became a tenfold silence, right in the middle of the Loop. My windows look toward Grant Park. Now and then I rested my eyes on the lakefront, where Cousin Karger had sheared away the flowering shrubs to deprive sex maniacs of their cover, and set up narrow single-occupancy toilets. The monumental park, and the yacht basin, with sleek boats owned by lawyers and corporate executives. Sexual brutalities weekdays, at anchor; on Sundays the same frenzied erotomaniacs sail peacefully with the wife and kids. And whether we are preparing a new birth of spirit or the agonies of final dissolution (and this is the *suspense* referred to some pages back) depends on what you think, feel, and will about such manifestations or apparitions, on the kabbalistic skill you develop in the interpretation of these contemporary formations. My intuition is that the Koryak and the Chukchee lead me in the right direction.

So I go into trances over Bogoras and Jochelson at the office. Nobody bothers me much. At conference time I wake up. I become seerlike and the associates like to listen to my analyses. I was right about Brazil, right about Iran. I foresaw the revolution of the mullahs, which the president's advisers did not. But my views had to be rejected. Returns so huge for the lending institutions, and protected by government guarantees—I couldn't expect my recommendations to be accepted. My reward is to be praised as "deep" and "brilliant." Where the kids in Logan Square used to see the eyes of an orangutan, my colleagues see the gaze of a clairvoyant. Nobody comes right out with it, but everybody reads my reports and the main thing is that I am left alone to pursue my spiritual investigation. I pore over an old photograph of Yukaghir women on the bank of the Nalemna River. The far shore barren—snow, rocks, spindling trees. The women are squatting, stringing a catch of big whitefish piled in the foreground, working with needle and thread at thirty degrees below zero, Fahrenheit. Their labor makes them sweat so that they take off their fur bodices and are half naked. They even "thrust large cakes of snow into their bosoms." Primitive women overheating at thirty below and cooling their breasts with snow lumps. As I read I ask myself who in this building, this up-up-upward skyscraper containing thousands, has the strangest imaginations. Who knows what secret ideas others are having, the dreams of these bankers, lawyers, career women—their fancies and mantic visions? They themselves couldn't bring them out, frightened by their crazy intensity. Human beings, by definition, half the time mad.

So who will mind if I eat up these books? Actually, I am rereading them. My first acquaintance with them goes back many years. I was piano player in a bar near the capitol in Madison, Wisconsin. I even sang some specialty numbers, one of which was "The Princess Papooli Has Plenty Papaya." I was rooming with my cousin Ezekiel on the wrong side of the tracks. Zeke, called Seckel in the family, was then lecturing in primitive languages at the state university, but his main enterprise took him to the north woods every week. He drove off each Wednesday in his dusty Plymouth to record Mohican folktales. He had found some Mohican survivors and, in the upper peninsula, he did just as Jochelson had done, with the assistance of his wife, Dr. Dina Brodsky, in eastern Siberia. Seckel assured me that this Dr. Brodsky was a cousin. At the turn of the century, the two Jochelsons had come to New York City to work at the American Museum of Natural History with Franz Boas. Seckel insisted that at that time Dr. Brodsky had looked up the family.

Why were the Jews such avid anthropologists? Among the founders of the science were Durkheim and Lévy-Bruhl, Marcel Mauss, Boas, Sapir, Lowie. They may have believed that they were demystifiers, that science was their motive and that their ultimate aim was to increase universalism. I don't see it that way myself. A truer explanation is the nearness of ghettos to the sphere of Revelation, an easy move for the mind from rotting streets and rancid dishes, a direct ascent into transcendence. This of course was the situation of Eastern Jews. The Western ones were prancing and preening like learned Germans. And were Polish and Russian Jews (in disgrace with civilized judgment, afflicted with tuberculosis and diseased eyes) so far from the imagination of savage practices? They didn't have to make a Symbolist decision to derange their senses; they were born that way. Exotics going out to do science upon exotics. And then it all came out in Rabbinic-Germanic or Cartesian-Talmudic forms.

Cousin Seckel, by the way, had no theorizing bent. His talent was for picking up strange languages. He went down to the Louisiana bayou country to learn an Indian dialect from its last speaker, who was moribund. In a matter of months he spoke the language perfectly. So on his deathbed, the old Indian at last had somebody to talk to, and when he was gone there was only Seckel in possession of the words. The tribe lived on in him alone. I learned one of the Indian love songs from him: "*Hai y'hee, y'hee y'ho*—Kiss me before you go." He urged me to play it in the cocktail lounge. He passed on to me also a recipe for Creole jambalaya (ham, rice, crawfish, peppers, chicken, and tomatoes), which as a single man I have no occasion to cook. He had great skill also as a maker of primitive cat's cradles, and had a learned paper on Indian string-figures to his credit. Some of these cat's cradles I can still manage myself, when there are kids to entertain.

A stout young man, round-backed, Seckel had a Hasidic pallor. His plump face wore earnest lines, and the creases of his forehead resembled the frets of a musical instrument. Dark hair covered his head in virile curls, somewhat dusty from his five-hundred-mile weekly trips to Indian country. Seckel didn't bathe much, didn't often change his underclothes. It didn't matter to the woman who loved him. She was Dutch, Jennie Bouwsma, and carried her books in a rucksack. She appears in my memory wearing a tam and knee socks, legs half bare and looking inflamed in the Wisconsin winter. While in the sack with Seckel, she shouted out loudly. There were no doors, only curtains in our little rooms. Seckel hurried back and forth. His calves and buttocks were strongly developed, white, muscular. I wonder how this classic musculature got into the family.

We rented from the widow of a locomotive engineer. We had the ground floor of an old frame house.

The only book that Seckel picked up that year was *The Last of the Mohicans,* of which he would read the first chapter to put himself to sleep. On the theoretical side, he said he was a pluralist. Marxism was *out.* He also denied the possibility of a science of history—he took a strong position on this. He described himself as a Diffusionist. All culture was invented *once,* and spread from a single source. He had actually read G. Elliot Smith and was committed to a theory of the Egyptian origins of everything.

His sleepy eyes were deceiving. Their dazed look was a screen for labors of linguistics that never stopped. His dimples did double duty, for they were sometimes critical (I refer here to the modern crisis, the source of the *suspense*). I ran into Seckel in Mexico City in 1947, not too long before he died. He was leading a delegation of Indians who knew no Spanish, and since no one in the Mexican civil service could speak their lingo, Seckel was their interpreter and no doubt the instigator of their complaints as well. These silent Indians, men in sombreros and white droopy drawers, the black hair growing at the corners of their lips, came out of the sun, which was their element, into the colonnades of the government building.

All this I remember. The one thing I forget is what I myself was doing in Mexico.

It was through Seckel, via Dr. Dina Brodsky, that I learned of the work of Waldemar Jochelson (presumably a cousin by marriage) on the Koryak. At a ladies' auxiliary sale I bought a charming book called *To the Ends of the Earth* (by John Perkins and the American Museum of Natural History), and found in it a chapter on the tribes of eastern Siberia. Then I recalled the monographs I had first seen years ago in Madison, Wisconsin, and borrowed the two Jesup volumes from the Regenstein Library. The women of Koryak myth, I read, were able to detach their genitalia when necessary and hang them up on the trees;

and Raven, an unearthly comedian, the mythic father of the tribe, when he explored his wife's innards, entering her from behind, found himself first of all standing in a vast chamber. In contemplating such inventions or fantasies, one should bear in mind how hard a life the Koryak led, how they struggled to survive. In winter the fishermen had to hack holes in solid ice to a depth of six feet to drop their lines in the river. Overnight these holes were filled and frozen again. Koryak huts were cramped. A woman, however, was roomy. The tribe's mythic mother was palatial.

Very sympathetic to me (I'm sure she isn't being merely nosy), my assistant, Miss Rodinson, comes into the office to ask why I have been bent over at the window for an hour, apparently staring down into Monroe Street. It's only that these giant mat-green monographs borrowed from the Regenstein are hard to hold, and I rest them on the windowsill. In the eagerness of her sympathy Miss Rodinson perhaps wishes she might enter my thoughts, make herself useful. But what help can she be? Better not enter this lusterless pelagic green, the gateway to a savage Siberia that no longer exists.

Two weeks from now, I am being sent to a conference in Europe, on the rescheduling of debts, and she wants approval for travel arrangements. Will I be landing first in Paris? I say, vaguely, yes. And putting up for two nights at the Montalembert? Then Geneva, and returning via London. All this is routine. She is aware that she isn't getting to me. Then, because I have spoken to her about Tokyo Joe Eto (my interest in such items having increased since Tanky's patron, Dorfman, was murdered), she hands me a clipping from the *Tribune*. The two men who botched the execution of Tokyo Joe have themselves been executed. Their bodies were found in the trunk of a Buick parked in residential Naperville. A terrible stink had been rising from the car and there were flies parading over the lid of the trunk, denser than May Day in Red Square.

Eunice called me again, not about her brother this time but about her Uncle Mordecai, my father's first cousin—the head of the family, insofar as there is a family, and insofar as it has a head. Mordecai—Cousin Motty, as we called him—had been hurt in an automobile accident, and as he was nearly ninety it was a serious matter—and so I was on the telephone with Eunice, speaking from a dark corner of my dark apartment. Evidently I can't really say why I should have had it so dark. I have a clear preference for light and simple outlines, but I am stuck for the right atmosphere. I have made myself surroundings I was not ready for, a Holy Sepulchre atmosphere, far too many Oriental rugs bought from Mr. Hering at Marshall Field's (he recently retired and devotes himself to his horse farm), and books with old bindings, which I long ago stopped reading. My only reading matter for months has been the reports of the Jesup Expedition, and I am attracted to certain books by Heidegger. But you can't browse through Heidegger; Heidegger is hard work. Sometimes I read the poems of Auden as well, or biographies of Auden. That's neither here nor there. I suspect I created these dark and antipathetic surroundings in an effort to revise or rearrange myself at the core. The essentials are all present. What they need is proper arrangement.

Now, why anybody should pursue such a project in one of the great capitals of the American superpower is also a subject of interest. I have never discussed this with anyone, but I have had colleagues say to me (sensing that I was up to something out-of-the-way) that there was so much spectacular action in a city like Chicago, there were so many things going on in the *outer* world, the city itself was so rich in opportunities for *real* development, a center of such wealth, power, drama, rich even in crimes and vices, in diseases, and intrinsic—not accidental—monstrosities, that it was foolish, querulous, to concentrate on oneself. The common daily life was more absorbing than anybody's inmost anything. Well, yes, and I think I have fewer romantic illusions about this inmost stuff than most. Conscious inmosts when you come to look at them are mercifully vague. Besides, I avoid anything resembling a *grandiose initiative.* Also I am not isolated by choice. The problem is that I can't seem to find the contemporaries I require.

I'll get back to this presently. Cousin Mordecai has quite a lot to do with it.

Eunice, on the telephone, was telling me about the accident. Cousin Riva, Motty's wife, was at the wheel, Motty's license having been lifted years ago. Too bad. He had just discovered, after fifty years of driving, what a rearview mirror was for. Riva's license should have been taken away, too, said Eunice, who had never liked Riva (there had been a long war between Shana and Riva; it continued through Eunice). Riva overruled everybody and would not give up her Chrysler. She had become too small to drive that huge machine. Well, she had wrecked it, finally.

"Are they hurt?"

"She wasn't at all. *He* was—his nose and his right hand, pretty bad. In the hospital he developed pneumonia."

I felt a pang at this. Poor Motty, he was already in such a state of damage before the accident.

Eunice went on. News from the frontiers of science: "They can handle pneumonia now. It used to carry them off so fast that the doctors called it 'the old man's friend.' Now they've sent him home. . . ."

"Ah." We had gotten another stay. It couldn't be put off for long, but every reprieve was a relief. Mordecai was the eldest survivor of his generation, and extinction was close, and feelings had to be prepared.

Cousin Eunice had more to tell: "He doesn't like to leave his bed. Even before the accident they had that problem with him. After breakfast he'd get under the covers again. This was hard on Riva, because she likes to be active. She went to business with him every day of her life. She said it was spooky to have Motty covering himself up in bed. It was abnormal behavior, and she forced him to go to a family counselor in Skokie. The woman was very good. She said that all his life he had got up at five A.M. to go to the shop, and it was no wonder after all the sleep he had missed if he wanted to catch up."

I didn't go with this interpretation. I let it pass, however.

"Now let me tell you the very latest," said Eunice. "He still has fluid in the lungs and they have to make him sit up. They force him."

"How do they do it?"

"He has to be strapped into a chair."

"I think I'd rather skip this visit."

"You can't do that. You always were a pet of his."

This was true, and I saw now what I had done: claimed Motty's affection, given him my own, treated him with respect, observed his birthdays, extended to him the love I had felt for my own parents. By such actions, I had rejected certain revolutionary developments of the past centuries, the advanced views of the enlightened, the contempt for parents illustrated with such charm and sharpness by Samuel Butler, who had said that the way to be born was alone, with a twenty-thousand-pound note pinned to your diaper; I had missed the classic lessons of a Mirabeau and his father, of Frederick the Great, of Old Goriot and his daughters, of Dostoyevsky's parricides—shunning what Heidegger holds up before us as "the frightful," using the old Greek words *deinon* and *deinotaton* and telling us that the frightful is the gate to the sublime. The very masses are turning their backs on the family. Cousin Motty in his innocence was unaware of these changes. For these and other reasons—mixed reasons—I was reluctant to visit Cousin Motty, and Eunice was quite right to remind me that this put my affection in doubt. I was in a box. Once under way, these relationships have to be played to the end. I couldn't fink out on him. Now, Tanky, who was Motty's nephew, hadn't set eyes on the old man in twenty years. This was fully rational and consistent. When I last saw him the old man couldn't speak, or wouldn't. He was shrunken. He turned away from me.

"He always loved you, Ijah."

"And I love him."

Eunice said, "He's aware of everything."

"That's what I'm afraid of."

Self-examination, all theoretical considerations set aside, told me that I loved the old man. Imperfect love, I admit. Still, there it was. It had always been there.

Eunice, having discovered to what extent I was subject to cousinly feelings, was increasing her influence over me. So here I was picking her up in my car and driving her out to Lincolnwood, where Motty and Riva lived in a ranch-style house.

When we entered the door, Cousin Riva threw up her now crooked arms in a "hurrah" gesture and said, "Motty will be so happy. . . ."

Quite separate from this greeting was the look her shrewd blue eyes gave us. She didn't at all care for Eunice, and for fifty years she had taken a skeptical view of me, not lacking in sympathy but waiting for me to manifest trustworthy signs of normalcy. To me she had become a dear old lady who was also very tough-minded. I remembered Riva as a full-figured, dark-haired, plump, straight-legged woman. Now all the geometry of her figure had changed. She had come down in the knees like the jack of a car, to a diamond posture. She still made an effort to move with speed, as if she were dancing after the Riva she had once been. But that she was no longer. The round face had lengthened, and a Voltairean look had come into it. Her blue stare put it to you directly: Read me the riddle of this absurd transformation, the white hair, the cracked voice. My transformation, and for that matter yours. Where is your hair, and why are you stooped? And perhaps there were certain common premises. All these physical alterations seem to release the mind. For me there are further suggestions: that as the social order goes haywire and the constraints of centuries are removed, and the seams of history open, as it were, walls come apart at the corners, bonds dissolve, and we are freed to think for ourselves—provided we can find the strength to make use of the opportunity—to escape through the gaps, not succumbing in lamentations but getting on top of the collapsed pile.

There were children and grandchildren, and they satisfied Riva, undoubtedly, but she was not one of your grannies. She had been a businesswoman. She and Motty had built a large business out of a shop with two delivery wagons. Sixty years ago Cousin Motty and his brother Shimon, together with my father, their first cousin, and a small workforce of Polish bakers, had supplied a few hundred immigrant grocery stores with bread and kaiser rolls, and with cakes—fry cakes, layer cakes, coffee cakes, cream puffs, bismarcks, and eclairs. They had done it all in three ovens fired with scrap wood—mill edgings with the bark still on them, piled along the walls—and with sacks of flour and sugar, barrels of jelly, tubs of shortening, crates of eggs, long hod-shaped kneading vats, and fourteen-foot slender peels that slipped in and out of the heat to bring out loaves. Everybody was coated in flour except Cousin Riva, in an office under the staircase, where she kept the books and did the billing and the payroll. My father's title at the shop was Manager, as if the blasting ovens and the fragrance filling the whole block had anything to do with "Management." He could never Manage anything. Nerve Center of Anxieties would have been a better title, with the chief point of concentration in the middle of his forehead, like a third eye for all that might go wrong in the night, when he was in charge. They built a large business (not my father, who went out on his own and was never connected with any sizable success), and the business expanded until it reached the limits of its era, when it could not adapt itself to the conditions set by supermarkets—refrigerated long-distance shipping, uniformity of product, volume (demands for millions of dozens of kaiser rolls). So the company was liquidated. Nobody was to blame for that.

Life entered a new phase, a wonderful or supposedly wonderful period of retirement—Florida and all that, places where the warm climate favors dreaming, and people, if they haven't become too restless and distorted, may recover the exaltation of a prior state of being. Out of the question, as we all know. Well, Motty made an earnest effort to be a good American. A good American makes propaganda for whatever existence has forced him to become. In Chicago, Motty went to his downtown club for a daily swim. He was a "character" down there. For a decade he entertained the membership with jokes. These were excellent jokes. I had heard most of them from my father. Many of them required some knowledge of the old country—Hebrew texts, parables, proverbs. Much of it was fossil material, so that if you were unaware that in the shtetl the Orthodox, as they went about their tasks, recited the Psalms to themselves in an undertone, you had to ask for footnotes. Motty wished, and deserved, to be identified as a fine, cheerful old man who had had a distinguished career, perhaps the city's best baker, rich, magnanimous, a person of known integrity. But when the older members of the club died off, there was nobody to exchange such weighty values with. Motty, approaching ninety, still latched on to people to tell them funny things. These were his gift offerings. He repeated himself. The commodity brokers, politicians, personal-injury lawyers, bagmen and fixers, salesmen and promoters who worked out at the club lost patience with him. He was offensive in the locker room, wrapped in his sheet. Nobody knew what he was talking about. Too much Chinese in his cantos, too much Provençal. The club asked the family to keep him at home.

"Forty years a member," said Riva.

"Yes, but all his contemporaries are dead. The new people don't appreciate him."

I had always thought that Motty with his endless jokes was petitioning for acceptance, pleading his case, and that by entertaining in the locker room he suffered a disfigurement of his nature. He had spoken much less when he was younger. As a young boy at the Russian bath among grown men, I had admired Motty's size and strength when we squatted in the steam. Naked, he resembled an Indian brave. Crinkly hair grew down the center of his head. His dignity was a given of his nature. Now there was no band of hair down the middle. He had shrunk. His face was reduced. During his decade of cheer when he swam and beamed, pure affection, he was always delighted to see me. He said, "I have reached the *shmonim*"—eighties—"and I do twenty lengths a day in the pool." Then, "Have you heard this one?"

"I'm sure I haven't."

"Listen. A Jew enters a restaurant. Supposed to be good, but it's filthy."

"Yes."

"And there isn't any menu. You order your meal from the tablecloth, which is stained. You point to a spot and say, 'What's this? *Tzimmes?* Bring me some.' "

"Yes."

"And the waiter writes no check. The customer goes straight to the cashier. She picks up his necktie and says, 'You ate *tzimmes.*' But then the customer belches and she says, 'Ah, you had radishes, too.' "

This is no longer a joke but a staple of your mental life. When you've heard it a hundred times it becomes mythic, like Raven crawling into his wife's interior and finding himself in a vast chamber. All jokes, however, have now stopped.

Before we go upstairs, Cousin Riva says, "I see where the FBI has done a Greylord Sting operation on your entire profession and there will be hundreds of indictments."

No harm intended. Riva is being playful, without real wickedness, simply exercising her faculties. She likes to tease me, well aware that I don't practice law, don't play the piano, don't do any of the things I was famous for (with intramural fame). Then she says, her measured way of speaking unchanged, "We mustn't allow Motty to lie down, we have to force him to sit up, otherwise the fluid will accumulate in his lungs. The doctor has ordered us to strap him in."

"He can't take that well."

"Poor Motty, he hates it. He's escaped a couple of times. I feel bad about it. We all do. . . ."

Motty is belted into an armchair. The buckles are behind him. My first impulse is to release him, despite doctor's orders. Doctors prolong life, but how Motty feels about the rules they impose cannot be known. He acknowledges our visit with a curt sign, slighter than a nod, then turns his head away. It is humiliating to be seen like this. It occurs to me that in the letter to Judge Eiler it had crossed my mind that Tanky in his high chair had struggled in silence, determined to tear free from his straps.

Motty is not ready to talk—not able. So nothing at all is said. It is a visit and we stand visiting. What do I want with Motty anyway, and why have I made a trip from the Loop to molest him? His face is even smaller than when I saw him last—*genio* and *figura* making their last appearance, the components about to get lost. He is down to nature now, and reckons directly with death. It's no great kindness to come to witness this.

In my first recollections, Eunice stood low, sucking her thumb. Now Eunice is standing high, and it's Riva who is low. Cousin Riva's look is contracted. No way of guessing what she thinks. The TV is switched off. Its bulging glass is like the forehead of an intrusive somebody who has withdrawn into his evil secret, inside the cokey (brittle gray) cells of the polished screen. Behind the drawn drapes is North Richmond Street, static and empty like all other nice residential streets, all the human interest in them siphoned off by bigger forces, by the main action. Whatever is not plugged into the main action withers and is devoured by death. Motty became the patriarch-comedian when his business was liquidated. Now there are no forms left for life to assume.

Something has to be said at last, and Eunice calls upon her strengths, which are scientific and advisory. She seems, moreover, to be prompted by a kind of comic instinct. She says, "You ought to have physiotherapy for Uncle Motty's hand, otherwise he'll lose the use of it. I'm *very* surprised that this has been neglected."

Cousin Riva is furious at this. She already blames herself for the accident, she had been warned not to drive, and also for the strapped chair, but she will not allow Cousin Eunice to take such a critical tone. "I think I can be relied upon to look after my husband," she says, and leaves the room. Eunice follows her, and I can hear her making a fuller explanation to the "layman," persisting. The cure of her stutter fifty years ago sold her forever on professional help. "Send for the best" is her slogan.

To sit on the bed, I move aside Riva's books and magazines. It comes back to me that she used to like Edna Ferber, Fannie Hurst, and Mary Roberts Rinehart. Once at Lake Zurich, Illinois, she let me read her copy of *The Circular Staircase*. With this came all of the minute particulars, unnecessarily circumstantial. The family drove out one summer day in three cars and on the way out of town Cousin Motty stopped at a hardware store on Milwaukee Avenue and bought a clothesline to secure the picnic baskets on the roof of the Dodge. He stood on the bumpers and on the running board and lashed the baskets everywhich way, crisscross.

Like the dish in which you clean watercolor brushes, Lake Zurich is yellow-green, the ooze is deep, the reeds are thick, the air is close, and the grove smells not of nature but of sandwiches and summer bananas. At the picnic table there is a poker game presided over by Riva's mother, who has drawn down the veil of her big hat to keep off the mosquitoes and perhaps also to conceal her looks from the other players. Tanky, about two years old, escapes naked from his mother and the mashed potatoes she cries after him to eat. Shana's brothers, Motty and Shimon, walk in the picnic grounds, discussing bakery matters. Mountainous Shimon has a hump, but it is a hump of strength, not a disfigurement. Huge hands hang from his sleeves. He cares nothing for the seersucker jacket that covers his bulging back. He bought it, he owns it, but by the way he wears it he turns it against itself. It becomes some sort of anti-American joke. His powerful step destroys small vegetation. He is deadly shrewd and your adolescent secrets burn up in the blue fire of his negating gaze. Shimon didn't like me. My neck was too long, my eyes were too alien. I was studious. I held up a false standard, untrue to real life. Cousin Motty defended me. I can't say that he was entirely in the right. Cousin Shana used to say of me, "The boy has an open head." What she meant was that book learning was easy for me. As far as they went, Cousin Shimon's intuitions were more accurate. On the shore of Lake Zurich I should have been screaming in the ooze with the other kids, not reading a stupid book (it had an embossed monochrome brown binding) by Mary Roberts Rinehart. I was refusing to hand over my soul to "actual conditions," which are the conditions uncovered now by the FBI's sting. (The disclosures of corruption won't go very far; the worst of the bad guys have little to fear.)

Cousin Shana was on the wrong track. What she said is best interpreted as metaphysics. It wasn't the *head* that was open. It was something else. We enter the world without prior notice, we are manifested before we can be aware of manifestation. An original self exists or, if you prefer, an original soul. It may be as Goethe suggested, that the soul is a theater in which Nature can show itself, the only such theater that it has. And this makes sense when you attempt to account for some kinds of passionate observation—the observation of cousins, for example. If it were just observation in the usual sense of the term, what would it be worth? But if it is expressed "As a man is, so he sees. As the eye is formed, such are its powers," that is a different matter. When I ran into Tanky and his hoodlum colleague at O'Hare and thought what a disembodied William Blake eye above us might see, I was invoking my own fundamental perspective, that of a person who takes into reckoning distortion in the ordinary way of seeing but has never given up the habit of referring all truly important observations to that original self or soul.

I believed that Motty in his silence was consulting the "original person." The distorted one could die without regrets, perhaps was already dead.

The seams open, the bonds dissolve, and the untenability of existence releases you back again to the original self. Then you are free to look for real being under the debris of modern ideas, and in a magical trance, if you like, or with a lucidity altogether different from the lucidity of *approved* types of knowledge.

It was at about this moment that Cousin Motty beckoned me with his head. He had something to say. It was very little. Almost nothing. Certainly he said nothing that I was prepared to hear. I didn't expect him to ask to be unbuckled. As I bent toward him I put one hand on his shoulder, sensing that he would want me to. I'm sure he did. And perhaps it would have been appropriate to speak to him in his native language, as Seckel in the bayous had spoken to his Indian, the last of his people. The word Motty now spoke couldn't have been *"Shalom."* Why should he give such a conventional greeting? Seeing how he had puzzled me, he turned his eyes earnestly on me—they were very large. He tried again.

So I asked Riva why he was saying this, and she explained, "Oh, he's saying 'Scholem.' Over and over he reminds me that we've been receiving mail for you from Scholem Stavis. . . ."

"From Cousin Scholem? . . . Not *Shalom.*"

"He must not have an address for you."

"I'm unlisted. And we haven't seen each other in thirty years. You could have told him where to reach me."

"My dear, I had my hands full. I wish you would take all this stuff away. It fills a whole drawer in my pantry, and it's been on Motty's mind as unfinished business. He'll feel much better. When you take it."

As she said "take all this stuff away" she glanced toward Eunice. It was a heavy glance. "Take this cross from me" was her message. Sighing, she led me to the kitchen.

Scholem Stavis, a Brodsky on his mother's side, was one of the blue-eyed breed of cousins, like Shimon and Seckel. When Tanky in that memorable moment at O'Hare Airport had spoken of geniuses in the family—"We had a couple or three"—he was referring also to Scholem, holding the pair of us up to ridicule. "If you're so smart, how come you ain't rich?" was the category his remark fell into, together with "How many divisions does the Pope have?" Old-style immigrant families had looked eagerly for prodigies. Certain of the children had tried to gratify their hopes. You couldn't blame Tanky for grinning at the failure of such expectations.

Scholem and I, growing up on neighboring streets, attending the same schools, had traded books, and since Scholem had no trivial interests, it was Kant and Schelling all the way, it was Darwin and Nietzsche, Dostoyevsky and Tolstoy, and in our senior year in high school it was Oswald Spengler. A whole year was invested in *The Decline of the West*. In his letters (Riva gave me a Treasure Island shopping bag to carry them in) Scholem reminded me of these shared interests. He wrote with a dated dignity that I rather appreciated. He sounded just a little like the Constance Garnett translations of Dostoyevsky. He addressed me as "Brodsky." I still prefer the Garnett translations to all later ones. It isn't real Dostoyevsky if it doesn't say, "Just so, Porfiry Petrovitch," or "I worshipped Tanya, as it were." I take a more slam-bang approach to things myself. I have a weakness for modern speed and even a touch of blasphemy. I offer as an example Auden's remark about Rilke, "The greatest lesbian poet since Sappho." Just to emphasize that we can't afford to forget the dissolution of the bonds (announced at Jena, 1806). But of course I didn't dispute the superiority of Dostoyevsky or Beethoven, whom Scholem always mentioned as the Titans. Scholem had been and remained a Titanist. The documents I brought home from Riva's pantry kept me up until four in the morning. I didn't sleep at all.

It was Scholem's belief that he had made a discovery in biology that did with Darwin what Newton had done with Copernicus, and what Einstein had done with Newton, and the development and application of Scholem's discovery made possible a breakthrough in philosophy, the first major breakthrough since the *Critique of Pure Reason*. I might have predicted from my early recollections of him that Scholem wouldn't do anything by halves. He was made of durable stuff. Wear out? Well, in the course of nature we all wore out, but life would never crack him. In the old days we would walk all over Ravenswood. He could pack more words into a single breath than any talker I ever knew, and in fact he resisted breathing altogether, as an interruption. White-faced, thin, queerly elastic in his gait, thumbs hooked into the pockets of his pants, he was always ahead of me, in a pale fever. His breath had an odor like boiled milk. As he lectured, a white paste formed in the corners of his mouth. In his visionary state he hardly heard what you were saying, but ran galactic rings around you in a voice stifled with urgency. I thought of him later when I came to read Rimbaud, especially the "Bateau Ivre"—a similar intoxication and storming of the cosmos, only Scholem's way was abstruse, not sensuous. On our walks he would pursue some subject like Kant's death categories, and the walk-pursuit would take us west on Foster Avenue, then south to the great Bohemian Cemetery, then around and around North Park College and back and forth over the bridges of the drainage canal. Continuing our discussion in front of automobile showrooms on Lawrence Avenue, we were not likely to notice our gestures distorted in the plate-glass windows.

He looked altogether different in the color photo that accompanied the many documents he had mailed. His eyebrows were now thick and heavy, color dark, aspect grim, eyes narrowed, mouth compressed and set in deep folds. Scholem hadn't cracked, but you could see how much pressure he had had to withstand. It had driven hard into his face, flattened the hair to his skull. In one of the Holy Sepulchre corners of my apartment, I studied the picture closely. Here was a man really worth examining, an admirable cousin, a fighter made of stern stuff.

By contrast, I seemed to myself a slighter man. I could understand why I had tried my hand at the entertainment business instead, a seriocomic MC on Channel Seven—Second City cabaret stuff, dinner among the hoods and near-hoods at Fritzel's, even cutting a caper on Kupcinet's inane talk show before self-respect counseled me to knock it off. I now took a more balanced view of myself. Still, I recognized that in matters of the intellect I had yielded first honors to Cousin Scholem Stavis. Even now the unwavering intensity of his face, the dilation of his nose breathing fire earthward, tell you what sort of man this is. Since the snapshot was taken near his apartment house, you can see the scope of his challenge, for behind him is residential Chicago, a street of Chicago six-flats, a good address sixty years ago, with all the middle-class graces available to builders in the twenties—a terrifying setting for a man like Scholem. Was this a street to write philosophy in? It's because of places like this that I hate the evolutionism that tells us we must die in stages of boredom for the eventual perfection of our species.

But in these streets Cousin Scholem actually did write philosophy. Before he was twenty-five years old he had already broken new ground. He told me that he had made the first real advance since the eighteenth century. But before he could finish his masterpiece the Japanese attacked Pearl Harbor, and the logic of his revolutionary discoveries in biology, philosophy, and world history made it necessary for him to enter the armed forces—as a volunteer, of course. I worked hard over the pages he had sent, trying to understand the biological and world-historical grounds of all this. The evolution of gametes and zygotes; the splitting of plants in monocotyledons and dicotyledons, of the animals into annelids and vertebrates—these were familiar to me. When he moved from these into a discussion of the biological foundations of modern politics, it was only my good-will that he took with him, not my understanding. The great landmasses were held by passive, receptive nations. Smaller states were the aggressive impregnating forces. No résumé would help; I'd have to read the full text, he wrote. But Right and Left, he wished to tell me now, were epiphenomena. The main current would turn finally into a broad, centrist, free evolutionary continuum which was just beginning to reveal its promise in the Western democracies. From this it is easy to see why Scholem enlisted. He came to the defense not only of democracy but also of his theories.

He was an infantry rifleman and fought in France and Belgium. When American and Russian forces met on the Elbe and cut the German armies in two, Cousin Scholem was in one of the patrols that crossed the river. Russian and American fighting men cheered, drank, danced, wept, and embraced. Not hard to imagine the special state of a Northwest Side Chicago kid whose parents emigrated from Russia and who finds himself a fighter in Torgau, in the homeland of Kant and Beethoven, a nation that had organized and carried out the mass murder of Jews. I noted just a while ago that an Ijah Brodsky, his rapt soul given over to the Chukchee and the Koryak, could not be certain that his thoughts were the *most* curious in the mental mass gathered within the First National building, at the forefront of American capitalism in its subtlest contemporary phase. Well, neither can one be certain that among the embracing, weeping, boozing soldiers whooping it up in Torgau (nor do I omit the girls who were with the Russian troops, nor the old women who sat cooling their feet in the river—very swift at that point) there wasn't someone else equally preoccupied with biological and historical theories. But Cousin Scholem in the land of . . . well, Spengler—why should we leave out Spengler, whose parallels between antiquity and modernity had worked us up intolerably when we were boys in Ravenswood?—Cousin Scholem had not only read world history, not merely thought it and untied some of its most stupefying, paralyzing knots and tangles just before enlisting, he was also personally, effectively experiencing it as a rifleman. Soldiers of both armies, Scholem in the midst of them, took an oath to be friends forever, never to forget each other, and to build a peaceful world.

For years after this my cousin was busy with organizational work, appeals to governments, activities at the UN, and international conferences. He went to Russia with an American delegation and in the Kremlin handed to Khrushchev the map used by his patrol as it approached the Elbe—a gift from the American people to the Russian people, and an earnest of amity.

The completion and publication of his work, which he considered to be the only genuine contribution to pure philosophy in the twentieth century, had to be postponed.

For some twenty years Cousin Scholem was a taxicab driver in Chicago. He was now retired, a pensioner of the cab company, living on the North Side. He was not, however, living quietly. Recently he had undergone cancer surgery at the VA hospital. The doctors told him that he would soon be dead. This was why I had received so much mail from him, a pile of documents containing reproductions from *Stars and Stripes,* pictures of the embracing troops at Torgau, photostats of official letters, and final statements, both political and personal. I had a second and then a third look at the recent picture of Scholem—the inward squint of his narrow eyes, the emotional power of his face. He had meant to have a significant life. He believed that his death, too, would be significant. I myself sometimes think what humankind will be like when I am gone, and I can't say that I foresee any special effects from my final disappearance, whereas Cousin Scholem has an emotional conviction of achievement, and believes that his influence will continue for the honor and dignity of our species. I came presently to his valedictory statement. He makes many special requests, some of them ceremonial. He wants to be buried at Torgau on the Elbe, close to the monument commemorating the defeat of the Nazi forces. He asks that his burial service begin with a reading from the conclusion of *The Brothers Karamazov* in the Garnett translation. He asks that the burial service end with the playing of the second movement of Beethoven's Seventh Symphony, the Solti recording with the Vienna Philharmonic. He writes out the inscription for his headstone. It identifies him by the enduring intellectual gift he leaves to mankind, and by his participation in the historic oath. He concludes with John 12:24: "Verily, verily, I say unto you, Except a corn of wheat fall into the ground and die, it abideth alone; but if it die, it bringeth forth much fruit."

Appended to the valedictory is a letter from the Department of the Army, Office of the Adjutant General, advising Mr. Stavis that he will have to find out what rules the German Democratic Republic (East Germany) has governing the bringing into their country of human remains for the purpose of burial. Inquiries may be made at the GDR chancery in Washington, D.C. As for expenses, the liability of the U.S. government is unfortunately restricted, and it cannot pay for the transportation of Scholem's body, much less for the passage of his mourning family. Allowances for cemeteries and burial plots may be available through the Veterans Administration. The letter is decent and sympathetic.

Of course, the colonel who signs it can't be expected to know how remarkable a person Scholem Stavis is.

There is a final communication, concerning a gathering next year in Paris (September 1984) to commemorate the seventieth anniversary of the Battle of the Marne. This will honor the taxi drivers who took part in the defense of the city by carrying fighting men to the front. Cabbies from all countries have been invited to this event, even pedal-cab drivers from Southeast Asia. The grand procession will form near Napoleon's tomb and then follow the route taken in 1914. Scholem means to salute the last of the venerable taxicabs on display in the Invalides. As a member of the planning committee, he will soon go to Paris to take part in the preparations for this event. On the way home he will stop in New York City, where he will call upon the five permanent members of the Security Council to ask them to respect the spirit of the great day at Torgau, and to take a warm farewell of everybody. He will visit the French UN delegation at nine-thirty A.M., the Soviet Union at eleven, China at twelve-thirty, Great Britain at two P.M., the U.S.A. at half past three. At five P.M. he will pay his respects to the Secretary General. Then return to Chicago and a "new life"—the life promised in John 12:24.

He appeals for financial assistance in the name of mankind itself, referring again to the dignity of humanity in this century.

Lesser documents contain statements on nuclear disarmament and on the hopeful prospects for an eventual reconciliation between the superpowers, in the spirit of Torgau. At three A.M. my head is not clear enough to study them.

Sleep is out of the question, so instead of going to bed I make myself some strong coffee. No use sacking out; I'd only go on thinking.

Insomnia is not a word I apply to the sharp thrills of deep-night clarity that come to me. During the day the fusspot habits of a lifetime prevent real discovery. I have learned to be grateful for the night hours that harrow the nerves and tear up the veins—"lying in restless ecstasy." To want this, and to bear it, you need a strong soul.

I lie down with the coffee in one of my Syrian corners (I didn't intend to create this Oriental environment; how did it come into existence?), lie down in proximity to the smooth, lighted, empty moon surface of the Outer Drive to consider what I might do for Cousin Scholem. Why do anything? Why not just refer him to the good-intentions department? After he had been in the good-intentions chamber five or six times, I could almost feel that I had done something for him. The usual techniques of evasion would not, however, work in Cousin Scholem's case. The son of Jewish immigrants (his father was in the egg business in Fulton Market), Cousin Scholem was determined to find support in

Nature and History for freedom and to mitigate, check, or banish the fear of death that governs the species—convulses it. He was, moreover, a patriotic American (a terribly antiquated affect) and a world citizen. Above all he wanted to affirm that all would be well, to make a distinguished gift, to bless mankind. In all this Scholem fitted the classical norm for Jews of the diaspora. Against the Chicago background of boardrooms and back rooms, of fraud, arson, assassination, hit men, bag men, the ideology of decency disseminated from unseen sources of power—the moral law, never thicker, in Chicago, than onionskin or tissue paper—was now a gas as rare as argon. Anyway, think of him, perhaps the most powerful mind ever to be placed behind the wheel of a cab, his passengers descendants of Belial who made II Corinthians look sick, and Scholem amid unparalleled decadence being ever more pure in thought. The effort gave him a malignant tumor. I have also been convinced always that the strain of driving ten hours a day in city traffic is enough to give you cancer. It's the enforced immobility that does it; and there's also the aggravated ill will, the reflux of fury released by organisms, and perhaps by mechanisms, too.

But what could I do for Scholem? I couldn't go running to his house and ring the bell after thirty years of estrangement. I couldn't bring financial assistance— I don't have the money to print so many thousands of pages. He would need a hundred thousand at least, and he might expect Ijah to conjure it out of the barren air of the Loop. Didn't Ijah belong to a crack team of elite financial analysts? But Cousin Ijah was not one of the operators who had grabbed off any of the big money available for "intellectual" projects or enlightened reforms, the political grant-getters who have millions to play with.

Also I shrank from sitting down with him in his six-flat parlor to discuss his life's work. I didn't have the language it required. My college biology would be of no use. My Spengler was deader than the Bohemian Cemetery where we discussed the great questions (dignified surroundings, massy tombs, decaying flowers).

I didn't have a language to share with Cousin Motty, either, to open my full mind to him; and from his side Cousin Scholem couldn't enlist my support for his philosophical system until I had qualified myself by years of study. So little time was left that it was out of the question. In the circumstances, all I could do was to try to raise funds to have him buried in East Germany. The Communists, needing hard currency so badly, would not turn down a reasonable proposition. And toward morning, as I washed and shaved, I remembered that there was a cousin in Elgin, Illinois—not a close cousin, but one with whom I had always had friendly and even affectionate relations. He might be able to help. The affections have to manage as they can at a time so abnormal. They are kept alive in storage, as it were, for one doesn't often see their objects. These mental hydroponic growths can, however, be curiously durable and tenacious. People seem able to keep one another on "hold" for decades or scores of years. Separations like these have a flavor of eternity. One interpretation of "having no contemporaries" is that all valuable associations are kept in a time-arrested state. Those who are absent seem to sense that they have not lost their value for you. The relationship is played *ritardando* on a trance instrument of which the rest of the orchestra is only subliminally aware.

The person I refer to was still there, in Elgin. Mendy Eckstine, once a freelance journalist and advertising man, was now semiretired. He and Scholem Stavis were from altogether different spheres. Eckstine had been my pool-hall, boxing, jazz-club cousin. Mendy had had a peculiar relish for being an American of his time. Born in Muskingum, Ohio, where his father ran a gents' furnishings shop, he attended a Chicago high school and grew up a lively, slangy man who specialized in baseball players, vaudeville performers, trumpeters and boogie-woogie musicians, gamblers, con artists, city hall small-rackets types. The rube shrewdie was a type he dearly loved—"Aaron Slick from Punkin Crick." Mendy's densely curled hair was combed straight up, his cheeks were high, damaged by acne, healed to a patchy whiteness. He had a wonderful start of the head, to declare that he was about to set the record straight. He used to make this movement when he laid down his cigarette on the edge of the pool table of the University of Wisconsin Rathskeller and picked up his cue to study his next shot. From Mendy as from Seckel I had learned songs. He loved hick jazz numbers like "Sounds a Little Goofus to Me," and in particular,

> *Oh, the cows went dry and the hens wouldn't lay*
> *When he played on his ole cornet.*

Altogether an admirable person, and a complete American, as formal, as total in his fashion as a work of art. The model on which he formed himself has been wiped out. In the late thirties he and I went to the fights together, or the Club de Lisa for jazz.

Cousin Mendy was the man to approach on Scholem's behalf because there was a fund, somewhere, set up by a relative dead these many years, the last of his branch. As I understood its provisions, this fund was set up to make essential family loans and also to pay for the education of poor relations, if they were gifted, perhaps even for their higher cultural activities. Vague about it myself, I was sure that Mendy would know, and I quickly got hold of him on the telephone. He said he would come downtown next day, delighted, he told me, to have a talk. "Been far too long, old buddy."

The fund was the legacy of an older Eckstine, Arcadius, called Artie. Artie, of whom nothing was expected and who had never in his life tied his shoelaces, not because he was too stout (he was only plump) but because he announced to the world that he was *dégagé,* had come into some money toward the end of his life.

Before the Revolution, he had brought to America a Russian schoolboy's version of Pushkin's life, and he gave Pushkin recitations incomprehensible to us. Modern experience had never touched him. Viewed from above, Artie's round, brownish-fair head was the head of a boy, combed with boyish innocence. He grew somewhat puffy in the cheeks and eyelids. His eyes were kiwi green. He lost one of his fingers in a barbed-wire factory in 1917. Perhaps he sacrificed it to avoid the draft. There is a "cabinet portrait" of Artie and his widowed mother, taken about seventy years ago. He poses with his thumb under his lapel. His mother, Tanya, is stout, short, and Oriental. Although she looks composed, her face is in reality inflated with laughter. Why? Well, if her legs are so plump and short that they don't reach the floor, the cause is a comical deficiency in the physical world, ludicrously incapable of adapting itself to Aunt Tanya. Tanya's second marriage was to a millionaire junkman, prominent in his synagogue, a plain man and strictly Orthodox. Tanya, a movie fan, loved Clark Gable and never missed a performance of *Gone with the Wind.* "Oy, Clark Gebble, I love him so!"

Her old husband was the first to die. She followed in her mideighties, five years later. At the time of her death, Artie was a traveler in dehydrated applesauce and was demonstrating his product in a small downstate department store when the news came. He and his wife, a childless couple, retired at once. He said he would resume his study of philosophy, in which he had majored at Ann Arbor God knows how many years ago, but the management of his property and money kept him from the books. He used to say to me, "Ijah, wot is your opinion of Chon Dewey—ha?"

When these Eckstine cousins died, it was learned that a fund for higher studies had been set up under the will—a sort of foundation, said Mendy.

"And has it been used?"

"Very little."

"Could we get money out of it for Scholem Stavis?"

He said, "That depends," implying that he might be able to swing it.

I had prepared an exhibit for him. He quickly grasped the essentials of Scholem's case. "There wouldn't be money enough to publish his life's work. And how do we find out whether he really is to Darwin what Newton was to Copernicus?"

"It would be hard for us to decide."

"Who would you ask?" said Mendy

"We'd have to retain a few specialists. My confidence in academics is not too great."

"You think they'd steal from a defenseless genius-amateur?"

"Contact with inspiration often disturbs your steady worker. . . ."

"Assuming that Scholem is inspired. Artie and his missis didn't live long enough to enjoy their inheritance. I wouldn't like to blow too much of their dough on a brainstorm," said Mendy. "I'd have more confidence in Scholem if he weren't so statuesque."

People nowadays don't trust you if you don't show them your trivial humanity—Leopold Bloom in the outhouse, his rising stink, his wife's goat udders, or whatever. The chosen standards for common humanity have moved toward this lower range of facts.

"Besides," said Mendy, "what's all this Christianity? Why does he have to quote from the most anti-Semitic of the Gospels? After what we've been through, that's not the direction to take."

"For all I know, he may be the heir of Immanuel Kant and can't accept an all-Jewish outlook. He's also an American claiming his natural right to an important position in the history of knowledge."

"Even so," said Mendy, "what's this asking to be buried behind the iron curtain? Doesn't he know what Jew-haters those Russians are—right up there with the Germans? Does he think by lying there that he'll soak up all that hate like blotting paper? Cure them? Maybe he thinks he can—he and nobody else."

He was working himself up to accuse Scholem of megalomania. These psychological terms lying around, tempting us to use them, are a menace. They should all be shoveled into trucks and taken to the dump.

It was interesting to consider Mendy's own development. He was very intelligent, though you might not think so if you had observed how he had dramatized himself as a middle American of the Hoover or early Roosevelt period. He pursued the idiocies and even the pains of his Protestant models, misfortunes like the estrangement of husbands and wives, sexual self-punishment. He would get drunk in the Loop and arrive swacked on the commuter train, like other Americans. He bought an English bulldog that irritated his wife to madness. He and his mother-in-law elaborated all the comical American eccentricities of mutual dislike. She went down to the cellar when he was at home and after he had gone to bed she came up to make herself a cup of cocoa in the kitchen. He would say to me, "I sent her to a nutritionist because I couldn't understand how she could look so well and rosy on a diet of sweet rolls and cocoa." (Histrionics, I guess, had kept her in splendid condition.) Mendy made an ally of his young son; they went on fishing trips and visited Civil War battlegrounds. He was a man-and-boy Midwesterner, living out of a W. C. Fields script. And yet in the eyes under that snap-brim fedora there had always been a mixture of Jewish lights, and in his sixties he was visibly more Jewish. And, as I have said, the American model he had adopted was now utterly obsolete. The patriarchs of the Old Testament were infinitely more modern than the Punkin Crick smart alecks. Mendy was not returning to the religion of his fathers, far from it, but in semiretirement, stuck out there in Elgin, he must have been as hard up for comprehension as Cousin Motty had been in the locker room of his club.

Accordingly, it didn't surprise him that I should take so much interest in cousins. His own interest was stirred. Unless I misinterpreted the expression of his now malformed, lumpy, warm face, he was appealing to me to extend this interest to him. He wished to draw nearer.

"You aren't being sentimental, are you, Ijah, because you and Scholem went on such wonderful walks together? You'd probably be able to judge if you read his blockbusting book. They didn't hire dummies at the Rand Corporation—someday I'll ask you to tell me about that super think tank."

"I'd rather call it sympathy, not soft sentiment."

In the moral sphere, a wild ignorance, utter anarchy.

Mendy said, "If you tried talking to him, he'd lecture you from on high, wouldn't he? Since you don't understand about these zygotes and gametes, you'd be forced to sit and listen. . . ."

What Mendy intended to say was that he and I—*we* could understand each other, owing to our common ilk. Jews who had grown up on the sidewalks of America, we were in no sense foreigners, and we had brought so much enthusiasm, verve, love to this American life that we had become *it*. Odd that *it* should begin to roll toward oblivion just as we were perfecting ourselves in this admirable democracy. However, our democracy was passé. The *new* democracy with its *new* abstractions was cruelly disheartening. Being an American always had been something of an abstract project. You came as an immigrant. You were offered a most reasonable proposition and you said yes to it. You were *found*. With the new abstractions you were *lost*. They demanded a shocking abandonment of personal judgment. Take Eunice's letter to the medical school as an example. By using the word "integrity" you could cheat with a good conscience. Schooled in the new abstractions, you no longer had to worry about truth and falsehood, good and evil. What excused you from good and evil was the effort you put into schooling. You worked hard at your limited lesson, you learned it, and you were forever in the clear. You could say, for instance, "Guilt has to die. Human beings are entitled to guiltless pleasure." Having learned this valuable lesson, you could now accept the fucking of your daughters, which in the past would have choked you. You were compensated by the gratification of a lesson well learned. Well, there's the new thoughtfulness for you. And it's possibly on our capacity for thoughtfulness that our survival depends—all the rational decisions that have to be made. And listen here, I am not digressing at all. Cousin Scholem was a noble creature who lived in the forests of *old* thoughtfulness. An excellent kind of creature, if indeed he was the real thing. Cousin Mendy suggested that he was not. Cousin Mendy wished to remind me that he and I were representatives of a peculiar Jewish and American development (wiped out by history) and had infinitely more in common than any superannuated prodigy could ever understand.

"I want to do something for Scholem, Mendy."

"I'm not sure we can spend Cousin Artie's money to bury him in East Germany."

"Fair enough. Now, suppose you raise the money to have his great work read . . . find a biologist to vet it. And a philosopher and a historian."

"Maybe so. I'll take it up with the executors. I'll get back to you," said Mendy.

I divined from this that he himself was all of the executors.

"I have to go abroad," I said. "I may even see Scholem in Paris. His valedictory letter mentions a trip to plan the taxis-of-the-Marne business."

I gave Mendy Miss Rodinson's number.

"Flying the Concorde, I suppose," said Mendy. Devoid of envy. I would have been glad of his company.

I stopped in Washington to confer with International Monetary Fund people about the intended resumption of loans from commercial banks to the Brazilians. I found time to spend a few hours at the Library of Congress, looking for Bogoras and Jochelson material, and to get inquiries under way at the East German chancery. Then I telephoned my former wife at National Public Radio. Isabel has become one of its most familiar voices. After three marriages, she has resumed her maiden name. I sometimes hear it after the prancing music of the program's signature: "We will now hear from our correspondent Isabel Greenspan in Washington." I invited her to have dinner with me. She said no, offended perhaps that I hadn't called earlier from Chicago. She said she would come to the Hay-Adams Hotel to have a drink with me.

The thought persistently suggested by Isabel when we meet is that man is the not-yet-stabilized animal. By this I mean not only that defective, diseased, abortive types are common (Isabel is neither defective nor sick, by the way) but that the majority of human beings will never attain equilibrium and that they are by nature captious, fretful, irritable, uncomfortable, looking for relief from their travail and angry that it does not come. A woman like Isabel, determined to make an impression of perfect balance, reflects this unhappy instability. She identifies me with errors she has freed herself from; she measures her progress by our ever-more-apparent divergence. Clever enough to be a member of the Mensa (high-IQ) society, and, on the air, a charming person, she is always somewhat somber with me, as if she weren't altogether satisfied with her "insights." As a national figure in a program offering enlightened interpretation to millions of listeners, Sable is "committed," "engaged"; but as an intelligent woman, she is secretly rueful about this enlightenment.

She talked to me about Chicago, with which, in certain respects, she identified me. "White machine aldermen tying the black mayor in knots while they strip the city of its last buck. While you, of course, see it all. You always see it all. But you'd rather go on mooning." There was a noteworthy difference in Sable this afternoon. At cocktail time, she was made up like the dawn of day. Her dark color was the departing night. She was more perfumed than the dawn. It was otherwise a very good resemblance. No denying that she is an attractive woman. She was dressed in dark, tea-colored silk with a formal design in scarlet. She didn't always make herself so attractive for our meetings.

Vain to pretend that I "see it all," but what she meant when she said "mooning" was quite clear. It had two distinct and associated meanings: (1) my special preoccupations, and (2) my lifelong dream-connection with Virgie Dunton née Miletas, the eight-fingered concert harpist. Despite her congenital defect, Virgie had mastered the entire harp repertoire, omitting a few impossible works, and had a successful career. It's perfectly true that I had never been cured of my feeling for Virgie—her black eyes, her round face, its whiteness, its frontal tendency, its feminine emanations, the assurances of humanity or pledges of kindness which came from it. Even the slight mutilation of her short nose—it was the result of a car accident; she refused plastic surgery—was an attraction. It's perfectly true that for me the word "female" had its most significant representation in her. Whenever possible, I attended her concerts; I walked in her neighborhood in hopes of running into her, imagined that I saw her in department stores. Chance meetings—five in thirty years—were remembered in minute actuality. When her husband, a heavy drinker, lent me Galbraith's book on his accomplishments in India, I read every word of it, and this can only be explained by the swollen affect or cathexis that had developed. Virgie Miletas, the Venus of rudimentary thumbs, with her electric binding power, was the real object of Sable's "you'd rather go on mooning." The perfect happiness I might have known with Mrs. Miletas-Dunton, like the longed-for union of sundered beings in the love myth of Aristophanes—I refrain from invoking the higher Eros described by Socrates during the long runs of the blatting El trains that used to carry me, the inspired philosophy student, from Van Buren Street and its hockshops to Sixty-third Street and its throng of junkies—was an artificial love dream and Sable was quite right to despise it.

At the Hay-Adams, where we were drinking gin and tonic, Sable now made a comment which was surprising, nothing like her usual insights, which were not. She said, "I don't think mooning is such a satisfactory word. To be more exact, you have an exuberance that you keep to yourself. You have a crazy high energy absolutely peculiar to you. Because of this high charge you can defy the plain dirty facts that other people have to suffer through, whether they like it or not. What you are is an exuberance-hoarder, Ijah. You live on your exuberant hoard. It would kill you to be depressed, as others are."

This was a curious attack. There was something to it. I gave her full credit for this. I preferred, however, to think it over at leisure instead of answering at once. So I started to talk to her about Cousin Scholem. I described his case to her. If he were to be interviewed on National Public Radio and received the attention he deserved (the war hero–philosopher–cabby), he might succeed in stimulating the interest and, more important, the queer generosity of the public. Sable rejected this immediately. She said he'd be too heavy. If he announced that in him Kant and Darwin had a successor at last, listeners would say, Who is this nut! She admitted that the taxis of the Marne would be rich in human interest, but the celebration would not take place until 1984; it was still a year away. She also observed that her program didn't encourage fund-raising initiatives. She said, "Are you sure the man is really dying? You have only his word for it."

"That's a heartless question," I said.

"Maybe it is. You've always been soft about cousins, though. The immediate family threw a chill on your exuberance, and you simply turned to the cousins. I used to think you'd open every drawer in the morgue if somebody told you that there was a cousin to be found. Ask yourself how many of them would come looking for you."

This made me smile. Sable always had had a strong sense of humor.

She said also, "At a time when the nuclear family is breaking up, what's this excitement about collateral relatives?"

The only answer I could make came from left field. I said, "Before the First World War, Europe was governed by a royalty of cousins."

"Yes? That came out real good, didn't it?"

"There are people who think of that time as a golden age—the last of the old *douceur de vivre,* and so on."

But I didn't really mean it. The millennial history of nihilism culminated in 1914, and the brutality of Verdun and Tannenberg was a prelude to the even greater destruction that began in 1939. So here again is the all-pervading *suspense*—the seams of history opening, the bonds in dissolution (Hegel), the constraints of centuries removed. Unless your head is hard, this will give you nothing but dizzy fits, but if you don't yield to fits you may be carried into a kind of freedom. Disorder, if it doesn't murder you, brings certain opportunities. You wouldn't guess that when I sit in my Holy Sepulchre apartment at night (the surroundings that puzzled Eunice's mind when she came to visit: "All these Oriental rugs and lamps, and so many books," she said), wouldn't guess that I am concentrating on strategies for pouncing passionately on the freedom made possible by dissolution. Hundreds of books, but only half a shelf of those that matter. You don't get more goodness from more knowledge. One of the writers I often turn to concentrates on passion. He invites you to consider love and hate. He denies that hate is blind. On the contrary, hate is perspicuous. If you let hate germinate, it will eat its way inward and consume your very being, it will intensify reflection. It doesn't blind, it increases lucidity, it opens a man up; it makes him reach out and concentrates his being so that he is able to grasp himself. Love, too, is clear-eyed and not blind. True love is not delusive. Like hate, it is a primal source. But love is hard to come by. Hate is in tremendous supply. And evidently you endanger your being by waiting for the rarer passion. So you must have confidence in hate, which is so abundant, and embrace it with your whole soul, if you hope to achieve any clarity at all.

I wasn't about to take this up with Sable, although she would be capable of discussing it. She was still talking about my weakness for cousins. She said, "If you had cared about me as you do about all those goofy, half-assed cousins, and such, we never would have divorced."

"Such" was a dig at Virgie.

Was Sable hinting that we try again? Was this why she had come painted like the dawn and so beautifully dressed? I felt quite flattered.

In the morning I went to Dulles and flew out on the Concorde. The International Monetary Fund was waiting for the Brazilian parliament to make up its mind. I jotted some notes toward my report and then I was free to think of other matters. I considered whether Sable was priming me to make her a proposal. I liked what she had said about hoarded exuberance. Her opinion was that, through the cousins, through Virgie, I indulged my taste for the easier affects. I lacked true modern severity. Maybe she believed that I satisfied an artist's needs by visits to old galleries, walking through museums of beauty, happy with the charms of kinship, quite contented with painted relics, not tough enough for rapture in its strongest forms, not purified by nihilistic fire.

And about marriage . . . single life was tiresome. There were, however, unpleasant considerations in marriage that must not be avoided. What would I do in Washington? What would Sable do if she came to live in Chicago? No, she wouldn't be willing to move. We'd be flying back and forth, commuting. To spell the matter out, item by item, Sable had become a public-opinion molder. Public opinion is power. She belonged to a group that held great power. It was not the kind of power I cared about. While her people were not worse jerks than their conservative opposites, they were nevertheless jerks, more numerous in her profession than in other fields, and disagreeably influential.

I was now in Paris, pulling up in front of the Montalembert. I had given up a hotel I liked better when I found cockroaches in my luggage, black ones that had recrossed the Atlantic with me and came out all set to conquer Chicago.

I inspected the room at the Montalembert and then walked down the rue du Bac to the Seine. Marvelous how much good these monumental capitals can do an American, still. I almost felt that here the sun itself should take a monumental form, something like the Mexican calendar stone, to shine on the Sainte-Chapelle, the Conciergerie, the Pont Neuf, and other medieval relics.

Returning to the hotel after dinner, I found a message from Miss Rodinson in Chicago. "Eckstine fund will grant ten thousand dollars to Mr. Stavis."

Good for Cousin Mendy! I now had news for Scholem, and since he would be at the Invalides tomorrow if he was alive and had made it to Paris for the planning session, I would have more than mere sympathy to offer when we met after so many decades. Mendy meant the grant to be used to determine whether Scholem's pure philosophy, grounded in science, was all that he claimed it to be, an advance on the *Critique of Pure Reason*. Immediately I began to devise ways to get around Mendy. I could choose Scholem's readers myself. I would offer them small sums—they didn't deserve fat fees anyway, those academic nitwits. (Angry with them, you see, because they had done so little to prevent the U.S. from sinking into decadence; I blamed them, in fact, for hastening our degradation.) Five experts at two hundred bucks apiece, whom I would pay myself, would allow me to give the entire ten grand to Scholem. By using my clout in Washington, I might get a burial permit out of the East Germans for two or three thousand, bribes included. That would leave money enough for transportation and last rites. For if Scholem had a clairvoyant conviction that his burial at Torgau would shrink the world's swollen madness to a small pellet, it might be worth a try. Interred at Waldheim in Chicago, beside the pounding truck traffic of Harlem Avenue, one could not hope to have any effect.

To catch up with European time, I stayed up late playing solitaire with a pack of outsized cards that made eyeglasses unnecessary and this put me in a frame of mind to get into bed without a fit of exuberance. Given calm and poise, I *can* understand my situation. Musing back and forth over the cards, I understood Sable's complaint that I had ruined our marriage by denying it a transfusion of exuberance. Speaking of my sentiments for the cousins, she referred indirectly to the mystery of being a Jew. Sable had a handsome Jewish nose, perhaps a little too much of one. Also, she had conspicuously offered her legs to my gaze, knowing my weakness for them. She had a well-turned bosom, a smooth throat, good hips, and legs still capable of kicking in the bedroom—I used to refer to "your skip-rope legs." Now, then, had Sable continued through three marriages to think of me as her only true husband, or was she trying her strength one last time against her rival from (Egyptian) Alexandria? Guiltless Virgie was the hate of her life, and hate made you perspicuous, failing love. Heidegger would have approved. His idea had, as it were, infected me. I was beginning to be obsessed with the two passions that made you perspicuous. Love there isn't too much of; hate is as ubiquitous as nitrogen or carbon. Maybe hate is inherent in matter itself and is therefore a component of our bones; our very blood is perhaps swollen with it. For moral coldness in the arctic range I had found a physical image in the Siberian environment of the Koryak and the Chukchee—the subpolar desert whose frosts are as severe as fire, a fit location for slave-labor camps. Put all this together, and my idyll of Virgie Miletas might be construed as a fainthearted evasion of the reigning coldness.

Well, I could have told Sable that she couldn't win against an unconsummated *amour* of so many years. It's after all the woman you *didn't* have whose effect is mortal.

I concede, however, that the real challenge is to capture and tame wickedness. Without this you remain suspended. At the mercy of the suspense over the new emergence of spirit . . .

But on this I sacked out.

In the morning on my breakfast tray was an express envelope from Miss Rodinson. I was in no mood to open it now; it might contain information about a professional engagement, and I didn't want that. I was on my way to the Invalides to meet with Scholem, if he had made it there. The world cabbies' organizing session, attended, as I noted in *Le Monde,* by some two hundred delegates from fifty countries, would begin at eleven o'clock. I put Miss Rodinson's mail in my pocket with my wallet and my passport.

I was rushed to the great dome in a cab, and went in. A wonderful work of religious architecture—Bruant in the seventeenth century, Mansart in the eighteenth. I took note of its grandeur intermittently. There were gaps in which the dome was no more to me than an egg cup, owing to my hectic excitement— derangement. The stains were growing under my arms. Loss of moisture dried my throat. I went to get information about the taxis of the Marne and had the corner pointed out to me. The drivers had not yet begun to arrive. I had to wander about for half an hour or so, and I climbed up to the first *étage* to look down in the crypt of the Chapelle Saint-Jérôme. Hoo! what grandeur, what beauties! Such arches and columns and statuary, and floating and galloping frescoes. And the floor so sweetly tessellated. I wanted to kiss it. And also the mournful words of Napoleon from Saint Helena. "*Je désire que mes cendres reposent sur les bords de la Seine* in the middle of that nation, *ce peuple Français,* that I loved so much." Now Napoleon was crammed under thirty-five tons of polished porphyry or alizarin in a shape suggestive of Roman pomp.

As I was descending the stairs I took out Miss Rodinson's envelope, and I felt distinctly topsy-turvy, somewhat intoxicated, as I read the letter from Eunice— that was all it contained. Here came Tanky's third wish: that I write once again to Judge Eiler to request that the final months of his prison term be served in a halfway house in Las Vegas. In a halfway house, Eunice explained, you had minimal supervision. You signed out in the morning, and signed in again at night. The day was your own, to attend to private business. Eunice wrote, "I think that prison has been a tremendous learning experience for my brother. As he is very intelligent, under it all, he has already absorbed everything there was to absorb from jail. You might try that on the judge, phrasing it in your own way."

Well, to phrase it in my own way, the great fish tottered on the grandiose staircase, filled with drunken darkness and hearing the turbulent seas. An inner voice told him, "This is it!" and he felt like opening a great crimson mouth and tearing the paper with his teeth.

I wanted to send back a message, too: "I am not Cousin Schmuck, I am a great fish who can grant wishes and in whom there are colossal powers!"

Instead I calmed myself by tearing Eunice's notepaper six, eight, ten times, and then seeking discipline in a wastepaper basket. By the time I reached the gathering place, my emotions were more settled, although not entirely normal. There was a certain amount of looping and veering still.

Upward of a hundred delegates had gathered in the taxi corner, if gathered is the word to apply to such a crowd of restless exotics. There were people from all the corners of the earth. They wore caps, uniforms, military insignia, batik pants, Peruvian hats, pantaloons, wrinkled Indian breeches, crimson gowns from Africa, kilts from Scotland, skirts from Greece, Sikh turbans. The whole gathering reminded me of the great UN meeting that Khrushchev and Castro had attended, and where I had seen Nehru in his lovely white garments with a red rose in his lapel and a sort of baker's cap on his head—I had been present when Khrushchev pulled off his shoe to bang his desk in anger.

Then it came to me how geography had been taught in the Chicago schools when I was a kid. We were issued a series of booklets: "Our Little Japanese Cousins," "Our Little Moroccan Cousins," "Our Little Russian Cousins," "Our Little Spanish Cousins." I read all these gentle descriptions about little Ivan and tiny Conchita, and my eager heart opened to them. Why, we were close, we were one under it all (as Tanky was very intelligent "under it all"). We were not guineas, dagos, krauts; we were cousins. It was a splendid conception, and those of us who opened our excited hearts to the world union of cousins were happy, as I was, to give our candy pennies to a fund for the rebuilding of Tokyo after the earthquake of the twenties. After Pearl Harbor, we were obliged to bomb the hell out of the place. It's unlikely that Japanese children had been provided with books about their little American cousins. The Chicago Board of Education had never thought to look into this.

Two French nonagenarians were present, survivors of 1914. They were the center of much eager attention. A most agreeable occasion, I thought, or would have thought if I had been less agitated.

I didn't see Scholem anywhere. I suppose I should have told Miss Rodinson to phone his Chicago number for information, but they would have asked who was calling, and for what purpose. I wasn't sorry to have come to this mighty hall. In fact I wouldn't have missed it. But I was emotionally primed for a meeting with Scholem. I had even prepared some words to say to him. I couldn't bear to miss him. I came out of the crowd and circled it. The delegates were already being conducted to their meeting place, and I stationed myself strategically near a door. The gorgeous costumes increased the confusion.

In any case, it wasn't I who found Scholem. I couldn't have. He was too greatly changed—emaciated. It was he who spotted me. A man being helped by a young woman—his daughter, as it turned out—glanced up into my face. He stopped and said, "I don't dream much because I don't sleep much, but if I'm not having hallucinations, this is my cousin Ijah."

Yes yes! It was Ijah! And here was Scholem. He no longer resembled the older man of the Instamatic color photo, the person who squinted inward under heavy brows. Because he had lost much weight his face was wasted, and the tightening of the skin brought back his youthful look. Much less doomed and fanatical than the man in the picture, who breathed prophetic fire. There seemed a kind of clear innocence about him. The size of his eyes was exceptional—like the eyes of a newborn infant in the first presentation of *genio* and *figura*. And suddenly I thought: What have I done? How do you tell a man like this that you have money for him? Am I supposed to say that I bring him the money he can bury himself with?

Scholem was speaking, saying to his daughter, "My cousin!" And to me he said, "You live abroad, Ijah? You got my mailings? Now I understand—you didn't answer because you wanted to surprise me. I have to make a speech, to greet the delegates. You'll sit with my daughter. We'll talk later."

"Of course. . . ."

I'd get the girl's help; I'd inform her of the Eckstine grant. She'd prepare her father for the news.

Then I felt robbed of strength, all at once. Doesn't existence lay too much on us? I had remembered, observed, studied the cousins, and these studies seemed to fix my own essence and to keep me as I had been. I had failed to include myself among them, and suddenly I was billed for this oversight. At the presentation of this bill, I became bizarrely weak in the legs. And when the girl, noticing that I seemed unable to walk, offered me her arm, I wanted to say, "What d'you mean? I need no help. I still play a full set of tennis every day." Instead I passed my arm through hers and she led us both down the corridor.

ZETLAND: BY A
CHARACTER WITNESS

YES, I KNEW THE GUY. We were boys in Chicago. He was wonderful. At fourteen, when we became friends, he had things already worked out and would
willingly tell you how everything had come about. It went like this: First the
earth was molten elements and glowed in space. Then hot rains fell. Steaming
seas were formed. For half the earth's history, the seas were azoic, and then life
began. In other words, first there was astronomy, and then geology, and by and
by there was biology, and biology was followed by evolution. Next came pre-
history and then history—epics and epic heroes, great ages, great men; then
smaller ages with smaller men; then classical antiquity, the Hebrews, Rome, feudalism, papacy, renascence, rationalism, the industrial revolution, science, democracy, and so on. All this Zetland got out of books in the late twenties, in the
Midwest. He was a clever kid. His bookishness pleased everyone. Over pale-blue
eyes, which sometimes looked strained, he wore big goggles. He had full lips
and big boyish teeth, widely spaced. Sandy hair, combed straight back, exposed
a large forehead. The skin of his round face often looked tight. He was short,
heavyish, strongly built but not in good health. At seven years old he had had
peritonitis and pneumonia at the same time, followed by pleurisy, emphysema,
and TB. His recovery was complete, but he was never free from minor ailments.
His skin was peculiar. He was not allowed to be in the sun for long. Exposure to
sunlight caused cloudy brown subcutaneous bruises, brownish iridescences. So,
often, while the sun shone, he drew the shades and read in his room by lamp-
light. But he was not at all an invalid. Though he played only on cloudy days,
his tennis was good, and he swam a thoughtful breast-stroke with frog motions
and a froggy underlip. He played the fiddle and was a good sight reader.

The neighborhood was largely Polish and Ukrainian, Swedish, Catholic, Orthodox, and Evangelical Lutheran. The Jews were few and the streets tough. Bungalows and brick three-flats were the buildings. Back stairs and porches were made of crude gray lumber. The trees were cottonwood elms and ailanthus, the grass was crabgrass, the bushes lilacs, the flowers sunflowers and elephant-ears. The heat was corrosive, the cold like a guillotine as you waited for the streetcar. The family, Zet's bullheaded father and two maiden aunts who were "practical nurses" with housebound patients (dying, usually), read Russian novels, Yiddish poetry, and were mad about culture. He was encouraged to be a little intellectual. So, in short pants, he was a junior Immanuel Kant. Musical (like Frederick the Great or the Esterhazys), witty (like Voltaire), a sentimental radical (like Rousseau), bereft of gods (like Nietzsche), devoted to the heart and to the law of love (like Tolstoy). He was earnest (the early shadow of his father's grimness), but he was playful, too. Not only did he study Hume and Kant but he discovered Dada and Surrealism as his voice was changing. The mischievous project of covering the great monuments of Paris in mattress ticking appealed to him. He talked about the importance of the ridiculous, the paradox of playful sublimity. Dostoyevsky, he lectured me, had it right. The intellectual (petty bourgeois–plebeian) was a megalomaniac. Living in a kennel, his thoughts embraced the universe. Hence the funny agonies. And remember Nietzsche, the *gai savoir.* And Heine and the "Aristophanes of Heaven." He was a learned adolescent, was Zetland.

Books in Chicago were obtainable. The public library in the twenties had many storefront branches along the car lines. Summers, under flipping gutta-percha fan blades, boys and girls read in the hard chairs. Crimson trolley cars swayed, cowbellied, on the rails. The country went broke in 1929. On the public lagoon, rowing, we read Keats to each other while the weeds bound the oars. Chicago was nowhere. It had no setting. It was something released into American space. It was where trains arrived; where mail orders were dispatched. But on the lagoon, with turning boats, the water and the sky clear green, pure blue, the boring power of a great manufacturing center arrested (there was no smoke, the mills were crippled—industrial distress benefited the atmosphere), Zet recited "Upon the honeyed middle of the night . . ." Polack children threw rocks and crab apples from the shore.

Studying his French, German, math, and music. In his room a bust of Beethoven, a lithograph of Schubert (also with round specs) sitting at the piano, moving his friends' hearts. The shades were drawn, the lamp burned. In the alley, peddlers' horses wore straw hats to ward off sunstroke. Zet warded off the prairies, the real estate, the business and labor of Chicago. He boned away at his Kant. Just as assiduously, he read Breton and Tristan Tzara. He quoted, "The earth is blue, like an orange." And he propounded questions of all sorts.

Had Lenin really expected democratic centralism to work within the Bolshevik party? Was Dewey's argument in *Human Nature and Conduct* unassailable? Was the "significant form" position fruitful for painting? What was the future of primitivism in art?

Zetland wrote surrealist poems of his own:

> *Plum lips suck the green of sleeping hills . . .*

or:

> *Foaming rabbis rub electrical fish!*

The Zetland apartment was roomy, inconvenient, in the standard gloomy style of 1910. Built-in buffets and china closets, a wainscot in the dining room with Dutch platters, a gas log in the fireplace, and two stained-glass small windows above the mantelpiece. A windup Victrola played "Eli, Eli," the *Peer Gynt* Suite. Chaliapin sang "The Flea" from *Faust,* Galli-Curci the "Bell Song" from *Lakmé,* and there were Russian soldiers' choruses. Surly Max Zetland gave his family "everything," he said. Old Zetland had been an immigrant. His start in life was slow. He learned the egg business in the poultry market on Fulton Street. But he rose to be assistant buyer in a large department store downtown: imported cheeses, Czech ham, British biscuits and jams—fancy goods. He was built like a fullback, with a black cleft in the chin and a long mouth. You would wear yourself out to win this mouth from its permanent expression of disapproval. He disapproved because he *knew life.* His first wife, Elias's mother, died in the flu epidemic of 1918. By his second wife old Zetland had a feebleminded daughter. The second Mrs. Zetland died of cancer of the brain. The third wife, a cousin of the second, was much younger. She came from New York; she had worked on Seventh Avenue; she had a *past.* Because of this *past* Max Zetland gave way to jealousy and made nasty scenes, breaking dishes and shouting brutally. *"Des histoiress,"* said Zet, then practicing his French. Max Zetland was a muscular man who weighed two hundred pounds, but these were only scenes— not dangerous. As usual, the morning after, he stood at the bathroom mirror and shaved with his painstaking brass Gillette, made neat his reprehending face, flattened his hair like an American executive, with military brushes. Then, Russian style, he drank his tea through a sugar cube, glancing at the *Tribune,* and went off to his position in the Loop, more or less *in Ordnung.* A normal day. Descending the back stairs, a short cut to the El, he looked through the window of the first floor at his Orthodox parents in the kitchen. Grandfather sprayed his bearded mouth with an atomizer—he had asthma. Grandmother made orange-peel candy. Peels dried all winter on the steam radiators. The candy was kept in shoeboxes and served with tea.

Sitting in the El, Max Zetland wet his finger on his tongue to turn the pages of the thick newspaper. The tracks looked down on small brick houses. The El ran like the bridge of the elect over the damnation of the slums. In those little bungalows Poles, Swedes, micks, spics, Greeks, and niggers lived out their foolish dramas of drunkenness, gambling, rape, bastardy, syphilis, and roaring death. Max Zetland didn't even have to look; he could read about it in the *Trib.* The little trains had yellow cane seats. Hand-operated gates of bent metal, waist-high, let you out of the car. Tin pagoda roofs covered the El platforms. Each riser of the long staircase advertised Lydia Pinkham's Vegetable Compound. Iron loss made young girls pale. Max Zetland himself had a white face, white-jowled, a sarcastic bear, but acceptably pleasant, entering the merchandising palace on Wabash Avenue, neat in his office, smart on the telephone, fluent except for a slight Russian difficulty with initial aitches, releasing a mellow grumble when he spoke, his mind factual, tabular, prices and contracts memorized. He held in the smoke of his cigarettes as he stood by his desk. The smoke drifted narrowly from his nose. With a lowered face, he looked about. He judged with furious Jewish snobbery the laxity and brainlessness of the golf-playing goy who could afford to walk in knickers on the restricted fairway, who could be what he seemed, who had no buried fury, married no lascivious New York girls, had no idiot orphans, no house of death. Max Zetland's hard paunch subdued by the cut of his jacket, the tense muscles of his calves showing through trouser legs, the smoke-retentive nose, the rage of taciturnity—well, in the business world one must be a nice fellow. He was an executive in a great retail organization and he *was* a nice fellow. He was a short-headed man whose skull had no great depth. But his face was broad, heavily masculine, self-consciously centered between the shoulders. His hair was parted in the middle and brushed flat. There was a wide space between his front teeth, which Zet inherited. Only the unshavable pucker in his father's chin was a sign of pathos, and this hint of the pitiful Max Zetland was defied by the Russian military stoutness of his bearing, by his curt style of smoking, by the snap with which he drank a glass of schnapps. Among friends his son had various names for him. The General, the Commissar, Osipovich, Ozymandias, he often called him. "My name is Ozymandias, king of kings: Look on my works, ye Mighty, and despair!"

Before his third marriage, Ozymandias the widower would come home from the Loop with the *Evening American,* printed on peach-colored paper. He took a glass of whiskey before dinner and saw his daughter. Perhaps she was not feeble-minded, only temporarily retarded. His bright son tried to tell him that Casanova was hydrocephalic until he was eight and considered an imbecile, and that Einstein was a backward child. Max hoped she might be taught to sew. He started with table manners. Meals, for a time, were horrible. She was unteachable. In her the family face was compressed, reduced, condensed into a cat's face. She stammered, she tottered, her legs were long and undeveloped. She picked up her skirt in company, she trickled on the toilet without closing the door. The kid gave away all the weaknesses of the breed. Relatives were sympathetic, but this sympathy of aunts and cousins Max sensed to be self-congratulatory. He coldly rejected it, looking straight before him and lengthening his straight mouth. When people spoke sympathetically to him about his daughter, he seemed to be considering the best way to put them to death.

Father Zetland read Russian and Yiddish poetry. He preferred the company of musical people and artists, bohemian garment workers, Tolstoyans, followers of Emma Goldman and of Isadora Duncan, revolutionists who wore pince-nez, Russian blouses, Lenin or Trotsky beards. He attended lectures, debates, concerts, and readings; the utopians amused him; he respected brains and was sold on high culture. It was obtainable in Chicago, in those days.

Facing Humboldt Park, on California Avenue, the Chicago anarchists and Wobblies had their forum; the Scandinavians had their fraternal lodges, churches, a dance hall; the Galician Jews a synagogue; the Daughters of Zion their charity day nursery. On Division Street, after 1929, little savings banks crashed. One became a fish store. A tank for live carp was made of the bank marble. The vault became an icebox. A movie house turned into a funeral parlor. Nearby, the red carbarn rose from slummy weeds. The vegetarians had a grand photo of old Count Tolstoy in the window of the Tolstoy Vegetarian Restaurant. What a beard, what eyes, and what a nose! Great men repudiated the triviality of ordinary and merely human things, including what was merely human in themselves. What was a nose? Cartilage. A beard? Cellulose. A count? A caste figure, a thing produced by epochs of oppression. Only Love, Nature, and God are good and great.

In one-hundred-percent-industrial contemporary Chicago, where shadows of loveliness were lacking, a flat wheel of land meeting a flat wheel of fresh water, intelligent boys like Zet, though fond of the world, too, were not long detained by surface phenomena. No one took Zet fishing. He did not go to the woods, was not taught to shoot, nor to clean a carburetor, nor even to play billiards or to dance. Zet concentrated on his books—his astronomy, geology, etc. First the blazing mass of matter, then the lifeless seas, then pulpy creatures crawling ashore, simple forms, more complex forms, and so on; then Greece, then Rome, then Arabian algebra, then history, poetry, philosophy, painting. Still wearing knickers, he was invited by neighborhood study groups to speak on the élan vital, on the differences between Kant and Hegel. He was professorial, Germanic, the wunderkind, Max Zetland's secret weapon. Old Zet would be the *man* of the family and young Zet its *genius*.

"He wanted me to be a John Stuart Mill," said Zet. "Or some shrunken little Itzkowitz of a prodigy—Greek and calculus at the age of eight, damn him!" Zet believed he had been cheated of his childhood, robbed of the angelic birthright.

He believed all that old stuff about the sufferings of childhood, the lost paradise, the crucifixion of innocence. Why was he sickly, why was he myopic, why did he have a greenish color? Why, grim old Zet wanted him to be all marrow, no bone. He caged him in reprehending punitive silence, he demanded that he dazzle the world. And he never—but never—approved of anything.

To be an intellectual was the next stage of human development, the historical fate of mankind, if you prefer. Now the masses were reading, and we were off in all directions, Zet believed. The early phases of this expansion of mind could not fail to produce excesses, crime, madness. Wasn't that, said Zet, the meaning of books like *The Brothers Karamazov,* the decay produced by rationalism in the feudal peasant Russian? And parricide the first result of revolution? The resistance to the modern condition and the modern theme? The terrible wrestling of Sin and Freedom? The megalomania of the pioneers? To be an intellectual was to be a parvenu. The business of these parvenus was to purge themselves of their first wild impulses and of their crazy baseness, to change themselves, to become disinterested. To love truth. To become great.

Naturally Zetland was sent to college. College was waiting for him. He won prizes in poetry, essay contests. He joined a literary society, and a Marxist study group. Agreeing with Trotsky that Stalin had betrayed the October Revolution, he joined the Spartacus Youth League, but as a revolutionist he was fairly vague. He studied logic under Carnap, and later with Bertrand Russell and Morris R. Cohen.

The best of it was that he got away from home and lived in rooming houses, the filthier the better. The best was a whitewashed former coalbin on Woodlawn Avenue. Soft coal, still stored in the adjoining shed, trickled between the whitewashed planks. There was no window. On the cement floor was a rag rug, worried together out of tatters and coming unbound. An old oak library table with cigarette burns and a shadeless floorlamp were provided. The meters for the whole house were over Zet's cot. Rent was $2.50 a week. The place was jolly—it was bohemian, it was European. Best of all, it was Russian! The landlord, Perchik, said that he had been game-beater for Grand Duke Cyril. Abandoned in Kamchatka when the Japanese War began, he trudged back across Siberia. With him Zet had Russian conversations. Long in the teeth, Perchik wore a meager beard, and the wires of his dime-store specs were twisted. In the back he had built a little house out of pop bottles, collected in a coaster in the alleys. Rags and garbage were burned in the furnace, and the fumes blew through the hot-air registers. The landlord sang old ballads and hymns, falsetto. Really, the place couldn't have been better. Disorderly, dirty, irregular, free, and you could talk all night and sleep late. Just what you wanted for thought, for feeling, for invention. In his happiness, Zet entertained the Perchik house with his charades, speeches, jokes, and songs. He was a laundry mangle, a time clock, a tractor, a telescope. He did *Don Giovanni* in all parts and voices—*"Non sperar, se non m'uccidi . . . Donna folle, indarno gridi."* He reproduced the harpsichord background in the recitatives or the oboe weeping when the Commendatore's soul left his body. To follow up he might do Stalin addressing a party congress, a Fuller Brush salesman in German, or a submarine commander sinking an *amerikanische* freighter. Zet also was practically useful. He helped people to move. He minded kids for married graduate students. He cooked for the sick. He looked after people's dogs and cats when they went out of town, and shopped for old women in the house when it snowed. Now he was something between the stout boy and the nearsighted young man with odd ideas and exotic motives. Loving, virtually Franciscan, a simpleton for God's sake, easy to cheat. An ingenu. At the age of nineteen he had a great deal of Dickensian heart. When he earned a little money mopping floors at Billings Hospital, he shared it with clinic patients, bought them cigarettes and sandwiches, lent them carfare, walked them across the Midway. Sensitive to suffering and to symbols of suffering and misery, his eyes filled when he went into some Depression grocery. The withered potatoes, the sprouting onions, the unhappy face of the storekeeper got him. His cat had a miscarriage, and he wept about that, too, because the mother cat was grieving. I flushed the stillborn cats down the boardless grimy toilet in the cellar. He made me testy, carrying on like that. Practicing his feelings on everyone, I said. He warned me not to be hard-hearted. I said he exaggerated everything. He accused me of a lack of sensibility. It was an odd argument for two adolescents. I suppose the power of Americanization faltered during the Depression. We broke away, and seized the opportunity to be more *foreign.* We were a laughable pair of university highbrows who couldn't have a spat without citing William James and Karl Marx, or Villiers de l'Isle-Adam or Whitehead. We decided that we were the tender-minded and tough-minded of William James, respectively. But James had said that to know everything that happened in one city on a single day would crush the toughest mind. No one could be as tough as he needed to be. "You'll be barren of sympathy if you don't look out," Zet said. That was the way he talked. His language was always elegant. Lord knows where his patrician style came from—Lord Bacon, perhaps, plus Hume and a certain amount of Santayana. He debated with his friends in the whitewashed cellar. His language was very pure and musical.

But then he was musical. He didn't walk down the street without practicing a Haydn quartet, or Borodin or Prokofiev. Overcoat buttoned at the neck, he hauled his briefcase and made the violin stops inside his fuzz-lined gloves and puffed the music in his throat and cheeks. In good heart, with skin the color of yellow grapes, he did the cello in his chest and the violins high in the nose. The trees were posted in the broom-swept, dust-mixed snow and were bound to the subpavement soil and enriched by sewer seepage. Zetland and the squirrels enjoyed the privileges of motility.

Heat overpowered him when he entered Cobb Hall. Its interior was Baptist brown, austere, varnished, very like old churches. The building was kept very hot, and he felt the heat on his face immediately. It struck him on the cheeks. His goggles fogged up. He dropped the slow movement of his Borodin quartet and sighed. After the sigh he wore an intellectual, not a musical, expression. He now was ready for semiotics, symbolic logic—the reader of Tarski, Carnap, Feigl, and Dewey. A stoutish young man whose color was poor, whose sandy hair, brushed flat, had greenish lights, he sat in the hard seminar chair and fetched out his cigarettes. Playing parts, he was here a Brain. With Skinny Jones in his raveled sweater and missing front teeth, with Tisewitch whose eyebrows were kinky, with Dark Devvie—a lovely, acid, pale girl—and Miss Krehayn, a redhead and hard stutterer, he was a leading logical positivist.

For a while. In the way of mental work, he could do anything, but he was not about to become a logician. He was, however, attracted by rational analysis. The emotional struggles of mankind were never resolved. The same things were done over and over, with passion, with passionate stupidity, insectlike, the same emotional struggles repeated in daily reality—urge, drive, desire, self-preservation, aggrandizement, the search for happiness, the search for justification, the experience of coming to be and of passing away, from nothingness to nothingness. Very boring. Frightening. Doom. Now, mathematical logic could extricate you from all this nonsensical existence. "See here," said Zet in his soiled canvas Bauhaus chair, the dropped glasses shortening his short nose. "As propositions are either true or false, whatever *is* is right. Leibnitz was no fool. Provided that you really know that what is, indeed *is*. Still, I haven't entirely made up my mind about the religious question, as a true positivist should."

Just then from straight-ruled Chicago, blue with winter, brown with evening, crystal with frost, the factory whistles went off. Five o'clock. The mouse-gray snow and the hutchy bungalows, the furnace blasting, and Perchik's shovel gritting in the coalbin. The radio boomed through the floors, to us below. It was the *Anschluss*—Schuschnigg and Hitler. Vienna was just as cold as Chicago now; much gloomier.

"Lottie is expecting me," said Zetland.

Lottie was pretty. She was also, in her own way, theatrical—the party girl, the pagan beauty with hibiscus in her teeth. She was a witty young woman, and she loved an amusing man. She visited his coalbin. He stayed in her room. They found an English basement together which they furnished with an oak table and rose velvet junk. They kept cats and dogs, a squirrel, and a pet crow. After their first quarrel Lottie smeared her breasts with honey as a peace gesture. And before graduation she borrowed an automobile and they drove to Michigan City and were married. Zet had gotten a fellowship in philosophy at Columbia. There was a wedding and good-bye party for them on Kimbark Avenue, in an old flat. After being separated for five minutes, Zet and Lottie ran the whole length of the corridor, embracing, trembling, and kissing. "Darling, suddenly you weren't there!"

"Sweetheart, I'm always there. I'll always be there!"

Two young people from the sticks, overdoing the thing, acting out their love in public. But there was more to it than display. They adored each other. Besides, they had already lived as man and wife for a year with all their dogs and cats and birds and fishes and plants and fiddles and books. Ingeniously, Zet mimicked animals. He washed himself like a cat and bit fleas on his haunch like a dog, and made goldfish faces, wagging his fingertips like fins. When they went to the Orthodox church for the Easter service, he learned to genuflect and make the sign of the cross Eastern style. Charlotte kept time with her head when he played the violin, just a bit off, his loving metronome. Zet was forever acting something out and Lottie was also demonstrative. There is probably no way for human beings to avoid playacting, Zet said. As long as you know where the soul is, there is no harm in being Socrates. It is when the soul can't be located that the play of being someone turns desperate.

So Zet and Lottie were not simply married but delightfully married. Instead of a poor Macedonian girl whose muttering immigrant mother laid spells and curses on Zet and whose father sharpened knives and scissors, and went up and down alleys ringing a hand bell, Zet had *das Ewig-Weibliche,* a natural, universal, gorgeous power. As for Lottie, she said, "There's no one in the world like Zet." She added, "In every way." Then she dropped her voice, speaking from the side of her mouth with absurd Dietrich charm, in tough Chicago style, saying, "I'm not exactly inexperienced, I want you to know." That was no secret. She had lived with a fellow named Huram, an educational psychologist, who had a mended harelip, over which he grew a mustache. Before that there had been someone else. But now she was a wife and overflowed with wifely love. She ironed his shirts and buttered his toast, lit his cigarette, and gazed like a little Spanish virgin at him, all aglow. It amused some, this melting and *Schwärmerei.* Others were irritated. Father Zetland was enraged.

The couple departed from La Salle Street Station for New York, by day coach. The depot looked archaic, mineral. The steam foamed up to the sooty skylights. The El pillars vibrated on Van Buren Street, where the hockshops and the army-navy stores and the two-bit barbershops were. The redcap took the valises. Zet tried to say something to Ozymandias about the kingly airs of the black porters. The aunts were also there. They didn't easily follow when Zet made one of his odd statements about the black of the station and the black redcaps and their ceremonious African style. The look that went between the old girls agreed that he was not making sense, poor Elias. They blamed Lottie. Excited at starting out in life, married, a fellow at Columbia University, he felt that his father was casting his own glumness on him, making him heavy-hearted. Zet had grown a large brown mustache. His big boyish teeth, wide-spaced, combined oddly with these mature whiskers. The low, chesty, almost burly figure was a shorter version of his father's. But Ozymandias had a Russian military posture. He did not believe in grinning and ducking and darting and mimicry. He stood erect. Lottie cried out affectionate things to everyone. She wore an apple-blossom dress and matching turban and apple-blossom high-heeled shoes. The trains clashed and huffed, but you could hear the rapid stamping of Lottie's gaudy heels. Her Oriental eyes, her humorous peasant nose, her pleasant bosom, her smooth sexual rear with which Zet's hand kept contact all the while, drew the silent, harsh attention of Ozymandias. She called him "Pa." He strained cigarette smoke between his teeth with an expression that passed for a smile. Yes, he managed to look pleasant through it all. The Macedonian in-laws didn't show up at all. They were on a streetcar and caught in a traffic jam.

On this sad, jolly occasion Ozymandias restrained himself. He looked very European despite the straw summer skimmer he was wearing, with a red-white-and-blue band. The downtown buyer, well trained in dissembling, subdued the snarls of his heart and by pressing down his chin with the black hole in it cooled his rage. Temporarily he was losing his son. Lottie kissed her father-in-law. She kissed the aunts, the two practical nurses who read Romain Rolland and Warwick Deeping beside the wheelchair and the deathbed. Their opinion was that Lottie might be more fastidious in her feminine hygiene. Aunt Masha thought the herringy odor was due to dysmenorrhea. Virginal, Aunt Masha was unfamiliar with the odor of a woman who had been making love on a warm day. The young people took every opportunity to strengthen each other.

Imitating their brother, the aunts, too, gave false kisses with inexperienced lips. Lottie then cried with joy. They were leaving Chicago, the most boring place in the world, and getting rid of surly Ozymandias and of her mother the witch and her poor daddy the knife grinder. She was married to Zet, who had a million times more charm and warmth and brains than anyone else.

"Oh, Pa! Good-bye!" Zet emotionally took his iron father in his arms.

"Do right. Study. Make something of yourself. If you get in trouble, wire for money."

"Dear Pa, I love you. Masha, Dounia, I love you, too," said Lottie, now red-faced with tears. She gave them all sobbing kisses. Then at the coach window, waving, the young people embraced and the train slid off.

As the *Pacemaker* departed, Father Zetland shook his fist at the observation car. He stamped his feet. At Lottie, who was ruining his son, he cried, "You wait! I'll get you. Five years, ten years, but I'll get you." He shouted, "You bitch—you nasty cunt."

Russian in his rage, he cried out, *"Cont!"* His sisters did not understand.

Zet and Lottie swam into New York City from the skies—that was how it felt in the *Pacemaker*, rushing along the Hudson at sunrise. First many blue twigs overhanging the water, then a rosy color, and then the heavy flashing of the river under the morning sun. They were in the dining car, their eyes weary with an overflow of impressions. They were drained by a night of broken sleep in the day coach, and they were dazzled. They drank coffee from cups as grainy as soapstone, and poured from New York Central pewter. They were in the East, where everything was better, where objects were different. Here there was deeper meaning in the air.

After changing at Harmon to an electric locomotive, they began a more quick and eager ride. Trees, water, sky, and the sky raced off, floating, and there came bridges, structures, and at last the tunnel, where the air brakes gasped and the streamliner was checked. There were yellow bulbs in wire mesh, and subterranean air came through the vents. The doors opened, the passengers, pulling their clothing straight, flowed out and got their luggage, and Zet and Lottie, reaching Forty-second Street, refugees from arid and inhibited Chicago, from Emptyland, embraced at the curb and kissed each other repeatedly on the mouth. They had come to the World City, where all behavior was deeper and more resonant, where they could freely be themselves, as demonstrative as they liked. Intellect, art, the transcendent, needed no excuses here. Any cabdriver understood, Zet believed.

"Ah, darling, darling—thank God," said Zet. "A place where it's normal to be a human being."

"Oh, Zet, amen!" said Lottie with tremors and tears.

At first they lived uptown, on the West Side. The small, chinging trolleys still rolled on slant Broadway. Lottie chose a room described as a studio, at the rear of a brownstone. There was a studio bedroom, and the bathroom was also the kitchen. Covered with a heavy, smooth board, the tub became the kitchen table. You could reach the gas ring from the bath. Zet liked that. Frying your eggs while you sat in the water. You could hear the largo of the drain as you drank your coffee, or watch the cockroaches come and go about the cupboards. The toaster spring was tight. It snapped out the bread. Sometimes a toasted cockroach was flung out. The ceilings were high. There was little daylight. The fireplace was made of small tiles. You could bring home an apple crate from Broadway and have a ten-minute fire, which left a little ash and many hooked nails. The studio turned into a Zet habitat, a Zet-and-Lottie place: dark, dirty portieres, thriftshop carpets, upholstered chairs with bald arms that shone, said Zetland, like gorilla hide. The window opened on an air shaft, but Zet had lived even in Chicago behind drawn shades or in a whitewashed coalbin. Lottie bought lamps with pink porcelain shades flounced at the edges like ancient butter dishes. The room had the agreeable dimness of a chapel, the gloom of a sanctuary. When I visited Byzantine churches in Yugoslavia, I thought I had found the master model, the archetypal Zet habitat.

The Zetlands settled in. Crusts, butts, coffee grounds, dishes of dog food, books, journals, music stands, odors of Macedonian cookery (mutton, yogurt, lemon, rice), and white Chilean wine in bulbous bottles. Zetland reconnoitered the philosophy department, brought home loads of books from the library, and put himself to work. His industry might have pleased Ozymandias. But nothing, he would say, could really please the old guy. Or perhaps his ultimate pleasure was never to be pleased, and never to approve. With an M.A. of her own in sociology, Lottie went to work in an office. Look at her, said Zet, such an impulsive young woman, and so efficient, such a crack executive secretary. See how steady she was, how uncomplaining about getting up in the dark, and what a dependable employee this Balkan Gypsy had turned out to be. He found a sort of sadness in this, and he was astonished. Office work would have killed him. He had tried that. Ozymandias had found jobs for him. But routine and paperwork paralyzed him. He had worked in the company warehouse helping the zoologist to see what ailed the filberts and the figs and the raisins, keeping parasites in check. That was interesting, but not for long. And one week he had worked in the shops of the Field Museum, learning to make plastic leaves for habitats. Dead animals, he learned, were preserved in many poisons and that, he said, was how he felt about being an employee—a toxic condition.

So it was Lottie who worked, and the afternoons were very long. Zet and the dog waited for her at five o'clock. At last she came, with groceries, hurrying westward from Broadway. In the street Zet and Miss Katusha ran toward her. Zet called out, "Lottie!" and the brown dog scrabbled on the pavement and whined. Lottie was wan from the subway, and warm, and made contralto sounds in her throat when she was kissed. She brought home hamburger meat and yogurt, bones for Katusha, and small gifts for Zetland. They were still honeymooners. They were ecstatic in New York. They had the animal ecstasies of the dog for emphasis or analogy. They made friends in the building with a pulp writer and his wife—Giddings and Gertrude. Giddings wrote Westerns: the Balzac of the Badlands, Zet named him. Giddings called him the Wittgenstein of the West Side. Zetland thus had an audience for his cheerful inventions. He read aloud funny sentences from the *Encyclopedia of Unified Sciences* and put H. Rider Haggard, Gidding's favorite novelist, into the language of symbolic logic. Evenings, Lottie became again a Macedonian Gypsy, her mama's daughter. Mama was a necromancer from Skoplje, said Zetland, and made spells with cats' urine and snakes' navels. She knew the erotic secrets of antiquity. Evidently Lottie knew them, too. It was established that Lottie's female qualities were rich, and deep and sweet. Romantic Zetland said fervent and grateful things about them.

From so much sweetness, this chocolate life, nerves glowing too hotly, came pangs of anxiety. In its own way the anxiety was also delicious, he said. He explained that he had two kinds of ecstasy, sensuous and sick. Those early months in New York were too much for him. His lung trouble came back, and he ran a fever; he ached, passed urine painfully, and he lay in bed, the faded wine-colored pajamas binding him at the crotch and under the plump arms. His skin developed its old irritability.

It was his invalid childhood all over again for a few weeks. It was awful that he should fall into it, a grown man, just married, but it was delectable, too. He remembered the hospital very well, the booming in his head when he was etherized and the horrible open wound in his belly. It was infected and wouldn't heal. He drained through a rubber tube which an ordinary diaper pin secured. He understood that he was going to die, but he read the funny papers. All the kids in the ward had to read were funny papers and the Bible: Slim Jim, Boob McNutt, Noah's ark, Hagar, Ishmael ran into each other like the many colors of the funnies. It was a harsh Chicago winter, there were golden icon rays at the frosted windows in the morning, and the streetcars droned and ground, clanged. Somehow he had made it out of the hospital, and his aunts nursed him at home with marrow broth and scalded milk and melted butter, soda biscuits as big as playing cards. His illness in New York brought back the open wound with its rotten smell and the rubber tube which a diaper pin kept from falling into his belly, and bedsores and his having to learn again at the age of eight how to walk. A very early and truthful sense of the seizure of matter by life energies, the painful, difficult, intricate chemical-electrical transformation and organization, gorgeous, streaming with radiant colors, and all the scent and the stinking. This combination was too harsh. It whirled too much. It troubled and intimidated the soul too much. What were we here for, of all strange beings and creatures the strangest? Clear colloid eyes to see with, for a while, and see so finely, and a palpitating universe to see, and so many human messages to give and to receive. And the bony box for thinking and for the storage of thoughts, and a cloudy heart for feelings. Ephemerids, grinding up other creatures, flavoring and heating their flesh, devouring this flesh. A kind of being filled with death-knowledge, and also filled with infinite longings. These peculiar internal phrases were not intentional. That was just it, they simply came to Zetland, naturally, involuntarily, as he was consulting with himself about this tangle of bright and terrifying qualities.

So Zet laid aside his logic books. They had lost their usefulness. They joined the funny papers he had put away when he was eight years old. He had no more use for Rudolf Carnap than for Boob McNutt. He said to Lottie, "What other books are there?" She went to the shelf and read off the titles. He stopped her at *Moby Dick,* and she handed him the large volume. After reading a few pages he knew that he would never be a Ph.D. in philosophy. The sea came into his inland, Lake Michigan soul, he told me. Oceanic cold was just the thing for his fever. He felt polluted, but he read about purity. He had reached a bad stage of limited selfhood, disaffection, unwillingness to be; he was sick; he wanted *out.* Then he read this dazzling book. It rushed over him. He thought he would drown. But he didn't drown; he floated.

The creature of flesh and blood, and ill, went to the toilet. Because of his intestines he shuffled to sit on the board and over the porcelain, over the sewer-connected hole and its water—the necessary disgrace. And when the dizzy floor tiles wavered under his sick eyes like chicken wire, the amethyst of the ocean was also there in the bevels of the medicine-chest mirror, and the white power of the whale, to which the bathtub gave a fleeting gauge. The cloaca was there, the nausea, and also the coziness of bowel smells going back to childhood, the old brown colors. And the dismay and sweetness of ragged coughing and the tropical swampiness of the fever. But also there rose up the seas. Straight through the air shaft, west, and turn left at the Hudson. The Atlantic was there.

The real business of his life was with comprehensive vision, he decided. He had been working in philosophy with the resemblance theory of universals. He had an original approach to the predicate "resemble." But that was finished. When sick, he was decisive. He had the weak sweats and was coughing up blue phlegm with his fist to his mouth and his eyes swelling. He cleared his throat and said to Lottie, who sat on the bed holding his tea for him during this coughing fit, "I don't think I can go on in the philosophy department."

"It's really worrying you, isn't it? You were talking philosophy in your sleep the other night."

"Was I?"

"Talking in your sleep about epistemology or something. I don't understand that stuff, you know that."

"Ah, well, it's not really for me, either."

"But, honey, you don't have to do anything you don't like. Switch to something else. I'll back you all the way."

"Ah, you're a dear woman. But we'll have to get along without the fellowship."

"What's it worth? Those cheap bastards don't give you enough to live on anyway. Zet, dear, screw the money. I can see you've gone through a change of heart because of that book."

"Oh, Lottie, it's a miracle, that book. It takes you out of this human world."

"What do you mean?"

"I mean it takes you out of the universe of mental projections or insulating fictions of ordinary social practice or psychological habit. It gives you elemental liberty. What really frees you from these insulating social and psychological fictions is the other fiction, of art. There really is no human life without this poetry. Ah, Lottie, I've been starving on symbolic logic."

"I've *got* to read that book now," she said.

But she didn't get far with it. Sea books were for men, and anyway she wasn't bookish; she was too impulsive to sit long with any book. That was Zet's department. He would tell her all she needed to know about *Moby Dick*.

"I'll have to go and talk to Professor Edman."

"As soon as you're strong enough, go on down and quit. Just quit. All the better. What the hell do you want to be a professor for? Oh, that dog!" Katusha had gotten into a barking duel with an animal in the next yard. "Shut up, you bitch! Sometimes I really hate that lousy dog. I feel her barking right in the middle of my head."

"Give her to the Chinese laundryman; he likes her."

"Likes her? He'd cook her. Now look, Zet, don't you worry about a thing. Screw that logic. Okay? You can do a hundred things. You know French, Russian, German, and you're a real brain. We don't need much to live on. No fancy stuff for me. I shop on Union Square. So what?"

"With that beautiful Macedonian body," said Zet, "Klein's is just as good as haute couture. Blessings on your bust, your belly, and your bottom."

"If your fever goes down by the weekend, we'll go to the country, to Giddings and Gertrude."

"Pa will be upset when he hears I've dropped out of Columbia."

"So what? I know you love him, but he's such a grudger, you can't please him anyway. Well, screw him, too."

They moved downtown in 1940 and lived on Bleecker Street for a dozen years. They were soon prominent in Greenwich Village. In Chicago they had been bohemians without knowing it. In the Village Zet was identified with the avant-garde in literature and with radical politics. When the Russians invaded Finland, radical politics became absurd. Marxists debated whether the workers' state could be imperialistic. This was too nonsensical for Zetland. Then there was the Nazi-Soviet pact, there was the war. Constantine was born during the war—Lottie wanted him to have a Balkan name. Zetland wanted to enter the service. When he behaved with spirit, Lottie was always for him, and she supported him against his father, who of course disapproved.

LEAVING THE YELLOW HOUSE

THE NEIGHBORS—there were in all six white people who lived at Sego Desert Lake—told one another that old Hattie could no longer make it alone. The desert life, even with a forced-air furnace in the house and butane gas brought from town in a truck, was still too difficult for her. There were women even older than Hattie in the county. Twenty miles away was Amy Walters, the gold miner's widow. She was a hardy old girl, more wiry and tough than Hattie. Every day of the year she took a bath in the icy lake. And Amy was crazy about money and knew how to manage it, as Hattie did not. Hattie was not exactly a drunkard, but she hit the bottle pretty hard, and now she was in trouble and there was a limit to the help she could expect from even the best of neighbors.

They were fond of her, though. You couldn't help being fond of Hattie. She was big and cheerful, puffy, comic, boastful, with a big round back and stiff, rather long legs. Before the century began she had graduated from finishing school and studied the organ in Paris. But now she didn't know a note from a skillet. She had tantrums when she played canasta. And all that remained of her fine fair hair was frizzled along her forehead in small gray curls. Her forehead was not much wrinkled, but the skin was bluish, the color of skim milk. She walked with long strides in spite of the heaviness of her hips. With her shoulders, she pushed on, round-backed, showing the flat rubber bottoms of her shoes.

Once a week, in the same cheerful, plugging but absent way, she took off her short skirt and the dirty aviator's jacket with the wool collar and put on a girdle, a dress, and high-heeled shoes. When she stood on these heels her fat old body trembled. She wore a big brown Rembrandt-like tam with a ten-cent-store brooch, eyelike, carefully centered. She drew a straight line with lipstick on her mouth, leaving part of the upper lip pale. At the wheel of her old turret-shaped car, she drove, seemingly methodical but speeding dangerously, across forty miles of mountainous desert to buy frozen meat pies and whiskey. She went to the Laundromat and the hairdresser, and then had lunch with two martinis at the Arlington. Afterward she would often visit Marian Nabot's Silvermine Hotel at Miller Street near skid row and pass the rest of the day gossiping and drinking with her cronies, old divorcées like herself who had settled in the West. Hattie never gambled anymore and she didn't care for the movies. And at five o'clock she drove back at the same speed, calmly, partly blinded by the smoke of her cigarette. The fixed cigarette gave her a watering eye.

The Rolfes and the Paces were her only white neighbors at Sego Desert Lake. There was Sam Jervis too, but he was only an old gandy walker who did odd jobs in her garden, and she did not count him. Nor did she count among her neighbors Darly, the dudes' cowboy who worked for the Paces, nor Swede, the telegrapher. Pace had a guest ranch, and Rolfe and his wife were rich and had retired. Thus there were three good houses at the lake, Hattie's yellow house, Pace's, and the Rolfes'. All the rest of the population—Sam, Swede, Watchtah the section foreman, and the Mexicans and Indians and Negroes—lived in shacks and boxcars. There were very few trees, cottonwoods and box elders. Everything else, down to the shores, was sagebrush and juniper. The lake was what remained of an old sea that had covered the volcanic mountains. To the north there were some tungsten mines; to the south, fifteen miles, was an Indian village—shacks built of plywood or railroad ties.

In this barren place Hattie had lived for more than twenty years. Her first summer was spent not in a house but in an Indian wickiup on the shore. She used to say that she had watched the stars from this almost roofless shelter. After her divorce she took up with a cowboy named Wicks. Neither of them had any money—it was the Depression—and they had lived on the range, trapping coyotes for a living. Once a month they would come into town and rent a room and go on a bender. Hattie told this sadly, but also gloatingly, and with many trimmings. A thing no sooner happened to her than it was transformed into something else. "We were caught in a storm," she said, "and we rode hard, down to the lake, and knocked on the door of the yellow house"—now her house. "Alice Parmenter took us in and let us sleep on the floor." What had actually happened was that the wind was blowing—there had been no storm—and they were not far from the house anyway; and Alice Parmenter, who knew that Hattie and Wicks were not married, offered them separate beds; but Hattie, swaggering, had said in a loud voice, "Why get two sets of sheets dirty?" And she and her cowboy had slept in Alice's bed while Alice had taken the sofa.

Then Wicks went away. There was never anybody like him in the sack; he was brought up in a whorehouse and the girls had taught him everything, said Hattie. She didn't really understand what she was saying but believed that she was being Western. More than anything else she wanted to be thought of as a rough, experienced woman of the West. Still, she was a lady, too. She had good silver and good china and engraved stationery, but she kept canned beans and A-1 sauce and tuna fish and bottles of catsup and fruit salad on the library shelves of her living room. On her night table was the Bible her pious brother Angus—the other brother was a heller—had given her; but behind the little door of the commode was a bottle of bourbon. When she awoke in the night she tippled herself back to sleep. In the glove compartment of her old car she kept little sample bottles for emergencies on the road. Old Darly found them after her accident.

The accident did not happen far out in the desert as she had always feared, but very near home. She had had a few martinis with the Rolfes one evening, and as she was driving home over the railroad crossing she lost control of the car and veered off the crossing onto the tracks. The explanation she gave was that she had sneezed, and the sneeze had blinded her and made her twist the wheel. The motor was killed and all four wheels of the car sat smack on the rails. Hattie crept down from the door, high off the roadbed. A great fear took hold of her—for the car, for the future, and not only for the future but spreading back into the past—and she began to hurry on stiff legs through the sagebrush to Pace's ranch.

Now the Paces were away on a hunting trip and had left Darly in charge; he was tending bar in the old cabin that went back to the days of the pony express, when Hattie burst in. There were two customers, a tungsten miner and his girl.

"Darly, I'm in trouble. Help me. I've had an accident," said Hattie.

How the face of a man will alter when a woman has bad news to tell him! It happened now to lean old Darly; his eyes went flat and looked unwilling, his jaw moved in and out, his wrinkled cheeks began to flush, and he said, "What's the matter—what's happened to you now?"

"I'm stuck on the tracks. I sneezed. I lost control of the car. Tow me off, Darly. With the pickup. Before the train comes."

Darly threw down his towel and stamped his high-heeled boots. "Now what have you gone and done?" he said. "I told you to stay home after dark."

"Where's Pace? Ring the fire bell and fetch Pace."

"There's nobody on the property except me," said the lean old man. "And I'm not supposed to close the bar and you know it as well as I do."

"Please, Darly. I can't leave my car on the tracks."

"Too bad!" he said. Nevertheless he moved from behind the bar. "How did you say it happened?"

"I told you, I sneezed," said Hattie.

Everyone, as she later told it, was as drunk as sixteen thousand dollars: Darly, the miner, and the miner's girl.

Darly was limping as he locked the door of the bar. A year before, a kick from one of Pace's mares had broken his ribs as he was loading her into the trailer, and he hadn't recovered from it. He was too old. But he dissembled the pain. The high-heeled narrow boots helped, and his painful bending looked like the ordinary stooping posture of a cowboy. However, Darly was not a genuine cowboy, like Pace who had grown up in the saddle. He was a latecomer from the East and until the age of forty had never been on horseback. In this respect he and Hattie were alike. They were not genuine Westerners.

Hattie hurried after him through the ranch yard.

"Damn you!" he said to her. "I got thirty bucks out of that sucker and I would have skinned him out of his whole paycheck if you minded your business. Pace is going to be sore as hell."

"You've got to help me. We're neighbors," said Hattie.

"You're not fit to be living out here. You can't do it anymore. Besides, you're swacked all the time."

Hattie couldn't afford to talk back. The thought of her car on the tracks made her frantic. If a freight came now and smashed it, her life at Sego Desert Lake would be finished. And where would she go then? She was not fit to live in this place. She had never made the grade at all, only seemed to have made it. And Darly—why did he say such hurtful things to her? Because he himself was sixty-eight years old, and he had no other place to go, either; he took bad treatment from Pace besides. Darly stayed because his only alternative was to go to the soldiers' home. Moreover, the dude women would still crawl into his sack. They wanted a cowboy and they thought he was one. Why, he couldn't even raise himself out of his bunk in the morning. And where else would he get women? "After the dude season," she wanted to say to him, "you always have to go to the Veterans' Hospital to get fixed up again." But she didn't dare offend him now.

The moon was due to rise. It appeared as they drove over the ungraded dirt road toward the crossing where Hattie's turret-shaped car was sitting on the rails. Driving very fast, Darly wheeled the pickup around, spraying dirt on the miner and his girl, who had followed in their car.

"You get behind the wheel and steer," Darly told Hattie.

She climbed into the seat. Waiting at the wheel, she lifted up her face and said, "Please God, I didn't bend the axle or crack the oil pan."

When Darly crawled under the bumper of Hattie's car the pain in his ribs suddenly cut off his breath, so instead of doubling the tow chain he fastened it at full length. He rose and trotted back to the truck on the tight boots. Motion seemed the only remedy for the pain; not even booze did the trick anymore. He put the pickup into towing gear and began to pull. One side of Hattie's car dropped into the roadbed with a heave of springs. She sat with a stormy, frightened, conscience-stricken face, racing the motor until she flooded it.

The tungsten miner yelled, "Your chain's too long."

Hattie was raised high in the air by the pitch of the wheels. She had to roll down the window to let herself out because the door handle had been jammed from inside for years. Hattie struggled out on the uplifted side crying, "I better call the Swede. I better have him signal. There's a train due."

"Go on, then," said Darly. "You're no good here."

"Darly, be careful with my car. Be careful."

The ancient sea bed at this place was flat and low, and the lights of her car and of the truck and of the tungsten miner's Chevrolet were bright and big at twenty miles. Hattie was too frightened to think of this. All she could think was that she was a procrastinating old woman; she had lived by delays; she had meant to stop drinking; she had put off the time, and now she had smashed her car—a terrible end, a terrible judgment on her. She got to the ground and, drawing up her skirt, she started to get over the tow chain. To prove that the chain didn't have to be shortened, and to get the whole thing over with, Darly threw the pickup forward again. The chain jerked up and struck Hattie in the knee and she fell forward and broke her arm.

She cried, "Darly, Darly, I'm hurt. I fell."

"The old lady tripped on the chain," said the miner. "Back up here and I'll double it for you. You're getting nowheres."

Drunkenly the miner lay down on his back in the dark, soft red cinders of the roadbed. Darly had backed up to slacken the chain.

Darly hurt the miner, too. He tore some skin from his fingers by racing ahead before the chain was secure. Without complaining, the miner wrapped his hand in his shirttail saying, "She'll do it now." The old car came down from the tracks and stood on the shoulder of the road.

"There's your goddamn car," said Darly to Hattie.

"Is it all right?" she said. Her left side was covered with dirt, but she managed to pick herself up and stand, round-backed and heavy, on her stiff legs. "I'm hurt, Darly." She tried to convince him of it.

"Hell if you are," he said. He believed she was putting on an act to escape blame. The pain in his ribs made him especially impatient with her. "Christ, if you can't look after yourself anymore you've got no business out here."

"You're old yourself," she said. "Look what you did to me. You can't hold your liquor."

This offended him greatly. He said, "I'll take you to the Rolfes. They let you booze it up in the first place, so let them worry about you. I'm tired of your bunk, Hattie."

He raced uphill. Chains, spade, and crowbar clashed on the sides of the pickup. She was frightened and held her arm and cried. Rolfe's dogs jumped at her to lick her when she went through the gate. She shrank from them crying, "Down, down."

"Darly," she cried in the darkness, "take care of my car. Don't leave it standing there on the road. Darly, take care of it, please."

But Darly in his ten-gallon hat, his chin-bent face wrinkled, small and angry, a furious pain in his ribs, tore away at high speed.

"Oh, God, what will I do," she said.

The Rolfes were having a last drink before dinner, sitting at their fire of pitchy railroad ties, when Hattie opened the door. Her knee was bleeding, her eyes were tiny with shock, her face gray with dust.

"I'm hurt," she said desperately. "I had an accident. I sneezed and lost control of the wheel. Jerry, look after the car. It's on the road."

They bandaged her knee and took her home and put her to bed. Helen Rolfe wrapped a heating pad around her arm.

"I can't have the pad," Hattie complained. "The switch goes on and off, and every time it does it starts my generator and uses up the gas."

"Ah, now, Hattie," Rolfe said, "this is not the time to be stingy. We'll take you to town in the morning and have you looked over. Helen will phone Dr. Stroud."

Hattie wanted to say, "Stingy! Why you're the stingy ones. I just haven't got anything. You and Helen are ready to hit each other over two bits in canasta." But the Rolfes were good to her; they were her only real friends here. Darly would have let her lie in the yard all night, and Pace would have sold her to the bone man. He'd give her to the knacker for a buck.

So she didn't talk back to the Rolfes, but as soon as they left the yellow house and walked through the superclear moonlight under the great skirt of box-elder shadows to their new station wagon, Hattie turned off the switch, and the heavy swirling and battering of the generator stopped. Presently she became aware of real pain, deeper pain, in her arm, and she sat rigid, warming the injured place with her hand. It seemed to her that she could feel the bone sticking out. Before leaving, Helen Rolfe had thrown over her a comforter that had belonged to Hattie's dead friend India, from whom she had inherited the small house and everything in it. Had the comforter lain on India's bed the night she died? Hattie tried to remember, but her thoughts were mixed up. She was fairly sure the deathbed pillow was in the loft, and she believed she had put the death bedding in a trunk. Then how had this comforter got out? She couldn't do anything about it now but draw it away from contact with her skin. It kept her legs warm. This she accepted, but she didn't want it any nearer.

More and more Hattie saw her own life as though, from birth to the present, every moment had been filmed. Her fancy was that when she died she would see the film in the next world. Then she would know how she had appeared from the back, watering the plants, in the bathroom, asleep, playing the organ, embracing—everything, even tonight, in pain, almost the last pain, perhaps, for she couldn't take much more. How many twists and angles had life to show her yet? There couldn't be much film left. To lie awake and think such thoughts was the worst thing in the world. Better death than insomnia. Hattie not only loved sleep, she believed in it.

The first attempt to set the bone was not successful. "Look what they've done to me," said Hattie and showed visitors the discolored breast. After the second operation her mind wandered. The sides of her bed had to be raised, for in her delirium she roamed the wards. She cursed at the nurses when they shut her in. "You can't make people prisoners in a democracy without a trial, you bitches." She had learned from Wicks how to swear. "*He* was profane," she used to say. "I picked it up unconsciously."

For several weeks her mind was not clear. Asleep, her face was lifeless; her cheeks were puffed out and her mouth, no longer wide and grinning, was drawn round and small. Helen sighed when she saw her.

"Shall we get in touch with her family?" Helen asked the doctor. His skin was white and thick. He had chestnut hair, abundant but very dry. He sometimes explained to his patients, "I had a tropical disease during the war."

He asked, "Is there a family?"

"Old brothers. Cousins' children," said Helen. She tried to think who would be called to her own bedside (she was old enough for that). Rolfe would see that she was cared for. He would hire private nurses. Hattie could not afford that. She had already gone beyond her means. A trust company in Philadelphia paid her eighty dollars a month. She had a small savings account.

"I suppose it'll be up to us to get her out of hock," said Rolfe. "Unless the brother down in Mexico comes across. We may have to phone one of those old guys."

In the end, no relations had to be called. Hattie began to recover. At last she could recognize visitors, though her mind was still in disorder. Much that had happened she couldn't recall.

"How many quarts of blood did they have to give me?" she kept asking. "I seem to remember five, six, eight different transfusions. Daylight, electric light . . ." She tried to smile, but she couldn't make a pleasant face as yet. "How am I going to pay?" she said. "At twenty-five bucks a quart. My little bit of money is just about wiped out."

Blood became her constant topic, her preoccupation. She told everyone who came to see her, "—have to replace all that blood. They poured gallons into me. Gallons. I hope it was all good." And, though very weak, she began to grin and laugh again. There was more hissing in her laughter than formerly; the illness had affected her chest.

"No cigarettes, no booze," the doctor told Helen.

"Doctor," Helen asked him, "do you expect her to change?"

"All the same, I am obliged to say it."

"Life sober may not be much of a temptation to her," said Helen.

Her husband laughed. When Rolfe's laughter was intense it blinded one of his eyes. His short Irish face turned red; on the bridge of his small, sharp nose the skin whitened. "Hattie's like me," he said. "She'll be in business till she's cleaned out. And if Sego Lake turned to whisky she'd use her last strength to knock her old yellow house down to build a raft of it. She'd float away on whisky. So why talk temperance?"

Hattie recognized the similarity between them. When he came to see her she said, "Jerry, you're the only one I can really talk to about my troubles. What am I going to do for money? I have Hotchkiss Insurance. I paid eight dollars a month."

"That won't do you much good, Hat. No Blue Cross?"

"I let it drop ten years ago. Maybe I could sell some of my valuables."

"What valuables have you got?" he said. His eye began to droop with laughter.

"Why," she said defiantly, "there's plenty. First there's the beautiful, precious Persian rug that India left me."

"Coals from the fireplace have been burning it for years, Hat!"

"The rug is in *perfect* condition," she said with an angry sway of the shoulders. "A beautiful object like that never loses its value. And the oak table from the Spanish monastery is three hundred years old."

"With luck you could get twenty bucks for it. It would cost fifty to haul it out of here. It's the house you ought to sell."

"The house?" she said. Yes, that had been in her mind. "I'd have to get twenty thousand for it."

"Eight is a fair price."

"Fifteen. . . ." She was offended, and her voice recovered its strength. "India put eight into it in two years. And don't forget that Sego Lake is one of the most beautiful places in the world."

"But where is it? Five hundred and some miles to San Francisco and two hundred to Salt Lake City. Who wants to live way out here but a few eccentrics like you and India? And me?"

"There are things you can't put a price tag on. Beautiful things."

"Oh, bull, Hattie! You don't know squat about beautiful things. Any more than I do. I live here because it figures for me, and you because India left you the house. And just in the nick of time, too. Without it you wouldn't have had a pot of your own."

His words offended Hattie; more than that, they frightened her. She was silent and then grew thoughtful, for she was fond of Jerry Rolfe and he of her. He had good sense and, moreover, he only expressed her own thoughts. He spoke no more than the truth about India's death and the house. But she told herself, He doesn't know everything. You'd have to pay a San Francisco architect ten thousand just to *think* of such a house. Before he drew a line.

"Jerry," the old woman said, "what am I going to do about replacing the blood in the blood bank?"

"Do you want a quart from me, Hat?" His eye began to fall shut.

"You won't do. You had that tumor, two years ago. I think Darly ought to give some."

"The old man?" Rolfe laughed at her. "You want to kill him?"

"Why!" said Hattie with anger, lifting up her massive face. Fever and perspiration had frayed the fringe of curls; at the back of the head the hair had knotted and matted so that it had to be shaved. "Darly almost killed me. It's his fault that I'm in this condition. He must have *some* blood in him. He runs after all the chicks—all of them—young and old."

"Come, you were drunk, too," said Rolfe.

"I've driven drunk for forty years. It was the sneeze. Oh, Jerry, I feel wrung out," said Hattie, haggard, sitting forward in bed. But her face was cleft by her nonsensically happy grin. She was not one to be miserable for long; she had the expression of a perennial survivor.

Every other day she went to the therapist. The young woman worked her arm for her; it was a pleasure and a comfort to Hattie, who would have been glad to leave the whole cure to her. However, she was given other exercises to do, and these were not so easy. They rigged a pulley for her and Hattie had to hold both ends of a rope and saw it back and forth through the scraping little wheel. She bent heavily from the hips and coughed over her cigarette. But the most important exercise of all she shirked. This required her to put the flat of her hand to the wall at the level of her hips and, by working her finger tips slowly, to make the hand ascend to the height of her shoulder. That was painful; she often forgot to do it, although the doctor warned her, "Hattie, you don't want adhesions, do you?"

A light of despair crossed Hattie's eyes. Then she said, "Oh, Dr. Stroud, buy my house from me."

"I'm a bachelor. What would I do with a house?"

"I know just the girl for you—my cousin's daughter. Perfectly charming and very brainy. Just about got her Ph.D."

"You must get quite a few proposals yourself," said the doctor.

"From crazy desert rats. They chase me. But," she said, "after I pay my bills I'll be in pretty punk shape. If at least I could replace that blood in the blood bank I'd feel easier."

"If you don't do as the therapist tells you, Hattie, you'll need another operation. Do you know what adhesions are?"

She knew. But Hattie thought, *How long must I go on taking care of myself?* It made her angry to hear him speak of another operation. She had a moment of panic, but she covered it up. With him, this young man whose skin was already as thick as buttermilk and whose chestnut hair was as dry as death, she always assumed the part of a child. In a small voice she said, "Yes, doctor." But her heart was in a fury.

Night and day, however, she repeated, "I was in the Valley of the Shadow. But I'm alive." She was weak, she was old, she couldn't follow a train of thought very easily, she felt faint in the head. But she was still here; here was her body, it filled space, a great body. And though she had worries and perplexities, and once in a while her arm felt as though it was about to give her the last stab of all; and though her hair was scrappy and old, like onion roots, and scattered like nothing under the comb, yet she sat and amused herself with visitors; her great grin split her face; her heart warmed with every kind word.

And she thought, People will help me out. It never did me any good to worry. At the last minute something turned up, when I wasn't looking for it. Marian loves me. Helen and Jerry love me. Half Pint loves me. They would never let me go to the ground. And I love them. If it were the other way around, I'd never let them go down.

Above the horizon, in a baggy vastness which Hattie by herself occasionally visited, the features of India, her *shade,* sometimes rose. India was indignant and scolding. Not mean. Not really mean. Few people had ever been really mean to Hattie. But India was annoyed with her. "The garden is going to hell, Hattie," she said. "Those lilac bushes are all shriveled."

"But what can I do? The hose is rotten. It broke. It won't reach."

"Then dig a trench," said the phantom of India. "Have old Sam dig a trench. But save the bushes."

Am I thy servant still? said Hattie to herself. *No,* she thought, *let the dead bury their dead.*

But she didn't defy India now any more than she had done when they lived together. Hattie was supposed to keep India off the bottle, but often both of them began to get drunk after breakfast. They forgot to dress, and in their slips the two of them wandered drunkenly around the house and blundered into each other, and they were in despair at having been so weak. Late in the afternoon they would be sitting in the living room, waiting for the sun to set. It shrank, burning itself out on the crumbling edges of the mountains. When the sun passed, the fury of the daylight ended and the mountain surfaces were more blue, broken, like cliffs of coal. They no longer suggested faces. The east began to look simple, and the lake less inhuman and haughty. At last India would say, "Hattie—it's time for the lights." And Hattie would pull the switch chains of the lamps, several of them, to give the generator a good shove. She would turn on some of the wobbling eighteenth-century-style lamps whose shades stood out from their slender bodies like dragonflies' wings. The little engine in the shed would shuffle, then spit, then charge and bang, and the first weak light would rise unevenly in the bulbs.

"Hettie!" cried India. After she drank she was penitent, but her penitence too was a hardship to Hattie, and the worse her temper the more British her accent became. *"Where the hell ah you Het-tie!"* After India's death Hattie found some poems she had written in which she, Hattie, was affectionately and even touchingly mentioned. That was a good thing—Literature. Education. Breeding. But Hattie's interest in ideas was very small, whereas India had been all over the world. India was used to brilliant society. India wanted her to discuss Eastern religion, Bergson and Proust, and Hattie had no head for this, and so India blamed her drinking on Hattie. "I can't talk to you," she would say. "You don't understand religion or culture. And I'm here because I'm not fit to be anywhere else. I can't live in New York anymore. It's too dangerous for a woman my age to be drunk in the street at night."

And Hattie, talking to her Western friends about India, would say, "She is a lady" (implying that they made a pair). "She is a creative person" (this was why they found each other so congenial). "But helpless? Completely. Why she can't even get her own girdle on."

"Hettie! Come here. Het-tie! Do you know what sloth is?"

Undressed, India sat on her bed and with the cigarette in her drunken, wrinkled, ringed hand she burned holes in the blankets. On Hattie's pride she left many small scars, too. She treated her like a servant.

Weeping, India begged Hattie afterward to forgive her. *"Hettie, please don't condemn me in your heart. Forgive me, dear, I know I am bad. But I hurt myself more in my evil than I hurt you."*

Hattie would keep a stiff bearing. She would lift up her face with its incurved nose and puffy eyes and say, "I am a Christian person. I never bear a grudge." And by repeating this she actually brought herself to forgive India.

But of course Hattie had no husband, no child, no skill, no savings. And what she would have done if India had not died and left her the yellow house nobody knows.

Jerry Rolfe said privately to Hattie's friend Marian, a businesswoman in town, "Hattie can't do anything for herself. If I hadn't been around during the forty-four blizzard she and India both would have starved. She's always been careless and lazy and now she can't even chase a cow out of the yard. She's too feeble. The thing for her to do is to go east to her damn brother. Hattie would have ended at the poor farm if it hadn't been for India. But besides the damn house India should have left her some dough. She didn't use her goddamn head."

When Hattie returned to the lake she stayed with the Rolfes. "Well, old shell-back," said Jerry, "there's a little more life in you now."

Indeed, with joyous eyes, the cigarette in her mouth and her hair newly frizzed and overhanging her forehead, she seemed to have triumphed again. She was pale, but she grinned, she chuckled, and she held a bourbon old-fashioned with a cherry and a slice of orange in it. She was on rations; the Rolfes allowed her two a day. Her back, Helen noted, was more bent than before. Her knees went outward a little weakly; her feet, however, came close together at the ankles.

"Oh, Helen dear and Jerry dear, I am so thankful, so glad to be back at the lake. I can look after my place again, and I'm here to see the spring. It's more gorgeous than ever."

Heavy rains had fallen while Hattie was away. The sego lilies, which bloomed only after a wet winter, came up from the loose dust, especially around the marl pit; but even on the burnt granite they seemed to grow. Desert peach was beginning to appear, and in Hattie's yard the rosebushes were filling out. The roses were yellow and abundant, and the odor they gave off was like that of damp tea leaves.

"Before it gets hot enough for the rattlesnakes," said Hattie to Helen, "we ought to drive up to Marky's ranch and gather watercress."

Hattie was going to attend to lots of things, but the heat came early that year and, as there was no television to keep her awake, she slept most of the day. She was now able to dress herself, though there was little more that she could do. Sam Jervis rigged the pulley for her on the porch and she remembered once in a while to use it. Mornings when she had her strength she rambled over to her own house, examining things, being important and giving orders to Sam Jervis and Wanda Gingham. At ninety, Wanda, a Shoshone, was still an excellent seamstress and housecleaner.

Hattie looked over the car, which was parked under a cottonwood tree. She tested the engine. Yes, the old pot would still go. Proudly, happily, she listened to the noise of tappets; the dry old pipe shook as the smoke went out at the rear.

She tried to work the shift, turn the wheel. That, as yet, she couldn't do. But it would come soon, she was confident.

At the back of the house the soil had caved in a little over the cesspool and a few of the old railroad ties over the top had rotted. Otherwise things were in good shape. Sam had looked after the garden. He had fixed a new catch for the gate after Pace's horses—maybe because he could never afford to keep them in hay—had broken in and Sam found them grazing and drove them out. Luckily, they hadn't damaged many of her plants. Hattie felt a moment of wild rage against Pace. He had brought the horses into her garden for a free feed, she was sure. But her anger didn't last long. It was reabsorbed into the feeling of golden pleasure that enveloped her. She had little strength, but all that she had was a pleasure to her. So she forgave even Pace, who would have liked to do her out of the house, who had always used her, embarrassed her, cheated her at cards, swindled her. All that he did he did for the sake of his quarter horses. He was a fool about horses. They were ruining him. Racing horses was a millionaire's amusement.

She saw his animals in the distance, feeding. Unsaddled, the mares appeared undressed; they reminded her of naked women walking with their glossy flanks in the sego lilies which curled on the ground. The flowers were yellowish, like winter wool, but fragrant; the mares, naked and gentle, walked through them. Their strolling, their perfect beauty, the sound of their hoofs on stone touched a deep place in Hattie's nature. Her love for horses, birds, and dogs was well known. Dogs led the list. And now a piece cut from a green blanket reminded Hattie of her dog Richie. The blanket was one he had torn, and she had cut it into strips and placed them under the doors to keep out the drafts. In the house she found more traces of him: hair he had shed on the furniture. Hattie was going to borrow Helen's vacuum cleaner, but there wasn't really enough current to make it pull as it should. On the doorknob of India's room hung the dog collar.

Hattie had decided that she would have herself moved into India's bed when it was time to die. Why should there be two deathbeds? A perilous look came into her eyes, her lips were pressed together forbiddingly. *I follow,* she said, speaking to India with an inner voice, *so never mind.* Presently—before long— she would have to leave the yellow house in her turn. And as she went into the parlor, thinking of the will, she sighed. Pretty soon she would have to attend to it. India's lawyer, Claiborne, helped her with such things. She had phoned him in town, while she was staying with Marian, and talked matters over with him. He had promised to try to sell the house for her. Fifteen thousand was her bottom price, she said. If he couldn't find a buyer, perhaps he could find a tenant. Two hundred dollars a month was the rental she set. Rolfe laughed. Hattie turned toward him one of those proud, dulled looks she always took on when he angered her. Haughtily she said, "For summer on Sego Lake? That's reasonable."

"You're competing with Pace's ranch."

"Why, the food is stinking down there. And he cheats the dudes," said Hattie. "He really cheats them at cards. You'll never catch me playing blackjack with him again."

And what would she do, thought Hattie, if Claiborne could neither rent nor sell the house? This question she shook off as regularly as it returned. *I don't have to be a burden on anybody,* thought Hattie. *It's looked bad many a time before, but when push came to shove, I made it. Somehow I got by.* But she argued with herself: *How many times? How long, O God—an old thing, feeble, no use to anyone?* Who said she had any right to own property?

She was sitting on her sofa, which was very old—India's sofa—eight feet long, kidney-shaped, puffy, and bald. An underlying pink shone through the green; the upholstered tufts were like the pads of dogs' paws; between them rose bunches of hair. Here Hattie slouched, resting, with knees wide apart and a cigarette in her mouth, eyes half shut but farseeing. The mountains seemed not fifteen miles but fifteen hundred feet away, the lake a blue band; the tealike odor of the roses, though they were still unopened, was already in the air, for Sam was watering them in the heat. Gratefully Hattie yelled, "Sam!"

Sam was very old, and all shanks. His feet looked big. His old railroad jacket was made tight across the back by his stoop. A crooked finger with its great broad nail over the mouth of the hose made the water spray and sparkle. Happy to see Hattie, he turned his long jaw, empty of teeth, and his long blue eyes, which seemed to bend back to penetrate into his temples (it was his face that turned, not his body), and he said, "Oh, there, Hattie. You've made it home today? Welcome, Hattie."

"Have a beer, Sam. Come around the kitchen door and I'll give you a beer."

She never had Sam in the house, owing to his skin disease. There were raw patches on his chin and behind his ears. Hattie feared infection from his touch, having decided that he had impetigo. She gave him the beer can, never a glass, and she put on gloves before she used the garden tools. Since he would take no money from her—Wanda Gingham charged a dollar a day—she got Marian to find old clothes for him in town and she left food for him at the door of the damp-wood-smelling boxcar where he lived.

"How's the old wing, Hat?" he said.

"It's coming. I'll be driving the car again before you know it," she told him. "By the first of May I'll be driving again." Every week she moved the date forward. "By Decoration Day I expect to be on my own again," she said.

In mid-June, however, she was still unable to drive. Helen Rolfe said to her, "Hattie, Jerry and I are due in Seattle the first week of July."

"Why, you never told me that," said Hattie.

"You don't mean to tell me this is the first you heard of it," said Helen. "You've known about it from the first—since Christmas."

It wasn't easy for Hattie to meet her eyes. She presently put her head down. Her face became very dry, especially the lips. "Well, don't you worry about me. I'll be all right here," she said.

"Who's going to look after you?" said Jerry. He evaded nothing himself and tolerated no evasion in others. Except that, as Hattie knew, he made every possible allowance for her. But who would help her? She couldn't count on her friend Half Pint, she couldn't really count on Marian either. She had had only the Rolfes to turn to. Helen, trying to be steady, gazed at her and made sad, involuntary movements with her head, sometimes nodding, sometimes seeming as if she disagreed. Hattie, with her inner voice, swore at her: *Bitch-eyes. I can't make it the way she does because I'm old. Is that fair?* And yet she admired Helen's eyes. Even the skin about them, slightly wrinkled, heavy underneath, was touching, beautiful. There was a heaviness in her bust that went, as if by attachment, with the heaviness of her eyes. Her head, her hands and feet should have taken a more slender body. Helen, said Hattie, was the nearest thing she had on earth to a sister. But there was no reason to go to Seattle—no genuine business. Why the hell Seattle? It was only idleness, only a holiday. The only reason was Hattie herself; this was their way of telling her that there was a limit to what she could expect them to do for her. Helen's nervous head wavered, but her thoughts were steady. She knew what was passing through Hattie's mind. Like Hattie, she was an idle woman. Why was her right to idleness better?

Because of money? thought Hattie. Because of age? Because she has a husband? Because she had a daughter in Swarthmore College? But an interesting thing occurred to her. Helen disliked being idle, whereas Hattie herself had never made any bones about it: an idle life was all she was good for. But for her it had been uphill all the way, because when Waggoner divorced her she didn't have a cent. She even had to support Wicks for seven or eight years. Except with horses, Wicks had no sense. And then she had had to take tons of dirt from India. *I am the one,* Hattie asserted to herself. *I would know what to do with Helen's advantages. She only suffers from them. And if she wants to stop being an idle woman why can't she start with me, her neighbor?* Hattie's skin, for all its puffiness, burned with anger. She said to Rolfe and Helen, "Don't worry. I'll make out. But if I have to leave the lake you'll be ten times more lonely than before. Now I'm going back to my house."

She lifted up her broad old face, and her lips were childlike with suffering. She would never take back what she had said.

But the trouble was no ordinary trouble. Hattie was herself aware that she rambled, forgot names, and answered when no one spoke.

"We can't just take charge of her," Rolfe said. "What's more, she ought to be near a doctor. She keeps her shotgun loaded so she can fire it if anything happens to her in the house. But who knows what she'll shoot? I don't believe it was Jacamares who killed that Doberman of hers."

Rolfe drove into the yard the day after she moved back to the yellow house and said, "I'm going into town. I can bring you some chow if you like."

She couldn't afford to refuse his offer, angry though she was, and she said, "Yes, bring me some stuff from the Mountain Street Market. Charge it." She had only some frozen shrimp and a few cans of beer in the icebox. When Rolfe had gone she put out the package of shrimp to thaw.

People really used to stick by one another in the West. Hattie now saw herself as one of the pioneers. The modern breed had come later. After all, she had lived on the range like an old-timer. Wicks had had to shoot their Christmas dinner and she had cooked it—venison. He killed it on the reservation, and if the Indians had caught them, there would have been hell to pay.

The weather was hot, the clouds were heavy and calm in a large sky. The horizon was so huge that in it the lake must have seemed like a saucer of milk. *Some milk!* Hattie thought. Two thousand feet down in the middle, so deep no corpse could ever be recovered. A body, they said, went around with the currents. And there were rocks like eyeteeth, and hot springs, and colorless fish at the bottom which were never caught. Now that the white pelicans were nesting they patrolled the rocks for snakes and other egg thieves. They were so big and flew so slow you might imagine they were angels. Hattie no longer visited the lake shore; the walk exhausted her. She saved her strength to go to Pace's bar in the afternoon.

She took off her shoes and stockings and walked on bare feet from one end of her house to the other. On the land side she saw Wanda Gingham sitting near the tracks while her great-grandson played in the soft red gravel. Wanda wore a large purple shawl and her black head was bare. All about her was—was nothing, Hattie thought; for she had taken a drink, breaking her rule. Nothing but mountains, thrust out like men's bodies; the sagebrush was the hair on their chests.

The warm wind blew dust from the marl pit. This white powder made her sky less blue. On the water side were the pelicans, pure as spirits, slow as angels, blessing the air as they flew with great wings.

Should she or should she not have Sam do something about the vine on the chimney? Sparrows nested in it, and she was glad of that. But all summer long the king snakes were after them and she was afraid to walk in the garden. When the sparrows scratched the ground for seed they took a funny bound; they held their legs stiff and flung back the dust with both feet. Hattie sat down at her old Spanish monastery table, watching them in the cloudy warmth of the day, clasping her hands, chuckling and sad. The bushes were crowded with yellow roses, half of them now rotted. The lizards scrambled from shadow to shadow. The water was smooth as air, gaudy as silk. The mountains succumbed, falling asleep in the heat. Drowsy, Hattie lay down on her sofa, its pads to her always like dogs' paws. She gave in to sleep and when she woke it was midnight;

she did not want to alarm the Rolfes by putting on her lights, so she took advantage of the moon to eat a few thawed shrimps and go to the bathroom. She undressed and lifted herself into bed and lay there feeling her sore arm. Now she knew how much she missed her dog. The whole matter of the dog weighed heavily on her soul. She came close to tears, thinking about him, and she went to sleep oppressed by her secret.

I suppose I had better try to pull myself together a little, thought Hattie nervously in the morning. *I can't just sleep my way through.* She knew what her difficulty was. Before any serious question her mind gave way. It scattered or diffused. She said to herself, *I can see bright, but I feel dim. I guess I'm not so lively anymore. Maybe I'm becoming a little touched in the head, as Mother was.* But she was not so old as her mother was when she did those strange things. At eighty-five, her mother had to be kept from going naked in the street. *I'm not as bad as that yet. Thank God! Yes, I walked into the men's wards, but that was when I had a fever, and my nightie was on.*

She drank a cup of Nescafé and it strengthened her determination to do something for herself. In all the world she had only her brother Angus to go to. Her brother Will had led a rough life; he was an old heller, and now he drove everyone away. He was too crabby, thought Hattie. Besides he was angry because she had lived so long with Wicks. Angus would forgive her. But then he and his wife were not her kind. With them she couldn't drink, she couldn't smoke, she had to make herself small-mouthed, and she would have to wait while they read a chapter of the Bible before breakfast. Hattie could not bear to sit at table waiting for meals. Besides, she had a house of her own at last. Why should she have to leave it? She had never owned a thing before. And now she was not allowed to enjoy her yellow house. *But I'll keep it,* she said to herself rebelliously. *I swear to God I'll keep it. Why, I barely just got it. I haven't had time.* And she went out on the porch to work the pulley and do something about the adhesions in her arm. She was sure now that they were there. *And what will I do?* she cried to herself. *What will I do? Why did I ever go to Rolfe's that night—and why did I lose control on the crossing?* She couldn't say, now, "I sneezed." She couldn't even remember what had happened, except that she saw the boulders and the twisting blue rails and Darly. It was Darly's fault. He was sick and old himself. *He* couldn't make it. He envied her the house, and her woman's peaceful life. Since she returned from the hospital he hadn't even come to visit her. He only said, "Hell, I'm sorry for her, but it was her fault." What hurt him most was that she had said he couldn't hold his liquor.

Fierceness, swearing to God did no good. She was still the same procrastinating old woman. She had a letter to answer from Hotchkiss Insurance and it drifted out of sight. She was going to phone Claiborne the lawyer, but it slipped her mind. One morning she announced to Helen that she believed she would apply to an institution in Los Angeles that took over the property of old people and managed it for them. They gave you an apartment right on the ocean, and your meals and medical care. You had to sign over half of your estate. "It's fair enough," said Hattie. "They take a gamble. I may live to be a hundred."

"I wouldn't be surprised," said Helen.

However, Hattie never got around to sending to Los Angeles for the brochure. But Jerry Rolfe took it on himself to write a letter to her brother Angus about her condition. And he drove over also to have a talk with Amy Walters, the gold miner's widow at Fort Walters—as the ancient woman called it. The fort was an old tar-paper building over the mine. The shaft made a cesspool unnecessary. Since the death of her second husband no one had dug for gold. On a heap of stones near the road a crimson sign FORT WALTERS was placed. Behind it was a flagpole. The American flag was raised every day.

Amy was working in the garden in one of dead Bill's shirts. Bill had brought water down from the mountains for her in a homemade aqueduct so she could raise her own peaches and vegetables.

"Amy," Rolfe said, "Hattie's back from the hospital and living all alone. You have no folks and neither has she. Not to beat around the bush about it, why don't you live together?"

Amy's face had great delicacy. Her winter baths in the lake, her vegetable soups, the waltzes she played for herself alone on the grand piano that stood beside her woodstove, the murder stories she read till darkness obliged her to close the book—this life of hers had made her remote. She looked delicate, yet there was no way to affect her composure, she couldn't be touched. It was very strange.

"Hattie and me have different habits, Jerry," said Amy. "And Hattie wouldn't like my company. I can't drink with her. I'm a teetotaler."

"That's true," said Rolfe, recalling that Hattie referred to Amy as if she were a ghost. He couldn't speak to Amy of the solitary death in store for her. There was not a cloud in the arid sky today, and there was no shadow of death on Amy. She was tranquil, she seemed to be supplied with a sort of pure fluid that would feed her life slowly for years to come.

He said, "All kinds of things could happen to a woman like Hattie in that yellow house, and nobody would know."

"That's a fact. She doesn't know how to take care of herself."

"She can't. Her arm hasn't healed."

Amy didn't say that she was sorry to hear it. In the place of those words came a silence which might have meant that. Then she said, "I might go over there a few hours a day, but she would have to pay me."

"Now, Amy, you must know as well as I do that Hattie has no money—not much more than her pension. Just the house."

At once Amy said, no pause coming between his words and hers, "I would take care of her if she'd agree to leave the house to me."

"Leave it in your hands, you mean?" said Rolfe. "To manage?"

"In her will. To belong to me."

"Why, Amy, what would you do with Hattie's house?" he said.

"It would be my property, that's all. I'd have it."

"Maybe you would leave Fort Walters to her in your will," he said.

"Oh, no," she said. "Why should I? I'm not asking Hattie for her help. I don't need it. Hattie is a city woman."

Rolfe could not carry this proposal back to Hattie. He was too wise ever to mention her will to her.

But Pace was not so careful of her feelings. By mid-June Hattie had begun to visit his bar regularly. She had so many things to think about she couldn't stay at home. When Pace came in from the yard one day—he had been packing the wheels of his horse trailer and was wiping grease from his fingers—he said with his usual bluntness, "How would you like it if I paid you fifty bucks a month for the rest of your life, Hat?"

Hattie was holding her second old-fashioned of the day. At the bar she made it appear that she observed the limit; but she had started drinking at home. One before lunch, one during, one after lunch. She began to grin, expecting Pace to make one of his jokes. But he was wearing his scoop-shaped Western hat as level as a Quaker, and he had drawn down his chin, a sign that he was not fooling. She said, "That would be nice, but what's the catch?"

"No catch," he said. "This is what we'd do. I'd give you five hundred dollars cash, and fifty bucks a month for life, and you let me sleep some dudes in the yellow house, and you'd leave the house to me in your will."

"What kind of a deal is that?" said Hattie, her look changing. "I thought we were friends."

"It's the best deal you'll ever get," he said.

The weather was sultry, but Hattie till now had thought that it was nice. She had been dreamy but comfortable, about to begin to enjoy the cool of the day; but now she felt that such cruelty and injustice had been waiting to attack her, that it would have been better to die in the hospital than be so disillusioned.

She cried, "Everybody wants to push me out. You're a cheater, Pace. God! I know you. Pick on somebody else. Why do you have to pick on me? Just because I happen to be around?"

"Why, no, Hattie," he said, trying now to be careful. "It was just a business offer."

"Why don't you give me some blood for the bank if you're such a friend of mine?"

"Well, Hattie, you drink too much and you oughtn't to have been driving anyway."

"I sneezed, and you know it. The whole thing happened because I sneezed. Everybody knows that. I wouldn't sell you my house. I'd give it away to the lepers first. You'd let me go away and never send me a cent. You never pay anybody. You can't even buy wholesale in town anymore because nobody trusts you. I'm stuck, that's all, just stuck. I keep on saying that this is my only home in all the world, this is where my friends are, and the weather is always perfect and the lake is beautiful. But I wish the whole damn empty old place were in hell. It's not human and neither are you. But I'll be here the day the sheriff takes away your horses—you never mind! I'll be clapping and applauding!"

He told her then that she was drunk again, and so she was, but she was more than that, and though her head was spinning she decided to go back to the house at once and take care of some things she had been putting off. This very day she was going to write to the lawyer, Claiborne, and make sure that Pace never got her property. She wouldn't put it past him to swear in court that India had promised him the yellow house.

She sat at the table with pen and paper, trying to think how to put it.

"I want this on record," she wrote. "I could kick myself in the head when I think of how he's led me on. I have been his patsy ten thousand times. As when that drunk crashed his Cub plane on the lake shore. At the coroner's jury he let me take the whole blame. He said he had instructed me when I was working for him never to take in any drunks. And this flier was drunk. He had nothing on but a T-shirt and Bermuda shorts and he was flying from Sacramento to Salt Lake City. At the inquest Pace said I had disobeyed his instructions. The same was true when the cook went haywire. She was a tramp. He never hires decent help. He cheated her on the bar bill and blamed me and she went after me with a meat cleaver. She disliked me because I criticized her for drinking at the bar in her one-piece white bathing suit with the dude guests. But he turned her loose on me. He hints that he did certain services for India. She would never have let him touch one single finger. He was too common for her. It can never be said about India that she was not a lady in every way. He thinks he is the greatest sack-artist in the world. He only loves horses, as a fact. He has no claims at all, oral or written, on this yellow house. I want you to have this over my signature. He was cruel to Pickle-Tits who was his first wife, and he's no better to the charming woman who is his present one. I don't know why she takes it. It must be despair." Hattie said to herself, *I don't suppose I'd better send that.*

She was still angry. Her heart was knocking within; the deep pulses, as after a hot bath, beat at the back of her thighs. The air outside was dotted with transparent particles. The mountains were as red as furnace clinkers. The iris leaves were fan sticks—they stuck out like Jiggs's hair.

She always ended by looking out of the window at the desert and lake. *They drew you from yourself. But after they had drawn you, what did they do with you? It was too late to find out. I'll never know. I wasn't meant to. I'm not the type,* Hattie reflected. *Maybe something too cruel for women, young or old.*

So she stood up and, rising, she had the sensation that she had gradually become a container for herself. You get old, your heart, your liver, your lungs seem to expand in size, and the walls of the body give way outward, swelling, she thought, and you take the shape of an old jug, wider and wider toward the top. You swell up with tears and fat. She no longer even smelled to herself like a woman. Her face with its much-slept-upon skin was only faintly like her own— like a cloud that has changed. It was a face. It became a ball of yarn. It had drifted open. It had scattered.

I was never one single thing anyway, she thought. *Never my own. I was only loaned to myself.*

But the thing wasn't over yet. And in fact she didn't know for certain that it was ever going to be over. You only had other people's word for it that death was such-and-such. How do I know? she asked herself challengingly. Her anger had sobered her for a little while. Now she was again drunk. . . . *It was strange. It is strange. It may continue being strange.* She further thought, *I used to wish for death more than I do now. Because I didn't have anything at all. I changed when I got a roof of my own over me. And now? Do I have to go? I thought Marian loved me, but she already has a sister. And I thought Helen and Jerry would never desert me, but they've beat it. And now Pace has insulted me. They think I'm not going to make it.*

She went to the cupboard—she kept the bourbon bottle there; she drank less if each time she had to rise and open the cupboard door. And, as if she were being watched, she poured a drink and swallowed it.

The notion that in this emptiness someone saw her was connected with the other notion that she was being filmed from birth to death. That this was done for everyone. And afterward you could view your life. A hereafter movie.

Hattie wanted to see some of it now, and she sat down on the dogs'-paw cushions of her sofa and, with her knees far apart and a smile of yearning and of fright, she bent her round back, burned a cigarette at the corner of her mouth and saw—the Church of Saint Sulpice in Paris where her organ teacher used to bring her. It looked like country walls of stone, but rising high and leaning outward were towers. She was very young. She knew music. How she could ever have been so clever was beyond her. But she did know it. She could read all those notes. The sky was gray. After this she saw some entertaining things she liked to tell people about. She was a young wife. She was in Aix-les-Bains with her mother-in-law, and they played bridge in a mud bath with a British general and his aide. There were artificial waves in the swimming pool. She lost her bathing suit because it was a size too big. How did she get out? Ah, you got out of everything.

She saw her husband, James John Waggoner IV. They were snowbound together in New Hampshire. "Jimmy, Jimmy, how can you fling a wife away?" she asked him. "Have you forgotten love? Did I drink too much—did I bore you?" He had married again and had two children. He had gotten tired of her. And though he was a vain man with nothing to be vain about—no looks, not too much intelligence, nothing but an old Philadelphia family—she had loved him. She too had been a snob about her Philadelphia connections. Give up the name of Waggoner? How could she? For this reason she had never married Wicks. "How dare you," she had said to Wicks, "come without a shave in a dirty shirt and muck on you, come and ask me to marry! If you want to propose, go and clean up first." But his dirt was only a pretext.

Trade Waggoner for Wicks? she asked herself again with a swing of her shoulders. She wouldn't think of it. Wicks was an excellent man. But he was a cowboy. Socially nothing. He couldn't even read. But she saw this on her film. They were in Athens Canyon, in a cratelike house, and she was reading aloud to him from *The Count of Monte Cristo.* He wouldn't let her stop. While walking to stretch her legs, she read, and he followed her about to catch each word. After all, he was very dear to her. Such a man! Now she saw him jump from his horse. They were living on the range, trapping coyotes. It was just the second gray of evening, cloudy, moments after the sun had gone down. There was an animal in the trap, and he went toward it to kill it. He wouldn't waste a bullet on the creatures but killed them with a kick, with his boot. And then Hattie saw that this coyote was all white—snarling teeth, white scruff. "Wicks, he's white! White as a polar bear. You're not going to kill him, are you?" The animal flattened to the ground. He snarled and cried. He couldn't pull away because of the heavy trap. And Wicks killed him. What else could he have done? The white beast lay dead. The dust of Wicks's boots hardly showed on its head and jaws. Blood ran from the muzzle.

And now came something on Hattie's film she tried to shun. It was she herself who had killed her dog, Richie. Just as Rolfe and Pace had warned her, he was vicious, his brain was turned. She, because she was on the side of all dumb creatures, defended him when he bit the trashy woman Jacamares was living with. Perhaps if she had had Richie from a puppy he wouldn't have turned on her. When she got him he was already a year and a half old and she couldn't break him of his habits. But she thought that only she understood him. And Rolfe had warned her, "You'll be sued, do you know that? The dog will take out after somebody smarter than that Jacamares's woman, and you'll be in for it."

Hattie saw herself as she swayed her shoulders and said, "Nonsense."

But what fear she had felt when the dog went for her on the porch. Suddenly she could see, by his skull, by his eyes that he was evil. She screamed at him, "Richie!" And what had she done to him? He had lain under the gas range all day growling and wouldn't come out. She tried to urge him out with the broom, and he snatched it in his teeth. She pulled him out, and he left the stick and tore at her. Now, as the spectator of this, her eyes opened, beyond the pregnant curtain and the air-wave of marl dust, summer's snow, drifting over the water. "Oh, my God! Richie!" Her thigh was snatched by his jaws. His teeth went through her skirt. She felt she would fall. Would she go down? Then the dog would rush at her throat—then black night, bad-odored mouth, the blood pouring from her neck, from torn veins. Her heart shriveled as the teeth went into her thigh, and she couldn't delay another second but took her kindling hatchet from the nail, strengthened her grip on the smooth wood, and hit the dog. She saw the blow. She saw him die at once. And then in fear and shame she hid the body. And at night she buried him in the yard. Next day she accused Jacamares. On him she laid the blame for the disappearance of her dog.

She stood up; she spoke to herself in silence, as was her habit. *God, what shall I do? I have taken life. I have lied. I have borne false witness. I have stalled. And now what shall I do? Nobody will help me.*

And suddenly she made up her mind that she should go and do what she had been putting off for weeks, namely, test herself with the car, and she slipped on her shoes and went outside. Lizards ran before her in the thirsty dust. She opened the hot, broad door of the car. She lifted her lame hand onto the wheel. With her right hand she reached far to the left and turned the wheel with all her might. Then she started the motor and tried to drive out of the yard. But she could not release the emergency brake with its rasplike rod. She reached with her good hand, the right, under the steering wheel and pressed her bosom on it and strained. No, she could not shift the gears and steer. She couldn't even reach down to the hand brake. The sweat broke out on her skin. Her efforts were too much. She was deeply wounded by the pain in her arm. The door of the car fell open again and she turned from the wheel and with her stiff legs hanging from the door she wept. What could she do now? And when she had wept over the ruin of her life she got out of the old car and went back to the house. She took the bourbon from the cupboard and picked up the ink bottle and a pad of paper and sat down to write her will.

"My Will," she wrote, and sobbed to herself.

Since the death of India she had numberless times asked the question, To Whom? Who will get this when I die? She had unconsciously put people to the test to find out whether they were worthy. It made her more severe than before.

Now she wrote, "I Harriet Simmons Waggoner, being of sound mind and not knowing what may be in store for me at the age of seventy-two (born 1885), living alone at Sego Desert Lake, instruct my lawyer, Harold Claiborne, Paiute County Court Building, to draw my last will and testament upon the following terms."

She sat perfectly still now to hear from within who would be the lucky one, who would inherit the yellow house. For which she had waited. Yes, waited for India's death, choking on her bread because she was a rich woman's servant and whipping girl. But who had done for her, Hattie, what she had done for India? And who, apart from India, had ever held out a hand to her? Kindness, yes. Here and there people had been kind. But the word in her head was not kindness, it was succor. And who had given her that? *Succor?* Only India. If at least, next best after succor, someone had given her a shake and said, "Stop stalling. Don't be such a slow, old, procrastinating sit-stiller." Again, it was only India who had done her good. She had offered her succor. "Het-tie!" said that drunken mask. "Do you know what sloth is? Demn you! poky old demned thing!"

But I was waiting, Hattie realized. *I was waiting, thinking, "Youth is terrible, frightening. I will wait it out. And men? Men are cruel and strong. They want things I haven't got to give."* *There were no kids in me,* thought Hattie. *Not that I wouldn't have loved them, but such my nature was. And who can blame me for having it? My nature?*

She drank from an old-fashioned glass. There was no orange in it, no ice, no bitters or sugar, only the stinging, clear bourbon.

So then, she continued, looking at the dry sun-stamped dust and the last freckled flowers of red wild peach, *to live with Angus and his wife? And to have to hear a chapter from the Bible before breakfast? Once more in the house—not of a stranger, perhaps, but not far from it either?* In other houses, in someone else's house, to wait for mealtimes was her lifelong punishment. She always felt it in the throat and stomach. And so she would again, and to the very end. However, she must think of someone to leave the house to.

And first of all she wanted to do right by her family. None of them had ever dreamed that she, Hattie, would ever have something to bequeath. Until a few years ago it had certainly looked as if she would die a pauper. So now she could keep her head up with the proudest of them. And, as this occurred to her, she actually lifted up her face with its broad nose and victorious eyes; if her hair had become shabby as onion roots, if, at the back, her head was round and bald as a newel post, what did that matter? Her heart experienced a childish glory, not yet tired of it after seventy-two years. She, too, had amounted to something. *I'll do some good by going,* she thought. *Now I believe I should leave it to, to . . .* She returned to the old point of struggle. She had decided many times and many times changed her mind. She tried to think, *Who would get the most out of this yellow house?* It was a tearing thing to go through. If it had not been the house but, instead, some brittle thing she could hold in her hand, then her last action would be to throw and smash it, and so the thing and she herself would be demolished together. But it was vain to think such thoughts. To whom should she leave it? Her brothers? Not they. Nephews? One was a submarine commander. The other was a bachelor in the State Department. Then began the roll call of cousins. Merton? He owned an estate in Connecticut. Anna? She had a face like a hot-water bottle. That left Joyce, the orphaned daughter of her cousin Wilfred. Joyce was the most likely heiress. Hattie had already written to her and had her out to the lake at Thanksgiving, two years ago. But this Joyce was another odd one; over thirty, good, yes, but placid, running to fat, a scholar—ten years in Eugene, Oregon, working for her degree. In Hattie's opinion this was only another form of sloth. Nevertheless, Joyce yet hoped to marry. Whom? Not Dr. Stroud. He wouldn't. And still Joyce had vague hopes. Hattie knew how that could be. At least have a man she could argue with.

She was now more drunk than at any time since her accident. Again she filled her glass. *Have ye eyes and see not? Sleepers awake!*

Knees wide apart she sat in the twilight, thinking. Marian? Marian didn't need another house. Half Pint? She wouldn't know what to do with it. Brother Louis came up for consideration next. He was an old actor who had a church for the Indians at Athens Canyon. Hollywood stars of the silent days sent him their negligees; he altered them and wore them in the pulpit. The Indians loved his show. But when Billy Shawah blew his brains out after his two-week bender, they still tore his shack down and turned the boards inside out to get rid of his ghost. They had their old religion. No, not Brother Louis. He'd show movies in the yellow house to the tribe or make a nursery out of it for the Indian brats.

And now she began to consider Wicks. When last heard from he was south of Bishop, California, a handyman in a saloon off toward Death Valley. It wasn't she who heard from him but Pace. Herself, she hadn't actually seen Wicks since—how low she had sunk then!—she had kept the hamburger stand on Route 158. The little lunchroom had supported them both. Wicks hung around on the end stool, rolling cigarettes (she saw it on the film). Then there was a quarrel. Things had been going from bad to worse. He'd begun to grouse now about this and now about that. He beefed about the food, at last. She saw and heard him. "Hat," he said, "I'm good and tired of hamburger." "Well, what do you think I eat?" she said with that round, defiant movement of her shoulders which she herself recognized as characteristic (*me all over,* she thought). But he opened the cash register and took out thirty cents and crossed the street to the butcher's and brought back a steak. He threw it on the griddle. "Fry it," he said. She did, and watched him eat.

And when he was through she could bear her rage no longer. "Now," she said, "you've had your meat. Get out. Never come back." She kept a pistol under the counter. She picked it up, cocked it, pointed it at his heart. "If you ever come in that door again, I'll kill you," she said.

She saw it all. *I couldn't bear to fall so low,* she thought, *to be slave to a shiftless cowboy.*

Wicks said, "Don't do that, Hat. Guess I went too far. You're right."

"You'll never have a chance to make it up," she cried. "Get out!"

On that cry he disappeared, and since then she had never seen him.

"Wicks, dear," she said. "Please! I'm sorry. Don't condemn me in your heart. Forgive me. I hurt myself in my evil. I always had a thick idiot head. I was born with a thick head."

Again she wept, for Wicks. She was too proud. A snob. Now they might have lived together in this house, old friends, simple and plain.

She thought, *He really was my good friend.*

But what would Wicks do with a house like this, alone, if he was alive and survived her? He was too wiry for soft beds or easy chairs.

And she was the one who had said stiffly to India, "I'm a Christian person. I do not bear a grudge."

Ah yes, she said to herself. *I have caught myself out too often. How long can this go on?* And she began to think, or try to think, of Joyce, her cousin's daughter. Joyce was like herself, a woman alone, getting on in years, clumsy. Probably never been laid. Too bad. She would have given much, now, to succor Joyce.

But it seemed to her now that that too, the succor, had been a story. First you heard the pure story. Then you heard the impure story. Both stories. She had paid out years, now to one shadow, now to another shadow.

Joyce would come here to the house. She had a little income and could manage. She would live as Hattie had lived, alone. Here she would rot, start to drink, maybe, and day after day read, day after day sleep. See how beautiful it was here? It burned you out. How empty! It turned you into ash.

How can I doom a younger person to the same life? asked Hattie. It's for somebody like me. When I was younger it wasn't right. But now it is, exactly. Only I fit in here. It was made for my old age, to spend my last years peacefully. If I hadn't let Jerry make me drunk that night—if I hadn't sneezed! Because of this arm, I'll have to live with Angus. My heart will break there away from my only home.

She was now very drunk, and she said to herself, *Take what God brings. He gives no gifts unmixed. He makes loans.*

She resumed her letter of instructions to lawyer Claiborne: "Upon the following terms," she wrote a second time. "Because I have suffered much. Because I only lately received what I have to give away, I can't bear it." The drunken blood was soaring to her head. But her hand was clear enough. She wrote, "It is too soon! Too soon! Because I do not find it in my heart to care for anyone as I would wish. Being cast off and lonely, and doing no harm where I am. Why should it be? This breaks my heart. In addition to everything else, why must I worry about this, which I must leave? I am tormented out of my mind. Even though by my own fault I have put myself into this position. And I am not ready to give up on this. No, not yet. And so I'll tell you what, I leave this property, land, house, garden, and water rights, to Hattie Simmons Waggoner. Me! I realize this is bad and wrong. Not possible. Yet it is the only thing I really wish to do, so may God have mercy on my soul."

How could that happen? She studied what she had written (and finally acknowledged there was no alternative). "I'm drunk," she said, "and don't know what I'm doing. I'll die, and end. Like India. Dead as that lilac bush."

Then she thought that there was a beginning, and a middle. She shrank from the last term. She began once more—a beginning. After that, there was the early middle, then middle middle, late middle middle, quite late middle. In fact the middle is all I know. The rest is just a rumor.

Only tonight I can't give the house away. I'm drunk and so I need it. And tomorrow, she promised herself, I'll think again. I'll work it out, for sure.

WHAT KIND OF DAY
DID YOU HAVE?

DIZZY WITH PERPLEXITIES, seduced by a restless spirit, Katrina Goliger took a trip she shouldn't have taken. What was the matter with her, why was she jumping around like this? A divorced suburban matron with two young kids, was she losing ground, were her looks going or her options shrinking so fast that it made her reckless? Looks were not her problem; she was pretty enough, dark hair, nice eyes. She had a full figure, a little on the plump side, but she handled it with some skill. Victor Wulpy, the man in her life, liked her just as she was. The worst you could say of her was that she was clumsy. Clumsiness, however, might come out as girlishness if it was well managed. But there were few things which Trina managed well. The truth, to make a summary of it, was that she was passably pretty, she was awkward, and she was wildly restless.

In all fairness, her options were increasingly limited by Wulpy. It wasn't that he was being capricious. He had very special difficulties to deal with—the state of his health, certain physical disabilities, his advanced age, and, in addition to the rest, his prominence. He was a major figure, a world-class intellectual, big in the art world, and he had been a bohemian long before bohemianism was absorbed into everyday life. The civilized world knew very well who Victor Wulpy was. You couldn't discuss modern painting, poetry—any number of important topics—without referring to him.

Well, then, toward midnight, and in the dead of winter—Evanston, Illinois, where she lives at the bottom of a continental deep freeze—Katrina's phone rings and Victor asks her—in effect he tells her—"I have to have you here first thing in the morning."

"Here" is Buffalo, New York, where Victor has been lecturing.

And Katrina, setting aside all considerations of common sense or of self-respect, says, "I'll get an early flight out."

If she had been having an affair with a younger man, Katrina might have passed it off with a laugh, saying, "That's a real brainstorm. It would be a gas, wouldn't it, and just what this zero weather calls for. But what am I supposed to do with my kids on such short notice?" She might also have mentioned that her divorced husband was suing for custody of the little girls, and that she had a date downtown tomorrow with the court-appointed psychiatrist who was reporting on her fitness. She would have mixed these excuses with banter, and combined them with a come-on: "Let's do it Thursday. I'll make it up to you." With Victor refusal was not one of her options. It was almost impossible, nowadays, to say no to him. Poor health was a euphemism. He had nearly died last year.

Various forces—and she wasn't altogether sorry—robbed her of the strength to resist. Victor was such a monument, and he went back so far in modern cultural history. You had to remember that he had begun to publish in *transition,* an avant-garde magazine, and always in lowercase, and *Hound and Horn* before she was born. He was beginning to have an avant-garde reputation while she was still in her playpen. And if you thought he was not tired out and had no more surprises up his sleeve, you were thinking of the usual three-score and ten, not of Victor Wulpy. Even his bitterest detractors, the diehard grudgers, had to admit that he was still first-rate. And about how many Americans had leaders of thought like Sartre, Merleau-Ponty, and Hannah Arendt said, "*Chapeau bas!* This is a man of genius." Merleau-Ponty was especially impressed with Victor's essays on Karl Marx.

Besides, Victor was personally so impressive—he had such a face, such stature; without putting it on, he was so commanding that he often struck people as being a king, of an odd kind. A New York–style king, thoroughly American—good-natured, approachable, but making it plain that he was a sovereign; he took no crap from anybody. But last year—it was that time of life for him, the midseventies—he went down with a crash. It happened at Harvard, and he was taken to Mass. General for surgery. The doctors there had dragged him from the edge of the grave. Or maybe he had spurned the grave himself, wrapped in bandages as he was and with pipes up his nose and drugged to the limit. Seeing him on his back, you would never have believed that he would walk through the door again. But he did just that.

Suppose, however, that Victor had died, what would Katrina have done? To think of it confused her. But Katrina's sister, Dorothea, who never spared anybody, spelled out the consequences of Victor's death. Dorothea, in plain truth, couldn't let the subject alone. "This has been the main event of your life. This time, kid, you really came out swinging." (An odd figure for Katrina, who was pretty and plump and seldom so much as raised her voice.) "You're going to be up against it when it finally happens. You must have known you could only have a short run." Katrina knew all that Dotey had to say. The résumé ran as follows: You dumped your husband to have this unusual affair. Sexual excitement and social ambition went together. You aimed to break into high cultural circles. I don't know what you thought *you* had to offer. If you took Daddy's word for it, and he'd repeat it from the next world, you're just an average Dumb Dora from north-suburban Chicagoland.

Quite true, the late Billy Weigal had called his daughters Dumb Dora One and Dumb Dora Two. He sent them down to the state university at Champaign-Urbana, where they joined a sorority and studied Romance languages. The girls wanted French? Good. Theater arts? Sure, why not. Old Doc Weigal pretended to think that it was all jibber-jabber. He had been a politician, mainly a tax fixer with high connections in the Chicago Democratic machine. His wife, too, was a mental lightweight. It was part of the convention that the womenfolk be birdbrains. It pleased his corrupt, protective heart. As Victor pointed out (all higher interpretation came from him), this was plain old middle-class ideology, the erotic components of which were easy to make out. Ignorance in women, a strong stimulus for men who considered themselves rough. On an infinitely higher level, Baudelaire had advised staying away from learned ladies. Bluestockings and bourgeois ladies caused sexual paralysis. Artists could trust only women of the people.

Anyway, Katrina had been raised to consider herself a nitwit. That she knew she was not one was an important secret postulate of her feminine science. And she didn't really object to Dorothea's way of discussing her intricate and fascinating problem with Victor. Dorothea said, "I want to get you to look at it from every angle." What this really meant was that Dotey would try to shaft her from every side. "Let's start with the fact that as Mrs. Alfred Goliger nobody in Chicago would take notice of you. When Mr. Goliger invited people to look at his wonderful collections of ivory, jade, semiprecious stones, and while he did all the talking, he only wanted you to serve the drinks and eats. And to the people with whom he tried to make time, the Lyric Opera types, the contemporary arts crowd, the academics, and those other shits, you were just a humdrum housewife. Then all of a sudden, through Wulpy, you're meeting all the Motherwells and Rauschenbergs and Ashberys and Frankenthalers, and you leave the local culture creeps groveling in the dust. However, when your old wizard dies, what then? Widows are forgotten pretty fast, except those with promotional talent. So what happens to girlfriends?"

Arriving at Northwestern University to give his seminars on American painting, Victor had been lionized by the Goligers. Alfred Goliger, who, flying to Bombay and to Rio, had branched out from gems to antiques and objets d'art and bought estate jewelry and also china, sterling, pottery, statuary in all continents, longed to be a part of the art world. He wasn't one of your hobbled husbands; he did pretty much as he liked in Brazil and India. He misjudged Katrina if he thought that in her he had a homebody who spent her time choosing wallpapers and attending PTA meetings. Victor, the perfect lion, relaxing among Evanston admirers while he drank martinis and ate hors d'oeuvres, took in the eager husband, aggressively on the make, and then considered the pretty wife—in every sense of the word a dark lady. He perceived that she was darkest where darkness counted most. Circumstances had made Katrina look commonplace. She did what forceful characters do with such imposed circumstances; she used them as camouflage. Thus she approached Wulpy like a nearsighted person, one who has to draw close to study you. She drew so near that you could feel her breath. And then her lowering, almost stubborn look rested on you for just that extra beat that carried a sexual message. It was the incompetency with which she presented herself, the nearsighted puzzled frown, that made the final difference. Her first handshake informed him of a disposition, an inclination. He saw that all her preparations had been set. With a kind of engraved silence about the mouth under the wide bar of his mustache, Wulpy registered all this information. All he had to do was give the countersign. He intended to do just that.

At first it was little more than the fooling of a visiting fireman, an elderly, somewhat spoiled celebrity. But Wulpy was too big a man for crotchets. He was a disciplined intellectual. He stood for something. At the age of seventy, he had arranged his ideas in well-nigh final order: none of the weakness, none of the drift that made supposedly educated people contemptible. How can you call yourself a modern thinker if you lack the realism to identify a weak marriage quickly, if you don't know what hypocrisy is, if you haven't come to terms with lying—if, in certain connections, people can still say about you, "He's a sweetheart!"? Nobody would dream of calling Victor "a sweetheart." Wickedness? No, well-seasoned judgment. But whatever his first intentions might have been, the affair became permanent. And how do you assess a woman who knows how to bind such a wizard to her? She's got to be more than a dumpy suburbanite sexpot with clumsy ankles. And this is something more than the cruel absurdity, the decline and erotic enslavement, of a distinguished man grown (how suddenly!) old.

The divorce was ugly. Goliger was angry, vengeful. When he moved, he stripped the house, taking away his Oriental treasures, the jade collection, the crystal, the hangings, the painted gilded elephants, the bone china, even some of the valuable jewelry he had given her and which she hadn't had the foresight to put in the bank. He was determined to evict her from the house, too, a fine old house. He could do that if he obtained custody of the kids. The kids took little notice of the disappearance of the Indian and Venetian objects, although Trina's lawyer argued in court that they were disoriented. Dorothea said about her nieces, "I'll be interested to find out what gives with those two mysterious characters. As for Alfred, this is all-out war." She thought that Katrina was too absentminded to be a warrior. "Are you taking notice, or not?"

"Of course I'm taking notice. He was always flying to an auction. Never at home. What did *he* do, away in India?"

Katrina was still at the dinner table when Victor's call came. Her guest was Lieutenant Krieggstein, a member of the police force. He arrived late, because of the fierce weather, and told a story about skidding into a snowdrift and waiting for a tow truck. He had almost lost his voice and said it would take him an hour to thaw. A friend of the family, he needed no permission to bring up wood from the cellar and build a fire. The house had been built in the best age of Chicago architecture (made like a Stradivarius, said Krieggstein), and the curved tiles of the fireplace ("the old craftsmanship!") were kingfisher blue.

"I've seen rough weather before, but this beats everything," he said, and he asked for Red Devil sauce to sprinkle on his curry and drank vodka from a beer mug. His face still burned with the frost, and his eyes went on watering at the table. He said, "Oh, what a luxury that fire is on my back."

"I hope it doesn't set off your ammunition."

The Lieutenant carried at least three guns. Were all plainclothes ("softclothes") men armed to the teeth, or did he have more weapons because he was a little guy? He set himself up as gracious but formidable. Just challenge him and you'd see fatal action. Victor said about him that he was just this side of sanity but was always crossing the line. "A lone cowhand on both sides of the Rio Grande simultaneously." On the whole, he took an indulgent view of Krieggstein.

It was nearly midnight in Buffalo. Katrina hadn't expected Victor to call just yet. Thoroughly familiar with his ways, Katrina knew that her old giant must have had a disappointing evening, had probably thrown himself disgusted on the bed in the Hilton, more than half his clothing on the floor and a pint of Black Label nearby to "keep the auxiliary engines going." The trip was harder than he was willing to admit. Beila, his wife, had advised him not to take it, but her opinions didn't count. A subordinate plant manager didn't tell the chairman of the board what to do. He was off to see Katrina. Lecturing, of course, was his pretext. "I promised those guys," he said. Not entirely a pretext, however. Greatly in demand, he got high fees. Tonight he had spoken at the state university, and tomorrow he was speaking to a group of executives in Chicago. Buffalo was a combined operation. The Wulpys' youngest daughter, Vanessa, who was an undergraduate there, was having problems. For Victor, family problems could never be what they were for other people—he wouldn't *have* them. Vanessa was being provocative and he was irritated.

Well, when the phone rang, Katrina said, "There's Victor. A little early. This may take a while." With Krieggstein you needn't stand on ceremony. Dinner had ended, and if she was too long on the phone he could let himself out. A large heavy beauty, shapely (only just within the limits), Katrina left the dining room as rapidly as her style of movement allowed. She released the catch of the swinging kitchen door. Of course Krieggstein meant to stay and to eavesdrop. Her affair was no secret and he considered himself her confidant. He had every qualification for this: he was a cop, and cops saw it all; he was a Pacific-war hero; and he was her scout's-honor friend. Listening, he turned his thick parboiled face to the fire, made his plump legs comfortable, crossed his short arms over his cardigan.

"How has it been, Victor?" said Katrina. How tired winter travel had made him was what she had to determine from the pitch of his voice and his choice of words. This must have been an exceptionally hard trip. It was strenuous labor for a man of his size, and with a surgically fused knee, to pole his way upon a walking stick against the human tides of airports. Wearing his Greek sea captain's cap, he was all the more conspicuous. He made his way everywhere with a look of willing acceptance and wit. He was on good terms with his handicaps (a lifelong, daily familiarity with pain) and did not complain about going it alone. Other famous old men had helpers. She had heard that Henry Moore kept no fewer than six assistants. Victor had nobody. His life had assumed a crazy intensity that could not be shared. Secrecy was necessary, obviously. At the heart of so much that was obvious was an unyielding mystery: Why *did* he? Katrina's answer was Love. Victor wouldn't say, declined to give an answer. Perhaps he hadn't yet found the core of the question.

Katrina thought him mysterious-looking, too. Beneath the bill of the Greek or Lenin-style cap there was a sort of millipede tangle about the eyes. His eyes were long, extending curiously into the temples. His cheeks were as red in sickness as in health; he was almost never pale. He carried himself with admirable, nonposturing, tilted grace, big but without heaviness. Not a bulky figure. He had style. You could, if you liked, call him an old bohemian, but such classifications did not take you far. No category could hold Victor.

The traveling-celebrity bit was very tiring. You flew in and you were met at the airport by people you didn't know and who put you under a strain because they wanted to be memorable individually, catch your attention, ingratiate themselves, provoke, flatter—it all came to the same thing. Driving from the airport, you were locked in a car with them for nearly an hour. Then there were drinks—a cocktail hubbub. After four or five martinis you went in to dinner and were seated between two women, not always attractive. You had to remember their names, make conversation, give them equal time. You might as well be running for office, you had to shake so many hands. You ate your prime rib and drank wine, and before you had unfolded your speech on the lectern, you were already tuckered out. You shouldn't fight all this, said Victor; to fight it only tired you more. But normally Victor thrived on noise, drink, and the conversation of strangers. He had so much to say that he overwhelmed everybody who approached him. In the full blast of a cocktail party he was able to hear everything and to make himself heard; his tenor voice was positively fifelike when he made an important point, and he was superarticulate.

If after his lecture a good discussion developed, he'd be up half the night drinking and talking. That was what he loved, and to be abed before midnight was a defeat. So he was either uncharacteristically fatigued or the evening had been a drag. Stupid things must have been said to him. And here he was, a man who had associated with André Breton, Duchamp, the stars of his generation, weary to the bone, in frozen Buffalo (you could picture Niagara Falls more than half iced over), checking in with a girlfriend in Evanston, Illinois. Add to the list of bad circumstances his detestation of empty hours in hotel rooms. Add also that he had probably taken off his pants, as she had seen him do in this mood, and thrown them at the wall, plus his big shoes, and his shirt made into a ball. He had his dudgeons, especially when there hadn't been a single sign of intelligence or entertainment. Now for comfort (or was it out of irritation) he telephoned Katrina. Most likely he had had a couple of drinks, lying naked, passing his hand over the hair of his chest, which sometimes seemed to soothe him. Except for his socks, he would then resemble the old men that Picasso had put into his late erotic engravings. Victor himself had written about the painter-and-model series done at Mougins in 1968, ferocious scribbles of satyr artists and wide-open odalisques. Through peepholes aged wrinkled kings spied on gigantic copulations. (Victor was by turns the painter-partner and the aged king.) Katrina's pretty lopsidedness might have suited Picasso's taste. (Victor, by the way, was no great admirer of Picasso.)

"So Buffalo wasn't a success?"

"Buffalo! Hell, I can't see any reason why it exists."

"But you said you had to stop to see Vanessa."

"That's another ordeal I can do without. We're having breakfast at seven."

"And your lecture?"

"I read them my paper on Marx's *The Eighteenth Brumaire.* I thought, for a university crowd . . ."

"Well, tomorrow will be more important, more interesting," said Katrina.

Victor had been invited to address the Executives Association, an organization of bankers, economists, former presidential advisers, National Security Council types. Victor assured her that this was a far more important outfit than the overpublicized Trilateral Commission, which, he said, was a front organization using ex-presidents and other exploded stars to divert attention from real operations. The guys who were bringing him to Chicago wanted him to talk about "Culture and Politics, East and West." Much they cared about art and culture, said Victor. But they sensed that it had to be dealt with; challenging powers were ascribed to it, nothing immediate or worrisome, but one ought to know what intellectuals were up to. "They've listened to professors and other pseudoexperts," said Victor, "and maybe they believe they should send for an old Jewish character. Pay him his price and he'll tell you without fakery what it's all about." The power of big-shot executives wouldn't overawe him. Those people, he said, were made of Styrofoam. He was gratified nevertheless. They had asked for the best, and that was himself—a realistic judgment, and virtually free from vanity. Katrina estimated that he would pick up a ten-thousand-dollar fee. "I don't expect the kind of dough that Kissinger gets, or Haig, although I'll give better value," he told her. He didn't mention a figure, though. Dotey, no bad observer, said that he'd talk freely about anything in the world but money—*his* money.

Dotey's observations, however, were commonplace. She spoke with what Katrina had learned to call *ressentiment*—from behind a screen of grievances. What could a person like Dotey understand about a man like Victor, whom she called "that gimpy giant"? What if this giant should have been in his time one of the handsomest men ever made? What if he should still have exquisite toes and fingers; a silken scrotum that he might even now (as he held the phone) be touching, leading out the longest hairs—his unconscious habit when he lay in bed? What, moreover, if he should be a mine of knowledge, a treasury of insights in all matters concerning the real needs and interests of modern human beings? Could a Dorothea evaluate the *release* offered to a woman by such an extraordinary person, the independence? Could she feel what it meant to be free from so much *junk?*

"By the way, Victor," said Katrina. "Do you remember the notes you dictated over the phone for use, maybe, tomorrow? I typed them up for you. If you need them, I'll have them with me when I meet you at O'Hare in the morning."

"I've had a different thought," said Victor. "How would it be if you were to fly here?"

"Me? Fly to Buffalo?"

"That's right. You join me, and we'll go on to Chicago together."

Immediately all of Katrina's warmest expectations were reversed, and up from the bottom there seeped instead every kind of dreariness imaginable. While Victor was in the air in the morning, she wouldn't be preparing, treating herself to a long bath, then putting on her pine-green knitted Vivanti suit and applying the Cabochard, his favorite perfume. She would be up until two A.M., improvising, trying to make arrangements, canceling her appointment downtown, setting her clock for five A.M. She hated to get up while it was still night.

There must be a sensible explanation for this, but Katrina couldn't bring herself to ask what it was—like "What's wrong? Are you sick?" She had unbearable questions to put to herself, too: Will I have to take him to the hospital? . . . Why me? His daughter is there. Does he need emergency surgery? Back to all the horrible stuff that had happened at Mass. General? A love that began with passionate embraces ending with barium X rays, heavy drugs, bad smells? The grim wife coming back to take control?

Don't go so fast, Katrina checked herself. She regrouped and reentered her feelings at a different place. He was completely by himself and was afraid that he might start to crumble in his plane seat: a man like Victor, who was as close to being a prince as you could be (in what he described as "this bungled age"), such a man having to telephone a girl—and to Victor, when you came right down to it, she was *a* girl, one of many (although she was pretty sure she had beaten the rest of the field). He had to appeal to a girl ("I've had a different thought") and expose his weakness to her.

What was necessary now was to speak as usual, so that when he said, "I had the travel desk make a reservation for you, if you want to use it—are you there?" she answered, "Let me find a pen that writes." A perfectly good pen hung on a string. What she needed was to collect herself while she thought of an alternative. She wasn't clever enough to come up with anything, so she began to print out the numbers he gave her. Heavyhearted? Of course she was. She was forced to consider her position from a "worst case" point of view. A North Shore mother of two, in a bad, a deteriorating marriage, had begun to be available sexually to visitors. Selectively. It was true that a couple of wild mistakes had occurred. But then a godsend, Victor, turned up.

In long discussions with her analyst (whom she no longer needed), she had learned how central her father was in all this, in the formation or deformation of her character. Until she was ten years old she had known nothing but kindness from her daddy. Then, with the first hints of puberty, her troubles began. Exasperated with her, he said she was putting on a guinea-pig look. He called her a con artist. She was doing the farmer's-daughter-traveling-salesman bit. "That puzzled expression, as if you can't remember whether a dozen is eleven or thirteen. And what do you suppose happens with the thirteenth egg, hey? Pretty soon you'll let a stranger lead you into the broom closet and take off your panties." Well! Thank you, Daddy, for all the suggestions you planted in a child's mind. Predictably she began to be sly and steal pleasure, and she did play the farmer's daughter, adapting and modifying until she became the mature Katrina. In the end (a blessed miracle) it worked out for the best, for the result was just what had attracted Victor—an avant-garde personality who happened to be crazy about just this erotic mixture. Petty bourgeois sexuality, and retrograde petty bourgeois at that, happened to turn Victor on. So here was this suburban broad, the cliché of her father's loaded forebodings: call her what you liked—voluptuary, luxurious beauty, confused sexpot, carnal idiot with piano legs, her looks (mouth half open or half shut) meaning everything or nothing. Just this grace-in-clumsiness was the aphrodisiac of one of the intellectual captains of the modern world. She dismissed the suggestion (Dotey's suggestion) that it was his decline that had brought her into his life, that she appeared when he was old, failing, in a state of desperation or erotic bondage. And it was true that any day now the earth would open underfoot and he'd be gone.

Meanwhile, if he wasn't so powerful as he once had been (as if some dust had settled on his surface), he was powerful still. His color was fresh and his hair vigorous. Now and then for an instant he might look pinched, but when he sat with a drink in his hand, talking away, his voice was so strong and his opinions so confident that it was inconceivable that he should ever disappear. The way she sometimes put it to herself was he was more than her lover. He was also retraining her. She had been admitted to his master class. Nobody else was getting such instruction.

"I've got all the numbers now."

"You'll have to catch the eight o'clock flight."

"I'll park at the Orrington, because while I'm gone for the day I don't want the car sitting in front of the house."

"Okay. And you'll find me in the VIP lounge. There should be time for a drink before we catch the one P.M. flight."

"Just as long as I'm back by midafternoon. And I can bring the notes you dictated."

"Well," said Victor, "I *could* have told you they were indispensable."

"I see."

"I ask you to meet me, and it sounds like an Oriental proposition, as if the Sultan were telling his concubine to come out beyond the city walls with the elephants and the musicians. . . ."

"How nice that you should mention elephants," said Katrina, alert at once.

"Whereas it's just Chicago–Buffalo–Chicago."

That he should refer by a single word to her elephant puzzle, her poor attempt to do something on an elephant theme, was an unusual concession. She had stopped mentioning it because it made Victor go cross-eyed with good-humored boredom. But now he had dropped a hint that ordering her to fly to Buffalo was just as tedious, just as bad art, as her floundering attempt to be creative with an elephant.

Katrina pushed this no further. She said, "I wish I could attend your talk tomorrow. I'd love to hear what you'll say to those executives."

"Completely unnecessary," Victor said. "You hear better things from me in bed than I'll ever say to those guys."

He did say remarkable things during their hours of high intimacy. God only knows how much intelligence he credited her with. But he was a talker, he *had* to talk, and during those wide-ranging bed conversations (monologues) when he let himself go, he didn't stop to explain himself; it was blind trust, it was faute de mieux, that made him confide in her. As he went on, he was more salty, scandalous, he was murderous. Reputations were destroyed when he got going, and people torn to bits. So-and-so was a plagiarist who didn't know what to steal; X who was a philosopher was a chorus boy at heart; Y had a mind like a lazy Susan—six spoiled appetizers and no main course. Abed, Victor and Katrina smoked, drank, touched each other (tenderness from complicity), laughed; they *thought*—my God, they thought! Victor carried her into utterly foreign spheres of speculation. He lived for ideas. And he didn't count on Katrina's comprehension; he couldn't. Incomprehension darkened his life sadly. But it was a fixed condition, a given. And when he was wicked she understood him well enough. He wasn't wasting his wit on her, as when he said about Fonstine, a rival who tried to do him in, "He runs a Procrustean flophouse for bum ideas"; Katrina made notes later, and prayed that she was being accurate. So as usual Victor had it right—she did hear better things in bed than he could possibly say in public. When he took an entire afternoon off for such recreation, he gave himself over to it entirely—he was a daylong deep loller. When on the other hand he sat down to his papers, he was a daylong worker, and she didn't exist for him. Nobody did.

Arrangements for tomorrow having been made, he was ready to hang up. "You'll have to phone around to clear the decks," he said. "The TV shows nasty weather around Chicago."

"Yes, Krieggstein drove into a snowdrift."

"Didn't you say you were having him to dinner? Is he still there? Let him make himself useful."

"Like what?"

"Like walking the dog. There's a chore he can spare you."

"Oh, he'll volunteer to do that. Well, good night, then. And we'll have a wingding when you get here."

Hanging up, she wondered whether she hadn't said "wingding" too loudly (Krieggstein) and also whether Victor might not be put off by such dated words, sorority sex slang going back to the sixties. Hints from the past wouldn't faze him—what did he care about her college sex life? But he was unnervingly fastidious about language. As others were turned off by grossness, he was sensitive to bad style. She got into trouble in San Francisco when she insisted that he see *M*A*S*H*. "I've been to it, Vic. You mustn't miss this picture." Afterward, he could hardly bear to talk to her, an unforgettable disgrace. Eventually she made it up with him, after long days of coolness. Her conclusion was, "I can't afford to be like the rest."

Now back to Krieggstein: how different a corner within the human edifice Krieggstein occupied. "So you have to go out of town," he said. At the fireside, somber and solid, he was giving his fullest attention to her problem. She often suspected that he might be an out-and-out kook. If he *was* a kook, how had he become her great friend? Well, there was a position to fill and nobody else to fill it with. And he was, remember, a true war hero. It was no easy matter to figure out who or what Sammy Krieggstein really was. Short, broad, bald, rugged, he apparently belonged to the police force. Sometimes he said he was on the vice squad, and sometimes homicide or narcotics; and now and then he wouldn't say at all, as if his work were top-secret, superclassified. "This much I'll tell you, dear—there are times on the street when I could use the good old flamethrower." He had boxed in the Golden Gloves tournament, way back before the Pacific war, and had scar tissue on his face to prove it. Still earlier he had been a street fighter. He made himself out to be very tough—a terrifying person who was also a gentleman and a tender friend. The first time she invited him for a drink he asked for a cup of tea, but he laid out all his guns on the tea table. Under his arm he carried a Magnum, in his belt was stuck a flat small gun, and he had another pistol strapped to his leg. He had entertained the little girls with these weapons. Perfectly safe, he said. "Why should we give the whole weapon monopoly to the wild element on the streets?" He told Katrina when he took her to Le Perroquet about stabbings and disembowelments, car chases and shoot-outs. When a bruiser in a bar recently took him for a poor schnook, he showed him one of the guns and said, "All right, pal, how would you like a second asshole right between your eyes." Drawing a theoretical conclusion from this anecdote, Krieggstein said to Katrina, "You people"—his interpretations were directed mainly at Victor—"ought to have a better idea than you do of how savage it is out there. When Mr. Wulpy wrote about *The House of the Dead,* he referred to 'absolute criminals.' In America we are now far out on a worse track. A hundred years ago Russia was still a religious country. We haven't got the saints that are supposed to go with the sinners. . . ." The Lieutenant valued his acquaintance with the famous man. He himself, in his sixties, was working on a Ph.D. in criminology. On any topic of general interest Krieggstein was prepared to take a position immediately.

Victor called him the Santa Claus of threats. He was amused by him. He also said, "Krieggstein belongs to the Golden Age of American Platitudes."

"What do you mean by that, Victor?"

"I'm thinking first of all about the ladies he takes out, the divorcées he's so attentive to. He sends them candy and flowers, Gucci scarves, Jewish New Year's cards. He keeps track of their birthdays."

"I see. Yes, he does that."

"He's part Whitehat, part Heavy. He tries to be like one of those Balzac characters, like what's-his-name—Vautrin."

"Only, what is he *really?*" said Katrina. For Victor, what a Krieggstein was really wasn't worth thinking about. Yet when she returned to the dining room, the flapping of the double-hinged door at her back was also the sound of her dependency. She *needed* somebody, and here was Krieggstein who offered himself. At least he gave the appearance of offering. Not many went as far as *that.* Didn't even make the gesture. Here she was thinking of her sister Dorothea.

"Bad moment, eh?" said Krieggstein gravely. "You have to go. Is he sick again?"

"He didn't say that."

"He wouldn't." Krieggstein, contracted with seriousness, had a look of new paint over old—rust painted over in red.

"I have to go."

"You certainly must, if it's like that. But it's not so bad, is it? You're lucky to have that old Negro lady taking care of the little girls the way she took care of you and your sister."

"That sounds better than it really is. By now Ysole ought to be completely trustworthy. You would think . . ."

"Isn't she?"

"The old woman is very complex, and as she grows older she's even harder to interpret. She always was satirical and sharp."

"She's taking sides; you've told me so before. She disapproves of the divorce. She keeps an eye on you. You suspect she takes money from Alfred and gives him information. But she had no children of her own."

"She was fond of us when we were kids. . . ."

"But transferred her loyalty to your children? I haven't got what it takes to track her motives with."

Katrina thought: But whom am I having this conversation with? Krieggstein's bare head, bare face, by firelight had the shapes you saw in Edward Lear's books of nonsense verse—distorted eggs. He meant to wear an expression of Churchillian concern—the Hinge of Fate. He was saying it wouldn't be a good idea to lose your head. The big artists, big minds, didn't peter out like average guys. Think of Casals in his nineties, or Bertrand Russell, et cetera. Even Francisco Franco on his deathbed. When they told the old fellow that some General García was there to say good-bye to him, he said, "Why, is García going on a trip?"

Katrina wanted to smile at this but, in the crowding forward of anxious difficulties, smiling was ruled out.

The Lieutenant said, "You can be sure I'll help all I can. *Anything* you need done." Krieggstein, always tactfully and with respect, hinted that he would like to figure more personally in her life. The humblest of suitors, he was a suitor nonetheless. This, too, took skillful managing, and Trina didn't always know what to do with him.

She said, "I have to call off a date with the court psychiatrist."

"A second time?"

"Alfred has dragged Victor into it. He said our relationship was harming the kids. This headshrink was very rude to me. Parents are criminals to these people. He was so rude that Dorothea suspected he was fixed."

"Sometimes the shrinkers prove their impartiality by being rough on both parties," said the Lieutenant. "Still, it's a realistic suspicion. Did you mention to your lawyer what your sister suggested?"

"He wouldn't answer. Lawyers level only among themselves. If ever."

"This doctor may be ethical. That's still another cause of confusion. As a buddy used to say on Guadalcanal, the individual in the woodpile may be Honesty in person—I could take this appointment for you. I have all the right credentials."

"Oh, please don't do that!" said Katrina.

"Objectively, I could make a wonderful case for you."

"If you'd only call his appointment secretary and set a time later in the week."

Dorothea was forever warning Trina against Krieggstein, whom she had met at one of the gun-display tea parties. "I wouldn't have him around. I think he's bananas. Is he really a cop, or some imaginary Kojak?"

"Why shouldn't he be real?" said Katrina.

"He could be a night watchman. No—if he worked nights he wouldn't be dating so many lonely middle-aged women. Still taking them to the senior prom. Have you had him checked out? Does he have a permit for those three guns?"

"The guns are nothing."

"Maybe he's a transit cop. I'm sure he's a nutcase."

Krieggstein was asking Katrina, "Did you tell the psychiatrist that you were writing a book for children?"

"I didn't. It never occurred to me."

"You see? You don't do yourself justice—put your best foot forward."

"What would really help, Sam, would be to walk the dog. Poor old thing, she hasn't been out."

"Oh, of course," said Krieggstein. "I should have thought of that."

The snow creaked under his weight as he led big Sukie across the wooden porch. The new street lamps were graceful, beautiful, everybody agreed, golden and pure. In summer, however, their light confused the birds, who thought the sun had risen and wore themselves out twittering. In winter the lights seemed to have descended from outer space. Packed into his storm coat, Krieggstein followed the stout, slow dog. Victor called him a "fantast." Who else would use such a word? "A fantast lacking in invention," he said. But the Lieutenant was a safe escort. He took Trina to see Yul Brynner at McCormick Place.

The three guns in fact made her feel safe. She was protected. He was her loyal friend.

She found herself affirming this to Dorothea later, after he was gone. She and her sister often had a midnight chat on the telephone.

After her husband died, Dorothea sold the big house in Highland Park and moved into fashionable Oldtown, bringing with her the Chinese bridal bed she and Winslow had bought at Gump's in San Francisco. The bedroom was small. A single window opened on the back alley. But she wouldn't part with her Chinese bed, and now she lay with her telephone inside the carved frame. To Katrina all that carving was like the crown of thorns. No wonder Dotey complained of insomnia and migraines. And *she* was setting *Katrina* straight? "You're locked into this futureless love affair, isolated, and the only man safe enough to see is this dumdum cop. Now you're hopping off to Buffalo."

"Krieggstein is a decent fellow."

"He's three-quarters off the screen."

Poodle-haired, thin, restless, with what Daddy used to call "neurasthenic stick" arms and legs, and large black eyes ready to soar out of her face, Dorothea was a spiky person, a sharp complainer.

"The children will go to school as usual with the older kid next door. Ysole comes at ten."

"You have to rush away and tumble through the clouds because the great man says you must. You claim you have no choice, but I think you like it. You remind me of that woman from Sunday school—'her foot abides not in her house.' A year's study in France was a wonderful privilege for you and me after graduation, but it was damaging, too, if you ask me. Dad was getting rid of some of the money he raked in through the tax assessor's office, and it was nicer to make Parisian demoiselles of us than to launder his dough in the usual ways. He was showing off. We were lost in Paris. Nobody to pay us any attention. Today I could really use those dollars."

O Dotey! bragging and deploring in the same breath. Dotey's husband had owned a small plastics factory. It was already going under when he died. So now she had to hustle plastic products. Her son was working for an MBA but not at a first-rate school. A woman in her situation needed a good address, and the rent she paid in Oldtown was outrageous. "For this kind of dough they could exterminate the rats. But I signed a two-year lease, and the landlord laughs at me." Forced into the business world, she sounded more and more like Father. But she hated the hustling. It was death to Dorothea to have to go anywhere, to have to do anything. To get out of bed in the morning was more than she could bear. Filtering her coffee, she cursed blindly, the soaring eyes filled with rage when the kettle whistled. To drag the comb through her hair she had to muster all her strength. As she herself said, "Like the lady in Racine: *'Tout me nuit, et conspire à me nuire.'*" (Taking a Chicago dig at her French education, a French dig at Chicago.) "Only Phèdre is you, baby, sick with love."

Dorothea drove herself, trembling, out of the house. Think how hard it was for her to call on chain-store buyers and institutional purchasing agents. She even managed to get on the tube to promote her product, wangling invitations from UHF ethnic and Moral Majority stations as a Woman Executive. Sometimes she seemed to be fainting under her burdens, purple lids closing. On the air, however, she was unfailingly vivacious and put on a charming act. And when she was aroused, she was very tough. "Let Wulpy go home if he's sick. Why doesn't his wife come fetch him?"

"Don't forget, I almost lost Victor last year," said Katrina.

"*You* almost . . . almost lost *him*."

"It's true you had surgery the same week, and I had to be away, but you weren't on the critical list, Dotey."

"I wasn't referring to me but to his wife, that poor woman, and what she suffered from you and other lady friends. . . . If she had to leave the room, this ding-a-ling broad from Evanston would rush in and throw herself on the sick man."

No use telling Dotey not to be so rude and vulgar. Katrina listened to her with a certain passivity, even with satisfaction—it amounted, almost, to pleasure. You might call it perturbation-pleasure. Dotey continued: "It isn't right that the man should use his mighty prestige on a poor lady from the suburbs. It's shooting fish in a barrel. You'll tell me that you have the magical secret, how to turn him on. . . ."

"I don't think that it's what I *do*, Dotey. It happens simply to be *me*. He even loves my varicose veins, which I would try to hide from somebody else. Or my uneven gum line, and that was my lifelong embarrassment. And when my eyes are puffy, even that draws him."

"Christ, that's it then," said Dorothea, testy. "You hold the lucky number. With you he gets it up."

Katrina thought: Why should we talk so intimately if there isn't going to be any sympathy? It was sad. But on a more reasonable view you couldn't blame Dorothea for being irritable, angry, and envious. She had a failing business to run. She needed a husband. She had no prospects to speak of. She hates the fact that I'm now completely out of her league, Katrina told herself. Over these four years I've met people like John Cage, Bucky Fuller, de Kooning. I come home and tell her how I chatted with Jackie Onassis or Françoise de la Renta. All she has to tell me is how hard it is to push her plastic bags, and how nasty and evil-minded those purchasing agents are.

Dorothea had lost patience. When she thought that the affair with Victor was a flash in the pan, she had been more tolerant, willing to listen. Katrina had even persuaded her to read some of Victor's articles. They had started with an easy one, "From Apollinaire to E. E. Cummings," but then went on to more difficult texts, like "Paul Valéry and the Complete Mind," "Marxism in Modern French Thought." They didn't tackle Marx himself, but they had French enough between them to do Valéry's *Monsieur Teste,* and they met for lunch at Old Orchard Shopping Center to discuss this strange book. First they looked at clothes, for with so many acres of luxurious merchandise about them it would have been impossible to concentrate immediately on *Teste.* Katrina had always tried to widen her horizons. For many years she had taken flying lessons. She was licensed to pilot a single-engine plane. After a lapse of twenty years she had tried to resume piano lessons. She had studied the guitar, she kept up her French at the center on Ontario Street. Once, during the worst of times, she had taken up foreign sports cars, driving round and round the north suburbs with no destination. She had learned lots of Latin, for which she had no special use. At one time she considered going into law, and had passed the aptitude test with high marks. Trying to zero in on some kind of perfection. And then in a booth at Old Orchard, Katrina and Dorothea had smoked cigarettes and examined Valéry: What was the meaning of the complete mind, "man as full consciousness"? Why did it make Madame Teste happy to be studied by her husband, as happy to be studied as to be loved? Why did she speak of him as "the angel of pure consciousness"? To grasp Valéry was hard enough. Wulpy *on* Valéry was utterly inaccessible to Dorothea, and she demanded that Trina explain. "Here he compares Monsieur Teste to Karl Marx—what does he mean by that?"

"Well," said Katrina, trying hard, "let's go back to this statement. It says, 'Minds that come from the void into this strange carnival and bring lucidity from outside . . .'"

Then Dotey cried, "*Which* void?" She wore the poodle hairdo as a cover for or an admission of the limitations of her bony head. But even this may have been a ruse, as she was really very clever in her way. Only her bosom was filled with a boiling mixture of sisterly feelings, vexation, resentment. She would bear with Katrina for a while and then she would say, "What is it with you and the intelligentsia? Because we went to the Pont Royal bar and none of those philosophers tried to pick us up? Or are you competing intellectually with the man's wife?"

No, Beila Wulpy had no such pretensions. The role of the great man's wife was what she played. She did it with dignity. Dark and stout, beautiful in her way, she reminded you of Catherine of Aragon—abused majesty. Although she was not herself an intellectual, she knew very well what it was to be one— the real thing. She was a clever woman.

Katrina tried to answer. "The strange carnival is the history of civilization as it strikes a detached mind. . . ."

"We don't play in this league," said Dotey at last. "It's not for types like us, Trina. And your brain is not the organ he's interested in."

"And I believe I'm equal to this, too, in a way of my own," said Katrina, obstinate. Trying to keep the discussion under control. "Types like us" wounded her, and she felt that her eyes were turning turbid. She met the threat of tears, or of sobs, by sinking into what she had always called her "flesh state": her cheeks grew thick, and she felt physically incompetent, gross. Dotey spoke with a harshness acquired from her City Hall father: "I'm just a broad who has to hustle plastic bags to creeps who proposition me." Katrina understood well enough that when Dotey said, "I'm a broad," she was telling her, "That's what you are, too." Then Dotey said, "Don't give me the 'strange carnival' bit." She added, "What about your elephant?"

This was a cheap shot. Katrina had been trying for some time to write a children's story about an elephant. She hoped to make some money by it, and to establish her independence. It had been a mistake to mention this to Dotey. She had done it because it was a story often told in the family. "That old elephant thing that Dad used to tell us? I'm going to put it to use." But for one reason and another she hadn't yet worked out the details. It was mean of Dotey to get at her through the elephant. The Valéry discussions at Old Orchard had ended with this dig.

But of course she had to tell Dotey that she was flying to Buffalo, and Dotey, sitting upright with the telephone in her carved Chinese bed, said, "So if any hitch develops, what you'd like is that I should cover for you with Alfred."

"I don't expect it to come to that. Just to be on the safe side, give me a number where I can reach you during the afternoon."

"I have to be all over the city. Competitors are trying to steal my chemist from me. Without him I'll have to fold. I'm near the breaking point, and I can do without extra burdens. And listen now, Trina, do you really care so much? Suppose the court does give Alfred the kids."

"I won't accept that."

"You might not mind too much. Mother's interest in you and me was minimal. She cared more about the pleats in her skirt. To this day, down on Bay Harbor Island, she's like that. You'll say you aren't Mother, but things do rub off."

"What has this got to do with Mother?"

"I'm only reckoning the way people actually do. You aren't getting anywhere with those kids. The house is a burden. Alfred took away all the pretty things. It eats up too much money in maintenance. Suppose Alfred did get custody? You'd move east with all the painters and curators. It would be nothing but arts and letters. Victor's set . . ."

"There isn't any set."

"There are crowds of people after him. You could insist on being together more openly, because Victor would *owe* you if you lost the kids. While he lasted . . ."

"In the midst of such conversations, Dotey, I think how often I've heard women say, 'I wish I had a sister.' "

Dorothea laughed. "Women who have sisters don't say it! Well, my way of being a good sister is to come in and turn on all the lights. You put off having children until you were almost too old. Alfred was upset about it. He's a quick-acting decisive type. Jewelers have to be. In his milieu he's somebody. Glance at a diamond, quote you a price. You didn't want kids by him? You tried to keep your options open? You were waiting for the main chance? Naturally Alfred will do you in if he can."

That's right, Katrina commented silently, scare me good. I'll never regret what I've done. She said, "I'd better go and set the alarm clock."

"I'll give you a couple of numbers where you might find me late in the afternoon," said Dorothea.

At five-thirty the alarm went off. Katrina never had liked this black winter hour. Her heart was low as she slid back the closet door and began to dress. To go with the green suit she chose a black cashmere sweater and matching hose. She rolled backward clumsily on the chaise longue, legs in the air, to pull the hose on. Her boots were of ostrich skin and came from the urban cowboy specialty shop on South State Street which catered to Negro dudes and dudesses. The pockmarked leather, roughly smooth and beautiful, was meant for slimmer legs than her own. What did that matter? They—she herself—gave Victor the greatest possible satisfaction.

She had set aside fifteen minutes for the dog. In the winter Ysole wouldn't walk her. At her age a fall on the ice was all she needed. ("Will *you* take care of me if I break my hip?" asked the old woman.) But Katrina liked taking Sukie out. It was partly as Dorothea had said: "Her feet abide not in her house." But the house, from which Alfred had removed the best carpets and chairs, the porcelain elephants from India and the curly gilt Chinese lions, did give Katrina vacancy heartaches. However, she had never really liked housekeeping. She needed action, and there was some action even in dog walking. You could talk to other dog owners. Astonishing, the things they sometimes said—the kinky proposals that were made. Since she need not take them seriously, she was in a position simply to enjoy them. As for Sukie, she had had it. The vet kept hinting that a sick, blind dog should be put down. Maybe Krieggstein would do her a favor—take the animal to the Forest Preserve and shoot her. Would the little girls grieve? They might or might not. You couldn't get much out of those silent kids. They studied their mother without comment. Krieggstein said they were great little girls, but Katrina doubted that they were the sort of children a friend of the family could dote on. One who belonged to the Golden Age of Platitudes, maybe. One of Krieggstein's odder suggestions was that the girls be enrolled in a martial arts course; Katrina should encourage them to be more aggressive. Also he tried to persuade Katrina to let him take them to the police pistol-practice range. She said they'd be scared out of their wits by the noise. He insisted on the contrary that it would do them a world of good. Dorothea referred to her nieces as "those mystery kids."

You couldn't hurry the dog. Black-haired, swaybacked, gentle, she sniffed every dog stain in the snow. She circled, then changed her mind. Where to do it? Done in the wrong place, it would unsettle the balance of things. All have their parts to play in the great symphony of the instincts (Victor). And even on a shattering cold day, gritting ice underfoot, the dog took her time. A hoarse sun rolled up. For a few minutes the circling snow particles sparkled, and then a wall of cloud came down. It would be a gray day.

Katrina woke the girls and told them to dress and come downstairs for their granola. Mother had to go to a meeting. Kitty from next door would come at eight to walk them to school. The girls seemed hardly to hear her. In what ways are they like me? Katrina sometimes wondered. Their mouths had the same half-open (or half-closed) charm. Victor didn't like to speak of kids. He especially avoided discussing her children. But he did make theoretical observations about the younger generation. He said they had been given a warrant to ravage their seniors with guilt. Kids were considered pitiable because their parents were powerless nobodies. As soon as they were able, they distanced themselves from their elders, whom they considered to be failed children. You would have thought that such opinions would depress Victor. No, he was spirited and cheerful. Not sporadically, either; he had a level temper.

When Katrina, ready to go, came into the kitchen in her fleece-lined coat, the girls were still sitting over their granola. The milk had turned brown while they dawdled. "I'm leaving a list on the bulletin board, tell Ysole. I'll see you after school." No reply. Katrina left the house half unwilling to admit how good it was to go away, how glad she would be to reach O'Hare, how wonderful it would be to make a flight even though Victor, waiting in Buffalo, might be sick.

The jet engines sucked and snarled up the frozen air; the huge plane lifted; the gray ground skidded away and you rose past hangars, over factories, ponds, bungalows, football fields, the stitched incisions of railroad tracks curving through the snow. And then the skyscraper community to the south. On an invisible sidewalk beneath, your little daughters walking to school might hear the engines, unaware that their mummy overflew them. Now the gray water of the great lake appeared below with all its stresses, wind patterns, whitecaps. Good-bye. Being above the clouds always made Katrina tranquil. Then—*bing!*—the lucid sunlight coming through infinite space (refrigerated blackness, they said) filled the cabin with warmth and color. In a book by Kandinsky she had once picked up in Victor's room, she had learned that the painter, in a remote part of Russia where the interiors of houses were decorated in an icon style, had concluded that a painting, too, ought to be an interior, and that the artist should induce the viewer to enter in. Who wouldn't rather? she thought. Drinking coffee above the state of Michigan, Katrina had her single hour of calm and luxury. The plane was almost empty.

There were even some thoughts about her elephant project. Would she or wouldn't she finish it?

In Katrina's story the elephant, a female, had been leased as a smart promotional idea to push the sale of Indian toys on the fifth floor of a department store. The animal's trainer had had trouble getting her into the freight elevator. After testing the floor with one foot and finding it shaky, she had balked, but Nirad, the Indian mahout, had persuaded her at last to get in. Once in the toy department she had had a heavenly time. Sales were out of sight. Margey was the creature's name, but the papers, which were full of her, called her Largey. The management was enthusiastic. But when the month ended and Margey-Largey was led again to the freight elevator and made the hoof test, nothing could induce her to enter. Now there was an elephant in the top story of a department store on Wabash Avenue, and no one could think of a way to get her out. There were management conferences and powwows. Experts were called in. Legions of inventive cranks flooded the lines with suggestions. Open the roof and lift out the animal with a crane? Remove a wall and have her lowered by piano movers? Drug her and stow her unconscious in the freight elevator? But how could you pick her up when she was etherized? The Humane Society objected. The circus from which Margey-Largey had been rented had to leave town and held the department store to its contract. Nirad the mahout was frantic. The great creature was in misery, suffered from insomnia. Were there no solutions? Katrina wasn't quite inventive enough to bring it off. Inspiration simply wouldn't come. Krieggstein wondered whether the armed forces might not have a jumbo-sized helicopter. Or if the store had a central gallery or well like Marshall Field's. Katrina after two or three attempts had stopped trying to discuss this with Victor. You didn't pester him with your nonsense. There was a measure of the difference between Victor and Krieggstein.

If he had been sick in earnest, Victor would have canceled the lecture, so he must have sent for her because he longed to see her (the most desirable maximum), or simply because he needed company. These reasonable conclusions made her comfortable, and for about an hour she rode through the bright sky as if she *were* inside a painting. Then, just east of Cleveland, the light began to die away, which meant that the plane was descending. Darkness returned. Beneath her was Lake Erie—an open toilet, she had heard an environmentalist call it. And now the jet was gliding into gray Buffalo, and she was growing agitated. Why was she sent for? Because he was sick and old, in spite of the immortality that he seemed wrapped in, and it was Katrina's fault that he was on the road. He did it for her sake. He didn't travel with assistants (like Henry Moore or other dignitaries of the same rank) because a sexual romance imposed secrecy; because Alfred was gunning for her—Alfred who had always outclassed and out-smarted her and who was incensed by this turnaround. And if Alfred were to win his case, Victor would have Katrina on his hands. But would he accept her? She felt it would never come to that.

After landing in Buffalo, she stopped in the ladies' room and when she looked herself over she was far from satisfied with the thickness of her face and her agitated eyes. She put on lipstick (Alfred's rage was burning and smoking on the horizon and she was applying lipstick). She did what she could with her comb and went out to get directions to the first-class lounge.

Victor never flew first-class—why waste money? He only used the facilities. The executives in first were not his type. He had always lived like an artist, and therefore belonged in the rear cabin. Owing to his bum knee, he did claim early seating, together with nursing infants and paraplegics. No display of in-firmity, but he needed an aisle seat for his rigid leg. What was true was that he assumed a kind of presidential immunity from all inconveniences. For some reason this was especially galling to Dorothea, and she took a Who-the-hell-is-he! tone when she said, "He takes everything for granted. When he came to Northwestern—that fatal visit!—he borrowed a jalopy and wouldn't even put out fifty bucks for a battery, but every day phoned some sucker to come with ca-bles and give him a jump. And here's a man who must be worth upward of a million in modern paintings alone."

"I don't know," said Katrina. (At her stubbornest she lowered her eyes, and when she looked as if she were submitting, she resisted most.) "Victor *really* be-lieves in equality. But I don't think that special consideration, in his case, is out of line."

When Victor appeared at a party, true enough, people cleared a path for him, and a hassock was brought and a drink put in his hand. As he took it, there was no break in his conversation. Even his super-rich friends were glad to put them-selves out for him. Cars were sent. Apartments (in places like the Waldorf) were available, of which he seldom availed himself. An old-style Villager, he kept a room to write in on Sullivan Street, among Italian neighbors, and while he was working he would pick up a lump of provolone and scraps from the bread box, drink whiskey or coffee from his Pyrex measuring cup, lie on his bed (the sheets were maybe changed annually) to refine his thoughts, passing them through his mind as if the mind were a succession of high-energy chambers. It was the thinking that mattered. He had those thinking dark eyes shining inside the densely fringed lids, big diabolical brows, authoritative not unkindly. The eyes were set, or *let* into his cheeks, at an odd angle. The motif of the odd angle appeared in many forms. And on Sullivan Street he required no special consideration. He bought his own salami and cheese, cigarettes, in the Italian grocery, carried them to his third-floor walk-up (rear), working until drink time, perfectly independent. Uptown, he might accept a lift in a limousine. In the soundproof glass cabinet of a Rolls, Katrina had once heard him talking during a half-hour ride downtown with a billionaire Berliner. (Escaped from the Nazis in the thirties with patents for synthetic rubber, he had bought dozens of Matisses, cheap.) Victor was being serious with him, and Katrina had tried to keep track of the subjects covered between Seventy-sixth Street and Washington Square: the politics of modern Germany from the Holy Roman Empire through the Molotov-Ribbentrop Pact; what surrealist communism had *really* been about; Kiesler's architecture; Hans Hofmann's influence; what limits were set by liberal democracy for the development of the arts. Three or four other wonderful topics she couldn't remember. Various views on the crises in economics, cold war, metaphysics, sexaphysics. The clever, lucky old Berlin Jew, whose head was like a round sourdough loaf, all uneven and dusted with flour, had asked the right questions. It wasn't as if Victor had been singing for his ride. He didn't do that sort of thing.

Dorothea tried, and tried too hard, to find the worst possible word for Victor. She would say, "He's a Tartuffe."

"You called me Madame Bovary," said Katrina. "What kind of a pair does that make us?"

Dotey, you got your B.A. fair and square. Now stick to plastic bags.

Such comments, tactfully censored, seemed to swell out Katrina's lips. You often saw a sort of silent play about her mouth. Interpreted, it told you that Victor was a real big shot, and that she was proud of—well, of their special intimacy. He confided in her. She knew his true opinions. They were conspirators. She was with him in his lighthearted, quick-moving detachment from everything that people (almost all of them) were attached to. In a public-opinion country, he made his own opinions. Katrina was enrolled as his only pupil. She paid her tuition with joy.

This at least was one possible summary of their relations, the one she liked best.

Passing down the glass-walled corridors of the airport, Katrina didn't like the look of the sky—a kind of colic in the clouds, and snow gusts spitting and twisting on the fields of concrete. Traffic, however, was normal. Planes were rolling in, trundling toward the runways. The look of the sky was wicked, but you didn't want to translate your anxieties into weather conditions. Anyway, the weather was shut out when you entered the VIP lounge. First-class lounges were always inner rooms, low-lighted, zones of quiet and repose. Drinks were free, and Victor, holding a glass, rested his legs on a coffee table. His stick was wedged beside him in sofa cushions. The action of the whiskey wasn't sufficient, for his yellow-green corduroy car coat was zippered and buttoned for warmth. As she kissed him the Cabochard fragrance puffed from her dress, scarf, throat—she could smell it herself. Then they looked each other in the face to see what was up. She wouldn't have said that he was sick—he didn't look it, and he didn't have about him the sick flavor that had become familiar to her during his illness. *That* at least! So there was no cause for panic. He was, however, out of sorts, definitely—something was working at him, like vexation, disgust. She knew the power of his silent glooms. Several objects had been deposited at the side of the sofa. His duffel bag she knew; heavy canvas, stained, it might have contained a plumber's tools, but there was something else with it, just around the corner.

Well, I was sent for, and I came. Was I needed, or was it extreme tetchiness?

"Right on the dot," she said, turning her watch on the wrist.

"Good."

"All I have to do is make it back."

"I see no reason why you shouldn't. It didn't give you a lot of trouble to arrange, did it?"

"Only ducking a date with the court psychiatrist, and chancing the usual heat from Alfred."

"Such behavior in this day and age," said Victor. "Why does your husband have to interpose himself as if *he* were a principal, and behave like a grand-opera lunatic?"

"Well, you know, Victor. Alfred always had lots of assurance, but rivalry with you was more than his self-esteem could bear."

Victor was not the type to be interested in personality troubles. Insofar as they were nothing but personal, he cared for nobody's troubles. That included his own.

"What have you got there, with your duffel bag?"

"I'll tell you as soon as we've ordered you some whiskey." Early drinking was unusual; it meant he needed an extra boost. When his arm was raised, the signal couldn't be overlooked, and the hostess came right over. In the old Mediterranean or in Asia, you might have found examples of Victor's physical type. He towered. He also tilted, on account of the leg. Katrina had never determined exactly what was the matter with it, medically. For drainage it was punctured in two places, right through the flesh. Sometimes there was a deposit around the holes, and it was granular, like brown sugar. That took getting used to, just a little. He made jokes about his size. He said he was too big for the subtler human operations. He would point out the mammoths, they hadn't made it, and he would note how many geniuses were little guys. But that was just talk. At heart he was pleased with the way he was. Nothing like a mammoth. He was still one of the most dramatic-looking men in the world, and besides, as she had reason to know, his nervous reactions were very fine. A face like Victor's might have been put on the cover of a book about the ancient world: the powerful horizontal planes—forehead, cheekbones, the intelligent long eyes, the brows kinky with age now, and with tufts that could be wicked. His mouth was large, and the cropped mustache was broad. By the way the entire face expanded when he spoke emphatically, you recognized that he was a kind of tyrant in thought. His cheekbones were red, like those of an actor in makeup; the sharp color hadn't left him even when he was on the critical list. It seemed a mistake that he should be dying. Besides, he was so big that you wondered what he was doing in a bed meant for ordinary patients, but when he opened his eyes, those narrow visual canals, the message was, "I'm dying!" Still, only a couple of months later he was back in circulation, eating and drinking, writing critical pieces—in full charge. A formidable person, Victor Wulpy. Even the way he gimped was formidable, not as if he was dragging his leg but as if he were kicking things out of the way. All of Victor's respect was reserved for people who lived out their *idea*. For whether or not you were aware of it, you had one, high or low, keen or stupid. He came on like the king of something—of the Jews perhaps. By and by, you became aware of a top-and-bottom contrast in Victor; he was not above as he was below. In the simplest terms, his shoes were used up and he wore his pants negligently, but when his second drink had warmed him and he took off the corduroy coat, he uncovered one of his typical shirts. It resembled one of Paul Klee's canvases, those that were filled with tiny rectilinear forms—green, ruby, yellow, violet, washed out but still beautiful. His large trunk was one warm artwork. After all, he was a chieftain and pundit in the art world, a powerful man; even his oddities (naturally) had power. Kingly, artistic, democratic, he had been around forever. He was withering, though. But women were after him, even now.

His voice strengthened by the drink, he began to talk. He said, "Vanessa says her teachers put heat on her to bring me for a lecture, but it was mostly her own idea. Then she didn't attend. She had to play chamber music."

"Did you meet her Cuban boyfriend?"

"I'm coming to that. He's a lot better than the others."

"So there's no more religion?"

"After all the noise about becoming a rabbi, and the trouble of getting her into Hebrew Union College, she dropped out. Her idea seems to have been to boss Jews—adult Jews—in their temples and holler at them from the pulpit.

Plenty of them are so broken-down that they would not only acquiesce but brag about it. Nowadays you abuse people and then they turn around and take ads in the paper to say how progressive it is to be kicked in the face."

"Now she's fallen in love with this Cuban student. Are they still Catholics, under Castro? She books you for a lecture and plays a concert the same night."

"Not only that," said Victor. "She has me carry her violin to Chicago for repairs. It's a valuable instrument, and I have to bring it to Bein and Fushi in the Fine Arts Building. Can't let it be botched in Buffalo. A Guarnerius."

"So you met for breakfast?"

"Yes. And then I was taken to meet the boy's family. He turns out to be a young Archimedes type, a prodigy. They're refugees, probably on welfare. Fair enough, that among all the criminals the Cubans stuck us with there should be a genius or two. . . ."

"By the way, are you sure he's such a genius?"

"You can't go by me. He got a fat four-year scholarship in physiology. His brothers are busboys, if that. And that's where Nessa is meddling. The mother is in a state."

"Then she gave you her violin—an errand to do?"

"I accepted to avoid something worse. I paid a fair price for the instrument and by now it's quintupled in value. I want an appraisal from Bein and Fushi, just in case it enters Nessa's head to sell the fiddle and buy this Raul from his mother. Elope. Who knows what. . . . We can go to Bein together."

More errands for Katrina. Victor had sent Vanessa away to avoid a meeting with his lady friend, his Madame Bovary.

"We can lay the fiddle under a seat. I suppose that left-wing students came to your talk."

"Why so? I had a bigger crowd than that. The application of *The Eighteenth Brumaire* to American politics and society . . . the farce of the Second Empire. Very timely."

"It doesn't sound too American to me."

"What, more exotic than Japanese electronics, German automobiles, French cuisine? Or Laotian exiles settled in Kansas?"

Yes, she could see that, and see also how the subject would appear natural to Victor Wulpy from New York, of East Side origin, a street boy, sympathetic to mixed, immigrant and alien America; broadly tolerant of the Cuban boyfriend; exotic himself, with a face like his, and the Greek cap probably manufactured in Taiwan.

Victor had gone on talking. He was telling her now about a note he had received at the hotel from a fellow he had known years ago—a surprise that did not please him. "He takes the tone of an old chum. Wonderful to meet again after thirty years. He happens to be in town. And good old Greenwich Village—I hate the revival of these relationships that never were. Meantime, it's true, he's become quite a celebrity."

"Would I know the name?"

"Larry Wrangel. He had a recent success with a film called *The Kronos Factor.* Same type as *2001* or *Star Wars.*"

"Of course," said Katrina. "That's the Wrangel who was featured in *People* magazine. A late-in-life success, they called him. Ten years ago he was still making porno movies. Interesting." She spoke cautiously, having disgraced herself in San Francisco. Even now she couldn't be sure that Victor had forgiven her for dragging him to see *M*A*S*H.* Somewhere in his mental accounts there was a black mark still. Bad taste approaching criminality, he had once said. "He must be very rich. The piece in *People* said that his picture grossed four hundred million. Did he attend your lecture?"

"He wrote that he had an engagement, so he might be a bit late, and could we have a drink afterward. He gave a number, but I didn't call."

"You were what—tired? disgruntled?"

"In the old days he was bearable for about ten minutes at a time—just a character who longed to be taken seriously. The type that bores you most when he's most earnest. He came from the Midwest to study philosophy at NYU and he took up with the painters at the Cedar Bar and the writers on Hudson Street. I remember him, all right—a little guy, quirky, shrewd, offbeat. I think he supported himself by writing continuity for the comic books—Buck Rogers, Batman, Flash Gordon. He carried a scribbler in his zipper jacket and jotted down plot ideas. I lost track of him, and I don't care to find the track again—Trina, I was disturbed by some discoveries I made about my invitation from the Executives Association."

"What is this about the Executives?"

"I found out that a guy named Bruce Beidell is the main adviser to the speakers committee, and it turns out that he was the one who set up the invitation, and saw to it that I'd be told. He knows I don't like him. He's a rat, an English Department academic who became a culture politician in Washington. In the early Nixon years he built big expectations on Spiro Agnew; he used to tell me that Agnew was always studying serious worthy books, asking him for bigger and better classics. Reading! To read Beidell's mind you'd need a proctoscope. Suddenly I find that he'll be on the panel tonight, one of the speakers. And that's not all. It's even more curious. The man who will introduce me is Ludwig Felsher. The name won't mean much to you, but he's an old oldtimer. Before 1917 there was a group of Russian immigrants in the U.S., and Lenin used some of these people after the revolution to do business for him—Armand Hammer types who made ingenious combinations of big money with Communist world politics and became colossally rich. Felsher brought over masterpieces from the Hermitage to raise currency for the Bolsheviks. Duveen and Berenson put in a cheap bid for those treasures." Victor had been personally offended by Berenson and detested him posthumously.

"So you're in bad company. You never do like to share the platform."

He used both hands to move his leg to a more comfortable position. After this effort he was very sharp. "I've been among pimps before. I can bear it. But it's annoying to appear with these pricks. For a few thousand bucks: contemptible. I know this Felsher. From GPU to KGB, and his standing with American capitalists is impeccable. He's old, puffy, bald, red in the face, looks like an unlanced boil. No matter who you are, if you've got enough dough you'll get bear hugs from the chief executive. You've made campaign contributions, you carry unofficial messages to Moscow, and you're hugged in the Oval Office."

Fretful. Fallen among thieves. That was why he had sent for her, not because he suddenly suspected a metastasis.

"I'll hate seeing Beidell. Nothing but a fish bladder in his head, and the rest of him all malice and intrigue. Why are these corporation types so dumb?"

Katrina encouraged him to say more. She crossed her booted legs and offered him a listening face. Her chin was supported on bent fingers.

"Under these auspices, I don't mind telling you my teeth are on edge," he said.

"But, Victor, you could turn the tables on them all. You could let them have it."

Naturally he could. If he had a mind to. It would take a lot out of him, though. But he was not one of your (nowadays) neurotic, gutless, conniving intellectual types. From those he curtly dissociated himself. Katrina saw him in two aspects, mainly. In one aspect Victor reminded her comically of the huge bad guy in a silent Chaplin movie, the bully who bent gas lamps in the street to light his cigar and had huge greasepaint eyebrows. At the same time, he was a person of intensest delicacy and of more shadings than she would ever be able to distinguish. More and more often since he became sick, he had been saying that he needed to save his strength for what mattered. And did those executives matter? They didn't matter a damn. The Chase Manhattan, World Bank, National Security Council connections meant zilch to him, he said. He hadn't sought *them* out. And it wasn't as if they didn't know his views. He had more than once written, on the subject announced for tonight, that true personality was not to be found at the top of either hierarchy, East or West. Between them the superpowers had the capacity to kill everybody, but there was no evidence of higher human faculties to be found in the top leadership. On both sides power was in the hands of comedians and pseudopersons. The neglect, abasement, dismissal of art was a primary cause of this degeneration. If Victor were sufficiently fired

up, the executives would hear bold and unusual things from him about the valuing of life when it was bound up with the active valuing of art. But he was ailing, ruffled; his mind was tarnished. This was the condition of Victor himself.
He was thinking that he shouldn't even be here. What was he doing here in the
Buffalo airport in midwinter? In this lounge? Bound for Chicago? He was not at
the exact center of his own experience on days like this. There were sensations
which should absolutely be turned off. And he couldn't do that, either. He felt
himself being held hostage by oblique, unidentifiable forces.

He said, "One agreeable recollection I do have of this man Wrangel. He
played the fiddle in reverse. Being left-handed, he had the instrument restrung,
the sound posts moved. Back then, it was important to have your little specialty.
He went a long way, considering the small scale of his ingenuity. Became a big-
time illusionist."

The attendant had brought Katrina a small bottle of Dewar's. Pouring it, she
held the glass to the light to look at the powerful spirit of the spirit, like a spiral,
finer than smoke. Then she said, "It may do some good to look at the notes I
typed for you."

"Yes, let's."

She used reading glasses; Victor had no need of them. In some respects he
hadn't aged at all. For a big man he was graceful, and for an old one he was
youthful. Krieggstein might be right, and the excitement of thought did prevent
decay—her policeman friend must have overheard this somewhere, or picked it
up in the "Feminique" section of the *Tribune*. On his own he couldn't make
such observations.

The fixtures in the lounge were like those in the cabin of a plane, and Victor
had to hold up the paper to catch the slanted ceiling-light beam. "A quick once-
over," he said. "I don't expect much. 'Why people have taken to saying that
truth is stranger'—or did I say 'stronger'?—'than fiction. Because liberal democracy makes for enfeebled forms of self-consciousness—who was the fellow who
said that speaking for himself he would never exchange the public world, for all
its harshness and imperfections, for the stuffiness of a private world? Weak self-
conceptions, poor fictions. Lack of an *Idea*. Collective preemption of *Ideas* by
professional groups (lawyers, doctors, engineers). They make a simulacrum of
"standards," and this simulacrum becomes the morality of their profession. All
sense of individual cheating disappears. First step toward "stability," for them, is
to cancel individual moral judgments. Leadership can then be assumed by fictional personages.' "

"Would you say our leaders are fictional personages?" said Katrina.

"Wouldn't you?"

Victor didn't look well now. The red in his cheeks was an irritable red, and
there were other dangerous signs of distemper. He stared at her in that way he

had of seeming, once more, to review her credentials. It was humiliating. But she joined him in his doubts and was sorry for him. It was best for him now to talk. Even when he had to forgo the certainty of being understood. He lowered his head like a bull deciding whether or not to gore, and then he went on talking. She liked it best when his talk was mischievous and mean—when he said that a man had no brain but a fish bladder in his skull. Seriousness was more worrisome, and at present he was being serious. He told Katrina now that he didn't think these were useful notes. He had said the same things in his Marx lecture and said them better. Marx connected individual wakefulness with class struggle. When social classes found themselves prevented from acting politically, and class struggle fell into abeyance, temporarily, consciousness also became confused—waking, sleeping, dreaming, all mixed up.

Did he still consider himself a Marxist? Katrina wanted to know. She was scared by her own temerity, but even more afraid of being dumb. "I ask because you speak of class struggle. But also because you consider the Communist countries such a failure."

He said that, well, he had trained his mind on hard Marxist texts in his formative years and was permanently influenced—and why not? After reading *The Eighteenth Brumaire* again, he was convinced that Marx had America's present number. Here Victor, his leg extended like one of Admiral Nelson's cannon under wraps, gave a characteristically dazzling glance from beneath the primeval tangle of his brows and said that the Buffalo talk and the Chicago one would be connected. When wage earners, the middle class, the professions, lose track of their true material interests, they step outside history, so to speak, and then non-class interests take over, and when that happens society itself collapses into neuroses. An era of playacting begins. Vast revolutionary changes are concealed by the trivialities of the actors. Clowns and ham actors govern, or seem to. Superficially, it looks like farce. The deeper reality is anything but.

He was such an exceptional being altogether that because of the vast difference (to lesser people, Katrina meant), he himself might strike you as an actor. The interval of serious conversation had made him look more like himself—it had revived him. Katrina now admitted, "I was worried about you, Vic."

"Why? Because I asked you to come? I'm sore at those guys in Chicago and I wanted to tell you about it. I felt frustrated and depleted."

He can tell me things he's too dignified to say otherwise. He can be the child, Katrina concluded. Which not even my own kids will be with me. As a mother I seem to be an artificial product. Would that be because I can't put any sex into being a mother? She said to Victor, "My guess was that the bleak weather and the travel were getting you down."

Oh, as for bleakness. Examining her, he established that "bleak" was a different thing for him. Nor did he mean low spirits when he said "depleted." He wasn't low, he was higher than he liked, very high, in danger of being disconnected. He was superlucid, which he always wanted to be, but this lucidity had its price: clear ideas becoming ever more clear the more the ground opened under your feet—illumination increasing together with your physiological progress toward death. I never expected to live forever, but neither did I expect *this*. And there was no saying what *this* was, precisely. It was both definite and cloudy. And here Katrina gave him support, materially. Katrina, a lady with a full body, sat on her swelling bottom line. She wore a knitted dark-green costume. She had strong legs in black boots. Where the ostrich quills once grew, the surface of the leather was bubbled. Very plain to him in her figure were the great physical forces of the human trunk and the weight of the backswell, the separation of the thighs. The composure of her posture had a whore effect on him—did she know this or not? Was she aware that her neatness made him horny? He kept it from her, so that she had no idea of the attraction of her hands, especially the knuckle folds and the tips of what he called, to himself only, her touch-cock fingers. Katrina was his manifest Eros, this worried, comical lady for whom he had such complex emotions, for the sake of which he put up with so many idiocies, struggled with so many irritations. She could irritate him to the point of heartbreak, so that he asked was it worth it, and why didn't he spin off this stupid cunt; and couldn't he spend his old age better, or had his stars run out of influence altogether? He used to be able to take his business where he liked. That pagan availability was closing out. At first, she had been his lump of love. He counted the stages. At first, just fun. The next stage was laughable, as he recognized through her that his erotic epoch might after all be the Victorian, with its special doodads. Then there seemed to be a kind of Baudelairean phase,

> *. . . tu connais la caresse*
> *Qui fait revivre les morts . . .*

Only he didn't in fact buy that. His wasn't an example of clinically disturbed sexuality. He felt detached from all such fancy stuff. She *did* in fact have the touch that brought back the dead—his dead. But there was no witchery or sadic darkness about it. Evidently, whether he liked it or not, his was a common sexual type. He was beyond feeling the disgrace of its commonness. She kept him going, and he had to confess that he wouldn't know what to do at all if he didn't keep going. Therefore he went flying around. He was not ready to succumb. He paid no more attention to death than to a litter of puppies pulling at the cuffs of his pants.

About bleak winter, he was saying to Katrina, "I have trouble staying warm. I've heard that capsicum helps. For the capillaries. Last night was bad. I put my feet in hot water. I had to wear double socks and still was cold."

"I can take care of that."

Wonderful, what powers women will claim.

"And Vanessa, this morning—what was she like?"

"Well," he said, "what these kids really want is to make you obey the same powers that *they* have to serve. The older generation, it happens, cooperates with them. The Cuban mother was puzzled. I could read it in her eyes—'What in hell are you people *up* to?' "

"Oh, you met her."

"You bet I did. This morning I was sitting in her kitchen, and the boy was our interpreter. The kid's IQ must be out of sight. The woman says she has nothing against Vanessa. Nessa has made herself part of the family. She's moved in on them. She peels potatoes and washes pots. She and the boy don't go to restaurants and movies because he has no money and won't let her pay. So they study day and night, and they're both on the dean's list. But my daughter is just meddling. She abducted the genius of the family who was supposed to be the salvation of his siblings and his mama."

"But she says she loves him, and looks at you with those long eyes she inherited from you."

"She's a little bitch. I found out that she was giving her mother sex advice. How a modern wife can please a husband better. And you have to find new ways to humor an old man. She told Beila all about some homosexual encyclopedia. She said not to buy it, but gave her the address of a shop where she could read some passages on foreplay."

Katrina saw nothing funny in this. She was stabbed with anger. "Were you approached? That way?"

"By Beila? Everybody would have to go mad altogether."

No, not Beila. You had only to think about it to see how impossible it would be. Beila carried herself with the pride of the presiding woman, the wife. Her rights were maintained with Native American dignity. She was a gloomy person. (Victor had made her gloomy—one could understand that.) She was like the wife of a Cherokee chieftain, or again Catherine of Aragon. There was something of each type of woman in the gaudy-gloomy costumes she designed for herself. Tremendous, her silent air of self-respect. For such a proud person to experiment along lines suggested by a gay handbook was out of the question, totally. Still, Katrina felt the hurt of it. Disrespect. Ill will. It was disrespectful also of Beila. Beila was long-suffering. At heart, Beila was a generous woman. Katrina really did know the score. .

"So there's the new generation," said Victor. "When you consider the facts, they seem sometimes to add up to an argument for abortion. My youngest child! The wildest of all three. Now she's abandoned her plan to be a rabbi and she looks more Jewish than ever, with those twists of hair beside her ears."

Curious how impersonal Victor could be. Categories like wife, parent, child never could affect his judgment. He could discuss a daughter like any other subject submitted to his concentrated, radiant consideration—with the same generalizing detachment. It wasn't unkindness. It wasn't ordinary egotism. Katrina didn't have the word for it.

Anyway, they were together in the lounge, and to have him to herself was one of her best pleasures. He was always being identified on New York streets, buttonholed by readers, bugged by painters (and there were millions of people who painted), but here in this sequestered corner Katrina did not expect to be molested. She was wrong. A man appeared; he entered obviously looking for someone. That someone could only be Victor. She gave a warning signal—lift of the head—and Victor cautiously turned and then said in a low voice, somewhat morose, "It's him—I mean the character who wrote me the note."

"Oh-oh."

"He's a determined little guy. . . . That's quite a fur coat he's wearing. It must have been designed by F. A. O. Schwarz." It seemed to sweeten his temper to have said this. He smiled a little.

"*That* is an expensive garment," said Katrina.

It was a showy thing, beautifully made but worn carelessly. In circles of fur, something like the Michelin tire circles, it reached almost to the floor. Larry Wrangel was slight, slender, his bald head was unusually long. The grizzled side hair, unbrushed, looked as if he had slept on it when it was damp. A long soiled white scarf, heavy silk, drooped over the fur. Under the scarf a Woolworth's red bandanna was knotted. The white fur must have been his travel coat. For it wouldn't have been of any use in Southern California. His tanned face was lean, the skin stretched—perhaps a face-lift? Katrina speculated. His scalp was spotted with California freckles. The dark eyebrows were nicely arched. His mouth was thin, shy and also astute.

Victor said as they were shaking hands, "I couldn't get back to you last night."

"I didn't really expect it."

Wrangel pulled over one of the Swedish-modern chairs and sat forward in his rolls of white fur. Not removing the coat was perhaps his way of dealing with the difference in their sizes—bulk against height.

He said, "I guessed you would be surrounded, and also bushed by late evening. Considering the weather, you had a good crowd."

Wrangel did not ignore women. As he spoke he inspected Katrina. He might have been trying to determine why Victor should have taken up with this one. Whole graduating classes of girls on the make used to pursue Victor.

Katrina quickly reconciled herself to Wrangel—a little, smart man, not snooty with her, no enemy. He was eager only to have a talk, long anticipated, a serious first-class talk. Victor, unwell, feeling damaged, was certainly thinking how to get rid of the man.

Wrangel was chatting rapidly, wanting to strike the right offering while avoiding loss of time. His next move was to try the Cedar Bar and the Artists'

Club on Eighth Street. He spoke of Baziotes and of Arshile Gorky, of Gorky's loft on Union Square. He recalled that Gorky couldn't get Walt Whitman's name straight and that he spoke of him as "Vooterman." He mentioned Parker Tyler, and Tyler's book on Pavel Tchelitchew, naming also Edith Sitwell, who had been in love with Tchelitchew (Wulpy grimaced at Edith Sitwell and said, "Tinkle poems, like harness bells"). Wrangel laughed, betraying much tension in his laughter. Shyness and shrewdness made him seem to squint and even to jeer. He wished to become expansive, to make himself agreeable. But he didn't have the knack for this. An expert in pleasing Victor, Katrina could have told him where he was going wrong. Victor's attitude was one of angry restraint and thinly dissimulated impatience. Trina felt that he was being too severe. This Wrangel fellow should be given half a chance. He was being put down too hard because he was a celebrity.

On closer inspection, the white furs which should have been immaculate were spotted by food and drink; nor was there any reason (he was so rich!) why the silk scarf should be so soiled. She took a liking to Wrangel, though, because he made a point of including her in the conversation. If he mentioned a name like Chiaromonte or Barrett, he would say, aside, "A top intellectual in that circle," or, "The fellow who introduced Americans to German phenomenology."

But Victor wouldn't have any of this nostalgia, and he said, "What are you doing in Buffalo anyway? This is a hell of a season to leave California."

"I have a screwy kind of motive," said Wrangel. "Clinical psychologists, you see, often send me suggestions for films, inspired by the fantasies of crazy patients. So once a year I make a swing of selected funny farms. And here in Buffalo I saw some young fellows who were computer bugs—now institutionalized."

"That's a new wrinkle," said Victor. "I would have thought that you didn't need to leave California, then."

"The maddest mad are on the Coast? Do you think so?"

"Well, not now, maybe," Victor said. Then he made one of his characteristic statements: "It takes a serious political life to keep reality real. So there are sections of the country where brain softening is accelerated. And Southern California from the first has been set up for the maximum exploitation of whatever goes wrong with the American mind. They farm the kinks as much as they do lettuces and oranges."

"Yes, I suppose so," said Wrangel.

"As for the part played by intellectuals . . . Well, I suppose in this respect there's not much difference between California and Massachusetts. They're in the act together with everybody else. I mean intellectuals. Impossible for them to hold out. Besides, they're so badly educated they can't even identify the evils. Even Vespasian when he collected his toilet tax had to justify himself: *Pecunia non olet*. But we've come to a point where it's *only* money that doesn't stink."

"True, intellectuals are in shameful shape. . . ."

Katrina observed that Wrangel's eyes were iodine-colored. There was an io-dine tinge even to the whites.

"The main money people despise the intelligentsia, I mean especially the fellows that bring the entertainment industry suggestions for deepening the general catalepsy. Or the hysteria."

Wrangel took this meekly enough. He seemed to have thought it all through for himself and then passed on to further considerations. "The banks, of course . . ." he said. "It can take about twenty million bucks to make one of these big pictures, and they need a profit in the neighborhood of three hundred percent. But as for money, I can remember when Jackson Pollock was driving at top speed in and out of the trees at East Hampton while loving up a girl in his jeep. He wouldn't have been on welfare and food stamps, if he had lived. He played with girls, with art, with death, and wound up with dollars. What do those drip canvases fetch now?" Wrangel said this in a tone so moderate that he got away with it. "Sure, the investment golems think of me as a gold mine, and they detest me. I detest them right back, in spades." He said to Katrina, "Did you hear Victor's lecture last night? It was the first time in forty years that I actually found myself taking notes like a student."

Katrina couldn't quite decide what opinion Victor was forming of this Wrangel. When he'd had enough, he would get up and go. No boring end-men would ever trap him in the middle. As yet there was no sign that he was about to brush the man off. She was glad of that; she found Wrangel entertaining, and she was as discreet as could be in working the band of her watch forward on her wrist. Tactful, she drew back her sleeve to see the time. Very soon now the kids would be having their snack. Silent Pearl, wordless Soolie. She had failed to get a rise out of them with the elephant story. A lively response would have helped her to finish it. But you simply couldn't get them to react. Not even Lieutenant Krieggstein with his display of guns impressed them. Krieggstein may have confused them when he pulled up his trousers and showed the holster strapped to his stout short leg. Then, too, he sometimes wore his wig and sometimes not. That also might have been confusing.

Victor had decided to give Wrangel a hearing. If this proved to be a waste of time, he would start forward, assemble his limbs, take his stick upside down like a polo mallet, and set off, as silent as Pearl, as wordless as Soolie. Since he loved conversation, his cutting out would be a dreadful judgment on the man. "You gave me a lot to think about during the night," said Wrangel. "Your comments on the nonrevolution of Louis Napoleon and his rabble of deadbeats, and especially the application of that to the present moment—what you called the proletarianized present." He took out a small notebook, which Trina identified as a Gucci product, and read out one of his notes. " 'Proletarianization: people deprived of everything that formerly defined humanity to itself as human.' "

Never mind the fellow's thoughts of the night, Victor was trying to adjust himself to the day, shifting his frame, looking for a position that didn't shoot pains down the back of his thigh. Since the operation, his belly was particularly tender, distended and lumpy, and the small hairs stuck him like burning darts. As if turned inward. The nerve endings along the scar were like the tip of a copper wire with the strands undone. For his part, Wrangel seemed fit—youthfully elderly, durably fragile, probably a vegetarian. As he was trying to fix Wrangel's position, somewhere between classics of thought (Hegel) and the funny papers, there came before Victor the figures of Happy Hooligan and the Captain from *The Katzenjammer Kids* with the usual detached colors, streaks of Chinese vermilion and blocks of forest green. Looking regal, feeling jangled, Victor sat and listened. Wrangel's eyes were inflamed; it must really have been a bad night for him. He had a wry, wistful, starveling expression on his face, and his silk banner made you think of the scarf that had broken Isadora's neck. His main pitch was now beginning. He had read *The Eighteenth Brumaire,* and he could prove it. Why had the French Revolution been made in the Roman style? All the revolutionists had read Plutarch. Marx noted that they had been inspired by "old poetry." "Ancient traditions lying like a nightmare on the brains of the living."

"I see that you boned up on your Marx."

"It's marvelous stuff." Wrangel refused to take offense. All of Katrina's sympathies were with him. He was behaving well. He said, "Now let's see if I can put it together with *your* conjectures. It's still a struggle with the burden of history. *Le mort saisit le vif.* And you suggest that the modern avant-garde hoped to be free from this death grip of tradition. Art becoming an activity in which life brings raw material to the artists, and the artist using his imagination to bring forth a world of his own, owing nothing to the old humanism."

"Well, okay. What of it?" said Victor.

Katrina's impression was that Wrangel was pleased with himself. He thought he was passing his orals. "Then you said that the parody of a revolution in 1851—history as farce—might be seen as a prelude to today's politics of deception—government by comedians who use mass-entertainment techniques. Concocted personalities, pseudoevents."

Worried for him now, Katrina moved to the edge of her seat. She thought it might be necessary to rise soon, get going, break it up. "So you fly around the country and talk to psychiatrists," she said.

Her intervention was not welcome, although Wrangel was polite. "Yes."

"A sound approach to popular entertainment," said Victor. "Enlist the psychopaths."

"Try leaving them out, at any level," said Wrangel, only slightly stiff. He said, "In Detroit I'm seeing a party named Fox. He has published a document by a certain D'Amiens, who is sometimes also Boryshinski. The author is supposed to have disappeared without a trace. He had made the dangerous discovery that the planet is controlled by powers from other worlds. All this according to Mr. Fox's book. These other-world powers have programmed the transformation and control of the human species through something called CORP-ORG-THINK. They work through a central data bank and they already have control of the biggest corporations, banking circles, and political elites. Some of their leading people are David Rockefeller, Whitney Stone of Stone and Webster, Robert Anderson of Arco. And the overall plan is to destroy our life-support system, and then to evacuate the planet. The human race will be moved to a more suitable location."

"And what becomes of this earth?" said Katrina.

"It becomes hell, the hell of the unfit whom CORP plans to leave behind. When the long reign of Quantification begins, says Boryshinski, mankind will accept a purely artificial mentality, and the divine mind will be overthrown by the technocratic mind."

"Does this sound to you like a possible film?" said Katrina.

"If they don't ask too much for the rights, I might be interested."

"How would you go about saving us—in the picture, I mean?" Victor said. "Maybe Marx suggests some angle that you can link up with the divine mind."

Katrina hoped that Wrangel would stand up to Victor, and he did. Being deferential got you nowhere; you had to fight him if you wanted his good opinion. Wrangel said, "I'd forgotten how grand a writer Marx was. What marvelous images! The ghosts of Rome surrounding the cradle of the new epoch. The bourgeois revolution storming from success to success. 'Ecstasy the everyday spirit.' 'Men and things set in sparkling brilliants.' But a revolution that draws its poetry from the past is condemned to end in depression and dullness. A real revolution is not imitative or histrionic. It's a *real* event."

"Oh, all right," said Victor. "You're dying to tell me what *you* think. So why don't you tell me and get it over with."

"My problem is with class struggle," said Wrangel, "the destiny of social classes. You argue that class paralysis produces these effects of delusion—lying, cheating, false appearances. It all seems real, but what's really real is the unseen convulsion under the apparitions. You're imposing European conceptions of class on Americans."

Katrina's thought was: Ah, he wants to play with the big boys. She was afraid he might be hurt.

"And what's your idea?" said Victor.

"Well," said Wrangel, "I have a friend who says that the created souls of people, of the Americans, have been removed. The created soul has been replaced by an artificial one, so there's nothing real that human beings can refer to when they try to judge any matter for themselves. They live mainly by *rationales*. They have made-up guidance systems."

"That's the artificial mentality of your Boryshinski," said Victor.

"It has nothing to do with Boryshinski. Boryshinski came much later."

"Is this friend of yours a California friend? Is he a guru?" said Victor.

"I wish we had had time for a real talk," said Wrangel. "You always set a high value on ideas, Victor. I remember that. Well, I've considered this from many sides, and I am convinced that most ideas are trivial. A thought of the real is also an image of the real; if it's a true thought, it's a true picture and is accompanied also by a true feeling. Without this, our ideas are corpses. . . ."

"Well, by God!" Victor took up his stick, and Katrina was afraid that he might take a swipe at Wrangel, whack him with it. But no, he planted the stick before him and began to rise. It was a complicated operation. Shifting forward, he braced himself upon his knuckles. He lifted up the bum leg; his color was hectic. Remember (Katrina remembered) that he was almost always in pain.

Katrina explained as she was picking up the duffel bag and the violin case, "We have a plane to catch."

Wrangel answered with a sad smile. "I see. Can't fight flight schedules, can we?"

Victor righted his cap from the back and made for the door, stepping wide in his crippled energetic gait.

Outside the lounge Katrina said, "We still have about half an hour to kill."

"Driven out."

"He was terribly disappointed."

"Sure he was. He came east just to take me on. Maybe his guru told him that he was strong enough, at last. He gave himself away when he mentioned Parker Tyler and Tchelitchew. Tchelitchew, you see, attacked me. He said *he* had a vision of the world, whereas the abstract painting that I advocated was like a crazy lady expecting a visit from the doctor and smearing herself with excrement to make herself attractive—like a love potion. Wrangel was trying to stick me with this insult."

Threatening weather, the wicked Canadian north wind crossing the border in white gusts, didn't delay boarding. The first to get on the plane was Victor. His special need, an aisle seat at the back, made this legitimate. It depressed Katrina to enter the empty dark cabin. The sky looked dirty, and she was anxious. Their seats were in the tail, next to the rest rooms. She stowed the violin overhead and the zipper bag under the seat. Victor lowered himself into place, arranged his body, leaned backward, and shut his eyes. Either he was very tired or he wanted to be alone with his thoughts.

The plane filled up. It was some comfort that despite the mean look of the weather, practical-minded people never doubted that they would lift off from Buffalo and land in Chicago—business as usual. In the hand of God, but also routine. Katrina, who looked sensible along with the rest of the passengers, didn't know what to do about her anxious doubts, couldn't collect them in a single corner and turn the key on them. In one respect Dotey was dead right: Katrina jumped at any chance to rush off and be with Victor. Victor, even if he was ailing, even if no life with him was really possible—he couldn't last long—was entirely different from other people. Other people mostly stood in a kind of bleakness. They had the marks of privation upon them. There was a lack of space and air about them, they were humanly bare, whereas Victor gave off a big light. Strange little Wrangel may have been a pretentious twerp. He wanted to exchange serious thoughts; he might be puffing himself up absurdly, a faker, as Victor suspected. But when he had talked about ecstasy as the everyday spirit or men and things set in brilliants, she had understood exactly what he was saying. She had understood even better when he said that when the current stopped, the dullness and depression were worse than ever. To spell it out further, she herself could never generate any brilliancy. If she had somebody to get her going, she could join in and perhaps make a contribution. This contribution would be feminine and sexual. It would be important, it might even be indispensable, but it would not be inventive. She could, however, be inventive in deceit. And she had made an effort to branch out with the elephant story. She had, nevertheless, had that serious setback with *M*A*S*H*. The movie house itself had been part of her misfortune. They were surrounded by hippies, not very young ones, and in the row ahead there was a bearded guy slurping Popsicles and raising himself to one cheek, letting off loud farts. Victor said, "There's change from the general for the caviar it's eaten." Katrina hadn't yet figured out *that* one. Then Victor stood up and said, "I won't sit in this stink!" When they reached the street, the disgrace and horror of being *exposed* by *M*A*S*H* and associated with San Francisco degenerates made Katrina want to throw herself in front of a cable car rushing downhill from the Mark Hopkins.

Now she made a shelf of her hand on her brow and looked away from Victor, who was staring out at the field. Was there anything she could do about that goddamn elephant? Suppose a man turned up who hypnotized ball players and could do the same with an animal. They were now discovering new mental powers in the bigger mammals. Whales, for example, sang to one another; they were even thought to be capable of rhyming. Whales built walls out of air bubbles and could encircle and entrap millions of shrimp. What if an eccentric zoologist were to visit the management with a new idea? Meanwhile the management had to send for fodder while the elephant dropped whole pyramids of dung. The creature was melancholy and wept tears as big as apricots. The mahout demanded mud. If Margey didn't have a good wallow soon, she'd go berserk and wreck the entire fifth floor. Abercrombie & Fitch (were they still in Chicago?) offered to send over a big-game hunter. For them it would be terrific publicity to shoot her. Humane people would be outraged. Suppose a pretty high school girl were to come forward with the solution? And what if she were to be a Chinese girl? In Chinese myth, elephants and not men had once been the masters of the world. And then?

Victor's mind was also at work, although you couldn't say that he was thinking. Something soft and heavy seemed to have been spread over his body. It resembled the lead apron laid over you by X-ray technicians. Victor was stretched under this suave deadly weight and feeling as you felt when waking from a deep sleep—unable to lift your arm. On the field, in the winter light, the standing machines were paler than the air, and the entire airport stood in a frame of snow, looking like a steel engraving. It reminded him of the Lower East Side in—oh, about 1912. The boys (ancients today, those who were alive) were reading the Pentateuch. The street, the stained pavement, was also like a page of Hebrew text, something you might translate if you knew how. Jacob lay dreaming of a ladder which rose into heaven. *V'hinei malachi elohim*—behold the angels of God going up and down. This had caused Victor no surprise. What age was he, about six? It was not a dream to him. *Jacob* was dreaming, while Victor was awake, reading. There was no "long ago." It was all now. The cellar classroom had a narrow window at sidewalk level, just enough to permit a restricted upward glance showing fire escapes under snow, the gold shop sign of the Chinese laundry hanging from the ironwork, and angels climbing up and down. This did not have to be interpreted. It came about in a trance, as if under the leaden weight of the flexible apron. Now the plane was starting its takeoff run, and soon the NO SMOKING sign would be turned off. Victor would have liked to smoke, but the weight of his hands made any movement impossible.

It wasn't like him to cherish such recollections, although he had them, and they had lately been more frequent. He began now to remember that his mother had given him the windpipe of a goose after drying it in the Dutch oven of the coal stove, and that he had cut a notch in the windpipe with his father's straight razor and made a whistle of it. When it was done, he disliked it. Even when dry it had kept its terrible red color, and it was very harsh to the touch and had left an unpleasant taste in his mouth. This was not exactly Marx's nightmare of history from which mankind had to be liberated. The raw fowl taste was nasty. The angels on the fire escape, however, were very pleasing, and his consciousness of them, while it was four thousand years old, had also been exactly contemporary. Different ideas of time and space had not yet been imposed upon him. One comprehensive light contained everybody. Among the rest—parents, patriarchs, angels, God—there was yourself. Victor did not feel bound to get to the bottom of this; it was only a trance, probably an effect of fatigue and injury. He gave a side thought to Mass. General, where a tumor had been lifted out of a well of blood in his belly, and he reminded himself that he was still a convalescent—reminded himself also that Baudelaire had believed the artist to be always in a spiritually convalescent state. (This really was Baudelaire Day; just a while ago it had been the touch that brought the dead to life.) Only just returned from the shadow of death, the convalescent inhaled with delight the close human odors of the plane. Pollution didn't matter, the state of a convalescent being the state of a child drunk with impressions. Genius *must* be the recovery of the powers of childhood by an act of the creative *will*. Victor knew all this like the palm of his hand or the nose on his face. By combining the strength of a man (analytic power) with the ecstasy of a child you could discover the New. What God's Revelation implied was that the Jews (his children) would obstinately will (with mature intelligence) the divine adult promise. This would earn them the hatred of the whole world. They were always archaic, *and* they were always contemporary—we could sort that out later.

But now suppose that this should *not* be convalescence but something else, and that he should be on the circuit not because he was recovering but because he was losing ground. Falling apart? This was where Katrina entered the picture. Hers was the touch that resurrected, or that reunited, reintegrated his otherwise separating physical powers. He asked himself: That she turns me on, does that mean that I love her, or does it simply mean that she belongs to the class of women that turn me on? He didn't like the question he was asking. But he was having many difficult sensations, innumerable impressions of winter, winters of seven decades superimposed. The winter world even brought him a sound, not for the ear but for some other organ. And none of this was clearly communicable, nor indeed worth communicating. It was simply part of the continuing life of every human being. Everybody was filled with visions that had been repressed, and amassed involuntarily, and when you were sick they were harder to disperse.

"I can tell you, now that we're in the air, Victor, that I am *relieved*. I wasn't sure we'd get back." The banking plane gave them a single glimpse of Lake Erie slanting green to the right, and then rose into dark-gray snow clouds. It was a bumpy flight. The headwind was strong. "Have I ever told you about my housekeeper's husband? He's a handsome old Negro who used to be a dining-car waiter. Now he gambles. Impressive to look at. Ysole's afraid of him."

"Why are we discussing him?"

"I wonder if I shouldn't have a talk with her husband about Ysole. If she takes money from Alfred, my ex-husband, if she should testify against me in the case, it would be serious. Alfred's lawyer could bring out that she *raised* me, and therefore has my number."

"Would she want to harm you as much as that?"

"Well, she's always been somewhat cracked. She used to call herself a conjure-woman. She's shrewd and full of the devil."

"I wonder why we're flying at this altitude. By now we should have been above the clouds," said Victor.

They had fifteen minutes of open sky and then dropped back again into the darkness. "Yes, why are we so low?" said Katrina. "We're not getting anywhere."

The seat-belt sign went on and the pilot announced, "Owing to the weather, O'Hare Airport is closed, briefly. We will be landing in Detroit in five minutes."

"I *can't* be stuck in Detroit!" said Katrina.

"Easy, Katrina. In Chicago it isn't even one o'clock. We'll probably sit on the ground awhile and take right off again."

Suddenly fields were visible beneath—warehouses, hangars, highways, water. The landing gear came into position as Katrina, watching from the ground, had often seen it do, when the belly of the Boeing opened and the black bristling innards descended. Victor was able to stop one of the busy stewardesses, and she told them that it was a bad scene in Chicago. "Blitzed by snow."

When they disembarked they found themselves immediately in a crowd of grounded passengers. Once you got into such a crowd your fear was that you'd never get out. How lucky that Victor was not fazed. He was going forward in that rising-falling gait of his, his brows resembling the shelf mushrooms that grow on old tree trunks. For her part, Katrina was paralyzed by tension. Signs signified little. BAGGAGE CLAIM: there was no baggage. She was carrying Vanessa's precious fiddle. TERMINAL: Why should Victor limp all the way to the terminal only to be sent back to some gate? "There should be agents here to give information."

"No way. They're not organized for this," said Victor. "And we can't get near the phones. They're lined up ten deep. Let's see if we can find two seats and try to figure out what to do."

It was slow going. Alternate blasts of chill from the gates and heat from the blowers caught them about the legs and in the face. They found a single seat, and Victor sat himself down. He had that superlative imperturbability in the face of accident and local disturbances that Katrina was welcome to share if she could. Beila seemed to have learned how to do it. Trina had not acquired the knack. Victor laid his heel on the duffel bag. The violin case he took between his legs. With his stick he improvised a barrier to keep people from tripping over him.

Going off to gather information, Katrina found a man in a blue-gray uniform who looked as if he might be a flight engineer. He was leaning, arms crossed, against the wall. She noticed how well shined his black shoes were, and that he had a fresh complexion. She thought that he should be able to direct her. But when she said, "Excuse me," he refused to take notice of her, he turned his face away. She said, "I wonder if you could tell me. My flight is grounded. Where can I find out what's happening?"

"How would I know!"

"Because you're in uniform, I thought . . ."

He put his hand to her chest and pushed her away. "What are you *doing?*" she said. She felt her eyes flooding, growing turbid, smarting. "What's the *matter* with you?" What followed was even worse. While he looked into her face, not downward, his heel ground her instep. He was stomping her foot. And this was not being done in anger. It didn't seem anger at all; it was a different kind of intensity. She tried to read the name on the bar clipped to his chest, but he was gone before she could make it out. She thought: I've put myself in a position where people can hurt me and get away with it. As if I came out of Evanston to do wrong and it's written all over me. It might have been a misogynist, or other psychopath in uniform. A bitter hot current came from low underneath, going through her bowels like fainting heat, then moved up her chest and into her throat and cheeks. Hurt as she was, she conjectured that it might have been disrespect for his profession that put him in a fury, an engineer being approached like a cabin steward. Or he might have been putting out waves of hate magnetism and praying for somebody to approach, to give the works to. Victor, if he had been there, would have hit the guy on the head with his stick. Sick or well, he had presence of mind.

While she waited in a flight information line, Katrina concentrated on shrinking down the incident and restoring scale. He was just a person from a nice family in the suburbs probably, average comfortable people, judging from the way he wore his uniform—what Victor, when he got going, called the "animal human average" and, quoting one of his writers, "the dark equivocal crowd saturated with falsity." He liked such strong expressions. Good thing she had on the ostrich boots. Otherwise the man might have broken something.

When her turn came, the woman behind the counter had little information to give. New flights would be announced as soon as O'Hare opened its runways. "There'll be a rush for seats. Maybe I'd better buy first-class tickets," said Katrina.

"I can't reserve for you. The computer has no information, no matter how I punch it."

"Still, I'll buy two open first-class flights. On my credit card. They can be turned in if I don't use them."

As she approached Victor from the side, he looked pleasant enough in his cap—silent, bemused, amused. It was in the lower face that the signs of aging were most advanced, in the shortening of his jaw and the sharpening of its corners. In profile the signs were more noticeable, touched off more worry, inspired more sorrow. Katrina did not think that her full face, the just-repainted mouth, and the carriage of her bosom gave it away, but she was in low spirits: his condition, the jam of passengers, the spite of the man who had stomped her, the agony of being stuck here. From the front Victor was as "rich" in looks as ever. Yet she could not borrow much strength from him. There were Wulpy fans even here in Detroit who would have rushed out to the airport in a fleet of cars if they had known that he was here. They were better qualified to appreciate him than a woman who had twisted his arm to see *M*A*S*H*. These fans from the city would talk, drink, or take him home. All she could do was to stand on Square One—a woman from Evanston, not vivid with desperation but dull with it, without a particle of invention to her.

You seldom saw Victor in a flap. He wasn't greatly disturbed—not yet anyway. "Aren't you getting hungry? I am," he said.

"We should eat, I suppose."

"I guess we could find a fast-food spot."

"Something more substantial than a hamburger."

". . . Not to spoil tonight's banquet," he said.

Their march through the concourse began. Normally Victor was a fair walker, patient with his infirmity. But a solid mass like this was daunting. Movement was further complicated by baggage carts, sweepers, and wheelchairs, and Katrina soon said, "We aren't getting anywhere. It's after one o'clock in Chicago."

Victor said, "I wouldn't panic just yet. The housekeeper is there. Your sister. Your friend the cop."

"My sister isn't exactly in sympathy."

"You often say how critical she is. Still, she may not let you down."

"Even through bad times, I stood by her. Last summer she drove up with a shovel in the trunk of her car and said she was on her way to the cemetery to dig up her husband. She said she just had to see him again. I took her into the garden and made her drunk. Then she told me I had let her down, that I had gone to Boston to be with you when *she* was having surgery. They removed that tumor from the cervix."

Victor, far from shocked, nodded as she spoke—grieving wives, hysterical sisters. To read about such matters in a well-written book might have been of interest; to hear about them, no. Katrina could not convey how awful it had been to get her sister plastered—the damp heat, Dotey's thin face sweating. Because of the smell of clay underfoot you were reminded of graves. Just try to picture Dotey with neurasthenic stick arms, digging. She would have passed out in a matter of minutes.

Victor was filled with scenes from world history, fully documented knowledge of evil, battles, deportations to the murder camps from the *Umschlagplatz* in Warsaw, the terrible scenes during the evacuation from Saigon, and certainly he could imagine Dorothea trying to dig up her husband's corpse. But when to turn your imagination to phenomena of this class remained unclear. He had written about the "inhuman" as an element of the Modern, about the feebleness, meanness, drunkenness of modern man and of the consequences of this for art and for politics. His reputation was based upon the analyses he had made of Modernist extremism. He was the teacher of famous painters and writers. She had pored over his admirable books, yet she, you see, had to deal with him on the personal level. And on the personal level, well, he had more to say about art as a remedy for the bareness, as a cover for modern nakedness, than about the filling of *personal* gaps, or deficiencies. Yet even there he was not entirely predictable. He never ran out of surprises.

"I see you favoring your left foot. Does the boot pinch?"

"It was stepped on."

"You bumped into somebody?"

"A nice fair-haired young man rushed away from me when I stopped to get information, but before he rushed away he stomped me."

Victor stopped, looking at her from his height. "Why didn't you report him?"

"He disappeared."

"More and more new kinds of crazies coming at you. How changed everything is! . . . It was women and children first when the *Titanic* went down. Middle-class gallantry is gone with the Biedermeier."

"There's no real damage. It just aches some. But, Vic, think of the time lost to eat bad food. Is there nothing we can do to get out of here?"

"I might try to telephone the guy in charge of tonight's arrangements. Let me look in my wallet." Hooking his cane over his shoulder, he examined his hip-pocket army-navy billfold. "Yes. Continental Bank. Horace Kinglake. Why don't we phone him? If he wants me to speak tonight, he'd better organize our rescue. Why don't you call him, Katrina?"

"You want me to do the talking?"

"Why not? He must have top-level contacts with United or American. I hope you brought your telephone credit card."

"I did," said Katrina.

"Airports used to have good central services. Even Grand Central had telephone operators. Let's see if we can get hold of a phone." They had just begun to move forward when Victor stopped Katrina, saying, "I see our buddy Wrangel. He's coming toward us."

"He's sure to see us. You're pretty conspicuous."

"What if he does? . . . He did say he was flying to Detroit, didn't he?"

"When you walked out, I was embarrassed," said Katrina.

"He had no business to pursue me to the lounge."

"A different way to view it is that he came all the way from California to hear your lecture and to engage in conversation."

"To settle an old score, I think. This is a day when events have a dream tendency," said Victor. "There's a line about *'les revenants qui vous raccrochent en plein jour.'*"

"You'd better give me the card with that Kinglake's number."

Victor, curiously, didn't try to avoid Wrangel, and Wrangel, to Katrina's surprise, was terribly pleased to find them in the concourse. He might justifiably have been a little huffy. Not at all. In his own shy way he was delighted. "You didn't say you were going to Detroit, too."

"We weren't. We're grounded by the bad weather in Chicago."

"Oh, you have to wait. In that case why don't you have lunch with me?"

"I wish we could," said Katrina. "But we have to get to a telephone. It's urgent."

"Phoning would be much easier from a restaurant. Just a minute ago I passed a decent-looking bar and grill."

It was a big dark place, under a low ceiling, Tudor decor. As soon as the hostess appeared, Katrina saw money changing hands. It looked like a ten-dollar bill that Wrangel slipped the woman. Why not, if *The Kronos Factor* had grossed four hundred million? A leather booth was instantly available. Victor occupied the corner, laying his leg along the settee on the left. "Shall we drink?" said Wrangel. "Shall we order before you make your call? Miss," he said to the hostess, "please let this lady use your telephone. What shall we get for you, my dear?"

"A turkey sandwich, white meat, on toast."

"Duck à l'orange," said Victor. In a lounge as dark as this, where you couldn't see what you were eating, Katrina would have chosen a simpler meal for him as well. Amber light descended from a fixture upon Wrangel's head and on the thick white furs.

"Better make that call person-to-person," Victor advised Katrina.

It was good advice, for Horace Kinglake was hard to reach. The call went through many transfers. By his voice when he said "Kinglake," she recognized that he was an adroit, managerial type. From Victor she had picked up a certain contempt for polished executives. Still, it was comforting to talk even to a man whose courtesies were artificial. "Stuck in Detroit? Oh, we can't have that, can we? Some two hundred acceptances have come in. An audience from all parts of the country. It would be a disaster if Mr. Wulpy . . . I am really concerned. And so sorry. Wasn't there an earlier flight?" Cursing Victor, probably, for this last-minute fuck-up.

"Is the Chicago weather so ferocious?" Katrina asked for facts to go with her forebodings.

But Mr. Kinglake was taking her call in a private dining room, and what would a senior executive in his seventieth-story offices know about weather in the streets? He had heard some reports of a freak storm. "We'll get Mr. Wulpy here, regardless. I'll put my ace troubleshooter on this. Give me about half an hour."

"You can reach us at this number in Detroit. . . . I wonder, is O'Hare closed down for the day?"

"There is Midway and also Meigs Field."

Half reassured, she went back to the booth. A woman in her position, taking chances, playing outlaw in order to be at Victor's side—the big man's consort; but when she had seen him in profile (just after the flight engineer had stomped her instep, and when she had felt that there were unsobbed sobs in her chest), she had had a new view of the deterioration he had suffered since he had taken up with her.

The double shot of booze he had drunk apparently had done him good. He held a thick wide glass in his hand—a refill. This was what his system needed, food and drink and a booth to rest in. He could well have afforded to bring her here himself, and to slip the hostess ten bucks and to have the use of the telephone. But he would never have done that. It would have been a sacrifice of principle. And this was why he had been glad to see Wrangel. Wrangel had got him off his feet. The duck à l'orange would be awful. A servitor, an aide, was necessary to satisfy his psyche. Also somebody to pick up the tab. She admitted that this was important to him.

Trina made her report, and Victor said, "Well, we can just take it easy until he calls back. I'll talk to him myself, about tonight's program. Sit down, kid, and have a drink." Katrina shared the corner beside him. Vanessa's fiddle stood upright behind them. Katrina was grateful to Wrangel just then. She needed help with Victor. He seemed to her unstable, off center. The term often used in *Psychology Today* was "labile." He was labile. And he was more pleased than not to have Wrangel's company now. He seemed to have forgotten the poisonous dig about Tchelitchew. Katrina thought it likely that Wrangel had never heard about Tchelitchew's offensive statement. Of course, Victor believed that movies of the kind made by Wrangel infected the mental life of the country (and the international community), but they weren't considering Wrangel's movies just now. Evidently, though, they had been talking about erotic films, for Wrangel was saying that he hadn't personally been involved in that business. "Productions of that kind don't need scriptwriters."

"No?" said Victor. "Just interracial couples balling away?"

"I wonder if you can get the waitress to bring me a Bloody Mary," said Katrina.

"Certainly," said Wrangel. "Now, to fill you in on my career since the Village days, I had many kinds of writing jobs. One of the more curious was with the crew in Texas that helped to put together the memoirs of President Johnson."

"How did that come about?" said Katrina.

"Out of the Bread Loaf Conference, where I met some Washington journalists. Also Robert Frost—and a few gentleman types from Harvard. And I was recommended by Dick Goodwin, so there I was in Austin on Johnson's staff of writers. He had retired by then."

"How was that done—the work?" said Victor.

"It began with a course of brainwashing. We used to gather atop the Federal Building in Austin built by LBJ toward the end of his administration. He had his own suite, and he landed by helicopter, from his ranch, and came down from the rooftop to spend the day with us. He repeated his version of every event until it was grafted on our minds. You often come across these legend builders who hypnotize you by repetition. You become the receptacle of their story. Robert Frost was another of those authorized-version fellows. They do all of the talking, and they repeat themselves until your mind begins to reject alternative versions. Johnson brought us to his ranch, too. He drove over the pastures in his Lincoln, and the bodyguards followed in their Lincoln. When he needed more to drink, he rolled down his window and the guards pulled up alongside and poured him more whiskey. Most of us were intimidated by him—easier to do with a person like me, Victor, than with you."

"Oh, it's been tried. Once at Berenson's villa. The famous mummy was brought out—another Litvak, like myself. I was raised to respect my elders, but I didn't care to have so many cultural flourishes made over me."

"The Latin quotations . . ." Katrina reminded him.

"The *lacrimae rerum*. Wow! If it could have been done by ass-kissing his patrons and patronesses, B.B. would have dried away a good many tears. Then he said that he understood I was a considerable person in the bohemian life of New York. And I said that to call me a bohemian was like describing John the Baptist as a hydrotherapist. I had hoped to get the discussion around to modern painting, but of course that never happened."

A friendly chat. It was now half past two. At noon Katrina had been afraid that Victor might hit Wrangel on the head with his stick for saying "Most ideas are trivial." How well they were getting along now.

"You didn't mean that you were any kind of John the Baptist?" said Wrangel.

"No, it just drove me wild to be patronized."

For the moment, Victor was being charming. "Most people know better than to lack charm," he had once told Katrina. "Even harsh people have their own harsh charm. Some are *all* charm, like Franklin D. Roosevelt. Some repudiate all charm, like Stalin. When all-charm and no-charm met at Yalta, no-charm won hands down." Victor in his heart of hearts dismissed charm. Style, yes; style was essential; but charm tended to blur your thoughts. And if Victor was now charming with Wrangel, joking about John the Baptist, it was because he wanted to prevent Wrangel from bringing out his Gucci appointment book with its topic sentences on *The Eighteenth Brumaire*.

It was plainly Wrangel's purpose to resume—to develop a serious conversation. It was the drive for serious conversation that had made him cross the continent from L.A. to Buffalo. Trina was beginning to see a certain efficiency and toughness in Wrangel. It was not by accident that he had earned so many millions. While he seemed "humbly happy" in Victor's company, he was also opinionated, obstinate. In the past, and even today, Victor had dismissed him—not a mind of the A category—and Wrangel was determined to win a higher rating. He thought he deserved it. That was Katrina's view. The shy, astute man in the arctic fox coat had Victor Wulpy to himself—a failing Victor, but Wrangel would not know that, since Victor carried himself so firmly, and after a few slugs of Scotch he sat up as princely as ever. He was, however, very far from himself. He was in one of those badly lighted (on purpose) no-man's-land restaurants that airports specialize in; he had eaten all the sesame sticks and crackers on the table, and when he put one of his hands under the back of Katrina's sweater she felt an icy pang through her silk slip.

The food was served just as Victor was called to the phone, and Wrangel asked the waiter to take it back to the kitchen and keep it warm.

Tilting to the right to avoid the hanging ornaments, fixtures with gilt chains, Victor followed the hostess to the telephone.

"Do you know," said Katrina, partly to forestall a conversation about Victor, "I was interested to hear that you started out by inventing plots for science comics. You must be very quick at it. I've been trying and trying to do a children's story about an elephant stuck on the top floor of a Chicago department store, and you have no idea how it drags and bothers me. When the animal was taken up in the freight elevator, she tested the floor, and she was reluctant to trust it. Her mahout—the trainer—sweet-talked her into it. She was a great success in the store, but when it came time to go down and she tested the elevator again with her foot, she wouldn't enter."

"They're stuck with her? How to get her out?" He gave one of his intense but restricted smiles. "What have you thought of?"

"Piano movers; the fire department; drugging the elephant; hypnotism; dismantling a wall; a wooden ramp down the staircase."

"A builders' crane?" said Wrangel.

"Sure, but the roof would have to be opened."

"Of course it would. Even if there were a hatch. But look here—suppose they braced the floor of the elevator from beneath. Temporary steel beams. She goes in. Maybe some person she trusts is inside and gives her hay mixed with marshmallows while the supports are being removed by mechanic commandos at top speed. So they get her down and parade her on Michigan Boulevard."

"Oh, that's a perfectly angelic solution!" said Katrina.

"As long as the floor is firm when she tests it."

"Fabulous! Do elephants have a weakness for marshmallows? You are a wizard plotter. I think I may be able to handle it now. Totally inexperienced, you see."

"I'd be only too happy to help. If you get stuck, this card of mine has all the numbers where I can be reached."

"That's awfully decent. Thanks."

"And it's a very bright idea for a kids' book. Charming. I hope it goes over big."

Trina for a moment considered telling him what a difference an independent success would make to her. He looked now, despite his own success and celebrity, like a man who had had very bad times, ugly defeats, choking disappointments, and so she was tempted to talk openly to him. It would bring some light and warmth into this dark frozen day, some emotional truth. But it wouldn't be prudent to open up. He had helped with the elephant. However, there was Victor to think of. This Wrangel might be eager to make use of what she would tell him about herself to obtain privileged knowledge of Victor, for which he perhaps had an unusual, a ravenous, a kinky appetite.

"Victor is a marvelous man," said Wrangel. "I always admired him enormously. I was just a kid when I met him, and he couldn't possibly take me seriously. For a long time I've had a relationship to him of which he couldn't be aware. I made a study of him, you see. I've put a tremendous lot of thought into him. I'm afraid I have to confess that he's been an obsession. I've read all his books, collected his articles."

"He thinks you came East on purpose, to talk to him."

"It's true, and I'm not surprised that he guessed it. He was sick last year, wasn't he?"

"Near death."

"I can see he's not his old self."

"I hope you don't have some idea about straightening out his thinking, Mr. Wrangel."

"Who, me? Do I think he'd listen to *me*? I know better than that."

"And I don't want you to think that if you tell me your opinions I'm going to transmit them."

"Why would I do that? It would be just as easy to send him my opinions in writing. Believe it or not, Miss Gallagher, it's more a matter of affection."

"Although you haven't even seen him in thirty years?"

"The psyche has a different calendar," he said. "Anyway, you haven't got it quite right. Anybody who knows Victor naturally wants to talk about him. There's so much to him."

"There are a hundred people you could discuss him with—the famous painters he influenced, or types like Clement Greenberg or Kenneth Burke or Harold Rosenberg—or any of the big-time art theorists. Plus a whole regiment of other people's wives."

"You must be a musician, Miss Gallagher. You carry a violin."

"It belongs to Victor's youngest daughter and we're taking it to Chicago for repair. If I were a violinist, why would I write a story about an elephant? I understand that you used to fiddle yourself."

"Did Victor remember my left-handed fooling—my trick instrument?"

"Anyway, what were you going to say about Victor, Mr. Wrangel?"

"Victor was meant to be a great man. Very, very smart. A powerful mind. A subtle mind. Completely independent. Not really a Marxist, either. I went to visit Sidney Hook last week, who used to be my teacher at NYU, and we were talking about the radicals of the older generation in New York. Sidney pooh-poohed them. They never had been serious, never organized themselves to take control as the European left did. They were happy enough, talking. Talk about Lenin, talk about Rosa Luxemburg, or German fascism, or the Popular Front, or Léon Blum, or Trotsky's interpretation of the Molotov-Ribbentrop Pact, or about James Burnham or whomever. They spent their lives discussing every-thing. If they felt their ideas were correct, they were satisfied. They were a bunch of mental hummingbirds. The flowers were certainly red, but there couldn't have been any nectar in them. Still, it was enough if they were very ingenious, and if they drew a big, big picture—the very biggest picture. Now apply this to what Victor said one plane hop back, in Buffalo, that it takes a serious political life to keep reality real. . . ."

Katrina pretended that he was saying this to the wrong party. "I don't have any theoretical ability at all," she said, and she bent toward him as if to call at-tention to her forehead, which couldn't possibly have had real thoughts behind it. She was the farmer's daughter who couldn't remember how many made a dozen. But she saw from Wrangel's silent laugh—his skin was so taut, had he or hadn't he had a face-lift in California?—saw from the genial scoff lines around his mouth that she wasn't fooling him for a minute.

"Victor was one of those writers who took command of a lot of painters, told them what they were doing, what they should do. Society didn't care about art anyway, it was busy with other things, and art became the plaything of intellec-tuals. Real painters, real painting, those are very rare. There are masses of edu-cated people, and they'll tell you that they're all for poetry, philosophy, or painting, but they don't know them, don't do them, don't really care about them, sacrifice nothing for them, and really can't spare them the time of day—can't read, can't see, and can't hear. Their real interests are commercial, profes-sional, political, sexual, financial. They don't live by art, with art, through art. But they're willing in a way to be imposed upon, and that's what the pundits do. They do it to the artists as well. The brush people are led by the word peo-ple. It's like some General Booth with a big brass band leading artists to an ab-stract heaven."

"You have clever ways of expressing yourself, Mr. Wrangel. Are you saying that Victor is nothing but a promoter?"

"Not for a minute. He's a colorful, powerful, intricate man. Unlike the other critic crumb-bums, he has a soul. Really. As for being a promoter, I can't see how he could hold the forefront if he didn't do a certain amount of promoting and operating. Well, what's the status of innocence, anyway, and can you get anywhere without hypocrisy? I'm not calling Victor a hypocrite; I'm saying that he has no time to waste on patsies, and he's perfectly aware that America is one place where being a patsy won't kill you. We can afford confusion of mind, in a safe, comfortable country. Of course, it's been fatal to art and culture. . . ."

"Is this your way of asking *me* how corrupt Victor is?" Katrina asked. Heavy distress, all the more distressing because of its mixed elements, came over her. Should she tell Wrangel off? Was it disloyal to listen to him? But she was fascinated and hungry for more. And Victor himself would have thought her a patsy for raising the question of loyalty at all. Too big for trivial kinds of morality, he waved them off. And Wrangel was taking advantage of Victor's brief absence, crowding in as many comments as he could. He was very smart, and she now felt like a dope for bothering him with her elephant.

He was trying to impress her, strutting a little (was he trying also to make time with her?), but his passion for understanding Victor was genuinely a passion.

"Victor is a promoter. He did well by himself, solidly. But he hasn't faked anything. He really studied the important questions of art—art and technology, art and science, art in the era of the mass life. He understands how the artistic faculties are hampered in America, which isn't really an art land. Here art isn't serious. Not in the way a vaccine for herpes is *serious*. And even for professionals, critics, curators, editors, art is just *blah!* And it should be like the air you breathe, the water you drink, basic, like nutrition or truth. Victor knows what the real questions are, and if you ask him what's the matter here he would tell you that without art we can't judge what life is, we can't sort anything out at all. Then the 'practical sphere' itself, where 'planners,' generals, opinion makers, and presidents operate, is no more real than the lint under your bed. But even Victor's real interest is politics. Sometimes his politics are idiotic, too, as they were during the French student crisis, when he agreed with Sartre that we were on the verge of an inspiring and true revolution. He got carried away. His politics would have made bad art. In politics Victor is still something of a sentimentalist. Some godlike ideas he has, and a rich appreciation of human complexities. But he couldn't be engrossed in the colors of the sky around Combray, as Proust was. He's not big on hawthorn blossoms and church steeples, and he'll never get killed crossing the street because he's having visions."

Katrina said, "In Victor's place, I don't know how I'd feel about such a close study."

"Shall I tell you something? There was more than one hint of Victor Wulpy in the adventures of Buck Rogers."

This little guy, the celebrity covered by *People*—opinionated, sensitive, emotional—was definitely an oddball. Under the flame-shaped bulbs with their incandescent saffron threads, delicacy, obstinacy, and bliss were mingled in his face.

He began now to tell her about his son, an only child. "By my second wife," he said. "A younger woman. My Hank is now twenty-one. A problem from the beginning. He was born to startle. Some kids are dropping acid, stealing cars—that was the least of it. If he signed checks with my name, I could handle it by keeping my checking account low. He made the house so terrible that he drove his mother out. She couldn't take it, and she's now living with someone else. Illegal dealings started when Hank was about fourteen. Chased on the highway by the police. He held out money on dope dealers and they tried to kill him. No communication between me and the boy—too much sea-noise in his head. He's in a correctional prison now where I'm not allowed to visit. There the recidivists are treated like infants. Their diet is infantile—farina—and they're forced to wear diapers. The theory must be that the problem lies in infancy, so there's a program of compulsory regression. That's how human life is interpreted by psychological specialists."

"Heartbreaking," said Katrina.

"Oh, I can't afford to be heartbroken. He's my crazy Absalom. His mother is finished with him. She'll talk to me. To him, never. He resembles her physically: fair-haired and slight, the boy is. A born mechanic, and a genius with engines, only he'd take apart my Porsche and leave the parts lying on the ground."

"Does he hate you?"

"He doesn't use such language."

Why, the boy may kill him in the end, Katrina thought. The one who's loyal may be the one who pays with his life.

"Enough of that," said Wrangel. "Getting back to Victor. It wasn't by his opinions that he influenced my attitudes toward art, but by the way he was. I don't really *like* his ideas. In the old days I would compare him mentally to Franklin D. Roosevelt, whom I personally admired although critical of his policies."

Like Roosevelt! Of course! Both handicapped men. Katrina made some rapid comparisons. Beila was like Eleanor Roosevelt. She, Trina, was like Missy LeHand. Katrina remembered hearing that Missy LeHand, with whom Roosevelt had had a love affair, fell ill and crept away to die, and Roosevelt, busy with the war, had no time to think about her, didn't ask what had become of her. FDR was as cold as he was great. Victor, too, talked about the coldness and isolation of people—the mark of the Modern. The Modern truth was severe. Making love to a middle-class woman, it was necessary to indulge her sentiments of warmth, but to a hard judgment these had no historical reality. There was monstrousness and horror in Modern man. Useless to deny dehumanization. That was how Victor would talk, when he lay in bed like one of Picasso's naked old satyrs. But you, spread beside him—the full woman, perhaps the fat woman, woman-smelling—you perhaps knew more about him than he knew himself.

They now saw Victor working his way back to the booth, and Wrangel signaled to the waitress to serve their lunch. The glazed orange duck looked downright dangerous. Circles of fat swam in the spiced gravy. Famished, Victor attacked his food. His whiskey glass was soon fingerprinted with grease. He tore up his rolls over the dish and spooned up the fatty sops. He was irritable. Wrangel tried to make conversation, as a host should do. Victor gave him a gloomy if not sinister look—a glare, to be more accurate—when Wrangel began to point out connections between cartoons and abstract ideas. When people spoke of ideas as "clear," didn't they mean reductive? Human beings, in reduction, represented as *things*. Acceptable enough if they were funny. But suppose the intention wasn't funny, as shorthand representations of the human often were, then you got an abstract condensation of the Modern theme. Take Picasso and Daumier as caricaturists (much deference in this to Victor, the expert). It might be fair to say that Daumier treated a social subject: the middle class, the courtroom. Picasso didn't. In Picasso you had the flavor of nihilism that went with increased abstraction. Wrangel in his rolls of fur and his chin supported by silk scarf and cotton bandanna was nervous, insecure of tone, twitching.

"What's this about reason?" said Victor. "First you tell me that ideas are trivial, they're dead, and then what do you do but discuss ideas with me?"

"There's no contradiction, is there, if I say that abstract ideas and caricature go together?"

"I have little interest in discussing this," said Victor. "It'll keep until you get back to California, won't it?"

"I suppose it will."

"Well, then, stow it. Skip it. Stuff it."

"It's a pity that my success in sci-fi should be held against me. Actually I've had a better than average training in philosophy."

"Well, I'm not in the mood for philosophy. And I don't want to discuss the nihilism that goes with reason. I figure you've done enough to fuck up the consciousness of millions of people with this mishmash of astrophysics and divinity that has made you so famous. Your trouble is that you'd like to sneak up on real seriousness. Well, you've already made your contribution. Your statement is on record."

"You yourself have written about 'divine sickness,' Victor. I would suppose that any creature, regardless of his worldly status, had one ticket good for a single admission if he has suffered—if he paid his price."

But Victor wouldn't hear him out. He made a face so satirical, violent, so killing that Katrina would have turned away from it if it hadn't been so extraordinary—an aspect of Victor never manifested before. He drew his lips over his teeth to imitate bare gums. He gabbled in pantomime, not a sound coming out. He let out his tongue like a dog panting. He squeezed his eyes so tight that you couldn't see anything except the millipede brows and lashes. He put his thumbs to the sides of his head and waggled his fingers. Then he slid himself out of the booth, took up the duffel, and started for the door. Katrina, too, stood up. She held Vanessa's fiddle in her arms, saying, "I'd apologize for him if you didn't also know him. He's in very bad shape, Mr. Wrangel, you can see that for yourself. Last year we nearly lost him. And he's in pain every day. Try to remember that. I'm sorry about this. Don't let him get to you."

"Well, this is a lesson. Of course, it makes me very sad. Yes, I see he's in bad shape. Yes, it's a pity."

It had cut him up, and Katrina's heart went out to Wrangel. "Thank you," she said, drawing away, turning. She hoped she didn't look too clumsy from the rear.

Victor was waiting for her in the concourse and she spoke to him angrily. "That was bad behavior. I didn't like being a party to it."

"When he started on me with Daumier and Picasso, I couldn't stand it, not a minute more of it."

"You feel rotten and you took it out on him."

He conceded this in silence.

"You didn't behave well with me, either. You never said a word about your conversation with Kinglake, and whether we're getting out of here or not."

"He's sending a corporate plane for us. He says it can get through."

"Now, you know I'm in trouble if I'm stuck in Detroit overnight."

"You're not going to be stuck. A plane is coming for us."

Once more, thousands of people. Nothing she could think of accounted for the sorrow she was feeling in the crowd-crazed concourse. Victor stopped beside the blazing window of a costume jewelry boutique and stared down into her face. He was speaking to her. She could not hear. Her ears seemed plugged.

"You should have told me sooner. You know my anxiety about being stuck."

"Why *should* I put up with a guy like Wrangel?" he said. "Thousands of people zero in on me. They come to clean up their act, or make a bid to change their act altogether. They want better clichés to live by. A man like Wrangel has to achieve another 'self' because he's in a position he never expected to reach. When he turned up in the Village long ago, he made himself striking by re-stringing his violin or by being a comic-strip plot spinner whose *real* life was with Hegel and Pascal. Now he's become a big pop symbol, so he's completely lost. Wears arctic fox. All right, if you don't stand up to the real conditions of life and stand up to them with strength and shrewdness, you are condemned to live by one poor fiction or another, of which you are the commonplace interpreter.

Their commonplaces sting these guys without mercy, and drive them to try to be original. See how hard Wrangel was trying. He wanted me to adopt him and be his spiritual uncle or something—too old for a father. A while back I got a letter from a guy, an artist, who works in fire extinguishers. He said he was guarding the human soul from the arsonists of evil. He would never paint anything except fire extinguishers. He demanded my blessing. *I* have no Secret Service to protect me. I have to fend 'em off myself."

"All right. . . . Now, what are we supposed to do until the plane arrives?"

"There's a hotel on these premises, upstairs, out of this madhouse. Kinglake has reserved a room for us."

"Thank God! I can't face any more shoving and pushing up and down the corridors," said Katrina. "What kind of plane are they sending?"

"A plane. How should I know? You're overreacting. This is not such an awful crisis. The Negro woman wouldn't desert the kids, and there's your sister."

"I've been trying to tell you. My sister is half bonkers."

"I had words with Kinglake about Felsher, the man who is supposed to introduce me. I said he was an old Stalinist bum, and he'd give a low tone to the occasion. It's too late to change the program, but I put my objection on record."

"Can we go up to the room, Victor? You have a rest. I have to use the phone."

They made their way to the hotel desk. They were expected. Victor signed the card and he refused a bellhop. "We don't want help. Nothing to carry. We're just waiting for our plane." Why should it cost a buck to put the key in the lock?

When he came into the room, Victor pitched himself heavily on the bed and Katrina removed his shoes. They must have been size sixteen. Nevertheless, his feet were delicate in shape. A human warmth was released from these shoes when she pulled them off. She stacked pillows behind his head. As he made himself comfortable, he was aware again of the bristling of nerve ends in the belly. Surgical damage. The frayed ends of copper wires. Hair-darts ingrown.

"I'm calling my sister. Don't worry, I'll tell the operator to cut in."

She went down the list of numbers Dotey had given her. People answered who were rude and hung up—behavior was getting worse and worse. At last she reached her sister, who said she was on the far South Side, fifteen miles from home, twenty-five from Evanston. Hazardous driving. "Too bad about all this snow," she said. It was, however, satisfaction and not sympathy that her voice expressed.

"Did you call Evanston? Is Ysole there?"

"Ysole wanted me to tell her where you were. She didn't believe you were in Schaumburg. She said that Krieggstein phoned in several times. He does stand by you, doesn't he? He's in love with you, Trina."

"He's a friend to me."

"Where are you, by the way?"

"We had to land in Detroit."

"Detroit! Jesus! I heard that O'Hare was closing. Can you get back?"

"A little late. Not too much. Did Ysole say that Alfred had called? By now the psychiatrist has told the lawyer about the canceled appointment, and if his lawyer has heard, so has mine."

"You encourage Krieggstein too much," said Dotey.

"I'm one of many. He courts ten ladies at a time."

"So he says. It's you he's fascinated by. After Victor goes, he'll close in. You may be too beat to resist him."

"You're being very ugly to me, Dorothea."

Victor had pulled a pillow over the top of his head like a cowl. His eyes were closed, and he said, "Don't tangle with her. Bottle up your feelings."

"Let's conclude. I'm tying up a customer's line," said Dotey.

"I count on you to stand by. . . ."

"To go to Evanston tonight is out of the question. I've accepted a dinner invitation."

"You didn't mention that last night."

"I'm sitting with business associates," Dotey was saying. "You can reach me at home between six and eight."

"All right," said Katrina. Very quietly, obedient to Victor, she put down the phone.

"Be a sweetheart and turn off the air-conditioning, Katrina. I hate this fucking false airflow in hotels. The motor gets me down. These places more and more resemble funeral parlors."

Katrina's face as she turned the switch was blotched with the stings her sister had inflicted on her. "Dotey has like an instinct against me. When I'm in trouble she's always ready to give me more lumps."

"You'll manage without her. We'll fly back in an executive jet. You'll go to Evanston in a limousine." To these words of comfort Victor added, "The kids love a snowfall. They're out playing, and they're happy. I'd give you odds." Even he was somewhat surprised by the gentleness of his tone. He was in a melting mood. It seemed to him that even when making faces at Wrangel he hadn't felt harsh—playful rather. How to see such an occurrence: Chief Iffucan, the Indian in his caftan, the old man with henna hackles. Barbarous charm. It was possible for Wulpy to take such a view. The irritation of his scars had abated. He did not listen to Katrina's next conversation, which was with Ysole. What he was led to consider (again, a frequent subject) was the limits he had never until lately reckoned with. Now he touched limits on every side: "Thou hast appointed his bounds that he cannot pass." For the representative of American energy and action these omnipresent touchable bounds were funny-lamentable. What was a *weak* "barbarian"? Newfangled men needed strength. Philosophers of action must be able to act. Of course, Wulpy had had his intimations of helplessness (the biblical "appointed bounds" didn't count, those were from another life—the *yivrach katzail,* "he fleeth as a shadow," he had studied as a boy). The bad leg had not been a limitation. It had been an aid to ascendancy. As perhaps the foot of Oedipus had been. But no longer than three years ago he had had his mother lying in the backseat of his beat-up Pontiac, serving for the afternoon as an ambulance. An old cousin had telephoned to say that his mother was virtually speechless in the nursing home where he kept her. He had finally gone to inspect this unspeakable tenement. He packed her bag and checked her out of there. That afternoon, a day of killing heat, he drove from one joint to another and tried to place her. He visited nursing homes, locking her in the car (bad neighborhoods) while he climbed stairs—the torment of getting two feet on each tread—to look at bedrooms, enter kitchens and bathrooms, and discuss terms with a bedlam population of "administrators," otherwise "dollar psychotics," who tore the money from you. (Not that he didn't fight for every buck. "Licensed abuse," he told them. "A horrible rip-off.") At four o'clock he had still not found the right place for her, that semiconscious regal monument in the backseat of his jalopy. And while he drove around Astoria and Jackson Heights, Katrina—in fantasy—drove her car behind him, tailgating him between red walls of dead brick. This imaginary Katrina wore nothing but a coat, under which she was naked, in a state of sexual readiness. When he parked and hobbled into a building, he imagined that she had pulled up behind, invisibly, and that she was streaming under the buckled Aquascutum coat. That this was a commonplace fantasy, he knew well. But he accepted it. Apparently he needed to imagine the woman-slime odor—that swamp-smell—and the fever that came with it was peculiarly his. At last Wulpy had found a good place, or maybe just gave up, and his mother was carried in while he wrote the check. The old girl seemed indifferent by now. In a matter of months she was dead, leaving Victor with his ideas and his travels, his erotic activities—the whole vivid stir: an important man, making important statements, publishing important articles. Shortly after his mother died, he himself entered Mass. General. There he escaped death, but became aware that it was necessary to consider the appointed bounds. Something like a great river was going to change its course. A Mississippi was about to find a new bed. Whole cities would drown. Mansions would float across the Gulf of Mexico, lifted from their foundations, and come aground on the sands of Venezuela.

"Where are you anyway, Trina?" said Ysole.

"I had to attend a meeting in Schaumburg, and I'm stuck out here."

"All right," said Ysole. "Give me that suburban number where you're at." When Katrina made no answer, Ysole said, "You never would tell the truth if you could lie instead."

Look at it this way: There was a howling winter space between them. The squat Negro woman with her low deformed hips who pressed the telephone to her ear, framed in white hair, was far shrewder than Katrina and was (with a black nose and brown mouth formed by nature for amusement) amused by her lies and antics. Katrina considered. Suppose that I told her, "I'm in a Detroit motel with Victor Wulpy. And right now he's getting out of bed to go to the bathroom." What use could such facts be to her? Ysole said, "Your friend the cop and your sister both checked in with me."

"If I'm not home by five, when Lilburn comes, give him a drink, and have dinner there, too."

"This is our regular night for bingo. We go to the church supper."

"I'll pay you fifty bucks, which is more than you can win at the church."

Ysole said no.

Katrina again felt: Everybody has power over me. Alfred, punishing me, the judge, the lawyers, the psychiatrist, Dotey—even the kids. They all apply standards nobody has any use for, except to stick you with. That's what drew me to Victor, that he wouldn't let anybody set conditions for him. Let others make the concessions. That's how I'd like to be. Except that I haven't got his kind of ego, which is a whole mountain of ego. Now it's Ysole's turn. "Are you holding me up, Ysole?" she said.

"Trina, I wouldn't stay for five hundred. I had to fight Lilburn for this one night of the week. When do you figure to get home?"

"As fast as I can."

"Well, the kids will be all right. I'll lock the doors, and they can watch TV."

They hate us, said Trina to herself, after Ysole had hung up. They hate us terribly.

She needed Visine to ease the burning of her eyes. In the winter she was subject to eye inflammation. She thought it was because exhaust gases clung closer to the ground in zero weather and the winter air stank more. She opened her purse and sat on the edge of the bed raking through keys, compacts, paper tissues, dollar bills, credit cards, emery boards.

"You got nowhere with the telephone, I see," said Victor. He was now standing above her, and he passed his hand through her hair. There was always some skepticism mixed with his tenderness when he approached her, as if he were sorry for her, sorry for all that she would never understand, that he would never do. Then he made a few distracted observations—unusual for him. Again he mentioned the air-conditioning unit. He couldn't find the switch that turned it off. It reminded him of the machinery he had heard for the first time when he was etherized as a kid for surgery on his leg. Unconscious, he saw a full, brilliant moon. An old woman tried to climb over a bar—the diameter of this throbbing moon. If she had made it he would have died. "Those engines may have been my own heartbeats. Invisible machinery has affected me ever since. And you know how much invisible machinery there is in a place like this—all the jets, all the silicon-chip computers. . . . Now, Katrina, do something for me. Reach under my belt. Put your delicious hand down there. I need a touch from you. It's one of the few things I can count on."

She did it. It was not too much to ask of a woman of mature years. A matter between human friends. Signs of eagerness were always instantaneous. Never failing.

"What about a quickie, Trina?"

"But the phone will ring."

"All the better, under pressure."

"In these boots?"

"Just pull down your things."

Victor lowered himself toward her. To all that was exposed he applied his cheeks, warmth to warmth, to her thighs, on her belly with its faint trail of hairs below the navel. The telephone was silent. It didn't ring. They were winning, winning, winning, winning. They won!

That was what Victor said to her. "We got some of our own back."

"We were due for *one* break," said Katrina. "Dizzy luck. I'm spinning around."

"Let's stay put awhile. Don't get up. There's a Russian proverb: If late for an appointment, walk slower. We're best off just as we are. Kinglake would have rung us if the plane weren't on its way."

"Do you think it's after sundown, Victor?"

"How would we know from here? We're on the inside of the inside of the inside. Why worry? You'll be only a little late. They have to get me there. No Wulpy, no festival. It's a test for *them,* a challenge they've accepted."

They rested on the edge of the bed, legs hanging. He took Katrina's hand, kissed her fingers. He was a masterful, cynical man, but with her at times like these he put aside his cynicism. She took it as a sign—how much he cared for her. He enjoyed talking when they lay together like this. She could recall many memorable things he had said on such occasions: "You could write better than Fonstine"—one of his enemies—"if you took off your shoes and pounded the keyboard with your rosy heels. Or just by lifting your skirts and sitting on the machine with your beautiful bottom. The results would be more inspiring."

Victor now mentioned Wrangel. "He wanted to establish a relationship."

"He has great respect—admiration for you," said Katrina. "He said that to him when he came to the Village in the fifties—just a kid—you were in a class with Franklin D. Roosevelt. Meant to be a great man."

"I was sure he would do lots of talking while I was on the telephone. Well, not to be modest about it, Katrina . . ." (And what was there to be modest about? They lay together at the foot of the bed, bare between the waist and the knees. His arm was still under her shoulders.) "In some respects I can see . . . I thought what I would do with power. It gave me an edge over intellectuals who never tried to imagine power. This was why they couldn't *think*. I have more iron in me. My ideas had more authority because I conceived what I would do in authority. It's my nature. . . ." He paused. "It *was* my nature. I'm going to have to part with my nature presently. All the more reason to increase the dispassionate view I always preferred."

"Talking like this, just after sex?" said Katrina.

"I would have done well in a commanding situation. I have the temperamental qualifications. Don't flinch from being a reprobate. Naturally political, and I have a natural contempt for people in private life who have no power-stir. Let it be in thought, let it be in painting. It has to be a powerful reading of the truth of existence. Metaphysical passion. You get as much truth as you have the courage to approach."

Having nobody but me to tell this to. This was one of Katrina's frequent thoughts—she was disappointed for his sake. If there had been a pad to the right of her she might have taken notes. She did have *some* idea what he was saying.

"Some of the sharpest pains we feel come from the silence imposed on the deepest inward mining that we do. The most unlikely-looking people may be the most deep miners. I've often thought, 'He, or she, is intensely at work, digging in a different gallery, but the galleries are far apart, in parallels which never meet, and the diggers are deaf to one another's work.' It must be one of the wickedest forms of human suffering. And it could explain the horrible shapes often taken by what we call 'originality.'"

"Was there nothing Wrangel said that had any value?"

"I might have been interested by his guru. I had a sense of secondhand views. I don't think Wrangel had any hot news for me. If this is something like the end of time—for this civilization—everything already is quite clear and intelligible to alert minds. In our *real* thoughts, and I don't mean what we say—what's said is largely hokum—in the real thoughts, alert persons recognize what is happening. There may have been something in what Wrangel said—still echoing his guru—about the connections made by real thoughts: a true thought may have a true image corresponding to it. Do you know why communication broke down with Wrangel? It was uncomfortable to hear a California parody of things that I had been thinking myself. I've been very troubled, Katrina. And the ideas I've developed over sixty years don't seem to help me to cope with the trouble. I made an extreme commitment to lucidity. . . ."

"But aren't you lucid?"

"That's my *mental* lucidity. I've been having lucid impressions—like dreams, visions—instead of lucid ideas."

"What's this about?"

"Well, there's shared knowledge that we don't talk about. That deaf deep mining."

"Like what?"

"Cryptic persistent suggestions: the dead are not really *dead*. Or, we don't create thoughts, as that movie drip suggested. A thought *is* real, already created, and a real thought can pay you a visit. I think I understand why this happens to me. After so many years in the arts, you begin to assume that the value of life is bound up with the value of art. And there is no rational basis for this. Then you begin to suspect that it's the 'rational' that lacks real meaning. Rationality would argue back that it's the weakening of the organism that suggests this. A stupid argument." Victor refrained from speaking of the erotic side of this—magical, aesthetic, erotic—or of what this final flare-up of eroticism might mean. It might mean that he was paying out from his last fibers for lucidity of impression and for sexual confirmation of the fact that he still existed. But full strength, strong fibers, only made you more capable of lying to yourself, of maintaining the *mauvaise foi,* the false description of your personal reality. He didn't mention to Katrina the underground music which signified (had signified to Mark Antony) that the god Hercules was going away.

He changed the subject. He said to Katrina, "It's a real laugh that Wrangel should mix me up in his mind with FDR."

Roosevelt, too, was dying at a moment when to have strength was more necessary than ever. And hadn't there been a woman with him at Warm Springs when he had his brain hemorrhage?

"Didn't it ever occur to you?" said Katrina.

"It occurred, but I didn't encourage the thought. Stalin made a complete fool of the man. Those trips to Teheran and Yalta must have been the death of him. They were ruinous physically. I'm certain that Stalin meant to hasten his death. Terrible journeys. Roosevelt felt challenged to demonstrate his vigor. Stalin didn't budge. Roosevelt let himself be destroyed, proving his strength as chief of a great power, and also his 'nobility.' "

Katrina, who had moved her round face closer—a girl posing for a "sweetheart snapshot," cheek to cheek—said, "Aren't you cold? Wouldn't you like me to pull the covers over you? No? At least slide your fingers under me to warm up."

To encourage him she turned on her side. A gambit she could always count on—the smooth shape of her buttocks, their crème de Chantilly whiteness. He always laughed when she offered herself this way, and put out his big, delicate hands. Something of a tough guy he really was, and particularly with age distortions—the wrecked Picasso Silenus reaching toward the nude beauty. She felt a sort of aristocratic delicacy from him even when he was manipulating these round forms of hers. It was really a bit crazy, the pride she took in her bottom. He matched up the freckles on each cheek—she had two prominent birthmarks—as if they were eyes. "Now you're squinting. Now you're cross-eyed. Now you're planning a conspiracy." Victor paused and said, "This is what little Wrangel was saying about cartoons and abstractions, isn't it? Making these faces?" Then he smoothed her gently and said, "It's no figure of speech to say that your figure leaves me speechless."

It was at this moment that the telephone began to ring, again and again—merciless. It was the desk. Their plane was just now landing. The limousine had started out. They were to be downstairs in five minutes.

They waited in the cold, under the bright lights. Victor had his stick and the mariner's cap—the broad mustache, the wonderful face, the noble ease in all circumstances. The Thinker Prince. Never quite up to his great standard, she felt just a little clumsy beside him. She was in charge of the damned fiddle, too. To hold an instrument she couldn't play. It turned her into a native bearer. She should set it on her head. And there they were on the edges of Detroit, standing on one of its crusts of light. Just like the other blasted cities of the northern constellation—Buffalo, Cleveland, Chicago, St. Louis—all those fields of ruin that looked so golden and beautiful by night.

"*This* is no limousine," said Victor, irritated, when the car stopped. "It's a goddamn compact Honda."

But he made no further fuss about it. Opening the door of the car and taking a grip on the edge of the roof, he began to install himself in the front seat. First there was the stiff leg to get in, over on the driver's end, by the brake, and then he eased in his head and his huge back so that, as he turned, the car was crammed to the top. Then he descended into the seat with patient, clever labor. It was like a difficult intromission. But as soon as he was in place, and while Katrina was settling herself in the back, he was already talking. Nerving himself for the approaching lecture, tuning up? "Did you ever get through the Céline book I gave you?"

"The *Journey*? I did, finally."

"It's not agreeable, but it is important. It's one of those French things I've had on my mind."

"Like the Baudelaire?"

"Right." The driver had taken off swiftly by a dark side road, along fences. Victor made an effort to turn in the small seat; he wanted to look at her. Apparently he wished to make a statement not only in words but also with his face. "Didn't you think Céline was truly terrifying? He uses the language that people everywhere really use. He expresses the ideas and feelings they really share."

"Last time we spoke about it you said those were the ideas that made France collapse in 1940. And that the Germans also had those same ideas."

"I don't think that was exactly what I said. Talking about nihilism . . ."

Why had he asked her to read that book? Toward the end of it—a nightmare—a certain adventurer named Robinson refused to tell a woman that he loved her, and this "loving" woman, enraged, had shot him dead. Not even when she pointed the gun at him in the taxicab could she make him say the words "I love you." The "loving" woman was really a maniac, while the man, the "lover," although he was himself a crook, a deadbeat, a murderer, had one shred of honor left, and that, too, was in the terminal stage. Better dead than carried off for life by this loony ogress whom he would have to pretend to "love." It wasn't so much the book that had shocked Katrina—a book was only a book—but the fact that he, Victor, had told her to read it. Of course, he was always pushing the widest possible perspective of historical reality. The whole universe was his field of operations. A cosmopolitan in the fullest sense, a giant of comprehension, he was located in the central command post of comprehension. "Face the destructive facts. No palliatives," was the kind of thing he said.

"That book was next door to the murder camps," she said.

"I don't deny it."

"Well, back at the hotel you said that alert people everywhere were recognizing the same facts. But same isn't quite the way it was in the Céline book. Not even for you, Victor."

There was no time to answer. The car had stopped at the small private-aircraft building. When the driver ran from the front seat to open her door, she thought his face was distorted. Maybe it was only the cold that made him grimace. Extricating himself from the car, Victor again caught at the roof and hopped backward, drawing out the bad leg.

They entered the overilluminated shack. At the counter, where phones were jingling, Trina gave the name Wulpy to the dispatcher. The man said, "Yes, your Cessna is on the ground. It'll taxi up in a few minutes."

She passed the news to Victor, who nodded but went on talking. "I'll grant you, the French had been had by their ideology. An ideology is a spell cast by the ruling class, a net of binding falsehoods, and the discovery of this can throw people into a rage. That's why Céline is violent."

"People? *Some* people."

You have a love affair and then you ask your ladylove to read a book to discredit love, and it's the most extreme book you can select. That's some valentine.

Her ostrich boots gave her no sense of elegance as she preceded him into the Cessna. She felt clumsy and thick, every graceless thing that a woman can be, and she carried Vanessa's instrument across her chest. By the light of the lurid revolving bubble on the fuselage, she watched Victor being assisted into the plane. The two-man crew received Victor and Katrina with particular consideration. This was how the personnel were trained for these executive ferrying jobs.

Passengers were guests. Would they care for coffee? And fresh doughnuts, or powdered bismarcks? Or would they prefer whiskey? The afternoon papers hadn't been available when they left Chicago. They did, however, have *Barron's* and the *Wall Street Journal*. The seats were luxurious—as much legroom as you liked, excellent reading lights. Here was the panel with its many switches. Neither of the passengers cared to read just now.

The pilot said, "We'll be landing at Midway, and you'll get a helicopter ride to Meigs."

"Well, this is more like it," said Victor. "You see?" She translated "You see?" as an assertion that he had not misled her. He had sent for her, and he was returning her to Chicago. He had the power to make good all assurances. He raised his whiskey glass. We'll drink to you and me. Something like a smile passed over his face, but he was also ruffled, moody. His eyes, those narrow canals, were black with mortal injury. None of these powers—summoning special machines, commanding special privileges—really seemed to mean a thing. Doodads for a canary's cage. "Oh, yes, you're a pilot yourself," he remembered.

"Not one of these planes," said Katrina. She held up her wristwatch to the light. Ysole would have left the house by now.

Suddenly the silence of the cabin was torn by a furious roar. Nothing could be heard. The plane bumped across the icy seams of the field. Then came the clean run and they were (thank God!) airborne. Their course would take them southwest across Lake Michigan. It was just as well in this weather that the water should be invisible. The parlorlike neatness of the cabin was meant to give a sense of safety. She tasted the coffee—it was freeze-dried, it was not hot. When she bit into the jelly doughnut, she liked the fragrance of the fried dough but not the cold jelly that gushed out.

He may have had no special intention in giving her the Céline book to read. If so, why did he bring it up now? And what of the dowager Beila, to whom Vanessa had recommended the book on homosexual foreplay? They *were* a bookish family, weren't they. But this was to misread Beila completely. You could no more think of her that way than you could think of Queen Victoria. And Victor did not encourage discussions of Beila. Sometimes he spoke of "wives of a certain kind." "Perfect happiness for wives of a certain kind is to immobilize their husbands." The suggestion was that a man in his seventies who had barely survived Mass. General and had a bad leg was a candidate for immobilization. You could as easily immobilize Niagara Falls. A perfectly objective judgment of Beila, removing all rivalry and guilt, was that she behaved with dignity. When it looked as if Victor was not going to make it at Mass. General, Beila had asked him whether he wanted to see Katrina, who was hiding in one of the waiting rooms. Victor did want to see her, and Beila had sent for her, and had withdrawn from the room also, to let them take leave of each other. Then

Katrina and Victor had gripped hands. He seemed unable to speak. She wept with heartbreak. She told him that she would always love him. He held her hand fast and said, "This is it, kid." His tongue was impeded, but he was earnest and clear, she remembered. And since then, she thought how important it was that her claim to access should be affirmed, and that his feeling for her should be acknowledged. It wasn't just another adultery. She wasn't one of his casual women. Before death, his emotions were open, and she came—when she rushed in she was bursting. Her suffering was conceded its rights. Their relationship was certified; it took a sort of formal imprint from the sickroom. Last farewells. He was dying. When he released her hand, meaning that it was time to go—too much for him, perhaps, too painful—and she went out sobbing, she saw the distant significant figure of Beila down the corridor, watching or studying her.

Well, what had Beila's generosity achieved, when Victor was on his feet again? It only made matters simpler for the lovers. Then this creepy, rabbinical, fiddling, meddling, and bratty daughter advised a mother in her late sixties to learn to tickle and to suck, use advanced techniques of lewdness. ("For two cents I'd throw her fiddle right into the lake! Little bitch!") Beila needed all the dignity she could muster. And especially with a husband whose description might be: "Others abide our judgment, thou art free!" Finally Victor himself bringing up the ultimate, hellish judgment on "love"—that love was something *dégueulasse.* Like spoiled meat; dogs would walk away from it, but "lovers" poured out some "tenderness sauce" and then it became a dainty dish to set before the king—handing Katrina such a book to read.

That wasn't what he had been like in Mass. General, with death on top of him.

It occurred to her that his aim was to desensitize her feelings so that when he died—and he felt it coming—she would suffer less.

But he did play rough. A few years ago he had suggested that Joe So-and-so, a nice young poet, very pretty, too, no ball of fire, though, was attentive to her. "Do you think you might like him?" That may have been a test. Just as possibly it was an attempt to get rid of her, and his estimation of So-and-so's talent (no secret that there *was* no talent) also told Katrina how he ranked her on a realistic scale—a dumpy sexpot, varicose veins, uneven gum line, crème de Chantilly inner thighs but otherwise no great shakes. Her oddities happened to suit him, Victor. But there were idiosyncrasies, and then there were real standards. Since his miraculous recovery he had made no offensive matchmaking suggestions. He even seemed to suspect, jealously, that she was looking around, in the glamour world to which he had introduced her. She wouldn't have been surprised if, by insulting Wrangel and trying to make her a party to the insult, Victor had tried to eliminate this celebrity producer as a rival. He was a very cunning man, Victor. This afternoon's sex, for instance, had it been desire or had it been payola? No, no; even Dotey said, "You're his only turn-on." That was the truth. She brought Victor to life again. The *caresse qui fait revivre les morts.* The man's sexual resurrection.

The door of the cockpit was open. Beyond the shoulders of the pilots were the lights of the instrument panel. The copilot occasionally glanced back at the passengers. Then he said, "It's getting a little bumpy. Better fasten those belts." A patch of rough air? It was far worse than that. The plane was knocked, thumped like a speeding speedboat by the waves. Victor, who had been savagely silent, finally took notice. He reached for Katrina's hand. The pilots now closed the door to the cockpit. Underfoot, plastic cups, liquor bottles, doughnuts were sliding leftward.

"You realize how tilted we are, Victor?"

"They must be trying to climb out of this turbulence. In a big plane you wouldn't notice. We've both flown through worse weather."

"I don't believe that."

The overhead light became dimmer and dimmer. Various shades of darkness were what you saw in Katrina's face. On Victor's cheekbones the red color seemed laid on with a brush. "They couldn't be having a power failure—what do you think, Victor?"

"I don't believe that." As was his custom, he sketched out a summary. It included Katrina and took the widest possible overview. They were in a Cessna because he had accepted a lecture invitation, a trip not strictly necessary and which (for himself he took it calmly) might be fatal. For Katrina it was even less than necessary. For her he was sorry. She was here because of him. But then it came home to him that he didn't understand a life so different from his own. Why did anybody want to live such a life as she lived? I know why I did mine. Why does she do hers? It was a wicked question, even put comically, for it had its tinge of comedy. But when he had put the question he felt exposed, without any notice at all, to a kind of painful judgment. Supposedly, his life had had real scale, it produced genuine ideas, and these had caused significant intellectual and artistic innovations. All of that was serious. Katrina? Not serious. Divorcing, and then pursuing a prominent figure—the pursuit of passion, high pleasure? Such old stuff—*not* serious! Nevertheless, they were together now, both leaning far over in the banking plane; same destiny for them both. He was her reason for being here, and she was (indirectly) his. Vanessa, for female reasons, put Katrina in a rage, but her knees (sexual even now) gripped the violin protectively. He had often said, conceded, that the obscurest and most powerful question, deeper than politics, was that of an understanding between man and woman. And he knew very well that Katrina had formed absurd visions of what she would do with him—take him away from Beila, then serve him for the rest of his life, then achieve unbelievable social elevation, preside over a salon, then become known after his death as a legendary woman of wide knowledge and great subtlety. This mixed Katrina, a flutter of images, both commonplace and magical. Before her this man of words *was,* at times, speechless. He doted on her *because! Because* she was just within the line separating grace from clumsiness, *because* of the sensual effect, on him, of her fingers, *because* of the pathos of her knees holding the violin. She held him better than any fiddle. And now will you tell me what *any* of this has to do with the *ideas* of Victor Wulpy! What had made him really angry with Wrangel was that he had said most ideas were trivial—meaning, principally, that Victor's own ideas were trivial. And if Victor could not explain Katrina's sexual drawing power, the Eros that (only just) kept him from disintegrating, Wrangel did have a point, didn't he? Katrina, as a subject for thought, was the least trivial of all. Of all that might be omitted in thinking, the worst was to omit your own being. You had lost, then. You heard the underground music of your ancestor Hercules growing fainter as he abandoned you. All you were left with was lucidity, final superlucidity, which was delayed until you reached the border of death. Any minute now he might discover what the other side of the border was like.

He had heard planes making stress noises before, but nothing like the crackling of metal about him now, as if the rivets were going to pop like old-time collar buttons. Wings after all were very slight. Even in calm blue daylight, when they quivered, you thought: A pair of ironing boards, that's all.

"Victor, we're banking the other way. . . . I've never seen it so bad."

No comment. No denying the obvious. The plane tumbled like a playing card.

"If we go down . . ."

"It'll be my fault. *I* got you into this."

There was a moment of level flight. Victor wondered why his heart rate had not increased. He didn't hold his breath, he was not sweating, when the plane dropped again.

"You don't even mind too much," said Katrina.

"Of course I mind."

"Now listen, Victor. If it's death any minute, if we're going to end in the water . . . I'm going to ask you to tell me something."

"Don't start that, Katrina."

"It's very simple. I just want you to say it. . . ."

"Come off it, Katrina. With so much to think about, at a time like this, you ask me *that?* Love?" Temper made his voice fifelike again. His mouth expanded, the mustache widening also. He was about to speak even more violently.

She cut him off. "Don't be awful with me now, Victor. If we're going to crash, why shouldn't you say it? . . ."

"You grab this opportunity to twist my arm."

"If we don't love each other, what are we doing? How did we get here?"

"We got here because you're a woman and I'm a man, and that's how we got here."

An odd thought he had: Atheists accept extreme unction. The wife urges, and the dying man nods. Why not?

In the next interval they felt the controlled lift of the aircraft. They had found smoother air again and were sailing more calmly. Katrina, still in suspense, began to think about gathering her storm-scattered spirits.

"We may be okay," said Victor.

She felt that she was less okay than she had ever been. My God! what a lot of ground I lost, she was thinking.

The cockpit door slid back, and the copilot said, "All right? That was a bad patch. But we're coming up on South Chicago in a minute." A spatter of words, an incomprehensible crackle, came from the control tower at Midway.

Victor was silent, but he looked good-humored. What a man he was for composure! And he didn't hold ridiculous things against you. He was really very decent that way. *M*A*S*H,* for instance. He couldn't say, "I love you." It would have been *mauvaise foi.* Death staring you in the face was no excuse. She was going back and forth over her words, his words, while the plane made its approach and its landing. She was mulling all of it over even when they whirled off in the helicopter, under the slapping blades. The way girls were indoctrinated: Don't worry, dear, love will solve your problems. Make yourself deserving, and you'll be loved. People are crazy, but they're not *too* crazy. So you won't actually be murdered. You'll be okay. And with this explanation from a dopey mother (and Mother really was stupid), you went into action.

Victor said to her, "You see how these executives do things?"

"What is it, about six o'clock? I'll be two hours late back to Evanston."

"After they drop me, they can run you home. I'll tell them to. Do me a favor and take the fiddle home with you."

"All right, I will." Tomorrow she'd have to bring it to Bein and Fushi.

She didn't like the look of him at Meigs Field. Another time it might have excited her to land here. The blues of the ground lights were so bright, and the revolving reds so vivid and clear against the snow. But Victor was very slow getting out of the machine, which made her sore at heart. A fellow shook hands with him. That was Mr. Kinglake, who handed them into a big car. They came out between the aquarium and the museum and proceeded, all power and luxury like a funeral livery, to Randolph Street, and north on Michigan Boulevard to the 333 Building. Victor, keeping his own counsel all this while, squeezed her fingers before he got out.

"Tomorrow?" he said.

"Sure, tomorrow. And *merde* for luck. Don't let those people throw you."

"Not to worry. I'm on top of this," said Victor.

So he was. He had gotten her back to Chicago, too.

In the cushioned warmth of the limousine, northward bound, Katrina, as she pictured Victor in the swift, rich-men's gilded elevator rushing upward, upward, felt a clawing at her heart and innards—pity for the man, which he didn't feel for himself. Really, he did not. Pressed for time. He had too much to think about. All that unfinished mental business to keep him busy forever and ever. He wouldn't have liked it that she should feel clawed around the heart for his sake.

And then, had it been right to turn on a man of his stature and stick him with a cliché? But one good thing about Victor was that he was very light on your venial sins, especially the feminine ones. Still, in that case, he might have obliged her, might have spoken the words she wanted to hear. He didn't need to worry that she might make use of them later, against him.

The lake came very close to shore along the Outer Drive and made mad charges on the pilings and the beaches, rushing horribly white out of the hundreds of miles of darkness they had just crossed in the Cessna.

At Howard Street the white mausoleums and enormous Celtic crosses faced the water. It was a shame to spoil such fine real estate with graves. She disliked this stretch of the road and said to the driver, "This is a favorite speed trap for the cops." He didn't wish to answer. "Now please take me to the Orrington," she said.

She drove her car home from the garage, and had to park in a rut some distance from the curb because her driveway hadn't been cleared.

The house was dark. Nobody there. Her first fear was that Alfred had come and taken the girls away. She let herself into the warm hallway, pushing the handsome heavy white door against the resistance of a living creature: Sukie, of course, the poor old thing, not too deaf to hear the scratch of Katrina's key.

Lighted, the living room showed that Soolie and Pearl had been cutting composition paper after school. Probably Ysole had ordered them to do it. Their habit was to force you to give them commands. But where had they gone? Katrina looked in the kitchen for a message. Nothing on the bulletin board. Nothing on the dining-room table. She rang Alfred's number. If he was there, he didn't answer. She telephoned Dorothea and after two rings there came Dotey's little recording, which Katrina had never heard with such dislike—Dotey being playful: "When the vibrations of the gong subside, kindly leave your name and message." The gong, to go with the bed, was also Chinese. Katrina said, "Dotey, where the hell are my kids?" Immediately she depressed the button, and when the dial tone resumed, she dialed Lieutenant Krieggstein. No one there. She considered next whether to try her lawyer. He sharply disliked being bothered at home. Just now this was not a consideration. What did matter was that she had nothing to tell him except that she feared her children had been abducted by their father while she was gone. . . . Gone where? Flying with her lover.

Sukie had followed her to the kitchen and pressed against her, needing to be taken out. Absentmindedly tender, Katrina stroked the animal's black neck. The fur was thick, but it was flimsy to the touch. Might as well walk her while I think what to do, Katrina decided, and clipped the leash to Sukie's collar. All the neighbors had been shoveled out; only the Goliger house was still under snow. The dog relieved herself at once. Obviously, no one had thought of her all day. Katrina went to the corner in her slow, hip-rich gait, the hat pushed back from her forehead—so very tired she hardly noticed the cold. Her face was aching with the strains of the day. Had Ysole taken the girls home with her? To the church bingo? That was the least likely conjecture of all.

Turning back from the corner, she saw a car parking in front of her house. Because its lights shone into her eyes, she couldn't identify it. She began trotting in her ostrich-skin boots, pulling the dog by the leash, saying, "Come on, girl. Come on."

The children were being lifted over the snow heaps and set down on the sidewalk. She recognized Krieggstein by his fedora. Also his storm coat, bulky and hampering, and his movements.

"Where did you go? Where have you been? There was no message."

"I took the children to dinner."

"Soolie. Pearl. . . . What kind of day did you have?" said Katrina.

They answered nothing at all, but Krieggstein said, "We had a great outing at Burger King. They don't fry like the other fast-food joints, they grill their meat. Then we stopped at Baskin-Robbins and bought a quart of chocolate marshmallow mousse. Good stuff."

"Did you just walk in and find them?"

"No, I took over from your Negro woman. You called her, didn't you?"

"Of course I did."

"I arranged to come by," said Krieggstein. "Didn't she tell you that?"

"She let me think she was taking off at five o'clock."

"Her idea of a joke," said Krieggstein. "I asked her to tell you that I'd be here."

"Oh, thank you, Sam."

In the hallway he helped her off with her coat. They removed it from her weary body.

Katrina's mind at that moment made an important connection. Why should Victor declare, "I love you"? For her sake, he went on the road. Would he have made such a journey for any other reason? If he was like FDR, whose death Stalin had hastened by forcing him to come to Yalta, to Teheran, why would a woman who claimed to love him impose such hardships on him?

"Whose violin is this?" said Krieggstein. "I never saw a fiddle here before."

He was taking off his storm coat, pulling down his gun-bulging jacket, smoothing his parboiled face, rubbing his frost-red eyes.

She had been right when she had said in the Cessna, "You don't even mind too much." Victor had denied it. But he could do nothing else. Her guess was that he longed to be dying. Dying would illuminate. There were ideas closely associated with dying which only dying could reveal. He probably felt that he had postponed too long; although he loved her, he couldn't postpone much longer.

"Did you call the psychiatrist?" she said.

"I did better than that, Trina. The receptionist said you were going to be charged for the hour anyway, so I went and had a talk with the guy."

"*Me* charged? *Alfred* will be charged. Did he talk to you?"

"Give me some credit. You don't make the grade of police lieutenant by dumb bungling. I gave him an impression of stability. He and I speak the same language. Working on my Ph.D. in criminology, we understood each other. I said you couldn't come because you had a female-type emergency. You had to go to the gynecologist. I came instead, as a friend of the family. *I* know what bad mothers are. My experiences as police officer: cocaine mothers, nymphomaniacs, armed prostitutes, alcoholic mothers. He could take it from me what a stable person you are."

"I'll go to the kitchen. The girls want their dessert."

They had set out the bowls and spoons. She took the scoop to the chocolate marshmallow mousse. They didn't say, "Where have you been, Mother?" She was not called upon for any alibis. Their small faces with identical bangs communicated nothing. They did have curious eyes, science-fiction eyes that dazzled and also threatened from afar. Wrangel might have seen that, too. Emissaries from another planet, grown from seeds that dropped from outer space, little invaders with iridium in their skulls. Victor was right, you know, about the way that *Star Wars* flicks corrupted everybody, implanted mistrust of your own flesh and blood. Well, okay, but now I see how to extricate my elephant.

She returned to Krieggstein to thank him, and to get rid of him. He wanted to stay and bask in her gratitude. "How good it was of you to stand by me," she said. "Ysole gave me a scare, and I thought that Alfred would come and snatch the kids."

"I'd do anything for you, Katrina," said Krieggstein. "Just now you're all wrapped up in Victor—how is he, by the way?—and I don't expect anything for my loyalty. No strings attached. . . ."

Well, Katrina had to admit that Dotey was right on target. Krieggstein was presenting himself as a successor, humble but determined. Maybe he *was* a cop, and not a loony with guns. Give him the benefit of the doubt. Let's assume he was the real thing. He was getting his degree in criminology. He was going to be chief of police, head of the FBI, he might make J. Edgar Hoover himself look insignificant—he was off the wall, nevertheless. Since Alfred had removed all the art objects, the house had felt very bare, but with a man like Krieggstein she'd learn what bareness could really be.

"Right now, the most considerate thing you could do, Sam, would be to slip out of the house and let me be. I'll just lock the door and I'll take a bath. I have to have a bath, then send the kids to bed and take a sleeping pill."

"Sorry," said Krieggstein. "In the present state of your emotions I have no business to say anything of an intimate nature. . . ."

She rose, and handed him his storm coat. "Anything of an intimate nature now, Sam, and I'll break down completely." She put her hands over her ears, saying, "I'll go to pieces under your very eyes."

MOSBY'S MEMOIRS

THE BIRDS CHIRPED AWAY. Fweet, Fweet, Bootchee-Fweet. Doing all the
things naturalists say they do. Expressing abysmal depths of aggression, which
only Man—Stupid Man—heard as innocence. We feel everything is so
innocent—because our wickedness is so fearful. Oh, very fearful!

Mr. Willis Mosby, after his siesta, gazing down-mountain at the town of
Oaxaca where all were snoozing still—mouths, rumps, long black Indian hair,
the antique beauty photographically celebrated by Eisenstein in *Thunder over
Mexico*. Mr. Mosby—Dr. Mosby really; erudite, maybe even profound; thought
much, accomplished much—had made some of the most interesting mistakes a
man could make in the twentieth century. He was in Oaxaca now to write his
memoirs. He had a grant for the purpose, from the Guggenheim Foundation.
And why not?

Bougainvillea poured down the hillside, and the hummingbirds were spinning. Mosby felt ill with all this whirling, these colors, fragrances, ready to topple on him. Liveliness, beauty, seemed very dangerous. Mortal danger. Maybe
he had drunk too much mescal at lunch (beer, also). Behind the green and red
of Nature, dull black seemed to be thickly laid like mirror backing.

Mosby did not feel quite well; his teeth, gripped tight, made the muscles
stand out in his handsome, elderly tanned jaws. He had fine blue eyes, light-
pained, direct, intelligent, disbelieving; hair still thick, parted in the middle; and
strong vertical grooves between the brows, beneath the nostrils, and at the back
of the neck.

The time had come to put some humor into the memoirs. So far it had
been: Fundamentalist family in Missouri—Father the successful builder—
Early schooling—The State University—Rhodes Scholarship—Intellectual

friendships—What I learned from Professor Collingwood—Empire and the mental vigor of Britain—My unorthodox interpretation of John Locke—I work for William Randolph Hearst in Spain—The personality of General Franco—Radical friendships in New York—Wartime service with the OSS—The limited vision of Franklin D. Roosevelt—Comte, Proudhon, and Marx revisited—de Tocqueville once again.

Nothing very funny here. And yet thousands of students and others would tell you, "Mosby had a great sense of humor." Would tell their children, "This Mosby in the OSS," or "Willis Mosby, who was in Toledo with me when the Alcázar fell, made me die laughing." "I shall never forget Mosby's observations on Harold Laski." "On packing the Supreme Court." "On the Russian purge trials." "On Hitler."

So it was certainly high time to do something. He had given it some consideration. He would say, when they sent down his ice from the hotel bar (he was in a cottage below the main building, flowers heaped upon it; envying a little the unencumbered mountains of the Sierra Madre) and when he had chilled his mescal—warm, it tasted rotten—he would write that in 1947, when he was living in Paris, he knew any number of singular people. He knew the Comte de la Mine-Crevée, who sheltered Gary Davis the World Citizen after the World Citizen had burnt his passport publicly. He knew Mr. Julian Huxley at UNESCO. He discussed social theory with Mr. Lévi-Straus but was not invited to dinner—they ate at the Musée de l'Homme. Sartre refused to meet with him; he thought all Americans, Negroes excepted, were secret agents. Mosby for his part suspected all Russians abroad of working for the GPU. Mosby knew French well; extremely fluent in Spanish; quite good in German. But the French cannot identify originality in foreigners. That is the curse of an old civilization. It is a heavier planet. Its best minds must double their horsepower to overcome the gravitational field of tradition. Only a few will ever fly. To fly away from Descartes. To fly away from the political anachronisms of left, center, and right persisting since 1789. Mosby found these French exceedingly banal. These French found him lean and tight. In well-tailored clothes, elegant and dry, his good Western skin, pale eyes, strong nose, handsome mouth, and virile creases. *Un type sec.*

Both sides—Mosby and the French, that is—with highly developed attitudes. Both, he was lately beginning to concede, quite wrong. Possibly equidistant from the truth, but lying in different sectors of error. The French were worse off because their errors were collective. Mine, Mosby believed, were at least peculiar. The French were furious over the collapse in 1940 of *La France Pourrie,* their lack of military will, the extensive collaboration, the massive deportations unopposed (the Danes, even the *Bulgarians* resisted Jewish deportations), and, finally, over the humiliation of liberation by the Allies. Mosby, in the OSS, had information to support such views. Within the State Department, too, he had university colleagues—former students and old acquaintances. He had expected a high postwar appointment, for which, as director of counterespionage in Latin America, he was ideally qualified. But Dean Acheson personally disliked him. Nor did Dulles approve. Mosby, a fanatic about *ideas,* displeased the institutional gentry. He had said that the Foreign Service was staffed by rejects of the power structure. Young gentlemen from good Eastern colleges who couldn't make it as Wall Street lawyers were allowed to interpret the alleged interests of their class in the State Department bureaucracy. In foreign consulates they could be rude to displaced persons and indulge their country-club anti-Semitism, which was dying out even in the country clubs. Besides, Mosby had sympathized with the Burnham position on managerialism, declaring, during the war, that the Nazis were winning because they had made their managerial revolution first. No Allied combination could conquer, with its obsolete industrialism, a nation which had reached a new state of history and tapped the power of the inevitable, etc. And then Mosby, holding forth in Washington, among the elite Scotch drinkers, stated absolutely that however deplorable the concentration camps had been, they showed at least the rationality of German political ideas. The Americans had no such ideas. They didn't know what they were doing. No design existed. The British were not much better. The Hamburg fire-bombing, he argued in his clipped style, in full declarative phrases, betrayed the idiotic emptiness and planlessness of Western leadership. Finally, he said that when Acheson blew his nose there were maggots in his handkerchief.

Among the defeated French, Mosby admitted that he had a galled spirit. (His jokes were not too bad.) And of course he drank a lot. He worked on Marx and Tocqueville, and he drank. He would not cease from mental strife. The Comte de la Mine-Crevée (Mosby's own improvisation on a noble and ancient name) kept him in PX booze and exchanged his money on the black market for him. He described his swindles and was very entertaining.

Mosby now wished to say, in the vein of Sir Harold Nicolson or Santayana or Bertrand Russell, writers for whose memoirs he had the greatest admiration, that Paris in 1947, like half a Noah's ark, was waiting for the second of each kind to arrive. There was one of everything. Something of this sort. Especially among Americans. The city was very bitter, grim; the Seine looked and smelled like medicine. At an American party, a former student of French from Minnesota, now running a shady enterprise, an agency which specialized in bribery, private undercover investigations, and procuring broads for VIPs, said something highly emotional about the City of Man, about the meaning of Europe for Americans, the American failure to preserve human scale. Not omitting to work in Man the Measure. And every other tag he could bring back from Randall's *Making of the Modern Mind* or *Readings in the Intellectual History of*

Europe. "I was tempted," Mosby meant to say (the ice arrived in a glass jar with tongs; the natives no longer wore the dirty white drawers of the past). "Tempted . . ." He rubbed his forehead, which projected like the back of an observation car. "To tell this sententious little drunkard and gyp artist, formerly a pacifist and vegetarian, follower of Gandhi at the University of Minnesota, now driving a very handsome Bentley to the Tour d'Argent to eat duck à l'orange. Tempted to say, 'Yes, but we come here across the Atlantic to relax a bit in the past. To recall what Ezra Pound had once said. That we would make another Venice, just for the hell of it, in the Jersey marshes any time we liked. Toying. To divert ourselves in the time of colossal mastery to come. Reproducing anything, for fun. Baboons trained to row will bring us in gondolas to discussions of astrophysics. Where folks burn garbage now, and fatten pigs and junk their old machines, we will debark to hear a concert.' "

Mosby the thinker, like other busy men, never had time for music. Poetry was not his cup of tea. Members of Congress, cabinet officers, organization men, Pentagon planners, party leaders, presidents had no such interests. They could not be what they were and read Eliot, hear Vivaldi, Cimarosa. But they planned that others might enjoy these things and benefit by their power. Mosby perhaps had more in common with political leaders and joint chiefs and presidents. At least, they were in his thoughts more often than Cimarosa and Eliot. With hate, he pondered their mistakes, their shallowness. Lectured on Locke to show them up. Except by the will of the majority, unambiguously expressed, there was no legitimate power. The only absolute democrat in America (perhaps in the world—although who can know what there is in the world, among so many billions of minds and souls) was Willis Mosby. Notwithstanding his terse, dry, intolerant style of conversation (more precisely, examination), his lank dignity of person, his aristocratic bones. Dark long nostrils hinting at the afflictions that needed the strength you could see in his jaws. And, finally, the light-pained eyes.

A most peculiar, ingenious, hungry, aspiring, and heartbroken animal, who, by calling himself Man, thinks he can escape being what he really is. Not a matter of his definition, in the last analysis, but of his being. Let him say what he likes.

> *Kingdoms are clay: our dungy earth alike*
> *Feeds beast as man; the nobleness of life*
> *Is to do thus.*

Thus being love. Or any other sublime option. (Mosby knew his Shakespeare anyway. *There* was a difference from the president. And of the vice president he said, "I wouldn't trust him to make me a pill. A has-been druggist!")

With sober lips he sipped the mescal, the servant in the coarse orange shirt enriched by metal buttons reminding him that the car was coming at four o'clock to take him to Mitla, to visit the ruins.

"Yo mismo soy una ruina," Mosby joked.

The stout Indian, giving only so much of a smile—no more—withdrew with quiet courtesy. Perhaps I was fishing, Mosby considered. Wanted him to say I was *not* a ruin. But how could he? Seeing that for him I *am* one.

Perhaps Mosby did not have a light touch. Still, he thought he did have an eye for certain kinds of comedy. And he *must* find a way to relieve the rigor of this account of his mental wars. Besides, he could really remember that in Paris at that time people, one after another, revealed themselves in a comic light. He was then seeing things that way. Rue Jacob, rue Bonaparte, rue du Bac, rue de Verneuil, Hôtel de l'Université—filled with funny people.

He began by setting down a name: Lustgarten. Yes, there was the man he wanted. Hymen Lustgarten, a Marxist, or former Marxist, from New Jersey. From Newark, I think. He had been a shoe salesman, and belonged to any number of heretical, fanatical, Bolshevistic groups. He had been a Leninist, a Trotskyist, then a follower of Hugo Oehler, then of Thomas Stamm, and finally of an Italian named Salemme who gave up politics to become a painter, an abstractionist. Lustgarten also gave up politics. He wanted now to be successful in business—rich. Believing that the nights he had spent poring over *Das Kapital* and Lenin's *State and Revolution* would give him an edge in business dealings. We were staying in the same hotel. I couldn't at first make out what he and his wife were doing. Presently I understood. The black market. This was not then reprehensible. Postwar Europe was like that. Refugees, adventurers, GIs. Even the Comte de la M.-C. Europe still shuddering from the blows it had received. Governments new, uncertain, infirm. No reason to respect their authority. American soldiers led the way. Flamboyant business schemes. Machines, whole factories, stolen, treasures shipped home. An American colonel in the lumber business started to saw up the Black Forest and send it to Wisconsin. And, of course, Nazis concealing their concentration-camp loot. Jewels sunk in Austrian lakes. Artworks hidden. Gold extracted from teeth in extermination camps, melted into ingots and mortared like bricks into the walls of houses. Incredibly huge fortunes to be made, and Lustgarten intended to make one of them. Unfortunately, he was incompetent.

You could see at once that there was no harm in him. Despite the bold revolutionary associations, and fierceness of doctrine. Theoretical willingness to slay class enemies. But Lustgarten could not even hold his own with pushy people in a *pissoir*. Strangely meek, stout, swarthy, kindly, grinning with mulberry lips, a froggy, curving mouth which produced wrinkles like gills between the ears and the grin. And perhaps, Mosby thought, he comes to mind in Mexico because of his Toltec, Mixtec, Zapotec look, squat and black-haired, the tip of his nose turned downward and the black nostrils shyly widening when his friendly smile was accepted. And a bit sick with the treachery, the awfulness of life but, respectfully persistent, bound to get his share. Efficiency was his style—action, determination, but a wicked incompetence trembled within. Wrong calling. Wrong choice. A bad mistake. But he was persistent.

His conversation amused me, in the dining room. He was proud of his revolutionary activities, which had consisted mainly of cranking the mimeograph machine. Internal Bulletins. Thousands of pages of recondite examination of fine points of doctrine for the membership. Whether the American working class should give *material* aid to the Loyalist Government of Spain, controlled as that was by Stalinists and other class enemies and traitors. You had to fight Franco, and you had to fight Stalin as well. There was, of course, no material aid to give. But *had* there been any, *should* it have been given? This purely theoretical problem caused splits and expulsions. I always kept myself informed of these curious agonies of sectarianism, Mosby wrote. The single effort made by Spanish Republicans to purchase arms in the United States was thwarted by that friend of liberty Franklin Delano Roosevelt, who allowed one ship, the *Mar Cantábrico,* to be loaded but set the Coast Guard after it to turn it back to port. It was, I believe, that *genius* of diplomacy, Mr. Cordell Hull, who was responsible, but the decision, of course, was referred to FDR whom Huey Long amusingly called Franklin de la *No!* But perhaps the most refined of these internal discussions left of left, the documents for which were turned out on the machine by that Jimmy Higgins, the tubby devoted party-worker Mr. Lustgarten, had to do with the Finnish war. Here the painful point of doctrine to be resolved was whether a Workers' State like the Soviet Union, even if it was a *degenerate* Workers' State, a product of the Thermidorian Reaction following the glorious Proletarian Revolution of 1917, could wage an Imperialistic War. For only the bourgeoisie could be Imperialistic. Technically, Stalinism could not be Imperialism. By definition. What then should a Revolutionary Party say to the Finns? Should they resist Russia or not? The Russians were monsters but they would expropriate the Mannerheim White-Guardist landowners and move, painful though it might be, in the correct historical direction. This, as a sect-watcher, I greatly relished. But it was too foreign a subtlety for many of the sectarians. Who were, after all, Americans. Pragmatists at heart. It was *too* far out for Lustgarten. He decided, after the war, to become (it shouldn't be hard) a rich man. Took his savings and, I believe his wife said, his mother's savings, and went abroad to build a fortune.

Within a year he had lost it all. He was cheated. By a German partner, in particular. But also he was caught smuggling by Belgian authorities.

When Mosby met him (Mosby speaking of himself in the third person as Henry Adams had done in *The Education of Henry Adams*)—when Mosby met

him, Lustgarten was working for the American army, employed by Graves Registration. Something to do with the procurement of crosses. Or with supervision
of the lawns. Official employment gave Lustgarten PX privileges. He was rebuilding his financial foundations by the illegal sale of cigarettes. He dealt also
in gas-ration coupons which the French government, anxious to obtain dollars,
would give you if you exchanged your money at the legal rate. The gas coupons
were sold on the black market. The Lustgartens, husband and wife, persuaded
Mosby to do this once. For them, he cashed his dollars at the bank, not with la
Mine-Crevée. The occasion seemed important. Mosby gathered that Lustgarten
had to drive at once to Munich. He had gone into the dental-supply business
there with a German dentist who now denied that they had ever been partners.

Many consultations between Lustgarten (in his international intriguer's
trench coat, ill-fitting; head, neck, and shoulders sloping backward in a froggy
curve) and his wife, a young woman in an eyelet-lace blouse and black velveteen
skirt, a velveteen ribbon tied on her round, healthy neck. Lustgarten, on the circular floor of the bank, explaining as they stood apart. And sweating blood; being reasonable with Trudy, detail by tortuous detail. It grated away poor
Lustgarten's patience. Hands feebly remonstrating. For she asked female questions or raised objections which gave him agonies of patient rationality. Only
there was nothing rational to begin with. That is, he had had no legal right to go
into business with the German. All such arrangements had to be licensed by the
military government. It was a black-market partnership and when it began to
show a profit, the German threw Lustgarten out. With what they call impunity.
Germany as a whole having discerned the limits of all civilized systems of punishment as compared with the unbounded possibilities of crime. The bank
in Paris, where these explanations between Lustgarten and Trudy were taking
place, had an interior of some sort of red porphyry. Like raw meat. A color
which bourgeois France seemed to have vested with ideas of potency, mettle,
and grandeur. In the Invalides also, Napoleon's sarcophagus was of polished red
stone, a great, swooping, polished cradle containing the little green corpse. (We
have the testimony of M. Rideau, the Bonapartist historian, as to the color.) As
for the living Bonaparte, Mosby felt, with Auguste Comte, that he had been an
anachronism. The Revolution was historically necessary. It was socially justified.
Politically, economically, it was a move toward industrial democracy. But the
Napoleonic drama itself belonged to an archaic category of personal ambitions,
feudal ideas of war. Older than feudalism. Older than Rome. The commander
at the head of armies—nothing rational to recommend it. Society, increasingly
rational in its organization, did not need it. But humankind evidently desired it.
War is a luxurious pleasure. Grant the first premise of hedonism and you must
accept the rest also. Rational foundations of modernity are cunningly accepted
by man as the launching platform of ever wilder irrationalities.

Mosby, writing these reflections in a blue-green color of ink which might have been extracted from the landscape. As his liquor had been extracted from the green spikes of the mescal, the curious sharp, dark-green fleshy limbs of the plant covering the fields.

The dollars, the francs, the gas rations, the bank like the beefsteak mine in which W. C. Fields invested, and shrinking but persistent dark Lustgarten getting into his little car on the sodden Parisian street. There were few cars then in Paris. Plenty of parking space. And the streets were so yellow, gray, wrinkled, dismal. But the French were even then ferociously telling the world that they had the *savoir-vivre,* the *gai savoir.* Especially Americans, haunted by their Protestant ethic, had to hear this. My God—sit down, sip wine, taste cheese, break bread, hear music, know love, stop running, and learn ancient life-wisdom from Europe. At any rate, Lustgarten buckled up his trench coat, pulled down his big hoodlum's fedora. He was bunched up in the seat. Small brown hands holding the steering wheel of the Simca Huit, and the grinning despair with which he waved.

"Bon voyage, Lustgarten."

His Zapotec nose, his teeth like white pomegranate seeds. With a sob of the gears he took off for devastated Germany.

Reconstruction is big business. You demolish a society, you decrease the population, and off you go again. New fortunes. Lustgarten may have felt, *qua* Jew, that he had a right to grow rich in the German boom. That all Jews had natural claims beyond the Rhine. On land enriched by Jewish ashes. And you never could be sure, seated on a sofa, that it was not stuffed or upholstered with Jewish hair. And he would not use German soap. He washed his hands, Trudy told Mosby, with Lifebuoy from the PX.

Trudy, a graduate of Montclair Teachers' College in New Jersey, knew French, studied composition, had hoped to work with someone like Nadia Boulanger, but was obliged to settle for less. From the bank, as Lustgarten drove away in a kind of doomed, latently tearful daring in the rain-drenched street, Trudy invited Mosby to the Salle Pleyel, to hear a Czech pianist performing Schönberg. This man, with muscular baldness, worked very hard upon the keys. The difficulty of his enterprise alone came through—the labor of culture, the trouble it took to preserve art in tragic Europe, the devoted drill. Trudy had a nice face for concerts. Her odor was agreeable. She shone. In the left half of her countenance, one eye kept wandering. Stone-hearted Mosby, making fun of flesh and blood, of these little humanities with their short inventories of bad and good. The poor Czech in his blazer with chased buttons and the muscles of his forehead rising in protest against tabula rasa—the bare skull.

Mosby could abstract himself on such occasions. Shut out the piano. Continue thinking about Comte. Begone, old priests and feudal soldiers! Go, with Theology and Metaphysics! And in the Positive Epoch Enlightened Woman would begin to play her part, vigilant, preventing the managers of the new society from abusing their powers. Over Labor, the Supreme Good.

Embroidering the trees, the birds of Mexico, looking at Mosby, and the hummingbird, so neat in its lust, vibrating tinily, and the lizard on the soil drinking heat with its belly. To bless small creatures is supposed to be real good.

Yes, this Lustgarten was a funny man. Cheated in Germany, licked by the partner, and impatient with his slow progress in Graves Registration, he decided to import a Cadillac. Among the new postwar millionaires of Europe there was a big demand for Cadillacs. The French government, moving slowly, had not yet taken measures against such imports for rapid resale. In 1947, no tax prevented such transactions. Lustgarten got his family in Newark to ship a new Cadillac. Something like four thousand dollars was raised by his brother, his mother, his mother's brother for the purpose. The car was sent. The customer was waiting. A down payment had already been given. A double profit was expected. Only, on the day the car was unloaded at Le Havre new regulations went into effect. The Cadillac could not be sold. Lustgarten was stuck with it. He couldn't even afford to buy gas. The Lustgartens were seen one day moving out of the hotel, into the car. Mrs. Lustgarten went to live with musical friends. Mosby offered Lustgarten the use of his sink for washing and shaving. Weary Lustgarten, defeated, depressed, frightened at last by his own plunging, scraped at his bristles, mornings, with a modest cricket noise, while sighing. All that money—mother's savings, brother's pension. No wonder his eyelids turned blue. And his smile, like a spinster's sachet, the last fragrance ebbed out long ago in the trousseau never used. But the long batrachian lips continued smiling.

Mosby realized that compassion should be felt. But passing in the night the locked, gleaming car, and seeing huddled Lustgarten, sleeping, covered with two coats, on the majestic seat, like Jonah inside Leviathan, Mosby could not say in candor that what he experienced was sympathy. Rather he reflected that this shoe salesman, in America attached to foreign doctrines, who could not relinquish Europe in the New World, was now, in Paris, sleeping in the Cadillac, encased in this gorgeous Fisher Body from Detroit. At home exotic, in Europe a Yankee. His timing was off. He recognized this himself. But believed, in general, that he was too early. A pioneer. For instance, he said, in a voice that creaked with shy assertiveness, the French were only now beginning to be Marxians. He had gone through it all years ago. What did these people know! Ask them about the Shakhty Engineers! About Lenin's Democratic Centralism! About the Moscow Trials! About "Social Fascism"! They were ignorant. The Revolution having been totally betrayed, these Europeans suddenly discovered Marx and Lenin. "Eureka!" he said in a high voice. And it was the cold war, beneath it all.

For should America lose, the French intellectuals were preparing to collaborate with Russia. And should America win they could still be free, defiant radicals under American protection.

"You sound like a patriot," said Mosby.

"Well, in a way I am," said Lustgarten. "But I am getting to be objective. Sometimes I say to myself, 'If you were outside the world, if you, Lustgarten, didn't exist as a man, what would your opinion be of this or that?' "

"Disembodied truth."

"I guess that's what it is."

"And what are you going to do about the Cadillac?" said Mosby.

"I'm sending it to Spain. We can sell it in Barcelona."

"But you have to get it there."

"Through Andorra. It's all arranged. Klonsky is driving it."

Klonsky was a Polish Belgian in the hotel. One of Lustgarten's associates, congenitally dishonest, Mosby thought. Kinky hair, wrinkled eyes like Greek olives, and a cat nose and cat lips. He wore Russian boots.

But no sooner had Klonsky departed for Andorra than Lustgarten received a marvelous offer for the car. A capitalist in Utrecht wanted it at once and would take care of all excise problems. He had all the necessary *tuyaux,* unlimited drag. Lustgarten wired Klonsky in Andorra to stop. He raced down on the night train, recovered the Cadillac, and started driving back at once. There was no time to lose. But after sitting up all night on the *rapide,* Lustgarten was drowsy in the warmth of the Pyrenees and fell asleep at the wheel. He was lucky, he later said, for the car went down a mountainside and might have missed the stone wall that stopped it. He was only a foot or two from death when he was awakened by the crash. The car was destroyed. It was not insured.

Still faintly smiling, Lustgarten, with his sling and cane, came to Mosby's café table on the boulevard Saint-Germain. Sat down. Removed his hat from dazzling black hair. Asked permission to rest his injured foot on a chair. "Is this a private conversation?" he said.

Mosby had been chatting with Alfred Ruskin, an American poet. Ruskin, though some of his front teeth were missing, spoke very clearly and swiftly. A perfectly charming man. Inveterately theoretical. He had been saying, for instance, that France had shot its collaborationist poets. America, which had no poets to spare, put Ezra Pound in Saint Elizabeth's. He then went on to say, barely acknowledging Lustgarten, that America had had no history, was not a historical society. His proof was from Hegel. According to Hegel, history was the history of wars and revolutions. The United States had had only one revolution and very few wars. Therefore it was historically empty. Practically a vacuum.

Ruskin also used Mosby's conveniences at the hotel, being too fastidious for his own latrine in the Algerian backstreets of the Left Bank. And when he emerged from the bathroom he invariably had a topic sentence.

"I have discovered the main defect of Kierkegaard."

Or, "Pascal was terrified by universal emptiness, but Valéry says the difference between empty space and space in a bottle is only quantitative, and there is nothing intrinsically terrifying about quantity. What is your view?"

We do not live in bottles—Mosby's reply.

Lustgarten said, when Ruskin left us, "Who is that fellow? He mooched you for the coffee."

"Ruskin," said Mosby.

"*That* is Ruskin?"

"Yes, why?"

"I hear my wife was going out with Ruskin while I was in the hospital."

"Oh, I wouldn't believe such rumors," said Mosby. "A cup of coffee, an apéritif together, maybe."

"When a man is down on his luck," said Lustgarten, "it's the rare woman who won't give him hell in addition."

"Sorry to hear it," Mosby replied.

And then, as Mosby in Oaxaca recalled, shifting his seat from the sun—for he was already far too red, and his face, bones, eyes, seemed curiously thirsty—Lustgarten had said, "It's been a terrible experience."

"Undoubtedly so, Lustgarten. It must have been frightening."

"What crashed was my last stake. It involved family. Too bad in a way that I wasn't killed. My insurance would at least have covered my kid brother's loss. And my mother and uncle."

Mosby had no wish to see a man in tears. He did not care to sit through these moments of suffering. Such unmastered emotion was abhorrent. Though perhaps the violence of this abomination might have told Mosby something about his own moral constitution. Perhaps Lustgarten did not want his face to be working. Or tried to subdue his agitation, seeing from Mosby's austere, though not unkind, silence that this was not his way. Mosby was by taste a Senecan. At least he admired Spanish masculinity—the *varonil* of Lorca. The *clavel varonil,* the manly red carnation, the clear classic hardness of honorable control.

"You sold the wreck for junk, I assume?"

"Klonsky took care of it. Now look, Mosby. I'm through with that. I was reading, thinking, in the hospital. I came over to make a pile. Like the gold rush. I really don't know what got into me. Trudy and I were just sitting around during the war. I was too old for the draft. And we both wanted action. She in music. Or life. Excitement. You know, dreaming at Montclair Teachers' College of the Big Time. I wanted to make it possible for her. Keep up with the world, or something. But really—in my hospital bed I realized—I was right the first time. I am a socialist. A natural idealist. Reading about Attlee, I felt at home again. It became clear that I am still a political animal."

Mosby wished to say, "No, Lustgarten. You're a dandler of swarthy little babies. You're a piggyback man—a giddyap horsie. You're a sweet old Jewish Daddy." But he said nothing.

"And I also read," said Lustgarten, "about Tito. Maybe the Tito alternative is the real one. Perhaps there is hope for socialism somewhere between the Labour Party and the Yugoslav type of leadership. I feel it my duty," Lustgarten told Mosby, "to investigate. I'm thinking of going to Belgrade."

"As what?"

"As a matter of fact, that's where you could come in," said Lustgarten. "If you would be so kind. You're not *just* a scholar. You wrote a book on Plato, I've been told."

"On the *Laws*."

"And other books. But in addition you know the Movement. Lots of people. More connections than a switchboard. . . ."

The slang of the forties.

"You know people at the *New Leader*?"

"Not my type of paper," said Mosby. "I'm actually a political conservative. Not what you would call a Rotten Liberal but an out-and-out conservative. I shook Franco's hand, you know."

"Did you?"

"This very hand shook the hand of the Caudillo. Would you like to touch it for yourself?"

"Why should I?"

"Go on," said Mosby. "It may mean something. Shake the hand that shook the hand."

Very strangely, then, Lustgarten extended padded, swarthy fingers. He looked partly subtle, partly ill. Grinning, he said, "Now I've made contact with real politics at last. But I'm serious about the *New Leader*. You probably know Bohn. I need credentials for Yugoslavia."

"Have you ever written for the papers?"

"For the *Militant*."

"What did you write?"

Guilty Lustgarten did not lie well. It was heartless of Mosby to amuse himself in this way.

"I have a scrapbook somewhere," said Lustgarten.

But it was not necessary to write to the *New Leader*. Lustgarten, encountered two days later on the boulevard, near the pork butcher, had taken off the sling and scarcely needed the cane. He said, "I'm going to Yugoslavia. I've been invited."

"By whom?"

"Tito. The government. They're asking interested people to come as guests to tour the country and see how they're building socialism. Oh, I know," he quickly said, anticipating standard doctrinal objection, "you don't build socialism in one country, but it's no longer the same situation. And I really believe Tito may redeem Marxism by actually transforming the dictatorship of the proletariat. This brings me back to my first love—the radical movement. I was never meant to be an entrepreneur."

"Probably not."

"I feel some hope," Lustgarten shyly said. "And then also, it's getting to be spring." He was wearing his heavy moose-colored bristling hat, and bore many other signs of interminable winter. A candidate for resurrection. An opportunity for the grace of life to reveal itself. But perhaps, Mosby thought, a man like Lustgarten would never, except with supernatural aid, exist in a suitable form.

"Also," said Lustgarten touchingly, "this will give Trudy time to reconsider."

"Is that the way things are with you two? I'm sorry."

"I wish I could take her with me, but I can't swing that with the Yugoslavs. It's sort of a VIP deal. I guess they want to affect foreign radicals. There'll be seminars in dialectics, and so on. I love it. But it's not Trudy's dish."

Steady-handed, Mosby on his patio took ice with tongs, and poured more mescal flavored with *gusano de maguey*—a worm or slug of delicate flavor. These notes on Lustgarten pleased him. It was essential, at this point in his memoirs, to disclose new depths. The preceding chapters had been heavy. Many unconventional things were said about the state of political theory. The weakness of conservative doctrine, the lack, in America, of conservative alternatives, of resistance to the prevailing liberalism. As one who had personally tried to create a more rigorous environment for slovenly intellectuals, to force them to do their homework, to harden the categories of political thought, he was aware that on the right as on the left the results were barren. Absurdly, the college-bred dunces of America had longed for a true left-wing movement on the European model. They still dreamed of it. No less absurd were the right-wing idiots. You cannot grow a rose in a coal mine. Mosby's own right-wing graduate students had disappointed him. Just a lot of television actors. Bad guys for the Susskind interview programs. They had transformed the master's manner of acid elegance, logical tightness, factual punctiliousness, and merciless laceration in debate into a sort of shallow Noël Coward style. The real, the original Mosby approach brought Mosby hatred, got Mosby fired. Princeton University had offered Mosby a lump sum to retire seven years early. One hundred and forty thousand dollars. Because his mode of discourse was so upsetting to the academic community. Mosby was invited to no television programs. He was like the Guerrilla Mosby of the Civil War. When he galloped in, all were slaughtered.

Most carefully, Mosby had studied the memoirs of Santayana, Malraux, Sartre, Lord Russell, and others. Unfortunately, no one was reliably or consistently great. Men whose lives had been devoted to thought, who had tried mightily to govern the disorder of public life, to put it under some sort of intellectual authority, to get ideas to save mankind or to offer it mental aid in saving itself, would suddenly turn into gruesome idiots. Wanting to kill everyone. For instance, Sartre calling for the Russians to drop A-bombs on American bases in the Pacific because America was now presumably monstrous. And exhorting the blacks to butcher the whites. This moral philosopher! Or Russell, the Pacifist of World War I, urging the West to annihilate Russia after World War II. And sometimes, in his memoirs—perhaps he was gaga—strangely illogical. When, over London, a Zeppelin was shot down, the bodies of Germans were seen to fall, and the brutal men in the street horribly cheered, Russell wept, and had there not been a beautiful woman to console him in bed that night, this heartlessness of mankind would have broken him utterly. What was omitted was the fact that these same Germans who fell from the Zeppelin had come to bomb the city. They were going to blow up the brutes in the street, explode the lovers. This Mosby saw.

It was earnestly to be hoped—this was the mescal attempting to invade his language—that Mosby would avoid the common fate of intellectuals. The Lustgarten digression should help. The correction of pride by laughter.

There were twenty minutes yet before the chauffeur came to take the party to Mitla, to the ruins. Mosby had time to continue. To say that in September the Lustgarten who reappeared looked frightful. He had lost no less than fifty pounds. Sun-blackened, creased, in a filthy stained suit, his eyes infected. He said he had had diarrhea all summer.

"What did they feed their foreign VIPs?"

And Lustgarten shyly bitter—the lean face and inflamed eyes materializing from a spiritual region very different from any heretofore associated with Lustgarten by Mosby—said, "It was just a chain gang. It was hard labor. I didn't understand the deal. I thought we were invited, as I told you. But we turned out to be foreign volunteers-of-construction. A labor brigade. And up in the mountains. Never saw the Dalmatian coast. Hardly even shelter for the night. We slept on the ground and ate shit fried in rancid oil."

"Why didn't you run away?" asked Mosby.

"How? Where?"

"Back to Belgrade. To the American embassy at least?"

"How could I? I was a guest. Came at their expense. They held the return ticket."

"And no money?"

"Are you kidding? Dead broke. In Macedonia. Near Skoplje. Bug-stung, starved, and running to the latrine all night. Laboring on the roads all day, with pus in my eyes, too."

"No first aid?"

"They may have had the first, but they didn't have the second."

Mosby though it best to say nothing of Trudy. She had divorced Lustgarten. Commiseration, of course.

Mosby shaking his head.

Lustgarten with a certain skinny dignity walking away. He himself seemed amused by his encounters with capitalism and socialism.

The end? Not quite. There was a coda: The thing had quite good form.

Lustgarten and Mosby met again. Five years later. Mosby enters an elevator in New York. Express to the forty-seventh floor, the executive dining room of the Rangeley Foundation. There is one other passenger, and it is Lustgarten. Grinning. He is himself again, filled out once more.

"Lustgarten!"

"Willis Mosby!"

"How are you, Lustgarten?"

"I'm great. Things are completely different. I'm happy. Successful. Married. Children."

"In New York?"

"Wouldn't live in the U.S. again. It's godawful. Inhuman. I'm visiting."

Without a blink in its brilliancy, without a hitch in its smooth, regulated power, the elevator containing only the two of us was going up. The same Lustgarten. Strong words, vocal insufficiency, the Zapotec nose, and under it the frog smile, the kindly gills.

"Where are you going now?"

"Up to *Fortune*," said Lustgarten. "I want to sell them a story."

He was on the wrong elevator. This one was not going to *Fortune*. I told him so. Perhaps I had not changed either. A voice which for many years had informed people of their errors said, "You'll have to go down again. The other bank of elevators."

At the forty-seventh floor we emerged together.

"Where are you settled now?"

"In Algiers," said Lustgarten. "We have a Laundromat there."

"We?"

"Klonsky and I. You remember Klonsky?"

They had gone legitimate. They were washing burnooses. He was married to Klonsky's sister. I saw her picture. The image of Klonsky, a cat-faced woman, head ferociously encased in kinky hair, Picasso eyes at different levels, sharp teeth. If fish, dozing in the reefs, had nightmares, they would be of such teeth. The children also were young Klonskys. Lustgarten had the snapshots in his wallet of North African leather. As he beamed, Mosby recognized that pride in his success was Lustgarten's opiate, his artificial paradise.

"I thought," said Lustgarten, "that *Fortune* might like a piece on how we made it in North Africa."

We then shook hands again. Mine the hand that had shaken Franco's hand—his that had slept on the wheel of the Cadillac. The lighted case opened for him. He entered in. It shut.

Thereafter, of course, the Algerians threw out the French, expelled the Jews. And Jewish-Daddy-Lustgarten must have moved on. Passionate fatherhood. He loved those children. For Plato this child-breeding is the lowest level of creativity.

Still, Mosby thought, under the influence of mescal, my parents begot me like a committee of two.

From a feeling of remotion, though he realized that the car for Mitla had arrived, a shining conveyance waited, he noted the following as he gazed at the afternoon mountains:

> *Until he was some years old*
> *People took care of him*
> *Cooled his soup, sang, chirked,*
> *Drew on his long stockings,*
> *Carried him upstairs sleeping.*
> *He recalls at the green lakeside*
> *His father's solemn navel,*
> *Nipples like dog's eyes in the hair*
> *Mother's thigh with wisteria of blue veins.*
>
> *After they retired to death,*
> *He conducted his own business*
> *Not too modestly, not too well.*
> *But here he is, smoking in Mexico*
> *Considering the brown mountains*
> *Whose fat laps are rolling*
> *On the skulls of whole families.*

Two Welsh women were his companions. One was very ancient, lank. The Wellington of lady travelers. Or like C. Aubrey Smith, the actor who used to command Gurkha regiments in movies about India. A great nose, a gaunt jaw, a pleated lip, a considerable mustache. The other was younger. She had a small dewlap, but her cheeks were round and dark eyes witty. A very satisfactory pair. Decent was the word. English traits. Like many Americans, Mosby desired such traits for himself. Yes, he was pleased with the Welsh ladies. Though the guide was unsuitable. Overweening. His fat cheeks a red pottery color. And he drove too fast.

The first stop was at Tule. They got out to inspect the celebrated Tule tree in the churchyard. This monument of vegetation, intricately and densely convoluted, a green cypress, more than two thousand years old, roots in a vanished lake bottom, older than the religion of this little heap of white and gloom, this charming peasant church. In the comfortable dust, a dog slept. Disrespectful. But unconscious. The old lady, quietly dauntless, tied on a scarf and entered the church. Her stiff genuflection had real quality. She must be Christian. Mosby looked into the depths of the Tule tree. A world in itself! It could contain communities. In fact, if he recalled his Gerald Heard, there was supposed to be a primal tree occupied by early ancestors, the human horde housed in such appealing, dappled, commodious, altogether beautiful organisms. The facts seemed not to support this golden myth of an encompassing paradise. Earliest man probably ran about on the ground, horribly violent, killing everything. Still, this dream of gentleness, this aspiration for arboreal peace was no small achievement for the descendants of so many killers. For his religion, this tree would do, thought Mosby. No church for him.

He was sorry to go. *He* could have lived up there. On top, of course. The excrements would drop on you below. But the Welsh ladies were already in the car, and the bossy guide began to toot the horn. Waiting was hot.

The road to Mitla was empty. The heat made the landscape beautifully crooked. The driver knew geology, archaeology. He was quite ugly with his information. The Water Table, the Caverns, the Triassic Period. Inform me no further! Vex not my soul with more detail. I cannot use what I have! And now Mitla appeared. The right fork continued to Tehuantepec. The left brought you to the Town of Souls. Old Mrs. Parsons (Elsie Clews Parsons, as Mosby's mental retrieval system told him) had done ethnography here, studied the Indians in these baked streets of adobe and fruit garbage. In the shade, a dark urinous tang. A long-legged pig struggling on a tether. A sow. From behind, observant Mosby identified its pink small female opening. The dungy earth feeding beast as man.

But here were the fascinating temples, almost intact. This place the Spanish priests had not destroyed. All others they had razed, building churches on the same sites, using the same stones.

A tourist market. Coarse cotton dresses, Indian embroidery, hung under flour-white tarpaulins, the dust settling on the pottery of the region, black saxophones, black trays of glazed clay.

Following the British travelers and the guide, Mosby was going once more through an odd and complex fantasy. It was that he was dead. He had died. He continued, however, to live. His doom was to live life to the end as Mosby. In the fantasy, he considered this his purgatory. And when had death occurred? In a collision years ago. He had thought it a near thing then. The cars were demolished. The actual Mosby was killed. But another Mosby was pulled from the car. A trooper asked, "You okay?"

Yes, he was okay. Walked away from the wreck. But he still had the whole thing to do, step by step, moment by moment. And now he heard a parrot blabbing, and children panhandled him and women made their pitch, and he was getting his shoes covered with dust. He had been working at his memoirs and had provided a diverting recollection of a funny man—Lustgarten. In the manner of Sir Harold Nicolson. Much less polished, admittedly, but in accordance with a certain protocol, the language of diplomacy, of mandarin irony. However, certain facts had been omitted. Mosby had arranged, for instance, that Trudy should be seen with Alfred Ruskin. For when Lustgarten was crossing the Rhine, Mosby was embracing Trudy in bed. Unlike Lord Russell's beautiful friend, she did not comfort Mosby for the disasters he had (by intellectual commitment) to confront. But Mosby had not advised her about leaving Lustgarten. He did not mean to interfere. However, his vision of Lustgarten as a funny man was transmitted to Trudy. She could not be the wife of such a funny man. But he *was,* he *was* a funny man! He was, like Napoleon in the eyes of Comte, an anachronism. Inept, he wished to be a colossus, something of a Napoleon himself, make millions, conquer Europe, retrieve from Hitler's fall a colossal fortune. Poorly imagined, unoriginal, the rerun of old ideas, and so inefficient. Lustgarten didn't have to happen. And so he *was* funny. Trudy too was funny, however. What a large belly she had. Since individuals are sometimes born from a twin impregnation, the organism carrying the undeveloped brother or sister in vestigial form—at times no more than an extra organ, a rudimentary eye buried in the leg, or a kidney or the beginnings of an ear somewhere in the back—Mosby often thought that Trudy had a little sister inside her. And to him she was a clown. This need not mean contempt. No, he liked her. The eye seemed to wander in one hemisphere. She did not know how to use perfume. Her atonal compositions were foolish.

At this time, Mosby had been making fun of people.

"Why?"

"Because he had needed to."

"Why?"

"Because!"

The guide explained that the buildings were raised without mortar. The mathematical calculations of the priests had been perfect. The precision of the cut stone was absolute. After centuries you could not find a chink, you could not insert a razor blade anywhere. These geometrical masses were balanced by their own weight. Here the priests lived. The walls had been dyed. The cochineal or cactus louse provided the dye. Here were the altars. Spectators sat where you are standing. The priests used obsidian knives. The beautiful youths played on flutes. Then the flutes were broken. The bloody knife was wiped on the head of the executioner. Hair must have been clotted. And here, the tombs of the nobles. Stairs leading down. The Zapotecs, late in the day, had practiced this form of sacrifice, under Aztec influence.

How game this Welsh crone was. She was beautiful. Getting in and out of these pits, she required no assistance.

Of course you cannot make yourself an agreeable, desirable person. You can't will yourself into it without regard to the things to be done. Imperative tasks. Imperative comprehensions, monstrous compulsions of duty which deform. Men will grow ugly under such necessities. This one a director of espionage. That one a killer.

Mosby had evoked, to lighten the dense texture of his memoirs, a Lustgarten whose doom was this gaping comedy. A Lustgarten who didn't have to happen. But himself, Mosby, also a separate creation, a finished product, standing under the sun on large blocks of stone, on the stairs descending into this pit, he was complete. He had completed himself in this cogitating, unlaughing, stone, iron, nonsensical form.

Having disposed of all things human, he should have encountered God.

Would this occur?

But having so disposed, what God was there to encounter?

But they had now been led below, into the tomb. There was a heavy grille, the gate. The stones were huge. The vault was close. He was oppressed. He was afraid. It was very damp. On the elaborately zigzag-carved walls were thin, thin pipings of fluorescent light. Flat boxes of ground lime were here to absorb moisture. His heart was paralyzed. His lungs would not draw. Jesus! I cannot catch my breath! To be shut in here! To be dead here! Suppose one were! Not as in accidents which ended, but did not quite end, existence. *Dead*-dead. Stooping, he looked for daylight. Yes, it was there. The light was there. The grace of life still there. Or, if not grace, air. Go while you can.

"I must get out," he told the guide. "Ladies, I find it very hard to breathe."

HIM WITH HIS FOOT
IN HIS MOUTH

DEAR MISS ROSE: I almost began "My Dear Child," because in a sense what I did to you thirty-five years ago makes us the children of each other. I have from time to time remembered that I long ago made a bad joke at your expense and have felt uneasy about it, but it was spelled out to me recently that what I said to you was so wicked, so lousy, gross, insulting, unfeeling, and savage that you could never in a thousand years get over it. I wounded you for life, so I am given to understand, and I am the more greatly to blame because this attack was so gratuitous. We had met in passing only, we scarcely knew each other. Now, the person who charges me with this cruelty is not without prejudice toward me, he is out to get me, obviously. Nevertheless, I have been in a tizzy since reading his accusations. I wasn't exactly in great shape when his letter arrived. Like many elderly men, I have to swallow all sorts of pills. I take Inderal and quinidine for hypertension and cardiac disorders, and I am also, for a variety of psychological reasons, deeply distressed and for the moment without ego defenses.

It may give more substance to my motive in writing to you now if I tell you that for some months I have been visiting an old woman who reads Swedenborg and other occult authors. She tells me (and a man in his sixties can't easily close his mind to such suggestions) that there is a life to come—wait and see—and that in the life to come we will feel the pains that we inflicted on others. We will suffer all that we made them suffer, for after death all experience is reversed. We enter into the souls of those whom we knew in life. They enter also into us and feel and judge us from within. On the outside chance that this old Canadian woman has it right, I must try to take up this matter with you. It's not as though I had tried to murder you, but my offense is palpable all the same.

I will say it all and then revise, send Miss Rose only the suitable parts.

. . . In this life between birth and death, while it is still possible to make amends . . .

I wonder whether you remember me at all, other than as the person who wounded you—a tall man and, in those days, dark on the whole, with a mustache (not worn thick), physically a singular individual, a touch of the camel about him, something amusing in his composition. If you can recall the Shawmut of those days, you should see him now. *Edad con Sus Disgracias* is the title Goya gave to the etching of an old man who struggles to rise from the chamber pot, his pants dropped to his ankles. "Together with most weak hams," as Hamlet wickedly says to Polonius, being merciless about old men. To the disorders aforementioned I must add teeth with cracked roots, periodontia requiring antibiotics that gave me the runs and resulted in a hemorrhoid the size of a walnut, plus creeping arthritis of the hands. Winter is gloomy and wet in British Columbia, and when I awoke one morning in this land of exile from which I face extradition, I discovered that something had gone wrong with the middle finger of the right hand. The hinge had stopped working and the finger was curled like a snail—a painful new affliction. Quite a joke on me. And the extradition is real. I have been served with papers.

So at the very least I can try to reduce the torments of the afterlife by one.

It may appear that I come groveling with hard-luck stories after thirty-five years, but as you will see, such is not the case.

I traced you through Miss Da Sousa at Ribier College, where we were all colleagues in the late forties. She has remained there, in Massachusetts, where so much of the nineteenth century still stands, and she wrote to me when my embarrassing and foolish troubles were printed in the papers. She is a kindly, intelligent woman who *like yourself, should I say that?* never married. Answering with gratitude, I asked what had become of you and was told that you were a retired librarian living in Orlando, Florida.

I never thought that I would envy people who had retired, but that was when retirement was still an option. For me it's not in the cards now. The death of my brother leaves me in a deep legal-financial hole. I won't molest you with the facts of the case, garbled in the newspapers. Enough to say that his felonies and my own faults or vices have wiped me out. On bad legal advice I took refuge in Canada, and the courts will be rough because I tried to escape. I may not be sent to prison, but I will have to work for the rest of my natural life, will die in harness, and damn queer harness, hauling my load to a peculiar peak. One of my father's favorite parables was about a feeble horse flogged cruelly by its driver. A bystander tries to intercede: "The load is too heavy, the hill is steep, it's useless to beat your old horse on the face, why do you do it?" "To be a horse was *his* idea," the driver says.

I have a lifelong weakness for this sort of Jewish humor, which may be alien to you not only because you are Scotch-Irish (so Miss Da Sousa says) but also because you as a (pre-computer) librarian were in another sphere—zone of quiet, within the circumference of the Dewey decimal system. It is possible that you may have disliked the life of a nun or shepherdess which the word "librarian" once suggested. You may resent it for keeping you out of the modern "action"—erotic, narcotic, dramatic, dangerous, salty. Maybe you have loathed circulating other people's lawless raptures, handling wicked books (for the most part fake, take it from me, Miss Rose). Allow me to presume that you are old-fashioned enough not to be furious at having led a useful life. If you aren't an old-fashioned person I haven't hurt you so badly after all. No modern woman would brood for forty years over a stupid wisecrack. She would say, "Get lost!"

Who is it that accuses me of having wounded you? Eddie Walish, that's who. He has become the main planner of college humanities surveys in the State of Missouri, I am given to understand. At such work he is wonderful, a man of genius. But although he now lives in Missouri, he seems to think of nothing but Massachusetts in the old days. He can't forget the evil I did. He was there when I did it (whatever *it* really was), and he writes, "I have to remind you of how you hurt Carla Rose. So characteristic of you, when she was trying to be agreeable, not just to miss her gentle intentions but to give her a shattering kick in the face. I happen to know that you traumatized her for life." (Notice how the liberal American vocabulary is used as a torture device: By "characteristic" he means: "You are not a *good person,* Shawmut.") Now, were you really traumatized, Miss Rose? How does Walish "happen to know"? Did you tell him? Or is it, as I conjecture, nothing but gossip? I wonder if you remember the occasion at all. It would be a mercy if you didn't. And I don't want to thrust unwanted recollections on you, but if I did indeed disfigure you so cruelly, is there any way to avoid remembering?

So let's go back again to Ribier College. Walish and I were great friends then, young instructors, he in literature, I in fine arts—my specialty music history. As if this were news to you; my book on Pergolesi is in all libraries. Impossible that you shouldn't have come across it. Besides, I've done those musicology programs on public television, which were quite popular.

But we are back in the forties. The term began just after Labor Day. My first teaching position. After seven or eight weeks I was still wildly excited. Let me start with the beautiful New England setting. Fresh from Chicago and from Bloomington, Indiana, where I took my degree, I had never seen birches, roadside ferns, deep pinewoods, little white steeples. What could I be but out of place? It made me scream with laughter to be called "Dr. Shawmut." I felt absurd here, a camel on the village green. I am a high-waisted and long-legged man, who is susceptible to paradoxical, ludicrous images of himself. I hadn't yet gotten the real picture of Ribier, either. It wasn't true New England, it was a bohemian college for rich kids from New York who were too nervous for the better schools, unadjusted.

Now then: Eddie Walish and I walking together past the college library. Sweet autumnal warmth against a background of chill from the surrounding woods—it's all there for me. The library is a Greek Revival building and the light in the porch is mossy and sunny—bright-green moss, leafy sunlight, lichen on the columns. I am turned on, manic, flying. My relations with Walish at this stage are easy to describe: very cheerful, not a kink in sight, not a touch of darkness. I am keen to learn from him, because I have never seen a progressive college, never lived in the East, never come in contact with the Eastern Establishment, of which I have heard so much. What is it all about? A girl to whom I was assigned as adviser has asked for another one because I haven't been psychoanalyzed and can't even begin to relate to her. And this very morning I have spent two hours in a committee meeting to determine whether a course in history should be obligatory for fine-arts majors. Tony Lemnitzer, professor of painting, said, "Let the kids read about the kings and the queens—what can it hoit them?" Brooklyn Tony, who had run away from home to be a circus roustabout, became a poster artist and eventually an Abstract Expressionist. "Don't ever feel sorry for Tony," Walish advises me. "The woman he married is a millionairess. She's built him a studio fit for Michelangelo. He's embarrassed to paint, he only whittles there. He carved out two wooden balls inside a birdcage." Walish himself, Early Hip with a Harvard background, suspected at first that my ignorance was a put-on. A limping short man, Walish looked at me—looked upward—with real shrewdness and traces of disbelief about the mouth. From Chicago, a Ph.D. out of Bloomington, Indiana, can I be as backward as I seem? But I am good company, and by and by he tells me (is it a secret?) that although he comes from Gloucester, Mass., he's not a real Yankee. His father, a second-generation American, is a machinist, retired, uneducated. One of the old man's letters reads, "Your poor mother—the doctor says she has a groweth on her virginia which he will have to operate. When she goes to surgery I expect you and your sister to be here to stand by me."

There were two limping men in the community, and their names were similar. The other limper, Edmund Welch, justice of the peace, walked with a cane. Our Ed, who suffered from curvature of the spine, would not carry a stick, much less wear a built-up shoe. He behaved with sporting nonchalance and defied the orthopedists when they warned that his spinal column would collapse like a stack of dominoes. His style was to be free and limber. You had to take him as he came, no concessions offered. I admired him for that.

Now, Miss Rose, you have come out of the library for a breath of air and are leaning, arms crossed, and resting your head against a Greek column. To give himself more height, Walish wears his hair thick. You couldn't cram a hat over it. But I have on a baseball cap. Then, Miss Rose, you say, smiling at me, "Oh, Dr. Shawmut, in that cap you look like an archaeologist." Before I can stop myself, I answer, "And you look like something I just dug up."

Awful!

The pair of us, Walish and I, hurried on. Eddie, whose hips were out of line, made an effort to walk more quickly, and when we were beyond your little library temple I saw that he was grinning at me, his warm face looking up into my face with joy, with accusing admiration. He had witnessed something extraordinary. What this something might be, whether it came under the heading of fun or psychopathology or wickedness, nobody could yet judge, but he was glad. Although he lost no time in clearing himself of guilt, it was exactly his kind of wisecrack. He loved to do the Groucho Marx bit, or give an S. J. Perelman turn to his sentences. As for me, I had become dead sober, as I generally do after making one of my cracks. I am as astonished by them as anybody else. They may be hysterical symptoms, in the clinical sense. I used to consider myself absolutely normal, but I became aware long ago that in certain moods my laughing bordered on hysteria. I myself could hear the abnormal note. Walish knew very well that I was subject to such seizures, and when he sensed that one of my fits was approaching, he egged me on. And after he had had his fun he would say, with a grin like Pan Satyrus, "What a bastard you are, Shawmut. The sadistic stabs you can give!" He took care, you see, not to be incriminated as an accessory.

And my joke wasn't even witty, just vile, no excuse for it, certainly not "inspiration." Why should inspiration be so idiotic? It was simply idiotic and wicked. Walish used to tell me, "You're a Surrealist in spite of yourself." His interpretation was that I had raised myself by painful efforts from immigrant origins to a middle-class level but that I avenged myself for the torments and falsifications of my healthy instincts, deformities imposed on me by this adaptation to respectability, the strain of social climbing. Clever, intricate analysis of this sort was popular in Greenwich Village at that time, and Walish had picked up the habit. His letter of last month was filled with insights of this kind. People seldom give up the mental capital accumulated in their "best" years. At sixty-odd, Eddie is still a youthful Villager and associates with young people, mainly. I have accepted old age.

It isn't easy to write with arthritic fingers. My lawyer, whose fatal advice I followed (he is the youngest brother of my wife, who passed away last year), urged me to go to British Columbia, where, because of the Japanese current, flowers grow in midwinter, and the air is purer. There are indeed primroses out in the snow, but my hands are crippled and I am afraid that I may have to take gold injections if they don't improve. Nevertheless, I build up the fire and sit concentrating in the rocker because I need to make it worth your while to consider these facts with me. If I am to believe Walish, you have trembled from that day onward like a flame on a middle-class altar of undeserved humiliation. One of the insulted and injured.

From my side I have to admit that it was hard for me to acquire decent manners, not because I was naturally rude but because I felt the strain of my position. I came to believe for a time that I couldn't get on in life until I, too, had a false self like everybody else and so I made special efforts to be considerate, deferential, civil. And of course I overdid things and wiped myself twice where people of better breeding only wiped once. But no such program of betterment could hold me for long. I set it up, and then I tore it down, and burned it in a raging bonfire.

Walish, I must tell you, gives me the business in his letter. Why was it, he asks, that when people groped in conversations I supplied the missing phrases and finished their sentences with greedy pedantry? Walish alleges that I was showing off, shuffling out of my vulgar origins, making up to the genteel and qualifying as the kind of Jew acceptable (just barely) to the Christian society of T. S. Eliot's dreams. Walish pictures me as an upwardly mobile pariah seeking bondage as one would seek salvation. In reaction, he says, I had rebellious fits and became wildly insulting. Walish notes all this well, but he did not come out with it during the years when we were close. He saved it all up. At Ribier College we liked each other. We were friends, somehow. But in the end, somehow, he intended to be a mortal enemy. All the while that he was making the gestures of a close and precious friend he was fattening my soul in a coop till it was ready for killing. My success in musicology may have been too much for him.

Eddie told his wife—he told everyone—what I had said to you. It certainly got around the campus. People laughed, but I was depressed. Remorse: you were a pale woman with thin arms, absorbing the colors of moss, lichen, and limestone into your skin. The heavy library doors were open, and within there were green reading lamps and polished heavy tables, and books massed up to the gallery and above. A few of these books were exalted, some were usefully informative, the majority of them would only congest the mind. My Swedenborgian old lady says that angels do not read books. Why should they? Nor, I imagine, can librarians be great readers. They have too many books, most of them burdensome. The crowded shelves give off an inviting, consoling, seductive odor that is also tinctured faintly with something pernicious, with poison and doom. Human beings can lose their lives in libraries. They ought to be warned. And you, an underpriestess of this temple stepping out to look at the sky, and Mr. Lubeck, your chief, a gentle refugee always stumbling over his big senile dog and apologizing to the animal, "Ach, excuse me!" (heavy on the sibilant).

Personal note: Miss Rose never was pretty, not even what the French call une belle laide, *or ugly beauty, a woman whose command of sexual forces makes ugliness itself contribute to her erotic power. A* belle laide *(it* would *be a French idea!) has to be a rolling-mill of lusts. Such force was lacking. No organic basis for it. Fifty years earlier Miss Rose would have been taking Lydia Pinkham's Vegetable Compound. Nevertheless, even if she looked green, a man might have loved her—loved her for her timid warmth, or for the courage she had had to muster to compliment me on my cap. Thirty-five years ago I might have bluffed out this embarrassment with compliments, saying, "Only think, Miss Rose, how many objects of rare beauty have been dug up by archaeologists—the Venus de Milo, Assyrian winged bulls with the faces of great kings. And Michelangelo even buried one of his statues to get the antique look and then exhumed it." But it's too late for rhetorical gallantries. I'd be ashamed. Unpretty, unmarried, the nasty little community laughing at my crack, Miss Rose, poor thing, must have been in despair.*

Eddie Walish, as I told you, would not act the cripple despite his spiral back. Even though he slouched and walked with an outslapping left foot, he carried himself with style. He wore good English tweeds and Lloyd & Haig brogans. He himself would say that there were enough masochistic women around to encourage any fellow to preen and cut a figure. Handicapped men did very well with girls of a certain type. You, Miss Rose, would have done better to save your compliment for him. But his wife was then expecting; I was the bachelor.

Almost daily during the first sunny days of the term we went out walking. I found him mysterious then.

I would think: Who is he, anyway, this (suddenly) close friend of mine? What is this strange figure, the big head low beside me, whose hair grows high and thick? With a different slant, like whipcord stripes, it grows thickly also from his ears. One of the campus ladies has suggested that I urge him to shave his ears, but why should I? She wouldn't like him better with shaven ears, she only dreams that she might. He has a sort of woodwind laugh, closer to oboe than to clarinet, and he releases his laugh from the wide end of his nose as well as from his carved pumpkin mouth. He grins like Alfred E. Neuman from the cover of *Mad* magazine, the successor to Peck's Bad Boy. His eyes, however, are warm and induce me to move closer and closer, but they withhold what I want most. I long for his affection, I distrust him and love him, I woo him with wisecracks. For he is a wise guy in an up-to-date postmodern existentialist sly manner. He also seems kindly. He seems all sorts of things. Fond of Brecht and Weill, he sings "Mackie Messer" and trounces out the tune on the upright piano. This, however, is merely period stuff—German cabaret jazz of the twenties, Berlin's answer to trench warfare and exploded humanism. Catch Eddie allowing himself to be dated like that! Up-to-the-minute Eddie has always been in the avant-garde. An early fan of the Beat poets, he was the first to quote me Allen Ginsberg's wonderful line "America I'm putting my queer shoulder to the wheel."

Eddie made me an appreciative reader of Ginsberg, from whom I learned much about wit. You may find it odd, Miss Rose (I myself do), that I should have kept up with Ginsberg from way back. Allow me, however, to offer a specimen statement from one of his recent books, which is memorable and also charming. Ginsberg writes that Walt Whitman slept with Edward Carpenter, the author of *Love's Coming-of-Age*; Carpenter afterward became the lover of the grandson of one of our obscurer presidents, Chester A. Arthur; Gavin Arthur when he was very old was the lover of a San Francisco homosexual who, when he embraced Ginsberg, completed the entire cycle and brought the Sage of Camden in touch with his only true successor and heir. It's all a little like Dr. Pangloss's account of how he came to be infected with syphilis.

Please forgive this, Miss Rose. It seems to me that we will need the broadest possible human background for this inquiry, which may so much affect your emotions and mine. You ought to know to whom you were speaking on that day when you got up your nerve, smiling and trembling, to pay me a compliment—to give me, us, your blessing. Which I repaid with a bad witticism drawn, characteristically, from the depths of my nature, that hoard of strange formulations. I had almost forgotten the event when Walish's letter reached me in Canada. That letter—a strange *megillah* of which I myself was the Haman. He must have brooded with *ressentiment* for decades on my character, drawing the profile of my inmost soul over and over and over. He compiled a list of all my faults, my sins, and the particulars are so fine, the inventory so extensive, the summary so condensed, that he must have been collecting, filing, formulating, and polishing furiously throughout the warmest, goldenest days of our friendship. To receive such a document—I ask you to imagine, Miss Rose, how it affected me at a time when I was coping with grief and gross wrongs, mourning my wife (and funnily enough, also my swindling brother), and experiencing *Edad con Sus Disgracias*, discovering that I could no longer straighten my middle finger, reckoning up the labor and sorrow of threescore and ten (rapidly approaching). At our age, my dear, nobody can be indignant or surprised when evil is manifested, but I ask myself again and again, why should Eddie Walish work up my faults for thirty-some years to cast them into my teeth? This is what excites my keenest interest, so keen it makes me scream inwardly. The whole comedy of it comes over me in the night with the intensity of labor pains. I lie in the back bedroom of this little box of a Canadian house, which is scarcely insulated, and bear down hard so as not to holler. All the neighbors need is to hear such noises at three in the morning. And there isn't a soul in British Columbia I can discuss this with. My only acquaintance is Mrs. Gracewell, the old woman (she is very old) who studies occult literature, and I can't bother her with so different a branch of experience. Our conversations are entirely theoretical. . . . One helpful remark she did make, and this was: "The lower self is what the Psalmist referred to when he wrote, 'I am a worm and no man.' The higher self, few people are equipped to observe. This is the reason they speak so unkindly of one another."

More than once Walish's document (denunciation) took off from Ginsberg's poetry and prose, and so I finally sent an order to City Lights in San Francisco and have spent many evenings studying books of his I had missed—he publishes so many tiny ones. Ginsberg takes a stand for true tenderness and full candor. Real candor means excremental and genital literalness. What Ginsberg opts for is the warmth of a freely copulating, manly, womanly, comradely, "open road" humanity which doesn't neglect to pray and to meditate. He speaks with horror of our "plastic culture," which he connects somewhat obsessively with the CIA. And in addition to the CIA there are other spydoms, linked with Exxon, Mobil, Standard Oil of California, sinister Occidental Petroleum with its Kremlin connections (that *is* a weird one to contemplate, undeniably). Supercapitalism and its carcinogenic petrochemical technology are linked through James Jesus Angleton, a high official of the Intelligence Community, to T. S. Eliot, one of his pals. Angleton, in his youth the editor of a literary magazine, had the declared aim of revitalizing the culture of the West against the "so-to-speak Stalinists." The ghost of T. S. Eliot, interviewed by Ginsberg on the fantail of a ship somewhere in death's waters, admits to having done little spy jobs for Angleton. Against these, the Children of Darkness, Ginsberg ranges the gurus, the bearded meditators, the poets loyal to Blake and Whitman, the "holy creeps," the lyrical, unsophisticated homosexuals whose little groups the secret police track on their computers, amongst whom they plant provocateurs, and whom they try to corrupt with heroin. This psychopathic vision, so touching because there is, realistically, so much to be afraid of, and also because of the hunger for goodness reflected in it, a screwball defense of beauty, I value more than my accuser, Walish, does. I truly understand. To Ginsberg's sexual Fourth of July fireworks I say, Tee-hee. But then I muse sympathetically over his obsessions, combing my mustache downward with my fingernails, my eyes feeling keen as I try to figure him. I am a more disinterested Ginsberg admirer than Eddie is. Eddie, so to speak, comes to the table with a croupier's rake. He works for the house. He skims from poetry.

One of Walish's long-standing problems was that he looked distinctly Jewy. Certain people were distrustful and took against him with gratuitous hostility, suspecting that he was trying to pass for a full American. They'd sometimes say, as if discovering how much force it gave them to be brazen (force is always welcome), "What was your name before it was Walish?"—a question of the type that Jews often hear. His parents were descended from north of Ireland Protestants, actually, and his mother's family name was Ballard. He signs himself Edward Ballard Walish. He pretended not to mind this. A taste of persecution made him friendly to Jews, or so he said. Uncritically delighted with his friendship, I chose to believe him.

It turns out that after many years of concealed teetering, Walish concluded that I was a fool. It was when the public began to take me seriously that he lost patience with me and his affection turned to rancor. My TV programs on music history were what did it. I can envision this—Walish watching the screen in a soiled woolen dressing gown, cupping one elbow in his hand and sucking a cigarette, assailing me while I go on about Haydn's last days, or Mozart and Salieri, developing themes on the harpsichord: "Superstar! What a horseshit idiot!" "Christ! How phony can you get!" "Huckleberry Fink!"

My own name, Shawmut, had obviously been tampered with. The tampering was done long years before my father landed in America by his brother Pinye, the one who wore a pince-nez and was a music copyist for Sholom Secunda. The family must have been called Shamus or, even more degrading, Untershamus. The *untershamus,* lowest of the low in the Old World synagogue, was a quasi-unemployable incompetent and hanger-on, tangle-bearded and cursed with comic ailments like a large hernia or scrofula, a pauper's pauper. *"Orm,"* as my father would say, *"auf steiffleivent."* Steiffleivent was the stiff linen-and-horsehair fabric that tailors would put into the lining of a jacket to give it shape. There was nothing cheaper. "He was so poor that he dressed in dummy cloth." Cheaper than a shroud. But in America Shawmut turns out to be the name of a chain of banks in Massachusetts. How do you like *them* apples! You may have heard charming, appealing, sentimental things about Yiddish, but Yiddish is a *hard* language, Miss Rose. Yiddish is severe and bears down without mercy. Yes, it is often delicate, lovely, but it can be explosive as well. "A face like a slop jar," "a face like a bucket of swill." (Pig connotations give special force to Yiddish epithets.) If there is a demiurge who inspires me to speak wildly, he may have been attracted to me by this violent unsparing language.

As I tell you this, I believe that you are willingly following, and I feel the greatest affection for you. I am very much alone in Vancouver, but that is my own fault, too. When I arrived, I was invited to a party by local musicians, and I failed to please. They gave me their Canadian test for U.S. visitors: Was I a Reaganite? I couldn't be that, but the key question was whether El Salvador might not be another Vietnam, and I lost half of the company at once by my reply: "Nothing of the kind. The North Vietnamese are seasoned soldiers with a military tradition of many centuries—*really* tough people. Salvadorans are Indian peasants." Why couldn't I have kept my mouth shut? What do I care about Vietnam? Two or three sympathetic guests remained, and these I drove away as follows: A professor from UBC observed that he agreed with Alexander Pope about the ultimate unreality of evil. Seen from the highest point of metaphysics. To a rational mind, nothing bad ever really happens. He was talking high-minded balls. Twaddle! I thought. I said, "Oh? Do you mean that every gas chamber has a silver lining?"

That did it, and now I take my daily walks alone.

It is very beautiful here, with snow mountains and still harbors. Port facilities are said to be limited and freighters have to wait (at a daily fee of $10,000). To see them at anchor is pleasant. They suggest the "Invitation au Voyage," and also "Anywhere, anywhere, Out of the world!" But what a clean and civilized city this is, with its clear northern waters and, beyond, the sense of an unlimited wilderness beginning where the forests bristle, spreading northward for millions of square miles and ending at ice whorls around the Pole.

Provincial academics took offense at my quirks. Too bad.

But lest it appear that I am always dishing it out, let me tell you, Miss Rose, that I have often been on the receiving end, put down by virtuosi, by artists greater than myself, in this line. The late Kippenberg, prince of musicologists, when we were at a conference in the Villa Serbelloni on Lake Como, invited me to his rooms one night to give him a preview of my paper. Well, he didn't actually invite me. I was eager. The suggestion was mine and he didn't have the heart to refuse. He was a huge man dressed in velvet dinner clothes, a copious costume, kelly green in color, upon which his large, pale, clever head seemed to have been deposited by a boom. Although he walked with two sticks, a sort of *diable boiteux,* there was no one faster with a word. He had published *the* great work on Rossini, and Rossini himself had made immortal wisecracks (like the one about Wagner: *"Il a de beaux moments mais de mauvais quarts d'heure"*). You have to imagine also the suite that Kippenberg occupied at the villa, eighteenth-century rooms, taffeta sofas, brocades, cool statuary, hot silk lamps. The servants had already shuttered the windows for the night, so the parlor was very close. Anyway, I was reading to the worldly-wise and learned Kippenberg, all swelled out in green, his long mouth agreeably composed. Funny eyes the man had, too, set at the sides of his head as if for bilateral vision, and eyebrows like caterpillars from the Tree of Knowledge. As I was reading he began to nod. I said, "I'm afraid I'm putting you to sleep, Professor." "No, no—on the contrary, you're keeping me awake," he said. That, and at my expense, was genius, and it was a privilege to have provoked it. He had been sitting, massive, with his two sticks, as if he were on a slope, skiing into profound sleep. But even at the brink, when it was being extinguished, the unique treasure of his consciousness could still dazzle. I would have gone around the world for such a put-down.

Let me, however, return to Walish for a moment. The Walishes lived in a small country house belonging to the college. It was down in the woods, which at that season were dusty. You may remember, in Florida, what New England woods are in a dry autumn—pollen, woodsmoke, decayed and mealy leaves, spiderwebs, perhaps the wing powder of dead moths. Arriving at the Walishes' stone gateposts, if we found bottles left by the milkman we'd grab them by the neck and, yelling, hurl them into the bushes. The milk was ordered for Peg Walish, who was pregnant but hated the stuff and wouldn't drink it anyway. Peg was socially above her husband. Anybody, in those days, could be; Walish had below him only Negroes and Jews, and owing to his Jewy look, was not secure even in this advantage. Bohemianism therefore gave him strength. Mrs. Walish enjoyed her husband's bohemian style, or said she did. My Pergolesi and Haydn made me less objectionable to her than I might otherwise have been. Besides, I was lively company for her husband. Believe me, he needed lively company. He was depressed; his wife was worried. When she looked at me I saw the remedy-light in her eyes.

Like Alice after she had emptied the DRINK ME bottle in Wonderland, Peg was very tall; bony but delicate, she resembled a silent-movie star named Colleen Moore, a round-eyed ingenue with bangs. In her fourth month of pregnancy, Peg was still working at Filene's, and Eddie, unwilling to get up in the morning to drive her to the station, spent long days in bed under the faded patchwork quilts. Pink, when it isn't fresh and lively, can be a desperate color. The pink of Walish's quilts sank my heart when I came looking for him. The cottage was paneled in walnut-stained boards, the rooms were sunless, the kitchen especially gloomy. I found him upstairs sleeping, his jaw undershot and his Jewish lip prominent. The impression he made was both brutal and innocent. In sleep he was bereft of the confidence into which he put so much effort. Not many of us are fully wakeful, but Walish took particular pride in being alert. That he was nobody's fool was his main premise. But in sleep he didn't look clever.

I got him up. He was embarrassed. He was not the complete bohemian after all. His muzziness late in the day distressed him, and he grumbled, putting his thin legs out of bed. We went to the kitchen and began to drink.

Peg insisted that he see a psychiatrist in Providence. He kept this from me awhile, finally admitting that he needed a tune-up, minor internal adjustments. Becoming a father rattled him. His wife eventually gave birth to male twins. The facts are trivial and I don't feel that I'm betraying a trust. Besides, I owe him nothing. His letter upset me badly. What a time he chose to send it! Thirty-five years without a cross word. He allows me to count on his affection. Then he lets me have it. When do you shaft a pal, when do you hand him the poison cup? Not while he's still young enough to recover. Walish waited till the very end—*my* end, of course. *He* is still youthful, he writes me. Evidence of this is that he takes a true interest in young lesbians out in Missouri, he alone knows their inmost hearts and they allow him to make love to them—Walish, the sole male exception. Like the explorer McGovern, who went to Lhasa in disguise, the only Westerner to penetrate the sacred precincts. They trust only youth, they trust him, so it's certain that he can't be old.

This document of his pulls me to pieces entirely. And I agree, objectively, that my character is not an outstanding success. I am inattentive, spiritually lazy, I tune out. I have tried to make this indolence of mine look good, he says. For example, I never would check a waiter's arithmetic; I refused to make out my own tax returns; I was too "unworldly" to manage my own investments, and hired experts (read "crooks"). Realistic Walish wasn't too good to fight over nickels; it was the principle that counted, as honor did with Shakespeare's great soldiers. When credit cards began to be used, Walish, after computing interest and service charges to the fourth decimal, cut up Peg's cards and threw them down the chute. Every year he fought it out with tax examiners, both federal and state. Nobody was going to get the better of Eddie Walish. By such hardness he connected himself with the skinflint rich—the founding Rockefeller, who wouldn't tip more than a dime, or Getty the billionaire, in whose mansion weekend guests were forced to use coin telephones. Walish wasn't being petty, he was being hard, strict, tighter than a frog's ass. It wasn't simply basic capitalism. Insofar as Walish was a Brecht fan, it was also Leninist or Stalinist hardness. And if I was, or appeared to be, misty about money, it was conceivably "a semiunconscious strategy," he said. Did he mean that I was trying to stand out as a Jew who disdained the dirty dollar? Wanting to be taken for one of my betters? In other words, assimilationism? Only I never admitted that anti-Semites of any degree were my betters.

I wasn't trying to be absentmindedly angelic about my finances. In fact, Miss Rose, I was really not with it. My ineptness with money was part of the same hysterical syndrome that caused me to put my foot in my mouth. I suffered from it genuinely, and continue to suffer. The Walish of today has forgotten that when he went to a psychiatrist to be cured of sleeping eighteen hours at a stretch, I told him how well I understood his problem. To console him, I said, "On a good day I can be acute for about half an hour, then I start to fade out and anybody can get the better of me." I was speaking of the dream condition or state of vague turbulence in which, with isolated moments of clarity, most of us exist. And it never occurred to me to adopt a strategy. I told you before that at one time it seemed a practical necessity to have a false self, but that I soon gave up on it. Walish, however, assumes that every clever modern man is his own avant-garde invention. To be avant-garde means to tamper with yourself, to have a personal project requiring a histrionic routine—in short, to put on an act. But what sort of act was it to trust a close relative who turned out to be a felon, or to let my late wife persuade me to hand over my legal problems to her youngest brother? It was the brother-in-law who did me in. Where others were simply unprincipled and crooked, he was in addition bananas. Patience, I am getting around to that.

Walish writes, "I thought it was time you knew what you were really like," and gives me a going-over such as few men ever face. I abused and badmouthed everybody, I couldn't bear that people should express themselves (this particularly irritated him; he mentions it several times) but put words into their mouths, finished their sentences for them, making them forget what they were about to say (supplied the platitudes they were groping for). I was, he says, "a mobile warehouse of middle-class spare parts," meaning that I was stocked with the irrelevant and actually insane information that makes the hateful social machine tick on toward the bottomless pit. And so forth. As for my supernal devotion to music, that was merely a cover. The real Shawmut was a canny promoter whose *Introduction to Music Appreciation* was adopted by a hundred colleges ("which doesn't happen of itself") and netted him a million in royalties. He compares me to Kissinger, a Jew who made himself strong in the Establishment, having no political base or constituency but succeeding through promotional genius, operating as a celebrity. . . . Impossible for Walish to understand the strength of character, even the constitutional, biological force such an achievement would require; to appreciate (his fur-covered ear sunk in his pillow, and his small figure thrice-bent, like a small fire escape, under the wads of pink quilt) what it takes for an educated man to establish a position of strength among semiliterate politicians. No, the comparison is far-fetched. Doing eighteenth-century music on PBS is not very much like taking charge of U.S. foreign policy and coping with drunkards and liars in the Congress or the executive branch.

An honest Jew? That would be Ginsberg the Confessor. Concealing no fact, Ginsberg appeals to Jew-haters by exaggerating everything that they ascribe to Jews in their pathological fantasies. He puts them on, I think, with crazy simple-mindedness, with his actual dreams of finding someone's anus in his sandwich or with his poems about sticking a dildo into himself. This bottom-line materialistic eroticism is most attractive to Americans, proof of sincerity and authenticity. It's on this level that they tell you they are "leveling" with you, although the deformities and obscenities that come out must of course be assigned to somebody else, some "morphodite" faggot or exotic junkie queer. When they tell you they're "leveling," put your money in your shoe at once, that's my advice.

I see something else in Ginsberg, however. True, he's playing a traditional

Jewish role with this comic self-degradation, just as it was played in ancient Rome, and probably earlier. But there's something else, equally traditional. Under all this all-revealing candor (or aggravated self-battery) is purity of heart. As an American Jew he must also affirm and justify democracy. The United States is destined to become one of the great achievements of humanity, a nation made up of many nations (not excluding the queer nation: how can anybody be left out?). The U.S.A. itself is to be the greatest of poems, as Whitman prophesied. And the only authentic living representative of American Transcendentalism is that fat-breasted, bald, bearded homosexual in smeared goggles, innocent in his uncleanness. Purity from foulness, Miss Rose. The man is a Jewish microcosm of this Midas earth whose buried corpses bring forth golden fruits. This is not a Jew who goes to Israel to do battle with Leviticus to justify homosexuality. He is a faithful faggot Buddhist in America, the land of his birth. The petrochemical capitalist enemy (an enemy that needs sexual and religious redemption) is right here at home. Who could help loving such a comedian! Besides, Ginsberg and I were born under the same birth sign, and both of us had crazy mothers and are given to inspired utterances. I, however, refuse to overvalue the erotic life. I do not believe that the path of truth must pass through all the zones of masturbation and buggery. He is consistent; to his credit, he goes all the way, which can't be said of me. Of the two of us, he is the more American. *He* is a member of the American Academy of Arts and Letters—I've never even been proposed as a candidate—and although he has suggested that some of our recent presidents were acidheads, he has never been asked to return his national prizes and medals. The more he libels them (did LBJ use LSD?), the more medals he is likely to get. Therefore I have to admit that he is closer to the American mainstream than I am. I don't even look like an American. (Nor does Ginsberg, for that matter.) Hammond, Indiana, was my birthplace (just before Prohibition my old man had a saloon there), but I might have come straight from Kiev. I certainly haven't got the build of a Hoosier—I am tall but I slouch, my buttocks are set higher than other people's, I have always had the impression that my legs are disproportionately long: it would take an engineer to work out the dynamics. Apart from Negroes and hillbillies, Hammond is mostly foreign, there are lots of Ukrainians and Finns there. These, however, look completely American, whereas I recognize features like my own in Russian church art—the compact faces, small round eyes, arched brows, and bald heads of the icons. And in highly structured situations in which champion American executive traits like prudence and discretion are required, I always lose control and I am, as Arabs say, a hostage to my tongue.

The preceding has been fun—by which I mean that I've avoided rigorous examination, Miss Rose. We need to get closer to the subject. I have to apologize to you, but there is also a mystery here (perhaps of karma, as old Mrs. Gracewell suggests) that cries out for investigation. Why does anybody *say* such things as I said to you? Well, it's as if a man were to go out on a beautiful day, a day so beautiful that it pressed him incomprehensibly to *do* something, to perform a commensurate action—or else he will feel like an invalid in a wheelchair by the seashore, a valetudinarian whose nurse says, "Sit here and watch the ripples."

My late wife was a gentle, slender woman, quite small, built on a narrow medieval principle. She had a way of bringing together her palms under her chin when I upset her, as if she were praying for me, and her pink color would deepen to red. She suffered extremely from my fits and assumed the duty of making amends for me, protecting my reputation and persuading people that I meant no harm. She was a brunette and her complexion was fresh. Whether she owed her color to health or excitability was an open question. Her eyes were slightly extruded, but there was no deformity in this; it was one of her beauties as far as I was concerned. She was Austrian by birth (Graz, not Vienna), a refugee. I never was attracted to women of my own build—two tall persons made an incomprehensible jumble together. Also I preferred to have to search for what I wanted. As a schoolboy, I took no sexual interest in teachers. I fell in love with the smallest girl in the class, and I followed my earliest taste in marrying a slender van der Weyden or Lucas Cranach woman. The rose color was not confined to her face. There was something not exactly contemporary about her complexion, and her conception of gracefulness also went back to a former age. She had a dipping way about her: her figure dipped when she walked, her hands dipped from the wrist while she was cooking, she was a dippy eater, she dipped her head attentively when you had anything serious to tell her and opened her mouth a little to appeal to you to make better sense. In matters of principle, however irrational, she was immovably obstinate. Death has taken Gerda out of circulation, and she has been wrapped up and put away for good. No more straight, flushed body and pink breasts, nor blue extruded eyes.

What I said to you in passing the library would have appalled her. She took it to heart that I should upset people. Let me cite an example. This occurred years later, at another university (a real one), one evening when Gerda put on a dinner for a large group of academics—all three leaves were in our cherrywood Scandinavian table. I didn't even know who the guests were. After the main course, a certain Professor Schulteiss was mentioned. Schulteiss was one of those bragging polymath types who gave everybody a pain in the ass. Whether it was Chinese cookery or particle physics or the connections of Bantu with Swahili (if any) or why Lord Nelson was so fond of William Beckford or the future of computer science, you couldn't interrupt him long enough to complain that he didn't let you get a word in edgewise. He was a big, bearded man with an assault-defying belly and fingers that turned back at the tips, so that if I had been a cartoonist I would have sketched him yodeling, with black whiskers and retroussé fingertips.

One of the guests said to me that Schulteiss was terribly worried that no one would be learned enough to write a proper obituary when he died. "I don't know if I'm qualified," I said, "but I'd be happy to do the job, if that would be of any comfort to him." Mrs. Schulteiss, hidden from me by Gerda's table flowers, was being helped just then to dessert. Whether she had actually heard me didn't matter, for five or six guests immediately repeated what I had said, and I saw her move aside the flowers to look at me.

In the night I tried to convince Gerda that no real harm had been done. Anna Schulteiss was not easy to wound. She and her husband were on the outs continually—why had she come without him? Besides, it was hard to guess what she was thinking and feeling; some of her particles (a reference to Schulteiss's learning in the field of particle physics) were surely out of place. This sort of comment only made matters worse. Gerda did not tell me that, but only lay stiff on her side of the bed. In the field of troubled breathing in the night she was an accomplished artist, and when she sighed heavily there was no sleeping. I yielded to the same stiffness and suffered with her. Adultery, which seldom tempted me, couldn't have caused more guilt. While I drank my morning coffee Gerda telephoned Anna Schulteiss and made a lunch date with her. Later in the week they went to a symphony concert together. Before the month was out we were baby-sitting for the Schulteisses in their dirty little university house, which they had turned into a Stone Age kitchen midden. When that stage of conciliation had been reached, Gerda felt better. My thought, however, was that a man who allowed himself to make such jokes should be brazen enough to follow through, not succumb to conscience as soon as the words were out. He should carry things off like the princely Kippenberg. Anyway, which was the real Shawmut, the man who made insulting jokes or the other one, who had married a wife who couldn't bear that anyone should be wounded by his insults?

You will ask: With a wife willing to struggle mortally to preserve you from the vindictiveness of the injured parties, weren't you perversely tempted to make trouble, just to set the wheels rolling? The answer is no, and the reason is not only that I loved Gerda (my love terribly confirmed by her death), but also that when I said things I said them for art's sake, i.e., without perversity or malice, nor as if malice had an effect like alcohol and I was made drunk on wickedness. I reject that. Yes, there has to be some provocation. But what happens when I am provoked happens because the earth heaves up underfoot, and then from opposite ends of the heavens I get a simultaneous shock to both ears. I am deafened, and I have to open my mouth. Gerda, in her simplicity, tried to neutralize the ill effects of the words that came out and laid plans to win back the friendship of all kinds of unlikely parties whose essential particles were missing and who had no capacity for friendship, no interest in it. To such people she sent azaleas, begonias, cut flowers, she took the wives to lunch. She came home and told me earnestly how many fascinating facts she had learned about them, how their husbands were underpaid, or that they had sick old parents, or madness in the family, or fifteen-year-old kids who burglarized houses or were into heroin.

I never said anything wicked to Gerda, only to provocative people. Yours is the only case I can remember where there was no provocation, Miss Rose—hence this letter of apology, the first I have ever written. You are the cause of my self-examination. I intend to get back to this later. But I am thinking now about Gerda. For her sake I tried to practice self-control, and eventually I began to learn the value of keeping one's mouth shut, and how it can give a man strength to block his inspired words and to let the wickedness (if wickedness is what it is) be absorbed into the system again. Like the "right speech" of Buddhists, I imagine. "Right speech" is sound physiology. And did it make much sense to utter choice words at a time when words have sunk into grossness and decadence? If a La Rochefoucauld were to show up, people would turn away from him in mid-sentence, and yawn. Who needs maxims now?

The Schulteisses were colleagues, and Gerda could work on them, she had access to them, but there were occasions when she couldn't protect me. We were, for instance, at a formal university dinner, and I was sitting beside an old woman who gave millions of dollars to opera companies and orchestras. I was something of a star that evening and wore tails, a white tie, because I had just conducted a performance of Pergolesi's *Stabat Mater,* surely one of the most moving works of the eighteenth century. You would have thought that such music had ennobled me, at least until bedtime. But no, I soon began to spoil for trouble. It was no accident that I was on Mrs. Pergamon's right. She was going to be hit for a big contribution. Somebody had dreamed up a schola cantorum, and I was supposed to push it (tactfully). The real pitch would come later. Frankly, I didn't like the fellows behind the plan. They were a bad lot, and a big grant would have given them more power than was good for anyone. Old Pergamon had left his wife a prodigious fortune. So much money was almost a sacred attribute. And also I had conducted sacred music, so it was sacred against sacred. Mrs. Pergamon talked money to me, she didn't mention the *Stabat Mater* or my interpretation of it. It's true that in the U.S., money leads all other topics by about a thousand to one, but this was one occasion when the music should not have been omitted. The old woman explained to me that the big philanthropists had an understanding, and how the fields were divided up among Carnegie, Rockefeller, Mellon, and Ford. Abroad there were the various Rothschild interests and the Volkswagen Foundation. The Pergamons did music, mainly. She mentioned the sums spent on electronic composers, computer music, which I detest, and I was boiling all the while that I bent a look of perfect courtesy from Kiev on her. I had seen her limousine in the street with campus cops on guard, supplementing the city police. The diamonds on her bosom lay like the Finger Lakes among their hills. I am obliged to say that the money conversation had curious effects on me. It reached very deep places. My late brother, whose whole life was devoted to money, had been my mother's favorite. He remains her favorite still, and she is in her nineties. Presently I heard Mrs. Pergamon say that she planned to write her memoirs. Then I asked—and Nietzsche might have described the question as springing from my inner *Fatum*—"Will you use a typewriter or an adding machine?"

Should I have said *that?* Did I actually *say* it? Too late to ask, the tempest had fallen. She looked at me, quite calm. Now, she was a great lady and I was from Bedlam. Because there was no visible reaction in her diffuse old face, and the blue of her eyes was wonderfully clarified and augmented by her glasses, I was tempted to believe that she didn't hear or else had failed to understand. But that didn't wash. I changed the subject. I understood that despite the almost exclusive interest in music, she had from time to time supported scientific research. The papers reported that she had endowed a project for research in epilepsy. Immediately I tried to steer her into epilepsy. I mentioned the Freud essay in which the theory was developed that an epileptic fit was a dramatization of the death of one's father. This was why it made you stiff. But finding that my struggle to get off the hook was only giving me a bloody lip, I went for the bottom and lay there coldly silent. With all my heart I concentrated on the *Fatum*. *Fatum* signifies that in each human being there is something that is inaccessible to revision. This something can be taught *nothing*. Maybe it is founded in the Will to Power, and the Will to Power is nothing less than Being itself. Moved, or as the young would say, stoned out of my head, by the *Stabat Mater* (the glorious mother who would not stand up for *me*), I had been led to speak from the depths of my *Fatum*. I believe that I misunderstood old Mrs. Pergamon entirely. To speak of money to me was kindness, even magnanimity on her part—a man who knew Pergolesi was as good as rich and might almost be addressed as an equal. And in spite of me she endowed the schola cantorum. You don't penalize an institution because a kook at dinner speaks wildly to you. She was so very old that she had seen every sort of maniac there is. Perhaps I startled myself more than I did her.

She was being gracious, Miss Rose, and I had been trying to go beyond her, to pass her on a dangerous curve. A power contest? What might that mean? Why did I need power? Well, I may have needed it because from a position of power you can say anything. Powerful men give offense with impunity. Take as an instance what Churchill said about an MP named Driberg: "He is the man who brought pederasty into disrepute." And Driberg instead of being outraged was flattered, so that when another member of Parliament claimed the remark for himself and insisted that his was the name Churchill had spoken, Driberg said, "*You?* Why would Winston take notice of an insignificant faggot like *you!*" This quarrel amused London for several weeks. But then Churchill was Churchill, the descendant of Marlborough, his great biographer, and also the savior of his country. To be insulted by him guaranteed your place in history. Churchill was, however, a holdover from a more civilized age. A less civilized case would be that of Stalin. Stalin, receiving a delegation of Polish Communists in the Kremlin, said, "But what has become of that fine, intelligent woman Comrade Z?" The Poles looked at their feet. Because, as Stalin himself had had Comrade Z murdered, there was nothing to say.

This is contempt, not wit. It is Oriental despotism, straight, Miss Rose. Churchill was human, Stalin merely a colossus. As for us, here in America, we are a demotic, hybrid civilization. We have our virtues but are ignorant of style. It's only because American society has no place for style (in the sense of Voltairean or Gibbonesque style, style in the manner of Saint-Simon or Heine) that it is possible for a man like me to make such statements as he makes, harming no one but himself. If people are offended, it's by the "hostile intent" they sense, not by the keenness of the words. They classify me then as a psychological curiosity, a warped personality. It never occurs to them to take a full or biographical view. In the real sense of the term, biography has fallen away from us. We all flutter like new-hatched chicks between the feet of the great idols, the monuments of power.

So what are words? A lawyer, the first one, the one who represented me in the case against my brother's estate (the second one was Gerda's brother)—lawyer number one, whose name was Klaussen, said to me when an important letter had to be drafted, "*You* do it, Shawmut. You're the man with the words."

"And you're the whore with ten cunts!"

But I didn't say this. He was too powerful. I needed him. I was afraid.

But it was inevitable that I should offend him, and presently I did.

I can't tell you *why.* It's a mystery. When I tried to discuss Freud's epilepsy essay with Mrs. Pergamon I wanted to hint that I myself was subject to strange seizures that resembled falling sickness. But it wasn't just brain pathology, lesions, grand mal chemistry. It was a kind of perversely happy *gaieté de coeur.* Elements of vengefulness, or blasphemy? Well, maybe. What about demonic inspiration, what about energumens, what about Dionysus the god? After a distressing luncheon with Klaussen the lawyer at his formidable club, where he bullied me in a dining room filled with bullies, a scene from Daumier (I had been beaten down ten or twelve times, my suggestions all dismissed, and I had paid him a twenty-five-thousand-dollar retainer, but Klaussen hadn't bothered yet to master the elementary facts of the case)—after lunch, I say, when we were walking through the lobby of the club, where federal judges, machine politicians, paving contractors, and chairmen of boards conferred in low voices, I heard a great noise. Workmen had torn down an entire wall. I said to the receptionist, "What's happening?" She answered, "The entire club is being re-wired. We've been having daily power failures from the old electrical system." I said, "While they're at it they might arrange to have people electrocuted in the dining room."

I was notified by Klaussen next day that for one reason or another he could no longer represent me. I was an incompatible client.

The intellect of man declaring its independence from worldly power—okay. But I had gone to Klaussen for protection. I chose him because he was big and arrogant, like the guys my brother's widow had hired. My late brother had swindled me. Did I want to recover my money or not? Was I fighting or doodling? Because in the courts you needed brazenness, it was big arrogance or nothing. And with Klaussen as with Mrs. Pergamon there was not a thing that Gerda could do—she couldn't send either of them flowers or ask them to lunch. Besides, she was already sick. Dying, she was concerned about my future. She remonstrated with me. "Did you have to needle him? He's a proud man."

"I gave in to my weakness. What's with me? Like, am I too good to be a hypocrite?"

"Hypocrisy is a big word. . . . A little lip service."

And again I said what I shouldn't have, especially given the state of her health: "It's a short step from lip service to ass kissing."

"Oh, my poor Herschel, you'll never change!"

She was then dying of leukemia, Miss Rose, and I had to promise her that I would put my case in the hands of her brother Hansl. She believed that for her sake Hansl would be loyal to me. Sure, his feeling for her was genuine. He loved his sister. But as a lawyer he was a disaster, not because he was disloyal but because he was in essence an inept conniver. Also he was plain crackers.

Lawyers, lawyers. Why did I need all these lawyers? you will ask. Because I loved my brother fondly. Because we did business, and business can't be done without lawyers. They have built a position for themselves at the very heart of money—strength at the core of what is strongest. Some of the cheerfulest passages in Walish's letter refer to my horrible litigation. He says, "I always knew you were a fool." Himself, he took the greatest pains never to be one. Not that any man can ever be absolutely certain that his prudence is perfect. But to retain lawyers is clear proof that you're a patsy. There I concede that Walish is right.

My brother, Philip, had offered me a business proposition, and that, too, was my fault. I made the mistake of telling him how much money my music-appreciation book had earned. He was impressed. He said to his wife, "Tracy, guess who's loaded!" Then he asked, "What are you doing with it? How do you protect yourself against taxes and inflation?"

I admired my brother, not because he was a "creative businessman," as they said in the family—that meant little to me—but because . . . Well, there is in fact no "because," there's only the *given,* a lifelong feeling, a mystery. His interest in my finances excited me. For once he spoke seriously to me, and this turned my head. I told him, "I never even tried to make money, and now I'm knee-deep in the stuff." Such a statement was a little disingenuous. It was, if you prefer, untrue. To take such a tone was also a mistake, for it implied that money wasn't so hard to make. Brother Philip had knocked himself out for it, while Brother Harry had earned heaps of it, incidentally, while fiddling. This, I now acknowledge, was a provocative booboo. He made a dark note of it. I even saw the note being made.

As a boy, Philip was very fat. We had to sleep together when we were children and it was like sharing the bed with a dugong. But since then he had firmed up quite a lot. In profile his face was large, with bags under the eyes, a sharp serious face upon a stout body. My late brother was a crafty man. He laid long-distance schemes. Over me he enjoyed the supreme advantage of detachment. My weakness was my fondness for him, contemptible in an adult male. He slightly resembled Spencer Tracy, but was more avid and sharp. He had a Texas tan, his hair was "styled," not barbered, and he wore Mexican rings on every one of his fingers.

Gerda and I were invited to visit his estate near Houston. Here he lived in grandeur, and when he showed me around the place he said to me, "Every morning when I open my eyes I say, 'Philip, you're living right in the middle of a park. You own a whole park.' "

I said, "It certainly is as big as Douglas Park in Chicago."

He cut me short, not wishing to hear about the old West Side, our dreary origins. Roosevelt Road with its chicken coops stacked on the sidewalks, the Talmudist horseradish grinder in the doorway of the fish store, or the daily drama of the Shawmut kitchen on Independence Boulevard. He abominated these reminiscences of mine, for he was thoroughly Americanized. On the other hand, he no more belonged on this Texas estate than I did. Perhaps no one belonged here. Numerous failed entrepreneurs had preceded him in this private park, the oilmen and land developers who had caused this monument to be built. You had the feeling that they must all have died in flophouses or on state funny farms, cursing the grandiose fata morgana that Philip now owned, or seemed to own. The truth was that he didn't like it, either; he was stuck with it. He had bought it for various symbolic reasons, and under pressure from his wife.

He told me in confidence that he had a foolproof investment for me. People were approaching him with hundreds of thousands, asking to be cut into the deal, but he would turn them all down for my sake. For once he was in a position to do something for me. Then he set his conditions. The first condition was that he was never to be questioned, that was how he did business, but I could be sure that he would protect me as a brother should and that there was nothing to fear. In the fragrant plantation gardens, he flew for one instant (no more) into Yiddish. He'd never let me lay my sound head in a sickbed. Then he flew out again. He said that his wife, who was the best woman in the world and the soul of honor, would respect his commitments and carry out his wishes with fanatical fidelity if anything were to happen to him. Her fanatical fidelity to him was fundamental. I didn't understand Tracy, he said. She was difficult to know but she was a true woman, and he wasn't going to have any clauses in our partnership agreement that would bind her formally. She would take offense at that and so would he. And you wouldn't believe, Miss Rose, how all these clichés moved me. I responded as if to an accelerator under his fat, elegantly shod foot, pumping blood, not gasoline, into my mortal engine. I was wild with feeling and said yes to it all. Yes, yes! The plan was to create an auto-wrecking center, the biggest in Texas, which would supply auto parts to the entire South and to Latin America as well. The big German and Italian exporters were notoriously short of replacement parts; I had experienced this myself—I had once had to wait four months for a BMW front-wheel stabilizer unobtainable in the U.S. But it wasn't the business proposition that carried me away, Miss Rose. What affected me was that my brother and I should be really associated for the first time in our lives. As our joint enterprise could never in the world be Pergolesi, it must necessarily be business. I was unreasonably stirred by emotions that had waited a lifetime for expression; they must have worked their way into my heart at a very early age, and now came out in full strength to drag me down.

"What have you got to do with wrecking automobiles?" said Gerda. "And grease, and metal, and all that noise?"

I said, "What has the IRS ever done for music that it should collect half my royalties?"

My wife was an educated woman, Miss Rose, and she began to reread certain books and to tell me about them, especially at bedtime. We went through much of Balzac. *Père Goriot* (what daughters can do to a father), *Cousin Pons* (how an elderly innocent was dragged down by relatives who coveted his art collection) . . . One swindling relative after another, and all of them merciless. She related the destruction of poor César Birotteau, the trusting perfumer. She also read me selections from Marx on the obliteration of the ties of kinship by capitalism. But it never occurred to me that such evils could affect a man who had read about them. I had read about venereal diseases and had never caught any. Besides, it was now too late to take a warning.

On my last trip to Texas I visited the vast, smoking wrecking grounds, and on our way back to the mansion Philip told me that his wife had become a breeder of pit bulldogs. You may have read about these creatures, which have scandalized American animal lovers. They are the most terrifying of all dogs. Part terrier, part English bulldog, smooth-skinned, broad-chested, immensely muscular, they attack all strangers, kids as well as grownups. As they do not bark, no warning is given. Their intent is always to kill, and once they have begun to tear at you they can't be called off. The police, if they arrive in time, have to shoot them. In the pit, the dogs fight and die in silence. Aficionados bet millions of dollars on the fights (which are illegal, but what of it?). Humane societies and civil liberties groups don't quite know how to defend these murderous animals or the legal rights of their owners. There is a Washington lobby trying to exterminate the breed, and meantime enthusiasts go on experimenting, doing everything possible to create the worst of all possible dogs.

Philip took an intense pride in his wife. "Tracy is a wonder, isn't she?" he said. "There's terrific money in these animals. Trust her to pick up a new trend. Guys are pouring in from all over the country to buy pups from her."

He took me to the dog-runs to show the pit bulls off. As we passed, they set their paws on the wire meshes and bared their teeth. I didn't enjoy visiting the pens. My own teeth were on edge. Philip himself wasn't comfortable with the animals, by any means. He owned them, they were assets, but he wasn't the master. Tracy, appearing among the dogs, gave me a silent nod. The Negro employees who brought meat were tolerated. "But Tracy," Philip said, "she's their goddess."

I must have been afraid, because nothing satirical or caustic came to mind. I couldn't even make up funny impressions to take home to Gerda, with whose amusement I was preoccupied in those sad days.

But as a reverberator, which it is my nature to be, I tried to connect the breeding of these terrible dogs with the mood of the country. The pros and cons of the matter add some curious lines to the spiritual profile of the U.S.A. Not long ago, a lady wrote to the *Boston Globe* that it had been a failure of judgment in the Founding Fathers not to consider the welfare of cats and dogs in our democracy, people being what they are. The Founders were too lenient with human viciousness, she said, and the Bill of Rights ought to have made provision for the safety of those innocents who are forced to depend upon us. The first connection to come to mind was that egalitarianism was now being extended to cats and dogs. But it's not simple egalitarianism, it's a merging of different species; the line between man and other animals is becoming blurred. A dog will give you such simple heart's truth as you will never get from a lover or a parent. I seem to recall from the thirties (or did I read this in the memoirs of Lionel Abel?) how scandalized the French Surrealist André Breton was when he visited

Leon Trotsky in exile. While the two men were discussing World Revolution, Trotsky's dog came up to be caressed and Trotsky said, "This is my only true friend." What? A dog the friend of this Marxist theoretician and hero of the October Revolution, the organizer of the Red Army? Symbolic Surrealist acts, like shooting at random into a crowd in the street, Breton could publicly recommend, but to be sentimental about a dog like any bourgeois was shocking. Today's psychiatrists would not be shocked. Asked whom they love best, their patients reply in increasing numbers, "My dog." At this rate, a dog in the White House becomes a real possibility. Not a pit bulldog, certainly, but a nice golden retriever whose veterinarian would become Secretary of State.

I didn't try these reflections out on Gerda. Nor, since it would have been unsettling, did I tell her that Philip, too, was unwell. He had been seeing a doctor. Tracy had him on a physical-fitness program. Mornings he entered the annex to the master bedroom, in which the latest gymnastic equipment had been set up. Wearing overlong silk boxer shorts (I reckon that their theme was the whiskey sour, since they were decorated with orange slices resembling wheels), he hung by his fat arms from the shining apparatus, he jogged on a treadmill with an odometer, and he tugged at the weights. When he worked out on the Exercycle, the orange-slice wheels of his underpants extended the vehicular fantasy, but he was going nowhere. The queer things he found himself doing as a rich man, the false position he was in! His adolescent children were rednecks. The druidic Spanish moss vibrated to the shocks of rock music. The dogs bred for cruelty bided their time. My brother, it appeared, was only the steward of his wife and children.

Still, he wanted me to observe him at his exercises and to impress me with his strength. As he did push-ups, his dipping titties touched the floor before his chin did, but his stern face censored any comical comments I might be inclined to make. I was called upon to witness that under the fat there was a block of primal powers, a strong heart in his torso, big veins in his neck, and bands of muscle across his back. "I can't do any of that," I told him, and indeed I couldn't, Miss Rose. My behind is like a rucksack that has slipped its straps.

I made no comments, because I was a general partner who had invested $600,000 in the wreckage of rusty automobiles. Two miles behind the private park, there were cranes and compactors, and hundreds of acres were filled with metallic pounding and dust. I understood by now that the real power behind this enterprise was Philip's wife, a short round blond of butch self-sufficiency, as dense as a meteorite and, somehow, as spacey. But no, it was I who was spacey, while she was intricately shrewd.

And most of my connubial ideas derived from the gentleness and solicitude of my own Gerda!

During this last visit with Brother Philip, I tried to get him to speak about

Mother. The interest he took in her was minimal. Family sentiment was not his dish. All that he had was for the new family; for the old family, nix. He said he couldn't recall Hammond, Indiana, or Independence Boulevard. "You were the only one I ever cared for," he said. He was aware that there were two departed sisters, but their names didn't come to him. Without half trying, he was far ahead of André Breton, and could never be overtaken. Surrealism wasn't a theory, it was an anticipation of the future.

"What was Chink's real name?" he said.

I laughed. "What, you've forgotten Helen's name? You're bluffing. Next you'll tell me you can't remember her husband, either. What about Kramm? He bought you your first pair of long pants. Or Sabina? She got you the job in the bucket shop in the Loop."

"They fade from my mind," he said. "Why should I keep those dusty memories? If I want details I can get you to fill me in. You've got such a memory hang-up—what use is it?"

As I grow older, Miss Rose, I don't dispute such views or opinions but tend instead to take them under consideration. True, I counted on Philip's memory. I wanted him to remember that we were brothers. I had hoped to invest my money safely and live on an income from wrecked cars—summers in Corsica, handy to London at the beginning of the musical season. Before the Arabs sent London real estate so high, Gerda and I discussed buying a flat in Kensington. But we waited and waited, and there was not a single distribution from the partnership. "We're doing great," said Philip. "By next year I'll be able to remortgage, and then you and I will have more than a million to cut up between us. Until then, you'll have to be satisfied with the tax write-offs."

I started to talk about our sister Chink, thinking my only expedient was to stir such family sentiments as might have survived in this atmosphere where the Spanish moss was electronicized by rock music (and, at the back, the pit bulldogs were drowning silently in the violence of their blood-instincts). I recalled that we had heard very different music on Independence Boulevard. Chink would play "Jimmy Had a Nickel" on the piano, and the rest of us would sing the chorus, or yell it out. Did Philip remember that Kramm, who drove a soda-pop truck (it was from affection, because he doted on Helen, that he called her Chink), could accurately pitch a case filled with bottles into a small opening at the very top of the pyramid? No, the pop truck wasn't exactly stacked like a pyramid, it was a ziggurat.

"What's a ziggurat?"

Assyrian or Babylonian, I explained, terraced, and not coming to a peak.

Philip said, "Sending you to college was a mistake, although I don't know what else you would have been fit for. Nobody else went past high school. . . . Kramm was okay, I guess."

Yes, I said, Chink got Kramm to pay my college tuition. Kramm had been a doughboy, did Philip remember that? Kramm was squat but powerful, full-faced, smooth-skinned like a Samoan, and wore his black hair combed flat to his head in the Valentino or George Raft style. He supported us all, paid the rent. Our dad, during the Depression, was peddling carpets to farm women in north-ern Michigan. *He* couldn't earn the rent. From top to bottom, the big household became Mother's responsibility, and if she had been a little tetched before, melo-dramatic, in her fifties she seemed to become crazed. There was something mili-tary about the way she took charge of the house. Her command post was the kitchen. Kramm had to be fed because he fed us, and he was an enormous eater. She cooked tubs of stuffed cabbage and of chop suey for him. He could swallow soup by the bucket, put down an entire pineapple upside-down cake by himself. Mother shopped, peeled, chopped, boiled, fried, roasted, and baked, served and washed. Kramm ate himself into a stupor and then, in the night, he might come out in his pajama bottoms, walking in his sleep. He went straight to the icebox. I recalled a summer's night when I watched him cutting oranges in half and rip-ping into them with his teeth. In his somnambulism he slurped away about a dozen of them, and then I saw him go back to bed, following his belly to the right door.

"And gambled in a joint called the Diamond Horseshoe, Kedzie and Law-rence," said Philip. He did not, however, intend to be drawn into any reminis-cences. He began, a little, to smile, but he remained basically gloomy, reserved.

Of course. He had entered upon one of his biggest swindles.

He changed the subject. He asked if I didn't admire the way Tracy ran this large estate. She was a magician. She didn't need interior decorators, she had done the whole place by herself. All the linens were Portuguese. The gardens were wonderful. Her roses won prizes. The appliances never gave trouble. She was a cordon bleu cook. It was true the kids were difficult, but that was how kids were nowadays. She was a terrific psychologist, and fundamentally the little bastards were well adjusted. They were just American youngsters. His greatest satisfaction was that everything was so American. It was, too—an all-American production.

For breakfast, if I called the kitchen persistently, I could have freeze-dried cof-fee and a slice of Wonder bread. They were brought to my room by a black per-son who answered no questions. Was there an egg, a piece of toast, a spoonful of jam? Nothing. It wounds me desperately not to be fed. As I sat waiting for the servant to come with the freeze-dried coffee and the absorbent-cotton bread, I prepared and polished remarks that I might make to her, considering how to strike a balance between satire and human appeal. It was a waste of time to try to reach a common human level with the servants. It was obvious that I was a guest of no importance, Miss Rose. No one would listen. I could almost hear the servants being instructed to "come slack of former services" or "Put on what weary negligence you please"—the words of Goneril in *King Lear*. Also the room they had given me had been occupied by one of the little girls, now too big for it. The wallpaper, illustrated with Simple Simon and Goosey Gander, at the time seemed inappropriate (it now seems sharply pertinent).

And I was obliged to listen to my brother's praise of his wife. Again and again he told me how wise and good she was, how clever and tender a mother, what a brilliant hostess, respected by the best people who owned the largest estates. And a shrewd counselor. (I could believe that!) Plus a warm sympathizer when he was anxious, an energetic lover, and she gave him what he had never had before—peace. And I, Miss Rose, with $600,000 sunk here, was constrained to go along, nodding like a dummy. Forced to underwrite all of his sustaining falsehoods, countersigning the bill of goods he sold himself, I muttered the words he needed to finish his sentences. (How Walish would have jeered!) Death breathing over both the odd brothers with the very fragrance of sub-tropical air—magnolia, honeysuckle, orange blossom, or whatever the hell it was, puffing into our faces. Oddest of all was Philip's final confidence (untrue!). For my ears only, he whispered in Yiddish that our sisters had shrieked like *papagayas* (parrots), that for the first time in his life he had quiet here, domestic tranquillity. Not true. There was amplified rock music.

After this lapse, he reversed himself with a vengeance. For a family dinner, we drove in two Jaguars to a Chinese restaurant, a huge showplace constructed in circles, or dining wells, with tables highlighted like symphonic kettledrums. Here Philip made a scene. He ordered far too many hors d'oeuvres, and when the table was jammed with dishes he summoned the manager to complain that he was being hustled, he hadn't asked for double portions of all these fried won-tons, egg rolls, and barbecued ribs. And when the manager refused to take them back Philip went from table to table with egg rolls and ribs, saying, "Here! Free! Be my guest!" Restaurants always did excite him, but this time Tracy called him to order. She said, "Enough, Philip, we're here to eat, not raise everybody's blood pressure." Yet a few minutes later he pretended that he had found a pebble in his salad. I had seen this before. He carried a pebble in his pocket for the purpose. Even the kids were on to him, and one of them said, "He's always doing this routine, Uncle." It gave me a start to have them call me Uncle.

Indulge me for a moment, Miss Rose. I am covering the ground as quickly as I can. There's not a soul to talk to in Vancouver except ancient Mrs. Gracewell, and with her I have to ride in esoteric clouds. Pretending that he had cracked his tooth, Philip had shifted from the Americanism of women's magazines (lovely wife, beautiful home, the highest standard of normalcy) to that of the rednecks—yelling at the Orientals, ordering his children to get his lawyer on the table tele-phone. The philistine idiosyncrasy of the rich American brute. But you can no longer be a philistine without high sophistication, matching the sophistication of what you hate. However, it's no use talking about "false consciousness" or any of that baloney. Philly had put himself into Tracy's hands for full Americanization. To achieve this (obsolete) privilege, he paid the price of his soul. But then he may never have been absolutely certain that there is any such thing as a soul. What he resented about me was that I wouldn't stop hinting that souls existed. What was I, a Reform rabbi or something? Except at a funeral service, Philip wouldn't have put up with Pergolesi for two minutes. And wasn't I—never mind Pergolesi—looking for a hot investment?

When Philip died soon afterward, you may have read in the papers that he was mixed up with chop-shop operators in the Midwest, with thieves who stole expensive cars and tore them apart for export piecemeal to Latin America and the whole of the third world. Chop shops, however, were not Philip's crime. On the credit established by my money, the partnership acquired and resold land, but much of the property lacked clear title, there were liens against it. Defrauded purchasers brought suit. Big trouble followed. Convicted, Philip appealed, and then he jumped bail and escaped to Mexico. There he was kidnapped while jogging in Chapultepec Park. His kidnappers were bounty hunters. The bonding companies he had left holding the bag when he skipped out had offered a bounty for his return. Specialists exist who will abduct people, Miss Rose, if the sums are big enough to make the risks worthwhile. After Philip was brought back to Texas, the Mexican government began extradition proceedings on the ground that he was snatched illegally, which he was, certainly. My poor brother died while doing push-ups in a San Antonio prison yard during the exercise hour. Such was the end of his picturesque struggles.

After we had mourned him, and I took measures to recover my losses from his estate, I discovered that his personal estate was devoid of assets. He had made all his wealth over to his wife and children.

I could not be charged with Philip's felonies, but since he had made me a general partner I was sued by the creditors. I retained Mr. Klaussen, whom I lost by the remark I made in the lobby of his club about electrocuting people in the dining room. The joke was harsh, I admit, although no harsher than what people often think, but nihilism, too, has its no-nos, and professional men can't allow their clients to make such cracks. Klaussen drew the line. Thus I found myself after Gerda's death in the hands of her energetic but unbalanced brother, Hansl. He decided, on sufficient grounds, that I was an incompetent, and as he is a believer in fast action, he took dramatic measures and soon placed me in my present position. Some position! Two brothers in flight, one to the south, the other northward and faced with extradition. No bonding company will set bounty hunters on me. I'm not worth it to them. And even though Hansl had promised that I would be safe in Canada, he didn't bother to check the law himself. One of his student clerks did it for him, and since she was a smart, sexy girl it didn't seem necessary to review her conclusions.

Knowledgeable sympathizers when they ask who represents me are impressed when I tell them. They say, "Hansl Genauer? Real smart fellow. You ought to do all right."

Hansl dresses very sharply, in Hong Kong suits and shirts. A slender man, he carries himself like a concert violinist and has a manner that, as a manner, is fully convincing. For his sister's sake ("She had a wonderful life with you, she said to the last"), he was, or intended to be, my protector. I was a poor old guy, bereaved, incompetent, accidentally prosperous, foolishly trusting, thoroughly swindled. "Your brother fucked you but good. He and his wife."

"She was a party to it?"

"Try giving it a little thought. Has she answered any of your letters?"

"No."

Not a single one, Miss Rose.

"Let me tell you how I reconstruct it, Harry," said Hansl. "Philip wanted to impress his wife. He was scared of her. Out of terror, he wanted to make her rich. She told him she was all the family he needed. To prove that he believed her, he had to sacrifice his old flesh and blood to the new flesh and blood. Like, 'I give you the life of your dreams, all you have to do is cut your brother's throat.' He did his part, he piled up dough, dough, and more dough—I don't suppose he liked you anyway—and he put all the loot in her name. So that when he died, which was *never* going to happen . . ."

Cleverness is Hansl's instrument; he plays it madly, bowing it with elegance as if he were laying out the structure of a sonata, phrase by phrase, for his backward brother-in-law. What did I need with his fiddling? Isn't there anybody, dear God, on *my* side? My brother picked me up by the trustful affections as one would lift up a rabbit by the ears. Hansl, now in charge of the case, analyzed the betrayal for me, down to the finest fibers of its brotherly bonds, and this demonstrated that he was completely on my side—right? He examined the books of the partnership, which I had never bothered to do, pointing out Philip's misdeeds. "You see? He was leasing land from his wife, the nominal owner, for use by the wrecking company, and every year that pig paid himself a rent of ninety-eight thousand dollars. There went your profits. More deals of the same kind all over these balance sheets. While you were planning summers in Corsica."

"I wasn't cut out for business. I see that."

"Your dear brother was a full-time con artist. He might have started a service called Dial-a-Fraud. But then you also provoke people. When Klaussen handed over your files to me, he told me what offensive, wicked things you said. He then decided he couldn't represent you anymore."

"But he didn't return the unused part of the fat retainer I gave him."

"*I'll* be looking out for you now. Gerda's gone, and that leaves me to see that things don't get worse—the one adult of us three. My clients who are the greatest readers are always in the biggest trouble. What they call culture, if you ask me, causes mostly confusion and stunts their development. I wonder if you'll ever understand why you let your brother do you in the way he did."

Philip's bad world borrowed me for purposes of its own. I had, however, approached him in the expectation of benefits, Miss Rose. I wasn't blameless. And if he and his people—accountants, managers, his wife—forced me to feel what they felt, colonized me with their realities, even with their daily moods, saw to it that I should suffer everything they had to suffer, it was after all *my* idea. I tried to make use of *them*.

I never again saw my brother's wife, his children, nor the park they lived in, nor the pit bulldogs.

"That woman is a legal genius," said Hansl.

Hansl said to me, "You'd better transfer what's left, your trust account, to my bank, where I can look after it. I'm on good terms with the officers over there. The guys are efficient, and no monkey business. You'll be taken care of."

I had been taken care of before, Miss Rose. Walish was dead right about "the life of feeling" and the people who lead it. Feelings are dreamlike, and dreaming is usually done in bed. Evidently I was forever looking for a safe place to lie down. Hansl offered to make secure arrangements for me so that I wouldn't have to wear myself out with finance and litigation, which were too stressful and labyrinthine and disruptive; so I accepted his proposal and we met with an officer of his bank. Actually the bank looked like a fine old institution, with Oriental rugs, heavy carved furniture, nineteenth-century paintings, and dozens of square acres of financial atmosphere above us. Hansl and the vice president who was going to take care of me began with small talk about the commodity market, the capers over at City Hall, the prospects for the Chicago Bears, intimacies with a couple of girls in a Rush Street bar. I saw that Hansl badly needed the points he was getting for bringing in my account. He wasn't doing well. Though nobody was supposed to say so, I was soon aware of it. Many forms were put before me, which I signed. Then two final cards were laid down just as my signing momentum seemed irreversible. But I applied the brake. I asked the vice president what these were for and he said, "If you're busy, or out of town, these will give Mr. Genauer the right to trade for you—buy or sell stocks for your account."

I slipped the cards into my pocket, saying that I'd take them home with me and mail them in. We passed to the next item of business.

Hansl made a scene in the street, pulling me away from the great gates of the bank and down a narrow Loop alley. Behind the kitchen of a hamburger joint he let me have it. He said, "You humiliated me."

I said, "We didn't discuss a power of attorney beforehand. You took me by surprise, completely. Why did you spring it on me like that?"

"You're accusing me of trying to pull a fast one? If you weren't Gerda's husband I'd tell you to beat it. You undermined me with a business associate. You weren't like this with your own brother, and I'm closer to you by affection than he was by blood, you nitwit. I wouldn't have traded your securities without notifying you."

He was tearful with rage.

"For God's sake, let's move away from this kitchen ventilator," I said. "I'm disgusted with these fumes."

He shouted, "You're out of it! Out!"

"And you're *in* it."

"Where the hell else is there to be?"

Miss Rose, you have understood us, I am sure of it. We were talking about the vortex. A nicer word for it is the French one, *le tourbillon,* or whirlwind. I was not out of it, it was only my project to *get* out. It's been a case of disorientation, my dear. I know that there's a right state for each of us. And as long as I'm not in the right state, the state of vision I was meant or destined to be in, I must assume responsibility for the unhappiness others suffer because of my disorientation. Until this ends there can only be errors. To put it another way, my dreams of orientation or true vision taunt me by suggesting that the world in which I—together with others—live my life is a fabrication, an amusement park that, however, does not amuse. It resembles, if you are following, my brother's private park, which was supposed to prove by external signs that he made his way into the very center of the real. Philip had prepared the setting, paid for by embezzlement, but he had nothing to set in it. He was forced to flee, pursued by bounty hunters who snatched him in Chapultepec, and so forth. At his weight, at that altitude, in the smog of Mexico City, to jog was suicidal.

Now Hansl explained himself, for when I said to him, "Those securities can't be traded anyway. Don't you see? The plaintiffs have legally taken a list of all my holdings," he was ready for me. "Bonds, mostly," he said. "That's just where I can outfox them. They copied that list two weeks ago, and now it's in their lawyers' file and they won't check it for months to come. They think they've got you, but here's what we do: we sell those old bonds off and buy new ones to replace them. We change all the numbers. All it costs you is brokerage fees. Then, when the time comes, they find out that what they've got sewed up is bonds you no longer own. How are they going to trace the new numbers? And by then I'll have you out of the country."

Here the skin of my head became intolerably tight, which meant even deeper error, greater horror anticipated. And, at the same time, temptation. People had kicked the hell out of me with, as yet, no reprisals. My thought was: It's time *I* made a bold move. We were in the narrow alley between two huge downtown institutions (the hamburger joint was crammed in tight). An armored Brink's truck could hardly have squeezed between the close colossal black walls.

"You mean I substitute new bonds for the old, and I can sell from abroad if I want to?"

Seeing that I was beginning to appreciate the exquisite sweetness of his scheme, Hansl gave a terrific smile and said, "And you will. That's the dough you'll live on."

"That's a dizzy idea," I said.

"Maybe it is, but do you want to spend the rest of your life battling in the courts? Why not leave the country and live abroad quietly on what's left of your assets? Pick a place where the dollar is strong and spend the rest of your life in musical studies or what you goddamn well please. Gerda, God bless her, is gone. What's to keep you?"

"Nobody but my old mother."

"Ninety-four years old? And a vegetable? You can put your textbook copyright in her name and the income will take care of her. So our next step is to check out some international law. There's a sensational chick in my office. She was on the *Yale Law Journal*. They don't come any smarter. She'll find you a country. I'll have her do a report on Canada. What about British Columbia, where old Canadians retire?"

"Whom do I know there? Whom will I talk to? And what if the creditors keep after me?"

"You haven't got so much dough left. There isn't all that much in it for them. They'll forget you."

I told Hansl I'd consider his proposal. I had to go and visit Mother in the nursing home.

The home was decorated with the intention of making everything seem normal. Her room was much like any hospital room, with plastic ferns and fireproof drapes. The chairs, resembling wrought-iron garden furniture, were also synthetic and light. I had trouble with the ferns. I disliked having to touch them to see if they were real. It was a reflection on my relation to reality that I couldn't tell at a glance. But then Mother didn't know me, either, which was a more complex matter than the ferns.

I preferred to come at mealtimes, for she had to be fed. To feed her was infinitely meaningful for me. I took over from the orderly. I had long given up telling her, "This is Harry." Nor did I expect to establish rapport by feeding her.

I used to feel that I had inherited something of her rich crazy nature and love of life, but it now was useless to think such thoughts. The tray was brought and the orderly tied her bib. She willingly swallowed the cream of carrot soup. When I encouraged her, she nodded. Recognition, nil. Two faces from ancient Kiev, similar bumps on the forehead. Dressed in her hospital gown, she wore a thread of lipstick on her mouth. The chapped skin of her cheeks gave her color also. By no means silent, she spoke of her family, but I was not mentioned.

"How many children have you got?" I said.

"Three: two daughters and a son, my son Philip."

All three were dead. Maybe she was already in communication with them. There was little enough of reality remaining in this life; perhaps they had made connections in another. In the census of the living, I wasn't counted.

"My son Philip is a clever businessman."

"Oh, I know."

She stared, but did not ask how I knew. My nod seemed to tell her that I was a fellow with plenty of contacts, and that was enough for her.

"Philip is very rich," she said.

"Is he?"

"A millionaire, and a wonderful son. He always used to give me money. I put it into Postal Savings. Have you got children?"

"No, I haven't."

"My daughters come to see me. But best of all is my son. He pays all my bills."

"Do you have friends in this place?"

"Nobody. And I don't like it. I hurt all the time, especially my hips and legs. I have so much misery that there are days when I think I should jump from the window."

"But you won't do that, will you?"

"Well, I think: What would Philip and the girls do with a mother a cripple?"

I let the spoon slip into the soup and uttered a high laugh. It was so abrupt and piercing that it roused her to examine me.

Our kitchen on Independence Boulevard had once been filled with such cockatoo cries, mostly feminine. In the old days the Shawmut women would sit in the kitchen while giant meals were cooked, tubs of stuffed cabbage, slabs of brisket. Pineapple cakes glazed with brown sugar came out of the oven. There were no low voices there. In that cage of birds you couldn't make yourself heard if you didn't shriek, too, and I had learned as a kid to shriek with the rest, like one of those operatic woman-birds. That was what Mother now heard from me, the sound of one of her daughters. But I had no bouffant hairdo, I was bald and wore a mustache, and there was no eyeliner on my lids. While she stared at me I dried her face with the napkin and continued to feed her.

"Don't jump, Mother, you'll hurt yourself."

But everyone here called her Mother; there was nothing personal about it. She asked me to switch on the TV set so that she could watch *Dallas.*

I said it wasn't time yet, and I entertained her by singing snatches of the *Stabat Mater.* I sang, *"Eja mater, fonsamo-o-ris."* Pergolesi's sacred chamber music (different from his formal masses for the Neapolitan church) was not to her taste. Of course I loved my mother, and she had once loved me. I well remember having my hair washed with a bulky bar of castile soap and how pained she was when I cried from the soap in my eyes. When she dressed me in a pongee suit (short pants of Chinese silk) to send me off to a surprise party, she kissed me ecstatically. These were events that might have occurred just before the time of the Boxer Rebellion or in the back streets of Siena six centuries ago. Bathing, combing, dressing, kissing—these now are remote antiquities. There was, as I grew older, no way to sustain them.

When I was in college (they sent me to study electrical engineering but I broke away into music) I used to enjoy saying, when students joked about their families, that because I was born just before the Sabbath, my mother was too busy in the kitchen to spare the time and my aunt had to give birth to me.

I kissed the old girl—she felt lighter to me than wickerwork. But I wondered what I had done to earn this oblivion, and why fat-assed Philip the evildoer should have been her favorite, the true son. Well, he didn't lie to her about *Dallas,* or try for his own sake to resuscitate her emotions, to appeal to her maternal memory with Christian music (fourteenth-century Latin of J. da Todi). My mother, two-thirds of her erased, and my brother—who knew where his wife had buried him?—had both been true to the present American world and its liveliest material interests. Philip therefore spoke to her understanding. I did not. By waving my long arms, conducting Mozart's *Great Mass* or Handel's *Solomon,* I wafted myself away into the sublime. So for many years I had not made sense, had talked strangely to my mother. What had she to remember me by? Half a century ago I had refused to enter into *her* kitchen performance. She had belonged to the universal regiment of Stanislavski mothers. During the twenties and thirties those women were going strong in thousands of kitchens across the civilized world from Salonika to San Diego. They had warned their daughters that the men they married would be rapists to whom they must submit in duty. And when I told her that I was going to marry Gerda, Mother opened her purse and gave me three dollars, saying, "If you need it so bad, go to a whorehouse." Nothing but histrionics, of course.

"Realizing how we suffer," as Ginsberg wrote in "Kaddish," I was wickedly tormented. I had come to make a decision about Ma, and it was possible that I was fiddling with the deck, stacking the cards, telling myself, Miss Rose, "It was always me that took care of this freaked-in-the-brain, afflicted, calamitous, shrill old mother, not Philip. Philip was too busy building himself up into an imperial

American." Yes, that was how I put it, Miss Rose, and I went even further. The consummation of Philip's upbuilding was to torpedo me. He got me under the waterline, a direct hit, and my fortunes exploded, a sacrifice to Tracy and his children. And now I'm supposed to be towed away for salvage.

I'll tell you the truth, Miss Rose, I was maddened by injustice. I think you'd have to agree not only that I'd been had but that I was singularly foolish, a burlesque figure. I could have modeled Simple Simon for the nursery-rhyme wallpaper of the little girl's room in Texas.

As I was brutally offensive to you without provocation, these disclosures, the record of my present state, may gratify you. Almost any elderly person, chosen at random, can provide such gratification to those he has offended. One has only to see the list of true facts, the painful inventory. Let me add, however, that while I, too, have reason to feel vengeful, I haven't experienced a Dionysian intoxication of vengefulness. In fact I have had feelings of increased calm and of enhanced strength—my emotional development has been steady, not fitful.

The Texas partnership, what was left of it, was being administered by my brother's lawyer, who answered all my inquiries with computer printouts. There were capital gains, only on paper, but I was obliged to pay taxes on them, too. The $300,000 remaining would be used up in litigation, if I stayed put, and so I decided to follow Hansl's plan even if it led to the *Götterdämmerung* of my remaining assets. All the better for your innocence and peace of mind if you don't understand these explanations. Time to hit back, said Hansl. His crafty looks were a study. That a man who was able to look so crafty shouldn't *really* be a genius of intrigue was the most unlikely thing in the world. His smiling wrinkles of deep cunning gave me confidence in Hansl. The bonds that the plaintiffs (creditors) had recorded were secretly traded for new ones. My tracks were covered, and I took off for Canada, a foreign country in which my own language, or something approaching it, is spoken. There I was to conclude my life in peace, and at an advantageous rate of exchange. I have developed a certain sympathy with Canada. It's no easy thing to share a border with the U.S.A. Canada's chief entertainment—it has no choice—is to watch (from a gorgeous setting) what happens in our country. The disaster is that there is no other show. Night after night they sit in darkness and watch us on the lighted screen.

"Now that you've made your arrangements, I can tell you," said Hansl, "how proud I am that you're hitting back. To go on taking punishment from those pricks would be a disgrace."

Busy Hansl really was crackers, and even before I took off for Vancouver I began to see that. I told myself that his private quirks didn't extend to his professional life. But before I fled, he came up with half a dozen unsettling ideas of what I had to do for him. He was a little bitter because, he said, I hadn't let him make use of my cultural prestige. I was puzzled and asked for an example. He said that for one thing I had never offered to put him up for membership in the University Club. I had had him to lunch there and it turned out that he was deeply impressed by the Ivy League class, the dignity of the bar, the leather seats, and the big windows of the dining room, decorated with the seals of the great universities in stained glass. He had graduated from De Paul, in Chicago. He had expected me to ask whether he'd like to join, but I had been too selfish or too snobbish to do that. Since he was now saving me, the least I could do was to use my influence with the membership committee. I saw his point and nominated him willingly, even with relish.

He next asked me to help him with one of his ladies. "They're Kenwood people, an old mail-order-house fortune. The family is musical and artistic. Babette is an attractive widow. The first guy had the Big C, and to tell the truth I'm a little nervous of getting in behind him, but I can fight that. I don't think I'll catch it, too. Now, Babette is impressed by you, she's heard you conduct and read some of your music criticism, watched you on Channel Eleven. Educated in Switzerland, knows languages, and this is a case where I can use your cultural clout. What I suggest is that you take us to Les Nomades—private dining without crockery noise. I gave her the best Italian food in town at the Roman Rooftop, but they not only bang the dishes there, they poisoned her with the sodium glutamate on the veal. So feed us at the Nomades. You can deduct the amount of the tab from my next bill. I always believed that the class you impressed people with you picked up from my sister. After all, you were a family of Russian peddlers and your brother was a lousy felon. My sister not only loved you, she taught you some style. Someday it'll be recognized that if that goddamn Roosevelt hadn't shut the doors on Jewish refugees from Germany, this country wouldn't be in such trouble today. We could have had ten Kissingers, and nobody will ever know how much scientific talent went up in smoke at the camps."

Well, at Les Nomades I did it again, Miss Rose. On the eve of my flight I was understandably in a state. Considered as a receptacle, I was tilted to the pouring point. The young widow he had designs on was attractive in ways that you had to come to terms with. It was fascinating to me that anybody with a Hapsburg lip could speak so rapidly, and I would have said that she was a little uncomfortably tall. Gerda, on whom my taste was formed, was a short, delicious woman. However, there was no reason to make comparisons.

When there are musical questions I always try earnestly to answer them. People have told me that I am comically woodenheaded in this respect, a straight man. Babette had studied music, her people were patrons of the Lyric Opera, but after she had asked for my opinion on the production of Monteverdi's *Coro-*

nation of Poppaea, she took over, answering all her own questions. Maybe her recent loss had made her nervously talkative. I am always glad to let somebody else carry the conversation, but this Babette, in spite of her big underlip, was too much for me. A relentless talker, she repeated for half an hour what she had heard from influential relatives about the politics surrounding cable-TV franchises in Chicago. She followed this up with a long conversation on films. I seldom go to the movies. My wife had no taste for them. Hansl, too, was lost in all this discussion about directors, actors, new developments in the treatment of the relations between the sexes, the progress of social and political ideas in the evolution of the medium. I had nothing at all to say. I thought about death, and also about the best topics for reflection appropriate to my age, the on the whole agreeable openness of things toward the end of the line, the outskirts of the City of Life. I didn't too much mind Babette's chatter, I admired her taste in clothing, the curved white and plum stripes of her enchanting blouse from Bergdorf's. She was well set up. Conceivably her shoulders were too heavy, proportional to the Hapsburg lip. It wouldn't matter to Hansl; he was thinking about Brains wedded to Money.

I hoped I wouldn't have a stroke in Canada. There would be no one to look after me, neither a discreet, gentle Gerda nor a gabby Babette.

I wasn't aware of the approach of one of my seizures, but when we were at the half-open door of the checkroom and Hansl was telling the attendant that the lady's coat was a three-quarter-length sable wrap, Babette said, "I realize now that I monopolized the conversation, I talked and talked all evening. I'm so sorry. . . ."

"That's all right," I told her. "You didn't say a thing."

You, Miss Rose, are in the best position to judge the effects of such a remark.

Hansl next day said to me, "You just can't be trusted, Harry, you're a born betrayer. I was feeling sorry for you, having to sell your car and furniture and books, and about your brother who shafted you, and your old mother, and my poor sister passing, but you have no gratitude or consideration in you. You insult everybody."

"I didn't realize that I was going to hurt the lady's feelings."

"I could have married the woman. I had it wrapped up. But I was an idiot. I had to bring *you* into it. And now, let me tell you, you've made one more enemy."

"Who, Babette?"

Hansl did not choose to answer. He preferred to lay a heavy, ambiguous silence on me. His eyes, narrowing and dilating with his discovery of my wicked habit, sent daft waves toward me. The message of those waves was that the foundations of his goodwill had been wiped out. In all the world, I had had only Hansl to turn to. Everybody else was estranged. And now I couldn't count on him, either. It was not a happy development for me, Miss Rose. I can't say that it didn't bother me, although I could no longer believe in my brother-in-law's dependability. By the standards of stability at the strong core of American business society, Hansl himself was a freak. Quite apart from his disjunctive habits of mind, he was disqualified by the violinist's figure he cut, the noble hands and the manicured filbert fingernails, his eyes, which were like the eyes you glimpse in the heated purple corners of the small-mammal house that reproduces the gloom of nocturnal tropics. Would any Aramco official have become his client? Hansl had no reasonable plans but only crafty fantasies, restless schemes. They puffed out like a lizard's throat and then collapsed like bubble gum.

As for insults, I never intentionally insulted anyone. I sometimes think that I don't have to say a word for people to be insulted by me, that my existence itself insults them. I come to this conclusion unwillingly, for God knows that I consider myself a man of normal social instincts and am not conscious of any will to offend. In various ways I have been trying to say this to you, using words like seizure, rapture, demonic possession, frenzy, *Fatum,* divine madness, or even solar storm—on a microcosmic scale. The better people are, the less they take offense at this gift, or curse, and I have a hunch that you will judge me less harshly than Walish. He, however, is right in one respect. You did nothing to offend me. You were the meekest, the only one of those I wounded whom I had no reason whatsoever to wound. That's what grieves me most of all. But there is still more. The writing of this letter has been the occasion of important discoveries about myself, so I am even more greatly in your debt, for I see that you have returned me good for the evil I did you. I opened my mouth to make a coarse joke at your expense and thirty-five years later the result is a communion.

But to return to what I literally am: a basically unimportant old party, ailing, cut off from all friendships, scheduled for extradition, and with a future of which the dimmest view is justified (shall I have an extra bed put in my mother's room and plead illness and incompetency?).

Wandering about Vancouver this winter, I have considered whether to edit an anthology of sharp sayings. Make my fate pay off. But I am too demoralized to do it. I can't pull myself together. Instead, fragments of things read or remembered come to me persistently while I go back and forth between my house and the supermarket. I shop to entertain myself, but Canadian supermarkets unsettle me. They aren't organized the way ours are. They carry fewer brands. Items like lettuce and bananas are priced out of sight while luxuries like frozen salmon are comparatively cheap. But how would I cope with a big frozen salmon? I couldn't fit it into my oven, and how, with arthritic hands, could I saw it into chunks?

Persistent fragments, inspired epigrams, or spontaneous expressions of ill will come and go. Clemenceau saying about Poincaré that he was a hydrocephalic in patent-leather boots. Or Churchill answering a question about the queen of Tonga as she passes in a barouche during the coronation of Elizabeth II: "Is that small gentleman in the admiral's uniform the queen's consort?" "I believe he is her lunch."

Disraeli on his deathbed, informed that Queen Victoria has come to see him and is in the anteroom, says to his manservant, "Her Majesty only wants me to carry a message to dear Albert."

Such items might be delicious if they were not so persistent and accompanied by a despairing sense that I am no longer in control.

"You look pale and exhausted, Professor X."

"I've been exchanging ideas with Professor Y, and I feel absolutely drained."

Worse than this is the nervous word game I am unable to stop playing.

"She is the woman who put the 'dish' into 'fiendish.' "

"He is the man who put the 'rat' into 'rational.' "

"The 'fruit' in 'fruitless.' "

"The 'con' in 'icon.' "

Recreations of a crumbling mind, Miss Rose. Symptoms perhaps of high blood pressure, or minor tokens of private resistance to the giant public hand of the law (that hand will be withdrawn only when I am dead).

No wonder, therefore, that I spend so much time with old Mrs. Gracewell. In her ticktock Meissen parlor with its uncomfortable chairs I am at home. Forty years a widow and holding curious views, she is happy in my company. Few visitors want to hear about the Divine Spirit, but I am seriously prepared to ponder the mysterious and intriguing descriptions she gives. The Divine Spirit, she tells me, has withdrawn in our time from the outer, visible world. You can see what it once wrought, you are surrounded by its created forms. But although natural processes continue, Divinity has absented itself. The wrought work is brightly divine but Divinity is not now active within it. The world's grandeur is fading. And this is our human setting, devoid of God, she says with great earnestness. But in this deserted beauty man himself still lives as a God-pervaded being. It will be up to him—to us—to bring back the light that has gone from these molded likenesses, if we are not prevented by the forces of darkness. Intellect, worshipped by all, brings us as far as natural science, and this science, although very great, is incomplete. Redemption from *mere* nature is the work of feeling and of the awakened eye of the Spirit. The body, she says, is subject to the forces of gravity. But the soul is ruled by levity, pure.

I listen to this and have no mischievous impulses. I shall miss the old girl. After much monkey business, dear Miss Rose, I am ready to listen to words of ultimate seriousness. There isn't much time left. The federal marshal, any day now, will be setting out from Seattle.

SOMETHING TO
REMEMBER ME BY

WHEN THERE IS too much going on, more than you can bear, you may choose to assume that nothing in particular is happening, that your life is going round and round like a turntable. Then one day you are aware that what you took to be a turntable, smooth, flat, and even, was in fact a whirlpool, a vortex. My first knowledge of the hidden work of uneventful days goes back to February 1933. The exact date won't matter much to you. I like to think, however, that you, my only child, will want to hear about this hidden work as it relates to me. When you were a small boy you were keen on family history. You will quickly understand that I couldn't tell a child what I am about to tell you now. You don't talk about deaths and vortices to a kid, not nowadays. In my time my parents didn't hesitate to speak of death and the dying. What they seldom mentioned was sex. We've got it the other way around.

My mother died when I was an adolescent. I've often told you that. What I didn't tell you was that I knew she was dying and didn't allow myself to think about it—there's your turntable.

The month was February, as I've said, adding that the exact date wouldn't matter to you. I should confess that I myself avoided fixing it.

Chicago in winter, armored in gray ice, the sky low, the going heavy.

I was a high school senior, an indifferent student, generally unpopular, a background figure in the school. It was only as a high jumper that I performed in public. I had no form at all; a curious last-minute spring or convulsion put me over the bar. But this was what the school turned out to see.

Unwilling to study, I was bookish nevertheless. I was secretive about my family life. The truth is that I didn't want to talk about my mother. Besides, I had no language as yet for the oddity of my peculiar interests.

But let me get on with that significant day in the early part of February.

It began like any other winter school day in Chicago—grimly ordinary. The temperature a few degrees above zero, botanical frost shapes on the window-pane, the snow swept up in heaps, the ice gritty and the streets, block after block, bound together by the iron of the sky. A breakfast of porridge, toast, and tea. Late as usual, I stopped for a moment to look into my mother's sickroom. I bent near and said, "It's Louie, going to school." She seemed to nod. Her eyelids were brown; the color of her face was much lighter. I hurried off with my books on a strap over my shoulder.

When I came to the boulevard on the edge of the park, two small men rushed out of a doorway with rifles, wheeled around aiming upward, and fired at pigeons near the rooftop. Several birds fell straight down, and the men scooped up the soft bodies and ran indoors, dark little guys in fluttering white shirts. Depression hunters and their city game. Moments before, the police car had loafed by at ten miles an hour. The men had waited it out.

This had nothing to do with me. I mention it merely because it happened. I stepped around the blood spots and crossed into the park.

To the right of the path, behind the wintry lilac twigs, the crust of the snow was broken. In the dead black night Stephanie and I had necked there, petted, my hands under her raccoon coat, under her sweater, under her skirt, adoles-cents kissing without restraint. Her coonskin cap had slipped to the back of her head. She opened the musky coat to me to have me closer.

Approaching the school building, I had to run to reach the doors before the last bell. I was on notice from the family—no trouble with teachers, no sum-mons from the principal at a time like this. And I did observe the rules, al-though I despised classwork. But I spent all the money I could lay hands on at Hammersmark's Bookstore. I read *Manhattan Transfer*, *The Enormous Room*, and *A Portrait of the Artist*. I belonged to the Cercle Français and the Senior Dis-cussion Club. The club's topic for this afternoon was Von Hindenburg's choice of Hitler to form a new government. But I couldn't go to meetings now; I had an after-school job. My father had insisted that I find one.

After classes, on my way to work, I stopped at home to cut myself a slice of bread and a wedge of Wisconsin cheese, and to see whether my mother might be awake. During her last days she was heavily sedated and rarely said anything. The tall, square-shouldered bottle at her bedside was filled with clear red Nem-butal. The color of this fluid was always the same, as if it could tolerate no shadow. Now that she could no longer sit up to have it washed, my mother's hair was cut short. This made her face more slender, and her lips were sober. Her breathing was dry and hard, obstructed. The window shade was halfway up. It was scalloped at the bottom and had white fringes. The street ice was dark gray. Snow was piled against the trees. Their trunks had a mineral-black look. Wait-ing out the winter in their alligator armor, they gathered coal soot.

Even when she was awake, my mother couldn't find the breath to speak. She sometimes made signs. Except for the nurse, there was nobody in the house. My father was at business, my sister had a downtown job, my brothers hustled. The eldest, Albert, clerked for a lawyer in the Loop. My brother Len had put me onto a job on the Northwestern commuter trains, and for a while I was a candy butcher, selling chocolate bars and evening papers. When my mother put a stop to this because it kept me too late, I had found other work. Just now I was delivering flowers for a shop on North Avenue and riding the streetcars carrying wreaths and bouquets to all parts of the city. Behrens the florist paid me fifty cents for an afternoon; with tips I could earn as much as a dollar. That gave me time to prepare my trigonometry lesson and, very late at night, after I had seen Stephanie, to read my books. I sat in the kitchen when everyone was sleeping, in deep silence, snowdrifts under the windows, and below, the janitor's shovel rasping on the cement and clanging on the furnace door. I read banned books circulated by my classmates, political pamphlets, read "Prufrock" and "Mauberley." I also studied arcane books, too far out to discuss with anyone.

I read on the streetcars (called trolleys elsewhere). Reading shut out the sights. In fact there *were* no sights—more of the same and then more of the same. Shop fronts, garages, warehouses, narrow brick bungalows.

The city was laid out on a colossal grid, eight blocks to the mile, every fourth street a car line. The days short, the streetlights weak, the soiled snowbanks toward evening became a source of light. I carried my carfare in my mitten, where the coins mixed with lint worn away from the lining. Today I was delivering lilies to an uptown address. They were wrapped and pinned in heavy paper. Behrens, spelling out my errand for me, was pale, a narrow-faced man who wore nose glasses. Amid the flowers, he alone had no color—something like the price he paid for being human. He wasted no words: "This delivery will take an hour each way in this traffic, so it'll be your only one. I carry these people on the books, but make sure you get a signature on the bill."

I couldn't say why it was such a relief to get out of the shop, the damp, warm-earth smell, the dense mosses, the prickling cactuses, the glass iceboxes with orchids, gardenias, and sickbed roses. I preferred the brick boredom of the street, the paving stones and steel rails. I drew down the three peaks of my racing-skater's cap and hauled the clumsy package to Robey Street. When the car came panting up there was room for me on the long seat next to the door. Passengers didn't undo their buttons. They were chilled, guarded, muffled, miserable. I had reading matter with me—the remains of a book, the cover gone, the pages held together by binder's thread and flakes of glue. I carried these fifty or sixty pages in the pocket of my short sheepskin. With the one hand I had free I couldn't manage this mutilated book. And on the Broadway–Clark car, reading was out of the question. I had to protect my lilies from the balancing straphangers and people pushing toward the front.

I got down at Ainslie Street holding high the package, which had the shape of a padded kite. The apartment house I was looking for had a courtyard with iron palings. The usual lobby: a floor sinking in the middle, kernels of tile, gaps stuffed with dirt, and a panel of brass mailboxes with earpiece-mouthpieces. No voice came down when I pushed the button; instead, the lock buzzed, jarred, rattled, and I went from the cold of the outer lobby to the overheated mustiness of the inner one. On the second floor one of the two doors on the landing was open, and overshoes and galoshes and rubbers were heaped along the wall. At once I found myself in a crowd of drinkers. All the lights in the house were on, although it was a good hour before dark. Coats were piled on chairs and sofas. All whiskey in those days was bootleg, of course. Holding the flowers high, I parted the mourners. I was quasi-official. The message went out: "Let the kid through. Go right on, buddy."

The long passageway was full too, but the dining room was entirely empty. There, a dead girl lay in her coffin. Over her a cut-glass luster was hanging from a taped, deformed artery of wire pulled through the broken plaster. I hadn't expected to find myself looking down into a coffin.

You saw her as she was, without undertaker's makeup, a girl older than Stephanie, not so plump, thin, fair, her straight hair arranged on her dead shoulders. All buoyancy gone, a weight that counted totally on support, not so much lying as sunk in this gray rectangle. I saw what I took to be the pressure mark of fingers on her cheek. Whether she had been pretty or not was no consideration.

A stout woman (certainly the mother), wearing black, opened the swing door from the kitchen and saw me standing over the corpse. I thought she was displeased when she made a fist signal to come forward. As I passed her she drew both fists against her bosom. She said to put the flowers on the sink, and then she pulled the pins and crackled the paper. Big arms, thick calves, a bun of hair, her short nose thin and red. It was Behrens's practice to tie the lily stalks to slender green sticks. There was never any damage.

On the drainboard of the sink was a baked ham with sliced bread around the platter, a jar of French's mustard and wooden tongue depressors to spread it. I saw and I saw and I saw.

I was on my most discreet and polite behavior with the woman. I looked at the floor to spare her my commiserating face. But why should she care at all about my discreetness; how did I come into this except as a messenger and menial? If she wouldn't observe my behavior, whom was I behaving for? All she wanted was to settle the bill and send me on my way. She picked up her purse, holding it to her body as she had held her fists. "What do I owe Behrens?" she asked me.

"He said you could sign for this."

However, she wasn't going to deal in kindnesses. She said, "No." She said, "I don't want debts following me later on." She gave me a five-dollar bill, she added a tip of fifty cents, and it was I who signed the receipt, as well as I could on the enameled grooves of the sink. I folded the bill small and felt under the sheepskin coat for my watch pocket, ashamed to take money from her within sight of her dead daughter. I wasn't the object of the woman's severity, but her face somewhat frightened me. She leveled the same look at the walls, the door. I didn't figure here, however; this was no death of mine.

As if to take another reading of the girl's plain face, I looked again into the coffin on my way out. And then on the staircase I began to extract the pages from my sheepskin pocket, and in the lobby I hunted for the sentences I had read the night before. Yes, here they were:

Nature cannot suffer the human form within her system of laws. When given to her charge, the human being before us is reduced to dust. Ours is the most perfect form to be found on earth. The visible world sustains us until life leaves, and then it must utterly destroy us. Where, then, is the world from which the human form comes?

If you swallowed some food and then died, that morsel of food that would have nourished you in life would hasten your disintegration in death.

This meant that nature didn't make life; it only housed it.

In those days I read many such books. But the one I had read the previous night went deeper than the rest. You, my only child, are only too familiar with my lifelong absorption in or craze for further worlds. I used to bore you when I spoke of spirit, or pneuma, and of a continuum of spirit and nature. You were too well educated, respectably rational, to take stock in such terms. I might add, citing a famous scholar, that what is plausible can do without proof. I am not about to pursue this. Still, there would be a gap in what I have to tell if I were to leave out my significant book, and this after all is a narrative, not an argument.

Anyway, I returned my pages to the pocket of my sheepskin, and then I didn't know quite what to do. At four o'clock, with no more errands, I was somehow not ready to go home. So I walked through the snow to Argyle Street, where my brother-in-law practiced dentistry, thinking that we might travel home together. I prepared an explanation for turning up at his office. "I was on the North Side delivering flowers, saw a dead girl laid out, realized how close I was, and came here." Why did I need to account for my innocent behavior when it *was* innocent? Perhaps because I was always contemplating illicit things. Because I was always being accused. Because I ran a little truck farm of deceits—but self-examination, once so fascinating to me, has become tiresome.

My brother-in-law's office was a high, second-floor walk-up: PHILIP HADDIS, D.D.S. Three bay windows at the rounded corner of the building gave you a full view of the street and of the lake, due east—the jagged flats of ice floating. The office door was open, and when I came through the tiny blind (windowless) waiting room and didn't see Philip at the big, back-tilted dentist's chair, I thought that he might have stepped into his lab. He was a good technician and did most of his own work, which was a big saving.

Philip wasn't tall, but he was very big, a burly man. The sleeves of his white coat fitted tightly on his bare, thick forearms. The strength of his arms counted when it came to pulling teeth. Lots of patients were referred to him for extractions.

When he had nothing in particular to do he would sit in the chair himself, studying the *Racing Form* between the bent mantis leg of the drill, the gas flame, and the water spurting round and round in the green glass spit-sink. The cigar smell was always thick. Standing in the center of the dental cabinet was a clock under a glass bell. Four gilt weights rotated at its base. This was a gift from my mother. The view from the middle window was divided by a chain that couldn't have been much smaller than the one that stopped the British fleet on the Hudson. This held the weight of the druggist's sign—a mortar and pestle outlined in electric bulbs. There wasn't much daylight left. At noon it was poured out; by four it had drained away. From one side the banked snow was growing blue, from the other the shops were shining warmth on it.

The dentist's lab was in a closet. Easygoing Philip peed in the sink sometimes. It was a long trek to the toilet at the far end of the building, and the hallway was nothing but two walls—a plaster tunnel and a carpet runner edged with brass tape. Philip hated going to the end of the hall.

There was nobody in the lab, either. Philip might have been taking a cup of coffee at the soda fountain in the drugstore below. It was possible also that he was passing the time with Marchek, the doctor with whom he shared the suite of offices. The connecting door was never locked, and I had occasionally sat in Marchek's swivel chair with a gynecology book, studying the colored illustrations and storing up the Latin names.

Marchek's starred glass pane was dark, and I assumed his office to be empty, but when I went in I saw a naked woman lying on the examining table. She wasn't asleep; she seemed to be resting. Becoming aware that I was there, she stirred, and then without haste, disturbing herself as little as possible, she reached for her clothing heaped on Dr. Marchek's desk. Picking out her slip, she put it on her belly—she didn't spread it. Was she dazed, drugged? No, she simply took her sweet time about everything, she behaved with exciting lassitude. Wires connected her nice wrists to a piece of medical apparatus on a wheeled stand.

The right thing would have been to withdraw, but it was already too late for that. Besides, the woman gave no sign that she cared one way or another. She didn't draw the slip over her breasts, she didn't even bring her thighs together. The covering hairs were parted. These were salt, acid, dark, sweet odors. These were immediately effective; I was strongly excited. There was a gloss on her forehead, an exhausted look about the eyes. I believed that I had guessed what she had been doing, but then the room was half dark, and I preferred to avoid any definite thought. Doubt seemed much better, or equivocation.

I remembered that Philip, in his offhand, lazy way, had mentioned a "research project" going on next door. Dr. Marchek was measuring the reactions of partners in the sexual act. "He takes people from the street, he hooks them up and pretends he's collecting graphs. This is for kicks; the science part is horseshit."

The naked woman, then, was an experimental subject.

I had prepared myself to tell Philip about the dead girl on Ainslie Street, but the coffin, the kitchen, the ham, the flowers were as distant from me now as the ice floes on the lake and the killing cold of the water.

"Where did you come from?" the woman said to me.

"From next door—the dentist's office."

"The doctor was about to unstrap me, and I need to get loose. Maybe you can figure out these wires."

If Marchek should be in the inner room, he wouldn't come in now that he heard voices. As the woman raised both her arms so that I could undo the buckles, her breasts swayed, and when I bent over her the odor of her upper body made me think of the frilled brown papers in a box after the chocolates had been eaten—a sweet aftersmell and acrid cardboard mixed. Although I tried hard to stop it, my mother's chest mutilated by cancer surgery passed through my mind. Its gnarled scar tissue. I also called in Stephanie's closed eyes and kissing face—anything to spoil the attraction of this naked young woman. It occurred to me as I undid the clasps that instead of disconnecting her I was hooking myself. We were alone in the darkening office, and I wanted her to reach under the sheepskin and undo my belt for me.

But when her hands were free she wiped the jelly from her wrists and began to dress. She started with her bra, several times lowering her breasts into the cups, and when her arms went backward to fasten the hooks she bent far forward, as if she were passing under a low bough. The cells of my body were like bees, drunker and drunker on sexual honey (I expect that this will change the figure of Grandfather Louie, the old man remembered as this or that but never as a hive of erotic bees).

But I couldn't be blind to the woman's behavior even now. It was very broad; she laid it on. I saw her face in profile, and although it was turned downward, there was no mistaking her smile. To use an expression from the thirties, she was giving me the works. She knew I was about to fall on my face. She buttoned every small button with deliberate slowness, and her blouse had at least twenty such buttons, yet she was still bare from the waist down. Though we were so minor, she and I, a schoolboy and a floozy, we had such major instruments to play. And if we were to go further, whatever happened would never get beyond this room. It would be between the two of us, and nobody would ever hear of it. Still, Marchek, that pseudoexperimenter, was probably biding his time in the next room. An old family doctor, he must have been embarrassed and angry. And at any moment, moreover, my brother-in-law Philip might come back.

When the woman slipped down from the leather table she gripped her leg and said she had pulled a muscle. She lifted one heel onto a chair and rubbed her calf, swearing under her breath and looking everywhere with swimming eyes. And then, after she had put on her skirt and fastened her stockings to the garter belt, she pushed her feet into her pumps and limped around the chair, holding it by the arm. She said, "Will you please reach me my coat? Just put it over my shoulders."

She, too, wore a raccoon. As I took it from the hook I wished it had been something else. But Stephanie's coat was newer than this one and twice as heavy. These pelts had dried out, and the fur was thin. The woman was already on her way out, and stooped as I laid the raccoon over over her back. Marchek's office had its own exit to the corridor.

At the top of the staircase, the woman asked me to help her down. I said that I would, of course, but I wanted to look once more for my brother-in-law. As she tied the woolen scarf under her chin she smiled at me, with an Oriental wrinkling of her eyes.

Not to check in with Philip wouldn't have been right. My hope was that he would be returning, coming down the narrow corridor in his burly, sauntering, careless way. You won't remember your Uncle Philip. He had played college football, and he still had the look of a tackle, with his swelling, compact forearms. (At Soldier Field today he'd be physically insignificant; in his time, however, he was something of a strongman.)

But there was the long strip of carpet down the middle of the wall-valley, and no one was coming to rescue me. I turned back to his office. If only a patient were sitting in the chair and I could see Philip looking into his mouth, I'd be on track again, excused from taking the woman's challenge. One alternative was to say that I couldn't go with her, that Philip expected me to ride back with him to the Northwest Side. In the empty office I considered this lie, bending my head so that I wouldn't confront the clock with its soundless measured weights revolving. Then I wrote on Philip's memo pad: "Louie, passing by." I left it on the seat of the chair.

The woman had put her arms through the sleeves of the collegiate, rah-rah raccoon and was resting her fur-bundled rear on the banister. She was passing her compact mirror back and forth, and when I came out she gave the compact a snap and dropped it into her purse.

"Still the charley horse?"

"My lower back too."

We descended, very slow, both feet on each tread. I wondered what she would do if I were to kiss her. Laugh at me, probably. We were no longer between the four walls where anything might have happened. In the street, space was unlimited. I had no idea how far we were going, how far I would be able to go. Although she was the one claiming to be in pain, it was I who felt sick. She asked me to support her lower back with my hand, and there I discovered what an extraordinary action her hips could perform. At a party I had overheard an older woman saying to another lady, "I know how to make them burn." Hearing this was enough for me.

No special art was necessary with a boy of seventeen, not even so much as being invited to support her with my hand—to feel that intricate, erotic working of her back. I had already *seen* the woman on Marchek's examining table and had also felt the full weight of her when she leaned—when she laid her female substance on me. Moreover, she fully knew my mind. She was the thing I was thinking continually, and how often does thought find its object in circumstances like these—the object *knowing* that it has been found? The woman knew my expectations. She *was,* in the flesh, those expectations. I couldn't have sworn that she was a hooker, a tramp. She might have been an ordinary family girl with a taste for trampishness, acting loose, amusing herself with me, doing a comic sex turn as in those days people sometimes did.

"Where are we headed?"

"If you have to go, I can make it on my own," she said. "It's just Winona Street, the other side of Sheridan Road."

"No, no. I'll walk you there."

She asked whether I was still at school, pointing to the printed pages in my coat pocket.

I observed when we were passing a fruit shop (a boy of my own age emptying bushels of oranges into the lighted window) that, despite the woman's thick-cream color, her eyes were Far Eastern, black.

"You should be about seventeen," she said.

"Just."

She was wearing pumps in the snow and placed each step with care.

"What are you going to be—have you picked your profession?"

I had no use for professions. Utterly none. There were accountants and engineers in the soup lines. In the world slump, professions were useless. You were free, therefore, to make something extraordinary of yourself. I might have said, if I hadn't been excited to the point of sickness, that I didn't ride around the city on the cars to make a buck or to be useful to the family, but to take a reading of this boring, depressed, ugly, endless, rotting city. I couldn't have thought it then, but I now understand that my purpose was to interpret this place. Its power was tremendous. But so was mine, potentially. I refused absolutely to believe for a moment that people here were doing what they thought they were doing. Beneath the apparent life of these streets was their real life, beneath each face the real face, beneath each voice and its words the true tone and the real message. Of course, I wasn't about to say such things. It was beyond me at that time to say them. I was, however, a high-toned kid, "La-di-dah," my critical, satirical brother Albert called me. A high purpose in adolescence will expose you to that.

At the moment, a glamorous, sexual girl had me in tow. I couldn't guess where I was being led, nor how far, nor what she would surprise me with, nor the consequences.

"So the dentist is your brother?"

"In-law—my sister's husband. They live with us. You're asking what he's like? He's a good guy. He likes to lock his office on Friday and go to the races. He takes me to the fights. Also, at the back of the drugstore there's a poker game. . . ."

"*He* doesn't go around with books in his pocket."

"Well, no, he doesn't. He says, 'What's the use? There's too much to keep up or catch up with. You could never in a thousand years do it, so why knock yourself out?' My sister wants him to open a Loop office, but that would be too much of a strain. I guess he's for inertia. He's not ready to do more than he's already doing."

"So what are you reading—what's it about?"

I didn't propose to discuss anything with her. I wasn't capable of it. What I had in mind just then was entirely different.

But suppose I had been able to explain. One does have a responsibility to answer genuine questions: "You see, miss, this is the visible world. We live in it, we breathe its air and eat its substance. When we die, however, matter goes to matter, and then we're annihilated. Now, which world do we really belong to, this world of matter or another world, from which matter takes its orders?"

Not many people were willing to talk about such notions. They made even Stephanie impatient. "When you die, that's it. Dead is dead," she would say. She loved a good time. And when I wouldn't take her downtown to the Oriental Theatre she didn't deny herself the company of other boys. She brought back off-color vaudeville jokes. I think the Oriental was part of a national entertainment circuit. Jimmy Savo, Lou Holtz, and Sophie Tucker played there. I was sometimes too solemn for Stephanie. When she gave imitations of Jimmy Savo singing "River, Stay Away from My Door," bringing her knees together and holding herself tight, she didn't break me up, and she was disappointed.

You would have thought that the book or book fragment in my pocket was a talisman from a fairy tale to open castle gates or carry me to mountaintops. Yet when the woman asked me what it was, I was too scattered to tell her. Remember, I still kept my hand as instructed on her lower back, tormented by that sexual grind of her movements. I was discovering what the lady at the party had meant by saying, "I know how to make them burn." So of course I was in no condition to talk about the Ego and the Will, or about the secrets of the blood. Yes, I believed that higher knowledge was shared out among all human beings. What else was there to hold us together but this force hidden behind daily consciousness? But to be coherent about it now was absolutely out of the question.

"Can't you tell me?" she said.

"I bought this for a nickel from a bargain table."

"That's how you spend your money?"

I assumed her to mean that I didn't spend it on girls.

"And the dentist is a good-natured, lazy guy," she went on. "What has he got to tell you?"

I tried to review the mental record. What did Phil Haddis say? He said that a stiff prick has no conscience. At the moment it was all I could think of. It amused Philip to talk to me. He was a chum. Where Philip was indulgent, my brother Albert, your late uncle, was harsh. Albert might have taught me something if he had trusted me. He was then a night-school law student clerking for Rowland, the racketeer congressman. He was Rowland's bagman, and Rowland hired him not to read law but to make collections. Philip suspected that Albert was skimming, for he dressed sharply. He wore a derby (called, in those days, a Baltimore heater) and a camel's-hair topcoat and pointed, mafioso shoes. Toward me, Albert was scornful. He said, "You don't understand fuck-all. You never will."

We were approaching Winona Street, and when we got to her building she'd have no further use for me and send me away. I'd see no more than the flash of the glass and then stare as she let herself in. She was already feeling in her purse for the keys. I was no longer supporting her back, preparing instead to mutter "Bye-bye," when she surprised me with a sideward nod, inviting me to enter. I think I had hoped (with sex-polluted hope) that she would leave me in the street. I followed her through another tile lobby and through the inner door. The staircase was fiercely heated by coal-fueled radiators, the skylight three stories up was wavering, the wallpaper had come unstuck and was curling and bulging. I swallowed my breath. I couldn't draw this heat into my lungs.

This had been a deluxe apartment house once, built for bankers, brokers, and well-to-do professionals. Now it was occupied by transients. In the big front room with its French windows there was a crap game. In the next room people were drinking or drowsing on the old chesterfields. The woman led me through what had once been a private bar—some of the fittings were still in place. Then I followed her through the kitchen—I would have gone anywhere, no questions asked. In the kitchen there were no signs of cooking, neither pots nor dishes. The linoleum was shredding, brown fibers standing like hairs. She led me into a narrower corridor, parallel to the main one. "I have what used to be a maid's room," she said. "It's got a nice view of the alley, but there is a private bathroom."

And here we were—an almost empty space. So this was how whores operated—assuming that she was a whore: a bare floor, a narrow cot, a chair by the window, a lopsided clothespress against the wall. I stopped under the light fixture while she passed behind, as if to observe me. Then from the back she gave me a hug and a small kiss on the cheek, more promissory than actual. Her face powder, or perhaps it was her lipstick, had a sort of green-banana fragrance. My heart had never beaten as hard as this.

She said, "Why don't I go into the bathroom awhile and get ready while you undress and lie down in bed. You look like you were brought up neat, so lay your clothes on the chair. You don't want to drop them on the floor."

Shivering (this seemed the one cold room in the house), I began to pull off my things, beginning with the winter-wrinkled boots. The sheepskin I hung over the back of the chair. I pushed my socks into the boots and then my bare feet recoiled from the grit underfoot. I took off everything, as if to disassociate my shirt, my underthings, from whatever it was that was about to happen, so that only my body could be guilty. The one thing that couldn't be excepted. When I pulled back the cover and got in, I was thinking that the beds in Bridewell prison would be like this. There was no pillowcase; my head lay on the ticking. What I saw of the outside were the utility wires hung between the poles like lines on music paper, only sagging, and the glass insulators like clumps of notes. The woman had said nothing about money. Because she liked me. I couldn't believe my luck—luck with a hint of disaster. I blinded myself to the Bridewell metal cot, not meant for two. I felt also that I couldn't hold out if she kept me waiting long. And what feminine thing was she doing in there—undressing, washing, perfuming, changing?

Abruptly, she came out. She had been waiting, nothing else. She still wore the raccoon coat, even the gloves. Without looking at me she walked very quickly, almost running, and opened the window. As soon as the window shot up, it let in a blast of cold air, and I stood up on the bed but it was too late to stop her. She took my clothes from the back of the chair and heaved them out. They fell into the alley. I shouted, "What are you doing!" She still refused to turn her head. As she ran away, tying the scarf under her chin, she left the door open. I could hear her pumps beating double time in the hallway.

I couldn't run after her, could I, and show myself naked to the people in the flat? She had banked on this. When we came in, she must have given the high sign to the man she worked with, and he had been waiting in the alley. When I ran to look out, my things had already been gathered up. All I saw was the back of somebody with a bundle under his arm hurrying in the walkway between two garages. I might have picked up my boots—those she had left me—and jumped from the first-floor window, but I couldn't chase the man very far, and in a few minutes I would have wound up on Sheridan Road naked and freezing.

I had seen a drunk in his union suit, bleeding from the head after he had been rolled and beaten, staggering and yelling in the street. I didn't even have a shirt and drawers. I was as naked as the woman herself had been in the doctor's office, stripped of everything, including the five dollars I had collected for the flowers. And the sheepskin my mother had bought for me last year. Plus the book, the fragment of an untitled book, author unknown. This may have been the most serious loss of all.

Now I could think on my own about the world I really belonged to, whether it was this one or another.

I pulled down the window, and then I went to shut the door. The room didn't seem lived in, but suppose it had a tenant, and what if he were to storm in now and rough me up? Luckily there was a bolt to the door. I pushed it into its loop and then I ran around the room to see what I could find to wear. In the lop-sided clothespress, nothing but wire hangers, and in the bathroom, only a cotton hand towel. I tore the blanket off the bed; if I were to slit it I might pull it over my head like a serape, but it was too thin to do me much good in freezing weather. When I dragged the chair over to the clothespress and stood on it, I found a woman's dress behind the molding, and a quilted bed jacket. In a brown paper bag there was a knitted brown tam. I had to put these things on. I had no choice.

It was now, I reckoned, about five o'clock. Philip had no fixed schedule. He didn't hang around the office on the off chance that somebody might turn up with a toothache. After his last appointment he locked up and left. He didn't necessarily set out for home; he was not too keen to return to the house. If I wanted to catch him I'd have to run. In boots, dress, tam, and jacket, I made my way out of the apartment. Nobody took the slightest interest in me. More people (Philip would have called them transients) had crowded in—it was even likely that the man who had snatched up my clothes in the alley had returned, was among them. The heat in the staircase now was stifling, and the wallpaper smelled scorched, as if it were on the point of catching fire. In the street I was struck by a north wind straight from the Pole, and the dress and sateen jacket counted for nothing. I was running, though, and had no time to feel it.

Philip would say, "Who was this floozy? Where did she pick you up?" Philip was unexcitable, always mild, amused by me. Anna would badger him with the example of her ambitious brothers—they hustled, they read books. You couldn't fault Philip for being pleased. I anticipated what he'd say—"Did you get in? Then at least you're not going to catch the clap." I depended on Philip now, for I had nothing, not even seven cents for carfare. I could be certain, however, that he wouldn't moralize at me, he'd set about dressing me, he'd scrounge a sweater among his neighborhood acquaintances or take me to the Salvation Army shop on Broadway if that was still open. He'd go about this in his slow-moving, thick-necked, deliberate way. Not even dancing would speed him up; he spaced out the music to suit him when he did the fox-trot and pressed his cheek to Anna's. He wore a long, calm grin. My private term for this particular expression was Pussy-Veleerum. I saw Philip as fat but strong, strong but cozy, purring but inserting a joking comment. He gave a little suck at the corner of the mouth when he was about to take a swipe at you, and it was then that he was Pussy-Veleerum. A name it never occurred to me to speak aloud.

I sprinted past the windows of the fruit store, the delicatessen, the tailor's shop. I could count on help from Philip. My father, however, was an intolerant, hasty man. Slighter than his sons, handsome, with muscles of white marble (so they seemed to me), laying down the law. It would put him in a rage to see me like this. And it was true that I had failed to consider: my mother dying, the ground frozen, a funeral coming, the dug grave, the packet of sand from the Holy Land to be scattered on the shroud. If I were to turn up in this filthy dress, the old man, breaking under his burdens, would come down on me in a blind, Old Testament rage. I never thought of this as cruelty but as archaic right ever-lasting. Even Albert, who was already a Loop lawyer, had to put up with the old man's blows—outraged, his eyes swollen and maddened, but he took it. It never seemed to any of us that my father was cruel. We had gone over the limit, and we were punished.

There were no lights in Philip's D.D.S. office. When I jumped up the stairs, the door with its blank starred glass was locked. Frosted panes were still rare. What we had was this star-marred product for toilets and other private windows. Marchek—whom nowadays we could call a voyeur—was also, angrily, gone. I had screwed up his experiment. I tried the doors, thinking that I could spend the night on the leather examining table where the beautiful nude had lain. From the office I could also make telephone calls. I did have a few friends, although there were none who might help me. I wouldn't have known how to explain my predicament to them. They'd think I was putting them on, that it was a practical joke—"This is Louie. A whore robbed me of my clothes and I'm stuck on the North Side without carfare. I'm wearing a dress. I lost my house keys. I can't get home."

I ran down to the drugstore to look for Philip there. He sometimes played five or six hands of poker in the druggist's back room, trying his luck before get-ting on the streetcar. I knew Kiyar, the druggist, by sight. He had no recollec-tion of me—why should he have? He said, "What can I do for you, young lady?"

Did he really take me for a girl, or a tramp off the street, or a Gypsy from one of the storefront fortune-teller camps? Those were now all over town. But not even a Gypsy would wear this blue sateen quilted boudoir jacket instead of a coat.

"I wonder, is Phil Haddis the dentist in the back?"

"What do you want with Dr. Haddis—have you got a toothache, or what?"

"I need to see him."

The druggist was a compact little guy, and his full round bald head was painfully sensitive looking. In its sensitivity it could pick up any degree of disturbance, I thought. Yet there was a canny glitter coming through his specs, and Kiyar had the mark of a man whose mind never would change once he had made it up. Oddly enough, he had a small mouth, baby's lips. He had been on the street—how long? Forty years? In forty years you've seen it all and nobody can tell you a single thing.

"Did Dr. Haddis have an appointment with you? Are you a patient?"

He knew this was a private connection. I was no patient. "No. But if I was out here he'd want to know it. Can I talk to him one minute?"

"He isn't here."

Kiyar had walked behind the grille of the prescription counter. I mustn't lose him. If he went, what would I do next? I said, "This is important, Mr. Kiyar." He waited for me to declare myself. I wasn't about to embarrass Philip by setting off rumors. Kiyar said nothing. He may have been waiting for me to speak up. Declare myself. I assume he took pride in running a tight operation, giving nothing away. To cut through to the man I said, "I'm in a spot. I left Dr. Haddis a note before, but when I came back I missed him."

At once I recognized my mistake. Druggists were always being appealed to. All those pills, remedy bottles, bright lights, medicine ads, drew wandering screwballs and moochers. They all said they were in bad trouble.

"You can go to the Foster Avenue station."

"The police, you mean."

I had thought of that too. I could always tell them my hard-luck story and they'd keep me until they checked it out and someone would come to fetch me. That would probably be Albert. Albert would love that. He'd say to me, "Well, aren't you the horny little bastard." He'd play up to the cops too, and amuse them.

"I'd freeze before I got to Foster Avenue" was my answer to Kiyar.

"There's always the squad car."

"Well, if Phil Haddis isn't in the back maybe he's still in the neighborhood. He doesn't always go straight home."

"Sometimes he goes over to the fights at Johnny Coulon's. It's a little early for that. You could try the speakeasy down the street, on Kenmore. It's an English basement, side entrance. You'll see a light by the fence. The guy at the slot is called Moose."

He didn't offer so much as a dime from his till. If I had said that I was in a scrape and that Phil was my sister's husband he'd probably have given me carfare. But I hadn't confessed, and there was a penalty for that.

Going out, I crossed my arms over the bed jacket and opened the door with my shoulder. I might as well have been wearing nothing at all. The wind cut at my legs, and I ran. Luckily I didn't have far to go. The iron pipe with the bulb at the end of it was halfway down the block. I saw it as soon as I crossed the street. These illegal drinking parlors were easy to find; they were meant to be. The steps were cement, four or five of them bringing me down to the door. The slot came open even before I knocked, and instead of the doorkeeper's eyes, I saw his teeth.

"You Moose?"

"Yah. Who?"

"Kiyar sent me."

"Come on."

I felt as though I were falling into a big, warm, paved cellar. There was little to see, almost nothing. A sort of bar was set up, a few hanging fixtures, some tables from an ice cream parlor, wire-backed chairs. If you looked through the window of an English basement your eyes were at ground level. Here the glass was tarred over. There would have been nothing to see anyway: a yard, a wooden porch, a clothesline, wires, a back alley with ash heaps.

"Where did you come from, sister?" said Moose.

But Moose was a nobody here. The bartender, the one who counted, called me over and said, "What is it, sweetheart? You got a message for somebody?"

"Not exactly."

"Oh? You needed a drink so bad that you jumped out of bed and ran straight over—you couldn't stop to dress?"

"No, sir. I'm looking for somebody—Phil Haddis? The dentist?"

"There's only one customer. Is that him?"

It wasn't. My heart sank into river mud.

"It's not a drunk you're looking for?"

"No."

The drunk was on a high stool, thin legs hanging down, arms forward, and his head lying sidewise on the bar. Bottles, glasses, a beer barrel. Behind the barkeeper was a sideboard pried from the wall of an apartment. It had a long mirror—an oval laid on its side. Paper streamers curled down from the pipes.

"Do you know the dentist I'm talking about?"

"I might. Might not," said the barkeeper. He was a sloppy, long-faced giant—something of a kangaroo look about him. That was the long face in combination with the belly. He told me, "This is not a busy time. It's dinner, you know, and we're just a neighborhood speak."

It was no more than a cellar, just as the barman was no more than a Greek, huge and bored. Just as I myself, Louie, was no more than a naked male in a woman's dress. When you had named objects in this elementary way, hardly anything remained in them. The barman, on whom everything now depended, held his bare arms out at full reach and braced on his spread hands. The place smelled of yeast sprinkled with booze. He said, "You live around here?"

"No, about an hour on the streetcar."

"Say more."

"Humboldt Park is my neighborhood."

"Then you got to be a Uke, a Polack, a Scandihoof, or a Jew."

"Jew."

"I know my Chicago. And you didn't set out dressed like that. You'da frozen to death inside of ten minutes. It's for the boudoir, not winter wear. You don't have the shape of a woman, neither. The hips aren't there. Are you covering a pair of knockers? I bet not. So what's the story, are you a morphodite? Let me tell you, you got to give this Depression credit. Without it you'd never find out what kind of funny stuff is going on. But one thing I'll never believe is that you're a young girl and still got her cherry."

"You're right as far as that goes, but the rest of it is that I haven't got a cent, and I need carfare."

"Who took you, a woman?"

"Up in her room when I undressed, she grabbed my things and threw them out the window."

"Left you naked so you couldn't chase her . . . I would have grabbed her and threw her on the bed. I bet you didn't even get in."

Not even, I repeated to myself. Why didn't I push her down while she was still in her coat, as soon as we entered the room—pull up her clothes, as he would have done? Because he was born to that. While I was not. I wasn't intended for it.

"So that's what happened. You got taken by a team of pros. She set you up. You were the mark. Jewish fellows aren't supposed to keep company with those bad cunts. But when you get out of your house, into the world, you want action like anybody else. So. And where did you dig up this dress with the fancy big roses? I guess you were standing with your sticker sticking out and were lucky to find anything to put on. Was she a good-looker?"

Her breasts, as she lay there, had kept their shape. They didn't slip sideward. The inward lines of her legs, thigh swelling toward thigh. The black crumpled hairs. Yes, a beauty, I would say.

Like the druggist, the barman saw the fun of the thing—an adolescent in a fix, a soiled dress, the rayon or sateen bed jacket. It was a lucky thing for me that business was at a standstill. If he had had customers, the barman wouldn't have given me the time of day. "In short, you got mixed up with a whore and she gave you the works."

For that matter, I had no sympathy for myself. I confessed that I had this coming, a high-minded Jewish schoolboy, too high-and-mighty to be Orthodox and with his eye on a special destiny. At home, inside the house, an archaic rule; outside, the facts of life. The facts of life were having their turn. Their first effect was ridicule. To throw my duds into the alley was the woman's joke on me. The druggist with his pain-sensitive head was all irony. And now the barman was going to get his fun out of my trouble before he, maybe, gave me the seven cents for carfare. Then I could have a full hour of shame on the streetcar. My mother, with whom I might never speak again, used to say that I had a line of pride straight down the bridge of my nose, a foolish stripe that she could see.

I had no way of anticipating what her death would signify.

The barman, having me in place, was giving me the business. And Moose ("Moosey," the Greek called him) had come away from the door so as not to miss the entertainment. The Greek's kangaroo mouth turned up at the corners. Presently his hand went up to his head and he rubbed his scalp under the black, spiky hair. Some said they drank olive oil by the glass, these Greeks, to keep their hair so rich. "Now give it to me again, about the dentist," said the barman.

"I came looking for him, but by now he's well on his way home."

He would by then be on the Broadway–Clark car, reading the Peach edition of the *Evening American,* a broad man with an innocent pout to his face, checking the race results. Anna had him dressed up as a professional man, but he let the fittings—shirt, tie, buttons—go their own way. His instep was fat and swelled inside the narrow shoe she had picked for him. He wore the fedora correctly. Toward the rest he admitted no obligation.

Anna cooked dinner after work, and when Philip came in, my father would begin to ask, "Where's Louie?" "Oh, he's out delivering flowers," they'd tell him. But the old man was nervous about his children after dark, and if they were late he waited up, walking—no, trotting—up and down the long apartment. When you tried to slip in, he caught you and twisted you tight by the neckband. He was small, neat, slender, a gentleman, but abrupt, not unworldly—he wasn't ignorant of vices; he had lived in Odessa and even longer in St. Petersburg—but he had no patience. The least thing might craze him. Seeing me in this dress, he'd lose his head at once. *I* lost *mine* when that woman showed me her snatch with all the pink layers, when she raised up her arm and asked me to disconnect the wires, when I felt her skin and her fragrance come upward.

"What's your family, what does your dad do?" asked the barman.

"His business is wood fuel for bakers' ovens. It comes by freight car from northern Michigan. Also from Birnamwood, Wisconsin. He has a yard off Lake Street, east of Halsted."

I made an effort to give the particulars. I couldn't afford to be suspected of invention now.

"I know where that is. Now, that's a neighborhood just full of hookers and cathouses. You think you can tell your old man what happened to you, that you got picked up by a cutie and she stole your clothes off you?"

The effect of this question was to make me tight in the face, dim in the ears. The whole cellar grew small and distant, toylike but not for play.

"How's your old man to deal with—tough?"

"Hard," I said.

"Slaps the kids around? This time you've got it coming. What's under the dress, a pair of bloomers?"

I shook my head.

"Your behind is bare? Now you know how it feels to go around like a woman."

The Greek's great muscles were dough-colored. You wouldn't have wanted him to take a headlock on you. That's the kind of man the Organization hired. The Capone people were now in charge. The customers would be like celluloid Kewpie dolls to the Greek. He looked like one of those boxing kangaroos in the movies, and he could do a standing jump over the bar. Yet he enjoyed playing zany. He could curve his long mouth up at the corners like the happy face in a cartoon.

"What were you doing on the North Side?"

"Delivering flowers."

"Hustling after school but with ramming on your brain. You got a lot to learn, buddy boy. Well, enough of that. Now, Moosey, take this flashlight and see if you can scrounge up a sweater or something in the back basement for this down-on-his-luck kid. I'd be surprised if the old janitor hasn't picked the stuff over pretty good. If mice have nested in it, shake out the turds. It'll help on the trip home."

I followed Moose into the hotter half of the cellar. His flashlight picked out the laundry tubs with the hand-operated wringers mounted on them, the pad-locked wooden storage bins. "Turn over some of these cardboard boxes. Mostly rags, is my guess. Dump 'em out, that's the easiest."

I emptied a couple of big cartons. Moose passed the light back and forth over the heaps. "Nothing much, like I said."

"Here's a flannel shirt," I said. I wanted to get out. The smell of heated burlap was hard to take. This was the only wearable article. I could have used a pullover or a pair of pants. We returned to the bar. As I was putting on the shirt, which revolted me (I come of finicky people whose fetish is cleanliness), the bar-man said, "I tell you what, you take this drunk home—this is about time for him, isn't it, Moosey? He gets plastered here every night. See he gets home and it'll be worth half a buck to you."

"I'll do it," I said. "It all depends on how far away he lives. If it's far, I'll be frozen before I get there."

"It isn't far. Winona, west of Sheridan, isn't far. I'll give you the directions. This guy is a City Hall payroller. He has no special job, he works direct for the ward committeeman. He's a lush with two little girls to bring up. If he's sober enough he cooks their dinner. Probably they take more care of him than he does of them."

"First I'll take charge of his money," said the barman. "I don't want my buddy here to be rolled. I don't say you would do it, but I owe this to a customer."

Bristle-faced Moose began to empty the man's pockets—his wallet, some keys, crushed cigarettes, a red bandanna that looked foul, matchbooks, greenbacks, and change. All these were laid out on the bar.

When I look back at past moments, I carry with me an apperceptive mass that ripens and perhaps distorts, mixing what is memorable with what may not be worth mentioning. Thus I see the barman with one big hand gathering in the valuables as if they were his winnings, the pot in a poker game. And then I think that if the kangaroo giant had taken this drunk on his back he might have bounded home with him in less time than it would have taken me to support him as far as the corner. But what the barman actually said was, "I got a nice escort for you, Jim."

Moose led the man back and forth to make sure his feet were operating. His swollen eyes now opened and then closed again. "McKern," Moose said, briefing me. "Southwest corner of Winona and Sheridan, the second building on the south side of the street, and it's the second floor."

"You'll be paid when you get back," said the barman.

The freeze was now so hard that the snow underfoot sounded like metal foil. Though McKern may have sobered up in the frigid street, he couldn't move very fast. Since I had to hold on to him, I borrowed his gloves. He had a coat with pockets to put his hands in. I tried to keep behind him and get some shelter from the wind. That didn't work. He wasn't up to walking. I had to hold him. Instead of a desirable woman, I had a drunkard in my arms. This disgrace, you see, while my mother was surrendering to death. At about this hour, upstairs neighbors came down and relatives arrived and filled the kitchen and the dining room—a deathwatch. I should have been there, not on the far North Side. When I had earned the carfare, I'd still be an hour from home on a streetcar making four stops to the mile.

Toward the last, I was dragging McKern. I kept the street door open with my back while I pulled him into the dim lobby by the arms.

The little girls had been waiting and came down at once. They held the inner door for me while I brought their daddy upstairs with a fireman's-carry and laid him on his bed. The children had had plenty of practice at this. They undressed him down to the long johns and then stood silent on either side of the room.

This, for them, was how things were. They took deep oddities calmly, as children generally will. I had spread his winter coat over him.

I had little sympathy for McKern, in the circumstances. I believe I can tell you why: He had surely passed out many times, and he would pass out again, dozens of times before he died. Drunkenness was common and familiar, and therefore accepted, and drunks could count on acceptance and support and relied on it. Whereas if your troubles were uncommon, unfamiliar, you could count on nothing. There was a convention about drunkenness, established in part by drunkards. The founding proposition was that consciousness is terrible. Its lower, impoverished forms are perhaps the worst. Flesh and blood are poor and weak, susceptible to human shock. Here my descendant will hear the voice of Grandfather Louie giving one of his sermons on higher consciousness and interrupting the story he promised to tell. You will hold him to his word, as you have every right to do.

The older girl now spoke to me. She said, "The fellow phoned and said a man was bringing Daddy home, and you'd help with supper if Daddy couldn't cook it."

"Yes. Well . . . ?"

"Only you're not a man—you've got a dress on."

"It looks like it, doesn't it. Don't you worry; I'll come to the kitchen with you."

"Are you a lady?"

"What do you mean—what does it look like? All right, I'm a lady."

"You can eat with us."

"Then show me where the kitchen is."

I followed them down a corridor narrowed by clutter—boxes of canned groceries, soda biscuits, sardines, pop bottles. When I passed the bathroom, I slipped in for quick relief. The door had neither a hook nor a bolt; the string of the ceiling fixture had snapped off. A tiny night-light was plugged into the baseboard. I thanked God it was so dim. I put up the board while raising my skirt, and when I had begun I heard one of the children behind me. Over my shoulder I saw that it was the younger one, and as I turned my back (*everything* was happening today) I said, "Don't come in here." But she squeezed past and sat on the edge of the tub. She grinned at me. She was expecting her second teeth. Today all females were making sexual fun of me, and even the infants were looking lewd. I stopped, letting the dress fall, and said to her, "What are you laughing about?"

"If you were a girl, you'd of sat down."

The kid wanted me to understand that she knew what she had seen. She pressed her fingers over her mouth, and I turned and went to the kitchen.

There the older girl was lifting the black cast-iron skillet with both hands.

On dripping paper, the pork chops were laid out—nearby, a Mason jar of grease. I was competent enough at the gas range, which shone with old filth. Loath to touch the pork with my fingers, I forked the meat into the spitting fat. The chops turned my stomach. My thought was, "I'm into it now, up to the ears." The drunk in his bed, the dim secret toilet, the glaring tungsten twist over the gas range, the sputtering droplets stinging the hands. The older girl said, "There's plenty for you. Daddy won't be eating dinner."

"No, not me. I'm not hungry," I said.

All that my upbringing held in horror geysered up, my throat filling with it, my guts griping.

The children sat at the table, an enamel rectangle. Thick plates and glasses, a waxed package of sliced white bread, a milk bottle, a stick of butter, the burning fat clouding the room. The girls sat beneath the smoke, slicing their meat. I brought them salt and pepper from the range. They ate without conversation. My chore (my duty) done, there was nothing to keep me. I said, "I have to go."

I looked in at McKern, who had thrown down the coat and taken off his drawers. The parboiled face, the short nose pointed sharply, the life signs in the throat, the broken look of his neck, the black hair of his belly, the short cylinder between his legs ending in a spiral of loose skin, the white shine of the shins, the tragic expression of his feet. There was a stack of pennies on his bedside table. I helped myself to carfare but had no pocket for the coins. I opened the hall closet feeling quickly for a coat I might borrow, a pair of slacks. Whatever I took, Philip could return to the Greek barman tomorrow. I pulled a trench coat from a hanger, and a pair of trousers. For the third time I put on stranger's clothing— this is no time to mention stripes or checks or make exquisite notations. Escaping, desperate, I struggled into the pants on the landing, tucking in the dress, and pulled on the coat as I jumped down the stairs, knotting tight the belt and sticking the pennies, a fistful of them, into my pocket.

But still I went back to the alley under the woman's window to see if her light was on, and also to look for pages. The thief or pimp perhaps had chucked them away, or maybe they had dropped out when he snatched the sheepskin. Her window was dark. I found nothing on the ground. You may think this obsessive crankiness, a crazy dependency on words, on printed matter. But remember, there were no redeemers in the streets, no guides, no confessors, comforters, en- lighteners, communicants to turn to. You had to take teaching wherever you could find it. Under the library dome downtown, in mosaic letters, there was a message from Milton, so moving but perhaps of no utility, perhaps aggravating difficulties: A GOOD BOOK, it said, IS THE PRECIOUS LIFE'S BLOOD OF A MASTER SPIRIT.

These are the plain facts, they have to be uttered. This, remember, is the New World, and we live in one of its mysterious cities. I should have hurried directly, to catch a car. Instead I was in a back alley hunting pages that would in any case have blown away.

I went back to Broadway—it *was* very broad—and waited on a safety island. Then the car came clanging, red, swaying on its trucks, a piece of Iron Age technology, double cane seats framed in brass. Rush hour was long past. I sat by a window, homebound, with flashes of thought like tracer bullets slanting into distant darkness. Like London in wartime. At home, what story would I tell? I wouldn't tell any. I never did. It was assumed anyway that I was lying. While I believed in honor, I did often lie. Is a life without lying conceivable? It was easier to lie than to explain myself. My father had one set of assumptions, I had another. Corresponding premises were not to be found.

I owed five dollars to Behrens. But I knew where my mother secretly hid her savings. Because I looked into all books, I had found the money in her *mahzor,* the prayer book for the High Holidays, the days of awe. As yet I hadn't taken anything. She had hoped until this final illness to buy passage to Europe to see her mother and her sister. When she died I would turn the money over to my father, except for ten dollars, five for the florist and the rest for Von Hügel's *Eternal Life* and *The World as Will and Idea.*

The after-dinner guests and cousins would be gone when I reached home. My father would be on the lookout for me. It was the rear porch door that was locked after dark. The kitchen door was generally off the latch. I could climb over the wooden partition between the stairs and the porch. I often did that. Once you got your foot on the doorknob you could pull yourself over the partition and drop to the porch without noise. Then I could see into the kitchen and slip in as soon as my patrolling father had left it. The bedroom shared by all three brothers was just off the kitchen. I could borrow my brother Len's cast-off winter coat tomorrow. I knew which closet it hung in. If my father should catch me I could expect hard blows on my shoulders, on the top of my head, on my face. But if my mother had, tonight, just died, he wouldn't hit me.

This was when the measured, reassuring, sleep-inducing turntable of days became a whirlpool, a vortex darkening toward the bottom. I had had only the anonymous pages in the pocket of my lost sheepskin to interpret it to me. They told me that the truth of the universe was inscribed into our very bones. That the human skeleton was itself a hieroglyph. That everything we had ever known on earth was shown to us in the first days after death. That our experience of the world was desired by the cosmos, and needed by it for its own renewal.

I do not think that these pages, if I hadn't lost them, would have persuaded me forever or made the life I led a different one.

I am writing this account, or statement, in response to an eccentric urge swelling toward me from the earth itself.

Failed my mother! That may mean, will mean, little or nothing to you, my only child, reading this document.

I myself know the power of nonpathos, in these low, devious days.

On the streetcar, heading home, I braced myself, but all my preparations caved in like sand diggings. I got down at the North Avenue stop, avoiding my reflection in the shopwindows. After a death, mirrors were immediately covered. I can't say what this pious superstition means. Will the soul of your dead be reflected in a looking glass, or is this custom a check to the vanity of the living?

I ran home, approached by the back alley, made no noise on the wooden backstairs, reached for the top of the partition, placed my foot on the white porcelain doorknob, went over the top without noise, and dropped down on our porch. I didn't follow the plan I had laid for avoiding my father. There were people sitting at the kitchen table. I went straight in. My father rose from his chair and hurried toward me. His fist was ready. I took off my tam or woolen beret and when he hit me on the head the blow filled me with gratitude. If my mother had already died, he would have embraced me instead.

Well, they're all gone now, and I have made my preparations. I haven't left a large estate, and this is why I have written this memoir, a sort of addition to your legacy.

AFTERWORD

A Japanese sage—I forget his name—told his disciples, "Write as short as you can." Sydney Smith, an English clergyman and wit of the last century, also spoke out for brevity: "Short views, for God's sake, short views!" he said. And Miss Ferguson, the lively spinster who was my composition teacher in Chicago some sixty years ago, would dance before the class, clap her hands, and chant (her music borrowed from Handel's "Hallelujah" Chorus):

> *Be*
> *speci-*
> *fic!*

Miss Ferguson would not put up with redundancy, prolixity, periphrasis, or bombast. She taught us to stick to the necessary and avoid the superfluous. Did I heed her warnings, follow her teaching? Not absolutely, I'm afraid, for in my early years I wrote more than one fat book. It's difficult for me now to read those early novels, not because they lack interest but because I find myself editing them, slimming down my sentences and cutting whole paragraphs.

Men who loved stout women used to say (how long ago *that* was!), "You can't have too much of a good thing." Everyone does understand, however, that a good thing can be overdone. Those devoted men, it should be added, didn't invent the obese ladies whom they loved; they discovered them.

Some of our greatest novels are very thick. Fiction is a loose popular art, and many of the classic novelists get their effects by heaping up masses of words. Decades ago, Somerset Maugham was inspired to publish pared-down versions of some of the very best. His experiment didn't succeed. Something went out of the books when their bulk was reduced. It would be mad to edit a novel like *Little Dorrit*. That sea of words *is* a sea, a force of nature. We want it that way, ample, capable of breeding life. When its amplitude tires us we readily forgive it. We wouldn't want it any other way.

Yet we respond with approval when Chekhov tells us, "Odd, I have now a mania for shortness. Whatever I read—my own or other people's works—it all seems to me not short enough." I find myself emphatically agreeing with this. There is a modern taste for brevity and condensation. Kafka, Beckett, and Borges wrote short. People of course do write long, and write successfully, but to write short is felt by a growing public to be a very good thing—perhaps the best. At once a multitude of possible reasons for this feeling comes to mind: This is the end of the millennium. We have heard it all. We have no time. We have more significant fish to fry. We require a wider understanding, new terms, a deeper penetration.

Of course, to obtain attention is harder than it used to be. The more leisure we have, the stiffer the competition for eyes and ears and mental space. On the front page of this morning's national edition of the *New York Times*, Michael Jackson, with hundreds of millions of fans worldwide, has signed a new contract worth a billion with Sony Software "to create feature films, theatrical shorts, television programming and a new record label for the Japanese conglomerate's American entertainment subsidiaries." Writers do not have such expectations and are not directly affected by the entertainment world. What is of interest to us here is that these are facts involving multitudes, that the news is commented upon by a leading "communications analyst," and that the article is continued in the Living Arts section of the paper, where the Trump divorce is also prominently featured, together with the usual television stuff, bridge, gardening, and Paris fashions. A new novel is reviewed on page B2.

I don't want to be understood as saying that writers should be concerned about the existence of these other publics.

There is a wonderful Daumier caricature of a bluestocking, a severe lady stormily looking through the newspaper at a café table. "Nothing but sports, snipe-hunting. And not a single word about my novel!" she complains.

What I do say is that we (we writers, I mean) must cope with a plethora of attractions and excitements—world crises, hot and cold wars, threats to survival, famines, unspeakable crimes. To conceive of these as "rivals" would be absurd—even monstrous. I say no more than that these crises produce states of mind and attitudes toward existence that artists must take into account.

The subject is not an easy one. I shall try to make a new beginning: Years ago Robert Frost and I exchanged signed copies. I gave him a novel respectfully dedicated. He signed a copy of his collected poems for me, adding, "To read if I will read him." A great tease, Frost. He couldn't promise to read my novel. I already knew his poems. You couldn't get a high school certificate in Chicago without memorizing "Mending Wall." What Frost hinted, perhaps, was that my novel might not stand high on his list of priorities. Why should he read mine, why not another? And why should I read *his* poems? I had my choice of dozens of other poets.

It's perfectly plain that we are astray in forests of printed matter. The daily papers are thick. Giant newsstands are virtually thatched with magazines. As for books—well, the English scholar F. L. Lucas wrote in the fifties: "With nearly twenty thousand volumes published yearly in Britain alone, there is a danger of good books, both new and old, being buried under the bad. If the process went on indefinitely we should finally be pushed into the sea by our libraries. Yet there are few of these books that might not at least be shorter, and all the better for being shorter; and most of them could, I believe, be most effectively shortened, not by cutting out whole chapters but by purging their sentences of useless words and paragraphs of their useless sentences." Answer the problem of quantity with improved quality—a touching idea, but Utopian. Too late, thirty years ago we had already been pushed into the sea.

The modern reader (or viewer, or listener: let's include everybody) is perilously overloaded. His attention is, to use the latest lingo, "targeted" by powerful forces. I hate to make lists of these forces, but I suppose that some of them had better be mentioned. Okay, then: automobile and pharmaceutical giants, cable TV, politicians, entertainers, academics, opinion makers, porn videos, Ninja Turtles, et cetera. The list is tedious because it is an inventory of what is put into our heads day in, day out. Our consciousness is a staging area, a field of operations for all kinds of enterprises, which make free use of it. True, we are at liberty to think our own thoughts, but our independent ideas, such as they may be, must live with thousands of ideas and notions inculcated by influential teachers or floated by "idea men," advertisers, communications people, columnists, anchormen, et cetera. Better-regulated (educated) minds are less easily overcome by these gas clouds of opinion. But no one can have an easy time of it. In all fields we are forced to seek special instruction, expert guidance to the interpretation of the seeming facts we are stuffed with. This is in itself a full-time occupation. A part of every mind, perhaps the major portion, is open to public matters. Without being actively conscious of it we somehow keep track of the Middle East, Japan, South Africa, reunified Germany, oil, munitions, the New York subways, the homeless, the markets, the banks, the major leagues, news from Washington; and also, pell-mell, films, trials, medical discoveries, rap groups, racial clashes, congressional scandals, the spread of AIDS, child murders—a crowd of horrors. Public life in the United States is a mass of distractions.

By some this is seen as a challenge to their ability to maintain internal order. Others have acquired a taste for distraction, and they freely consent to be addled. It may even seem to many that by being agitated they are satisfying the claims of society. The scope of the disorder can even be oddly flattering: "Just look—this tremendous noisy frantic monstrous agglomeration. There's never been anything like it. And we are *it!* This is *us!*"

Vast organizations exist to get our attention. They make cunning plans. They bite us with their ten-second bites. Our consciousness is their staple; they live on it. Think of consciousness as a territory just opening to settlement and exploitation, something like an Oklahoma land rush. Put it in color, set it to music, frame it in images—but even this fails to do justice to the vision. Obviously consciousness is infinitely bigger than Oklahoma.

Now what of writers? They materialize, somehow, and they ask the public (more accurately, *a* public) for its attention. Perhaps the writer has no actual public in mind. Often his only assumption is that he participates in a state of psychic unity with others not distinctly known to him. The mental condition of these others is understood by him, for it is his condition also. One way or another he understands, or intuits, what the effort, often a secret and hidden effort to put the distracted consciousness in order, is costing. These unidentified or partially identified others are his readers. They have been waiting for him. He must assure them immediately that reading him will be worth their while. They have many times been cheated by writers who promised good value but delivered nothing. Their attention has been abused. Nevertheless they long to give it. In his diaries Kafka says of a certain woman, "She holds herself by force below the level of her true human destiny and requires only . . . a tearing open of the door. . . ."

The reader will open his heart and mind to a writer who has understood this—has understood because in his person he has gone through it all, has experienced the same privations; who knows where the sore spots are; who has discerned the power of the need to come back to the level of one's true human destiny. Such a writer will trouble no one with his own vanities, will make no unnecessary gestures, indulge himself in no mannerisms, waste no reader's time. He will write as short as he can.

I offer this as a brief appendix to the stories in this volume.